The Magic

(October 1961–October 1967)
Ten Tales by Roger Zelazny

Hard Cover ISBN 13: 978-1-5154-3974-5
Trade Paperback ISBN 13: 978-1-5154-3975-2

The Magic

(October 1961–October 1967)
Ten Tales by Roger Zelazny

Selected and Introduced by
Samuel R. Delany
Cover art by Bob Eggleton

Acknowledgments

"Zelazny!" copyright © 2018 by Samuel R. Delany.

"Introduction" by Theodore Sturgeon originally appeared in *Four For Tomorrow* 1967. Copyright © 1967 by Theodore Sturgeon.

"When Zelazny was Magic" by Darrell Schweitzer copyright © 2018 by Darrell Schweitzer.

"A Rose for Ecclesiastes" originally appeared in *The Magazine of Fantasy and Science Fiction*, November 1963. Copyright © 1963 by Mercury Press.

"The Graveyard Heart" originally appeared in *Fantastic Stories of Imagination*, March 1964. Copyright © 1964 by Ziff-Davis Publishing Co.

"The Doors of His Face, The Lamps of His Mouth" originally appeared in *The Magazine of Fantasy and Science Fiction*, March 1965. Copyright © 1965 by Mercury Press.

"The Ides of Octember" originally appeared in *Amazing Stories*, January 1965 as "He Who Shapes." Copyright © 1965 by Ziff-Davis Publishing Co.

"The Furies" originally appeared in *Amazing Stories*, June 1965. Copyright © 1965 by Ziff-Davis Publishing Co.

"For a Breath I Tarry" originally appeared in *New Worlds*, March 1966. Copyright © 1966 by *New Worlds*.

"This Moment of the Storm" originally appeared in *The Magazine of Fantasy and Science Fiction*, June 1966. Copyright © 1966 by Mercury Press.

"The Keys to December" originally appeared in *New Worlds*, August 1966. Copyright © 1966 by *New Worlds*.

"This Mortal Mountain" originally appeared in *If*, March 1967. Copyright © 1967 by Galaxy Publishing Corporation.

"Damnation Alley" originally appeared in *Galaxy Magazine*, October 1967. Copyright © 1967 by Galaxy Publishing Corporation.

"A Word from Zelazny" and "Notes" following each story compiled by Christopher S. Kovacs. ©2009 by Christopher S. Kovacs, MD. Originally appeared in volumes 1, 2, and 3 of *The Collected Stories of Roger Zelazny*, NESFA Press, 2009. Revisions to the notes copyright © 2018.

Table of Contents

"A Word from Zelazny" and "Notes" following each story compiled by
Christopher S. Kovacs.

APPENDIX

Two Interviews with Roger Zelazny

Zelazny!

by Samuel R. Delany

In 1938, in what is probably one of the best books on writing I've ever read, Cyril Connelly wrote, "Those whom the gods would destroy, they first call promising."

Though I was not to hear of it till many years later, both Zelazny and I had early high school stories published in a national magazine called *Literary Cavalcade*–Roger's was a short-short called "Mr. Fuller's Revolt," from Vol. 7, October 1st, 1954.

A year before Connelly's *Enemies of Promise* appeared, Zelazny (May 13, 1937–June 14, 1995) was born in Euclid, Ohio.

In the October 1965 issue of *The Magazine of Fantasy and Science Fiction* the first half of his serialized novel . . . *And Call Me Conrad* appeared.

A young woman friend of mine named Ana Parez brought the issue to my apartment on East 7th Street, to show me. Ana was a folksinger, who, when I first met her, had been a student at the Bronx High School of Science, who had recently come from Boston Latin. When she arrived at Seventh Street, she explained: "This is it, what I told you about on the phone. Chip, who is this guy?" And that night I read it, and by the end I wanted to read not only the rest but everything he wrote or had published. And shortly I was able to find the November 1963 issue (with the glorious Hannes Bok cover) and read the first of the stories here, "A Rose for Ecclesiastes" (which would later be revealed to have been written a year before his first two professional sales, "Horseman" in the August 1962 issue of *Fantastic* and "Passion Play" in the August 1962 issue of *Amazing*). There is something about the early stories of Roger Zelazny that makes you want to analyze how they work, because they work so well.

The Magic

I wanted to meet him, and that year I went to my first SF convention, the Tricon, in Cleveland, Ohio, where . . . *And Call Me Conrad* tied for the Hugo Award with Frank Herbert's *Dune!* (For a while, in manuscript, Zelazny's novel had born three titles, typed or handwritten: *I Am Thinking of My Earth,* and *Good-Bye, My Darling, Good-Bye, Conrad* had been rejected; finally, *. . . And Call Me Conrad,* one of the handwritten ones, had—happily!—been chosen.) I recall sitting in the audience when the professionals who were in attendance were announced, and how we all applauded the known names when they came up. Zelazny's name received an incredibly enthusiastic, standing ovation—the only writer there who did, and—unlike the others—it went on and on and *on* . . .

I stood too, and felt good that I was there to applaud with the rest, and that, as well, I was lucky enough to belong to such a community that recognized the excellence of this writer. (I had read enough of *Dune* to know that, while I approved of what I had picked up as its ecological message, it was an unreadably poor novel and homophobic to boot.) That weekend, I sought out Roger (my own sixth novel, *Babel-17,* had been nominated for a Nebula Award), and he was free for dinner, and I was lucky enough to dine that night with him and his wife, Judith, at the hotel restaurant. We were both enthusiastic about each other's work, and I recall we reached our table over a transparent bridge above a fish pond in the floor, and we agreed that it looked like something one might find in an Alfred Bester novel. I also seem to remember that Judith said she didn't find science fiction that interesting, but that since everybody here seemed to like what Roger wrote, she guessed it was good.

As early as 1968, three years after . . . *And Call me Conrad,* I knew the stories I wanted to see together in this book. (One of his most satisfactory novels, *Doorways in the Sand* [1976] was still to come.) When, once again, we got a chance to sit down for a few moments together (in Baltimore?), I told him, "I didn't think 'Damnation Alley'—" which had been nominated for a Hugo award—"worked as well as it might." He grimaced a little.

Roger Zelazny and Samuel R. Delany

"Actually," he said, "I didn't think so either, Chip. But it's good to know you cared."

That was the last time we ever spoke directly, though we were in touch in other ways. In '68 in *The Magazine of Fantasy and Science Fiction* published my loving pastiche of what I felt to be Zelazny at his best, whose hero was a more realistic and, I hoped, a more heroic version of Hell Tanner. Only in 2012, did I hear—through a Facebook chat box of all places—Bruce Chrumka report "I once asked R. Zelazny what he thought of "We, in some Strange Power's Employ, Move on a Rigorous Line," [. . . and] he said he loved it and wished he'd written it. This was in front of perhaps 300 conventioneers in Edmonton, [Canada, in] the late '80s."

Although I didn't learn this until five years ago (twenty-two years after Roger's death), it was a high compliment.

When, in mid-June of 1995, Roger died in New Mexico of cancer, my old student, George R. R. Martin, phoned me with the news and also told me that Roger had wanted me to know he was thinking of me—another high compliment.

However lightweight I found some of the Amber novels that came to dominate Zelazny's output, through the 1970s, I could already reel off what I felt were Zelazny's strongest stories from his early works, which—if they were collected in a single volume—would foreground his strengths as a writer and storyteller: "A Rose for Ecclesiastes" (1961, pub 1963), "The Ides of Octember" (a.k.a, "He Who Shapes," 1965), "The Graveyard Heart" (1964), "The Doors of His Face, the Lamps of his Mouth" (1965), "The Furies" (1965), "The Keys to December" (1966), "For a Breath I Tarry" (1966), "This Moment of the Storm" (1966), "This Mortal Mountain" (1967), and the already discussed "Damnation Alley" (1967).

Both "The Ides of Octember" (under its alternate title) and "The Doors of His Face, the Lamps of His Mouth" won Nebula Awards as best long stories (novella and novelette) of their respective years.

An amazingly bad film was made "from" *Damnation Alley*, about which neither Zelazny nor I had anything to say at all. (I have to put "from" in quotes: The film's plot has nothing to do with Zelazny's tale, and then some special effects are added that have nothing to do with anything.) In his note on the story, Roger makes the point that the main character grew out of conversations with a real person (he does not tell us who), who actually rode a motorcycle, which is revealing; as he says, it's the only story he ever wrote in which this was the case. In the same note, he reveals his intention: "I wanted to do a straight, style-be-damned action story with the pieces fall (*sic*) wherever. Movement and menace. Splash and color is all."

Writers be warned: adventure, psychology, and even comprehension are before all else affects. It's impossible to achieve any of the three without at least grammar, whether acceded to or violated, or style of some kind under some control. Hell Tanner's realness produces only banality and an unearned confidence in the material that the reading experience doesn't support.

II

Speaking strictly, neither the Mars of "A Rose for Ecclesiastes" nor the Venus of "The Doors of His Face, the Lamps of His Mouth" is a science fiction construct. Both are fantasy worlds put together to *violate* what relatively recently had come to be known about each: this Mars has (a) a breathable atmosphere and (b) an ancient, matriarchal humanoid race put together precisely when we became sure that it didn't have either; Zelazny's Venus is a water-covered waste envisioned precisely when the returning Mariner probes made clear what was generally already known: the brightest planet in our sky—both the morning and evening star, as Parmenides had identified it, during the time of the Doric Greeks—was a world covered with hot, hydrocarbon gases completely enclosing a scalding desert. Life of any sort, much less a giant aquatic monster bigger than Roosevelt Island in the midst of the Hudson River—was not even reasonable speculation.

"The Lowlands of Venus lie between the Thumb and Forefinger of the continent known as Hand . . . Next you study Hand to lay its illusion: . . . the thumb is too short, and curls like the embryo tail of Cape Horn." In most reader's mind, with any familiarity with maps of earth, Hand begins to look like the tail end of Africa. This is a Venus that is a fantasy landscape, covered with water and a few islands, and clouds and a few small continents emerging.

"The Furies" is a mosaic story, in which the carefully described talents of the double named main characters make the escape of the super prey all but impossible, though it is indeed ingenious the way Zelazny sets it up. That it actually makes sense in the midst of all the fantasy creates an effect that suggests a *tour de force*.

"The Ides of Octember" and the "The Graveyard Heart" are actual science fiction tales—or they were when they were written. But have been rendered into fantasy by the passage of time. The irony is that the first scene of "Graveyard Heart" was thirty-five years in the future (and, as though Zelazny had learned his lesson: all right, stop trying to be poetic: call something nice and simple, and "Party Set" was the initial title; but by this point, readers were looking for poetic titles on Zelazny's tales: so it was changed to something "more poetic" and a much better title it is): " . . . the party of the millennium . . . in a few moments it would be Two Thousand."

The story turns on a famous quote from Shakespeare's Hamlet, only the first quarter of which is in the text:

> The Time is out of joint. O, curséd spite
> That ever I was born to set it right.

One reads the story, however, not as something that took place 17 years ago, but rather as something that, if we're lucky, might take place eighty odd years from now in our own future, if we have one.

The story was first published in 1964; that is, nine years before *Roe v. Wade*, when women's right to a safe abortion became the law. In my old neighborhood, there was a Planned Parenthood office half a block west and north of my front door—and there are regular Catholic protestors there, in larger or smaller numbers throughout the week, even today. Our twenty-seven year old point of view character, Alvin Moore, is in love with Leota Mathilde Mason. He dances with her on New Year's Eve, in the year 2000, so he must have be born in 1973—that is to say the story was written nine years before the right to a safe abortion for women was the law of the land, but none of the characters live in a world where this political/legal moment has yet come about.

This casts a strange light over the whole climatic scene, when a poet tries to drive a stake through the heart of a woman frozen in cold-sleep, which also takes out her baby (exactly how, I'm not sure), though the unsureness of the female anatomy is part of the confusion about female biology that goes along with the decade of the tale's composition. (It was within a decade of a great public debate about whether women had two types of orgasms or just one.) But it is very different reading this story as taking place in 1964 or post-1973, not to mention 18 years into the next century, even as it goes on to make its general point that the passions and technology work together to obliterate the damages that the other inflicts.

*

A figure whose influence must be taken into account, at least in his influence on his names in "The Furies," is Cordwainer Smith (1913–1966), pen name of the diminutive Dr. Paul Linebarger, who worked for the government writing on psychological warfare, and died of a heart attack at age 53, one of a number of writers who used science fiction to write about ideas that might not be so popular with the government he worked for. Another was James Tiptree Jr. (a. k. a. Alice Sheldon).

"The Furies" is Zelazny trying (and succeeding) to write a Cordwainer Smith story—about Sandor Sandor, Benedict Benedict, and Lynx Links—in their pursuit of Corgo. They succeed, and indeed it is an extremely good Cordwainer Smith story—done in brief mosaic sections and as memorable as any of Smith's stories of C'Mell, the cat girl, or D'Joan, the dog woman. But it is perhaps not the most interesting Zelazny story, which is perhaps the best analysis I can give of it here.

While he seemed to enjoy the attention lavished upon him in those years, the slim, dark man of Polish American extraction never did anything to seek it out, except write: the same humorous irony with which he confronted the

Roger Zelazny and Samuel R. Delany

most intense excitement about his work (from 1963 till approximately 1968), he would use to confront those people who, a few years later, were to declare his newer work was not as strong as his earlier productions. Zelazny went on to write more award-winning novels and stories, including *Lord of Light* and *Home is the Hangman*. His Amber novels, which began appearing in '70, were unremittingly popular, as the individual novels came out over the next twenty years, but the excitement within the SF community still centered on the ten long stories we have cited, coupled with a handful of those early novels: *This Immortal*, *The Dream Master* (an expansion of "He Who Shapes"), *Bridge of Ashes*, *Doorways in the Sand* (the last coming to be considered the best, with *This Immortal* close behind), while others would argue as intelligently and as passionately for *Isle of the Dead* and *Lord of light*, producing the conflict that is what must rumble about in the socio-aesthetic landscape for a century or so after the death of the author before any reputation can begin to settle.

"For a Breath I Tarry" (1966), and "The Keys to December" (1966), both first appeared in the English magazine, *New Worlds*, before its transition from digest size to tabloid size, but still locking Zelazny's reputation with that of the New Wave.

The first of them, Zelazny claims was his favorite novelette. (The second was developed for a film, at least as far as a completed script, but as is often the case on such projects, nothing materialized.) The title comes from A. E. Housman.

It is a retelling of the story of Job with all the characters taken by great artificial intelligences and their robots, long after humanity has vanished from the Solar System—Divcom, that burns like a blue star in the sky, and the Alternate, which is buried deep underground, in radio contact with each other and with a hoard of robots around a world, where only robots move and do destroy each other . . . each trying to undo what the other creates.

> Man had ceased to exist long before Frost had been created.
> Almost no trace of Man remained upon the Earth.
> Frost sought after all those traces which still existed.

The Magic

He employed constant visual monitoring through his machines, especially the diggers.

After a decade, he had accumulated portions of several bathtubs, a broken statue, and a collection of children's stories on a solid state record.

After a century, he had acquired a jewelry collection, eating utensils, several whole bathtubs, part of a symphony, seventeen buttons, three belt buckles, half a toilet seat, nine old coins, and the top part of an obelisk.

In this post-human world inhabited by only robots and A.I.s, the story of Frost is both the story of Job and the story of Faust, with Frost as the main character of both. Solcom and Divcom and the Alternate (as well as the Beta Machine and Mordel), are all god-like intelligences who seem to have no sense either of pain or their own eventual extinctions or even the meaning of the senses or the feelings that made them meaningful. ("The senses do not make a Man," said Mordel. "There have been many creatures possessing his sensory equivalence, but they were not Men.") They can measure the temperature, but have no awareness of what cold or warm means. They can perceive sunrises or sunsets and even artworks, but have no sense of what beauty is that distinguishes one from another.

Scattered throughout the story are bits of diction that recall passages from the Bible or poetry. ("Divcom created a crew of robots immune to the orders of Solcom and designed to go to and fro in the Earth and up and down in it . . . . For six days he worked at its shaping, and on the seventh he regarded it.") Divcom inhabits the air along with Solcom, which is sometimes perceived as "a blue star." The Alternate lives deep underground. Their conversations with each other seem to embody hostilities, and their first one in the fourth scene of the story ends with a line by Divcom that recalls another scriptural moment: "Do you know my servant Frost . . . ?"

In the course of the story, Frost, whose hobby has become the study of Man, is presented by Mordel three books, as the first of many others: *Human Physiology, An Outline of History* (by H. G. Wells), and *A Shropshire Lad* (by A.

16

E. Housman, in particular the XXXIInd poem "From far, from eve and morning"). The point of all of this is that without knowing the experiences that make the human physiology meaningful (hunger, thirst, desire, fear, pleasure . . .), true understanding of the others is finally impossible, even as what is called the Library of Man—the considerable number of books that remain in the world, though this is only a fraction of what once was there—is exposed to Frost's text scanners:

Load by load the surviving Library of Man passed beneath Frost's scanner. Frost was eager to have them all, and he complained because Divcom would not transmit their contents directly to him. Mordel explained it was because Divcom decided to do it that way. Frost decided it was so that he could not obtain a precise fix on Divcom's location.

Still, at the rate of one-hundred to one-hundred-fifty volumes a week, it took Frost only a little over a century to exhaust Divcom's supply of books.

At the end of the half-century, he laid himself open to monitoring, and there was no conclusion of failure.

During this time, Solcom made no comment upon the course of affairs. Frost decided this was not a matter of unawareness, but one of waiting. For what? He was not certain . . . "So few?" asked Frost. "Many of them contained bibliographies of books I have not yet scanned."

"Then those books no longer exist," said Mordel. "It is only by accident that my master succeeded in preserving as many as there are."

"Then there is nothing more to be learned from Man from his books. What else have you?"

"There were some films and tapes," said Mordel, "which my master transferred to solid state records. I could bring you those for viewing."

"Bring them," said Frost.

The Magic

Mordel departed and returned with the Complete Drama Critics Living Library. This could not be speeded up beyond twice natural time, so it took Frost a little over six months to view it in its entirety.

Then, "What else have you?" he asked.

"Some artifacts," said Mordel.

"Bring them."

He returned with pots and pans, game boards, and hand tools. He brought hairbrushes, combs, eyeglasses, human clothing. He showed Frost facsimiles of blueprints, paintings, newspapers, magazines, letters, and the scores of several pieces of music. He displayed a football, a baseball, a browning automatic rifle, a doorknob, a chain of keys, the tops to several mason jars, a model beehive. He played him the recorded music.

Then he returned with nothing. (pp 370)

Frost begins the processing of the material evaluation of what he has looked over, however poorly he does or does not understand it, and at least once, we see him decide to imitate what he thinks it is to be a Man when he tells Divcom, "Thank you."

Slowly, Frost begins to perceive what is left of the world as a factory for making humans, even though he does not quite understand what human beings are supposed to be. The working out of this process gives us the remainder of the story. By the same token, we realize Frost was destined to replace Man the moment he began obsessively studying Man in detail and taking Man as a "hobby," because the jobs he was supposed to be doing simply did not utilize his capacities anywhere near to the full.

III

"Not El Greco; nor Blake, no: Bosch. Without any question, Bosch—with his nightmare vision of the streets of hell. He would be the one to do justice to this moment of the storm."

Roger Zelazny and Samuel R. Delany

This is the story of "Godfrey Justin Holmes—'God' for short," and whose nickname is "Juss . . . " who has come to a watery world, and its single continent, "Terra del Cygnus, Land of the Swan—delightful name.

"Delightful place, too, for a while . . . "

Juss is a Hell Cop, a lookout with a hoard of 135 remote control eyes, which look over what at first seems to be a peaceful land, but as a great storm—far greater than any known on earth—raises up about the landscape a hoard of monsters in the streets. ("They say the job title comes from the name of an antique flying vehicle—a hellcopper, I think.") In this story, Zelazny's first person narrator returns to a cryogenic technique we last saw in "The Graveyard Heart," only here strung out to become the way to accomplish interstellar travel at slower than light speeds.

People smoke regularly—risking cancer. (It is what killed Zelazny in 1995 at the age of 58.) In the same story at one point sickness is said to come from "dampness" and "from cold," which is tantamount to earmarking the story as originating from before the increased awareness, which arrived with the age of AIDS, that sicknesses come from viruses and bacteria and that dampness, cold, and malnutrition can only lower one resistance *to* disease. Even dirt does not spread disease itself, if the proper pathogens are not present. The bag of hydrochloric that hangs at the bottom of the esophagus, commonly known as the belly, is not only an early step in the digestion process, it is also an early step in the immune system's fight against the pretty much ninety-five percent of all viruses and bacteria that might harm the human machine itself.

"Where are the rains of yesteryear?" Zelazny riffs on the line by Villon, "*Ou sont les nieges . . .* "

And another one of his Immortals moved off onto an uncertain future threaded across the stars: "Years have passed. I am not really counting them anymore. But I think of this thing often: Perhaps there *is* a Golden Age someplace, a Renaissance for me sometime, a special time somewhere, somewhere but a ticket, a visa, a diary-page away. I don't know where or when. Who does? Where are all the rains of yesterday?

The Magic

"In the invisible city?

Inside me . . . ?"

And in two more necessary sentences the story is done.

*

I seem to remember an editorial blurb at the beginning of Zelazny's story "This Mortal Mountain" that first appeared in the March 1967 edition of *Worlds of If* that said, in effect, that, as Dante knew, at the end of everything, there are stars. (John Ciardi's very serviceable translations of all three parts each ends with the word "stars.") This is a story about climbing the mount of Purgatory, and ironically, it begins with the protagonist, Jack Summers, looking down on that seven-tiered mountain from a space ship:

"A forty-mile-high mountain," I finally said, "is not a mountain. It is a world all by itself which some dumb deity forgot to bring into orbit."

The prospect of an ascent up the highest mountain in the explored section of the galaxy inspires Jack Summer to summon his posse from among the stars: Doc and Kelly and Stan and Mallardi and Vincent.

The discovery is that, at the top, is a woman who has been put into a sort of suspended animation who suffers from something called Dawson's Plague, by her husband (whose name was Carl, which is incidentally the name of the protagonist of "The Doors of His Face, the Lamps of His Mouth"), before he died. Illusions begin to confront them announcing that they should go back, in between other communications.

As Zelazny remarks, Dante had located the Earthly Paradise—Eden—on the top of Mount Purgatory (on the top level devoted to the Lustful). To go on beyond that point requires a miracle.

As they get closer and closer to the top, the mountain begins to look more and more like a Nordic version of a Night on Bald Mountain, with a three-headed dragon encircling its highest peak.

The seven chapters of the novelette correspond to the seven terraces that circle Dante's Mount of Purgatory, with the seven deadly sins that become more and more forgivable: pride, envy, ire, sloth, greed, gluttony, and finally lust or eros:

Roger Zelazny and Samuel R. Delany

The first chapter of the story establishes Jack Summer (Whitey) as the man who has climbed all the other great mountains in this universe, including Mt. Kasla on Litan, at 89,941 feet. As well, we learn that world, wherever it is, has a thin atmosphere, because the ceiling on a jet is 30-thousand feet, and the mountain is higher than that. And the beginning of the second chapter he sends out his call for his crew to join him: "If you want in on the biggest climb of all, come to Diesel. The Gray Sister eats Kasla for Breakfast.

The gravity of the planet is a little weaker. ("On Diesel, the pack and I together probably weighed about the same as me alone on Earth—for which I was grateful.") And as he does his early exploring of the mountain from the north face, now and again he hears the voice in his mind that says, "Go back." If there is envy, it would seem to be of the solidity of the mountain itself. In three days, we are told (in the way only science fiction can do), he has gotten higher than Everest—and that, indeed, on other islands nearby there are 12 and 15 mile high mountains, but nothing like the Gray Sister (a.k.a. The Lady).

Chapter III (which we might expect to be devoted to Ire) turns out to be the section that contains what first appears to be a burst of lyric madness; when his friends come and Whitey/Summer meets with them by themselves, he offers the proof that makes the story actually science fiction—a charred back pack he turns out to have brought back with him from his preliminary climb on the mountain while he was waiting for his crew to assemble. "Ire" is replaced by "Intelligence."

(It recalls a moment from Disch's *Camp Concentration* when the imprisoned poet Louis Sachetti recalls how his priest in his childhood would warn him to be beware of "Intellectual Pride," which Sacchetti finally decided was just a warning to deride intellect.)

Chapter IV finds the crew planning, mapping, charting, and studying photos—the only nod to "sloth" is that "Henry was on his way to fat," and that Doc and Stan, while in good condition, had not climbed in a while.

The Magic

In the course of this section, Summer meets with an embodied hallucination from the mountain—a woman—and the section ends with talk of tiredness and exhaustion.

Greed, Gluttony, and Lust lie ahead; and chapter V begins with two days of steady progress. ("We made slightly under ten thousand feet," pp 490.) They have made their way to the western side, where they break ninety thousand feet and stop "to congratulate ourselves that we had surpassed the Kalsa climb and to remind ourselves that we had still not hit the halfway mark." That takes them another two-and-a-half days.

A new hallucination materializes, then, which they all see: "the creature with the sword." Bits of logic are scattered throughout the tale:

The fires from the hallucination do not melt the ice it sits on. So the men can agree that, indeed, a hallucination is what it is. Things get colorful with scarlet serpents. "Rocks still fell periodically, but the boss seemed to be running low on them. The bird appeared, circled us and swooped on four different occasions. But this time we ignored it, and finally it went home to roost."

In Chapter VI (in which easily we might look for marks of gluttony), we find such statements as: "How does a man come to climb mountains? Is he drawn to the heights because he is afraid of the level land? Is he such a misfit in the society of man that he must flee and try to place himself above it? The way up is long and difficult, but if he succeeds they must grant him a garland of sorts. And if he falls, this too is a kind of glory. To end, hurled from the heights to the depths in hideous ruin and combustion down is a fitting climax for the loser for it too shakes mountains and minds, stirs things like thoughts below both is a kind of blasted garland of victory in defeat, and cold, so cold that final action that the movement is somewhere frozen forever into a statue-like rigidity of ultimate intent and purpose, thwarted only by the universal malevolence we all fear exists." The text has moved from a contemplation of the seven deadly sins to the classical problem of hubris itself.

Roger Zelazny and Samuel R. Delany

"I had known that I had to climb Kasla as I had climbed all the others, and I had known what the price would be. It cost me my only home. But Kasla was there, and my boots cried out for my feet. I knew as I did so, that somewhere I set them upon her summit and below me a world was ending." The world that is ending is the world in which the mountain has not been climbed, and the world that is beginning is the one in which the mountain has been conquered, and Jack Summer, a.k.a. Whitey, is the hero who has conquered it.

The climbers reach a hundred seventy-six thousand feet, making their way along a ledge, till one member of the climbing crew, Vince, calls out, "Look!"

> Up and up, and again further, blue-frosted and sharp, deadly and cold as Loki's dagger, slashing at the sky, it vibrated above us like electricity, hung like a piece of frozen thunder, and cut, cut, into the center of spirit that was desire twisted and become a fishhook to pull us on, to burn us with its barbs.
>
> Vince was the first to look up and see the top, the first to die. It happened so quickly and it was none of the terrors that achieved it.
>
> He slipped.
>
> That was all. It was a difficult piece of climbing. He was right behind me one second, was gone to the next. There was no body to recover. He had taken the long drop. The soundless blue was all around him and the great grey beneath. Then we were six. We shuddered and I suppose we all prayed in our own ways.

In the morning, one more crew member is gone:

"So we were five—Doc and Kelly and Henry and Mallardi and me—and that day we hit a hundred and eight thousand and felt very alone." (It suggests Kafka's parable "Fellowship": "We are five friends . . . and cannot be tolerated with this sixth one.") Once more the hallucination of the woman joins them. There is a conversation in which she seems strangely present and absent at the same time. "Why do you hate us?" Jack Summer asks.

"No hate, sir," she said.

"What then?"

"I protect."

"What? What is it that you protect?"

"The dying, that she may live."

"What? Who is dying? How?"

But her words went away somewhere, and I did not hear them. Then she went away too and there was nothing left but sleep for the rest of the night.

They climb for another week.

"I'm not worried about making it to the top," Henry says. "The clouds are like little wisps of cotton down there."

The purgatorial allegory results with approach of the uppermost level of the lustful—only the woman involved is as cold and stony as Leota Mathild Mason in cold-sleep in "The Graveyard Heart."

What the text recalls even more than the ascent of Purgatory is Sigfried breaking through the circle of fire surrounding Brunhilde, with the flames themselves taking on the aspect of demons and dragons.

I left Henry far below me. The creature was a moving light in the sky. I made two hundred feet in a hurry, and when I looked up again. I saw the creature had grown two more heads. Lightnings flashed from its nostrils, and its tail whipped around the mountain. I made an another hundred feet, and I could see Mallardi clearly by then, climbing steadily, outlined against the brilliance. I swung my pick, gasping, and I fought the mountain, following the trail he had cut. I began to gain on him because he was still pounding out his way and I didn't have that problem yet. Then I heard him talking:

"Not yet, big fella, not yet," he was saying, from behind a wall of static. "Here's a ledge . . . "

I looked up, and he vanished.

Roger Zelazny and Samuel R. Delany

The seventh and final section—the entrance into the cave at the mountain top—replays the entrance into the cold-sleep bunker at the end of "The Graveyard Heart" without the Grand Guignol of the stake through the heart/womb. The disease Linda's husband—Carl—is trying to help her survive until it is cured is something called Dawson's Plague.

A death . . .

A life . . .

A lot of technological hugger-mugger . . .

At the top of a mountain whose peak is forty-two miles high, above the atmosphere itself. Clearly Zelazny is aware of the Puragotrial allegory. ("Tell me what it was like to climb a mountain like this one. Why?"

("There is a certain madness involved," I said, "a certain envy of great and powerful natural forces, that some men have. Each mountain is a deity you know. Each mountain is an immortal power. If you make sacrifice upon its slopes, a mountain may grant you a certain grace, and for a time, you will share its power.")

I think the key to why "Damnation Alley" is less effective than it might be is in Zelazny's own note: "I wanted to do a straight, style-be-damned action story with the pieces fall[ing] wherever." Well, when the style is let go, the truth is there's not that much left to a Zelazny tale—though the results are still interesting.

Zelazny's own comments on the movie is instructive: there were two scripts, the first of which he was shown, and which was much better than the second which they actually used. It recalls Lessing's characterization of genius: the ability "to put talent wholly into the service of an idea," which is what the flexibility of voice that Zelazny's strives for in his various styles accomplishes in the passages where the style is most in evidence:

The stories, such as the ones here, where the full toolbox is used most artfully.

And that is why one should continue to read him.

—*Friday, February 8, 2018,*
Philadephia, PA.

Introduction

by Theodore Sturgeon

There has been nothing like Zelazny in the science fiction field since—
Thus began the first draft of this introduction and there it stayed for about
forty-eight hours while I maundered and chuntered on ways to finish that
sentence with justice and precision. The only possible way to do it is to
knock off the last word. And even then it misses the truth, for the term
"science fiction" gives the comment a kind of club membership which trims
verity. So much which is published as science fiction is nothing of the kind.
And more and more, science fiction is produced and not called science
fiction (and paid for heartily—i.e. On the Beach, Dr. Strangelove, Seven Days in
May, 1984, etc., etc., et al.—which makes the pro science fiction writers
candidates for persecution mania). Suffice it for now to say that you'll be
hard put to it to find a writer like Zelazny anywhere.

Genuine prose-poets we have seen, but quite often they fail when the
measures of pace and structure are applied. And we have certainly had truly
great storytellers, whose narrative architecture is solidly based, soundly built,
and well-braced clear to tower-tip; but more often than not, this is done
completely with a homogenized, nuts-and-bolts kind of prose. And there has
been a regrettably small handful of what I call "people experts"—those
especially gifted to create memorable characters, something more than real
ones well-photographed . . . living ones who change, as all living things
change, not only during the reading, but in the memory as the reader himself
lives and changes and becomes capable of bringing more of himself to that
which the writer has brought him. But there again, "people experts" have a
tendency to turn their rare gift into a preoccupation (and create small ardent
cliques who tend to the same thing) and skimp on matters of structure and
content. An apt analogy would be a play superbly cast and skillfully mounted,
for which somebody had forgotten to supply a script.

The Magic

And if you think I am about to say that Zelazny delivers all these treasures and avoids all these oversights, that he has full measures of substance and structure, means and ends, texture, cadence and pace, you are absolutely right.

Three factors in Zelazny's work call for isolation and examination; and the very cold-bloodedness of such a declamation demands amendment. Let me revise it to two and a pointing finger, a vague and inarticulate wave toward something Out (or Up, or In) There which can be analyzed about as effectively as the internal effect of watching the color-shift on the skin of a bubble or that silent explosion somewhere inside the midriff which is one of the recognitions of love.

First, Zelazny's stories are fabulous. I use this word in a special and absolutely accurate sense. Aesop did not, and did not intend to, convey a factual account of an improbably vegetarian fox equipped with speech and with human value judgments concerning a bunch of unreachable grapes. He was saying something else and something larger than what he said. And it has come to me over the years that the greatness of literature and the importance of literary entities (Captain Ahab, Billy Budd, Hamlet, Job, Uriah Heep) really lies in this fabulous quality. One may ponderously call them Jungian archetypes, but one recognizes them, and/or their situational predicaments, in one's own daily contacts with this landlord, that employer, and one's dearly beloved. A fable says more than it says, is bigger than its own parameters. Zelazny always says more than he says; all of his yarns have applications, illuminate truths, donate to the reader tools (and sometimes weapons) with which he was not equipped before, and for which he can find daily uses, quite outside the limits of his story.

Second, there is, as one reads more and more of this extraordinary writer's work, a growing sense of excitement, a gradual recognition of something which (in me, anyway) engenders an increasing awe. It comes, strangely enough, not from any of his many excellences, but from his flaws. For he has flaws—plenty of them. One feels at times that a few (a very few, I hasten to add) of his more vivid turns of phrase would benefit by an application of

Roger Zelazny and Samuel R. Delany

Dulcote (an artists' material, a transparent spray which uniformly pulls down brightness and gloss where applied). Not because they aren't beautiful—because most of them are, God knows—but because even so deft a wordsmith as Zelazny can forget from time to time that such a creation can keep a reader from his speedy progress from here to there, and that his furniture should be placed out of the traffic pattern. If I bang my shin on a coffee table it becomes a little beside the point that it is the most exquisitely crafted artifact this side of the Sun King. Especially since it was the author himself who put me in a dead run. And there is the matter of exotic references—the injection of one of those absolutely precise and therefore untranslatable German philosophic terms, or a citation from classical mythology. This is a difficult thing to criticize without being misunderstood. A really good writer has the right, if not the duty, of arrogance, and should feel free to say anything he damn pleases in any way he likes. On the other hand, writing, like elections, copulation, sonatas, or a punch in the mouth, is *communication,* an absolute necessity to the very existence of human beings in every area, concrete or abstract, which may be defined as that performed by human beings which evokes response *in kind* from other human beings. Communication is a double-ended, transmitter-receiver phenomenon or it doesn't exist. And if it evokes a response not in kind ("what the hell does *that* mean?" instead of "well of course!") it exists but it is crippled. There is a fine line, and hazy, between following the use of an exotic intrusion with a definition, which can be damned insulting to a reader who does understand it, and throwing him something knobby and hard to hold without warning or subsequent explanation. Yes, a reader *should* do part of the work; the more he does the more he participates, and the more he is led to participate the better the story (and writer). On the other hand, he shouldn't be stopped, thrown out of the current in which the author has placed him, by such menaces to navigation, however apt. It comes down to an awareness of who's listening—to whom the communication is addressed—and what he deserves. He deserves a great deal, because he's at the other end of something which could not exist without him. Those of him

The Magic

(for he is many) who need pampering do *not* deserve it. Those who can take anything a really good author can throw at him are an author's joy—but always a small part of that multifaceted and very human entity. The Reader. There is always, for a resourceful writer, a way to maximize communication by means acceptable to a writer's arrogance; all he has to do is to think of it. In a writer less resourceful than Zelazny we readily forgive his inability to think of it, but this writer doesn't have that excuse. Which brings this comment down to its point: Roger Zelazny is a writer of such merit that one judges him by higher standards than those one uses on others—a cross he will bear for all his writing life. Happily the shoulders that bear it are demonstrably well-muscled.

The larger point, derived from this consideration of flaws, has to do with the kind of flaws they are. For in none of the things I have mentioned, nor in the ones I could, is a single one stemming from inability. Every single one is the product of growth, expansion, trial, passage, flux. There is nothing so frightening to be said about a writer (although some writers are not frightened by it) as the laudatory comment "finish." A perfectly faceted diamond is beautiful to behold, and is by its very existence proof of high skill and hard work; but it has nowhere to go, intrinsically, from there. A great tree reaches its ultimate "finish" when it is killed; and it may then become toothpicks or temples, but as a tree it is dead and gone. Only that which is in constant, day-by-day, cell-by-cell change is alive. And it is in this area that I have detected and increasingly feel a sense of awe in Zelazny's work, for he is young and already a giant; he has the habit of hard work and of learning, and shows no slightest sign of slowing down or of being diverted. I do not know him personally, but if I did, if I ever do, I would want more than anything else to convey to him the fact that he can and has evoked this awe—that the curve he has drawn with his early work can be extended into true greatness, and that if he follows his star as a writer all other things will come to him. If ever anything seems more important to him—he must know that it isn't. If ever anything diverts him from writing, he must know to the marrow that whatever it is or appears to be, it is a lesser thing than his gift. He gives no evidence to date that he has stopped growing or that he ever will.

Do you know how rare this is?

*

The four stories in this book, listed here by my own intensely personal (and therefore, to you, perhaps fallible) system of ascending excellence, are all of that wondrous species which makes me envy anyone who has not read them and is about to.

"The Doors of His Face, the Lamps of His Mouth" is all size and speed, which would be a good story if told purely in a write-what-happens, this-is-the-plot style, and which would also be a good story if it confined itself to what went on in the heads and in the hearts of its people, and which is a good story on both counts.

"The Furies" is a *tour de force,* the easy accomplishment of what most writers would consider impossible, and a few very good ones insuperably difficult. Seemingly with the back of his hand, he has created *milieu,* characters and a narrative goal as far out as anyone need go; he makes you believe it all the way, and walks off breathing easily leaving you gasping with a fable in your hands.

"The Graveyard Heart" is in that wonderful category which is, probably, science fiction's greatest gift to literature and to human beings: the "feedback" story, the "if this goes on" story; an extension of some facet of the current scene which carries you out and away to times and places you've never imagined because you can't; and when it's finished, you turn about and look at the thing he extended for you, in its here-and-now reality, sharing this very day and planet with you; and you know he's told you something, given you something you didn't have before, and that you will never look at this aspect of your world with quite the same eyes again.

"A Rose for Ecclesiastes" is one of the most important stories I have read—perhaps I should say it is one of the most memorable experiences I have ever had. It happens (well, I *told* you this was an intensely personal assignment of rank!) that this particular fable, with all its truly astonishing twists and turns, up to and most painfully including its wrenching denouement, is an agonizing analogy of my own experience; and this astronomically unlikely happenstance may well make it what it is to me and may not reach you quite as poignantly. If it does it will chop you up into dog meat. But as objective as I can be, which isn't very, I still feel safe in stating that it is one of the most beautifully written, skillfully composed and passionately expressed works of art to appear anywhere, ever.

*

Briefly, let me commend to your attention two novels by Roger Zelazny, *This Immortal* and *The Dream Master*, and sum up everything I have said here, and a good many things I have not said; sum up all the thoughts and feelings I hold concerning the works of Roger Zelazny, past and to come; sum up what has struck me at each of the peaks of all of his narratives, and without fail, so far, at that regretful moment when I have turned down the last page of any and all of them; sum up all this in one word, which is:

Grateful.

Theodore Sturgeon
Sherman Oaks, California. 1967

When Zelazny was Magic

by Darrell Schweitzer

I remember when Roger Zelazny was magic. This is not to say that he was ever anything but an accomplished, fine writer or that he ever lacked an audience, but there was a period, around 1964–1970, when he was *magic*, and every new story of his was an event. He was a tremendously variable writer too, so that each event was not like the past one. "He Who Shapes" serialized in *Amazing* was very special indeed, a mind-blower. Not at all like the novella "Damnation Alley" in *Galaxy* a couple years later. Not at all like "A Rose for Ecclesiastes" or "The Graveyard Heart."

I enter the scene in the spring of 1967. Probably the first Zelazny story I ever read was "This Mortal Mountain" in the March *IF*. I then read "Dawn," an excerpt from the forthcoming *Lord of Light*, in the April *F&SF*. Then came "The Man Who Loved the Faoli" in the June *Galaxy*. This last, I realized later, a particularly remarkable achievement for Zelazny. The story was written around a cover, a painting by Gray Morrow which showed rectangular-bodied, tentacled robots wading through a valley of dry bones beneath a strange sun. This was clearly a reject or leftover from the Ace Books printings of Neil R. Jones's Professor Jameson series. (The "robots" were the star-traveling Zoromes. The professor's brain was housed in one of them.) This orphaned painting was shuffled over to *Galaxy* and then a popular contributor was given the assignment of writing a story around it, as was a common editorial practice at the time. But where most writers would have just typed some squib, Zelazny wrote a story which seemed, to me at least, stunningly beautiful.

Zelazny was a name I learned to watch for.

I was a little short of fifteen in June of 1967. I remember writing an excited high-school paper (possibly a couple years later) about the works of Roger Zelazny. I don't think my English teacher was too thrilled. He tended to discourage any interest in popular or imaginative literature, particularly science fiction. But Zelazny was the first writer who made me aware of the possibilities of prose.

He had style.

This was, in science fiction fandom, the era of the New Wave Wars. We talked about "style" a lot. Zelazny was claimed by both sides, but he certainly had style.

It was easy to imitate.

Lots of short sentences.

Asterisk breaks.

*

And a flourish of something you hoped was "poetic."

I wrote Zelazny imitations. I even sold a couple. I picked up on the concept we see in "The Keys to December" and "The Graveyard Heart" about a pair of lovers who go on through the ages, out of sync with everybody else, living a few years (or days) every century. I did it with time-dilation. But of course the difference between a Zelazny imitation by an apprentice writer and a real Zelazny story is like the difference between a kid in a garage band trying to sound like the Beatles and the actual Beatles. About the same time I received a review copy of a book from Doubleday, *The Exile of Ellendon* by William Marden (1974) which was very clearly somebody else's attempt to write a Zelazny novel and published by Zelazny's own publisher presumably on the assumption that it would sell to the same audience. I don't blame Marden, certainly. He was no doubt as Zelazny-struck as I was.

Imitating Zelazny is easy to do.

But it won't be the real thing. Art conceals art, and all that.

What Zelazny did was considerably more complex and accomplished. Which does bring us back to the story I am supposed to be commenting on, "The Keys to December."

I read this one much later, either in the collection *The Doors of His Face, The Lamps of His Mouth* (1971) or in *New Worlds* as by that point I had mastered the art of acquiring used science fiction, even from overseas, and those paperback-sized, Compact Books *New Worlds* (early Moorcock issues) were easy to get. This story had no American periodical appearance, but Zelazny, as a "new wave" writer, was a regular in *New Worlds* in those days, before he was summarily drummed out in early 1968 (presumably for the crime of being too popular; you can't be a rebel underdog if you are successful) with a nasty, trashing review of *Lord of Light*, which signaled that he would never appear there again.

This is another story that makes language sing. Its prose jumps through hoops. The 300-word description of a planet gives us a hint of what Zelazny is capable of. The concept of this story could have come out of the 1950s. Think of the pantropy stories (collected as *The Seedling Stars*) of James Blish, or Poul Anderson's "Call Me Joe." Then it would have been about tough, not-quite human pioneers struggling to make it on a planet to which they had been adapted. There would have been a lot of technical detail. I can envision that Kelly Freas cover, from mid-'50s *Astounding*. Would the central moral dilemma of the story have been addressed in the 1950s in *Astounding*? Yes, probably. How about the religious aspect, with the hero becoming a god to the natives and (one gets a sense) almost enjoying it? Maybe, but probably not. That is something Philip José Farmer might have edged toward, but not in *Astounding*. (Farmer never wrote for *Astounding*.) But certainly none of those writers would have described "stands of windblasted stones like frozen music."

There are elements here we see elsewhere in Zelazny. The essentially alienated protagonist. The background of an interstellar capitalism that enables people or corporations to buy planets. Men who become gods. (Think of Francis Sandow in *Isle of the Dead*.) The myth elements are here, not in this case a replaying of something out of past Earth literature and religion, but a myth that is coming to being due to Jarry Dark's intervention with the natives. His combat with the bear-thing will surely be retold down the generations and become the stuff of epics. The death of Sanza will become a deep Mystery, possibly to be re-enacted in mysterious rites, millennia in the future. The reader may be at first disturbed by what the December group is doing. They are of course, the invaders from space, changing the planet to their liking, to the detriment of the natives. There is no overt slaughter. There doesn't need to be. But the invasion is more extreme than that described in H.G. Wells' *The War of the Worlds*. About this same time (1965) Thomas M. Disch imagined aliens completely transforming the Earth for their own purposes. He called it *The Genocides*.

That the Worldchange machines are forcing the native lifeforms to evolve sounds like a corporate excuse. That this actually happens is intriguing, and of course it triggers the final crisis. Zelazny has *not* overlooked the moral implications of what is going on. Not all science fiction is that thoughtful. I remember reading a story in *Analog* once, by Christopher Anvil ("The Royal Road," June 1968), in which the superior Earthmen induce the benighted natives to labor long and hard, at the cost of immeasurable suffering and death, to build a massive, completely useless structure. When it is complete, we are told this was for their own good, because it united them with a sense of purpose and prevented wars, or some such nonsense. Of course the paternalistic humans decided what was for the natives' own good. Vile.

Zelazny is better than that. His character has to take radical action, then assume responsibility for what is happening. His is a far more nuanced, ambiguous solution. Yes, of course, this is one of the countless science fictions stories that prefigure the 2009 film *Avatar*. Its moral balance is considerably less black and white.

But mostly what we notice about this story is the style. Zelazny's voice, then and later, was unique. His prose sang. It still sings.

The Magic

(October 1961—October 1967)

Ten Tales by Roger Zelazny

A Rose for Ecclesiastes

I

I was busy translating one of my *Madrigals Macabre* into Martian on the morning I was found acceptable. The intercom had buzzed briefly, and I dropped my pencil and flipped on the toggle in a single motion.

"Mister G," piped Morton's youthful contralto, "the old man says I should 'get hold of that damned conceited rhymer' right away, and send him to his cabin. Since there's only one damned conceited rhymer . . . "

"Let not ambition mock thy useful toil." I cut him off.

So, the Martians had finally made up their minds! I knocked an inch and a half of ash from a smoldering butt, and took my first drag since I had lit it. The entire month's anticipation tried hard to crowd itself into the moment, but could not quite make it. I was frightened to walk those forty feet and hear Emory say the words I already knew he would say; and that feeling elbowed the other one into the background.

So I finished the stanza I was translating before I got up.

It took only a moment to reach Emory's door. I knocked twice and opened it, just as he growled, "Come in."

"You wanted to see me?" I sat down quickly to save him the trouble of offering me a seat.

"That was fast. What did you do, run?"

I regarded his paternal discontent:

Little fatty flecks beneath pale eyes, thinning hair, and an Irish nose; a voice a decibel louder than anyone else's . . . .

Hamlet to Claudius: "I was working."

"Hah!" he snorted. "Come off it. No one's ever seen you do any of that stuff."

I shrugged my shoulders and started to rise.

The Magic

"If that's what you called me down here—"

"Sit down!"

He stood up. He walked around his desk. He hovered above me and glared down. (A hard trick, even when I'm in a low chair.)

"You are undoubtably the most antagonistic bastard I've ever had to work with!" he bellowed, like a belly-stung buffalo. "Why the hell don't you act like a human being sometime and surprise everybody? I'm willing to admit you're smart, maybe even a genius, but—oh, hell!" He made a heaving gesture with both hands and walked back to his chair.

"Betty has finally talked them into letting you go in." His voice was normal again. "They'll receive you this afternoon. Draw one of the jeepsters after lunch, and get down there."

"Okay," I said.

"That's all, then."

I nodded, got to my feet. My hand was on the doorknob when he said:

"I don't have to tell you how important this is. Don't treat them the way you treat us."

I closed the door behind me.

*

I don't remember what I had for lunch. I was nervous, but I knew instinctively that I wouldn't muff it. My Boston publishers expected a Martian Idyll, or at least a Saint-Exupéry job on space flight. The National Science Association wanted a complete report on the Rise and Fall of the Martian Empire.

They would both be pleased. I knew.

That's the reason everyone is jealous—why they hate me. I always come through, and I can come through better than anyone else.

I shoveled in a final anthill of slop, and made my way to our car barn. I drew one jeepster and headed it toward Tirellian.

Flames of sand, lousy with iron oxide, set fire to the buggy. They swarmed over the open top and bit through my scarf; they set to work pitting my goggles.

Roger Zelazny and Samuel R. Delany

The jeepster, swaying and panting like a little donkey I once rode through the Himalayas, kept kicking me in the seat of the pants. The Mountains of Tirellian shuffled their feet and moved toward me at a cockeyed angle.

Suddenly I was heading uphill, and I shifted gears to accommodate the engine's braying. Not like Gobi, not like the Great Southwestern Desert, I mused. Just red, just dead . . . without even a cactus.

I reached the crest of the hill, but I had raised too much dust to see what was ahead. It didn't matter, though; I have a head full of maps. I bore to the left and downhill, adjusting the throttle. A crosswind and solid ground beat down the fires. I felt like Ulysses in Malebolge—with a terza-rima speech in one hand and an eye out for Dante.

I rounded a rock pagoda and arrived.

Betty waved as I crunched to a halt, then jumped down.

"Hi," I choked, unwinding my scarf and shaking out a pound and a half of grit. "Like, where do I go and who do I see?"

She permitted herself a brief Germanic giggle—more at my starting a sentence with "like" than at my discomfort—then she started talking. (She is a top linguist, so a word from the Village Idiom still tickles her!)

I appreciate her precise, furry talk; informational, and all that. I had enough in the way of social pleasantries before me to last at least the rest of my life. I looked at her chocolate-bar eyes and perfect teeth, at her sun-bleached hair, close-cropped to the head (I hate blondes!), and decided that she was in love with me.

"Mr. Gallinger, the Matriarch is waiting inside to be introduced. She has consented to open the Temple records for your study." She paused here to pat her hair and squirm a little. Did my gaze make her nervous?

"They are religious documents, as well as their only history," she continued, "sort of like the Mahabharata. She expects you to observe certain rituals in handling them, like repeating the sacred words when you turn pages—she will teach you the system."

I nodded quickly, several times.

"Fine, let's go in."

The Magic

"Uh—" She paused. "Do not forget their Eleven Forms of Politeness and Degree. They take matters of form quite seriously—and do not get into any discussions over the equality of the sexes—"

"I know all about their taboos," I broke in. "Don't worry. I've lived in the Orient, remember?"

She dropped her eyes and seized my hand. I almost jerked it away.

"It will look better if I enter leading you."

I swallowed my comments, and followed her, like Samson in Gaza.

*

Inside, my last thought met with a strange correspondence. The Matriarch's quarters were a rather abstract version of what I might imagine the tents of the tribes of Israel to have been like. Abstract, I say, because it was all frescoed brick, peaked like a huge tent, with animal-skin representations like gray-blue scars, that looked as if they had been laid on the walls with a palette knife.

The Matriarch, M'Cwyie, was short, white-haired, fifty-ish, and dressed like a queen. With her rainbow of voluminous skirts she looked like an inverted punch bowl set atop a cushion.

Accepting my obeisances, she regarded me as an owl might a rabbit. The lids of those black, black eyes jumped upwards as she discovered my perfect accent. —The tape recorder Betty had carried on her interviews had done its part, and I knew the language reports from the first two expeditions, verbatim. I'm all hell when it comes to picking up accents.

"You are the poet?"

"Yes," I replied.

"Recite one of your poems, please."

"I'm sorry, but nothing short of a thorough translating job would do justice to your language and my poetry, and I don't know enough of your language yet."

"Oh?"

"But I've been making such translations for my own amusement, as an exercise in grammar," I continued. "I'd be honored to bring a few of them along one of the times that I come here."

"Yes. Do so."

Score one for me!

She turned to Betty.

"You may go now."

Betty muttered the parting formalities, gave me a strange sideways look, and was gone. She apparently had expected to stay and "assist" me. She wanted a piece of the glory, like everyone else. But I was the Schliemann at this Troy, and there would be only one name on the Association report!

M'Cwyie rose, and I noticed that she gained very little height by standing. But then I'm six-six and look like a poplar in October; thin, bright red on top, and towering above everyone else.

"Our records are very, very old," she began. "Betty says that your word for that age is 'millennia.'"

I nodded appreciatively.

"I'm very eager to see them."

"They are not here. We will have to go into the Temple—they may not be removed."

I was suddenly wary.

"You have no objections to my copying them, do you?"

"No. I see that you respect them, or your desire would not be so great."

"Excellent."

She seemed amused. I asked her what was so funny.

"The High Tongue may not be so easy for a foreigner to learn."

It came through fast.

No one on the first expedition had gotten this close. I had had no way of knowing that this was a double-language deal—a classical as well as a vulgar. I knew some of their Prakrit, now I had to learn all their Sanskrit.

"Ouch, and damn!"

"Pardon, please?"

43

The Magic

"It's non-translatable, M'Cwyie. But imagine yourself having to learn the High Tongue in a hurry, and you can guess at the sentiment."

She seemed amused again, and told me to remove my shoes.

She guided me through an alcove . . .

. . . and into a burst of Byzantine brilliance!

*

No Earthman had ever been in this room before, or I would have heard about it. Carter, the first expedition's linguist, with the help of one Mary Allen, M.D., had learned all the grammar and vocabulary that I knew while sitting cross-legged in the antechamber.

We had had no idea this existed. Greedily, I cast my eyes about. A highly sophisticated system of esthetics lay behind the decor. We would have to revise our entire estimation of Martian culture.

For one thing, the ceiling was vaulted and corbeled; for another, there were side-columns with reverse flutings; for another—oh hell! The place was big. Posh. You could never have guessed it from the shaggy outsides.

I bent forward to study the gilt filigree on a ceremonial table. M'Cwyie seemed a bit smug at my intentness, but I'd still have hated to play poker with her.

The table was loaded with books.

With my toe, I traced a mosaic on the floor.

"Is your entire city within this one building?"

"Yes, it goes far back into the mountain."

"I see," I said, seeing nothing.

I couldn't ask her for a conducted tour, yet.

She moved to a small stool by the table.

"Shall we begin your friendship with the High Tongue?"

I was trying to photograph the hall with my eyes, knowing I would have to get a camera in here, somehow, sooner or later. I tore my gaze from a statuette and nodded, hard.

"Yes, introduce me."

I sat down.

Roger Zelazny and Samuel R. Delany

For the next three weeks alphabet-bugs chased each other behind my eyelids whenever I tried to sleep. The sky was an unclouded pool of turquoise that rippled calligraphies whenever I swept my eyes across it. I drank quarts of coffee while I worked and mixed cocktails of Benzedrine and champagne for my coffee breaks.

M'Cwyie tutored me two hours every morning, and occasionally for another two in the evening. I spent an additional fourteen hours a day on my own, once I had gotten up sufficient momentum to go ahead alone.

And at night the elevator of time dropped me to its bottom floors . . .

*

I was six again, learning my Hebrew, Greek, Latin, and Aramaic. I was ten, sneaking peeks at the *Iliad*. When Daddy wasn't spreading hellfire brimstone, and brotherly love, he was teaching me to dig the Word, like in the original.

Lord! There are so many originals and so *many* words! When I was twelve I started pointing out the little differences between what he was preaching and what I was reading.

The fundamentalist vigor of his reply brooked no debate. It was worse than any beating. I kept my mouth shut after that and learned to appreciate Old Testament poetry.

–Lord, I am sorry! Daddy–Sir–I am sorry! –It couldn't be! It couldn't be . . . .

On the day the boy graduated from high school, with the French, German, Spanish, and Latin awards, Dad Gallinger had told his fourteen-year old, six-foot scarecrow of a son that he wanted him to enter the ministry. I remember how his son was evasive:

"Sir," he had said, "I'd sort of like to study on my own for a year or so, and then take pre-theology courses at some liberal arts university. I feel I'm still sort of young to try a seminary, straight off."

The Voice of God: "But you have the gift of tongues, my son. You can preach the Gospel in all the lands of Babel. You were born to be a missionary. You say you are young, but time is rushing by you like a whirlwind. Start early, and you will enjoy added years of service."

The Magic

The added years of service were so many added tails to the cat repeatedly laid on my back. I can't see his face now; I never can. Maybe it was because I was always afraid to look at it then.

And years later, when he was dead, and laid out, in black, amidst bouquets, amidst weeping congregationalists, amidst prayers, red faces, handkerchiefs, hands patting your shoulders, solemn faced comforters . . . I looked at him and did not recognize him.

We had met nine months before my birth, this stranger and I. He had never been cruel—stern, demanding, with contempt for everyone's shortcomings—but never cruel. He was also all that I had had of a mother. And brothers. And sisters. He had tolerated my three years at St. John's, possibly because of its name, never knowing how liberal and delightful a place it really was.

But I never knew him, and the man atop the catafalque demanded nothing now; I was free not to preach the Word. But now I wanted to, in a different way. I wanted to preach a word that I could never have voiced while he lived.

I did not return for my senior year in the fall. I had a small inheritance coming, and a bit of trouble getting control of it, since I was still under eighteen. But I managed.

It was Greenwich Village I finally settled upon.

Not telling any well-meaning parishioners my new address, I entered into a daily routine of writing poetry and teaching myself Japanese and Hindustani. I grew a fiery beard, drank espresso, and learned to play chess. I wanted to try a couple of the other paths to salvation.

After that, it was two years in India with the Old Peace Corps—which broke me of my Buddhism, and gave me my *Pipes of Krishna* lyrics and the Pulitzer they deserved.

Then back to the States for my degree, grad work in linguistics, and more prizes.

Then one day a ship went to Mars. The vessel settling in its New Mexico nest of fires contained a new language. —It was fantastic, exotic, and esthetically overpowering. After I had learned all there was to know about it, and written my book, I was famous in new circles:

"Go, Gallinger. Dip your bucket in the well, and bring us a drink of Mars. Go, learn another world—but remain aloof, rail at it gently like Auden—and hand us its soul in iambics."

And I came to the land where the sun is a tarnished penny, where the wind is a whip, where two moons play at hot rod games, and a hell of sand gives you incendiary itches whenever you look at it.

*

I rose from my twisting on the bunk and crossed the darkened cabin to a port. The desert was a carpet of endless orange, bulging from the sweepings of centuries beneath it.

"I, a stranger, unafraid—This is the land—I've got it made!"

I laughed.

I had the High Tongue by the tail already—or the roots, if you want your puns anatomical, as well as correct.

The High and Low tongues were not so dissimilar as they had first seemed. I had enough of the one to get me through the murkier parts of the other. I had the grammar and all the commoner irregular verbs down cold; the dictionary I was constructing grew by the day, like a tulip, and would bloom shortly. Every time I played the tapes the stem lengthened.

Now was the time to tax my ingenuity, to really drive the lessons home. I had purposely refrained from plunging into the major texts until I could do justice to them. I had been reading minor commentaries, bits of verse, fragments of history. And one thing had impressed me strongly in all that I read.

They wrote about concrete things: rock, sand, water, winds; and the tenor couched within these elemental symbols was fiercely pessimistic. It reminded me of some Buddhists texts, but even more so, I realized from my recent *recherches*, it was like parts of the Old Testament. Specifically, it reminded me of the Book of Ecclesiastes.

The Magic

That, then, would be it. The sentiment, as well as the vocabulary, was so similar that it would be a perfect exercise. Like putting Poe into French. I would never be a convert to the Way of Malann, but I would show them that an Earthman had once thought the same thoughts, felt similarly.

I switched on my desk lamp and sought King James amidst my books.

Vanity of vanities, saith the Preacher, vanity of vanities; all if vanity. What profit hath a man . . .

*

My progress seemed to startle M'Cwyie. She peered at me, like Sartre's Other, across the tabletop. I ran through a chapter in the Book of Locar. I didn't look up, but I could feel the tight net her eyes were working about my head, shoulders, and rapid hands. I turned another page.

Was she weighing the net, judging the size of the catch? And what for? The books said nothing of fishers on Mars. Especially of men. They said that some god named Malann had spat, or had done something disgusting (depending on the version you read), and that life had gotten underway as a disease in inorganic matter. They said that movement was its first law, its first law, and that the dance was the only legitimate reply to the inorganic . . . the dance's quality its justification,—fication . . . and love is a disease in organic matter—Inorganic matter?

I shook my head. I had almost been asleep.

"M'narra."

I stood and stretched. Her eyes outlined me greedily now. So I met them, and they dropped.

"I grow tired. I want to rest for awhile. I didn't sleep much last night."

She nodded, Earth's shorthand for "yes," as she had learned from me.

"You wish to relax, and see the explicitness of the doctrine of Locar in its fullness?"

"Pardon me?"

"You wish to see a Dance of Locar?"

"Oh." Their damned circuits of form and periphrasis here ran worse than the Korean! "Yes. Surely. Any time it's going to be done I'd be happy to watch."

I continued, "In the meantime, I've been meaning to ask you whether I might take some pictures—"

"Now is the time. Sit down. Rest. I will call the musicians."

She bustled out through a door I had never been past.

Well now, the dance was the highest art, according to Locar, not to mention Havelock Ellis, and I was about to see how their centuries-dead philosopher felt it should be conducted. I rubbed my eyes and snapped over, touching my toes a few times.

The blood began pounding in my head, and I sucked in a couple deep breaths. I bent again and there was a flurry of motion at the door.

To the trio who entered with M'Cwyie I must have looked as if I were searching for the marbles I had just lost, bent over like that.

I grinned weakly and straightened up, my face red from more than exertion. I hadn't expected them *that* quickly.

Suddenly I thought of Havelock Ellis again in his area of greatest popularity.

The little redheaded doll, wearing, sari-like, a diaphanous piece of the Martian sky, looked up in wonder—as a child at some colorful flag on a high pole.

"Hello," I said, or its equivalent.

She bowed before replying. Evidently I had been promoted in status.

"I shall dance," said the red wound in that pale, pale cameo, her face. Eyes, the color of dream and her dress, pulled away from mine.

She drifted to the center of the room.

Standing there, like a figure in an Etruscan frieze, she was either meditating or regarding the design on the floor.

Was the mosaic symbolic of something? I studied it. If it was, it eluded me; it would make an attractive bathroom floor or patio, but I couldn't see much in it beyond that.

49

The Magic

The other two were paint-spattered sparrows like M'Cwyie, in their middle years. One settled to the floor with a triple-stringed instrument faintly resembling a *samisen*. The other held a simple woodblock and two drumsticks.

M'Cwyie disdained her stool and was seated upon the floor before I realized it. I followed suit.

The *samisen* player was still tuning it up, so I leaned toward M'Cwyie.

"What is the dancer's name?"

"Braxa," she replied, without looking at me, and raised her left hand, slowly, which meant yes, and go ahead, and let it begin.

The stringed-thing throbbed like a toothache, and a tick-tocking, like ghosts of all the clocks they had never invented, sprang from the block.

Braxa was a statue, both hands raised to her face, elbows high and outspread.

The music became a metaphor for fire.

Crackle, purr, snap . . .

She did not move.

The hissing altered to splashes. The cadence slowed. It was water now, the most precious thing in the world, gurgling clear then green over mossy rocks.

Still she did not move.

Glissandos. A pause.

Then, so faint I could hardly be sure at first, the tremble of winds began. Softly, gently, sighing and halting, uncertain. A pause, a sob, then a repetition of the first statement, only louder,

Were my eyes completely bugged from my reading, or was Braxa actually trembling, all over, head to foot?

She was.

She began a microscopic swaying. A fraction of an inch right, then left. Her fingers opened like the petals of a flower, and I could see that her eyes were closed.

Her eyes opened. They were distant, glassy, looking through me and the walls. Her swaying became more pronounced, merged with the beat.

50

Roger Zelazny and Samuel R. Delany

The wind was sweeping in from the desert now, falling against Tirellian like waves on a dike. Her fingers moved, they were the gusts. Her arms, slow pendulums, descended, began a counter-movement.

The gale was coming now. She began an axial movement and her hands caught up with the rest of her body, only now her shoulders commenced to writhe out a figure-eight.

The wind! The wind, I say. O wild, enigmatic! O muse of St. John Perse!

The cyclone was twisting around those eyes, its still center. Her head was thrown back, but I knew there was no ceiling between her gaze, passive as Buddha's, and the unchanging skies. Only the two moons, perhaps, interrupted their slumber in that elemental Nirvana of uninhabited turquoise.

Years ago, I had seen the Devadasis in India, the street-dancers, spinning their colorful webs, drawing in the male insect. But Braxa was more than this: she was a Ramadjany, like those votaries of Rama, incarnation of Vishnu, who had given the dance to man: the sacred dancers.

The clicking was monotonously steady now; the whine of the strings made me think of the stinging rays of the sun, their heat stolen by the wind's halations; the blue was Sarasvati and Mary, and a girl named Laura. I heard a sitar from somewhere, watched this statue come to life, and inhaled a divine afflatus.

I was again Rimbaud with his hashish, Baudelaire with his laudanum, Poe, De Quincy, Wilde, Mallarme and Aleister Crowley. I was, for a fleeting second, my father in his dark pulpit and darker suit, the hymns and the organ's wheeze transmuted to bright wind.

She was a spun weather vane, a feathered crucifix hovering in the air, a clothes-line holding one bright garment lashed parallel to the ground. Her shoulder was bare now, and her right breast moved up and down like a moon in the sky, its red nipple appearing momentarily above a fold and vanishing again. The music was as formal as Job's argument with God. Her dance was God's reply.

The Magic

The music slowed, settled; it had been met, matched, answered. Her garment, as if alive, crept back into the more sedate folds it originally held.

She dropped low, lower, to the floor. Her head fell upon her raised knees. She did not move.

There was silence.

*

I realized, from the ache across my shoulders, how tensely I had been sitting. My armpits were wet. Rivulets had been running down my sides. What did one do now? Applaud?

I sought M'Cwyie from the corner of my eye. She raised her right hand.

As if by telepathy the girl shuddered all over and stood. The musicians also rose. So did M'Cwyie.

I got to my feet, with a Charley Horse in my left leg, and said, "It was beautiful," inane as that sounds.

I received three different High Forms of "thank you."

There was a flurry of color and I was alone again with M'Cwyie.

"That is the one hundred-seventeenth of the two thousand, two hundred-twenty-four dances of Locar."

I looked down at her.

"Whether Locar was right or wrong, he worked out a fine reply to the inorganic."

She smiled.

"Are the dances of your world like this?"

"Some of them are similar. I was reminded of them as I watched Braxa—but I've never seen anything exactly like hers."

"She is good," M'Cwyie said. "She knows all the dances."

A hint of her earlier expression which had troubled me . . .

It was gone in an instant.

"I must tend my duties now." She moved to the table and closed the books. "M'narra."

"Good-bye." I slipped into my boots.

"Good-bye, Gallinger."

Roger Zelazny and Samuel R. Delany

I walked out the door, mounted the jeepster, and roared across the evening into night, my wings of risen desert flapping slowly behind me.

II

I had just closed the door behind Betty, after a brief grammar session, when I heard the voices in the hall. My vent was opened a fraction, so I stood there and eavesdropped:

Morton's fruity treble: "Guess what? He said 'hello' to me awhile ago."

"Hmmph!" Emory's elephant lungs exploded. "Either he's slipping, or you were standing in his way and he wanted you to move."

"Probably didn't recognize me. I don't think he sleeps any more, now he has that language to play with. I had night watch last week, and every night I passed his door at 0300—I always heard that recorder going. At 0500 when I got off, he was still at it."

"The guy *is* working hard," Emory admitted, grudgingly. "In fact, I think he's taking some kind of dope to keep awake. He looks sort of glassy-eyed these days. Maybe that's natural for a poet, though."

Betty had been standing there, because she broke in then:

"Regardless of what you think of him, it's going to take me at least a year to learn what he's picked up in three weeks. And I'm just a linguist, not a poet."

Morton must have been nursing a crush on her bovine charms. It's the only reason I can think of for his dropping his guns to say what he did.

"I took a course in modern poetry when I was back at the university," he began. "We read six authors—Yeats, Pound, Eliot, Crane, Stevens, and Gallinger—and on the last day of the semester, when the prof was feeling a little rhetorical, he said, 'These six names are written on the century, and all the gates of criticism and hell shall not prevail on them.'

"Myself," he continued, "I thought his *Pipes of Krishna* and his *Madrigals* were great. I was honored to be chosen for an expedition he was going on.

"I think he's spoken two dozen words to me since I met him," he finished.

The Magic

The Defense: "Did it ever occur to you," Betty said, "that he might be tremendously self-conscious about his appearance? He was also a precocious child, and probably never even had school friends. He's sensitive and very introverted."

"Sensitive? Self-conscious?" Emory choked and gagged. "The man is as proud as Lucifer, and he's a walking insult machine. You press a button like 'Hello' or 'Nice day' and he thumbs his nose at you. He's got it down to a reflex."

They muttered a few other pleasantries and drifted away.

Well bless you, Morton boy. You little pimple-faced, Ivy-bred connoisseur! I've never taken a course in my poetry, but I'm glad someone said that. The Gates of Hell. Well now! Maybe Daddy's prayers got heard somewhere, and I am a missionary, after all!

Only . . .

. . . Only a missionary needs something to convert people *to*. I have my private system of esthetics, and I suppose it oozes an ethical by-product somewhere. But if I ever had anything to preach, really, even in my poems, I wouldn't care to preach it to such low-lifes as you. If you think I'm a slob, I'm also a snob, and there's no room for you in my Heaven—it's a private place, where Swift, Shaw, and Petronius Arbiter come to dinner.

And oh, the feasts we have! The Trimalchios, the Emorys we dissect!

We finish you with the soup, Morton!

*

I turned and settled at my desk. I wanted to write something. Ecclesiastes could take a night off. I wanted to write a poem, a poem about the one hundred-seventeenth dance of Locar; about a rose following the light, traced by the wind, sick, like Blake's rose, dying . . .

I found a pencil and began.

When I had finished I was pleased. It wasn't great—at least, it was no greater than it needed to be—High Martian not being my strongest tongue. I groped, and put it into English, with partial rhymes. Maybe I'd stick it in my next book. I called it *Braxa*:

Roger Zelazny and Samuel R. Delany

In a land of wind and red,
where the icy evening of Time
freezes milk in the breasts of Life,
as two moons overhead—
cat and dog in alleyways of dream—
scratch and scramble agelessly my flight . . .
This final flower turns a burning head.

I put it away and found some phenobarbitol. I was suddenly tired.

*

When I showed my poem to M'Cwyie the next day, she read it through several times, very slowly.

"It is lovely," she said. "But you used three words from your own language. 'Cat' and 'dog,' I assume, are two small animals with a hereditary hatred for one another. But what is 'flower?'"

"Oh," I said. "I've never come across your word for 'flower,' but I was actually thinking of an Earth flower, the rose."

"What is it like?"

"Well, its petals are generally bright red. That's what I meant, on one level, by 'burning heads.' I also wanted it to imply fever, though, and red hair, and the fire of life. The rose, itself, has a thorny stem, green leaves, and a distinct, pleasing aroma."

"I wish I could see one."

"I suppose it could be arranged. I'll check."

"Do it, please. You are a—" She used the word for "prophet," or religious poet, like Isaias or Locar. "—and your poem is inspired. I shall tell Braxa of it."

I declined the nomination, but felt flattered.

The Magic

This, then, I decided, was the strategic day, the day on which to ask whether I might bring in the microfilm machine and the camera. I wanted to copy all their texts, I explained, and I couldn't write fast enough to do it.

She surprised me by agreeing immediately. But she bowled me over with her invitation.

"Would you like to come and stay here while you do this thing? Then you can work night and day, any time you want—except when the Temple is being used, of course."

I bowed.

"I should be honored."

"Good. Bring your machines when you want, and I will show you a room."

"Will this afternoon be all right?"

"Certainly."

"Then I will go now and get things ready. Until this afternoon . . . "

"Good-bye."

*

I anticipated a little trouble from Emory, but not much. Everyone back at the ship was anxious to see the Martians, poke needles in the Martians, ask them about Martian climate, diseases, soil chemistry, politics, and mushrooms (our botanist was a fungus nut, but a reasonably good guy)—and only four or five had actually gotten to see them. The crew had been spending most of its time excavating dead cities and their acropolises. We played the game by strict rules, and the natives were as fiercely insular as the nineteenth-century Japanese. I figured I would meet with little resistance, and I figured right.

In fact, I got the distinct impression that everyone was happy to see me move out.

I stopped in the hydroponics room to speak with our mushroom master.

"Hi, Kane. Grow any toadstools in the sand yet?"

He sniffed. He always sniffs. Maybe he's allergic to plants.

"Hello, Gallinger. No, I haven't had any success with toadstools, but look behind the car barn next time you're out there. I've got a few cacti going."

"Great," I observed. Doc Kane was about my only friend aboard, not counting Betty.

"Say, I came down to ask you a favor."

"Name it."

"I want a rose."

"A what?"

"A rose. You know, a nice red American Beauty job—thorns, pretty smelling—"

"I don't think it will take in this soil. *Sniff, sniff.*"

"No, you don't understand. I don't want to plant it, I just want the flower."

"I'd have to use the tanks." He scratched his hairless dome. "It would take at least three months to get you flowers, even under forced growth."

"Will you do it?"

"Sure, if you don't mind the wait."

"Not at all. In fact, three months will just make it before we leave." I looked about at the pools of crawling slime, at the trays of shoots. "—I'm moving up to Tirellian today, but I'll be in and out all the time. I'll be here when it blooms."

"Moving up there, eh? Moore said they're an in-group."

"I guess I'm 'in' then."

"Looks that way—I still don't see how you learned their language, though. Of course, I had trouble with French and German for my Ph.D, but last week I heard Betty demonstrate it at lunch. It just sounds like a lot of weird noises. She says speaking it is like working a *Times* crossword and trying to imitate birdcalls at the same time."

I laughed, and took the cigarette he offered me.

"It's complicated," I acknowledged. "But, well, it's as if you suddenly came across a whole new class of mycetae here—you'd dream about it at night."

His eyes were gleaming.

"Wouldn't that be something! I might, yet, you know."

"Maybe you will."

He chuckled as we walked to the door.

The Magic

"I'll start your roses tonight. Take it easy down there."

"You bet. Thanks."

Like I said, a fungus nut, but a fairly good guy.

*

My quarters in the Citadel of Tirellian were directly adjacent to the Temple, on the inward side and slightly to the left. They were a considerable improvement over my cramped cabin, and I was pleased that Martian culture had progressed sufficiently to discover the desirability of the mattress over the pallet. Also, the bed was long enough to accommodate me, which was surprising.

So I unpacked and took sixteen 35 mm. shots of the Temple, before starting on the books.

I took 'stats until I was sick of turning pages without knowing what they said. So I started translating a work of history.

"Lo. In the thirty-seventh year of the Process of Cillen the rains came, which gave way to rejoicing, for it was a rare and untoward occurrence, and commonly construed a blessing.

"But it was not the life-giving semen of Malann which fell from the heavens. It was the blood of the universe, spurting from an artery. And the last days were upon us. The final dance was to begin.

"The rains brought the plague that does not kill, and the last passes of Locar began with their drumming . . . . "

I asked myself what the hell Tamur meant, for he was an historian and supposedly committed to fact. This was not their Apocalypse.

Unless they could be one and the same . . . ?

Why not? I mused. Tirellian's handful of people were the remnant of what had obviously once been a highly developed culture. They had had wars, but no holocausts; science, but little technology. A plague, a plague that did not kill . . . ? Could that have done it? How, if it wasn't fatal?

I read on, but the nature of the plague was not discussed. I turned pages, skipped ahead, and drew a blank.

M'Cwyie! M'Cwyie! When I want to question you most, you are not around!

Would it be a *faux pas* to go looking for her? Yes, I decided. I was restricted to the rooms I had been shown, that had been an implicit understanding. I would have to wait to find out.

So I cursed long and loud, in many languages, doubtless burning Malann's sacred ears, there in his Temple.

He did not see fit to strike me dead, so I decided to call it a day and hit the sack.

*

I must have been asleep for several hours when Braxa entered my room with a tiny lamp. She dragged me awake by tugging at my pajama sleeve.

I said hello. Thinking back, there is not much else I could have said.

"Hello."

"I have come," she said, "to hear the poem."

"What poem?"

"Yours."

"Oh."

I yawned, sat up, and did things people usually do when awakened in the middle of the night to read poetry.

"That is very kind of you, but isn't the hour a trifle awkward?"

"I don't mind," she said.

Someday I am going to write an article for the *Journal of Semantics*, called "Tone of Voice: An Insufficient Vehicle for Irony."

However, I was awake, so I grabbed my robe.

"What sort of animal is that? she asked, pointing at the silk dragon on my lapel.

"Mythical," I replied. "Now look, it's late. I am tired. I have much to do in the morning. And M'Cwyie just might get the wrong idea if she learns you were here."

"Wrong idea?"

"You know damned well what I mean!" It was the first time I had had an opportunity to use Martian profanity, and it failed.

"No," she said, "I do not know."

The Magic

She seemed frightened, like a puppy dog being scolded without knowing what it has done wrong.

I softened. Her red cloak matched her hair and lips so perfectly, and those lips were trembling.

"Here now, I didn't mean to upset you. On my world there are certain, uh, mores, concerning people of different sex alone together in bedrooms, and not allied by marriage . . . . Um, I mean, you see what I mean?"

"No."

They were jade, her eyes.

"Well, it's sort of . . . Well, it's sex, that's what it is."

A light was switched on in those jade eyes.

"Oh, you mean having children!"

"Yes. That's it! Exactly!"

She laughed. It was the first time I had heard laughter in Tirellian. It sounded like a violinist striking his high strings with the bow, in short little chops. It was not an altogether pleasant thing to hear, especially because she laughed too long.

When she had finished she moved closer.

"I remember, now," she said. "We used to have such rules. Half a Process ago, when I was a child, we had such rules. But" —she looked as if she were ready to laugh again—"there is no need for them now."

My mind moved like a tape recorder playing at triple speed.

Half a Process! HalfaProcessa-ProcessaProcess! No! Yes! Half a Process was two hundred-forty-three years, roughly speaking!

—Time enough to learn the 2224 dances of Locar.

—Time enough to grow old, if you were human.

—Earth-style human, I mean.

I looked at her again, pale as the white queen in an ivory chess set.

She was human, I'd stake my soul—alive, normal, healthy. I'd stake my life—woman, my body . . .

But she was two and a half centuries old, which made M'Cwyie Methusala's grandma. It flattered me to think of their repeated complimenting of my skills, as linguist, as poet. These superior beings!

But what did she mean "there is no such need for them now"? Why the near-hysteria? Why all those funny looks I'd been getting from M'Cwyie?

I suddenly knew I was close to something important, besides a beautiful girl.

"Tell me," I said, in my Casual Voice, "did it have anything to do with 'the plague that does not kill,' of which Tamur wrote?"

"Yes," she replied, "the children born after the Rains could have no children of their own, and—"

"And what?" I was leaning forward, memory set at "record."

"—and the men had no desire to get any."

I sagged backward against the bedpost. Racial sterility, masculine impotence, following phenomenal weather. Had some vagabond cloud of radioactive junk from God knows where penetrated their weak atmosphere one day? One day long before Shiaparelli saw the canals, mythical as my dragon, before those "canals" had given rise to some correct guesses for all the wrong reasons, had Braxa been alive, dancing, here—damned in the womb since blind Milton had written of another paradise, equally lost?

I found a cigarette. Good thing I had thought to bring ashtrays. Mars had never had a tobacco industry either. Or booze. The ascetics I had met in India had been Dionysiac compared to this.

"What is that tube of fire?"

"A cigarette. Want one?"

"Yes, please."

She sat beside me, and I lighted it for her.

"It irritates the nose."

"Yes. Draw some into your lungs, hold it there, and exhale."

A moment passed.

"Ooh," she said.

A pause, then, "Is it sacred?"

The Magic

"No, it's nicotine," I answered, "a very *ersatz* form of divinity."
Another pause.

"Please don't ask me to translate 'ersatz.'"

"I won't. I get this feeling sometimes when I dance."

"It will pass in a moment."

"Tell me your poem now."

An idea hit me.

"Wait a minute," I said. "I may have something better."

I got up and rummaged through my notebooks, then I returned and sat beside her.

"These are the first three chapters of the Book of Ecclesiastes," I explained. "It is very similar to your own sacred books."

I started reading.

I got through eleven verses before she cried out, "Please don't read that! Tell me one of yours!"

I stopped and tossed the notebook onto a nearby table. She was shaking, not as she had quivered that day she danced as the wind, but with the jitter of unshed tears. She held her cigarette awkwardly, like a pencil. Clumsily, I put my arm about her shoulders.

"He is so sad," she said, "like all the others."

So I twisted my mind like a bright ribbon, folded it, and tied the crazy Christmas knots I love so well. From German to Martian, with love, I did an impromptu paraphrasal of a poem about a Spanish dancer. I thought it would please her. I was right.

"Ooh," she said again. "Did you write that?"

"No, it's by a better man than I."

"I don't believe it. You wrote it yourself."

"No, a man named Rilke did."

"But you brought it across to my language. Light another match, so I can see how she danced."

I did.

"The fires of forever," she mused, "and she stamped them out, 'with small, firm feet.' I wish I could dance like that."

"You're better than any Gypsy," I laughed, blowing it out.

"No, I'm not. I couldn't do that."

"Do you want me to dance for you?"

Her cigarette was burning down, so I removed it from her fingers and put it out, along with my own.

"No," I said. "Go to bed."

She smiled, and before I realized it, had unclasped the fold of red at her shoulder.

And everything fell away.

And I swallowed, with some difficulty.

"All right," she said.

So I kissed her, as the breath of fallen cloth extinguished the lamp.

III

The days were like Shelley's leaves: yellow, red, brown, whipped in bright gusts by the west wind. They swirled past me with the rattle of microfilm. Almost all of the books were recorded now. It would take scholars years to get through them, to properly assess their value. Mars was locked in my desk.

Ecclesiastes, abandoned and returned to a dozen times, was almost ready to speak in the High Tongue.

I whistled when I wasn't in the Temple. I wrote reams of poetry I would have been ashamed of before. Evenings I would walk with Braxa, across the dunes or up into the mountains. Sometimes she would dance for me; and I would read something long, and in dactylic hexameter. She still thought I was Rilke, and I almost kidded myself into believing it. Here I was, staying at the Caste Duino, writing his *Elegies*.

> . . . *It is strange to inhabit the Earth no more,*
> *to use no longer customs scarce acquired,*
> *nor interpret roses . . .*

The Magic

No! Never interpret roses! Don't. Smell them (sniff, Kane!), pick them, enjoy them. Live in the moment. Hold to it tightly. But charge not the gods to explain. So fast the leaves go by, are blown . . .

And no one ever noticed us. Or cared.

Laura. Laura and Braxa. They rhyme, you know, with a bit of clash. Tall, cool, and blonde was she (I hate blondes!), and Daddy had turned me inside out, like a pocket, and I thought she could fill me again. But the big, beat work-slinger, with Judas-beard and dog-trust in his eyes, oh, he had been a fine decoration at her parties. And that was all.

How the machine cursed me in the Temple! It blasphemed Malann and Gallinger. And the wild west wind went by and something was not far behind.

The last days were upon us.

*

A day went by and I did not see Braxa, and a night.

And a second. And a third.

I was half-mad. I hadn't realized how close we had become, how important she had been. With the dumb assurance of presence, I had fought against questioning the roses.

I had to ask. I didn't want to, but I had no choice.

"Where is she, M'Cwyie? Where is Braxa?"

"She is gone," she said.

"Where?"

"I do not know."

I looked at those devil-bird eyes. Anathema maranatha rose to my lips.

"I must know."

She looked through me.

"She has left us. She is gone. Up into the hills, I suppose. Or the desert. It does not matter. What does anything matter? The dance draws itself to a close. The Temple will soon be empty."

"Why? Why did she leave?"

"I do not know."

"I must see her again. We lift off in a matter of days."

"I am sorry, Gallinger."

"So am I," I said, and slammed shut a book without saying "m'narra."

I stood up.

"I will find her."

I left the Temple. M'Cwyie was a seated statue. My boots were still where I had left them.

*

All day I roared up and down the dunes, going nowhere. To the crew of the *Aspic* I must have looked like a sandstorm, all by myself. Finally, I had to return for more fuel.

Emory came stalking out.

"Okay, make it good. You look like the abominable dust man. Why the rodeo?"

"Why, I, uh, lost something."

"In the middle of the desert? Was it one of your sonnets? They're the only thing I can think of that you'd make such a fuss over."

"No, dammit! It was something personal."

George had finished filling the tank. I started to mount the jeepster again.

"Hold on there!" he grabbed my arm.

"You're not going back until you tell me what this is all about."

I could have broken his grip, but then he could order me dragged back by the heels, and quite a few people would enjoy doing the dragging. So I forced myself to speak slowly, softly:

"It's simply that I lost my watch. My mother gave it to me and it's a family heirloom. I want to find it before we leave."

"You sure it's not in your cabin, or down in Tirellian?"

"I've already checked."

"Maybe somebody hid it to irritate you. You know you're not the most popular guy around."

I shook my head.

The Magic

"I thought of that. But I always carry it in my right pocket. I think it might have bounced out going over the dunes."

He narrowed his eyes.

"I remember reading on a book jacket that your mother died when you were born."

"That's right," I said, biting my tongue. "The watch belonged to her father and she wanted me to have it. My father kept it for me."

"Hmph!" he snorted. "That's a pretty strange way to look for a watch, riding up and down in a jeepster."

"I could see the light shining off it that way," I offered, lamely.

"Well, it's starting to get dark," he observed. "No sense looking any more today.

"Throw a dust sheet over the jeepster," he directed a mechanic.

He patted my arm.

"Come on in and get a shower, and something to eat. You look as if you could use both."

Little fatty flecks beneath pale eyes, thinning hair, and an Irish nose; a voice a decibel louder than anyone else's . . .

His only qualification for leadership!

I stood there, hating him. Claudius! If only this were the fifth act!

But suddenly the idea of a shower, and food, came through to me. I could use both badly. If I insisted on hurrying back immediately I might arouse more suspicion.

So I brushed some sand from my sleeve.

"You're right. That sounds like a good idea."

"Come on, we'll eat in my cabin."

The shower was a blessing, clean khakis were the grace of God, and the food smelled like Heaven.

"Smells pretty good," I said.

We hacked up our steaks in silence. When we got to the dessert and coffee he suggested:

"Why don't you take the night off? Stay here and get some sleep."

I shook my head.

"I'm pretty busy. Finishing up. There's not much time left."

"A couple of days ago you said you were almost finished."

"Almost, but not quite."

"You also said they're be holding a service in the Temple tonight."

"That's right. I'm going to work in my room."

He shrugged his shoulders.

Finally, he said, "Gallinger," and I looked up because my name means trouble.

"It shouldn't be any of my business," he said, "but it is. Betty says you have a girl down there."

There was no question mark. It was a statement hanging in the air. Waiting.

Betty, you're a bitch. You're a cow and a bitch. And a jealous one, at that. Why didn't you keep your nose where it belonged, shut your eyes? You mouth?

"So?" I said, a statement with a question mark.

"So," he answered it, "it is my duty, as head of this expedition, to see that relations with the natives are carried on in a friendly, and diplomatic, manner."

"You speak of them," I said, "as though they are aborigines. Nothing could be further from the truth."

I rose.

"When my papers are published everyone on Earth will know that truth. I'll tell them things Doctor Moore never even guessed at. I'll tell the tragedy of a doomed race, waiting for death, resigned and disinterested. I'll tell why, and it will break hard, scholarly hearts. I'll write about it, and they will give me more prizes, and this time I won't want them.

"My God!" I exclaimed. "They had a culture when our ancestors were clubbing the saber-tooth and finding out how fire works!"

"*Do* you have a girl down there?"

The Magic

"Yes!" I said. Yes, *Claudius! Yes, Daddy! Yes, Emory!* "I do. but I'm going to let you in on a scholarly scoop now. They're already dead. They're sterile. In one more generation there won't be any Martians."

I paused, then added, "Except in my papers, except on a few pieces of microfilm and tape. And in some poems, about a girl who did give a damn and could only bitch about the unfairness of it all by dancing."

"Oh," he said.

After awhile:

"You *have* been behaving differently these past couple months. You've even been downright civil on occasion, you know. I couldn't help wondering what was happening. I didn't know anything mattered that strongly to you."

I bowed my head.

"Is she the reason you were racing around the desert?"

I nodded.

"Why?"

I looked up.

"Because she's out there, somewhere. I don't know where, or why. And I've got to find her before we go."

"Oh," he said again.

Then he leaned back, opened a drawer, and took out something wrapped in a towel. He unwound it. A framed photo of a woman lay on the table.

"My wife," he said.

It was an attractive face, with big, almond eyes.

"I'm a Navy man, you know," he began. "Young officer once. Met her in Japan."

"Where I come from it wasn't considered right to marry into another race, so we never did. But she was my wife. When she died I was on the other side of the world. They took my children, and I've never seen them since. I couldn't learn what orphanage, what home, they were put into. That was long ago. Very few people know about it."

"I'm sorry," I said.

"Don't be. Forget it. But"—he shifted in his chair and looked at me—"if you do want to take her back with you—do it. It'll mean my neck, but I'm too old to ever head another expedition like this one. So go ahead."

He gulped cold coffee.

"Get your jeepster."

He swiveled the chair around.

I tried to say "thank you" twice, but I couldn't. So I got up and walked out.

"Sayonara, and all that," he muttered behind me.

*

"Here it is, Gallinger!" I heard a shout.

I turned on my heel and looked back up the ramp.

"Kane!"

He was limned in the port, shadow against light, but I had heard him sniff.

I returned the few steps.

"Here what is?"

"Your rose."

He produced a plastic container, divided internally. The lower half was filled with liquid. The stem ran down into it. The other half, a glass of claret in this horrible night, was a large, newly opened rose.

"Thank you," I said, tucking it in my jacket.

"Going back to Tirellian, eh?"

"Yes."

"I saw you come aboard, so I got it ready. Just missed you at the Captain's cabin. He was busy. Hollered out that I could catch you at the barns."

"Thanks again."

"It's chemically treated. It will stay in bloom for weeks."

I nodded. I was gone.

*

Up into the mountains now. Far. Far. The sky was a bucket of ice in which no moons floated. The going became steeper, and the little donkey protested. I whipped him with the throttle and went on. Up. Up. I spotted a green, unwinking star, and felt a lump in my throat. The encased rose beat against

69

The Magic

my chest like an extra heart. The donkey brayed, long and loudly, then began to cough. I lashed him some more and he died.

I threw the emergency brake on and got out. I began to walk.

So cold, so cold it grows. Up here. At night? Why? Why did she do it? Why flee the campfire when night comes on?

And I was up, down, around, and through every chasm, gorge, and pass, with my long-legged strides and an ease of movement never known on Earth.

Barely two days remain, my love, and thou hast forsaken me. Why?

I crawled under overhangs. I leaped over ridges. I scraped my knees, an elbow. I heard my jacket tear.

No answer, Malann? Do you really hate your people this much? Then I'll try someone else. Vishnu, you're the Preserver. Preserve her, please! Let me find her.

Jehovah?

Adonis? Osiris? Thammuz? Manitou? Legba? Where is she?

I ranged far and high, and I slipped.

Stones ground underfoot and I dangled over an edge. My fingers so cold. It was hard to grip the rock.

I looked down.

Twelve feet or so. I let go and dropped, landed rolling.

Then I heard her scream.

*

I lay there, not moving, looking up. Against the night, above, she called.

"Gallinger!"

I lay still.

"Gallinger!"

And she was gone.

I heard stones rattle and knew she was coming down some path to the right of me.

I jumped up and ducked into the shadow of a boulder.

She rounded a cut-off, and picked her way, uncertainly, through the stones.

"Gallinger?"

I stepped out and seized her by the shoulders.

"Braxa."

She screamed again, then began to cry, crowding against me. It was the first time I had ever heard her cry.

"Why?" I asked. "Why?"

But she only clung to me and sobbed.

Finally, "I thought you had killed yourself."

"Maybe I would have," I said. "Why did you leave Tirellian? And me?"

"Didn't M'Cwyie tell you? Didn't you guess?"

"I didn't guess, and M'Cwyie said she didn't know."

"Then she lied. She knows."

"What? What is it she knows?"

She shook all over, then was silent for a long time. I realized suddenly that she was wearing only her flimsy dancer's costume. I pushed her from me, took off my jacket, and put it about her shoulders.

"Great Malann!" I cried. "You'll freeze to death!"

"No," she said, "I won't."

I was transferring the rose-case to my pocket.

"What is that?" she asked.

"A rose," I answered. "You can't make it out in the dark. I once compared you to one. Remember?"

"Yes—Yes. May I carry it?"

"Sure." I stuck it in the jacket pocket.

"Well? I'm still waiting for an explanation."

"You really do not know?" she asked.

"No!"

"When the Rains came," she said, "apparently only our men were affected, which was enough . . . . Because I—wasn't—affected—apparently—"

"Oh," I said. "Oh."

We stood there, and I thought.

"Well, why did you run? What's wrong with being pregnant on Mars? Tamur was mistaken. Your people can live again."

71

She laughed, again that wild violin played by a Paginini gone mad. I stopped her before it went too far.

"How?" she finally asked, rubbing her cheek.

"Your people can live longer than ours. If our child is normal it will mean our races can intermarry. There must still be other fertile women of your race. Why not?"

"You have read the Book of Locar," she said, "and yet you ask me that? Death was decided, voted upon, and passed, shortly after it appeared in this form. But long before, before the followers of Locar knew. They decided it long ago. 'We have done all things,' they said, 'we have seen all things, we have heard and felt all things. The dance was good. Now let it end.'"

"You can't believe that."

"What I believe does not matter," she replied. "M'Cwyie and the Mothers have decided we must die. Their very title is now a mockery, but their decisions will be upheld. There is only one prophecy left, and it is mistaken. We will die."

"No," I said.

"What, then?"

"Come back with me, to Earth."

"No."

"All right, then. Come with me now."

"Where?"

"Back to Tirellian. I'm going to talk to the Mothers."

"You can't! There is a Ceremony tonight!"

I laughed.

"A Ceremony for a god who knocks you down, and then kicks you in the teeth?"

"He is still Malann," she answered. "We are still his people."

"You and my father would have gotten along fine," I snarled. "But I am going, and you are coming with me, even if I have to carry you—and I'm bigger than you are."

"But you are not bigger than Ontro."

"Who the hell is Ontro?"

"He will stop you, Gallinger. He is the Fist of Malann."

IV

I scudded the jeepster to a halt in front of the only entrance I knew, M'Cwyie's. Braxa, who had seen the rose in a headlamp, now cradled it in her lap, like our child, and said nothing. There was a passive, lovely look on her face.

"Are they in the Temple now?" I wanted to know.

The Madonna-expression did not change. I repeated the question. She stirred.

"Yes," she said, from a distance, "but you cannot go in."

"We'll see."

I circled and helped her down.

I led her by the hand, and she moved as if in a trance. In the light of the new-risen moon, her eyes looked as they had the day I had met her, when she had danced. I snapped my fingers. Nothing happened.

So I pushed the door open and led her in. The room was half-lighted.

And she screamed for the third time that evening:

"Do not harm him, Ontro! It is Gallinger!"

I had never seen a Martian man before, only women. So I had no way of knowing whether he was a freak, though I suspected it strongly.

I looked up at him.

His half-naked body was covered with moles and swellings. Gland trouble, I guessed.

I had thought I was the tallest man on the planet, but he was seven feet tall and overweight. Now I knew where my giant bed had come from!

"Go back," he said. "She may enter. You may not."

"I must get my books and things."

He raised a huge left arm. I followed it. All my belonging lay neatly stacked in the corner.

"I must go in. I must talk with M'Cwyie and the Mothers."

The Magic

"You may not."

"The lives of your people depend on it."

"Go back," he boomed. "Go home to *your* people, Gallinger. Leave *us!*"

My name sounded so different on his lips, like someone else's. How old was he? I wondered. Three hundred? Four? Had he been a Temple guardian all his life? Why? Who was there to guard against? I didn't like the way he moved. I had seen men who moved like that before.

"Go back," he repeated.

If they had refined their martial arts as far as they had their dances, or worse yet, if their fighting arts were a part of the dance, I was in for trouble.

"Go on in," I said to Braxa. "Give the rose to M'Cwyie. Tell her that I sent it. Tell her I'll be there shortly."

"I will do as you ask. Remember me on Earth, Gallinger. Good-bye."

I did not answer her, and she walked past Ontro and into the next room, bearing her rose.

"Now will you leave?" he asked. "If you like, I will tell her that we fought and you almost beat me, but I knocked you unconscious and carried you back to your ship."

"No," I said, "either I go around you or go over you, but I am going through."

He dropped into a crouch, arms extended.

"It is a sin to lay hands on a holy man," he rumbled, "but I will stop you, Gallinger."

My memory was a fogged window, suddenly exposed to fresh air. Things cleared. I looked back six years.

I was a student of the Oriental Languages at the University of Tokyo. It was my twice-weekly night of recreation. I stood in a thirty-foot circle in the Kodokan, the *judogi* lashed about my high hips by a brown belt. I was *Ik-kyu*, one notch below the lowest degree of expert. A brown diamond above my right breast said "*Jiu-Jitsu*" in Japanese, and it meant *atemiwaza*, really, because of the one striking-technique I had worked out, found unbelievably suitable to my size, and won matches with.

74

Roger Zelazny and Samuel R. Delany

But I had never used it on a man, and it was five years since I had practiced. I was out of shape, I knew, but I tried hard to force my mind *tsuki no kokoro*, like the moon, reflecting the all of Ontro.

Somewhere, out of the past, a voice said, "*Hajime*, let it begin."

I snapped into my *neko-ashi-dachi* cat-stance, and his eyes burned strangely. He hurried to correct his own position—and I threw it at him!

My one trick!

My long left leg lashed up like a broken spring. Seven feet off the ground my foot connected with his jaw as he tried to leap backward.

His head snapped back and he fell. A soft moan escaped his lips. *That's all there is to it,* I thought. *Sorry, old fellow.*

And as I stepped over him, somehow, groggily, he tripped me, and I fell across his body. I couldn't believe he had strength enough to remain conscious after that blow, let alone move. I hated to punish him any more.

But he found my throat and slipped a forearm across it before I realized there was a purpose to his action.

No! Don't let it end like this!

It was a bar of steel across my windpipe, my carotids. Then I realized that he was still unconscious, and that this was a reflex instilled by countless years of training. I had seen it happen once, in *shiai*. The man had died because he had been choked unconscious and still fought on, and his opponent thought he had not been applying the choke properly. He tried harder.

But it was rare, so very rare!

I jammed my elbow into his ribs and threw my head back in his face. The grip eased, but not enough. I hated to do it, but I reached up and broke his little finger.

The arm went loose and I twisted free.

He lay there panting, face contorted. My heart went out to the fallen giant, defending his people, his religion, following his orders. I cursed myself as I had never cursed before, for walking over him, instead of around.

I staggered across the room to my little heap of possessions. I sat on the projector case and lit a cigarette.

The Magic

I couldn't go into the Temple until I got my breath back, until I thought of something to say.

How do you talk a race out of killing itself?

Suddenly—

—Could it happen! Would it work that way? If I read them the Book of Ecclesiastes—if I read them a greater piece of literature than any Locar ever wrote—and as somber—and as pessimistic—and showed them that our race had gone on despite one man's condemning all of life in the highest poetry—showed them that the vanity he had mocked had borne us to the Heavens—would they believe it—would they change their minds?

I ground out my cigarette on the beautiful floor, and found my notebook. A strange fury rose within me as I stood.

And I walked into the Temple to preach the Black Gospel according to Gallinger, from the Book of Life.

*

There was silence all about me.

M'Cwyie had been reading Locar, the rose set at her right hand, target of all eyes.

Until I entered.

Hundreds of people were seated on the floor, barefoot. The few men were as small as the women, I noted.

I had my boots on.

Go all the way, I figured. *You either lose or you win—everything!*

A dozen crones sat in a semicircle behind M'Cwyie. The Mothers.

The barren earth, the dry wombs, the fire-touched.

I moved to the table.

"Dying yourselves, you would condemn your people," I addressed them, "that they may not know the life you have known—the joys, the sorrows, the fullness. —But it is not true that you all must die." I addressed the multitude now. "Those who say this lie. Braxa knows, for she will bear a child—"

They sat there, like rows of Buddhas. M'Cwyie drew back into the semicircle.

"—my child!" I continued, wondering what my father would have thought of this sermon.

" . . . And all the women young enough may bear children. It is only your men who are sterile. —And if you permit the doctors of the next expedition to examine you, perhaps even the men may be helped. But if they cannot, you can mate with the men of Earth.

"And ours is not an insignificant people, an insignificant place," I went on. "Thousands of years ago, the Locar of our world wrote a book saying that it was. He spoke as Locar did, but we did not lie down, despite plagues, wars, and famines. We did not die. One by one we beat down the diseases, we fed the hungry, we fought the wars, and, recently, have gone a long time without them. We may finally have conquered them. I do not know.

"But we have crossed millions of miles of nothingness. We have visited another world. And our Locar had said 'Why bother? What is the worth of it? It is all vanity, anyhow.'

"And the secret is," I lowered my voice, as at a poetry reading, "he was right! It *is* vanity, it *is* pride! It is the hubris of rationalism to always attack the prophet, the mystic, the god. It is our blasphemy which has made us great, and will sustain us, and which the gods secretly admire in us. —All the truly sacred names of God are blasphemous things to speak!"

I was working up a sweat. I paused dizzily.

"Here is the Book of Ecclesiastes," I announced, and began:

"'Vanity of vanities, saith the Preacher, vanity of vanities; all is vanity. What profit hath a man . . . '"

I spotted Braxa in the back, mute, rapt.

I wondered what she was thinking.

And I wound the hours of the night about me, like black thread on a spool.

*

Oh, it was late! I had spoken till day came, and still I spoke. I finished Ecclesiastes and continued Gallinger.

And when I finished there was still only a silence.

The Magic

The Buddhas, all in a row, had not stirred through the night. And after a long while M'Cwyie raised her right hand. One by one the Mothers did the same.

And I knew what that meant.

It meant, no, do not, cease, and stop.

It meant that I had failed.

I walked slowly from the room and slumped beside my baggage.

Ontro was gone. Good that I had not killed him . . . .

After a thousand years M'Cwyie entered.

She said, "Your job is finished."

I did not move.

"The prophecy is fulfilled," she said. "My people are rejoicing. You have won, holy man. Now leave us quickly."

My mind was a deflated balloon. I pumped a little air back into it.

"I'm not a holy man," I said, "just a second-rate poet with a bad case of hubris."

I lit my last cigarette.

Finally, "All right, what prophecy?"

"The Promise of Locar," she replied, as though the explaining were unnecessary, "that a holy man would come from the Heavens to save us in our last hours, if all the dances of Locar were completed. He would defeat the Fist of Malann and bring us life."

"How?"

"As with Braxa, and as the example in the Temple."

"Example?"

"You read us his words, as great as Locar's. You read to us how there is 'nothing new under the sun.' And you mocked his words as you read them—showing us a new thing.

"There has never been a flower on Mars," she said, "but we will learn to grow them.

"You are the Sacred Scoffer," she finished. "He-Who-Must-Mock-in-the-Temple—you go shod on holy ground."

"But you voted 'no,'" I said.

"I voted not to carry out our original plan, and to let Braxa's child live instead."

"Oh." The cigarette fell from my fingers. How close it had been! How little I had known!

"And Braxa?"

"She was chosen half a Process ago to do the dances—to wait for you."

"But she said that Ontro would stop me."

M'Cwyie stood there for a long time.

"She had never believed the prophecy herself. Things are not well with her now. She ran away, fearing it was true. When you completed it, and we voted, she knew."

"Then she does not love me? Never did?"

"I am sorry, Gallinger. It was the one part of her duty she never managed."

"Duty," I said flatly . . . . Dutydutyduty! Tra-la!

"She has said good-bye, she does not wish to see you again.

" . . . and we will never forget your teachings," she added.

"Don't," I said automatically, suddenly knowing the great paradox which lies at the heart of all miracles. I did not believe a word of my own gospel, never had.

I stood, like a drunken man, and muttered "M'narra."

I went outside, into my last day on Mars.

I have conquered thee, Malann—and the victory is thine! Rest easy on thy starry bed. God damned!

I left the jeepster there and walked back to the *Aspic*, leaving the burden of life so many footsteps behind me. I went to my cabin, locked the door, and took forty-four sleeping pills.

*

But when I awakened I was in the dispensary, and alive.

I felt the throb of engines as I slowly stood up and somehow made it to the port.

The Magic

Blurred Mars hung like a swollen belly above me, until it dissolved, brimmed over, and streamed down my face.

A Word from Zelazny

"I had a strong sentimental attachment to what is now called 'space opera.' . . . I had long wanted to do something of that sort. When I began selling fiction in the sixties it was too late—almost. The space program had already invalidated the Mars and Venus of Edgar Rice Burroughs—almost . . . If I wanted to do homage . . . I would have to act quickly and do my best. I knew that I would only be allowed one shot at each world, and then I would have to leave the solar system. 'A Rose For Ecclesiastes' was my only word on Mars. 'The Doors of His Face, the Lamps of His Mouth' all that I would have to say on Venus. So I did it. I wrote them both and got in under the wire."[1]

Zelazny usually gave noncommittal answers when asked if the poet Gallinger had any resemblance to Zelazny himself, but he did give a very personal response to letter writer Clara on this very subject: "You ask me why I hated Gallinger so in 'A Rose For Ecclesiastes.' The answer is that I hated him because he was me. Once in my life I let a beautiful thing die, and now it can never be. Details are not important, in that they would add nothing. The story says what it must and stands or falls on its own merits. But you're right in your observation that it's a sad story, despite the fact that you felt crushed and even cheated. Life is full of these things, and one of them motivated this tale. I didn't want it to end that way, but it had to, because he was me. I felt pain along with him. He was a better linguist than I, and a better poet. He was a very good, misunderstood man. There is a sequel to the story which I will never write, where he goes back to Mars some years later. It is much sadder, believe me, and he doesn't deserve to be put through those paces. He's suffered enough. But sometimes things happen this way, and all that you can say is, 'Look. This is the way things are.' That's all."[2]

Zelazny was alluding to events that caused the breakup of his six month engagement to Hedy West; he wrote this story shortly after.

Roger Zelazny and Samuel R. Delany

This story was actually written in October 1961, five months prior to "Passion Play," but Zelazny had declined to submit it then because he knew that the Mars depicted within the story had lost all credibility by 1962. Critics and other authors greeted the story enthusiastically, assuming it reflected rapid maturation in his writing. In fact, he wrote it before his earlier published works.[3] It is unclear whether he'd revised it at all before submitting it.

Consistent with his intention to follow Hemingway's dictum to leave certain things unsaid, Zelazny did not reveal Gallinger's first name, Michael, in the story. "It wasn't important; I had no reason for using his first name . . . If the writer sees more of the story than he actually tells, it adds strength to the story. It makes the character seem more real."[4]

Notes

Theodore Sturgeon enthused that "'A Rose for Ecclesiastes' is one of the most important stories I have ever read—perhaps I should say it is one of the most memorable experiences I have ever had . . . as objective as I can be, which isn't very, I still feel safe in stating that it is one of the most beautifully written, skillfully composed and passionately expressed works of art to appear anywhere, ever."[5]

Fittingly, this story was included as one of the classic stories of "Martian literature" in the *Visions of Mars: First Library on Mars* silica glass mini- DVD that traveled to the Martian surface on May 25, 2008, aboard the lander *Phoenix*.

"A Rose for Ecclesiastes" appeared in *The Science Fiction Hall of Fame, Volume One*, ranked sixth among the 26 best stories from 1929–1964 (prior to the institution of the Nebula Awards), elected by the writers themselves.

The cover painting for this story was one of the very last works of Hannes Bok, and Zelazny later purchased the original painting.

*

The many references and allusions that enrich the text may benefit from identification or explanation. A **madrigal** is a musical form of secular text

81

composed for two voices, often in Italian. **Macabre** implies a grim or ghastly atmosphere with an emphasis on death. **"Let not ambition mock thy useful toil"** is a line from the poem "The Cotter's Saturday Night" by Robert Burns. **Hamlet** and his stepfather, King **Claudius**, despised and mistrusted each other. **Antoine de Saint-Exupery** was a writer and aviator who published several prominent novels pertaining to flight and is best known for the novel *The Little Prince*. **Malebolge** is the eighth circle of hell in Dante's *The Divine Comedy*, within which **Dante** discovers **Ulysses** standing in flames, doomed for three sins, but still capable of making a speech about his adventures. **Terza-rima** is a rhyming in triplets, specifically the style used in *The Divine Comedy*. The **Mahābhārata** is a lengthy Sanskrit epic of ancient India.

Samson was the Israelite whose immense strength lay in his uncut hair; his lover Delilah cut it off, the Philistines blinded him and imprisoned him in Gaza—but his hair grew again, and he pulled down the pillars of the temple, destroying himself and many Philistines. **Heinrich Schliemann** was a German treasure hunter who discovered and excavated Troy and fought with archaeologist Frank Calvert over it. In ancient India, **Prakrit** was the ordinary or vernacular speech while **Sanskrit** was the liturgical or high speech. **Vaulted and corbeled** means that the high ceiling is supported by projections from the walls. **Benzedrine** is a brand of amphetamine.

The *Iliad* by Homer describes the Trojan War and how Achilles killed Hector. **Added tails to the cat repeatedly laid on my back** suggests a cat-o'-nine-tails, a rope whip with nine knotted cords, formerly used to flog offenders (Gallinger must be speaking figuratively, not literally, because he later states that his father did not resort to physical punishment). A **catafalque** is a raised platform on which a dead body is carried or lies in state. **Greenwich Village** played an important role in the development of folk music in the 1960s (Dylan; Simon and Garfunkle; Peter, Paul and Mary; etc.) and was where Zelazny met his first fiancée, folk musician Hedy West. **W. H. Auden** was one of Zelazny's favorite poets. **Iambics** are meters in poetry consisting of one short (or unstressed) syllable followed by one long (or stressed) syllable.

I, a stranger, unafraid alludes to A. E. Housman's *Last Poems*, and the line "I, a stranger and afraid | | in a world I never made"—except that Gallinger reverses it into a boast. **This is the land** likely refers to Emily Dickinson's poem "This is the land the sunset washes." *Recherches* is French for researches. **Edgar Allan Poe** wrote poetry and horror stories such as "The Tell-Tale Heart." *Vanity of vanities . . .* is a quote from the Book of Ecclesiastes in the **King James** version of the Bible. **Jean-Paul Sartre** was an existentialist who dealt with the nature of human life and the structures of consciousness; **the Other** deals with the philosophical concept of how one consciousness deals with the existence of other minds. **Periphrasis** is the use of indirect and circumlocutory speech or writing.

Henry Havelock Ellis was a British doctor and sexual psychologist whose book *The Dance of Life* described that dancing and architecture are the two primary and essential arts. According to Ellis, dancing is the source of all arts that express themselves inside the person, and it came first; architecture is the beginning of all the arts that lie outside the person.

A **sari** is a garment worn by Hindu women, consisting of a long piece of cotton or silk wrapped around the body. An **Etruscan frieze** is a horizontal band of sculpted or painted decoration on a wall near the ceiling. The Etruscan civilization flourished circa 500 BC. The *samisen* is a Japanese three-stringed musical instrument played with a plectrum called a bachi. A **glissando** is a rapid slide through a series of scales on a musical instrument. **Saint-John Perse** was the pseudonym of a French poet who was awarded the Nobel Prize for Literature in 1960. **Devadasis** or "servants of God" were girls "married" to a deity or temple in a Hindu practice and who learned a sacred dance termed the Bharatanatyam. **Ramadjany** were sacred dancers.

Rama refers to any one of the three avatars of Vishnu, those being Balarama, Parashurama, or Ramachandra; **Vishnu** or "the Preserver" is the second member of the Trimurti, along with Brahma the Creator and Shiva the Destroyer. **Sarasvati** is the Hindu goddess of learning and the arts. The

sitar is a large, long-necked Indian lute with movable frets, played with a wire pick. **Afflatus** is a divine creative impulse or inspiration.

Arthur Rimbaud, Charles Baudelaire, Edgar Allan Poe, Thomas De Quincy, Oscar Wilde, Stephane Mallarme and Aleister Crowley were respected authors and poets. **Job** argued with God because conventional wisdom said that his suffering must be the just punishment for his sins, but he knew himself to be innocent of any crimes, and he wanted to meet God face to face rather than accept platitudes which he knew were untrue. A **charley horse** is localized pain or muscle stiffness following contusion or bruising of a muscle, or localized electrolyte imbalance.

William Butler Yeats, Ezra Pound, T. S. Eliot, Hart Crane, and Wallace Stevens were real poets whose work Zelazny admired, and Michael **Gallinger** is the protagonist and poet of this story. **Jonathan Swift** was an Irish poet and satirist best known for *Gulliver's Travels*, a satire on human society in the form of a fantastic tale of travels in imaginary lands. **George Bernard Shaw** was an Irish playwright whose plays (including *Pygmalion, Man and Superman*) combined comedy and an examination of conventional morals and thought. **Petronius Arbiter** was the author of *The Satyricon*, a work in prose and verse satirizing the excesses of Roman society. In *The Satyricon*, **Trimalchio** was a character known for throwing lavish dinner parties.

Blake's rose refers to "The Sick Rose," a poem by William Blake that begins "Oh Rose, thou art sick!" **Isaias** [variant of Isaiah] was a major prophet of Judah in the 8th century BC; the book of the Bible entitled *Isaiah* contains his prophecies. **Mycetae** are fungi. **Mores** are customs, practices, or ways of life in a culture. **Methuselah** was the grandfather of Noah and was said to have lived almost 1,000 years; the term also means a longlived or immortal man.

Giovanni Shiaparelli was an Italian astronomer who famously described the markings on Mars as canali (channels)—but this was mistranslated as "canals" and taken to mean evidence of a civilization on Mars. **John Milton** wrote *Paradise Lost* after he had gone blind. **Dionysiac** means sensual, spontaneous, and emotional. **Spanish Dancer** was a poem by German poet

Roger Zelazny and Samuel R. Delany

Rainer Maria **Rilke. Shelley's leaves** refers to Percy Shelley's poem "Ode to the West Wind." **Dactylic** refers to a metrical foot in poetry that consists of one stressed syllable followed by two unstressed syllables; **hexameter** means that each line contains six metrical feet.

Castle Duino sits on the rocky Carso high above the Gulf of Trieste and was frequented by Rilke; the quote ending "**nor interpret roses**" [not to give a meaning of human futurity to roses] is from the "First Elegy" within the Rilke's "Duino Elegies." **Anathema maranatha** is a curse for anyone who does not want to be saved because the Lord is coming. **Aspic** is an archaic word for *asp*, the Egyptian cobra; the usage may indicate that ship and crew were a snake in a Martian Eden.

Claudius! If only this were the fifth act! refers to the denouement of the play *Hamlet* in which Claudius and Hamlet are both killed. *Sayonara* is Japanese for goodbye. **Limned** means suffused or highlighted with a bright color. After receiving no aid from the fictional Martian god Malann, Gallinger calls on deities from various religions and mythologies—Hinduism (**Vishnu**), Christianity and Judaism (**Jehovah**), Greek (**Adonis**), Egyptian (**Osiris**), Sumerian (**Thammuz**), Algonquian (**Manitou**), and Haitian Vodou (**Legba**). **Niccolo Paganini** was an Italian violinist, violist and composer.

Kodokan ("A place for study and promotion of the way") is the headquarters of Japanese style judo. The *judogi* is the traditional uniform used for judo practice and competition. *Ik-kyu* is senior brown belt in judo. *Jiu-Jitsu* is a Japanese martial art. *Atemi-waza* are striking techniques rarely used at full force in judo because of the harm that they can inflict. *Tsuki no kokoro* ("A Mind Like the Moon") refers to the need to be constantly aware of the totality of the opponent and his or her movements, just as moonlight shines equally on everything in its range. *Hajime* means threshold or beginning. *Neko-ashi-dachi* ("Cat Stance") is a classic initial pose in judo and is often depicted in motion pictures. *Shiai* is a judo competition for a prize. **Hybris** is an alternate spelling for hubris, pride and arrogance.

[1] *Amber Dreams*, 1983.

The Magic

[2] *No-Eyed Monster* Summer 1968 #14, p 21–22.

[3] *Algol* 13(2):9–14. Summer 1976.

[4] *Roger Zelazny*, Theodore Krulik, 1986.

[5] *Four for Tomorrow*, 1967.

The Graveyard Heart

They were dancing.

—at the party of the century, the party of the millennium, and the Party of Parties,

—really, as well as calendar-wise,

—and he wanted to crush her, to tear her to pieces . . . .

Moore did not really see the pavilion through which they moved, nor regard the hundred faceless shadows that glided about them. He did not take particular note of the swimming globes of colored light that followed above and behind them.

He felt these things, but he did not necessarily sniff wilderness in that ever-green relic of Christmas past turning on its bright pedestal in the center of the room—shedding its fireproofed needles and traditions these six days after the fact.

All of these were abstracted and dismissed, inhaled and filed away . . . .

In a few more moments it would be Two Thousand.

Leota (*nee* Lilith) rested in the bow of his arm like a quivering arrow, until he wanted to break her or send her flying (he knew not where), to crush her into limpness, to make that samadhi, myopia, or whatever, go away from her gray-green eyes. At about that time, each time, she would lean against him and whisper something into his ear, something in French, a language he did not yet speak. She followed his inept lead so perfectly though, that it was not unwarranted that he should feel she could read his mind by pure kinesthesia.

Which made it all the worse then, whenever her breath collared his neck with a moist warmness that spread down under his jacket like an invisible infection. Then he would mutter "C'est vrai" or "Damn" or both and try to crush her bridal whiteness (overlaid with black webbing), and she would

The Magic

become an arrow once more. But she was dancing with him, which was a decided improvement over his last year/her yesterday.

It was almost Two Thousand.

Now . . .

The music broke itself apart and grew back together again as the globes blared daylight. Auld acquaintance, he was reminded, was not a thing to be trifled with.

He almost chuckled then, but the lights went out a moment later and he found himself occupied.

A voice speaking right beside him, beside everyone, stated:

"It is now Two Thousand. Happy New Year!"

He crushed her.

No one cared about Times Square. The crowds in the Square had been watching a relay of the Party on a jerry-screen the size of a football field. Even now the onlookers were being amused by blacklight close-ups of the couples on the dance floor. Perhaps at that very moment, Moore decided, they themselves were the subject of a hilarious sequence being served up before that overflowing Petri dish across the ocean. It was quite likely, considering his partner.

He did not care if they laughed at him, though. He had come too far to care.

"I love you," he said silently. (He used mental dittos to presume an answer, and this made him feel somewhat happier.) Then the lights fireflied once more and auld acquaintance was remembered. A blizzard compounded of a hundred smashed rainbows began falling about the couples; slow-melting spirals of confetti drifted through the lights, dissolving as they descended upon the dancers; furry-edged projections of Chinese dragon kites swam overhead, grinning their way through the storm.

They resumed dancing and he asked her the same question he had asked her the year before.

"Can't we be alone, together, somewhere, just for a moment?"

She smothered a yawn.

"No, I'm bored. I'm going to leave in half an hour."

If voices can be throaty and rich, hers was an opulent neckful. Her throat *was* golden, to a well-sunned turn.

"Then let's spend it talking—in one of the little dining rooms."

"Thank you, but I'm not hungry. I *must* be seen for the next half hour."

Primitive Moore, who had spent most of his life dozing at the back of Civilized Moore's brain, rose to his haunches then, with a growl. Civilized Moore muzzled him though, because he did not wish to spoil things.

"When can I see you again?" he asked grimly.

"Perhaps Bastille Day," she whispered. "There's the *Liberté, Egalité, Fraternité Fete Nue . . .* "

"Where?"

"In the New Versailles Dome, at nine. If you'd like an invitation, I'll see that you receive one."

"Yes, I do want one."

("She made you ask," jeered Primitive Moore.)

"Very well, you'll receive one in May."

"Won't you spare me a day or so now?"

She shook her head, her blue-blonde coif burning his face.

"Time is too dear," she whispered in mock-Camille pathos, "and the days of the Parties are without end. You ask me to cut years off my life and hand them to you."

"That's right."

"You ask too much," she smiled.

He wanted to curse her right then and walk away, but he wanted even more so to stay with her. He was twenty-seven, an age of which he did not approve in the first place, and he had spent all of the year 1999 wanting her. He had decided two years ago that he was going to fall in love and marry—because he could finally afford to do so without altering his standards of living. Lacking a woman who combined the better qualities of Aphrodite and a digital computer, he had spent an entire year on safari, trekking after the spoor of his starcrossed.

The Magic

The invitation to the Bledsoes' Orbiting New Year—which had hounded the old year around the world, chasing it over the International Dateline and off the Earth entirely, to wherever old years go—had set him back a month's pay, but had given him his first live glimpse of Leota Mathilde Mason, belle of the Sleepers. Forgetting about digital computers, he decided then and there to fall in love with her. He was old-fashioned in many respects.

He had spoken with her for precisely ninety-seven seconds, the first twenty of which had been Arctic. But he realized that she existed to be admired, so he insisted on admiring her. Finally, she consented to be seen dancing with him at the Millenium Party in Stockholm.

He had spent the following year anticipating her seduction back to a reasonable and human mode of existence. Now, in the most beautiful city in the world, she had just informed him that she was bored and was about to retire until Bastille Day. It was then that Primitive Moore realized what Civilized Moore must really have known all along: the next time that he saw her she would be approximately two days older and he would be going on twenty-nine. Time stands still for the Set, but the price of mortal existence is age. Money could buy her the most desirable of all narcissist indulgences: the cold bunk.

And he had not even had the chance of a Stockholm snowflake in the Congo to speak with her, to speak more than a few disjointed sentences, let alone to try talking her out of the ice-box club. (Even now, Setman laureate Wayne Unger was moving to cut in on him, with the expression of a golf pro about to give a lesson.)

"Hello, Leota. Sorry, Mister Uh."

Primitive Moore snarled and bashed him with his club; Civilized Moore released one of the most inaccessible women in the world to a god of the Set.

She was smiling. He was smiling. They were gone.

All the way around the world to San Francisco, sitting in the bar of the stratocruiser in the year of Our Lord Two Thousand—that is to say: two, zero, zero, zero—Moore felt that Time was out of joint.

*

90

Roger Zelazny and Samuel R. Delany

It was two days before he made up his mind what he was going to do about it.

He asked himself (from the blister balcony of his suite in the Hundred Towers of the Hilton-Frisco Complex) *Is* this the girl I want to marry?

He answered himself (looking alternately at the traffic capillaries below his shoetops and the Bay): Yes.

Why? he wanted to know.

Because she is beautiful, he answered, and the future will be lovely. I want her for my beautiful wife in the lovely future.

So he decided to join the Set.

He realized it was no mean feat he was mapping out. First, he required money, lots of money—green acres of Presidents, to be strewn properly in the proper places. The next requisite was distinction, recognition. Unfortunately, the world was full of electrical engineers, humming through their twenty-hour weeks, dallying with pet projects—competent, capable, even inspired—who did not have these things. So he knew it would be difficult.

He submerged himself into research with a unique will: forty, sixty, eighty hours a week he spent—reading, designing, studying taped courses in subjects he had never needed. He gave up on recreation.

By May, when he received his invitation, he stared at the engraved (not fac-copy) parchment (not jot-sheet) with bleary eyes. He had already had nine patents entered and three more were pending. He had sold one and was negotiating with Akwa Mining over a water purification process which he had, he felt, fallen into. Money he would have, he decided, if he could keep up the pace.

Possibly even some recognition. That part now depended mainly on his puro-process and what he did with the money. Leota (*nee* Lorelei) lurked beneath his pages of formulas, was cubed Braque-like in the lines on his sketcher; she burnt as he slept, slept as he burned.

In June he decided he needed a rest.

"Assistant Division Chief Moore," he told the face in the groomer (his laudatory attitude toward work had already earned him a promotion at the

The Magic

Seal-Lock Division of Pressure Units, Corporate), "you need more French and better dancing."

The groomer hands patted away at his sandy stubble and slashed smooth the shagginess above his ears. The weary eyes before him agreed bluely; they were tired of studying abstractions.

The intensity of his recreation, however, was as fatiguing in its own way as his work had been. His muscle tone *did* improve as he sprang weightlessly through the Young Men's Christian Association Satellite-3 Trampoline Room; his dance steps seemed more graceful after he had spun with a hundred robots and ten dozen women; he took the accelerated Berlitz drug-course in French (eschewing the faster electrocerebral-stimulation series, because of a rumored transference that might slow his reflexes later that summer); and he felt that he was beginning to *sound* better—he had hired a gabcoach, and he bake-ovened Restoration plays into his pillow (and hopefully, into his head) whenever he slept (generally every third day now)—so that, as the day of the Fête drew near, he began feeling like a Renaissance courtier (a tired one).

As he stared at Civilized Moore inside his groomer, Primitive Moore wondered how long that feeling would last.

Two days before Versailles he cultivated a uniform tan and decided what he was going to say to Leota this time:

—I love you? (Hell, no!)

—Will you quit the cold circuit? (Uh-uh.)

—If I join the Set, will you join me? (That seemed the best way to put it.)

Their third meeting, then, was to be on different terms. No more stakeouts in the wastes of the prosaic. The hunter was going to enter the brush. "Onward!" grinned Moore in the groomer, "and Excelsior!"

*

She was dressed in a pale blue, mutie orchid corsage. The revolving dome of the palace spun singing zodiacs and the floors fluoresced witch-fires. He had the uncomfortable feeling that the damned flowers were growing there, right above her left breast, like an exotic parasite; and he resented their intrusion with a parochial possessiveness that he knew was not of the Renaissance. Nevertheless . . .

"Good evening. How do your flowers grow?"

"Barely and quite contrary," she decided, sipping something green through a long straw, "but they cling to life."

"With an understandable passion," he noted, taking her hand which she did not withdraw. "Tell me, Eve of the Microprosopos—where are you headed?"

Interest flickered across her face and came to rest in her eyes.

"Your French has improved, Adam-Kadmon . . . ?" she noted. "I'm headed ahead. Where are you headed?"

"The same way."

"I doubt it—unfortunately."

"Doubt all you want, but we're parallel flows already."

"Is that a conceit drawn from some engineering laureate?"

"Watch me engineer a cold-bunk," he stated.

Her eyes shot X-rays through him, warming his bones.

"I knew you had something on your mind. If you were serious . . . "

"Us fallen spirits have to stick together here in Malkuth—I'm serious." He coughed and talked eyetalk. "Shall we stand together as though we're dancing. I see Unger; he sees us, and I want you."

"All right."

She placed her glass on a drifting tray and followed him out onto the floor and beneath the turning zodiac, leaving Setman Unger to face a labyrinth of flesh. Moore laughed at his predicament.

"It's harder to tell identities at an anti-costume party."

She smiled.

"You know, you dance differently today than last night."

"I know. Listen, how do I get a private iceberg and a key to Schleraffenland? I've decided it might be amusing. I know that it's not a matter of genealogy, or even money, for that matter, although both seem to help. I've read all the literature, but I could use some practical advice."

The Magic

Her hand quivered ever so slightly in his own.

"You know the Doyenne?" she said/asked.

"Mainly rumors," he replied, "to the effect that she's an old gargoyle they've frozen to frighten away the Beast come Armageddon."

Leota did not smile. Instead, she became an arrow again.

"More or less," she replied coldly. "She does keep beastly people out of the Set."

Civilized Moore bit his tongue.

"Although many do not like her," she continued, becoming slightly more animated as she reflected, "I've always found her a rare little piece of chinoiserie. I'd like to take her home, if I had a home, and set her on my mantel, if I had a mantel."

"I've heard that she'd fit right into the Victorian Room at the NAM Galleries," Moore ventured.

"She *was* born during Vicky's reign—and she *was* in her eighties when the cold-bunk was developed—but I can safely say that the matter goes no further."

"And she decided to go gallivanting through Time at that age?"

"Precisely," answered Leota, "inasmuch as she wishes to be the immortal arbiter of trans-society."

They turned with the music. Leota had relaxed once more.

"At one hundred and ten she's already on her way to becoming an archetype," Moore noted. "Is that one of the reasons interviews are so hard to come by?"

"One of the reasons . . . " she told him. "If, for example, you were to petition Party Set now, you would still have to wait until next summer for the interview—provided you reached that stage."

"How many are there on the roster of eligibles?"

She shut her eyes.

"I don't know. Thousands, I should say. She'll only see a few dozen, of course. The others will have been weeded out, pruned off, investigated away, and variously disqualified by the directors. Then, naturally, *she* will have the final say as to who is *in*."

Suddenly green and limpid—as the music, the lights, the ultrasonics, and the delicate narcotic fragrances of the air altered subtly—the room became a dark, cool place at the bottom of the sea, heady and nostalgic as the mind of a mermaid staring upon the ruins of Atlantis. The elegiac genius of the hall drew them closer together by a kind of subtle gravitation, and she was cool and adhesive as he continued:

"What is her power, really? I've read the tapes; I know she's a big stockholder, but so what? Why can't the directors vote around her. If I paid out—"

"They *wouldn't*," she said. "Her money means nothing. She is an institution.

"Hers is the quality of exclusiveness which keeps the Set the Set," she went on. "Imitators will always fail because they lack her discrimination. They'll take in any boorish body who'll pay. *That* is the reason that People Who Count" (she pronounced the capitals), "will neither attend nor sponsor any but Set functions. All exclusiveness would vanish from the Earth if the Set lowered its standards."

"Money is money," said Moore. "If others paid the same for their parties . . . "

" . . . Then the People who take their money would cease to Count. The Set would boycott them. They would lose their élan, be looked upon as hucksters."

"It sounds like a rather vicious moebius."

"It is a caste system with checks and balances. Nobody really wants it to break down."

"Even those who wash out?"

"Silly! They'd be the last. There's nothing to stop them from buying their own bunkers, if they can afford it, and waiting another five years to try again. They'd be wealthier anyhow for the wait, if they invest properly. Some have waited decades, and are still waiting. Some have made it after years of persisting. It makes the game more interesting, the achievement more satisfying. In a world of physical ease, brutal social equality, and reasonable economic equality, exclusiveness in frivolity becomes the most sought-after of all distinctions."

"'Commodities,'" he corrected.

"No," she stated, "it is not for sale. Try buying it if money is all you have to offer."

That brought his mind back to more immediate considerations.

"What *is* the cost, if all the other qualifications are met?"

"The rule on that is sufficiently malleable to permit an otherwise qualified person to meet his dues. He guarantees his tenure, bunk-wise or Party-wise, until such a time as his income offsets his debt. So if he only possesses a modest fortune, he may still be quite eligible. This is necessary if we are to preserve our democratic ideals."

She looked away, looked back.

"Usually a step-scale of percentages on the returns from his investments is arranged. In fact, a Set counselor will be right there when you liquidate your assets, and he'll recommend the best conversions."

"Set must clean up on this."

"*Certainement.* It is a business, and the Parties don't come cheaply. But then, you'd be a part of Set yourself—being a shareholder is one of the membership requirements—and we're a restricted corporation, paying high dividends. Your principal will grow. If you were to be accepted, join, and then quit after even one objective month, something like twenty actual years would have passed. You'd be a month older and much wealthier when you leave—and perhaps somewhat wiser."

"Where do I go to put my name on the list?"

He knew, but he had hopes.

"We can call it in tonight, from here. There is always someone in the office. You will be visited in a week or so, after the preliminary investigation."

"Investigation?"

"Nothing to worry about. Or have you a criminal record, a history of insanity, or a bad credit rating?"

Moore shook his head.

"No, no, and no."

"Then you'll pass."

"But will I actually have a chance of getting in, against all those others?"

It was as though a single drop of rain fell upon his chest.

"Yes," she replied, putting her cheek into the hollow of his neck and staring out over his shoulder so that he could not see her expression, "you'll make it all the way to the lair of Mary Maude Mullen with a member sponsoring you. That final hurdle will depend on yourself."

"Then I'll make it," he told her.

"The interview may only last seconds. She's quick; her decisions are almost instantaneous, and she's never wrong."

"Then I'll make it," he repeated, exulting.

Above them, the zodiac rippled.

*

Moore found Darryl Wilson in a barmat in the Poconos. The actor had gone to seed; he was not the man Moore remembered from the award-winning frontier threelie series. That man had been a crag-browed, bushy-faced Viking of the prairies. In four years' time a facial avalanche had occurred, leaving its gaps and runnels across his expensive frown and dusting the face fur a shade lighter. Wilson had left it that way and cauterized his craw with the fire water he had denied the Red Man weekly. Rumor had it he was well into his second liver.

Moore sat beside him and inserted his card into the counter slot. He punched out a Martini and waited. When he noticed that the man was unaware of his presence, he observed, "You're Darryl Wilson and I'm Alvin Moore. I want to ask you something."

The straight-shooting eyes did not focus.

"News media man?"

"No, an old fan of yours," he lied.

The Magic

"Ask away then," said the still-familiar voice. "You are a camera."

"Mary Maude Mullen, the bitch-goddess of the Set," he said. "What's she like?"

The eyes finally focused.

"You up for deification this session?"

"That's right"

"What do you think?"

Moore waited, but there were no more words, so he finally asked, "About what?"

"Anything. You name it."

Moore took a drink. He decided to play the game if it would make the man more tractable.

"I think I like Martinis," he stated. "Now—"

"Why?"

Moore growled. Perhaps Wilson was too far gone to be of any help. Still, one more try . . .

"Because they're relaxing and bracing, both at the same time, which is something I need after coming all this way."

"Why do you want to be relaxed and braced?"

"Because I prefer it to being tense and unbraced."

"Why?"

"What the hell is all this?"

"You lose. Go home."

Moore stood.

"Suppose I go out again and come back in and we start over? Okay?"

"Sit down. My wheels turn slowly but they still turn," said Wilson. "We're talking about the same thing. You want to know what Mary Maude is like? That's what she's like—all interrogatives. Useless ones. Attitudes are a disease that no one's immune to, and they vary so easily in the same person. In two minutes she'll have you stripped down to them, and your answers will depend on biochemistry and the weather. So will her decision. There's nothing I can tell you. She's pure caprice. She's life. She's ugly."

Roger Zelazny and Samuel R. Delany

"That's all?"

"She refuses the wrong people. That's enough. Go away."

Moore finished his Martini and went away.

That winter Moore made a fortune. A modest one, to be sure.

He quit his job for a position with the Akwa Mining Research Lab, Oahu Division. It added ten minutes to his commuting time, but the title, Processing Director, sounded better than Assistant Division Chief, and he was anxious for a new sound. He did not slacken the pace of his force fed social acceptability program, and one of its results was a January lawsuit.

The Set, he had been advised, preferred divorced male candidates to the perpetually single sort. For this reason, he had consulted a highly-rated firm of marriage contractors and entered into a three-month renewable, single partner drop-option contract, with Diane Demetrios, an unemployed model of Greek-Lebanese extraction.

One of the problems of modeling, he decided later, was that there were many surgically-perfected female eidolons in the labor force. It was a rough profession in which to stay employed. His newly-acquired status had been sufficient inducement to cause Diane to press a breach of promise suit on the basis of an alleged oral agreement that the option *would* be renewed.

Burgess Social Contracting Services of course sent a properly obsequious adjuster, and they paid the court costs as well as the medfees for Moore's broken nose. (Diane had hit him with *The Essentials of Dress Display*, a heavy, illustrated talisman of a manual which she carried about in a plastic case—as he slept beside their pool—plastic case and all.)

So, by the month of March Moore felt ready and wise and capable of facing down the last remaining citizen of the nineteenth century.

By May, though, he was beginning to feel he had overtrained. He was tempted to take a month's psychiatric leave from his work, but he recalled Leota's question about a history of insanity. He vetoed the notion and thought of Leota. The world stood still as his mind turned. Guiltily, he realized that he had not thought of her for months. He had been too busy with his autodidactics, his new job, and Diane Demetrios to think of the Setqueen, his love.

He chuckled.

Vanity, he decided; I want her because everyone wants her.

No, that wasn't true either; exactly . . . . He wanted—what?

He thought upon his motives, his desires.

He realized, then, that his goals had shifted; the act had become the actor. What he really wanted, first and foremost, impure and unsimple, was an in to the Set—that century-spanning stratocruiser, luxury class, jetting across tomorrow and tomorrow and all the days that followed after—to ride high, like those gods of old who appeared at the rites of the equinoxes, slept between processions, and were re-manifest with each new season, the bulk of humanity living through all those dreary days that lay between. To be a part of Leota was to be a part of the Set, and that was what he wanted now. So of course it was vanity. It was love.

He laughed aloud. His autosurf initialed the blue lens of the Pacific like a manned diamond, casting the sharp cold chips of its surface up and into his face.

*

Returning from absolute zero, Lazarus-like, is neither painful nor disconcerting, at first. There are no sensations at all until one achieves the temperature of a reasonably warm corpse. By that time though, an injection of nirvana flows within the body's thawed rivers.

It is only when consciousness begins to return, thought Mrs. Mullen, to return with sufficient strength so that one fully realizes what has occurred—that the wine has survived another season in an uncertain cellar, its vintage grown rarer still—only then does an unpronounceable fear enter into the mundane outlines of the bedroom furniture—for a moment.

It is more a superstitious attitude than anything, a mental quaking at the possibility that the stuff of life, one's own life, has in some indefinable way been tampered with. A microsecond passes, and then only the dim recollection of a bad dream remains.

She shivered, as though the cold was still locked within her bones, and she shook off the notion of nightmares past.

She turned her attention to the man in the white coat who stood at her elbow.

"What day is it?" she asked him

He was a handful of dust in the wines of Time . . . .

"August eighteen, two thousand-two," answered the handful of dust. "How do you feel?"

"Excellent, thank you," she decided. "I've just touched upon a new century—this makes three I've visited—so why shouldn't I feel excellent? I intend to visit many more."

"I'm sure you will, madam."

The small maps of her hands adjusted the counterpane. She raised her head.

"Tell me what is new in the world."

The doctor looked away from the sudden acetylene burst behind her eyes.

"We have finally visited Neptune and Pluto," he narrated. "They are quite uninhabitable. It appears that man is alone in the solar system. The Lake Sahara project has run into more difficulties but it seems that work may begin next spring now that those stupid French claims are near settlement . . . . " Her eyes fused his dust to planes of glass.

"Another competitor, Futuretime Gay, entered into the time-tank business three years ago," he recited, trying to smile, "but we met the enemy and they are ours—Set bought them out eight months ago. By the way, our own bunkers are now much more sophistica—"

"I repeat," she said, "what is new in the world, *doctor?*"

He shook his head, avoiding the look she gave him.

"We can lengthen the remissions now," he finally told her, "quite a time beyond what could be achieved by the older methods."

"A better delaying action?"

"Yes."

The Magic

"But not a cure?"

He shook his head.

"In my case," she told him, "it has already been abnormally delayed. The old nostrums have already worn thin. For how long are the new ones good?"

"We still don't know. You have an unusual variety of M.S. and it's complicated by other things."

"Does a cure seem any nearer?"

"It could take another twenty years. We might have one tomorrow."

"I see." The brightness subsided. "You may leave now, young man. Turn on my advice tape as you go,"

He was glad to let the machine take over.

*

Diane Demetrios dialed the library and requested the Setbook. She twirled the page-dial and stopped.

She studied the screen as though it were a mirror, her face undergoing a variety of expressions.

"I look just as good," she decided after a time. "Better, even. Your nose could be changed, and your browline . . .

"If they weren't facial fundamentalists," she told the picture, "if they didn't discriminate against surgery, lady —you'd be here and I'd be there.

"Bitch!"

*

The millionth barrel of converted seawater emerged, fresh and icy, from the Moore Purifier. Splashing from its chamber-tandem and flowing through the conduits, it was clean, useful, and singularly unaware of these virtues. Another transfusion of briny Pacific entered at the other hand.

The waste products were used in pseudoceramicware.

The man who designed the double-duty Purifier was rich.

The temperature was 82 in Oahu.

The million-first barrel splashed forth . . . .

*

They left Alvin Moore surrounded by china dogs.

Roger Zelazny and Samuel R. Delany

Two of the walls were shelved; floor to ceiling. The shelves were lined with blue, green, pink, russet (not to mention ochre, vermilion, mauve, and saffron) dogs, mainly glazed (although some were dry-rubbed primitives), ranging from the size of a largish cockroach up to that of a pigmy warthog. Across the room a veritable Hades of a wood fire roared its metaphysical challenge into the hot July of Bermuda.

Set above it was a mantelpiece bearing more dogs.

Set beside the hellplace was a desk, at which was seated Mary Maude Mullen, wrapped in a green and black tartan. She studied Moore's file, which lay open on the blotter. When she spoke to him she did not look up.

Moore stood beside the chair which had not been offered him and pretended to study the dogs and the heaps of Georgian kindling that filled the room to overflowing.

While not overly fond of live dogs, Moore bore them no malice. But when he closed his eyes for a moment he experienced a feeling of claustrophobia.

These were not dogs. These were the unblinking aliens staring through the bars of the last Earthman's cage. Moore promised himself that he would say nothing complimentary about the garish rainbow of a hound pack (fit, perhaps, for stalking a jade stag the size of a Chihuahua); he decided it could only have sprung from the mental crook of a monomaniac, or one possessed of a very feeble imagination and small respect for dogs.

After verifying all the generalities listed on his petition, Mrs. Mullen raised her pale eyes to his.

"How do you like my doggies?" she asked him.

She sat there, a narrow-faced, wrinkled woman with flaming hair, a snub nose, an innocent expression, and the lingering twist of the question quirking her thin lips.

Moore quickly played back his last thoughts and decided to maintain his integrity in regards china dogs by answering objectively.

"They're quite colorful," he noted.

The Magic

This was the wrong answer, he felt, as soon as be said it. The question had been too abrupt. He had entered the study ready to lie about anything but china dogs. So he smiled.

"There are a dreadful lot of them about. But of course they don't bark or bite or shed, or do other things . . . . "

She smiled back.

"My dear little, colorful little bitches and sons of bitches," she said. "They don't do anything. They're sort of symbolic. That's why I collect them too.

"Sit down"—she gestured—"and pretend you're comfortable."

"Thanks."

"It says here that you rose only recently from the happy ranks of anonymity to achieve some sort of esoteric distinction in the sciences. Why do you wish to resign it now?"

"I wanted money and prestige, both of which I was given to understand would be helpful to a Set candidate."

"Aha! Then they were a means rather than an end?"

"That is correct."

"Then tell me why you want to join the Set."

He had written out the answer to that one months ago. It had been bake-ovened into his brain, so that he could speak it with natural inflections. The words began forming themselves in his throat, but he let them die there. He had planned them for what he had thought would be maximum appeal to a fan of Tennyson's. Now he was not so sure.

Still . . . He broke down the argument and picked a neutral point—the part about following knowledge like a sinking star.

"There will be a lot of changes over the next several decades. I'd like to see them with a young man's eyes."

"As a member of the Set you will exist more to be seen than to see," she replied, making a note in his file. "And I think we'll have to dye your hair if we accept you."

"The hell you say! —Pardon me, that slipped out."

"Good." She made another note. "We can't have them too inhibited—nor too uninhibited, for that matter. Your reaction was rather quaint." She looked up again.

"Why do you want so badly to see the future?"

He felt uneasy. It seemed as though she knew he was lying.

"Plain human curiosity," he answered weakly, "as well as some professional interest. Being an engineer—"

"We're not running a seminar," she observed. "You'd not be wasting much time outside of attending Parties if you wanted to last very long with the Set. In twenty years—no, ten—you'll be back in kindergarten so far as engineering is concerned. It will all be hieroglyphics to you. You don't read hieroglyphics, do you?"

He shook his head.

"Good," she continued, "I have an inept comparison. —Yes, it will all be hieroglyphics, and if you should leave the Set you would be an unskilled draftsman—not that you'd have need to work. But if you were to want to work, you would have to be self-employed—which grows more and more difficult, almost too difficult to attempt, as time moves on. You would doubtless lose money."

He shrugged and raised his palms. He *had* been thinking of doing that. Fifty years, he had told himself, and we could kick the Set, be rich, and I could take refresher courses and try for a consultantship in marine engineering.

"I'd know enough to appreciate things, even if I couldn't participate," he explained.

"You'd be satisfied just to observe?"

"I think so," he lied.

"I doubt it." Her eyes nailed him again. "Do you think you are in love with Leota Mason? She nominated you, but of course that *is* her privilege."

"I don't know," he finally said. "I thought so at first, two years ago . . . . "

"Infatuation is fine," she told him. "It makes for good gossip. Love, on the other hand, I will not tolerate. Purge yourself of such notions. Nothing is so boring and ungay at a Set affair. It does not make for gossip; it makes for snickers.

"So is it infatuation or love?"

"Infatuation," he decided.

She glanced into the fire, glanced at her hands.

"You will have to develop a Buddhist's attitude toward the world around you. That world will change from day to day. Whenever you stop to look at it, it will be a different world—unreal."

He nodded.

"Therefore, if you are to maintain your stability, the Set must be the center of all things. Wherever your heart lies, there also shall reside your soul."

He nodded again.

" . . . And if you should happen not to like the future, whenever you do stop to take a look at it, remember you *cannot* come back. Don't just think about that, *feel* it!"

He felt it.

She began jotting. Her right hand began suddenly to tremble. She dropped the pen and too carefully drew her hand back within the shawl.

"You are not so colorful as most candidates," she told him, too naturally, "but then, we're short on the soulful type at present. Contrast adds depth and texture to our displays. Go view all the tapes of our past Parties."

"I already have."

" . . . And you can give your soul to that, or a significant part thereof?"

"Wherever my heart lies . . . "

"In that case, you may return to your lodgings, Mister Moore. You will receive our decision today."

Moore stood. There were so many questions he had not been asked, so many things he had wanted to say, had forgotten, or had not had opportunity to say . . . . Had she already decided to reject him? he wondered. Was that why the interview had been so brief? Still, her final remarks *had* been encouraging.

He escaped from the fragile kennel, all his pores feeling like fresh nail holes.

He lolled about the hotel pool all afternoon, and in the evening he moved into the bar. He did not eat dinner.

When he received the news that he had been accepted, he was also informed by the messenger that a small gift to his inquisitor was a thing of custom. Moore laughed drunkenly, foreseeing the nature of the gift.

Mary Maude Mullen received her first Pacificware dog from Oahu with a small, sad shrug that almost turned to a shudder. She began to tremble then, nearly dropping it from her fingers. Quickly, she placed it on the bottommost shelf behind her desk and reached for her pills; later, the flames caused it to crack.

*

They were dancing. The sea was an evergreen-gold sky above the dome. The day was strangely young.

Tired remnants of the Party's sixteen hours, they clung to one another, feet aching, shoulders sloped. There were eight couples still moving on the floor, and the weary musicians fed them the slowest music they could make. Sprawled at the edges of the world, where the green bowl of the sky joined with the blue tiles of the Earth, some five hundred people, garments loosened, mouths open, stared like goldfish on a tabletop at the water behind the wall.

"Think it'll rain?" he asked her.

"Yes," she answered.

"So do I. So much for the weather. Now, about that week on the moon—?"

"What's wrong with good old mother Earth?" she smiled.

Someone screamed. The sound of a slap occurred almost simultaneously. The screaming stopped.

"I've never been to the moon," he replied.

She seemed faintly amused.

"I have. I don't like it."

The Magic

"Why?"

"It's the cold, crazy lights outside the dome," she said, "and the dark, dead rocks everywhere around the dome," she winced. "They make it seem like a cemetery at the end of Time . . . . "

"Okay," he said, "forget it."

" . . . And the feeling of disembodied lightness as you move about inside the dome—"

"All right!"

"I'm sorry." She brushed his neck with her lips. He touched her forehead with his. "The Set has lost its shellac," she smiled.

"We're not on tape anymore. It doesn't matter now."

A woman began sobbing somewhere near the giant seahorse that had been the refreshment table. The musicians played more loudly. The sky was full of luminescent starfish, swimming moistly on their tractor beams. One of the starfish dripped salty water on them as it passed overhead.

"We'll leave tomorrow," he said.

"Yes, tomorrow," she said.

"How about Spain?" he said. "This is the season of the sherries. There'll be the Juegos Florales de la Vendimia Jerezana. It may be the last."

"Too noisy," she said, "with all those fireworks."

"But gay."

"Gay," she sighed with a crooked mouth. "Let's go to Switzerland and pretend we're old, or dying of something romantic."

"Necrophilist," he grinned, slipping on a patch of moisture and regaining his balance. "Better it be a quiet loch in the Highlands, where you can have your fog and miasma and I can have my milk and honeydew unblended."

"Nay,"she said, above a quick babble of drunken voices, "let's go to New Hampshire."

"What's wrong with Scotland?"

"I've never been to New Hampshire."

"I have, and I don't like it. It looks like your description of the moon."

A moth brushing against a candle flame, the tremor.

Roger Zelazny and Samuel R. Delany

The frozen bolt of black lightning lengthened slowly in the green heavens. A sprinkling of soft rain began.

As she kicked off her shoes he reached out for a glass on the floating tray above his left shoulder. He drained it and replaced it.

"Tastes like someone's watering the drinks."

"Set must be economizing," she said.

Moore saw Unger then, glass in hand, standing at the edge of the floor watching them.

"I see Unger."

"So do I. He's swaying."

"So are we," he laughed.

The fat bard's hair was a snowy chaos and his left eye was swollen nearly shut. He collapsed with a bubbling murmur, spilling his drink. No one moved to help him.

"I believe he's over indulged himself again."

" Alas, poor Unger," she said without expression, "I knew him well."

The rain continued to fall and the dancers moved about the floor like the figures in some amateur puppet show.

"They're coming!" cried a non-Setman, crimson cloak flapping. "They're coming down!"

The water streamed into their eyes as every conscious head in the Party Dome was turned upward. Three silver zeppelins grew in the cloudless green.

"They're coming for us," observed Moore.

"They're going to make it!"

The music had paused momentarily, like a pendulum at the end of its arc. It began again.

Good night, ladies, played the band, *good night, ladies . . .*

"We're going to live!"

"We'll go to Utah," he told her, eyes moist, "where they don't have seaquakes and tidal waves."

Good night ladies . . .

"We're going to live!"

109

The Magic

She squeezed his hand.

"*Merrily we roll along,*" the voices sang, "*roll along . . .* "

"'Roll along,'" she said.

"'Merrily,'" he answered.

"*O'er the deep blue sea!*"

*

A Set-month after the nearest thing to a Set disaster on record (that is to say, in the year of Our Lord and President Cambert 2019, twelve years after the quake), Setman Moore and Leota (*nee* Lachesis) stood outside the Hall of Sleep on Bermuda Island. It was almost morning.

"I believe I love you," he mentioned.

"Fortunately, love does not require an act of faith," she noted, accepting a light for her cigar, "because I don't believe in anything."

"Twenty years ago I saw a lovely woman at a Party and I danced with her."

"Five weeks ago," she amended.

"I wondered then if she would ever consider quitting the Set and going human again, and being heir to mortal ills."

"I have often wondered that myself," she said, "in idle moments. But she won't do it. Not until she is old and ugly."

"That means forever," he smiled sadly.

"You *are* noble." She blew smoke at the stars, touched the cold wall of the building. "Someday, when people no longer look at her, except for purposes of comparison with some fluffy child of the far future—or when the world's standards of beauty have changed—then she'll transfer from the express run to the local and let the rest of the world go by."

"Whatever the station, she will be all alone in a strange town," said Moore. "Every day, it seems, they remodel the world. I met a fraternity brother at that dinner last night—pardon me, last year—and he treated me as if he were my father. His every other word was 'son' or 'boy' or 'kid,' and he wasn't trying to be funny. He was responding to what he saw. My appetite was considerably diminished.

Roger Zelazny and Samuel R. Delany

"Do you realize where we're going?" he asked the back of her head as she turned away to look out over the gardens of sleeping flowers. "Away! That's where. We can never go back! The world moves on while we sleep."

"Refreshing, isn't it?" she finally said. "And stimulating, and awe-inspiring. Not being bound; I mean. Everything burning. Us remaining. Neither time nor space can hold us, unless we consent.

"And I do not consent to being bound," she declared.

"To anything?"

"To anything."

"Supposing it's all a big joke."

"What?"

"The world. —Supposing every man, woman, and child died last year in an invasion by creatures from Alpha Centauri, everyone but the frozen Set. Supposing it was a totally effective virus attack . . . . "

"There are no creatures in the Centauri System. I read that the other day."

"Okay, someplace else then. Supposing all the remains and all the traces of chaos were cleaned up, and then one creature gestured with a flipper at this building." Moore slapped the wall. "The creature said: 'Hey! There are some live ones inside, on ice. Ask one of the sociologists whether they're worth keeping, or if we should open the refrigerator door and let them spoil.' Then one of the sociologists came and looked at us, all in our coffins of ice, and he said: 'They might be worth a few laughs and a dozen pages in an obscure periodical. So let's fool them into thinking that everything is going on just as it was before the invasion. All their movements, according to these schedules, are preplanned, so it shouldn't be too difficult. We'll fill their Parties with human simulacra packed with recording machinery and we'll itemize their behavior patterns. We'll vary their circumstances and they'll attribute it to progress. We can watch them perform in all sorts of situations that way. Then, when we're finished, we can always break their bunktimers and let them sleep on—or open their doors and watch them spoil.'

The Magic

"So they agreed to do it," finished Moore, "and here we are, the last people alive on Earth, cavorting before machines operated by inhuman creatures who are watching us for incomprehensible reasons."

"Then we'll give them a good show," she replied, "and maybe they'll applaud us once before we spoil."

She snubbed out her cigar and kissed him good night. They returned to their refrigerators.

*

It was twelve weeks before Moore felt the need for a rest from the Party circuit. He was beginning to grow fearful. Leota had spent nonfunctional decades of her time vacationing with him, and she had recently been showing signs of sullenness, apparently regretting these expenditures on his behalf. So he decided to see something real, to take a stroll in the year 2078. After all, he was over a hundred years old.

The Queen Will Live Forever, said the faded clipping that hung in the main corridor of the Hall of Sleep. Beneath the bannerline was the old/recent story of the conquest of the final remaining problems of Multiple Sclerosis, and the medical ransom of one of its most notable victims. Moore had not seen the Doyenne since the day of his interview. He did not care whether he ever saw her again.

He donned a suit from his casualware style locker and strolled through the gardens and out to the airfield. There were no people about.

He did not really know where he wanted to go until he stood before a ticket booth and the speaker asked him, "Destination, please."

"Uh—Oahu. Akwa Labs, if they have a landing field of their own."

"Yes, they do. That will have to be a private charter though, for the final fifty-six miles—"

"Give me a private charter all the way, both ways."

"Insert your card, please."

He did.

After five minutes the card popped back into his waiting hand. He dropped it into his pocket.

"What time will I arrive?" he asked.

"Nine hundred thirty-two, if you leave on Dart Nine six minutes from now. Have you any luggage?"

"No."

"In that case, your Dart awaits you in area A-11."

Moore crossed the field to the VTO Dart numbered "Nine." It flew by tape. The flight pattern, since it was a specially chartered run, had been worked out back at the booth, within milliseconds of Moore's naming his destination. It was then broadcast-transferred to a blank tape inside Dart Nine; an auto-alternation brain permitted the Dart to correct its course in the face of unforeseen contingencies and later recorrect itself, landing precisely where it was scheduled to come down.

Moore mounted the ramp and stopped to slip his card into the slot beside the hatchway. The hatch swung open and he collected his card and entered. He selected a seat beside a port and snapped its belt around his middle. At this, the hatchway swung itself shut.

After a few minutes the belt unfastened itself and vanished into the arms of his seat. The Dart was cruising smoothly now.

"Do you wish to have the lights dimmed? Or would you prefer to have them brighter?" asked a voice at his side.

"They're fine just the way they are," he told the invisible entity.

"Would you care for something to eat? Or something to drink?"

"I'll have a Martini."

There was a sliding sound, followed by a muted click. A tiny compartment opened in the wall beside him. His Martini rested within.

He removed it and sipped a sip.

Beyond the port and toward the rear of the Dart, a faint blue nimbus arose from the sideplates.

"Would you care for anything else?" *Pause.* "Shall I read you an article on the subject of your choice?" *Pause.* "Or fiction?" *Pause.* "Or poetry?" *Pause.* "Would you care to view the catalog?" *Pause.* "Or perhaps you would prefer music?"

The Magic

"Poetry?" repeated Moore.

"Yes, I have many of—"

"I know a poet," he remembered "Have you anything by Wayne Unger?"

There followed a brief mechanical meditation, then:

"Wayne Unger. Yes," answered the voice. "On call are his *Paradise Unwanted*, *Fungi of Steel*, and *Chisel in the Sky*."

"Which is his most recent work?" asked Moore.

"*Chisel in the Sky*."

"Read it to me."

The voice began by reading him all the publishing data and copyright information. To Moore's protests it answered that it was a matter of law and cited a precedent case. Moore asked for another Martini and waited.

Finally, "'*Our Wintered Way Through Evening, and Burning Bushes Along It*,'" said the voice.

"Huh?"

"That is the title of the first poem."

"Oh, read on."

"'*(Where only the evergreens whiten . . .)*

Winter flaked ashes heighten
in towers of blizzard.
Silhouettes unseal an outline.
Darkness, like an absence of faces,
pours from the opened home;
it seeps through shattered pine
and flows the fractured maple.

Perhaps it is the essence senescent,
dreamculled from the sleepers,
that soaks upon this road
in weather-born excess.

Roger Zelazny and Samuel R. Delany

Or perhaps the great Anti-Life
learns to paint with a vengeance,
to run an icicle down the gargoyle's eye.

For properly speaking, though
no one can confront himself in toto,

I see your falling sky, gone gods,
as in a smoke-filled dream
of ancient statues burning,
soundlessly, down to the ground.

(. . . and never the everwhite's green.),"

There was a ten-second pause, then: "The next poem is entitled—"

"Wait a minute," asked Moore. "That first one—? Are you programmed to explain anything about it?"

"I am sorry, I am not. That would require a more complicated unit."

"Repeat the copyright date of the book."

"Two-thousand-sixteen, in the North American Union—"

"And it's his most recent work?"

"Yes; he is a member of the Party Set and there is generally a lapse of several decades between his books."

"Continue reading."

The machine read on. Moore knew little concerning verse, but he was struck by the continual references to ice and cold, to snow and sleep.

"Stop," he told the machine. "Have you anything of his from before he joined the Set?"

"*Paradise Unwanted* was published in 1981, two years after he became a member. According to its Foreword, however, most of it was written prior to his joining."

"Read it."

The Magic

Moore listened carefully. It contained little of ice, snow, or sleep. He shrugged at his minor discovery. His seat immediately adjusted and readjusted to the movement.

He barely knew Unger. He did not like his poetry. He did not like most poetry, though.

The reader began another.

"In the Dogged House," it said.

"The heart is a graveyard of crigas,
hid far from the hunter's eye,
where love wears death like enamel
and dogs crawl in to die . . . "

Moore smiled as it read the other stanzas. Recognizing its source, he liked that one somewhat better.

"Stop reading," he told the machine.

He ordered a light meal and thought about Unger. He had spoken with him once. When was it?

Two-thousand-seventeen . . . ? Yes, at the Free Workers Liberation Centennial in the Lenin Palace.

It was rivers of vodka . . . .

Fountains of juices, like inhuman arteries slashed, spurted their bright umbrellas of purple and lemon and green and orange. Jewels to ransom an Emir flashed near many hearts. Their host, Premier Korlov, seemed a happy frost giant in his display.

. . . In a dance pavilion of polaroid crystal, with the world outside blinking off and on, on and off—like an advertisement, Unger had commented, both elbows resting on the bar top and his foot on the indispensable rail.

116

Roger Zelazny and Samuel R. Delany

His head had swiveled as Moore approached. He was a bleary-eyed albino owl. "Albion Moore, I believe," he had said, extending a hand. "Quo vadis dammit?"

"Grape juice and wadka," said Moore to the unnecessary human standing beside the mix-machine. The uniformed man pressed two buttons and passed the glass across the two feet of frosty mahogany. Moore twitched it toward Unger in a small salute. "A happy Free Workers' Liberation Centennial to you."

"I'll drink to liberation." The poet leaned forward and poked his own combination of buttons. The man in the uniform sniffed audibly.

They drank a drink together.

"They accuse us" —Unger's gesture indicated the world at large—"of neither knowing nor caring anything about un-Set things, un-Set people."

"Well, it's true, isn't it?"

"Oh yes, but it might be expanded upon. We're the same way with our fellows. Be honest now, how many Setmen are you acquainted with?"

"Quite a few."

"I didn't ask how many names you knew."

"Well, I talk with them all the time. Our environment is suited to much movement and many words—and we have all the time in the world. How many friends do you have?" he asked.

"I just finished one," grunted the poet, leaning forward. "I'm going to mix me another."

Moore didn't feel like being depressed or joked with and he was not sure which category this fell into. He had been living inside a soap bubble since after the ill-starred Davy Jones Party, and he did not want anyone poking sharp things in his direction.

"So, you're your own man. If you're not happy in the Set, leave."

"You're not being a true *tovarisch*," said Unger, shaking a finger. "There was a time when a man could tell his troubles to bartenders and barfriends. You wouldn't remember, though—those days went out when the nickel-plated barmatics came in. Damn their exotic eyes and scientific mixing!"

117

The Magic

Suddenly he punched out three drinks in rapid succession. He slopped them across the dark, shiny surface.

"Taste them! Sip each of them!" he enjoined Moore. "Can't tell them apart without a scorecard, can you?"

"They're dependable that way."

"Dependable? Hell yes! Depend on them to create neurotics. One time a man could buy a beer and bend an ear. All that went out when the dependable mix-machines came in. Now we join a talk-out club of manic change and most unnatural! Oh, had the Mermaid been such!" he complained in false notes of frenzy. "Or the Bloody Lion of Stepney! What jaded jokes the fellows of Marlowe had been!"

He sagged.

"Aye! Drinking's not what it used to be."

The international language of his belch caused the mix-machine attendant to avert his face, which betrayed a pained expression before he did so.

"So I'll repeat my question," stated Moore, making conversation. "Why do you stay where you're unhappy? You could go open a real bar of your own, if that's what you like. It would probably be a success, now that I think of it—people serving drinks and all that."

"Go to! Go to! I shan't say where!" He stared at nothing. "Maybe that's what I'll do someday, though," he reflected, "open a real bar . . . "

Moore turned his back to him then, to watch Leota dancing with Korlov. He was happy.

"People join the Set for a variety of reasons," Unger was muttering, "but the main one is exhibitionism, with the titillating wraith of immortality lurking at the stage door, perhaps. Attracting attention to oneself gets harder and harder as time goes on. It's almost impossible in the sciences. In the nineteenth and twentieth centuries you could still name great names—now it's great research teams. The arts have been democratized out of existence—and where have all the audiences gone? I don't mean spectators either.

"So we have the Set," he continued. "Take our sleeping beauty there, dancing with Korlov—"

"Huh?"

"Pardon me, I didn't mean to awaken you abruptly. I was saying that if she wanted attention Miss Mason couldn't be a stripper today, so she had to join the Set. It's even better than being a threelie star, and it requires less work—"

"Stripper?"

"A folk artist who undressed to music."

"Yes, I recall hearing of them."

"That's gone too, though," sighed Unger, "and while I cannot disapprove of the present customs of dress and undress, it still seems to me as if something bright and frail died in the elder world."

"She is bright, isn't she?"

"Decidedly so."

They had taken a short walk then, outside, in the cold night of Moscow. Moore did not really want to leave, but he had had enough to drink so that he was easy to persuade. Besides that, he did not want the stumbling babbler at his side to fall into an excavation or wander off lost, to miss his flight or turn up injured. So they shuffled up bright avenues and down dim streets until they came to the Square. They stopped before a large, dilapidated monument. The poet broke a small limb from a shrub and bent it into a wreath. He tossed it against the wall.

"Poor fellow," he muttered.

"Who?"

"The guy inside."

"Who's that?"

Unger cocked his head at him.

"You really don't know?"

"I admit there are gaps in my education, if that's what you mean. I continually strive to fill them, but I always was weak on history. I specialized at an early age."

The Magic

Unger jerked his thumb at the monument.

"Noble Macbeth lies in state within," he said. "He was an ancient king who slew his predecessor, noble Duncan, most heinously. Lots of other people too. When he took the throne he promised he'd be nice to his subjects, though. But the Slavic temperament is a strange thing. He is best remembered for his many fine speeches, which were translated by a man named Pasternak. Nobody reads them anymore."

Unger sighed and seated himself on a stair. Moore joined him. He was too cold to be insulted by the arrogant mocking of the drunken poet.

"Back then, people used to fight wars," said Unger.

"I know," responded Moore, his fingers freezing; "Napoleon once burnt part of this city."

Unger tipped his hat.

Moore scanned the skyline. A bewildering range of structures hedged the Square—here, bright and functional, a ladderlike office building composed its heights and witnessed distances, as only the planned vantages of the very new can manage; there, a daytime aquarium of an agency was now a dark mirror, a place where the confidence-inspiring efficiencies of rehearsed officials were displayed before the onlooker; and across the Square, its purged youth fully restored by shadow, a deserted onion of a cupola poked its sharp topknot after soaring vehicles, a number of which, scuttling among the star fires, were indicated even now—and Moore blew upon his fingers and jammed his hands into his pockets.

"Yes, nations went to war," Unger was saying. "Artilleries thundered. Blood was spilled. People died. But we lived through it, crossing a shaky Shinvat word by word. Then one day there it was. Peace. It had been that way a long time before anyone noticed. We still don't know how we did it. Perpetual postponement and a short memory, I guess, as man's attention became occupied twenty-four hours a day with other things. Now there is nothing left to fight over, and everyone is showing off the fruits of peace—because everyone has some, by the roomful. All they want. More. These things that fill the rooms, though," he mused, "and the mind—how they have proliferated! Each month's version is better than the last, in some hypersophisticated manner. They seem to have absorbed the minds that are absorbed with them . . . . "

"We could all go live in the woods," said Moore, wishing he had taken the time to pocket a battery crystal and a thermostat for his suit.

"We could do lots of things, and we will, eventually—I suppose. Still, I guess we *could* wind up in the woods, at that."

"In that case, let's go back to the Palace while there's still time. I'm frozen."

"Why not?"

They climbed to their feet, began walking back.

"Why *did* you join the Set anyhow? So you could be discontent over the centuries?"

"Nay, son," the poet clapped him on the shoulder. "I'm an audience in search of an entertainment."

It took Moore an hour to get the chill out of his bones.

*

"Ahem. Ahem," said the voice. "We are about to land at Akwa Labs, Oahu."

The belt snaked out into Moore's lap. He snapped it tight.

A sudden feeling prompted him to ask: "Read me that last poem from *Chisel* again."

"*Future Be Not Impatient,*" stated the voice:

"*Someday, perhaps, but not this day.
Sometime; but then, not now.
Man is a monument-making mammal.
Never ask me how.*'"

He thought of Leota's description of the moon and he hated Unger for the forty-four seconds it took him to disembark. He was not certain why.

121

The Magic

He stood beside Dart Nine and watched the approach of a small man wearing a smile and gay tropical clothing. He shook hands automatically.

" . . . Very pleased," the man named Teng was saying, "and glad there's not much around for you to recognize anymore. We've been deciding what to show you ever since Bermuda called." Moore pretended to be aware of the call. " . . . Not many people remember their employers from as far back as you do," Teng was saying.

Moore smiled and fell into step with him, heading toward the Processing Complex.

"Yes, I was curious," he agreed, "to see what it all looks like now. My old office, my lab—"

"Gone, of course."

" . . . our first chamber-tandem, with its big-nozzled injectors—"

"Replaced, naturally."

"Naturally. And the big old pumps . . . "

"Shiny and new."

Moore brightened. The sun, which he had not seen for several days/years, felt good on his back, but the air conditioning felt even better as they entered the first building. There was something of beauty in the pure functional compactness of everything about them, something Unger might have called by a different name, he realized, but it was beauty to Moore. He ran his hand along the sides of the units he did not have time to study. He tapped the conduits and peered into the kilns which processed the by-product ceramicware; he nodded approval and paused to relight his pipe whenever the man at his side asked his opinion of something too technically remote for him to have any opinion.

They crossed catwalks, moved through the templelike innards of shut-down tanks, traversed alley ways where the silent, blinking panels indicated that unseen operations were in progress. Occasionally, they met a worker, seated before a sleeping trouble-board, watching a broadcast entertainment or reading something over his portable threelie. Moore shook hands and forgot names.

Roger Zelazny and Samuel R. Delany

Processing Director Teng could not help but be partly hypnotized—both by Moore's youthful appearance and the knowledge that he had developed a key process at some past date (as well as by his apparent understanding of present operations)—into believing that he was an engineer of his own breed, and up-to-date in his education. Actually, Mary Mullen's prediction that his profession would some day move beyond the range of his comprehension had not yet come to pass—but he could see that it was the direction in which he was headed. Appropriately, he had noticed his photo gathering dust in a small lobby, amid those of Teng's other dead and retired predecessors.

Sensing his feeling, Moore asked, "Say, do you think I could have my old job back?"

The man's head jerked about. Moore remained expressionless.

"Well—I suppose—something—could be worked . . . " he ended lamely as Moore broke into a grin and twisted the question back into casual conversation. It was somehow amusing to have produced that sudden, strange look of realization on the man's bored face, as he actually *saw* Moore for the first time. Frightening, too.

"Yes, seeing all this progress—is inspiring." Moore pronounced. "It's almost enough to make a man want to work again. —Glad I don't have to, of course. But there's a bit of nostalgia involved in coming back after all these years and seeing how this place grew out of the shoestring operation it seemed then—grew into more buildings than I could walk through in a week, and all of them packed with new hardware and working away to beat the band. Smooth. Efficient. I like it. I suppose you like working here?"

"Yes," sighed Teng, "as much as a man can like working. Say, were you planning on staying overnight? There's a weekly employees' luau and you'd be very welcome." He glanced at the wafer of a watchface clinging to his wrist. "In fact, it's already started," he added.

"Thanks," said Moore, "but I have a date and I have to be going. I just wanted to reaffirm my faith in progress. Thanks for the tour, and thanks for your time."

The Magic

"Any time," Teng steered him toward a lush Break Room. "You won't be wanting to Dart back for awhile yet, will you?" he said. "So while we're having a bite to eat in here I wonder if I could ask you some questions about the Set. Its entrance requirements in particular . . . ."

*

All the way around the world to Bermuda, getting happily drunk in the belly of Dart Nine, in the year of Our Lord 2078, Moore felt that Time had been put aright.

*

"So you want to have it?'" said/asked Mary Maude, uncoiling carefully from the caverns of her shawl.

"Yes."

"Why?" she asked.

"Because I do not destroy that which belongs to me. I possess so very little as it is."

The Doyenne snorted gently, perhaps in amusement. She tapped her favorite dog, as though seeking a reply from it.

"Though it sails upon a bottomless sea toward some fabulous orient," she mused, "the ship will still attempt to lower an anchor. I do not know why. Can you tell me? Is it simply carelessness on the part of the captain? Or the second mate?"

The dog did not answer. Neither did anything else.

"Or is it a mutineer's desire to turn around and go back?" she inquired. "To return home?"

There was a brief stillness. Finally:

"I live in a succession of homes. They are called hours. Each is lovely."

"But not lovely enough, and never to be revisited, eh? Permit me to anticipate your next words: 'I do not intend to marry. I do not intend to leave the Set. I shall have my child—' By the way, what will it be, a boy or a girl?"

"A girl."

"'—I shall have my daughter. I shall place her in a fine home, arrange her a glorious future, and be back in time for the Spring Festival.'" She rubbed her glazed dog as though it were a crystal and pretended to peer through its greenish opacity. "Am I not a veritable gypsy?" she asked.

"Indeed."

"And you think this will work out?"

"I fail to see why it should not."

"Tell me which her proud father will do," she inquired, "compose her a sonnet sequence, or design her mechanical toys?"

"Neither. He shall never know. He'll he asleep until spring, and I will not. *She* must never know either."

"So much the worse."

"Why, pray tell?"

"Because she will become a woman in less than two months, by the clocks of the Set—and a lovely woman, I daresay—because she will be able to afford loveliness."

"Of course."

"And, as the daughter of a member, she will be eminently eligible for Set candidacy."

"She may not want it."

"Only those who cannot achieve it allude to having those sentiments. No, she'll want it. Everyone does. And, if her beauty should be surgically obtained, I believe that I shall, in this instance, alter a rule of mine. I shall pass on her and admit her to the Set. She will then meet many interesting people—poets, engineers, her mother . . . . "

"No! I'd tell her, before I'd permit that to happen!"

"Aha! Tell me, is your fear of incest predicated upon your fear of competition, or is it really the other way around?"

"Please! Why are you saying these horrible things?"

"Because, unfortunately, you are something I can no longer afford to keep around. You have been an excellent symbol for a long time, but now your pleasures have ceased to be Olympian. Yours is a lapse into the mundane. You show that the gods are less sophisticated than schoolchildren—that they can be victimized by biology, despite the oceans of medical allies at our command. Princess, in the eyes of the world you are my daughter, for I am the Set. So take some motherly advice and retire. Do not attempt to renew your option. Get married first, and then to sleep for a few months—till spring, when your option is up. Sleep intermittently in the bunker, so that a year or so will pass. We'll play up the romantic aspects of your retirement. Wait a year or two to bear your child. The cold sleep won't do her any harm; there have been other cases such as yours. If you fail to agree to this, our motherly admonition is that you face present expulsion."

"You *can't!*"

"Read your contract."

"But no one need ever know!"

"You silly little dollface!" The acetylene blazed forth. "Your glimpses of the outside world have been fragmentary and extremely selective—for at least sixty years. Every news medium in the world watches almost every move every Setman makes, from the time he sits up in his bunker until he retires, exhausted, after the latest Party. Snoopers and newshounds today have more gimmicks and gadgets in their arsenals than your head has colorful hairs. We *can't* hide your daughter all her life, so we won't even try. We'd have trouble enough concealing matters if you decided not to have her—but I think we could outbribe and outdrug our own employees.

"Therefore, I call upon you for a decision."

"I am sorry."

"So am I," said the Doyenne.

The girl stood.

From somewhere, as she left, she seemed to hear the whimpering of a china dog.

*

Beyond the neat hedgerows of the garden and down a purposefully irregular slope ran the unpaved pathway which wandered, like an impulsive river, through neck-tickling straits of unkempt forsythia, past high islands of mobbed sumac, and by the shivering branches, like waves, of an occasional ginkgo, wagging at the overhead gulls, while dreaming of the high-flying Archaeopteryx about to break through its heart in a dive; and perhaps a thousand feet of twistings are required to negotiate the two hundred feet of planned wilderness that separates the gardens of the Hall of Sleep from the artificial ruins which occupy a full, hilly acre, dotted here and there by incipient jungles of lilac and the occasional bell of a great willow—which momentarily conceal, and then guide the eye on toward broken pediments, smashed friezes, half-standing, shred-topped columns, then fallen columns, then faceless, headless statues, and finally, seemingly random heaps of rubble which lay amid these things; here, the path over which they moved then forms a delta and promptly loses itself where the tides of Time chafe away the memento mori quality that the ruins first seem to spell, acting as a temporal entasis and in the eye of the beholding, Setman, so that he can look upon it all and say, "I am the older than this," and his companion can reply, "We will pass again some year and this too, will be gone," (even though she did not say it this time) feeling happier by feeling the less mortal by so doing; and crossing through the rubble, as they did, to a place where barbarously ruined Pan grins from inside the ring of a dry fountain, a new path is to be located, this time an unplanned and only recently formed way, where the grass is yellowed underfoot and the walkers must go single file because it leads them through a place of briars, until they reach the old breakwall over which they generally climb like commandos in order to gain access to a quarter mile strand of coved and deserted beach, where the sand is not quite so clean as the beaches of the town—which are generally sifted every third day—but where the shade is as intense, in its own way, as the sunlight, and there are flat rocks offshore for meditation.

"You're getting lazy," he commented, kicking off his shoes and digging his toes into the cool sand. "You didn't climb over."

"I'm getting lazy," she agreed.

They threw off their robes and walked to the water's edge.

"Don't push!"

"Come on. I'll race you to the rocks."

For once he won.

Loafing in the lap of the Atlantic, they could have been any two bathers in any place, in any time.

"I could stay here forever."

"It gets cold nights, and if there's a bad storm you might catch something or get washed away."

"I meant," she amended, "if it could always be like this."

"'*Verweile dock, du bist so schön,*'" he reminded. "Faust lost a bet that way, remember? So would a Sleeper. Unger's got me reading again—Hey! What's the matter?"

"Nothing!"

"There's something wrong, little girl. Even I can tell."

"So what if there is?"

"So a lot, that's what. Tell me."

Her hand bridged the narrow channel between their rocks and found his. He rolled onto his side and stared at her satin-wet hair and her stuck-together eyelashes, the dimpled deserts of her cheeks, and the bloodied oasis of her mouth. She squeezed his hand.

"Let's stay here forever—despite the chill, and being washed away."

"You are indicating that—?"

"We could get off at this stop."

"I suppose. But—"

"But you like it now? You like the big charade?"

He looked away.

"I think you were right," she told him, "that night—many years ago."

"What night?"

"The night you said it was all a joke—that we are the last people alive on Earth, performing before machines operated by inhuman creatures who watch us for incomprehensible purposes. What are we but wave-patterns of an oscilloscope? I'm sick of being an object of contemplation!"

He continued to stare into the sea.

Roger Zelazny and Samuel R. Delany

"I'm rather fond of the Set now," he finally responded. "At first I was ambivalent toward it. But a few weeks—years—ago I visited a place where I used to work. It was—different. Bigger. Better run. But more than that, actually. It wasn't just that it was filled with things I couldn't have guessed at fifty or sixty years ago. I had an odd feeling while I was there. I was with a little chatterbox of a Processing director named Teng, and he was yammering away worse than Unger, and I was just staring at all those tandem-tanks and tiers of machinery that had grown up inside the shell of that first old building—sort of like inside a womb—and I suddenly felt that someday something was going to be born, born out of steel and plastic and dancing electrons, in such a stainless, sunless place—and *that* something would be so fine that I would want to be there to see it. I couldn't dignify it by calling it a mystical experience or anything like that. It was just sort of a feeling I had. But if *that* moment could stay forever . . . Anyhow, the Set is my ticket to a performance I'd like to see."

"Darling," she began, "it is anticipation and recollection that fill the heart—never the sensation of the moment."

"Perhaps you are right . . . . "

His grip tightened on her hand as the tunnel between their eyes shortened. He leaned across the water and kissed the blood from her mouth.

"*Verweile loch . . .* "

" *. . . Du bist so schön.*"

*

It was the Party to end all Parties. The surprise announcement of Alvin Moore and Leota Mathilde Mason struck the Christmas Eve gathering of the Set as just the thing for the season. After an extensive dinner and the exchange of bright and costly trifles the lights were dimmed. The giant Christmas tree atop the transparent penthouse blazed like a compressed galaxy through the droplets of melted snow on the ceilingpane.

It was nine by all the clocks of London.

"Married on Christmas, divorced on Twelfth Night," said someone in the darkness.

129

The Magic

"What'll they do for an encore?" whispered someone else.

There were giggles and several off-key carols followed them. The backlight pickup was doubtless in action.

"Tonight we are quaint," said Moore.

"We danced in Davy Jones' Locker," answered Leota, "while they cringed and were sick on the floor."

"It's not the same Set," he told her, "not really. How many new faces have you counted? How many old ones have vanished? It's hard to tell. Where do old Setmen go?"

"The graveyard of the elephants," she suggested. "Who knows?"

"'The heart is a graveyard of crigas,'" recited Moore,

"'hid far from the hunter's eye,

"'where love wears death like enamel

"'and dogs crawl in to die.'"

"That's Unger's, isn't it?" she asked.

"That's right, I just happened to recall it."

"I wish you hadn't. I don't like it."

"Sorry."

"Where is Unger anyway?" she asked as the darkness retreated and the people arose.

"Probably at the punch bowl—or under the table."

"Not this early in the evening—for being under the table, I mean."

Moore shifted.

"What *are* we doing here anyhow?" he wanted to know. "Why did we have to attend this Party?"

"Because it is the season of charity."

"Faith and hope, too," he smirked. "You want to be maudlin or something? All right, I'll be maudlin with you. It *is* a pleasure, really."

He raised her hand to his lips.

"Stop that!"

"All right."

He kissed her on the mouth. There was laughter.

Roger Zelazny and Samuel R. Delany

She flushed but did not rise from his side.

"If you want to make a fool of me—of us," he said, "I'll go more than halfway. Tell me why we had to come to this Party and announce our un-Setness before everyone? We could have just faded away from the Parties, slept until spring, and let our options run out."

"No. I am a woman and I could not resist another Party—the last one of the year, the very last—and wear your gift on my finger and know that deep down inside, the others *do* envy us—our courage, if nothing else—and probably our happiness."

"Okay," he agreed, "I'll drink to it—to you, anyway." He raised his glass and downed it. There was no fireplace to throw it into, so as much as he admired the gesture he placed it back on the table.

"Shall we dance? I hear music."

"Not yet. Let's just sit here and drink."

"Fine."

When all the clocks in London said eleven, Leota wanted to know where Unger was.

"He left," a slim girl with purple hair told her, "right after dinner. Maybe indigestion"—she shrugged—"or maybe he went looking for the Globe."

She frowned and took another drink.

Then they danced. Moore did not really see the room through which they moved, nor the other dancers. They were all the featureless characters in a book he had already closed. Only the dance was real—and the woman with whom he was dancing.

Time's friction, he decided, and a raising of the sights. I have what I wanted and still I want more. I'll get over it.

It was a vasty hall of mirrors. There were hundreds of dancing Alvin Moores and Leotas (nee Mason) dancing. They were dancing at all their Parties of the past seventy—some years—from a Tibetan ski lodge to Davy Jones' Locker, from a New Years Eve in orbit to the floating Palace of Kanayasha, from a Halloween in the caverns of Carlsbad to a May Day at

The Magic

Delphi—they had danced everywhere, and tonight was the last Party, *good night, ladies.*

She leaned against him and said nothing and her breath collared his neck.

"Good night, good night, good night," he heard himself saying, and they left with the bells of midnight, early, early, and it was Christmas as they entered the hopcar and told the Set chauffeur that they were returning early.

And they passed over the stratocruiser and settled beside the Dart they had come in, and they crossed through the powdery fleece that lay on the ground and entered the smaller craft.

"Do you wish to have the lights dimmed? Or would you prefer to have them brighter?" asked a voice at their side, after London and its clocks and its Bridge had fallen, down.

"Dim them."

"Would you case for something to eat? Or to drink?"

"No."

"No."

"Shall I read you an article on the subject of your choice?" *Pause.* "Or fiction?" *Pause.* "Or poetry?" *Pause.* "Would you care to view the catalog?" *Pause.* "Or perhaps you would prefer music?"

"Music," she said. "Soft. Not the kind you listen to."

After about ten minutes of near-sleep, Moore heard the voice:

"Hilted of flame,
our frail phylactic blade
slits black
beneath Polestar's
pinprick comment,
foredging burrs
of mitigated hell,
spilling light without illumination.
Strands of song,

to share its stinging flight.
are shucked and scraped
to fit an idiot theme.
Here, through outlocked chaos,
climbed of migrant logic,
the forms of black notation
blackly dice a flame."

"Turn it off," said Moore. "We didn't ask you to read."

"I'm not reading," said the voice, "I'm composing."

"Who—?"

Moore came awake and turned in his seat, which promptly adjusted to the movement. A pair of feet projected over the arm of a double seat to the rear.

"Unger?"

"No, Santa Claus. Ho! Ho!"

"What are you doing going back this early?"

"You just answered your own question, didn't you?"

Moore snorted and settled back once more. At his side, Leota was snoring delicately, her seat collapsed into a couch.

He shut his eyes, but knowing they were not alone he could not regain the peaceful drifting sensation he had formerly achieved. He heard a sigh and the approach of lurching footfalls. He kept his eyes closed, hoping Unger would fall over and go to sleep. He didn't.

Abruptly, his voice rang out, a magnificently dreadful baritone:

"*I was down to Saint James' Infir-r-rmary,*" he sang. "*I saw my ba-a-aby there, stretched out on a long whi-i-ite ta-a-able-so sweet, so cold, so fair—*"

Moore swung his left hand, cross-body at the poet's midsection. He had plenty of target, but he was too slow. Unger blocked his fist and backed away, laughing.

Leota shook herself awake.

"What are you doing here?" she asked.

"Composing," he answered, "myself.

"Merry Christmas," he added.

"Go to hell," answered Moore.

"I congratulate you on your recent nuptials, Mister Moore."

"Thanks."

"Why wasn't I invited?"

"It was a simple ceremony."

He turned.

"Is that true, Leota? An old comrade-in-arms like me, not invited, just because it wasn't showy enough for my elaborate tastes?"

She nodded, fully awake now.

He struck his forehead.

"Oh, I am wounded!"

"Why don't you go back to wherever you came from?" asked Moore. "The drinks are on the house."

"I can't attend midnight mass in an inebriated condition."

Moore's fingers twitched back into fists.

"You may attend a mass for the dead without having to kneel."

"I believe you are hinting that you wish to be alone. I understand."

He withdrew to the rear of the Dart. After a time he began to snore.

"I hope we never see him again," she said.

"Why? He's a harmless drunk."

"No, he isn't. He hates us—because we're happy and he isn't."

"I think he's happiest when he's unhappy," smiled Moore, "and whenever the temperature drops. He loves the cold-bunk because it's like a little death to sleep in it. He once said, 'Each Setman dies many deaths. That's what I like about being a Setman.'

"You say more sleep won't be injurious—" he asked abruptly.

"No, there's no risk."

Below them, Time fled backward through the cold. Christmas was pushed out into the hallway and over the threshold of the front door to their

Roger Zelazny and Samuel R. Delany

world—Alvin's, Leota's, and Unger's world—to stand shivering on the doorsill of its own Eve, in Bermuda.

Inside the Dart, passing backward through Time, Moore recalled that New Year's Eve Party many years ago, recalled his desires of that day and reflected that they sat beside him now; recalled the Parties since then and reflected that he would miss all that were yet to come; recalled his work in the time before Time—a few months ago—and reflected that he could no longer do it properly—and that Time was indeed out of joint and that *he* could not set it aright; he recalled his old apartment, never revisited, all his old friends, including Diane Demetrios, now dead or senile, and reflected that, beyond the Set which he was leaving, he knew no one, save possibly the girl at his side. Only Wayne Unger was ageless, for he was an employee of the eternal. Given a month or two Unger could open up a bar, form his own circle of outcasts, and toy with a private renaissance, if he should ever decide to leave.

Moore suddenly felt very stale and tired, and he whispered to their ghostly servant for a Martini and reached across his dozing wife to fetch it from the cubicle. He sat there sipping it, wondering about the world below.

He should have kept up with life, he decided. He knew nothing of contemporary politics, or law, or art; his Standards were those grafted on by the Set, and concerned primarily with color, movement, gaiety, and clever speech; he was reduced again to childhood when it came to science. He knew he was wealthy, but the Set had been managing all his finances. All he had was an all-purpose card, good anywhere in the world for any sort of purchase, commodity or service-wise. Periodically, he had examined his file and seen balance sheets which told him he need never worry about being short of money. But he did not feel confident or competent when it came to meeting the people who resided in the world outside. Perhaps he would appear stodgy, old-fashioned, and "quaint" as he had felt tonight, without the glamor of the Set to mask his humanity.

Unger snored, Leota breathed deeply, and the world turned. When they reached Bermuda they returned to the Earth.

The Magic

They stood beside the Dart, just outside the flight terminal.

"Care to take a walk?" asked Moore.

"I am tired, my love," said Leota, staring in the direction of the Hall of Sleep. She looked back.

He shook his head. "I'm not quite ready."

She turned to him. He kissed her.

"I'll see you then in April, darling. Good night."

"April is the cruelest month," observed Unger. "Come, engineer, I'll walk with you as far as the shuttle stands."

They began walking. They moved across the roadway in the direction opposite the terminal, and they entered upon the broad, canopied walk that led to the ro-car garage.

It was a crystalline night, with stars like tinsel and a satellite beacon blazing like a gold piece deep within the pool of the sky. As they walked, their breath fumed into white wreathes that vanished before they were fully formed. Moore tried in vain to light his pipe. Finally, he stopped and hunched his shoulders against the wind until he got it going.

"A good night for walking," said Unger.

Moore grunted. A gust of wind lashed a fiery rain of loose tobacco upon his cheek. He smoked on, hands in the pockets of his jacket, collar raised. The poet clapped him on the shoulder.

"Come with me into the town," he suggested. "It's only over the hill. We can walk it."

"No," said Moore, through his teeth.

They strode on, and as they neared the garage Unger grew uneasy.

"I'd rather someone were with me tonight," he said abruptly. "I feel strange, as though I'd drunk the draught of the centuries and suddenly am wise in a time when wisdom is unnecessary. I—I'm afraid."

Moore hesitated.

"No," he finally repeated, "it's time to say good-bye. You're traveling on and we're getting off. Have fun."

Roger Zelazny and Samuel R. Delany

Neither offered to shake hands, and Moore watched him move into the shuttle stop.

Continuing behind the building, Moore cut diagonally across the wide lawns and into the garden. He strolled aimlessly for a few minutes, then found the path that led down to the ruins.

The going was slow and he wound his way through the cold wilderness. After a period of near-panic when he felt surrounded by trees and he had to backtrack, he emerged into the starlit clearing where menaces of shrubbery dappled the broken buildings with patterns of darkness, moving restlessly as the winds shifted.

The grass rustled about his ankles as he seated himself on a fallen pillar and got his pipe going once more.

He sat thinking himself into marble as his toes grew numb, and he felt very much a part of the place; an artificial scene, a ruin transplanted out of history onto unfamiliar grounds. He did not want to move. He just wanted to freeze into the landscape and become his own monument. He sat there making pacts with imaginary devils: he wanted to go back, to return with Leota to his Frisco town, to work again. Like Unger, he suddenly felt wise in time when wisdom was unnecessary. Knowledge was what he needed. Fear was what he had.

Pushed on by the wind, he picked his way across the plain. Within the circle of his fountain, Pan was either dead or sleeping. Perhaps it is the cold sleep of the gods, decided Moore, and Pan will one day awaken and blow upon his festival pipes and only the wind among high towers will answer, and the shuffling tread of an assessment robot be quickened to scan him— because the Party people will have forgotten the festival melodies, and the waxen ones will have isolated out the wisdom of the blood on their colored slides and inoculated mankind against it—and, programmed against emotions, a frivolity machine will perpetually generate the sensations of gaiety into the fever-dream of the delirious, so that they will not recognize his tunes—and there shall be none among the children of Phoebus to even repeat

The Magic

the Attic cry of his first passing, heard those many Christmases ago beyond the waters of the Mediterranean.

Moore wished that he had stayed a little longer with Unger; because he now felt that he had gained a glimpse of the man's perspective. It had taken the fear of a new world to generate these feelings, but he was beginning to understand the poet. Why did the man stay on in the Set, though? he wondered. Did he take a masochistic pleasure in seeing his ice-prophecies fulfilled, as he moved further and further away from his own times? Maybe that was it.

Moore stirred himself into one last pilgrimage. He walked along their old path down to the breakwall. The stones were cold beneath his fingers, so he used the stile to cross over to the beach.

He stood on a rim of rust at the star-reflecting bucket-bottom of the world. He stared out at the black humps of the rocks where they had held their sunny colloquy days/months ago. It was his machines he had spoken of then, before they had spoken of themselves. He had believed, still believed, in their inevitable fusion with the spirit of his kind, into greater and finer vessels for life. Now he feared, like Unger, that by the time this occurred something else might have been lost, and that the fine new vessels would only be partly filled, lacking some essential ingredient. He hoped Unger was wrong; he felt that the ups and downs of Time might at some future equinox restore all those drowsing verities of the soul's undersides that he was now feeling—and that there *would* be ears to hear the piped melody, and feet that would move with its sound. He tried to believe this. He hoped it would be true.

A star fell, and Moore looked at his watch. It was late. He scuffed his way back to the wall and crossed over it again.

*

Inside the pre-sleep clinic he met Jameson, who was already yawning from his prep-injection. Jameson was a tall, thin man with the hair of a cherub and the eyes of its opposite number.

"Moore," he grinned, watching him hang his jacket on the wall and roll up his sleeve. "You going to spend your honeymoon on ice?"

The hypogun sighed in the medic's husky hand and the prep-injection entered Moore's arm.

"That's right," he replied, leveling his gaze at the not completely sober Jameson. "Why?"

"It just doesn't seem the thing to do," Jameson explained, still grinning. "If I were married to Leota you wouldn't catch me going on ice. Unless—"

Moore took one step toward him, the sound in his throat like a snarl. Jameson drew back, his dark eyes widening.

"I was joking!" he said. "I didn't . . . "

There was a pain in Moore's injected arm as the big medic seized it and jerked him to a halt.

"Yeah," said Moore, "good night. Sleep tight, wake sober."

As he turned toward the door the medic released his arm. Moore rolled down his sleeve and donned his jacket as he left.

"You're off your rocker," Jameson called after him.

Moore had about half an hour before he had to hit his bunker. He did not feel like heading for it at the moment. He had planned on waiting in the clinic until the injection began to work, but Jameson's presence changed that.

He walked through the wide corridors of the Hall of Sleep, rode a lift up to the bunkers, then strode down the hallway until he came to his door. He hesitated, then passed on. He would sleep there for the next three and a half months; he did not feel like giving it half of the next hour also.

He refilled his pipe. He would smoke through a sentinel watch beside the ice goddess, his wife. He looked about for wandering medics. One is supposed to refrain from smoking after the prep-injection, but it had never bothered him yet, or anyone else he knew of.

An intermittent thumping sound reached his ears as he moved on up the hallway. It stopped as he rounded a corner, then began again, louder. It was coming from up ahead.

The Magic

After a moment there was another silence.

He paused outside Leota's door. Grinning around his pipe, he found a pen and drew a line through the last name on her plate. He printed" Moore" in above it. As he was forming the final letter the pounding began again.

It was coming from inside her room.

He opened the door, took a step, then stopped.

The man had his back to him. His right arm was raised. A mallet was clenched in his fist.

His panted mutterings, like an incantation, reached Moore's ears:

"'Strew on her roses, roses, and never spray a yew . . . In quiet she reposes—'"

Moore was across the chamber. He seized the mallet and managed to twist it away. Then he felt something break inside his hand as his fist connected with a jaw. The man collided with the opposite wall, then pitched forward onto the floor.

"Leota!" said Moore. "Leota . . . "

Cast of white Parian she lay, deep within the coils of the bunker. The canopy lead been raised high overhead. Her flesh was already firm as stone—because there was no blood on her breast where the stake had been driven in. Only cracks and fissures, as in stone.

"No," said Moore.

The stake was a very hard synthowood—like cocobolo, or quebracho, or perhaps lignum vitae—still to be unsplintered . . . .

"No," said Moore.

Her face had the relaxed expression of a dreamer, her hair was the color of aluminum. His ring was on her finger . . . .

There was a murmuring in the corner of the room.

"Unger," he said flatly, "why—did—you—do it?"

The man sucked air around his words. His eyes were focused on something nameless.

" . . . Vampire," he muttered, "luring men aboard her Flying Dutchman to drain them across the years . . . . She is the future—a goddess on the

140

outside and a thirsting vacuum within," he stated without emotion. "'Strew on her roses, roses . . . Her mirth the world required—She bathed it in smiles of glee . . . ' She was going to leave me way up here in the middle of the air. I can't get off the merry-go-round and I can't have the brass ring. But no one else will lose as I have lost, not now. ' . . . Her life was turning, turning, in mazes of heat and sound—' I thought she would come back to me, after she'd tired of you."

He raised his hand to cover his eyes as Moore advanced upon him.

"To the technician, the future—"

Moore hit him with the hammer, once, twice. After the third blow he lost count because his mind could not conceive of any number greater than three.

Then he was walking, running, the mallet still clutched in his hand—past doors like blind eyes, up corridors, down seldom—used stairwells.

As he lurched away from the Hall of Sleep he heard someone calling after him through the night. He kept running.

After a long while be began to walk again. His hand was aching and his breath burned within his lungs. He climbed a hill, paused at its top, then descended the other side.

Party Town, an expensive resort—owned and sponsored, though seldom patronized by the Set—was deserted, except for the Christmas lights in the windows, and the tinsel, and the boughs of holly. From some dim adytum the recorded carols of a private celebration could be heard, and some laughter. These things made Moore feel even more alone as he walked up one street and down another, his body seeming ever more a thing apart from him as the prep-injection took its inevitable effect. His feet were leaden. His eyes kept closing and he kept forcing them back open.

There were no services going on when he entered the church. It was warmer inside. He was alone there, too.

The interior of the church was dim, and he was attracted to an array of lights about the display at the foot of a statute. It was a manger scene. He leaned back against a pew and stared at the mother and the child, at the angels and the inquisitive cattle, at the father. Then he made a sound he had no words for and threw the mallet into the little stable and turned away. Clawing at the wall, he staggered off a dozen steps and collapsed, cursing and weeping, until he slept.

They found him at the foot of the cross.

*

Justice had become a thing of streamlined swiftness since the days of Moore's boyhood. The sheer force of world population had long ago crowded every docket of every court to impossible extremes, until measures were taken to waive as much of the paraphernalia as could be waived and hold court around the clock. That was why Moore faced judgment at ten o'clock in the evening, two days after Christmas.

The trial lasted less than a quarter of an hour. Moore waived representation; the charges were read; he entered a plea of guilty, and the judge sentenced him to death in the gas chamber without looking up from the stack of papers on his bench.

Numbly, Moore left the courtroom and was returned to a cell for his final meal, which he did not remember eating. He had no conception of the juridical process in this year in which he had come to rest. The Set attorney had simply looked bored as he told him his story, then mentioned "symbolic penalties" and told him to waive representation and enter a simple plea of "guilty to the homicide as described." He signed a statement to that effect. Then the attorney had left him and Moore had not spoken with anyone but his warders up until the time of the trial, and then only a few words before he went into court. And now—to receive a death sentence after he had admitted he was guilty of killing his wife's murderer—he could not conceive that justice had been done. Despite this, he felt an unnatural calm as he chewed mechanically upon whatever he had ordered. He was not afraid to die. He could not believe in it.

An hour later they came for him. He was led to a small, airtight room with a single, thick window set high in its metal door. He seated himself upon the bench within it and his gray-uniformed guards slammed the door behind him.

After an interminable time he heard the pellets breaking and he smelled the fumes. They grew stronger.

Finally, he was coughing and breathing fire and gasping and crying out, and he thought of her lying there in her bunker, the ironic strains of Unger's song during their Dart-flight recurring in his mind:

"I was down to Saint James' In fir-r-rmary.
I saw my ba-a-aby there,
Stretched out on a long whi-i-ite ta-a-able
So sweet, so cold, so fair . . . "

Had Unger been consciously contemplating her murder even then? he wondered. Or was it something lurking below his consciousness? Something he had felt stirring, so that he had wanted Moore to stay with him—to keep it from happening?

He would never know, he realized, as the fires reached into his skull and consumed his brain.

*

As he awoke, feeling very weak upon white linen, the voice within his earphones was saying to Alvin Moore: " . . . Let that be a lesson to you."

Moore tore off the earphones with what he thought was a strong gesture, but his muscles responded weakly. Still, the earphones came off.

He opened his eyes and stared.

He might be in the Set's Sick Ward, located high up in the Hall of Sleep, or in hell. Franz Andrews, the attorney who had advised him to plead guilty, sat at his bedside.

"How do you feel?" he asked.

"Oh, great! Care to play a set of tennis?"

The man smiled faintly.

"You have successfully discharged your debt to society," he stated, "through the symbolic penalty procedure."

"Oh, that explains everything," said Moore wryly. Finally: "I don't see why there had to be any penalty, symbolic or otherwise. That rhymer murdered my wife."

"He'll pay for it," said Andrews.

Moore rolled onto his side and studied the dispassionate, flat-featured face at his elbow. The attorney's short hair was somewhere between blond and gray and his gaze unflinchingly sober.

"Do you mind repeating what you just said?"

"Not at all. I said he'd pay for it."

"He's not dead!"

"No, he's quite alive—two floors above us. His head has to heal before he can stand trial. He's too ill to face execution."

"He's alive!" said Moore. "Alive? Then what the hell was I executed for?"

"Well, you *did* kill the man," said Andrews, somewhat annoyed. "The fact that the doctors were later able to revive him does not alter the fact that a homicide occurred. The symbolic penalty exists for all such cases. You'll think twice before ever doing it again."

Moore tried to rise. He failed.

"Take it easy. You're going to need several more days of rest before you can get up. Your own revival was only last night."

Moore chuckled weakly. Then he laughed for a long, long time. He stopped, ending with a little sob.

"Feel better now?"

"Sure, sure," he whispered hoarsely. "Like a million bucks, or whatever the crazy currency is these days. What kind of execution will Unger get for murder?"

"Gas," said the attorney, "the same as you, if the alleged—"

"Symbolic, or for keeps?"

"Symbolic, of course."

Roger Zelazny and Samuel R. Delany

Moore did not remember what happened next, except that he heard someone screaming and there was suddenly a medic whom he had not noticed doing something to his arm. He heard the soft hiss of an injection. Then he slept.

When he awakened he felt stronger and he noticed an insolent bar of sunlight streaking the wall opposite him. Andrews appeared not to have moved from his side.

He stared at the man and said nothing.

"I have been advised," said the attorney, "of your lack of knowledge concerning the present state of law in these matters. I did not stop to consider the length of your membership in the Set. These things so seldom occur—in fact, this is the first such case I've ever handled—that I simply assumed you knew what a symbolic penalty was when I spoke with you back in your cell. I apologize."

Moore nodded.

"Also," he continued, "I assumed that you had considered the circumstances under which Mister Unger allegedly committed a homicide—"

"'Allegedly,' hell! I was there. He drove a stake through her heart!" Moore's voice broke at that point.

"It *was* to have been a precedent-making decision," said Andrews, "as to whether he was to be indicated now for attempted homicide, or be detained until after the operation and face homicide charges if things do not go well. The matter of his detention then would have raised many more problems—which were fortunately resolved at his own suggestion. After his recovery he will retire to his bunker and remain there until the nature of the offense had been properly determined. He has volunteered to do this of his own free will, so no legal decision was delivered on the matter. His trial is postponed, therefore, until some of the surgical techniques have been refined—"

"What surgical techniques?" asked Moore, raising himself into a seated position and leaning against the head board. His mind was fully alert for the first time since Christmas. He felt what was coming next.

He said one word.

The Magic

"Explain."

Andrews shifted in his chair.

"Mister Unger," he began, "had a poet's conception as to the exact location of the human heart. He did not pierce it centrally, although the accidental angling of the stake did cause it to pass through the left ventricle. That can be repaired easily enough, according to the medics.

"Unfortunately, however, the slanting of the shaft caused it to strike against her spinal column," he said, "smashing two vertebrae and cracking several others. It appears that the spinal cord was severed . . . . "

Moore was numb again, numb with the realization that had dawned as the lawyer's words were filling the air between them. Of course she wasn't dead. Neither was she alive. She was sleeping the cold sleep. The spark of life would remain within her until the arousal began. *Then*, and only then, could she die. Unless—

" . . . Complicated by her pregnancy and the period of time necessary to raise her body temperature to an operable one," Andrews was saying.

"When are they going to operate?" Moore broke in.

"They can't say for certain, at this time," answered Andrews. "It will have to be a specially designed operation, as it raises problems for which there are answers in theory but not in practice. Any one of the factors could be treated at present, but the others couldn't be held in abeyance while the surgery is going on. Together, they are rather formidable—to repair the heart and fix the back, and to save the child, all at the same time, will require some new instrumentation and some new techniques."

"How long?" insisted Moore.

Andrews shrugged.

"They can't say. Months, years. She's all right as she is now, but—"

Moore asked him to go away, rather loudly, and he did.

*

The following day, feeling dizzy, he got to his feet and refused to return to bed until he could see Unger.

"He's in custody," said the medic who attended him.

Roger Zelazny and Samuel R. Delany

"No, he isn't," replied Moore. "You're not a lawyer, and I've already spoken with one. He won't be taken into legal custody until after he awakens from his next cold sleep—whenever that is."

It took over an hour for him to get permission to visit Unger. When he did, he was accompanied by Andrews and two orderlies.

"Don't you trust the symbolic penalty?" he smirked at Andrews. "You know that I'm supposed to think twice before I do it again."

Andrews looked away and did not answer him.

"Anyhow, I'm too weak and I don't have a hammer handy."

They knocked and entered.

Unger, his head turbaned in white, sat propped up by pillows. A closed book lay on the counterpane. He had been staring out of the window and into the garden. He turned his head toward them.

"Good morning, you son of a bitch," observed Moore.

"Please," said Unger.

Moore did not know what to say next. He had already expressed all that he felt. So he headed for the chair beside the bed and sat on it. He fished his pipe from the pocket of his robe and fumbled with it to hide his discomfort. Then he realized he had no tobacco with him. Neither Andrews nor the orderlies appeared to be watching them.

He placed the dry pipe between his teeth and looked up.

"I'm sorry," said Unger. "Can you believe that?"

"No," answered Moore.

"She's the future and she's yours," said Unger. "I drove a stake through her heart but she isn't really dead. They say they're working on the operating machines now. The doctors will fix up everything that I did, as good as new." He winced and looked down at the bedclothes.

"If it's any consolation to you," he continued, "I'm suffering and I'll suffer more. There is no Senta to save this Dutchman. I'm going to ride it out with the Set, or without it, in a bunker—die in some foreign place among strangers." He looked up, regarding Moore with a weak smile. Moore stared him back down. "They'll save her!" he insisted. "She'll sleep until they're

147

absolutely certain of the technique. Then you two will get off together and I'll keep on going. You'll never see me after that. I wish you happiness. I won't ask your forgiveness."

Moore got to his feet.

"We've got nothing left to say. We'll talk again some year, in a day or so."

He left the room wondering what else he could have said.

*

"An ethical question has been put before the Set—that is to say, myself," said Mary Maude. "Unfortunately, it was posed by government attorneys, so it cannot be treated as most ethical questions are to be treated. It requires an answer."

"Involving Moore and Unger?" asked Andrews.

"Not directly. Involving the entire Set, as a result of their escapade."

She indicated the fac-sheet on her desk. Andrews nodded.

"'Unto Us a Babe is Born,'" she read, considering the photo of the prostrate Setman in the church. "A front page editorial in this periodical has accused us of creating all varieties of neurotics—from necrophilists on down the line. Then there's that other photo—we still don't know who took it— here, on page three—"

"I've seen it."

"They now want assurances that ex-Setmen will remain frivolous and not turn into eminent undesirables."

"This is the first time it's ever happened—like this."

"Of course," she smiled. "They're usually decent enough to wait a few weeks before going anti—social—and wealth generally compensates for most normal maladjustments. But, according to the accusations, we are either selecting the wrong people—which is ridiculous—or not mustering them out properly when they leave—which is profoundly ridiculous. First, because I do all the interviewing, and second, because you *can't* boot a person half a century or so into the future and expect him to land on his feet as his normal, cheerful self, regardless of any orientation you may give him. Our people make a good show of it, though, because they don't generally do much of anything.

"But both Moore and Unger were reasonably normal, and they never knew each other particularly well. Both watched a little more closely than most Setmen as their worlds became history, and both were highly sensitive to those changes. Their problem, though, was interpersonal."

Andrews said nothing.

"By that, I mean it was a simple case of jealousy over a woman—an unpredictable human variable. I could not have foreseen their conflict. The changing times have nothing to do with it. Do they?"

Andrews did not answer.

" . . . Therefore, there is no problem," she continued. "We are not dumping Kaspar Hausers onto the street. We are simply transplanting wealthy people of good taste a few generations into the future—and they get on well. Our only misstep so far was predicated upon a male antagonism of the mutually accelerating variety, caused by a beautiful woman. That's all. Do you agree?"

"He thought that he was really going to die . . . " said Andrews. "I didn't stop to think that he knew nothing of the World Legal Code."

"A minor matter," she dismissed it. "He's still living."

"You should have seen his face when he came to in the Clinic."

"I'm not interested in faces. I've seen too many. Our problem now is to manufacture a problem and then to solve it to the government's satisfaction."

"The world changes so rapidly that I almost need to make a daily adjustment to it myself. These poor—"

"Some things do not change," said Mary Maude, "but I can see what you're driving at. Very clever. We'll hire us an independent Psych Team to do us a study indicating that what the Set needs is more adjustment, and they'll recommend that one day be set aside every year for therapeutic purposes. We'll hold each one in a different part of the world—at a non–Party locale. Lots of cities have been screaming for concessions. They'll all be days spent doing simple, adjustive things, mingling with un-Set people. Then, in the evening we'll have a light meal, followed by casual, restful entertainment, and then some dancing—dancing's good for the psyche, it relaxes tensions. —I'm sure that will satisfy all parties concerned." She smiled at the last.

"I believe you are right," said Andrews.

"Of course. After the Psych Team writes several thousand pages, you'll draft a few hundred of your own to summarize the findings and cast them into the form of a resolution to be put before the board."

He nodded.

"I thank you for your suggestions."

"Any time. That's what I'm paid for."

After he had left, Mary Maude donned her black glove and placed another log on the fire. Genuine logs cost more and more every year, but she did not trust flameless heaters.

*

It was three days before Moore had recovered sufficiently to enter the sleep again. As the prep-injection dulled his senses and his eyes closed, he wondered what alien judgment day would confront him when he awakened. He knew, though, that whatever else the new year brought, his credit would be good.

He slept, and the world passed by.

A Word from Zelazny

Zelazny acknowledged that the character of Mary Maude Mullen, the Victorian Doyenne of the Set, owes inspiration to the work of John Collier and the story "Evening Primrose." The Doyenne resembles Mrs. Vanderpants who rules the strange crew that live in the department store after closing hours in Collier's tale.[1]

Zelazny used some of his earlier poetry from *Chisel in the Sky* in this story. "Poetry had a way of creeping into a few of those early stories—and when I needed a poem I still had batches of them to draw upon, though I'd chucked hundreds when I'd made my decision for prose. A few of those remaining fit stories here and there."[2]

Notes

Theodore Sturgeon wrote, "'The Graveyard Heart' is in that wonderful category which is, probably, science fiction's greatest gift to literature and to human beings: the 'feedback' story, the 'if this goes on' story; an extension of some facet of the current scene which carries you out and away to times and places you've never imagined because you can't; and when it's finished, you turn about and look at the thing he extended for you, in its here-and-now reality, sharing this very day and planet with you; and you know he's told you something, given you something you didn't have before, and that you will never look at this aspect of your world with quite the same eyes again."[3]

In the story, Alvin Moore listens to excerpts from Wayne Unger's poetry collection, entitled *Chisel in the Sky*. This was the actual title of a poetry collection that Zelazny assembled and submitted to the Yale Younger Poets Competition in the late 1950s, but it did not win and was never published.[3] As noted above, the poems used within the story are Zelazny's own and were based on poems in Zelazny's manuscript *Chisel in the Sky*.

Leota is variously referred to by Alvin Moore as **nee Lilith, nee Lorelei; nee Lachesis; nee Mathilde Mason** during the story, and each of these names has significance. **Nee** means the maiden name follows, but **Lilith** refers to an evil Mesopotamian night demon and an evil force in the Kabbalah (Moore is describing Leota as evil). **Lorelei** was the Rhine maiden who used her songs to lure fishermen and navigators to their doom (Moore is describing Leota as his doom). **Lachesis** was the one of the three Fates who measured the length of thread that determined the span of a person's life and who decided upon that person's destiny (Moore is describing Leota as the determiner of his fate). **Mathilde** refers to the famous woman poet whose liaison with composer Richard Wagner made her his muse and inspired him to create *Tristan and Isolde* (a tale of fated love—see afterword to "The Ides of

The Magic

Octember"/"He Who Shapes" for details) and *The Valkyrie* (in Norse mythology, the strong warrior maidens who chose slain warriors for Odin)–thus, Moore is referring to Leota as his muse. **Mason** is apparently Leota's true surname in the context of the story.

Samadhi is a state of deep meditation in which a person experiences oneness with the universe. **Myopia** is nearsightedness. Leota has **graygreen eyes**, which is a recurrent motif in Zelazny's work. Although green eyes occur in less than 2% of people, at least 32 of his novels and short stories mention green, emerald, or jade eyes. **Kinesthesia** is the sensation of movement or strain in the muscles, tendons and joints. *C'est vrai* means 'that's true.' **Auld acquaintance** alludes to the song *Auld Lang Syne* which is often sung at New Year's Eve celebrations. **Bastille Day** is a national holiday on July 14 in France commemorating the storming of the Bastille on July 14, 1789. *Liberté, Egalité, Fraternité* (Liberty, Equality, Fraternity) was a motto of the French Revolution, was inscribed on the pediments of public buildings in 1880, and was eventually written into the 1958 French Constitution. **Fete Nue** means naked feast or holiday. **Camille** alludes to the novel *La Dame aux camelias* by Alexandre Dumas, fils, which is the tragic story of a young man who has an affair with a courtesan who later dies of tuberculosis. **Aphrodite** was the goddess of beauty, fertility, and sexual love. **The chance of a Stockholm snowflake in the Congo** paraphrases the saying "a snowflake's chance in hell"–an extremely unlikely event.

Green acres of Presidents refers to American paper money. **Georges Braque** was a French painter who developed Cubism with Picasso. **Berlitz** is a publisher of guides to learning languages. *Tovarisch* means comrade. A **courtier** attends at the court of a king or is a person who seeks favor by flattery and charm. **Excelsior!** (higher or ever upward) foreshadows doom because it refers to the poem by Henry Wadsworth Longfellow in which a young man passes through a town bearing the banner "Excelsior" and ignores all warnings, climbing higher until he is found "lifeless, but beautiful," frozen stiff and half-buried in the snow with the banner still clasped in his hands. An **orchid** is considered to have several meanings depending on context and country: purity or perfection; love, luxury and beauty; reproduction and fertility; aphrodisiac or sexual desire. **How do your flowers grow? . . . barely and contrary** refers to the nursery rhyme *Mary, Mary, Quite Contrary.*

Microprosopos refers to a microuniverse and to the Kabbalistic concept of nine of the ten manifestations (Sephiroth) of God in the universe; **Adam Kadmon** is Primal Man in Kabbal; **Malkuth** is the tenth Sephiroth and sits at the base of the Tree of Life. **Schleraffenland** is German for "the land of milk and honey." **Chinoiserie** means ornamental and elaborately or intricately decorated, in the style of Chinese. **Elegiac** means sorrowful or lamenting in tone. **Elan** is distinctive style or flair. **Moebius** or mobius is an object with one surface and one edge. *Certainement* means 'certainly.' **Poconos** refers to a mountain range in Pennsylvania. **Caprice** is a tendency to change one's mind unexpectedly, on a whim, for no apparent reason. **Diana** is the Greek goddess of the hunt, **Demeter** is the goddess of harvest and fertility; the name **Diane Demetrios** combines these two. An **eidolon** is an image of an ideal person or thing. **Autodidactics** are self-teachings or self-directed learnings, such as the self-training that Moore received (some of it while asleep) to be able to gossip and dance. **Those gods of old who appeared at the rites of the equinoxes** refers to the myth of the dying god, the contrast of immortality and suicide, which informed so much of Zelazny's writing. **Lazarus** was the man whom Jesus raised from the dead in the **New Testament**. **Nirvana** is a state of pure consciousness in which the mind is free of all contaminants, emotions and distractions. **He was a handful of dust in the winds of Time . . .** refers to T. S. Eliot's *The Waste Land: The Burial of the Dead.* **Nostrum** is a medication of unproven efficacy and secret ingredients; a quack medicine. **M.S.** is multiple sclerosis, a condition affecting the nervous system in which motor and sensory nerves lose their myelin sheaths (akin to insulation around an electrical wire), resulting in loss of function of that nerve.

Hades is hell or the underworld, the place of eternal flame and damnation. **Alfred, Lord Tennyson** was an important 19th century poet, a man of Mary Maude's time. A **Buddhist's attitude toward the world** is that everything changes, nothing is static or constant. In Spain, **Juegos Florales** are floral games at the **Fiesta de la Vendimia Jerezana** which is a fall festival that includes blessing of the grapes and must (the product of the initial crushing of the grapes) before an image of San Gines de la Jara, Patron Saint of vine growers. A **necrophilist** is someone who has an erotic fascination with death and corpses. **Miasma** is a foreboding, dangerous or poisonous atmosphere. **Alas, poor Unger . . . I knew him well** alludes to Hamlet's line "Alas, poor Yorick..." spoken as he contemplates the skull of his old acquaintance. **Merrily we roll along . . . deep blue sea!** are lyrics from the 1936 song "Merrily We Roll Along" which is best known as the theme music for Warner Bros.' Merrie Melodies cartoons. **Simulacra** are images or representations of someone or something. **Crigas** is an Indo-European word meaning fights, wars and strife.

An **Emir** is a chieftain, prince or head of state in some Islamic countries. *Quo vadis* is Latin for "where are you going?" and a famous phrase from the Bible in which Peter asks Jesus where he is going. Importantly, *Quo Vadis* is the title of a famous novel by Henryk Sienkiewicz and several motion picture adaptations, and it foreshadows aspects of the plot of "The Graveyard Heart"—a love triad, a death by stabbing in the heart, a couple set free to find happiness. **Davy Jones Party** refers to the earlier near-disaster of drownings in the story caused by an earthquake; Davy Jones' Locker means the bottom of the sea, and resting place of drowned sailors. **The Mermaid** was a seventeenth-century tavern on Cheapside in London, where Shakespeare and his colleagues reputedly met on the first Friday of every month (although scholars now doubt this). The **Red Lion in Stepney** was an inn/pub in Stepney (east end of London) which was later upgraded to a public playhouse just a few years after Shakespeare was born. **Christopher (Kit) Marlowe** was a poet and dramatist from the era of Shakespeare. **Noble Macbeth** and **Duncan** refers to Shakespeare's play *Macbeth*; the mausoleum or tomb they are leaning up against in the Red Square in Moscow is not Macbeth's, but Lenin's (Unger is having a joke with Moore's ignorance of history and their own present time: at that moment in the story, they were attending an event at Lenin's Palace in Moscow). **Boris Pasternak** was a Russian poet and writer, of which his novel *Doctor Zhivago* may be the best known; he also translated eight of Shakespeare's plays into Russian, including *Macbeth*. **Shinvat** is a legend from Iran: a bridge thin and sharp as a knife-blade, it divides the worlds and can only be crossed by the faithful and the just.

A **gingko** is a large tree with fan-shaped leaves which is thought to have survived from the Triassic Period, early in the age of dinosaurs. **Archaeopteryx** was a reptile-like fossil bird from the late Jurassic Period, having teeth and a long, feathered, vertebrate tail. **Memento mori** is something that reminds you that you are mortal and will die. **Entasis** is a slight convexity or swelling that is created in the shaft of a column, intended to compensate for the illusion of concavity that results from straight sides in a column. The quote *"Verweile doch, du bist so schön"* ["stay nevertheless, you are so beautiful"] is from Faust's moment of ecstasy and happiness with Helen of Troy—the very moment that he lost his bargain (and soul) to Mephistopheles, for he had bet that he would never achieve happiness. **Twelfth Night** means not only the 12th night of the Christmas season (the date of Epiphany), but the play *Twelfth Night* by Shakespeare which foreshadows events in "The Graveyard Heart": a pair of shipwrecked twins become ensnared in a carnival madness where love is as quickly caught as the plague, identities are mistaken, songs are sung, grown people make fools of themselves longing for what they cannot have, and one character ends up imprisoned and insane. **Maudlin** means tearful or foolishly sentimental, especially from drunkenness. **There was no fireplace to throw it into** refers to the Russian tradition of ending a toast by throwing the drained glasses against a wall or into a fireplace. The **Globe** refers to several theatres associated with the original performances of Shakespeare's plays; the first was built in 1599. The **Carlsbad** Caverns in New Mexico are the site of a bat sanctuary to which the bats return each spring. **Mayday** is the first day of May, celebrated with various festivities including the crowning of the May queen and dancing around the Maypole. **Delphi** was a city in ancient Greece and the location of one of the oracles of Apollo. **Good Night Ladies** is the original verse upon which *Merrily We Roll Along* was based. **Phylactic** means protecting from disease; a phylactic blade might be a sterilized scalpel. **St. James Infirmary Blues** is a folksong about a man going to the hospital to discover his girl is dead; Louis Armstrong recorded it.

Pan is the god of flocks and herds, and is typically represented with horns, ears, and legs of a goat on a man's body; he plays panpipes. **Phoebus** is another name for Apollo; he has many children by many different mates. **Attic** refers to Greece or Athens, or especially the ancient language of Greece. **Colloquy** is a formal conversation or dialogue. A **cherub** is an angelic, winged child with rosy cheeks. **"Strew on her roses..."** and **"Her life was turning, turning..."** quotes the funereal poem "Requiescat" by Matthew Arnold. **Parian** is unglazed porcelain that resembled white marble. **Cocobolo** is a hard, durable wood used for making knife handles and furniture. **Quebracho** is a south American tree with hard wood and a bark that is used as a source of tannin. **Lignum vitae** is a tropical wood that is very hard and used in making pulleys, mallet heads, bearings. The **Flying Dutchman** is a ghost ship that is doomed to sail the seven seas forever. A **Brass Ring** is a sought after prize or wealth. **Adytum** is the sacred part of a shrine that the public may not enter. **Juridical** means pertaining to law or justice. **Senta** is the character in Richard Wagner's **Flying Dutchman** who loves him, swears to be faithful until death, and drowns herself—an act that in turn saves him, resulting in both Senta and the Flying Dutchman ascending into heaven. **Kaspar Hauser** was a mysterious street orphan in 19th century Germany who was suspected to have ties to the royal house of Baden and to have been abandoned by them, but he was murdered before his identity could be confirmed.

[1] *Roger Zelazny*, Jane M. Lindskold, 1993.

[2] *When Pussywillows Last in the Catyard Bloomed*, 1980.

[3] *Four for Tomorrow*, 1967.

The Doors of His Face, The Lamps of His Mouth

I'm a baitman. No one is born a baitman, except in a French novel where everyone is. (In fact, I think that's the title, *We are All Bait*. Pfft!) How I got that way is barely worth the telling and has nothing to do with neo-exes, but the days of the beast deserve a few words, so here they are.

*

The Lowlands of Venus lie between the thumb and forefinger of the continent known as Hand. When you break into Cloud Alley it swings its silverblack bowling ball toward you without a warning. You jump then, inside that firetailed tenpin they ride you down in, but the straps keep you from making a fool of yourself. You generally chuckle afterwards, but you always jump first.

Next, you study Hand to lay its illusion and the two middle fingers become dozen-ringed archipelagoes as the outers resolve into greengray peninsulas; the thumb is too short, and curls like the embryo tail of Cape Horn.

You suck pure oxygen, sigh possibly, and begin the long topple back to the Lowlands.

There, you are caught like an infield fly at the Lifeline landing area—so named because of its nearness to the great delta in the Eastern Bay—located between the first peninsula and "thumb." For a minute it seems as if you're going to miss Lifeline and wind up as canned seafood, but afterwards—shaking off the metaphors—you descend to scorched concrete and present your middle-sized telephone directory of authorizations to the short, fat man in the gray cap. The papers show that you are not subject to mysterious inner rottings and etcetera. He then smiles you a short, fat, gray smile and motions you toward the bus which hauls you to the Reception Area. At the R.A. you spend three days proving that, indeed, you are not subject to mysterious inner rottings and etcetera.

Boredom, however, is another rot. When your three days are up, you generally hit Lifeline hard, and it returns the compliment as a matter of reflex. The effects of alcohol in variant atmospheres is a subject on which the connoisseurs have written numerous volumes, so I will confine my remarks to noting that a good binge is worthy of at least a week's time and often warrants a lifetime study.

I had been a student of exceptional promise (strictly undergraduate) for going on two years when the *Bright Water* fell through our marble ceiling and poured its people like targets into the city.

Pause. The Worlds Almanac re Lifeline: " . . . Port city on the eastern coast of Hand. Employees of the Agency for Non-terrestrial Research comprise approximately 85% of its 100,000 population (2010 Census). Its other residents are primarily personnel maintained by several industrial corporations engaged in basic research. Independent marine biologists, wealthy fishing enthusiasts, and waterfront entrepreneurs make up the remainder of its inhabitants."

I turned to Mike Dabis, a fellow entrepreneur, and commented on the lousy state of basic research.

"Not if the mumbled truth be known."

He paused behind his glass before continuing the slow swallowing process calculated to obtain my interest and a few oaths, before he continued.

"Carl," he finally observed, poker playing, "they're shaping Tensquare."

I could have hit him. I might have refilled his glass with sulfuric acid and looked on with glee as his lips blackened and cracked. Instead, I grunted a noncommittal.

"Who's fool enough to shell out fifty grand a day? ANR?"

He shook his head.

"Jean Luharich," he said, "the girl with the violet contacts and fifty or sixty perfect teeth. I understand her eyes are really brown."

"Isn't she selling enough face cream these days?"

He shrugged.

"Publicity makes the wheels go 'round. Luharich Enterprise jumped sixteen points when she picked up the Sun Trophy. You ever play golf on Mercury?"

I had, but I overlooked it and continued to press.

"So she's coming here with a blank check and a fishhook?"

"*Bright Water*, today," he nodded. "Should be down by now. Lots of cameras. She wants an Ikky, bad."

"Hmm," I hmmed. "How bad?"

"Sixty day contract. Tensquare. Indefinite extension clause. Million and a half deposit," he recited.

"You seem to know a lot about it."

"I'm Personnel Recruitment. Luharich Enterprises approached me last month. It helps to drink in the right places.

"Or own them." He smirked, after a moment.

I looked away, sipping my bitter brew. After awhile I swallowed several things and asked Mike what he expected to be asked, leaving myself open for his monthly temperance lecture.

"They told me to try getting you," he mentioned. "When's the last time you sailed?"

"Month and a half ago. The *Corning*."

"Small stuff," he snorted. "When have you been under, yourself?"

"It's been awhile."

"It's been over a year, hasn't it? That time you got cut by the screw, under the *Dolphin*?"

I turned to him.

"I was in the river last week, up at Angleford where the currents are strong. I can still get around."

"Sober," he added.

"I'd stay that way," I said, "on a job like this."

A doubting nod.

The Magic

"Straight union rates. Triple time for extraordinary circumstances," he narrated. "Be at Hangar Sixteen with your gear, Friday morning, five hundred hours. We push off Saturday, daybreak."

"You're sailing?"

"I'm sailing."

"How come?"

"Money."

"Ikky guano."

"The bar isn't doing so well and baby needs new minks."

"I repeat—"

" . . . And I want to get away from baby, renew my contract with basics—fresh air, exercise, make cash . . . "

"All right, sorry I asked."

I poured him a drink, concentrating on H_2SO_4, but it didn't transmute. Finally I got him soused and went out into the night to walk and think things over.

Around a dozen serious attempts to land *Ichthyform Leviosaurus Levianthus*, generally known as "Ikky", had been made over the past five years. When Ikky was first sighted, whaling techniques were employed. These proved either fruitless or disastrous, and a new procedure was inaugurated. Tensquare was constructed by a wealthy sportsman named Michael Jandt, who blew his entire roll on the project.

After a year on the Eastern Ocean, he returned to file bankruptcy. Carlton Davits, a playboy fishing enthusiast, then purchased the huge raft and laid a wake for Ikky's spawning grounds. On the nineteenth day out he had a strike and lost one hundred fifty bills' worth of untested gear, along with one *Ichthyform Levianthus*. Twelve days later, using tripled lines, he hooked, narcotized, and began to hoist the huge beast. It awakened then, destroyed a control tower, killed six men, and worked general hell over five square blocks of Tensquare. Carlton was left with partial hemiplegia and a bankruptcy suit of his own. He faded into waterfront atmosphere and

Roger Zelazny and Samuel R. Delany

Tensquare changed hands four more times, with less spectacular but equally expensive results.

Finally, the big raft, built only for one purpose was purchased at an auction by ANR for "marine research." Lloyd's still won't insure it, and the only marine research it has ever seen is an occasional rental at fifty bills a day—to people anxious to tell Leviathan fish stories. I've been a baitman on three of the voyages, and I've been close enough to count Ikky's fangs on two occasions. I want one of them to show my grandchildren, for personal reasons.

I faced the direction of the landing area and resolved a resolve.

"You want me for local coloring, gal. It'll look nice on the feature page and all that. But clear this—If anyone gets you an Ikky, it'll be me. I promise."

I stood in the empty Square. The foggy towers of Lifeline shared their mists.

*

Shoreline a couple eras ago, the western slope above Lifeline stretches as far as forty miles inland in some places. Its angle of rising is not a great one, but it achieves an elevation of several thousand feet before it meets the mountain range which separates us from the Highlands. About four miles inland and five hundred feet higher than Lifeline are set most of the surface airstrips and privately owned hangars. Hangar Sixteen houses Cal's Contract Cab, hop service, shore to ship. I do not like Cal, but he wasn't around when I climbed from the bus and waved to a mechanic.

Two of the hoppers tugged at the concrete, impatient beneath flywing haloes. The one on which Steve was working belched deep within its barrel carburetor and shuttered spasmodically.

"Bellyache?" I inquired.

"Yeah, gas pains and heartburn."

He twisted setscrews until it settled into an even keening, and turned to me.

"You're for out?"

I nodded.

The Magic

"Tensquare. Cosmetics. Monsters. Stuff like that."

He blinked into the beacons and wiped his freckles. The temperature was about twenty, but the big overhead spots served a double purpose.

"Luharich," he muttered. "Then you *are* the one. There's some people want to see you."

"What about?"

"Cameras. Microphones. Stuff like that."

"I'd better stow my gear. Which one am I riding?"

He poked the screwdriver at the other hopper.

"That one. You're on video tape now, by the way. They wanted to get you arriving."

He turned to the hangar, turned back.

"Say 'cheese.' They'll shoot the close-ups later."

I said something other than "cheese." They must have been using telelens and been able to read my lips, because that part of the tape was never shown.

I threw my junk in the back, climbed into a passenger seat, and lit a cigarette. Five minutes later, Cal himself emerged from the office Quonset, looking cold. He came over and pounded on the side of the hopper. He jerked a thumb back at the hangar.

"They want you in there!" he called through cupped hands. "Interview!"

"The show's over!" I yelled back. "Either that, or they can get themselves another baitman!"

His rustbrown eyes became nailheads under blond brows and his glare a spike before he jerked about and stalked off. I wondered how much they had paid him to be able to squat in his hangar and suck juice from his generator.

Enough, I guess, knowing Cal. I never liked the guy, anyway.

*

Venus at night is a field of sable waters. On the coasts, you can never tell where the sea ends and the sky begins. Dawn is like dumping milk into an inkwell. First, there are erratic curdles of white, then streamers. Shade the bottle for a gray colloid, then watch it whiten a little more. All of a sudden you've got day. Then start heating the mixture.

I had to shed my jacket as we flashed out over the bay. To our rear, the skyline could have been under water for the way it waved and rippled in the heatfall. A hopper can accommodate four people (five, if you want to bend Regs and underestimate weight), or three passengers with the sort of gear a baitman uses. I was the only fare, though, and the pilot was like his machine. He hummed and made no unnecessary noises. Lifeline turned a somersault and evaporated in the rear mirror at about the same time Tensquare broke the fore-horizon. The pilot stopped humming and shook his head.

I leaned forward. Feelings played flopdoodle in my guts. I knew every bloody inch of the big raft, but the feelings you once took for granted change when their source is out of reach. Truthfully, I'd had my doubts I'd ever board the hulk again. But now, now I could almost believe in predestination. There it was!

A tensquare football field of a ship. A-powered. Flat as a pancake, except for the plastic blisters in the middle and the "Rooks" fore and aft, port and starboard.

The Rook towers were named for their corner positions—and any two can work together to hoist, co-powering the graffles between them. The graffles—half gaff, half grapple—can raise enormous weights to near water level; their designer had only one thing in mind, though, which accounts for the gaff half. At water level, the Slider has to implement elevation for six to eight feet before the graffles are in a position to push upward, rather than pulling.

The Slider, essentially, is a mobile room—a big box capable of moving in any of Tensquare's crisscross groovings and "anchoring" on the strike side by means of a powerful electromagnetic bond. Its winches could hoist a battleship the necessary distance, and the whole craft would tilt, rather than the Slider come loose, if you want any idea of the strength of that bond.

The Slider houses a section operated control indicator which is the most sophisticated "reel" ever designed. Drawing broadcast power from the generator beside the center blister, it is connected by shortwave with the sonar room, where the movements of the quarry are recorded and repeated to the angler seated before the section control.

The fisherman might play his "lines" for hours, days even, without seeing any more than metal and an outline on the screen. Only when the beast is graffled and the extensor shelf, located twelve feet below waterline, slides out for support and begins to aid the winches, only then does the fisherman see his catch rising before him like a fallen Seraph. Then, as Davits learned, one looks into the Abyss itself and is required to act. He didn't, and a hundred meters of unimaginable tonnage, undernarcotized and hurting, broke the cables of the winch, snapped a graffle, and took a half-minute walk across Tensquare.

We circled till the mechanical flag took notice and waved us on down. We touched beside the personnel hatch and I jettisoned my gear and jumped to the deck.

"Luck," called the pilot as the door was sliding shut. Then he danced into the air and the flag clicked blank.

I shouldered my stuff and went below.

Signing in with Malvern, the de facto captain, I learned that most of the others wouldn't arrive for a good eight hours. They had wanted me alone at Cal's so they could pattern the pub footage along twentieth-century cinema lines.

Open: landing strip, dark. One mechanic prodding a contrary hopper. Stark-o-vision shot of slow bus pulling in. Heavily dressed baitman descends, looks about, limps across field. Close-up: he grins. Move in for words: "Do you think this is the time? The time he *will* be landed?" Embarrassment, taciturnity, a shrug. Dub something—"I see. And why do you think Miss Luharich has a better chance than any of the others? Is it because she's better equipped? [Grin.] Because more is known now about the creature's habits than when you were out before? Or is it because of her will to win, to be a champion? Is it any one of these things, or is it all of them?" Reply: "Yeah, all of them." "—Is that why you signed on with her? Because your instincts say, 'This one will be it'?" Answer: "She pays union rates. I couldn't rent that damned thing myself. And I want in." Erase. Dub something else. Fade-out as he moves toward hopper, etcetera.

"Cheese," I said, or something like that, and took a walk around Tensquare, by myself.

I mounted each Rook, checking out the controls and the underwater video eyes. Then I raised the main lift.

Malvern had no objections to my testing things this way. In fact, he encouraged it. We had sailed together before and our positions had even been reversed upon a time. So I wasn't surprised when I stepped off the lift into the Hopkins Locker and found him waiting. For the next ten minutes we inspected the big room in silence, walking through its copper coil chambers soon to be Arctic.

Finally, he slapped a wall.

"Well, will we find it?"

I shook my head.

"I'd like to, but I doubt it. I don't give two hoots and a damn who gets credit for the catch, so long as I have a part in it. But it won't happen. That gal's an egomaniac. She'll want to operate the Slider, and she can't."

"You ever meet her?"

"Yeah."

"How long ago?"

"Four, five years."

"She was a kid then. How do you know what she can do now?"

"I know. She'll have learned every switch and reading by this time. She'll be all up on theory. But do you remember one time we were together in the starboard Rook, forward, when Ikky broke water like a porpoise?"

"Well?"

He rubbed his emery chin.

"Maybe she can do it, Carl. She's raced torch ships and she's scubaed in bad waters back home." He glanced in the direction of invisible Hand. "And she's hunted in the Highlands. She might be wild enough to pull that horror into her lap without flinching.

The Magic

" . . . For Johns Hopkins to foot the bill and shell out seven figures for the corpus," he added. "That's money, even to a Luharich."

I ducked through a hatchway.

"Maybe you're right, but she was a rich witch when I knew her.

"And she wasn't blonde," I added, meanly.

He yawned.

"Let's find breakfast."

We did that.

*

When I was young I thought that being born a sea creature was the finest choice Nature could make for anyone. I grew up on the Pacific coast and spent my summers on the Gulf or the Mediterranean. I lived months of my life negotiating with coral, photographing trench dwellers, and playing tag with dolphins. I fished everywhere there are fish, resenting the fact that they can go places I can't. When I grew older I wanted a bigger fish, and there was nothing living that I knew of, excepting a Sequoia, that came any bigger than Ikky. That's part of it . . . .

I jammed a couple of extra rolls into a paper bag and filled a thermos with coffee. Excusing myself, I left the gallery and made my way to the Slider berth. It was just the way I remembered it. I threw a few switches and the shortwave hummed.

"That you, Carl?"

"That's right, Mike. Let me have some juice down here, you double-crossing rat."

He thought it over, then I felt the hull vibrate as the generators cut in. I poured my third cup of coffee and found a cigarette.

"So why am I a double-crossing rat this time?" came his voice again.

"You knew about the cameraman at Hangar Sixteen?"

"Yes."

"Then you're a double-crossing rat. The last thing I want is publicity. 'He who fouled up so often before is ready to try it, nobly, once more.' I can read it now."

"You're wrong. The spotlight's only big enough for one, and she's prettier than you."

My next comment was cut off as I threw the elevator switch and the elephant ears flapped above me. I rose, settling flush with the deck. Retracting the lateral rail, I cut forward into the groove. Amidships, I stopped at a juncture, dropped the lateral, and retracted the longitudinal rail.

I slid starboard, midway between the Rooks, halted, and threw on the coupler.

I hadn't spilled a drop of coffee.

"Show me pictures."

The screen glowed. I adjusted and got outlines of the bottom.

"Okay."

I threw a Status Blue switch and he matched it. The light went on.

The winch unlocked. I aimed out over the waters, extended an arm, and fired a cast.

"Clean one," he commented.

"Status Red. Call strike." I threw a switch.

"Status Red."

The baitman would be on his way with this, to make the barbs tempting.

It's not exactly a fishhook. The cables bear hollow tubes; the tubes convey enough dope for an army of hopheads; Ikky takes the bait, dandled before him by remote control, and the fisherman rams the barbs home.

My hands moved over the console, making the necessary adjustments. I checked the narco-tank reading. Empty. Good, they hadn't been filled yet. I thumbed the inject button.

"In the gullet," Mike murmured.

I released the cables. I played the beast imagined. I let him run, swinging the winch to simulate his sweep.

I had the air conditioner on and my shirt off and it was still uncomfortably hot, which is how I knew that morning had gone over into noon. I was dimly aware of the arrivals and departures of the hoppers. Some of the crew sat in the "shade" of the doors I had left open, watching the operation. I didn't see Jean arrive or I would have ended the session and gotten below.

She broke my concentration by slamming the door hard enough to shake the bond.

"Mind telling me who authorized you to bring up the Slider?" she asked.

"No one," I replied. "I'll take it below now."

"Just move aside."

I did, and she took my seat. She was wearing brown slacks and a baggy shirt and she had her hair pulled back in a practical manner. Her cheeks were flushed, but not necessarily from the heat. She attacked the panel with a nearly amusing intensity that I found disquieting.

"Status Blue," she snapped, breaking a violet fingernail on the toggle.

I forced a yawn and buttoned my shirt slowly. She threw a side glance my way, checked the registers, and fired a cast.

I monitored the lead on the screen. She turned to me for a second.

"Status Red," she said levelly.

I nodded my agreement.

She worked the winch sideways to show she knew how. I didn't doubt she knew how and she didn't doubt that I didn't doubt, but then—

"In case you're wondering," she said, "you're not going to be anywhere near this thing. You were hired as a baitman, remember? Not a Slider operator! A baitman! Your duties consist of swimming out and setting the table for our friend the monster. It's dangerous, but you're getting well paid for it. Any questions?"

She squashed the Inject button and I rubbed my throat.

"Nope," I smiled, "but I am qualified to run that thingamajigger—and if you need me I'll be available, at union rates."

"Mister Davits," she said, "I don't want a loser operating this panel."

"Miss Luharich, there has never been a winner at this game."

She started reeling in the cable and broke the bond at the same time, so that the whole Slider shook as the big yo-yo returned. We skidded a couple of feet backward. She raised the laterals and we shot back along the groove.

Slowing, she transferred rails and we jolted to a clanging halt, then shot off at a right angle. The crew scrambled away from the hatch as we skidded onto the elevator.

"In the future, Mister Davits, do not enter the Slider without being ordered," she told me.

"Don't worry. I won't even step inside if I am ordered," I answered. "I signed on as a baitman. Remember? If you want me in here, you'll have to *ask* me."

"That'll be the day," she smiled.

I agreed, as the doors closed above us. We dropped the subject and headed in our different directions after the Slider came to a halt in its berth. She did not say "good day," though, which I thought showed breeding as well as determination, in reply to my chuckle.

*

Later that night Mike and I stoked our pipes in Malvern's cabin. The winds were shuffling waves, and a steady pattering of rain and hail overhead turned the deck into a tin roof.

"Nasty," suggested Malvern.

I nodded. After two bourbons the room had become a familiar woodcut, with its mahogany furnishings (which I had transported from Earth long ago on a whim) and the dark walls, the seasoned face of Malvern, and the perpetually puzzled expression of Dabis set between the big pools of shadow that lay behind chairs and splashed in cornets, all cast by the tiny table light and seen through a glass, brownly.

"Glad I'm in here."

"What's it like underneath on a night like this?"

I puffed, thinking of my light cutting through the insides of a black diamond, shaken slightly. The meteor-dart of a suddenly illuminated fish, the swaying of grotesque ferns, like nebulae—shadow, then green, then gone— swam in a moment through my mind. I guess it's like a spaceship would feel, if a spaceship could feel, crossing between worlds—and quiet, uncannily, preternaturally quiet; and peaceful as sleep.

The Magic

"Dark," I said, "and not real choppy below a few fathoms."

"Another eight hours and we shove off," commented Mike.

"Ten, twelve days, we should be there," noted Malvern.

"What do you think Ikky's doing?"

"Sleeping on the bottom with Mrs. Ikky if he has any brains."

"He hasn't. I've seen ANR's skeletal extrapolation from the bones that have washed up—"

"Hasn't everyone?"

" . . . Fully fleshed, he'd be over a hundred meters long. That right, Carl?"

I agreed.

" . . . Not much of a brain box, though, for his bulk."

"Smart enough to stay out of our locker."

Chuckles, because nothing exists but this room, really. The world outside is an empty, sleet drummed deck. We lean back and make clouds.

"Boss lady does not approve of unauthorized fly fishing."

"Boss lady can walk north till her hat floats."

"What did she say in there?"

"She told me that my place, with fish manure, is on the bottom."

"You don't Slide?"

"I bait."

"We'll see."

"That's all I do. If she wants a Slideman she's going to have to ask nicely."

"You think she'll have to?"

"I think she'll have to."

"And if she does, can you do it?"

"A fair question," I puffed. "I don't know the answer, though."

I'd incorporate my soul and trade forty percent of the stock for the answer. I'd give a couple years off my life for the answer. But there doesn't seem to be a lineup of supernatural takers, because no one knows. Supposing when we get out there, luck being with us, we find ourselves an Ikky?

Roger Zelazny and Samuel R. Delany

Supposing we succeed in baiting him and get lines on him. What then? If we get him shipside, will she hold on or crack up? What if she's made of sterner stuff than Davits, who used to hunt sharks with poison-darted air pistols? Supposing she lands him and Davits has to stand there like a video extra.

Worse yet, supposing she asks for Davits and he still stands there like a video extra or something else—say, some yellowbellied embodiment named Cringe?

It was when I got him up above the eight-foot horizon of steel and looked out at all that body, sloping on and on till it dropped out of sight like a green mountain range . . . And that head. Small for the body, but still immense. Fat, craggy, with lidless roulettes that had spun black and red since before my forefathers decided to try the New Continent. And swaying.

Fresh narco-tanks had been connected. It needed another shot, fast. But I was paralyzed.

It had made a noise like God playing a Hammond organ . . .

And looked at me!

I don't know if seeing is even the same process in eyes like those. I doubt it. Maybe I was just a gray blur behind a black rock, with the plexi-reflected sky hurting its pupils. But it fixed on me. Perhaps the snake doesn't really paralyze the rabbit, perhaps it's just that rabbits are cowards by constitution. But it began to struggle and I still couldn't move, fascinated.

Fascinated by all that power, by those eyes, they found me there fifteen minutes later, a little broken about the head and shoulders, the Inject still unpushed.

And I dream about those eyes. I want to face them once more, even if their finding takes forever. I've got to know if there's something inside me that sets me apart from a rabbit, from notched plates of reflexes and instincts that always fall apart in exactly the same way whenever the proper combination is spun.

Looking down, I noticed that my hand was shaking. Glancing up, I noticed that no one else was noticing.

The Magic

I finished my drink and emptied my pipe. It was late and no songbirds were singing.

*

I sat whittling, my legs hanging over the aft edge, the chips spinning down into the furrow of our wake. Three days out. No action.

"You!"

"Me?"

"You."

Hair like the end of the rainbow, eyes like nothing in nature, fine teeth.

"Hello."

"There's a safety regulation against what you're doing, you know."

"I know. I've been worrying about it all morning."

A delicate curl climbed my knife then drifted out behind us. It settled into the foam and was plowed under. I watched her reflection in my blade, taking a secret pleasure in its distortion.

"Are you baiting me?" she finally asked.

I heard her laugh then, and turned, knowing it had been intentional.

"What, me?"

"I could push you off from here, very easily."

"I'd make it back."

"Would you push me off, then—some dark night, perhaps?"

"They're all dark, Miss Luharich. No, I'd rather make you a gift of my carving."

She seated herself beside me then, and I couldn't help but notice the dimples in her knees. She wore white shorts and a halter and still had an offworld tan to her which was awfully appealing. I almost felt a twinge of guilt at having planned the whole scene, but my right hand still blocked her view of the wooden animal.

"Okay, I'll bite. What have you got for me?"

"Just a second. It's almost finished."

Solemnly, I passed her the little wooden jackass I had been carving. I felt a little sorry and slightly jackass-ish myself, but I had to follow through. I always do. The mouth was split into a braying grin. The ears were upright.

She didn't smile and she didn't frown. She just studied it.

"It's very good," she finally said, "like most things you do—and appropriate, perhaps."

"Give it to me." I extended a palm.

She handed it back and I tossed it out over the water. It missed the white water and bobbed for awhile like a pigmy seahorse.

"Why did you do that?"

"It was a poor joke. I'm sorry."

"Maybe you are right, though. Perhaps this time I've bitten off a little too much."

I snorted.

"Then why not do something safer, like another race?"

She shook her end of the rainbow.

"No. It has to be an Ikky."

"Why?"

"Why did you want one so badly that you threw away a fortune?"

"Many reasons," I said. "An unfrocked analyst who held black therapy sessions in his basement once told me, 'Mister Davits, you need to reinforce the image of your masculinity by catching one of every kind of fish in existence.' Fish are a very ancient masculinity symbol, you know. So I set out to do it. I have one more to go. —Why do you want to reinforce *your* masculinity?"

"I don't," she said. "I don't want to reinforce anything but Luharich Enterprises. My chief statistician once said, 'Miss Luharich, sell all the cold cream and face powder in the System and you'll be a happy girl. Rich, too.' And he was right. I am the proof. I can look the way I do and do anything, and I sell most of the lipstick and face powder in the System—but I have to be *able* to do anything."

"You do look cool and efficient," I observed.

The Magic

"I don't feel cool," she said, rising. "Let's go for a swim."

"May I point out that we're making pretty good time?"

"If you want to indicate the obvious, you may. You said you could make it back to the ship, unassisted. Change your mind?"

"No."

"Then get us two scuba outfits and I'll race you under Tensquare.

"I'll win, too," she added.

I stood and looked down at her, because that usually makes me feel superior to women.

"Daughter of Lir, eyes of Picasso," I said, "you've got yourself a race. Meet me at the forward Rook, starboard, in ten minutes."

"Ten minutes," she agreed.

And ten minutes it was. From the center blister to the Rook took maybe two of them, with the load I was carrying. My sandals grew very hot and I was glad to shuck them for flippers when I reached the comparative cool of the corner.

We slid into harnesses and adjusted our gear. She had changed into a trim one-piece green job that made me shade my eyes and look away, then look back again.

I fastened a rope ladder and kicked it over the side. Then I pounded on the wall of the Rook.

"Yeah?"

"You talk to the port Rook, aft?" I called.

"They're all set up," came the answer. "There's ladders and draglines all over that end."

"You sure you want to do this?" asked the sunburnt little gink who was her publicity man, Anderson yclept.

He sat beside the Rook in a deckchair, sipping lemonade through a straw.

"It might be dangerous," he observed, sunken-mouthed. (His teeth were beside him, in another glass.)

"That's right," she smiled. "It *will* be dangerous. Not overly, though."

174

"Then why don't you let me get some pictures? We'd have them back to Lifeline in an hour. They'd be in New York by tonight. Good copy."

"No," she said, and turned away from both of us.

"Here, keep these for me."

She passed him a box full of her unseeing, and when she turned back to me they were the same brown that I remembered.

"Ready?"

"No," I said, tautly. "Listen carefully, Jean. If you're going to play this game there are a few rules. First," I counted, "we're going to be directly beneath the hull, so we have to start low and keep moving. If we bump the bottom, we could rupture an air tank . . . "

She began to protest that any moron knew that and I cut her down.

"Second," I went on, "there won't be much light, so we'll stay close together, and we will *both* carry torches."

Her wet eyes flashed.

"I dragged you out of Govino without—"

Then she stopped and turned away. She picked up a lamp.

"Okay. Torches. Sorry."

" . . . And watch out for the drive-screws," I finished. "There'll be strong currents for at least fifty meters behind them."

She wiped her eyes and adjusted the mask.

"All right, let's go."

We went.

She led the way, at my insistence. The surface layer was pleasantly warm. At two fathoms the water was bracing; at five it was nice and cold. At eight we let go the swinging stairway and struck out. Tensquare sped forward and we raced in the opposite direction, tattooing the hull yellow at ten-second intervals.

The hull stayed where it belonged, but we raced on like two darkside satellites. Periodically, I tickled her frog feet with my light and traced her antennae of bubbles. About a five meter lead was fine; I'd beat her in the home stretch, but I couldn't let her drop behind yet.

The Magic

Beneath us, black. Immense. Deep. The Mindanao of Venus, where eternity might eventually pass the dead to a rest in cities of unnamed fishes. I twisted my head away and touched the hull with a feeler of light; it told me we were about a quarter of the way along.

I increased my beat to match her stepped-up stroke, and narrowed the distance which she had suddenly opened by a couple of meters. She sped up again and I did, too. I spotted her with my beam.

She turned and it caught on her mask. I never knew whether she'd been smiling. Probably. She raised two fingers in a V-for-Victory and then cut ahead at full speed.

I should have known. I should have felt it coming. It was just a race to her, something else to win. Damn the torpedos!

So I leaned into it, hard. I don't shake in the water. Or, if I do it doesn't matter and I don't notice it. I began to close the gap again.

She looked back, sped on, looked back. Each time she looked it was nearer, until I'd narrowed it down to the original five meters.

Then she hit the jatoes.

That's what I had been fearing. We were about half-way under and she shouldn't have done it. The powerful jets of compressed air could easily rocket her upward into the hull, or tear something loose if she allowed her body to twist. Their main use is in tearing free from marine plants or fighting bad currents. I had wanted them along as a safety measure, because of the big suck-and-pull windmills behind.

She shot ahead like a meteorite, and I could feel a sudden tingle of perspiration leaping to meet and mix with the churning waters.

I swept ahead, not wanting to use my own guns, and she tripled, quadrupled the margin.

The jets died and she was still on course. Okay, I was an old fuddyduddy. She *could* have messed up and headed toward the top.

I plowed the sea and began to gather back my yardage, a foot at a time. I wouldn't be able to catch her or beat her now, but I'd be on the ropes before she hit deck.

Roger Zelazny and Samuel R. Delany

Then the spinning magnets began their insistence and she wavered. It was an awfully powerful drag, even at this distance. The call of the meat grinder.

I'd been scratched up by one once, under the *Dolphin*, a fishing boat of the middle-class. I *had* been drinking, but it was also a rough day, and the thing had been turned on prematurely. Fortunately, it was turned off in time, also, and a tendon-stapler made everything good as new, except in the log, where it only mentioned that I'd been drinking. Nothing about it being off-hours when I had the right to do as I damn well pleased.

She had slowed to half her speed, but she was still moving cross-wise, toward the port, aft corner. I began to feel the pull myself and had to slow down. She'd made it past the main one, but she seemed too far back. It's hard to gauge distances under water, but each red beat of time told me I was right. She was out of danger from the main one, but the smaller port screw, located about eighty meters in, was no longer a threat but a certainty.

She had turned and was pulling away from it now. Twenty meters separated us. She was standing still. Fifteen.

Slowly, she began a backward drifting. I hit my jatoes, aiming two meters behind her and about twenty back of the blades.

Straightline! Thankgod! Catching, softbelly, leadpipe on shoulder SWIMLIKEHELL! maskcracked, not broke though AND UP!

We caught a line and I remember brandy.

*

Into the cradle endlessly rocking I spit, pacing. Insomnia tonight and left shoulder sore again, so let it rain on me—they can cure rheumatism. Stupid as hell. What I said. In blankets and shivering. She: "Carl, I can't say it." Me: "Then call it square for that night in Govino, Miss Luharich. Huh?" She: nothing. Me: "Any more of that brandy?" She: "Give me another, too." Me: sounds of sipping. It had only lasted three months. No alimony. Many $ on both sides. Not sure whether they were happy or not. Wine-dark Aegean. Good fishing. Maybe he should have spent more time on shore. Or perhaps she shouldn't have. Good swimmer, though. Dragged him all the way to

The Magic

Vido to wring out his lungs. Young. Both. Strong. Both. Rich and spoiled as Hell. Ditto. Corfu should have brought them closer. Didn't. I think that mental cruelty was a trout. He wanted to go to Canada. She: "Go to hell if you want!" He: "Will you go along?" She: "No." But she did, anyhow. Many hells. Expensive. He lost a monster or two. She inherited a couple. Lot of lightning tonight. Stupid as hell. Civility's the coffin of a conned soul. By whom? —Sounds like a bloody neo-ex . . . . But I hate you, Anderson, with your glass full of teeth and her new eyes . . . . Can't keep this pipe lit, keep sucking tobacco. Spit again!

*

Seven days out and the scope showed Ikky.

Bells jangled, feet pounded, and some optimist set the thermostat in the Hopkins. Malvern wanted me to sit it out, but I slipped into my harness and waited for whatever came. The bruise looked worse than it felt. I had exercised every day and the shoulder hadn't stiffened on me.

A thousand meters ahead and thirty fathoms deep, it tunneled our path. Nothing showed on the surface.

"Will we chase him?" asked an excited crewman.

"Not unless she feels like using money for fuel." I shrugged.

Soon the scope was clear, and it stayed that way. We remained on alert and held our course.

I hadn't said over a dozen words to my boss since the last time we went drowning together, so I decided to raise the score.

"Good afternoon," I approached. "What's new?"

"He's going north-northeast. We'll have to let this one go. A few more days and we can afford some chasing. Not yet."

Sleek head . . .

I nodded. "No telling where this one's headed."

"How's your shoulder?"

"All right. How about you?"

Daughter of Lir . . .

"Fine. By the way, you're down for a nice bonus."

Roger Zelazny and Samuel R. Delany

Eyes of perdition!

"Don't mention it," I told her back.

Later that afternoon, and appropriately, a storm shattered. (I prefer "shattered" to "broke." It gives a more accurate idea of the behavior of tropical storms on Venus and saves a lot of words.) Remember that inkwell I mentioned earlier? Now take it between thumb and forefinger and hit its side with a hammer. Watch yourself! Don't get splashed or cut—

Dry, then drenched. The sky one million bright fractures as the hammer falls. And sounds of breaking.

"Everyone below?" suggested the loudspeakers to the already scurrying crew.

Where was I? Who do you think was doing the loudspeaking?

Everything loose went overboard when the water got to walking, but by then no people were loose. The Slider was the first thing below decks. Then the big lifts lowered their shacks.

I had hit it for the nearest Rook with a yell the moment I recognized the pre-brightening of the holocaust. From there I cut in the speakers and spent half a minute coaching the track team.

Minor injuries had occurred, Mike told me over the radio, but nothing serious. I, however, was marooned for the duration. The Rooks do not lead anywhere; they're set too far out over the hull to provide entry downwards, what with the extensor shelves below.

So I undressed myself of the tanks which I had worn for the past several hours, crossed my flippers on the table, and leaned back to watch the hurricane. The top was black as the bottom and we were in between, and somewhat illuminated because of all that flat, shiny space. The waters didn't rain down—they just sort of got together and dropped.

The Rooks were secure enough—they'd weathered any number of these onslaughts—it's just that their positions gave them a greater arc of rise and descent when Tensquare makes like the rocker of a very nervous grandma. I had used the belts from my rig to strap myself into the bolted-down chair, and I removed several years in purgatory from the soul of whoever left a pack of cigarettes in the table drawer.

I watched the water make teepees and mountains and hands and trees until I started seeing faces and people. So I called Mike.

"What are you doing down there?"

"Wondering what you're doing up there," he replied. "What's it like?"

"You're from the Midwest, aren't you?"

"Yeah."

"Get bad storms out there?"

"Sometimes."

"Try to think of the worst one you were ever in. Got a slide rule handy?"

"Right here."

"Then put a one under it, imagine a zero or two following after, and multiply the thing out."

"I can't imagine the zeros."

"Then retain the multiplicand—that's all you can do."

"So what are you doing up there?"

"I've strapped myself in the chair. I'm watching things roll around the floor right now."

I looked up and out again. I saw one darker shadow in the forest.

"Are you praying or swearing?"

"Damned if I know. But if this were the Slider—if only this were the Slider!"

"*He's out there?*"

I nodded, forgetting that he couldn't see me.

Big, as I remembered him. He'd only broken surface for a few moments, to look around. *There is no power on Earth that can be compared with him who was made to fear no one.* I dropped my cigarette. It was the same as before. Paralysis and an unborn scream.

"You all right, Carl?"

He had looked at me again. Or seemed to. Perhaps that mindless brute had been waiting half a millennium to ruin the life of a member of the most highly developed species in business . . . .

"You okay?"

. . . Or perhaps it had been ruined already, long before their encounter, and theirs was just a meeting of beasts, the stronger bumping the weaker aside, body to psyche . . . .

"Carl, dammit! Say something!"

He broke again, this time nearer. Did you ever see the trunk of a tornado? It seems like something alive, moving around in all that dark. Nothing has a right to be so big, so strong, and moving. It's a sickening sensation.

"Please answer me."

He was gone and did not come back that day. I finally made a couple of wisecracks at Mike, but I held my next cigarette in my right hand.

*

The next seventy or eighty thousand waves broke by with a monotonous similarity. The five days that held them were also without distinction. The morning of the thirteenth day out, though, our luck began to rise. The bells broke our coffee-drenched lethargy into small pieces, and we dashed from the gallery without hearing what might have been Mike's finest punchline.

"Aft!" cried someone. "Five hundred meters!"

I stripped to my trunks and started buckling. My stuff is always within grabbing distance.

I flipflopped across the deck, girding myself with a deflated squiggler.

"Five hundred meters, twenty fathoms!" boomed the speakers.

The big traps banged upward and the Slider grew to its full height, m'lady at the console. It rattled past me and took root ahead. Its one arm rose and lengthened.

I breasted the Slider as the speakers called, "Four-eight, twenty!"

"Status Red!"

The Magic

A belch like an emerging champagne cork and the line arced high over the waters.

"Four-eight, twenty!" it repeated, all Malvern and static. "Baitman, attend!"

I adjusted my mask and hand-over-handed it down the side. Then warm, then cool, then away.

Green, vast, down. Fast. This is the place where I am equal to a squiggler. If something big decides a baitman looks tastier than what he's carrying, then irony colors his title as well as the water about it.

I caught sight of the drifting cables and followed them down. Green to dark green to black. It had been a long cast, too long. I'd never had to follow one this far down before. I didn't want to switch on my torch.

But I had to.

Bad! I still had a long way to go. I clenched my teeth and stuffed my imagination into a straightjacket.

Finally the line came to an end.

I wrapped one arm about it and unfastened the squiggler. I attached it, working as fast as I could, and plugged in the little insulated connections which are the reason it can't be fired with the line. Ikky could break them, but by then it wouldn't matter.

My mechanical eel hooked up, I pulled its section plugs and watched it grow. I had been dragged deeper during this operation, which took about a minute and a half. I was near—too near—to where I never wanted to be.

Loathe as I had been to turn on my light, I was suddenly afraid to turn it off. Panic gripped me and I seized the cable with both hands. The squiggler began to glow, pinkly. It started to twist. It was twice as big as I am and doubtless twice as attractive to pink squiggler-eaters. I told myself this until I believed it, then I switched off my light and started up.

If I bumped into something enormous and steel-hided my heart had orders to stop beating immediately and release me—to dart fitfully forever along Acheron, and gibbering.

Ungibbering, I made it to green water and fled back to the nest.

Roger Zelazny and Samuel R. Delany

As soon as they hauled me aboard I made my mask a necklace, shaded my eyes, and monitored for surface turbulence. My first question, of course, was "Where is he?"

"Nowhere," said a crewman; "we lost him right after you went over. Can't pick him up on the scope now. Musta dived."

"Too bad."

The squiggler stayed down, enjoying its bath. My job ended for the time being, I headed back to warm my coffee with rum.

From behind me, a whisper: "Could you laugh like that afterwards?"

Perceptive Answer: "Depends on what he's laughing at."

Still chuckling, I made my way into the center blister with two cupfuls. "Still hell and gone?"

Mike nodded. His big hands were shaking, and mine were steady as a surgeon's when I set down the cups.

He jumped as I shrugged off the tanks and looked for a bench.

"Don't drip on that panel! You want to kill yourself and blow expensive fuses?"

I toweled down, then settled down to watching the unfilled eye on the wall. I yawned happily; my shoulder seemed good as new.

The little box that people talk through wanted to say something, so Mike lifted the switch and told it to go ahead.

"Is Carl there, Mister Dabis?"

"Yes, ma'am."

"Then let me talk to him."

Mike motioned and I moved.

"Talk," I said.

"Are you all right?"

"Yes, thanks. Shouldn't I be?"

"That was a long swim. I—I guess I overshot my cast."

"I'm happy," I said. "More triple-time for me. I really clean up on that hazardous duty clause."

The Magic

"I'll be more careful next time," she apologized. "I guess I was too eager. Sorry—" Something happened to the sentence, so she ended it there, leaving me with half a bagful of replies I'd been saving.

I lifted the cigarette from behind Mike's ear and got a light from the one in the ashtray.

"Carl, she was being nice," he said, after turning to study the panels.

"I know," I told him. "I wasn't."

"I mean, she's an awfully pretty kid, pleasant. Headstrong and all that. But what's she done to you?"

"Lately?" I asked.

He looked at me, then dropped his eyes to his cup.

"I know it's none of my bus—" he began.

"Cream and sugar?"

*

Ikky didn't return that day, or that night. We picked up some Dixieland out of Lifeline and let the muskrat ramble while Jean had her supper sent to the Slider. Later she had a bunk assembled inside. I piped in "Deep Water Blues" when it came over the air and waited for her to call up and cuss us out. She didn't though, so I decided she was sleeping.

Then I got Mike interested in a game of chess that went on until daylight. It limited conversation to several "checks," one "checkmate," and a "damn!" Since he's a poor loser it also effectively sabotaged subsequent talk, which was fine with me. I had a steak and fried potatoes for breakfast and went to bed.

Ten hours later someone shook me awake and I propped myself on one elbow, refusing to open my eyes.

"Whassamadder?"

"I'm sorry to get you up," said one of the younger crewmen, "but Miss Luharich wants you to disconnect the squiggler so we can move on."

I knuckled open one eye, still deciding whether I should be amused.

"Have it hauled to the side. Anyone can disconnect it."

"It's at the side now, sir. But she said it's in your contract and we'd better do things right."

"That's very considerate of her. I'm sure my Local appreciates her remembering."

"Uh, she also said to tell you to change your trunks and comb your hair, and shave, too. Mister Anderson's going to film it."

"Okay. Run along; tell her I'm on my way—and ask if she has some toenail polish I can borrow."

I'll save on details. It took three minutes in all, and I played it properly, even pardoning myself when I slipped and bumped into Anderson's white tropicals with the wet squiggler. He smiled, brushed it off; she smiled, even though Luharich Complectacolor couldn't completely mask the dark circles under her eyes; and I smiled, waving to all our fans out there in videoland. —Remember, Mrs. Universe, you, too, can look like a monster-catcher. Just use Luharich face cream.

I went below and made myself a tuna sandwich, with mayonnaise.

*

Two days like icebergs—bleak, blank, half-melting, all frigid, mainly out of sight, and definitely a threat to peace of mind—drifted by and were good to put behind. I experienced some old guilt feelings and had a few disturbing dreams. Then I called Lifeline and checked my bank balance.

"Going shopping?" asked Mike, who had put the call through for me.

"Going home," I answered.

"Huh?"

"I'm out of the baiting business after this one, Mike. The Devil with Ikky! The Devil with Venus and Luharich Enterprises! And the Devil with you!"

Up eyebrows.

"What brought that on?"

"I waited over a year for this job. Now that I'm here, I've decided the whole thing stinks."

"You knew what it was when you signed on. No matter what else you're doing, you're selling face cream when you work for face cream sellers."

185

The Magic

"Oh, that's not what's biting me. I admit the commercial angle irritates me, but Tensquare has always been a publicity spot, ever since the first time it sailed."

"What, then?"

"Five or six things, all added up. The main one being that I don't care any more. Once it meant more to me than anything else to hook that critter, and now it doesn't. I went broke on what started out as a lark and I wanted blood for what it had cost me. Now I realize that maybe I had it coming. I'm beginning to feel sorry for Ikky."

"And you don't want him now?"

"I'll take him if he comes peacefully, but I don't feel like sticking out my neck to make him crawl into the Hopkins."

"I'm inclined to think it's one of the four or five other things you said you added."

"Such as?"

He scrutinized the ceiling.

I growled.

"Okay, but I won't say it, not just to make you happy you guessed right."

He, smirking: "That look she wears isn't just for Ikky."

"No good, no good." I shook my head. "We're both fission chambers by nature. You can't have jets on both ends of the rocket and expect to go anywhere—what's in the middle just gets smashed."

"That's how it *was*. None of my business, of course—"

"Say that again and you'll say it without teeth."

"Any day, big man"—he looked up—"any place . . . "

"So go ahead. Get it said!"

"She doesn't care about that bloody reptile, she came here to drag you back where you belong. You're not the baitman this trip."

"Five years is too long."

"There must be something under that cruddy hide of yours that people like," he muttered, "or I wouldn't be talking like this. Maybe you remind us humans of some really ugly dog we felt sorry for when we were kids. Anyhow, someone wants to take you home and raise you—also, something about beggars not getting menus."

"Buddy," I chuckled, "do you know what I'm going to do when I hit Lifeline?"

"I can guess."

"You're wrong. I'm torching it to Mars, and then I'll cruise back home, first class. Venus bankruptcy provisions do not apply to Martian trust funds, and I've still got a wad tucked away where moth and corruption enter not. I'm going to pick up a big old mansion on the Gulf and if you're ever looking for a job you can stop around and open bottles for me."

"You are a yellowbellied fink," he commented.

"Okay," I admitted, "but it's her I'm thinking of, too."

"I've heard the stories about you both," he said. "So you're a heel and a goofoff and she's a bitch. That's called compatibility these days. I dare you, baitman, try keeping something you catch."

I turned.

"If you ever want that job, look me up."

I closed the door quietly behind me and left him sitting there waiting for it to slam.

*

The day of the beast dawned like any other. Two days after my gutless flight from empty waters I went down to rebait. Nothing on the scope. I was just making things ready for the routine attempt.

I hollered a "good morning" from outside the Slider and received an answer from inside before I pushed off. I had reappraised Mike's words, sans sound, sans fury, and while I did not approve of their sentiment or significance, I had opted for civility anyhow.

So down, under, and away. I followed a decent cast about two hundred-ninety meters out. The snaking cables burned black to my left and I paced their undulations from the yellowgreen down into the darkness. Soundless lay the wet night, and I bent my way through it like a cock-eyed comet, bright tail before.

The Magic

I caught the line, slick and smooth, and began baiting. An icy world swept by me then, ankles to head. It was a draft, as if someone had opened a big door beneath me. I wasn't drifting forwards that fast either.

Which meant that something might be moving up, something big enough to displace a lot of water. I still didn't think it was Ikky. A freak current of some sort, but not Ikky. Ha!

I had finished attaching the leads and pulled the first plug when a big, rugged, black island grew beneath me . . . .

I flicked the beam downward. His mouth was opened.

I was rabbit.

Waves of the death-fear passed downward. My stomach imploded. I grew dizzy.

Only one thing, and one thing only. Left to do. I managed it, finally. I pulled the rest of the plugs.

I could count the scaly articulations ridging his eyes by then.

The squiggler grew, pinked into phosphorescence . . . squiggled.

Then my lamp. I had to kill it, leaving just the bait before him.

One glance back as I jammed the jatoes to life.

He was so near that the squiggler reflected on his teeth, in his eyes. Four meters, and I kissed his lambent jowls with two jets of backwash as I soared. Then I didn't know whether he was following or had halted. I began to black out as I waited to be eaten.

The jatoes died and I kicked weakly.

Too fast, I felt a cramp coming on. One flick of the beam, cried rabbit. One second, to know . . .

Or end things up, I answered. No, rabbit, we don't dart before hunters. Stay dark.

Green waters, finally, to yellowgreen, then top.

Doubling, I beat off toward Tensquare. The waves from the explosion behind pushed me on ahead. The world closed in, and a screamed "He's alive!" in the distance.

A giant shadow and a shock wave. The line was alive, too. Happy Fishing Grounds. Maybe I did something wrong . . . .

Somewhere Hand was clenched. What's bait?

*

A few million years. I remember starting out as a one-celled organism and painfully becoming an amphibian, then an air-breather. From somewhere high in the treetops I heard a voice.

"He's coming around."

I evolved back into homosapience, then a step further into a hangover.

"Don't try to get up yet."

"Have we got him?" I slurred.

"Still fighting, but he's hooked. We thought he took you for an appetizer."

"So did I."

"Breathe some of this and shut up."

A funnel over my face. Good. Lift your cups and drink . . . .

"He was awfully deep. Below scope range. We didn't catch him till he started up. Too late, then."

I began to yawn.

"We'll get you inside now."

I managed to uncase my ankle knife.

"Try it and you'll be minus a thumb."

"You need rest."

"Then bring me a couple more blankets. I'm staying."

I fell back and closed my eyes.

*

Someone was shaking me. Gloom and cold. Spotlights bled yellow on the deck. I was in a jury-rigged bunk, bulked against the center blister. Swaddled in wool, I still shivered.

"It's been eleven hours. You're not going to see anything now."

I tasted blood.

"Drink this."

The Magic

Water. I had a remark but I couldn't mouth it.

"Don't ask me how I feel," I croaked. "I know that comes next, but don't ask me. Okay?"

"Okay. Want to go below now?"

"No. Just get me my jacket."

"Right here."

"What's he doing?"

"Nothing. He's deep, he's doped but he's staying down."

"How long since last time he showed?"

"Two hours, about."

"Jean?"

"She won't let anyone in the Slider. Listen, Mike says to come on in. He's right behind you in the blister."

I sat up and turned around. Mike was watching. He gestured; I gestured back.

I swung my feet over the edge and took a couple of deep breaths. Pains in my stomach. I got to my feet and made it into the blister.

"Howza gut?" queried Mike.

I checked the scope. No Ikky. Too deep.

"You buying?"

"Yeah, coffee."

"Not coffee."

"You're ill. Also, coffee is all that's allowed in here."

"Coffee is a brownish liquid that burns your stomach. You have some in the bottom drawer."

"No cups. You'll have to use a glass."

"Tough."

He poured.

"You do that well. Been practicing for that job?"

"What job?"

"The one I offered you—"

A blot on the scope!

"Rising, ma'am! Rising!" he yelled into the box.

"Thanks, Mike. I've got it in here," she crackled.

"Jean!"

"Shut up! She's busy!"

"Was that Carl?"

"Yeah," I called. "Talk later," and I cut it.

Why did I do that?

"Why did you do that?"

I didn't know.

"I don't know."

Damned echoes! I got up and walked outside.

Nothing. Nothing.

Something?

Tensquare actually rocked! He must have turned when he saw the hull and started downward again. White water to my left, and boiling. An endless spaghetti of cable roared hotly into the belly of the deep.

I stood awhile, then turned and went back inside.

Two hours sick. Four, and better.

"The dope's getting to him."

"Yeah."

"What about Miss Luharich?"

"What about her?"

"She must be half dead."

"Probably."

"What are you going to do about it?"

"She signed the contract for this. She knew what might happen. It did."

"I think you could land him."

"So do I."

"So does she."

"Then let her ask me."

Ikky was drifting lethargically, at thirty fathoms.

The Magic

I took another walk and happened to pass behind the Slider. She wasn't looking my way.

"Carl, come in here!"

Eyes of Picasso, that's what, and a conspiracy to make me Slide . . .

"Is that an order?"

"Yes—No! Please."

I dashed inside and monitored. He was rising.

"Push or pull?"

I slammed the "wind" and he came like a kitten.

"Make up your own mind now."

He balked at ten fathoms.

"Play him?"

"No!"

She wound him upwards—five fathoms, four . . .

She hit the extensors at two, and the caught him. Then the graffles.

Cries without and a heat of lightning of flashbulbs.

The crew saw Ikky.

He began to struggle. She kept the cables tight, raised the graffles.

Up.

Another two feet and the graffles began pulsing.

Screams and fast footfalls.

Giant beanstalk in the wind, his neck, waving. The green hills of his shoulders grew.

"He's big, Carl!" she cried.

And he grew, and grew, and grew uneasy . . .

"*Now!*"

He looked down.

He looked down, as the god of our most ancient ancestors might have looked down. Fear, shame, and mocking laughter rang in my head. Her head, too?

"*Now!*"

She looked up at the nascent earthquake.

"I can't!"

It was going to be so damnably simple this time, now the rabbit had died. I reached out.

I stopped.

"Push it yourself."

"I can't. You do it. Land him, Carl!"

"No. If I do, you'll wonder for the rest of your life whether you could have. You'll throw away your soul finding out. I know you will, because we're alike, and I did it that way. Find out now!"

She stared.

I gripped her shoulders.

"Could be that's me out there," I offered. "I am a green sea serpent, a hateful, monstrous beast, and out to destroy you. I am answerable to no one. Push the Inject."

Her hand moved to the button, jerked back.

"Now!"

She pushed it.

I lowered her still form to the floor and finished things up with Ikky.

It was a good seven hours before I awakened to the steady, sea-chewing grind of Tensquare's blades.

"You're sick," commented Mike.

"How's Jean?"

"The same."

"Where's the beast?"

"Here."

"Good." I rolled over. " . . . Didn't get away this time."

So that's the way it was. No one is born a baitman, I don't think, but the rings of Saturn sing epithalamium the sea-beast's dower.

A Word from Zelazny

Written in January 1963, according to correspondence with Gil Lamont.[1] Zelazny was well aware that the Mars and Venus of space opera no longer could exist as information came flooding in from the early space probes, but he wanted to write that kind of story before it went out of style. "I had a sentimental feeling for that kind of story, and at the time I wrote 'A Rose For Ecclesiastes' in late 1961, I decided to do something I always wanted to do—I had to do it then, because our knowledge of the solar system had changed so rapidly . . . that the sort of Mars of which Edgar Rice Burroughs wrote, or Leigh Brackett, [or Ray Bradbury], or the numerous Edmond Hamilton stories—that Mars, or that Venus—the great watery world with prehistoric creatures in its oceans—simply did not exist."[2,3]

"I realized that was the last point in time that anyone could write that sort of story. If I wanted to do it, I would have to do it immediately. So I wrote 'A Rose For Ecclesiastes' set on the old-fashioned Mars with the red deserts and the breathable atmosphere. It was just a composite of all my feelings. And I resolved very quickly to do one about Venus, which I did: 'The Doors of His Face, the Lamps of His Mouth.' That was it. I could never do another story of that sort again. But they were both, in a way, my tribute to a phase in the genre's history which had just closed and expressed my feelings towards it. So I wasn't actually making fun of it."[2] "Those were both, in a way, exercises in nostalgia for the earlier sort of science fiction that I had read."[3]

Concerning the two stories, he added, "It was, let's face it, a Byronic gesture, but I considered myself as a writer first, then an SF writer, and, as I said, I am sentimental."[4]

A writer told Zelazny that he used the Yellow Pages as a source of inspiration, and this idea caught on with Zelazny who would "project fifty years into the future the first half dozen entries to which I turned, and then I would ask myself how that business would be run fifty years from now . . . make some guesses about what society might be like . . . try the 'what if?' variations; e.g., what if some of the customers (or employees) aren't human . . . I would try shifting the business to another world, testing it in an even stranger setting. My story 'The Doors of His Face, the Lamps of His Mouth,' actually owed something to a bait-and-tackle ad."[5]

Roger Zelazny and Samuel R. Delany

Notes

While many readers greeted this story enthusiastically, some critics discarded it as a simple science fictional retelling of Herman Melville's *Moby Dick*—that comparison fails in several significant respects, including that Ahab never caught the whale that he was obsessed with but died trying, leaving Ishmael as the sole survivor of his crew. "The Doors of His Face, the Lamps of His Mouth" is a story of adventure, redemption and reconciliation, and self-introspection, told by a convincingly realized character in a convincingly realized setting despite the fact that it could only have been fantasy by the time it appeared.

The title is drawn from *The Book of Job* 41:14–19 in which the monstrous sea-creature known as the **Leviathan** is described: "Who can open the doors of his face? | | his teeth are terrible round about. | | His scales are his pride, | | shut together as with a close seal. | | Out of his mouth go burning lamps, | | and sparks of fire leap out." According to Robert Silverberg, *"We Are All Bait"* refers to *Nous sommes tous des assassins* [We Are All Assassins], a 1952 French film about several condemned men in a jail who are taken away one by one to be executed. Alternatively, another explanation is that Zelazny meant Emile Zola's 1890 novel *La bete humaine*. It certainly sounds like "the bait human" or "the human bait," and meets the criterion of being a French title. But correctly translated it means "the human beast." The novel concerned a man afflicted with a hereditary mania that causes him to desire to murder women, and he later kills his own wife. A recent discovery of a letter from Zelazny to his longtime friend Carl Yoke revealed that neither of these suppositions are correct. "I just have this thing about the existentialist novelists and think they're great to make fun of. So . . . The baitman reference to a French novel is a fabrication."[6]

In palmistry, the mount of **Venus** is the large area of the palm that borders the **thumb** and is fenced in by the **life line**, and which is believed to shows the passion and energy that a person has for life. The narrator is comparing the local geography of the continent of Hand on Venus, as viewed while descending from the sky, to the palm of his own hand. **Narcotized** is a slang

The Magic

term meaning put to sleep or made stuporous by use of a narcotic (an opioid or other pain-killing drug). **Hemiplegia** is paralysis on one side of the body due to a stroke (destruction of brain tissue by a blood clot or hemorrhage); Davits limps from a partial hemiplegia, the result of a stroke he experienced during his close-up encounter with Ikky. **Lloyd's** refers to Lloyd's of London, a group of insurance underwriters that originally formed in 1688 to insure, classify, register, and certify marine vessels.

A **gaff** is an iron hook with a handle for landing large fish, whereas a **grapple** or grapnel is an anchor with three or more flukes. A **Seraph** is a member of the highest of nine orders of angels. **Abyss** when capitalized refers to Hell or the primal Chaos before Creation. **De facto** means "in fact," as opposed to "in theory" or "in law." **Through a glass, brownly** alludes to the line "through a glass, darkly" in 1 Corinthians: 13 in the New Testament of the Bible; the line implies that humans have an imperfect perception of reality. **Daughter of Lir** refers to the Irish mythology of the Children of Lir, and specifically the beautiful daughter Fionnuala, who was cursed and changed into a swan by her stepmother. **Lir** himself is a god of the sea in Irish mythology and is alluded to in the story "The Horses of Lir." The phrase **Daughter of Lir, eyes of Picasso** is a quote from Ezra Pound's *Cantos II* in which he describes a seal: "Seal sports in the spray-whited circles of cliff wash, || Sleek head, daughter of Lir || eyes of Picasso || Under black fur hood, lithe daughter of ocean."

A **gink** is a foolish or contemptible person. **Yclept** means called or named. **Passed him a box full of her unseeing** means that she took out her colored contact lenses. **Govino** Bay is off the island of **Corfu**; the reference is to a time when Carlton Davits was rescued from near-drowning by Jean Luharich. **Mindanao** is the second-largest island in the Phillipines. **Jato** is an auxiliary jet-producing unit to provide thrust at takeoff. **Sleek head . . . Daughter of Lir . . . Eyes of . . .** quotes Cantos II again except **perdition** (damnation, eternal loss of soul) has been substituted for **Picasso**. **Vido** and **Corfu** are among the Greek islands. **There is no power on Earth that can be compared with him who was made to fear no one** is another quote from the Book of Job in which the Leviathan is described. **Acheron** is one of the rivers in Hades across which Charon ferries the newly dead. **Dart fitfully forever along Acheron** echoes poetry of Sappho and also a poem that Conrad quotes in *". . . And Call Me Conrad"/This Immortal.* **Dixieland** is a style of jazz music from New Orleans that features a rapid twobeat rhythm and solo improvisations. **Deep Water Blues** was performed by Louis Armstrong and the Dukes of Dixieland. **Sans** [without] **sound, sans fury** alludes to William Faulkner's novel *The Sound and the Fury* which, like this novella, features a stream-of-consciousness narrative. The original quote is from Shakespeare's *Macbeth—*" . . . a tale told by an idiot, full of sound and fury, signifying nothing . . . "—and suggests the narrator's self-deprecating humor, that he considers himself an idiot and that his tale is meaningless. An additional allusion in **"Sans sound, sans fury"** is to the "seven ages of man" monologue in *As You Like It*, which concludes "Sans teeth, sans eyes, sans taste, sans everything." **Epithalamium** means a bridal song, or an ode honoring the bride and groom; the usage implies that Carlton and Jean may be reconciling as a couple. **Dower** means the portion of a deceased man's property which is given to his widow, or it can mean a gift or endowment; in this case the deceased is the sea-beast.

[1] *Tightbeam* #37, May 1966.
[2] *Roger Zelazny*, Theodore Krulik, 1986.
[3] *Xignals* XVI Feb/Mar 1986.
[4] *Galaxie* #96 Mai 1972.
[5] *The Writer* 101(3):9–11. March 1988.
[6] Letter to Carl Yoke, February 28, 1974.

The Ides of Octember

Lovely as it was, with the blood and all, Render could sense that it was about to end.

Therefore, each microsecond would be better off as a minute, he decided—and perhaps the temperature should be increased . . . Somewhere, just at the periphery of everything, the darkness halted its constriction.

Something, like a crescendo of subliminal thunders, was arrested at one raging note. That note was a distillate of shame and pain and fear.

The Forum was stifling.

Caesar cowered outside the frantic circle. His forearm covered his eyes but it could not stop the seeing, not this time.

The senators had no faces and their garments were spattered with blood. All their voices were like the cries of birds. With an inhuman frenzy they plunged their daggers into the fallen figure.

All, that is, but Render.

The pool of blood in which he stood continued to widen. His arm seemed to be rising and falling with a mechanical regularity and his throat might have been shaping bird-cries, but he was simultaneously apart from and a part of the scene.

For he was Render, the Shaper.

Crouched, anguished and envious, Caesar wailed his protests.

"You have slain him! You have murdered Marcus Antonius—a blameless, useless fellow!"

Render turned to him and the dagger in his hand was quite enormous and quite gory.

"Aye," said he.

The blade moved from side to side. Caesar, fascinated by the sharpened steel, swayed to the same rhythm.

The Magic

"Why?" he cried. "Why?"

"Because," answered Render, "he was a far nobler Roman then yourself."

"You lie! It is not so!"

Render shrugged and returned to the stabbing.

"It is not true!" screamed Caesar. "Not true!"

Render turned to him again and waved the dagger. Puppetlike, Caesar mimicked the pendulum of the blade.

"Not true?" smiled Render. "And who are you to question an assassination such as this? You are no one! You detract from the dignity of this occasion! Begone!"

Jerkily, the pink-faced man rose to his feet, his hair half-wispy, half-wetplastered, a disarray of cotton. He turned, moved away; and as he walked, he looked back over his shoulder.

He had moved far from the circle of assassins, but the scene did not diminish in size. It retained an electric clarity. It made him feel even further removed, ever more alone and apart.

Render rounded a previously unnoticed corner and stood before him, a blind beggar.

Caesar grasped the front of his garment.

"Have you an ill omen for me this day?"

"Beware!" jeered Render.

"Yes! Yes!" cried Caesar. "'Beware!' That is good! Beware what?"

"The ides—"

"Yes? The ides—?"

"—of October."

He released the garment.

"What is that you say? What is Octember?"

"A month."

"You lie! There is no month of Octember!"

"And that is the date noble Caesar need fear—the non-existent time, the never-to-be-calendared occasion."

Render vanished around another sudden corner.

Roger Zelazny and Samuel R. Delany

"Wait! Come back!"

Render laughed, and the Forum laughed with him. The bird-cries became a chorus of inhuman jeers.

"You mock me!" wept Caesar.

The Forum was an oven, and the perspiration formed like a glassy mask over Caesar's narrow forehead, sharp nose and chinless jaw.

"I want to be assassinated too!" he sobbed. "It isn't fair!"

And Render tore the Forum and the senators and the grinning corpse of Antony to pieces and stuffed them into a black sack—with the unseen movement of a single finger—and last of all went Caesar.

*

Charles Render sat before the ninety white buttons and the two red ones, not really looking at any of them. His right arm moved in its soundless sling, across the lap-level surface of the console—pushing some of the buttons, skipping over others, moving on, retracing its path to press the next in the order of the Recall Series.

Sensations throttled, emotions reduced to nothing, Representative Erikson knew the oblivion of the womb.

There was a soft click.

Render's hand had glided to the end of the bottom row of buttons. An act of conscious intent—will, if you like—was required to push the red button.

Render freed his arm and lifted off his crown of Medusa-hair leads and microminiature circuitry. He slid from behind his desk-couch and raised the hood. He walked to the window and transpared it, fingering forth a cigarette.

One minute in the ro-womb, he decided. *No more. This is a crucial one . . . . Hope it doesn't snow till later—those clouds look mean . . . .*

It was smooth yellow trellises and high towers, glassy and gray, all smouldering into evening under a shale-colored sky; the city was squared volcanic islands, glowing in the end-of-day light, rumbling deep down under the earth; it was fat, incessant rivers of traffic, rushing.

Render turned away from the window and approached the great egg that lay beside his desk, smooth and glittering. It threw back a reflection that

The Magic

smashed all aquilinity from his nose, turned his eyes to gray saucers, transformed his hair into a light-streaked skyline; his reddish necktie became the wide tongue of a ghoul.

He smiled, reached across the desk. He pressed the second red button.

With a sigh, the egg lost its dazzling opacity and a horizontal crack appeared about its middle. Through the now-transparent shell. Render could see Erikson grimacing, squeezing his eyes tight, fighting against a return to consciousness and the thing it would contain. The upper half of the egg rose vertical to the base, exposing him knobby and pink on the half-shell. When his eyes opened he did not look at Render. He rose to his feet and began dressing. Render used this time to check the ro-womb.

He leaned back across his desk and pressed the buttons: temperature control, full range, *check*; exotic sounds—he raised the earphone—*check*, on bells, on buzzes, on violin notes and whistles, on squeals and moans, on traffic noises and the sound of surf; *check*, on the feedback circuit—holding the patient's own voice, trapped earlier in analysis; *check*, on the sound blanket, the moisture spray, the odor banks; *check*, on the couch agitator and the colored lights, the taste stimulants . . .

*

Render closed the egg and shut off its power. He pushed the unit into the closet, palmed shut the door. The tapes had registered a valid sequence.

"Sit down," he directed Erikson.

The man did so, fidgeting with his collar.

"You have full recall," said Render, "so there is no need for me to summarize what occurred. Nothing can be hidden from me. I was there."

Erikson nodded.

"The significance of the episode should be apparent to you."

Erikson nodded again, finally finding his voice. "But was it valid?" he asked. "I mean, you constructed the dream and you controlled it, all the way. I didn't really *dream* it—in the way I would normally dream. Your ability to make things happen stacks the deck for whatever you're going to say—doesn't it?"

Roger Zelazny and Samuel R. Delany

Render shook his head slowly, flicked an ash into the southern hemisphere of his globe-made-ashtray, and met Erikson's eyes.

"It is true that I supplied the format and modified the forms. You, however, filled them with an emotional significance, promoted them to the status of symbols corresponding to your problem. If the dream was not a valid analogue it would not have provoked the reactions it did. It would have been devoid of the anxiety-patterns which were registered on the tapes.

"You have been in analysis for many months now," he continued, "and everything I have learned thus far serves to convince me that your fears of assassination are without any basis in fact."

Erikson glared.

"Then why the hell do I have them?"

"Because," said Render, "you would like very much to be the subject of an assassination."

Erikson smiled then, his composure beginning to return.

"I assure you, doctor, I have never contemplated suicide, nor have I any desire to stop living."

He produced a cigar and applied a flame to it. His hand shook.

"When you came to me this summer," said Render, "you stated that you were in fear of an attempt on your life. You were quite vague as to why anyone should want to kill you—"

"My position! You can't be a Representative as long as I have and make no enemies!"

"Yet," replied Render, "it appears that you have managed it. When you permitted me to discuss this with your detectives I was informed that they could unearth nothing to indicate that your fears might have any real foundation. Nothing."

"They haven't looked far enough—or in the right places. They'll turn up something."

"I'm afraid not."

"Why?"

The Magic

"Because, I repeat, your feelings are without any objective basis. —Be honest with me. Have you any information whatsoever indicating that someone hates you enough to want to kill you?"

"I receive many threatening letters . . . . "

"As do all Representatives—and all of those directed to you during the past year have been investigated and found to be the work of cranks. Can you offer me *one* piece of evidence to substantiate your claims?"

Erikson studied the tip of his cigar.

"I came to you on the advice of a colleague," he said, "came to you to have you poke around inside my mind to find me something of that sort, to give my detectives something to work with. —Someone I've injured severely perhaps—or some damaging piece of legislation I've dealt with . . . "

"—And I found nothing," said Render, "nothing, that is, but the cause of your discontent. Now, of course, you are afraid to hear it, and you are attempting to divert me from explaining my diagnosis—"

"I am not!"

"Then listen. You can comment afterward if you want, but you've poked and dawdled around here for months, unwilling to accept what I presented to you in a dozen different forms. Now I am going to tell you outright what it is, and you can do what you want about it."

"Fine."

"First," he said, "you would like very much to have an enemy or enemies—"

"Ridiculous!"

"—Because it is the only alternative to having friends—"

"I have lots of friends!"

"—Because nobody wants to be completely ignored, to be an object for whom no one has really strong feelings. Hatred and love are the ultimate forms of human regard. Lacking one, and unable to achieve it, you sought the other. You wanted it so badly that you succeeded in convincing yourself it existed. But there is always a psychic pricetag on these things. Answering a genuine emotional need with a body of desire-surrogates does not produce real satisfaction, but anxiety, discomfort—because in these matters the psyche should be an open system. You did not seek outside yourself for human regard. You were closed off. You created that which you needed from the stuff of your own being. You are a man very much in need of strong relationships with other people."

"Manure!"

'Take it or leave it," said Render. "I suggest you take it."

"I've been paying you for half a year to help find out who wants to kill me. Now you sit there and tell me I made the whole thing up to satisfy a desire to have someone hate me."

"Hate you, or love you. That's right."

"It's absurd! I meet so many people that I carry a pocket recorder and a lapel-camera, just so I can recall them all . . . . "

"Meeting quantities of people is hardly what I was speaking of. —Tell me, *did* that dream sequence have a strong meaning for you?"

Erikson was silent for several tickings of the huge wall-clock.

"Yes," he finally conceded, "it did. But your interpretation of the matter is still absurd. Granting though, just for the sake of argument, that what you say is correct—what would I do to get out of this bind?"

Render leaned back in his chair.

"Rechannel the energies that went into producing the thing. Meet some people as yourself, Joe Erikson, rather than Representative Erikson. Take up something you can do with other people—something non-political, and perhaps somewhat competitive—and make some real friends or enemies, preferably the former. I've encouraged you to do this all along."

"Then tell me something else."

"Gladly."

"Assuming you *are* right, why is it that I am neither liked nor hated, and never have been? I have a responsible position in the Legislature. I meet people all the time. Why am I so neutral a—thing?"

Highly familiar now with Erikson's career. Render had to push aside his true thoughts on the matter, as they were of no operational value. He wanted to cite him Dante's observations concerning the trimmers—those souls who, denied heaven for their lack of virtue, were also denied entrance to hell for a lack of significant vices—in short, the ones who trimmed their sails to move them with every wind of the times, who lacked direction, who were not really concerned toward which ports they were pushed. Such was Erikson's long and colorless career of migrant loyalties, of political reversals.

Render said:

"More and more people find themselves in such circumstances these days. It is due largely to the increasing complexity of society and the depersonalization of the individual into a sociometric unit. Even the act of cathecting toward other persons has grown more forced as a result. There are so many of us these days."

Erikson nodded, and Render smiled inwardly.

Sometimes the gruff line, and then the lecture . . .

"I've got the feeling you could be right," said Erikson. "Sometimes I *do* feel like what you just described—a unit, something depersonalized . . . . "

Render glanced at the clock.

"What you choose to do about it from here is, of course, your own decision to make. I think you'd be wasting your time to remain in analysis any longer. We are now both aware of the cause of your complaint. I can't take you by the hand and show you how to lead your life. I can indicate, I can commiserate—but no more deep probing. Make an appointment as soon as you feel a need to discuss your activities and relate them to my diagnosis."

"I will," nodded Erikson, "and—damn that dream! It got to me. You can make them seem as vivid as waking life—more vivid . . . . It may be a long while before I can forget it."

"I hope so."

"Okay, doctor." He rose to his feet, extended a hand. "I'll probably be back in a couple weeks. I'll give this socializing a fair try." He grinned at the word he normally frowned upon. "In fact, I'll start now. May I buy you a drink around the corner, downstairs?"

Roger Zelazny and Samuel R. Delany

Render met the moist palm which seemed as weary of the performance as a lead actor in too successful a play. He felt almost sorry as he said, "Thank you, but I have an engagement."

Render helped him on with his coat then, handed him his hat, saw him to the door.

"Well, good night."

"Good night."

*

As the door closed soundlessly behind him. Render re-crossed the dark Astrakhan to his mahogany fortress and flipped his cigarette into the southern hemisphere of a globe ashtray. He leaned back in his chair, hands behind his head, eyes closed.

"Of course it was more real than life," he informed no one in particular, "I shaped it."

Smiling, he reviewed the dream sequence step by step, wishing some of his former instructors could have witnessed it. It had been well-constructed and powerfully executed, as well as being precisely appropriate for the case at hand. But then, he was Render, the Shaper—one of the two hundred or so special analysts whose own psychic makeup permitted them to enter into neurotic patterns without carrying away more than an esthetic gratification from the mimesis of aberrance—a Sane Hatter.

Render stirred his recollections. He had been analyzed himself, analyzed and passed upon as a granite-willed, ultra-stable outsider—tough enough to weather the basilisk gaze of a fixation, walk unscathed amidst the chimerae of perversions, force dark Mother Medusa to close her eyes before the caduceus of his art. His own analysis had not been difficult. Nine years before (it seemed much longer) he had suffered a willing injection of novocain into the most painful area of his spirit. It was after the auto wreck, after the death of Ruth, and of Miranda, their daughter, that he had begun to feel detached. Perhaps he did not want to recover certain empathies; perhaps his own world was now based upon a certain rigidity of feeling. If

The Magic

this was true, he was wise enough in the ways of the mind to realize it, and perhaps he had decided that such a world had its own compensations.

His son Peter was now ten years old. He was attending a school of quality, and he penned his father a letter every week. The letters were becoming progressively literate, showing signs of a precociousness of which Render could not but approve. He would take the boy with him to Europe in the summer.

As for Jill—Jill DeVille (what a luscious, ridiculous name!—he loved her for it)—she was growing if anything, more interesting to him. (He wondered if this was an indication of early middle age.) He was vastly taken by her unmusical nasal voice, her sudden interest in architecture, her concern with the unremovable mole on the right side of her otherwise well-designed nose. He should really call her immediately and go in search of a new restaurant. For some reason though, he did not feel like it.

It had been several weeks since he had visited his club, The Partridge and Scalpel, and he felt a strong desire to eat from an oaken table, alone, in the split-level dining room with the three fireplaces, beneath the artificial torches and the boars' heads like gin ads. So he pushed his perforated membership card into the phone-slot on his desk and there were two buzzes behind the voice-screen.

"Hello, Partridge and Scalpel," said the voice. "May I help you?"

"Charles Render," he said. "I'd like a table in about half an hour."

"How many will there be?"

"Just me."

"Very good, sir. Half an hour, then. —That's 'Render'?—R-e-n-d-er-?"

"Right."

"Thank you."

He broke the connection and rose from his desk. Outside, the day had vanished.

The monoliths and the towers gave forth their own light now. A soft snow, like sugar, was sifting down through the shadows and transforming itself into beads on the windowpane.

Render shrugged into his overcoat, turned off the lights, locked the inner office. There was a note on Mrs. Hedges' blotter.

Miss DeVille called, it said.

He crumpled the note and tossed it into the waste-chute. He would call her tomorrow and say he had been working until late on his lecture.

He switched off the final light, clapped his hat onto his head and passed through the outer door, locking it as he went. The drop took him to the sub-subcellar where his auto was parked.

*

It was chilly in the sub-sub, and his footsteps seemed loud on the concrete as he passed among the parked vehicles. Beneath the glare of the naked lights, his S-7 Spinner was a sleek gray cocoon from which it seemed turbulent wings might at any moment emerge. The double row of antennae which fanned forward from the slope of its hood added to this feeling. Render thumbed open the door.

He touched the ignition and there was the sound of a lone bee awakening in a great hive. The door swung soundlessly shut as he raised the steering wheel and locked it into place. He spun up the spiral ramp and came to a rolling stop before the big overhead.

As the door rattled upward he lighted his destination screen and turned the knob that shifted the broadcast map. —Left to right, top to bottom, section by section he shifted it, until he located the portion of Carnegie Avenue he desired. He punched out its coordinates and lowered the wheel. The car switched over to monitor and moved out onto the highway marginal. Render lit a cigarette.

Pushing his seat back into the centerspace, he left all the windows transparent. It was pleasant to half-recline and watch the oncoming cars drift past him like swarms of fireflies. He pushed his hat back on his head and stared upward.

He could remember a time when he had loved snow, when it had reminded him of novels by Thomas Mann and music by Scandinavian composers. In his mind now, though, there was another element from which it could never be wholly dissociated. He could visualize so clearly the eddies of milk-white coldness that swirled about his old manual-steer auto, flowing into its fire-charred interior to rewhiten that which had been blackened; so clearly—as though he had walked toward it across a chalky lakebottom—it, the sunken wreck, and he, the diver—unable to open his mouth to speak, for fear of drowning; and he knew, whenever he looked upon falling snow, that somewhere skulls were whitening. But nine years had washed away much of the pain, and he also knew that the night was lovely.

He was sped along the wide, wide roads, shot across high bridges, their surfaces slick and gleaming beneath his lights, was woven through frantic cloverleafs and plunged into a tunnel whose dimly glowing walls blurred by him like a mirage. Finally, he switched the windows to opaque and closed his eyes.

He could not remember whether he had dozed for a moment or not, which meant he probably had. He felt the car slowing, and he moved the seat forward and turned on the windows again. Almost simultaneously, the cut-off buzzer sounded. He raised the steering wheel and pulled into the parking dome, stepped out onto the ramp and left the car to the parking unit, receiving his ticket from that box-headed robot which took its solemn revenge on mankind by sticking forth a cardboard tongue at everyone it served.

*

As always, the noises were as subdued as the lighting. The place seemed to absorb sound and convert it into warmth, to lull the tongue with aromas strong enough to be tasted, to hypnotize the ear with the vivid crackle of the triple hearths.

Render was pleased to see that his favorite table, in the corner off to the right of the smaller fireplace, had been held for him. He knew the menu from memory, but he studied it with zeal as he sipped a Manhattan and worked up an order to match his appetite. Shaping sessions always left him ravenously hungry.

"Doctor Render . . . ?"

"Yes?" He looked up.

"Doctor Shallot would like to speak with you," said the waiter.

"I don't know anyone named Shallot," he said. "Are you sure he doesn't want Bender? He's a surgeon from Metro who sometimes eats here . . . . "

The waiter shook his head,

"No, sir—'Render.' See here?" He extended a three-by-five card on which Render's full name was typed in capital letters. "Doctor Shallot has dined here nearly every night for the past two weeks," he explained, "and on each occasion has asked to be notified if you came in."

"Hm?" mused Render. "That's odd. Why didn't he just call me at my office?"

The waiter smiled and made a vague gesture.

"Well, tell him to come on over," he said, gulping his Manhattan, "and bring me another of these."

"Unfortunately, Doctor Shallot is blind," explained the waiter. "It would be easier if you—"

"All right, sure." Render stood up, relinquishing his favorite table with a strong premonition that he would not be returning to it that evening.

"Lead on."

They threaded their way among the diners, heading up to the next level. A familiar face said "hello" from a table set back against the wall, and Render nodded a greeting to a former seminar pupil whose name was Jurgens or Jirkans or something like that.

He moved on, into the smaller dining room wherein only two tables were occupied. No, three. There was one set in the corner at the far end of the darkened bar, partly masked by an ancient suit of armor. The waiter was heading him in that direction.

They stopped before the table and Render stared down into the darkened glasses that had tilted upward as they approached. Doctor Shallot was a woman, somewhere in the vicinity of her early thirties. Her low bronze bangs did not fully conceal the spot of silver which she wore on her forehead like a caste-mark. Render inhaled, and her head jerked slightly as the tip of his cigarette flared. She appeared to be staring straight up into his eyes. It was an uncomfortable feeling, even knowing that all she could distinguish of him was that which her minute photoelectric cell transmitted to her visual cortex over the hair-fine wire implants attached to that oscillator converter: in short, the glow of his cigarette.

"Doctor Shallot, this is Doctor Render," the waiter was saying.

"Good evening," said Render.

"Good evening," she said. "My name is Eileen and I've wanted very badly to meet you." He thought he detected a slight quaver in her voice. "Will you join me for dinner?"

"My pleasure," he acknowledged, and the waiter drew out the chair.

Render sat down, noting that the woman across from him already had a drink. He reminded the waiter of his second Manhattan.

"Have you ordered yet?" he inquired.

"No."

" . . . And two menus—" he started to say, then bit his tongue.

"Only one," she smiled.

"Make it none," he amended, and recited the menu.

They ordered. Then:

"Do you always do that?"

"What?"

"Carry menus in your head."

"Only a few," he said, "for awkward occasions. What was it you wanted to see—talk to me about?"

"You're a neuroparticipant therapist," she stated, "a Shaper."

"And you are—?"

"—a resident in psychiatry at State Psych. I have a year remaining."

"You knew Sam Riscomb then."

"Yes, he helped me get my appointment. He was my adviser."

"He was a very good friend of mine. We studied together at Menninger."

She nodded.

"I'd often heard him speak of you—that's one of the reasons I wanted to meet you. He's responsible for encouraging me to go ahead with my plans, despite my handicap."

Render stared at her. She was wearing a dark green dress which appeared to be made of velvet. About three inches to the left of the bodice was a pin which might have been gold. It displayed a red stone which could have been a ruby, around which the outline of a goblet was cast. Or was it really two profiles that were outlined, staring through the stone at one another? It seemed vaguely familiar to him, but he could not place it at the moment. It glittered expensively in the dim light.

Render accepted his drink from the waiter.

"I want to become a neuroparticipant therapist," she told him.

And if she had possessed vision Render would have thought she was staring at him, hoping for some response in his expression. He could not quite calculate what she wanted him to say.

"I commend your choice," he said, "and I respect your ambition." He tried to put his smile into his voice. "It is not an easy thing, of course, not all of the requirements being academic ones."

"I know," she said, "But then, I have been blind since birth and it was not an easy thing to come this far."

"Since birth?" he repeated. "I thought you might have lost your sight recently. You did your undergrad work then, and went on through med school without eyes . . . . That's—rather impressive."

"Thank you," she said, "but it isn't. Not really. I heard about the first neuroparticipants—Bartelmetz and the rest—when I was a child, and I decided then that I wanted to be one. My life ever since has been governed by that desire."

"What did you do in the labs?" be inquired. "—Not being able to see a specimen, look through a microscope . . . ? Or all that reading?"

"I hired people to read my assignments to me. I taped everything. The school understood that I wanted to go into psychiatry and they permitted a special arrangement for labs. I've been guided through the dissection of cadavers by lab assistants, and I've had everything described to me. I can tell things by touch . . . and I have a memory like yours with the menu," she smiled. "'The quality of psychoparticipation phenomena can only be gauged by the therapist himself, at that moment outside of time and space as we normally know it, when he stands in the midst of a world erected from the stuff of another man's dreams, recognizes there the non-Euclidian architecture of aberrance, and then takes his patient by the hand and tours the landscape . . . . If he can lead him back to the common earth, then his judgments were sound, his actions valid.'"

"From *Why No Psychometrics in This Place*," reflected Render.

"—by Charles Render, M.D."

"Our dinner is already moving in this direction," he noted, picking up his drink as the speed-cooked meal was pushed toward them in the kitchen-buoy.

"That's one of the reasons I wanted to meet you," she continued, raising her glass as the dishes rattled before her. "I want you to help me become a Shaper."

Her shaded eyes, as vacant as a statue's, sought him again.

"Yours is a completely unique situation," he commented. "There has never been a congenitally blind neuroparticipant—for obvious reasons. I'd have to consider all the aspects of the situation before I could advise you. Let's eat now, though. I'm starved."

"All right. But my blindness does not mean that I have never seen."

He did not ask her what she meant by that, because prime ribs were standing in front of him now and there was a bottle of Chambertin at his elbow. He did pause long enough to notice though, as she raised her left hand from beneath the table, that she wore no rings.

*

"I wonder if it's still snowing," he commented as they drank their coffee. "It was coming down pretty hard when I pulled into the dome."

"I hope so," she said, "even though it diffuses the light and I can't 'see' anything at all through it. I like to feel it falling about me and blowing against my face."

"How do you get about?"

"My dog, Sigmund—I gave him the night off," she smiled, "—he can guide me anywhere. He's a mutie Shepherd."

"Oh?" Render grew curious. "Can he talk much?"

She nodded.

"That operation wasn't as successful on him as on some of them, though. He has a vocabulary of about four hundred words, but I think it causes him pain to speak. He's quite intelligent. You'll have to meet him sometime."

Render began speculating immediately. He had spoken with such animals at recent medical conferences, and had been startled by their combination of reasoning ability and their devotion to their handlers. Much chromosome tinkering, followed by delicate embryo-surgery, was required to give a dog a brain capacity greater than a chimpanzee's. Several followup operations were necessary to produce vocal abilities. Most such experiments ended in failure, and the dozen or so puppies a year on which they succeeded were valued in the neighborhood of a hundred thousand dollars each. He realized then, as he lit a cigarette and held the light for a moment, that the stone in Miss Shallot's medallion was a genuine ruby. He began to suspect that her admission to a medical school might, in addition to her academic record, have been based upon a sizeable endowment to the college of her choice. Perhaps he was being unfair though, he chided himself.

"Yes," he said, "we might do a paper on canine neuroses. Does he ever refer to his father as 'that son of a female Shepherd'?"

"He never met his father," she said, quite soberly. "He was raised apart from other dogs. His attitude could hardly be typical. I don't think you'll ever learn the functional psychology of the dog from a mutie."

"I imagine you're right," he dismissed it. "More coffee?"

"No, thanks."

Deciding it was time to continue the discussion, he said, "So you want to be a Shaper . . . . "

"Yes."

The Magic

"I hate to be the one to destroy anybody's high ambitions," he told her. "Like poison, I hate it. Unless they have no foundation at all in reality. Then I can be ruthless. So—honestly, frankly, and in all sincerity, I do not see how it could ever be managed. Perhaps you're a fine psychiatrist—but in my opinion, it is a physical and mental impossibility for you ever to become a neuroparticipant. As for my reasons—"

"Wait," she said. "Not here, please. Humor me. I'm tired of this stuffy place—take me somewhere else to talk. I think I might be able to convince you there *is* a way."

"Why not?" he shrugged. "I have plenty time. Sure—you call it. Where?"

"Blindspin?"

He suppressed an unwilling chuckle at the expression, but she laughed aloud.

"Fine," he said, "but I'm still thirsty."

A bottle of champagne was tallied and he signed the check despite her protests. It arrived in a colorful "Drink While You Drive" basket, and they stood then, and she was tall, but he was taller.

*

Blindspin.

A single name of a multitude of practices centered about the auto-driven auto. Flashing across the country in the sure hands of an invisible chauffeur, windows all opaque, night dark, sky high, tires assailing the road below like four phantom buzzsaws—and starting from scratch and ending in the same place, and never knowing where you are going or where you have been—it is possible, for a moment, to kindle some feeling of individuality in the coldest brainpan, to produce a momentary awareness of self by virtue of an apartness from all but a sense of motion. This is because movement through darkness is the ultimate abstraction of life itself—at least that's what one of the Vital Comedians said, and everybody in the place laughed.

Actually now, the phenomenon known as blindspin first became prevalent (as might be suspected) among certain younger members of the community, when monitored highways deprived them of the means to exercise their automobiles in some of the more individualistic ways which had come to be frowned upon by the National Traffic Control Authority. Something had to be done.

It was.

The first, disastrous reaction involved the simple engineering feat of disconnecting the broadcast control unit after one had entered onto a monitored highway. This resulted in the car's vanishing from the ken of the monitor and passing back into the control of its occupants. Jealous as a deity, a monitor will not tolerate that which denies its programmed omniscience: it will thunder and lightning in the Highway Control Station nearest the point of last contact, sending winged seraphs in search of that which has slipped from sight.

Often, however, this was too late in happening, for the roads are many and well-paved. Escape from detection was, at first, relatively easy to achieve.

Other vehicles, though, necessarily behave as if a rebel has no actual existence. Its presence cannot be allowed for.

Boxed-in on a heavily-traveled section of roadway, the offender is subject to immediate annihilation in the event of any overall speedup or shift in traffic pattern which involves movement through his theoretically vacant position. This, in the early days of monitor-controls, caused a rapid series of collisions. Monitoring devices later became far more sophisticated, and mechanized cutoffs reduced the collision incidence subsequent to such an action. The quality of the pulpefactions and contusions which did occur, however, remained unaltered.

The next reaction was based on a thing which had been overlooked because it was obvious. The monitors took people where they wanted to go only because people told them they wanted to go there. A person pressing a random series of coordinates, without reference to any map, would either be left with a stalled automobile and a "RECHECK YOUR COORDINATES" light, or would suddenly be whisked away in any direction. The latter possesses a certain romantic appeal in that it offers speed, unexpected sights, and free hands. Also, it is perfectly legal: and it is possible to navigate all over

The Magic

two continents in this manner, if one is possessed of sufficient wherewithal and gluteal stamina.

As is the case in all such matters, the practice diffused upwards through the age brackets. School teachers who only drove on Sundays fell into disrepute as selling points for used autos. Such is the way a world ends, said the entertainer.

End or no, the car designed to move on monitored highways is a mobile efficiency unit, complete with latrine, cupboard, refrigerator compartment and gaming table. It also sleeps two with ease and four with some crowding. On occasion, three can be a real crowd.

*

Render drove out of the dome and into the marginal aisle. He halted the car.

"Want to jab some coordinates?" he asked.

"You do it. My fingers know too many."

Render punched random buttons. The Spinner moved onto the highway. Render asked speed of the vehicle then, and it moved into the high-acceleration lane.

The Spinner's lights burnt holes in the darkness. The city backed away fast; it was a smouldering bonfire on both sides of the road, stirred by sudden gusts of wind, hidden by white swirlings, obscured by the steady fall of gray ash. Render knew his speed was only about sixty percent of what it would have been on a clear, dry night.

He did not blank the windows, but leaned back and stared out through them. Eileen "looked" ahead into what light there was. Neither of them said anything for ten or fifteen minutes.

The city shrank to sub-city as they sped on. After a time, short sections of open road began to appear.

"Tell me what it looks like outside," she said.

"Why didn't you ask me to describe your dinner, or the suit of armor beside our table?"

"Because I tasted one and felt the other. This is different."

"There is snow falling outside. Take it away and what you have left is black."

"What else?"

"There is slush on the road. When it starts to freeze, traffic will drop to a crawl unless we outrun this storm. The slush looks like an old, dark syrup, just starting to get sugary on top."

"Anything else?"

"That's it, lady."

"Is it snowing harder or less hard than when we left the club?"

"Harder, I should say."

"Would you pour me a drink?" she asked him.

"Certainly."

They turned their seats inward and Render raised the table. He fetched two glasses from the cupboard.

"Your health," said Render, after he had poured.

"Here's looking at you."

Render downed his drink. She sipped hers. He waited for her next comment. He knew that two cannot play at the Socratic game, and he expected more questions before she said what she wanted to say.

She said: "What is the most beautiful thing you have ever seen?"

Yes, he decided, he had guessed correctly.

He replied without hesitation: "The sinking of Atlantis."

"I was serious."

"So was I."

"Would you care to elaborate?"

"I sank Atlantis," he said, "personally.

"It was about three years ago. And God it was lovely! It was all ivory towers and golden minarets and silver balconies. There were bridges of opal, and crimson penants and a milk-white river flowing between lemon-colored banks. There were jade steeples, and trees as old as the world tickling the bellies of clouds, and ships in the great sea-harbor of Xanadu, as delicately constructed as musical instruments, all swaying with the tides. The twelve princes of the realm held court in the dozen-pillared Colliseum of the Zodiac, to listen to a Greek tenor sax play at sunset.

"The Greek, of course, was a patient of mine—paranoiac. The etiology of the thing is rather complicated, but that's what I wandered into inside his mind. I gave him free rein for awhile, and in the end I had to split Atlantis in half and sink it full fathom five. He's playing again and you've doubtless heard his sounds, if you like such sounds at all. He's good. I still see him periodically, but he is no longer the last descendent of the greatest minstrel of Atlantis. He's just a fine, late twentieth-century saxman.

"Sometimes though, as I look back on the apocalypse I worked within his vision of grandeur, I experience a fleeting sense of lost beauty—because, for a single moment, his abnormally intense feelings were my feelings, and he felt that his dream was the most beautiful thing in the world."

He refilled their glasses.

"That wasn't exactly what I meant," she said.

"I know."

"I meant something real."

"It was more real than real, I assure you."

"I don't doubt it, but . . . "

"—But I destroyed the foundation you were laying for your argument. Okay, I apologize. I'll hand it back to you. Here's something that could be real:

"We are moving along the edge of a great bowl of sand," he said. "Into it, the snow is gently drifting. In the spring the snow will melt, the waters will run down into the earth, or be evaporated away by the heat of the sun. Then only the sand will remain. Nothing grows in the sand, except for an occasional cactus. Nothing lives here but snakes, a few birds, insects, burrowing things, and a wandering coyote or two. In the afternoon these things will look for shade. Any place where there's an old fence post or a rock or a skull or a cactus to block out the sun, there you will witness life cowering before the elements. But the colors are beyond belief, and the elements are more lovely, almost, than the things they destroy."

"There is no such place near here," she said.

"If I say it, then there is. Isn't there? I've seen it."

"Yes . . . you're right."

"And it doesn't matter if it's a painting by a woman named O'Keefe, or something right outside our window, does it? If I've seen it?"

"I acknowledge the truth of the diagnosis," she said. "Do you want to speak it for me?"

"No, go ahead."

He refilled the small glasses once more.

"The damage is in my eyes," she told him, "not my brain."

He lit her cigarette.

"I can see with other eyes if I can enter other brains."

He lit his own cigarette.

"Neuroparticipation is based upon the fact that two nervous systems can share the same impulses, the same fantasies . . . . "

"*Controlled* fantasies."

"I could perform therapy and at the same time experience genuine visual impressions."

"No," said Render.

"You don't know what it's like to be cut off from a whole area of stimuli! To know that a Mongoloid idiot can experience something you can never know—and that he cannot appreciate it because, like you, he was condemned before birth in a court of biological hapstance, in a place where there is no justice—only fortuity, pure and simple."

"The universe did not invent justice. Man did. Unfortunately, man must reside in the universe."

"I'm not asking the universe to help me—I'm asking you."

"I'm sorry," said Render.

"Why won't you help me?"

"At this moment you are demonstrating my main reason."

"Which is . . . ?"

The Magic

"Emotion. This thing means far too much to you. When the therapist is in-phase with a patient he is narcoelectrically removed from most of his own bodily sensations. This is necessary—because his mind must be completely absorbed by the task at hand. It is also necessary that his emotions undergo a similar suspension. This, of course, is impossible in the one sense that a person always emotes to some degree. But the therapist's emotions are sublimated into a generalized feeling of exhilaration—or, as in my own case, into an artistic reverie. With you, however, the 'seeing' would be too much. You would be in constant danger of losing control of the dream."

"I disagree with you."

"Of course you do. But the fact remains that you would be dealing, and dealing constantly, with the abnormal. The power of a neurosis is unimaginable to ninety-nine point etcetera percent of the population, because we can never adequately judge the intensity of our own—let alone those of others, when we only see them from the outside. That is why no neuroparticipant will ever undertake to treat a full-blown psychotic. The few pioneers in that area are all themselves in therapy today. It would be like diving into a maelstrom. If the therapist loses the upper hand in an intense session, he becomes the Shaped rather than the Shaper. The synapses respond like a fission reaction when nervous impulses are artificially augmented. The transference effect is almost instantaneous.

"I did an awful lot of skiing five years ago. This is because I was a claustrophobe. I had to run and it took me six months to beat the thing—all because of one tiny lapse that occurred in a measureless fraction of an instant. I had to refer the patient to another therapist. And this was only a minor repercussion. —If you were to go gaga over the scenery, girl, you could wind up in a rest home for life."

She finished her drink and Render refilled the glass. The night raced by. They had left the city far behind them, and the road was open and clear. The darkness eased more and more of itself between the falling flakes. The Spinner picked up speed.

"All right," she admitted, "maybe you're right. Still, though, I think you can help me."

"How?" he asked.

"Accustom me to seeing, so that the images will lose their novelty, the emotions wear off. Accept me as a patient and rid me of my sight-anxiety. Then what you have said so far will cease to apply. I will be able to undertake the training then, and give my full attention to therapy. I'll be able to sublimate the sight-pleasure into something else."

Render wondered.

Perhaps it could be done. It would be a difficult undertaking, though.

It might also make therapeutic history.

No one was really qualified to try it, because no one had ever tried it before.

But Eileen Shallot was a rarity—no, a unique item—for it was likely she was the only person in the world who combined the necessary technical background with the unique problem.

He drained his glass, refilled it, refilled hers.

He was still considering the problem as the "RECOORDINATE" light came on and the car pulled into a cutoff and stood there. He switched off the buzzer and sat there for a long while, thinking.

It was not often that other persons heard him acknowledge his feelings regarding his skill. His colleagues considered him modest. Offhand, though, it might be noted that he was aware that the day a better neuroparticipant began practicing would be the day that a troubled homo sapien was to be treated by something but immeasurably less than angels.

Two drinks remained. Then he tossed the emptied bottle into the backbin.

"You know something?" he finally said.

"What?"

"It might be worth a try."

He swiveled about then and leaned forward to recoordinate, but she was there first. As he pressed the buttons and the S-7 swung around, she kissed him. Below her dark glasses her cheeks were moist.

The Magic

The suicide bothered him more than it should have, and Mrs. Lambert had called the day before to cancel her appointment. So Render decided to spend the morning being pensive. Accordingly, he entered the office wearing a cigar and a frown.

"Did you see . . . ?" asked Mrs. Hedges.

"Yes." He pitched his coat onto the table that stood in the far corner of the room. He crossed to the window, stared down. "Yes," he repeated, "I was driving by with my windows clear. They were still cleaning up when I passed."

"Did you know him?"

"I don't even know the name yet. How could I?"

"Priss Tully just called me—she's a receptionist for that engineering outfit up on the eighty-sixth. She says it was James Irizarry, an ad designer who had offices down the hall from them—That's a long way to fall. He must have been unconscious when he hit, huh? He bounced off the building. If you open the window and lean out you can see—off to the left there—where . . . "

"Never mind, Bennie. —Your friend have any idea why he did it?"

"Not really. His secretary came running up the hall, screaming. Seems she went in his office to see him about some drawings, just as he was getting up over the sill. There was a note on his board. 'I've had everything I wanted,' it said. 'Why wait around?' Sort of funny, huh? I don't mean *funny* . . . . "

"Yeah. —Know anything about his personal affairs?"

"Married. Coupla kids. Good professional rep. Lots of business. Sober as anybody. —He could afford an office in this building."

"Good Lord!" Render turned. "Have you got a case file there or something?"

"You know," she shrugged her thick shoulders, "I've got friends all over this hive. We always talk when things go slow. Prissy's my sister-in-law, anyhow—

"You mean that if I dived through this window right now, my current biography would make the rounds in the next five minutes?"

"Probably," she twisted her bright lips into a smile, "give or take a couple. But don't do it today, huh?—You know, it would be kind of anticlimactic, and it wouldn't get the same coverage as a solus.

"Anyhow," she continued, "you're a mind-mixer. You wouldn't do it."

"You're betting against statistics," he observed. "The medical profession, along with attorneys, manages about three times as many as most other work areas."

"Hey!" She looked worried. "Go 'way from my window!"

"I'd have to go to work for Doctor Hanson then," she added, "and he's a slob."

He moved to her desk.

"I never know when to take you seriously," she decided.

"I appreciate your concern," he nodded, "indeed I do. As a matter of fact, I have never been statistic-prone—I should have repercussed out of the neuropy game four years ago."

"You'd be a headline, though," she mused. "All those reporters asking me about you . . . Hey, why do they do it, huh?"

"Who?"

"Anybody."

"How should I know, Bennie? I'm only a humble psyche-stirrer. If I could pinpoint a general underlying cause—and then maybe figure a way to anticipate the thing—why, it might even be better than my jumping, for newscopy. But I can't do it, because there is no single simple reason—I don't think."

"Oh."

"About thirty-five years ago it was the ninth leading cause of death in the United States. Now it's number six for North and South America. I think it's seventh in Europe."

"And nobody will ever really know why Irizarry jumped?"

Reader swung a chair backward and seated himself. He knocked an ash into her petite and gleaming tray. She emptied it into the waste-chute, hastily, and coughed a significant cough.

The Magic

"Oh, one can always speculate," he said, "and one in my profession will. The first thing to consider would be the personality traits which might predispose a man to periods of depression. People who keep their emotions under rigid control, people who are conscientious and rather compulsively concerned with small matters . . . " He knocked another fleck of ash into her tray and watched as she reached out to dump it, then quickly drew her hand back again. He grinned an evil grin. "In short," he finished, "some of the characteristics of people in professions which require individual, rather than group performance—medicine, law, the arts."

She regarded him speculatively.

"Don't worry though," he chuckled, "I'm pleased as hell with life."

"You're kind of down in the mouth this morning."

"Pete called me. He broke his ankle yesterday in gym class. They ought to supervise those things more closely. I'm thinking of changing his school."

"Again?"

"Maybe. I'll see. The headmaster is going to call me this afternoon. I don't like to keep shuffling him, but I do want him to finish school in one piece."

"A kid can't grow up without an accident or two. It's—statistics."

"Statistics aren't the same thing as destiny, Bennie. Everybody makes his own."

"Statistics or destiny?"

"Both, I guess."

"I think that if something's going to happen, it's going to happen."

"I don't. I happen to think that the human will, backed by a sane mind, can exercise some measure of control over events. If I didn't think so, I wouldn't be in the racket I'm in."

"The world's a machine—you know—cause, effect. Statistics do imply the prob—"

"The human mind is not a machine, and I do not know cause and effect. Nobody does."

"You have a degree in chemistry, as I recall. You're a scientist, Doc."

"So I'm a Trotskyite deviationist," he smiled, stretching, "and you were once a ballet teacher." He got to his feet and picked up his coat.

"By the way. Miss DeVille called, left a message. She said: 'How about St. Moritz?'"

"Too ritzy," he decided aloud. "It's going to be Davos."

*

Because the suicide bothered him more than it should have, Render closed the door to his office and turned off the windows and turned on the phonograph. He put on the desk light only.

How has the quality of human life been changed, he wrote, *since the beginnings of the industrial revolution?*

He picked up the paper and reread the sentence. It was the topic he had been asked to discuss that coming Saturday. As was typical in such cases he did not know what to say because he had too much to say, and only an hour to say it in.

He got up and began to pace the office, now filled with Beethoven's Eighth Symphony.

"The power to hurt," he said, snapping on a lapel microphone and activating his recorder, "has evolved in a direct relationship to technological advancement." His imaginary audience grew quiet. He smiled. "Man's potential for working simple mayhem has been multiplied by mass-production; his capacity for injuring the psyche through personal contacts has expanded in an exact ratio to improved communication facilities. But these are all matters of common knowledge, and are not the things I wish to consider tonight. Rather, I should like to discuss what I choose to call autopsychomimesis—the self-generated anxiety complexes which on first scrutiny appear quite similar to classic patterns, but which actually represent radical dispersions of psychic energy. They are peculiar to our times . . . . "

He paused to dispose of his cigar and formulate his next words.

"Autopsychomimesis," he thought aloud, "a self-perpetuated imitation complex—almost an attention-getting affair. —A jazzman, for example, who acted hopped-up half the time, even though he had never used an addictive narcotic and only dimly remembered anyone who had—because all the stimulants and tranquilizers of today are quite benign. Like Quixote, he aspired after a legend when his music alone should have been sufficient outlet for his tensions.

"Or my Korean War Orphan, alive today by virtue of the Red Cross and UNICEF and foster parents whom he never met. He wanted a family so badly that be made one up. And what then?—He hated his imaginary father and be loved his imaginary mother quite dearly—for he was a highly intelligent boy, and he too longed after the half-true complexes of tradition. Why?

"Today, everyone is sophisticated enough to understand the time-honored patterns of psychic disturbance. Today, many of the reasons for those disturbances have been removed—not as radically as my now-adult war orphan's, but with as remarkable an effect. We are living in a neurotic past. —Again, why? Because our present times are geared to physical health, security and well-being. We have abolished hunger, though the backwoods orphan would still rather receive a package of food concentrates from a human being who cares for him than to obtain a warm meal from an automat unit in the middle of the jungle.

"Physical welfare is now every man's right in excess. The reaction to this has occurred in the area of mental health. Thanks to technology, the reasons for many of the old social problems have passed, and along with them went many of the reasons for psychic distress. But between the black of yesterday and the white of tomorrow is the great gray of today, filled with nostalgia and fear of the future, which cannot be expressed on a purely material plane, is now being represented by a willful seeking after historical anxiety-modes . . . . "

The phone-box buzzed briefly. Render did not hear it over the Eighth.

"We are afraid of what we do not know," he continued, "and tomorrow is a very great unknown. My own specialized area of psychiatry did not even exist thirty years ago. Science is capable of advancing itself so rapidly now that there is a genuine public uneasiness—I might even say 'distress'—as to the logical outcome: the total mechanization of everything in the world . . . . "

He passed near the desk as the phone buzzed again. He switched off his microphone and softened the Eighth.

"Hello?"

"Saint Moritz," she said.

"Davos," he replied firmly.

"Charlie, you are most exasperating!"

"Jill, dear—so are you."

"Shall we discuss it tonight?"

"There is nothing to discuss!"

"You'll pick me up at five, though?"

He hesitated, then:

"Yes, at five. How come the screen is blank?"

"I've had my hair fixed. I'm going to surprise you again."

He suppressed an idiot chuckle, said, "Pleasantly, I hope. Okay, see you then," waited for her "good-bye," and broke the connection.

He transpared the windows, turned off the light on his desk, and looked outside.

Gray again overhead, and many slow flakes of snow—wandering, not being blown about much—moving downward and then losing themselves in the tumult . . . .

He also saw, when he opened the window and leaned out, the place off to the left where Irizarry had left his next-to-last mark on the world.

He closed the window and listened to the rest of the symphony. It had been a week since he had gone blind-spinning with Eileen. Her appointment was for one o'clock.

*

He remembered her fingertips brushing over his face, like leaves, or the bodies of insects, learning his appearance in the ancient manner of the blind. The memory was not altogether pleasant. He wondered why.

The Magic

Far below, a patch of hosed pavement was blank once again; under a thin, fresh shroud of white, it was slippery as glass. A building custodian hurried outside and spread salt on it, before someone slipped and hurt himself.

*

Sigmund was the myth of Fenris come alive. After Render had instructed Mrs. Hedges, "Show them in," the door had begun to open, was suddenly pushed wider, and a pair of smoky-yellow eyes stared in at him. The eyes were set in a strangely misshapen dog-skull.

Sigmund's was not a low canine brow, slanting up slightly from the muzzle; it was a high, shaggy cranium making the eyes appear even more deep-set than they actually were. Render shivered slightly at the size and aspect of that head. The muties he had seen had all been puppies. Sigmund was full-grown, and his gray-black fur had a tendency to bristle, which made him appear somewhat larger than a normal specimen of the breed.

He stared in at Render in a very un-doglike way and made a growling noise which sounded too much like, "Hello, doctor," to have been an accident.

Render nodded and stood.

"Hello, Sigmund," he said. "Come in."

The dog turned his head, sniffing the air of the room—as though deciding whether or not to trust his ward within its confines. Then he returned his stare to Render, dipped his head in an affirmative, and shouldered the door open. Perhaps the entire encounter had taken only one disconcerting second.

Eileen followed him, holding lightly to the double-leashed harness. The dog padded soundlessly across the thick rug—head low, as though he were stalking something. His eyes never left Render's.

"So this is Sigmund . . . ? How are you, Eileen?"

"Fine. —Yes, he wanted very badly to come along, and I wanted you to meet him."

Render led her to a chair and seated her. She unsnapped the double guide from the dog's harness and placed it on the floor. Sigmund sat down beside it and continued to stare at Render.

"How is everything at State Psych?"

"Same as always. —May I bum a cigarette, doctor? I forgot mine."

He placed it between her fingers, furnished a light. She was wearing a dark blue suit and her glasses were flame blue. The silver spot on her forehead reflected the glow of his lighter; she continued to stare at that point in space after he had withdrawn his hand. Her shoulder-length hair appeared a trifle lighter than it had seemed on the night they met; today it was like a fresh-minted copper coin.

Render seated himself on the corner of his desk, drawing up his world-ashtray with his toe.

"You told me before that being blind did not mean that you had never seen. I didn't ask you to explain it then. But I'd like to ask you now."

"I had a neuroparticipation session with Doctor Riscomb," she told him, "before he had his accident. He wanted to accommodate my mind to visual impressions. Unfortunately, there was never a second session."

"I see. What did you do in that session?"

She crossed her ankles and Render noted they were well-turned.

"Colors, mostly. The experience was quite overwhelming."

"How well do you remember them? How long ago was it?"

"About six months ago—and I shall never forget them. I have even dreamed in color patterns since then."

"How often?"

"Several times a week."

"What sort of associations do they carry?"

"Nothing special. They just come into my mind along with other stimuli now—in a pretty haphazard way."

"How?"

"Well, for instance, when you ask me a question it's a sort of yellowish-orangish pattern that I 'see.' Your greeting was a kind of silvery thing. Now that you're just sitting there listening to me, saying nothing, I associate you with a deep, almost violet, blue."

Sigmund shifted his gaze to the desk and stared at the side panel.

The Magic

Can he hear the recorder spinning inside? wondered Render. *And if he can, can he guess what it is and what it's doing?*

If so, the dog would doubtless tell Eileen—not that she was unaware of what was now an accepted practice—and she might not like being reminded that he considered her case as therapy, rather than a mere mechanical adaptation process. If he thought it would do any good (he smiled inwardly at the notion), he would talk to the dog in private about it.

Inwardly, he shrugged.

"I'll construct a rather elementary fantasy world then," he said finally, "and introduce you to some basic forms today."

She smiled; and Render looked down at the myth who crouched by her side, its tongue a piece of beefsteak hanging over a picket fence.

Is he smiling too?

"Thank you," she said.

Sigmund wagged his tail.

"Well then," Render disposed of his cigarette near Madagascar, "I'll fetch out the 'egg' now and test it. In the meantime," he pressed an unobstrusive button, "perhaps some music would prove relaxing."

She started to reply, but a Wagnerian overture snuffed out the words. Render jammed the button again, and there was a moment of silence during which he said, "Heh heh. Thought Respighi was next."

It took two more pushes for him to locate some Roman pines.

"You could have left him on," she observed. "I'm quite fond of Wagner."

"No thanks," he said, opening the closet, "I'd keep stepping in all those piles of leitmotifs."

*

The great egg drifted out into the office, soundless as a cloud. Render heard a soft growl behind as he drew it toward the desk. He turned quickly.

Like the shadow of a bird, Sigmund had gotten to his feet, crossed the room, and was already circling the machine and sniffing at it—tail taut, ears flat, teeth bared.

"Easy, Sig," said Render. "It's an Omnichannel Neural T & R Unit. It won't bite or anything like that. It's just a machine, like a car, or a teevee, or a dishwasher. That's what we're going to use today to show Eileen what some things look like."

"Don't like it," rumbled the dog.

"Why?"

Sigmund had no reply, so he stalked back to Eileen and laid his head in her lap.

"Don't like it," he repeated, looking up at her.

"Why?"

"No words," he decided. "We go home now?"

"No," she answered him. "You're going to curl up in the corner and take a nap, and I'm going to curl up in that machine and do the same thing—sort of."

"No good," he said, tail drooping.

"Go on now," she pushed him, "lie down and behave yourself."

He acquiesced, but he whined when Render blanked the windows and touched the button which transformed his desk into the operator's seat.

He whined once more—when the egg, connected now to an outlet, broke in the middle and the top slid back and up, revealing the interior.

Render seated himself. His chair became a contour couch and moved in halfway beneath the console. He sat upright and it moved back again, becoming a chair. He touched a part of the desk and half the ceiling disengaged itself, reshaped itself, and lowered to hover overhead like a huge bell. He stood and moved around to the side of the ro-womb. Respighi spoke of pines and such, and Render disengaged an earphone from beneath the egg and leaned back across his desk. Blocking one ear with his shoulder and pressing the microphone to the other, he played upon the buttons with his free hand. Leagues of surf drowned the tone poem; miles of traffic overrode it; a great clanging bell sent fracture lines running through it; and the feedback said: " . . . Now that you are just sitting there listening to me, saying nothing, I associate you with a deep, almost violet, blue . . . . "

The Magic

He switched to the face mask and monitored, *one*—cinnamon, *two*—leaf mold, *three*—deep reptilian musk . . . and down through thirst, and the tastes of honey and vinegar and salt, and back on up through lilacs and wet concrete, a before-the-storm whiff of ozone, and all the basic olfactory and gustatory cues for morning, afternoon and evening in the town.

The couch floated normally in its pool of mercury, magnetically stabilized by the walls of the egg. He set the tapes.

The ro-womb was in perfect condition.

"Okay," said Render, turning, "everything checks."

She was just placing her glasses atop her folded garments. She had undressed while Render was testing the machine. He was perturbed by her narrow waist, her large, dark-pointed breasts, her long legs. She was too well-formed for a woman her height, he decided.

He realized though, as he stared at her, that his main annoyance was, of course, the fact that she was his patient.

"Ready here," she said, and he moved to her side.

He took her elbow and guided her to the machine. Her fingers explored its interior. As he helped her enter the unit, he saw that her eyes were a vivid seagreen. Of this, too, he disapproved.

"Comfortable?"

"Yes."

"Okay then, we're set. I'm going to close it now. Sweet dreams."

The upper shell dropped slowly. Closed, it grew opaque, then dazzling. Render was staring down at his own distorted reflection.

He moved back in the direction of his desk.

Sigmund was on his feet, blocking the way.

Render reached down to pat his head, but the dog jerked it aside.

"Take me, with," he growled.

"I'm afraid that can't be done, old fellow," said Render. "Besides, we're not really going anywhere. We'll just be dozing, right here, in this room."

The dog did not seem mollified.

"Why?"

Render sighed. An argument with a dog was about the most ludicrous thing he could imagine when sober.

"Sig," he said, "I'm trying to help her learn what things look like. You doubtless do a fine job guiding her around in this world which she cannot see—but she needs to know what it looks like now, and I'm going to show her."

"Then she, will not, need me."

"Of course she will." Render almost laughed. The pathetic thing was here bound so closely to the absurd thing that he could not help it. "I can't restore her sight," he explained. "I'm just going to transfer her some sight abstractions—sort of lend her my eyes for a short time. Savvy?"

"No," said the dog. "Take mine."

Render turned off the music.

The whole mutie-master relationship might be worth six volumes, he decided, *in German.*

He pointed to the far corner.

"Lie down, over there, like Eileen told you. This isn't going to take long, and when it's all over you're going to leave the same way you came—you leading. Okay?"

Sigmund did not answer, but he turned and moved off to the corner, tail drooping again.

Render seated himself and lowered the hood, the operator's modified version of the ro-womb. He was alone before the ninety white buttons and the two red ones. The world ended in the blackness beyond the console. He loosened his necktie and unbuttoned his collar.

He removed the helmet from its receptacle and checked its leads. Donning it then, he swung the half-mask up over his lower face and dropped the darksheet down to meet with it. He rested his right arm in the sling, and with a single tapping gesture, he eliminated his patient's consciousness.

A Shaper does not press white buttons consciously. He wills conditions. Then deeply-implanted muscular reflexes exert an almost imperceptible pressure against the sensitive arm-sling, which glides into the proper position and encourages an extended finger to move forward. A button is pressed. The sling moves on.

Render felt a tingling at the base of his skull; he smelled fresh-cut grass.

Suddenly he was moving up the great gray alley between the worlds.

After what seemed a long time. Render felt that he was footed on a strange Earth. He could see nothing; it was only a sense of presence that informed him he had arrived. It was the darkest of all the dark nights he had ever known.

He willed that the darkness disperse. Nothing happened.

A part of his mind came awake again, a part he had not realized was sleeping; he recalled whose world be had entered.

He listened for her presence. He heard fear and anticipation.

He willed color. First, red . . .

He felt a correspondence. Then there was an echo.

Everything became red; he inhabited the center of an infinite ruby.

Orange. Yellow . . .

He was caught in a piece of amber.

Green now, and he added the exhalations of a sultry sea. Blue, and the coolness of evening.

He stretched his mind then, producing all the colors at once. They came in great swirling plumes.

Then he tore them apart and forced a form upon them.

An incandescent rainbow arced across the black sky.

He fought for browns and grays below him. Self-luminescent, they appeared—in shimmering, shifting patches.

Somewhere, a sense of awe. There was no trace of hysteria though, so he continued with the Shaping.

He managed a horizon, and the blackness drained away beyond it. The sky grew faintly blue, and he ventured a herd of dark clouds. There was resistance to his efforts at creating distance and depth, so he reinforced the tableau with a very faint sound of surf. A transference from an auditory concept of distance came slowly then, as he pushed the clouds about. Quickly, he threw up a high forest to offset a rising wave of acrophobia.

The panic vanished.

Render focused his attention on tall trees—oaks and pines, poplars and sycamores. He hurled them about like spears, in ragged arrays of greens and browns and yellows, unrolled a thick mat of morning-moist grass, dropped a series of gray boulders and greenish logs at irregular intervals, and tangled and twined the branches overhead, casting a uniform shade throughout the glen.

The effect was staggering. It seemed as if the entire world was shaken with a sob, then silent.

Through the stillness he felt her presence. He had decided it would be best to lay the groundwork quickly, to set up a tangible headquarters, to prepare a field for operations. He could backtrack later, be could repair and amend the results of the trauma in the sessions yet to come; but this much, at least, was necessary for a beginning.

With a start, he realized that the silence was not a withdrawal. Eileen had made herself immanent in the trees and the grass, the stones and the bushes; she was personalizing their forms, relating them to tactile sensations, sounds, temperatures, aromas.

With a soft breeze, he stirred the branches of the trees. Just beyond the bounds of seeing he worked out the splashing sounds of a brook.

There was a feeling of joy. He shared it.

She was bearing it extremely well, so he decided to extend the scope of the exercise. He let his mind wander among the trees, experiencing a momentary doubling of vision, during which time he saw an enormous hand riding in an aluminum carriage toward a circle of white.

He was beside the brook now and he was seeking her, carefully.

He drifted with the water. He had not yet taken on a form. The splashes became a gurgling as he pushed the brook through shallow places and over rocks. At his insistence, the waters became more articulate.

"Where are you?" asked the brook.

The Magic

Here! Here!

Here!

. . . and here! replied the trees, the bushes, the stones, the grass.

"Choose one," said the brook, as it widened, rounded a mass of rock, then bent its way down a slope, heading toward a blue pool.

I cannot, was the answer from the wind.

"You must." The brook widened and poured into the pool, swirled about the surface, then stilled itself and reflected branches and dark clouds. "Now!"

Very well, echoed the wood, *in a moment.*

The mist rose above the lake and drifted to the bank of the pool.

"Now," tinkled the mist.

Here, then . . .

She had chosen a small willow. It swayed in the wind; it trailed its branches in the water.

"Eileen Shallot," he said, "regard the lake."

The breezes shifted; the willow bent.

It was not difficult for him to recall her face, her body. The tree spun as though rootless. Eileen stood in the midst of a quiet explosion of leaves; she stared, frightened, into the deep blue mirror of Render's mind, the lake.

She covered her face with her hands, but it could not stop the seeing.

"Behold yourself," said Render.

She lowered her hands and peered downward. Then she turned in every direction, slowly; she studied herself. Finally:

"I feel I am quite lovely," she said. "Do I feel so because you want me to, or is it true?"

She looked all about as she spoke, seeking the Shaper.

"It is true," said Render, from everywhere.

"Thank you."

There was a swirl of white and she was wearing a belted garment of damask. The light in the distance brightened almost imperceptibly. A faint touch of pink began at the base of the lowest cloudbank.

"What is happening there?" she asked, facing that direction.

"I am going to show you a sunrise," said Render, "and I shall probably botch it a bit—but then, it's my first professional sunrise under these circumstances."

"Where are you?" she asked.

"Everywhere," he replied.

"Please take on a form so that I can see you."

"All right."

"Your natural form."

He willed that he be beside her on the bank, and he was.

Startled by a metallic flash, he looked downward. The world receded for an instant, then grew stable once again. He laughed, and the laugh froze as he thought of something.

He was wearing the suit of armor which had stood beside their table in the Partridge and Scalpel on the night they met.

She reached out and touched it.

"The suit of armor by our table," she acknowledged, running her fingertips over the plates and the junctures. "I associated it with you that night."

" . . . And you stuffed me into it just now," he commented. "You're a strong-willed woman."

The armor vanished and he was wearing his gray-brown suit and looseknit bloodclot necktie and a professional expression.

"Behold the real me," he smiled faintly. "Now, to the sunset.[1] I'm going to use all the colors. Watch!"

They seated themselves on the green park bench which had appeared behind them, and Render pointed in the direction he had decided upon as east.

Slowly, the sun worked through its morning attitudes. For the first time in this particular world it shone down like a god, and reflected off the lake, and broke the clouds, and set the landscape to smouldering beneath the mist that arose from the moist wood.

The Magic

Watching, watching intently, staring directly into the ascending bonfire, Eileen did not move for a long while, nor speak. Render could sense her fascination.

She was staring at the source of all light; it reflected back from the gleaming coin on her brow, like a single drop of blood.

Render said, "That is the sun, and those are clouds," and he clapped his hands and the clouds covered the sun and there was a soft rumble overhead, "and that is thunder," he finished.

The rain fell then, shattering the lake and tickling their faces, making sharp striking sounds on the leaves, then soft tapping sounds, dripping down from the branches overhead, soaking their garments and plastering their hair. running down their necks and falling into their eyes, turning patches of brown earth to mud.

A splash of lightning covered the sky, and a second later there was another peal of thunder.

" . . . And this is a summer storm," he lectured. "You see how the rain affects the foliage and ourselves. What you just saw in the sky before the thunderclap was lightning."

" . . . Too much," she said. "Let up on it for a moment, please."

The rain stopped instantly and the sun broke through the clouds.

"I have the damndest desire for a cigarette," she said, "but I left mine in another world."

As she said it one appeared, already lighted, between her fingers.

"It's going to taste rather flat," said Render strangely.

He watched her for a moment, then:

"I didn't give you that cigarette," he noted. "You picked it from my mind."

The smoke laddered and spiraled upward, was swept away.

" . . . Which means that, for the second time today, I have underestimated the pull of that vacuum in your mind—in the place where sight ought to be. You are assimilating these new impressions very rapidly. You're even going to the extent of groping after new ones. Be careful. Try to contain that impulse."

"It's like a hunger," she said.

"Perhaps we had best conclude this session now."

Their clothing was dry again. A bird began to sing.

"No, wait! Please! I'll be careful. I want to see more things."

"There is always the next visit," said Render. "But I suppose we can manage one more. Is there something you want very badly to see?"

"Yes. Winter. Snow."

"Okay," smiled the Shaper, "then wrap yourself in that fur-piece . . . . "

*

The afternoon slipped by rapidly after the departure of his patient. Render was in a good mood. He felt emptied and filled again. He had come through the first trial without suffering any repercussions. He decided that he was going to succeed. His satisfaction was greater than his fear. It was with a sense of exhilaration that he returned to working on his speech.

" . . . And what is the power to hurt?" he inquired of the microphone.

"We live by pleasure and we live by pain," he answered himself. "Either can frustrate and either can encourage. But while pleasure and pain are rooted in biology, they are conditioned by society: thus are values to be derived. Because of the enormous masses of humanity, hectically changing positions in space every day throughout the cities of the world, there has come into necessary being a series of totally inhuman controls upon these movements. Every day they nibble their way into new areas—driving our cars, flying our planes, interviewing us, diagnosing our diseases—and I cannot even venture a moral judgment upon these intrusions. They have become necessary. Ultimately, they may prove salutary.

"The point I wish to make, however, is that we are often unaware of our own values. We cannot honestly tell what a thing means to us until it is removed from our life-situation. If an object of value ceases to exist, then the psychic energies which were bound up in it are released. We seek after new objects of value in which to invest this—mana, if you like, or libido, if you don't. And no one thing which has vanished during the past three or four or five decades was, in itself, massively significant; and no new thing which

241

came into being during that time is massively malicious toward the people it has replaced or the people it in some manner controls. A society, though, is made up of many things, and when these things are changed too rapidly the results are unpredictable. An intense study of mental illness is often quite revealing as to the nature of the stresses in the society where the illness was made. If anxiety-patterns fall into special groups and classes, then something of the discontent of society can be learned from them. Karl Jung pointed out that when consciousness is repeatedly frustrated in a quest for values it will turn its search to the unconscious; failing there, it will proceed to quarry its way into the hypothetical collective unconscious. He noted, in the postwar analyses of ex-Nazis, that the longer they searched for something to erect from the ruins of their lives—having lived through a period of classical iconoclasm, and then seen their new ideals topple as well—the longer they searched, the further back they seemed to reach into the collective unconscious of their people. Their dreams themselves came to take on patterns out of the Teutonic mythos.

"This, in a much less dramatic sense, is happening today. There are historical periods when the group tendency for the mind to turn in upon itself, to turn back, is greater than at other times. We are living in such a period of Quixotism, in the original sense of the term. This is because the power to hurt, in our time, is the power to ignore, to baffle—and it is no longer the exclusive property of human beings—"

A buzz interrupted him then. He switched off the recorder, touched the phone-box.

"Charles Render speaking," he told it.

"This is Paul Charter," lisped the box. "I am headmaster at Dilling."

"Yes?"

The picture cleared. Render saw a man whose eyes were set close together beneath a high forehead. The forehead was heavily creased; the mouth twitched as it spoke.

"Well, I want to apologize again for what happened. It was a faulty piece of equipment that caused—"

"Can't you afford proper facilities? Your fees are high enough."

"It was a *new* piece of equipment. It was a factory defect—"

"Wasn't there anybody in charge of the class?"

"Yes, but—"

"Why didn't he inspect the equipment? Why wasn't he on hand to prevent the fall?"

"He *was* on hand, but it happened too fast for him to do anything. As for inspecting the equipment for factory defects, that isn't his job. Look, I'm very sorry. I'm quite fond of your boy. I can assure you nothing like this will ever happen again."

"You're right, there. But that's because I'm picking him up tomorrow morning and enrolling him in a school that exercises proper safety precautions."

Render ended the conversation with a flick of his finger. After several minutes had passed he stood and crossed the room to his small wall safe, which was partly masked, though not concealed, by a shelf of books. It took only a moment for him to open it and withdraw a jewel box containing a cheap necklace and a framed photograph of a man resembling himself, though somewhat younger, and a woman whose upswept hair was dark and whose chin was small, and two youngsters between them—the girl holding the baby in her arms and forcing her bright bored smile on ahead. Render always stared for only a few seconds on such occasions, fondling the necklace, and then he shut the box and locked it away again for many months.

*

Whump! Whump! went the bass. *Tchg-tchg-tchga-tchg*, the gourds.

The gelatins splayed reds, greens, blues, and godawful yellows about the amazing metal dancers.

HUMAN? asked the marquee.

ROBOTS? (immediately below).

COME SEE FOR YOURSELF! (across the bottom, cryptically).

So they did.

The Magic

Render and Jill were sitting at a microscopic table, thankfully set back against a wall, beneath charcoal caricatures of personalities largely unknown (there being so many personalities among the subcultures of a city of fourteen million people). Nose crinkled with pleasure, Jill stared at the present focal point of this particular subculture, occasionally raising her shoulders to ear level to add emphasis to a silent laugh or a small squeal, because the performers were just *too* human—the way the ebon robot ran his fingers along the silver robot's forearm as they parted and passed . . . .

Render alternated his attention between Jill and the dancers and a wicked-looking decoction that resembled nothing so much as a small bucket of whiskey sours strewn with seaweed (through which the Kraken might at any moment arise to drag some hapless ship down to its doom).

"Charlie, I think they're really people!"

Render disentangled his gaze from her hair and bouncing earrings.

He studied the dancers down on the floor, somewhat below the table area, surrounded by music.

There *could* be humans within those metal shells. If so, their dance was a thing of extreme skill. Though the manufacture of sufficiently light alloys was no problem, it would be some trick for a dancer to cavort so freely—and for so long a period of time, and with such effortless-seeming ease—within a head-to-toe suit of armor, without so much as a grate or a click or a clank.

Soundless . . .

They glided like two gulls; the larger, the color of polished anthracite, and the other, like a moonbeam falling through a window upon a silk-wrapped manikin.

Even when they touched there was no sound—or if there was, it was wholly masked by the rhythms of the band.

Whump-whump! Tchga-tchg!

Render took another drink.

Slowly, it turned into an apache-dance. Render checked his watch. Too long for normal entertainers, he decided. They must be robots. As he looked up again the black robot hurled the silver robot perhaps ten feet and turned his back on her.

There was no sound of striking metal.

Wonder what a setup like that costs? he mused.

"Charlie! There was no sound! How do they do that?"

"I've no idea," said Render.

The gelatins were yellow again, then red, then blue, then green.

"You'd think it would damage their mechanisms, wouldn't you?"

The white robot crawled back and the other swiveled his wrist around and around, a lighted cigarette between the fingers. There was laughter as he pressed it mechanically to his lipless faceless face. The silver robot confronted him. He turned away again, dropped the cigarette, ground it out slowly, soundlessly, then suddenly turned back to his partner. Would he throw her again? No . . .

Slowly then. like the greatlegged birds of the East, they recommenced their movement, slowly, and with many turnings away.

Something deep within Render was amused, but he was too far gone to ask it what was funny. So he went looking for the Kraken in the bottom of the glass instead.

Jill was clutching his biceps then, drawing his attention back to the floor.

As the spotlight tortured the spectrum, the black robot raised the silver one high above his head, slowly, slowly, and then commenced spinning with her in that position—arms outstretched, back arched, legs scissored—very slowly, at first. Then faster.

Suddenly they were whirling with an unbelievable speed, and the gelatins rotated faster and faster.

Render shook his head to clear it.

They were moving so rapidly that they *had* to fall—human or robot. But they didn't. They were a mandala. They were a gray form uniformity. Render looked down.

Then slowing, and slower, slower. Stopped.

The music stopped.

The Magic

Blackness followed. Applause filled it.

When the lights came on again the two robots were standing statue-like, facing the audience. Very, very slowly, they bowed.

The applause increased.

Then they turned and were gone.

The music came on and the light was clear again. A babble of voices arose. Render slew the Kraken.

"What d'you think of that?" she asked him.

Render made his face serious and said: "Am I a man dreaming I am a robot, or a robot dreaming I am a man?" He grinned, then added: "I don't know."

She punched his shoulder gaily at that and he observed that she was drunk.

"I am not." she protested. "Not much, anyhow. Not as much as you."

"Still, I think you ought to see a doctor about it. Like me. Like now. Let's get out of here and go for a drive."

"Not yet, Charlie. I want to see them once more, huh? Please?"

"If I have another drink I won't be able to see that far."

"Then order a cup of coffee."

"Yaagh!"

"Then order a beer."

"I'll suffer without."

There were people on the dance floor now, but Render's feet felt like lead. He lit a cigarette.

"So you had a dog talk to you today?"

"Yes. Something very disconcerting about that . . . . "

"Was she pretty?"

"It was a boy dog. And boy, was he ugly!"

"Silly. I mean his mistress."

"You know I never discuss cases, Jill."

"You told me about her being blind and about the dog. All I want to know is if she's pretty."

"Well . . . Yes and no." He bumped her under the table and gestured vaguely. "Well, you know . . . "

"Same thing all the way around," she told the waiter who had appeared suddenly out of an adjacent pool of darkness, nodded, and vanished as abruptly.

"There go my good intentions," sighed Render. "See how you like being examined by a drunken sot, that's all I can say."

"You'll sober up fast, you always do. Hippocratics and all that."

He sniffed, glanced at his watch.

"I have to be in Connecticut tomorrow. Pulling Pete out of that damned school . . . . "

She sighed, already tired of the subject.

"I think you worry too much about him. Any kid can bust an ankle. It's part of growing up. I broke my wrist when I was seven. It was an accident. It's not the school's fault, those things sometimes happen."

"Like hell," said Render, accepting his dark drink from the dark tray the dark man carried. "If they can't do a good job, I'll find someone who can."

She shrugged.

"You're the boss. All I know is what I read in the papers.

"—And you're still set on Davos, even though you know you meet a better class of people at Saint Moritz?" she added.

"We're going there to ski, remember? I like the runs better at Davos."

"I can't score any tonight, can I?"

He squeezed her hand.

"You always score with me, honey."

And they drank their drinks and smoked their cigarettes and held their hands until the people left the dance floor and filed back to their microscopic tables, and the gelatins spun round and round, tinting clouds of smoke from hell to sunrise and back again, and the bass went whump!

Tchga-tchga!

"Oh, Charlie! Here they come again!"

*

The Magic

The sky was clear as crystal. The roads were clean. The snow had stopped.

Jill's breathing was the breathing of a sleeper. The S-7 raced across the bridges of the city. If Render sat very still he could convince himself that only his body was drunk; but whenever he moved his head the universe began to dance about him. As it did so, he imagined himself within a dream, and Shaper of it all.

For one instant this was true. He turned the big clock in the sky backward, smiling as he dozed. Another instant and he was awake again, and unsmiling.

The universe had taken revenge for his presumption. For one reknown moment with the helplessness which he had loved beyond helping, it had charged him the price of the lake-bottom vision once again; and as he had moved once more toward the wreck at the bottom of the world—like a swimmer, as unable to speak—he heard, from somewhere high over the Earth, and filtered down to him through the waters above the Earth, the howl of the Fenris Wolf as it prepared to devour the moon; and as this occurred, he knew that the sound was as like to the trump of a judgment as the lady by his side was unlike the moon. Every bit. In all ways. And he was afraid.

III

" . . . The plain, the direct, and the blunt. This is Winchester Cathedral," said the guidebook. "With its floor-to-ceiling shafts, like so many huge treetrunks, it achieves a ruthless control over its spaces: the ceilings are flat; each bay, separated by those shafts, is itself a thing of certainty and stability. It seems, indeed, to reflect something of the spirit of William the Conqueror. Its disdain of mere elaboration and its passionate dedication to the love of another world would make it seem, too, an appropriate setting for some tale out of Mallory . . . . "

"Observe the scalloped capitals," said the guide. "In their primitive fluting they anticipated what was later to become a common motif . . . . "

"Faugh!" said Render—softly though, because he was in a group inside a church.

Roger Zelazny and Samuel R. Delany

"Shh'" said Jill (Fotlock—that was her real last name) DeVille.

But Render was impressed as well as distressed.

Hating Jill's hobby though, had become so much of a reflex with him that he would sooner have taken his rest seated beneath an oriental device which dripped water onto his head than to admit he occasionally enjoyed walking through the arcades and the galleries, the passages and the tunnels, and getting all out of breath climbing up the high twisty stairways of towers.

So he ran his eyes over everything, burned everything down by shutting them, then built the place up again out of the still smouldering ashes of memory, all so that at a later date he would be able to repeat the performance, offering the vision to his one patient who could see only in this manner. This building he disliked less than most. Yes, he would take it back to her.

The camera in his mind photographing the surroundings, Render walked with the others, overcoat over his arm, his fingers anxious to reach after a cigarette. He kept busy ignoring his guide, realizing this to be the nadir of all forms of human protest. As he walked through Winchester he thought of his last two sessions with Eileen Shallot. He recalled his almost unwilling Adam-attitude as he had named all the animals passing before them, led of course by the *one* she had wanted to see, colored fearsome by his own unease. He had felt pleasantly bucolic after boning up on an old Botany text and then proceeding to Shape and name the flowers of the fields.

So far they had stayed out of the cities, far away from the machines. Her emotions were still too powerful at the sight of the simple, carefully introduced objects to risk plunging her into so complicated and chaotic a wilderness yet; he would build her city slowly.

Something passed rapidly, high above the cathedral, uttering a sonic boom. Render took Jill's hand in his for a moment and smiled as she looked up at him. Knowing she verged upon beauty, Jill normally took great pains to achieve it. But today her hair was simply drawn back and knotted behind her head, and her lips and her eyes were pale; and her exposed ears were tiny and white and somewhat pointed.

The Magic

"Observe the scalloped capitals," he whispered. "In their primitive fluting they anticipated what was later to become a common motif."

"Faugh!" said she.

"Shh!" said a sunburned little woman nearby, whose face seemed to crack and fall back together again as she pursed and unpursed her lips.

Later as they strolled back toward their hotel. Render said, "Okay on Winchester?"

"Okay on Winchester."

"Happy?"

"Happy."

"Good, then we can leave this afternoon."

"All right."

"For Switzerland . . . . "

She stopped and toyed with a button on his coat.

"Couldn't we just spend a day or two looking at some old chateaux first? After all, they're just across the channel, and you could be sampling all the local wines while I looked . . . "

"Okay," he said.

She looked up—a trifle surprised.

"What? No argument?" she smiled. "Where is your fighting spirit?—to let me push you around like this?"

She took his arm then and they walked on as he said, "Yesterday, while we were galloping about in the innards of that old castle, I heard a weak moan, and then a voice cried out, 'For the love of God, Montresor!' I think it was my fighting spirit, because I'm certain it was my voice. I've given up *der geist der stets verneint. Pax vobiscum!* Let us be gone to France. *Alors!*"

"Dear Rendy, it'll only be another day or two . . . . "

"Amen," he said. "though my skis that were waxed are already waning."

So they did that, and on the morn of the third day, when she spoke to him of castles in Spain, he reflected aloud that while psychologists drink and only grow angry, psychiatrists have been known to drink, grow angry and break things. Construing this as a veiled threat aimed at the Wedgewoods she had collected, she acquiesced to his desire to go skiing.

*

Free! Render almost screamed it.

His heart was pounding inside his head. He leaned hard. He cut to the left. The wind strapped at his face; a showed of ice crystals, like bullets of emery, fled by him, scraped against his cheek.

He was moving. Aye—the world had ended as Weissflujoch, and Dorftali led down and away from this portal.

His feet were two gleaming rivers which raced across the stark, curving plains; they could not be frozen in their course. Downward. He flowed. Away from all the rooms of the world. Away from the stifling lack of intensity, from the day's hundred spoon-fed welfares, from the killing pace of the forced amusements that hacked at the Hydra, leisure; away.

And as he fled down the run he felt a strong desire to look back over his shoulder, as though to see whether the world he had left behind and above had set one fearsome embodiment of itself, like a shadow, to trail along after him, hunt him down and drag him back to a warm and well-lit coffin in the sky, there to be laid to rest with a spike of aluminum driven through his will and a garland of alternating currents smothering his spirit.

"I hate you," he breathed between clenched teeth, and the wind carried the words back; and he laughed then, for he always analyzed his emotions, as a matter of reflex; and he added, "Exit Orestes, mad, pursued by the Furies . . . "

After a time the slope leveled out and he reached the bottom of the run and had to stop.

He smoked one cigarette then and rode back up to the top so that he could come down it again for nontherapeutic reasons.

*

That night he sat before a fire in the big lodge, feeling its warmth soaking into his tired muscles. Jill massaged his shoulders as he played Rorschach with the flames, and he came upon a blazing goblet which was snatched away from him in the same instant by the sound of his name being spoken somewhere across the Hall of the Nine Hearths.

"Charles Render!" said the voice (only it sounded more like "Sharlz Runder"), and his head instantly jerked in that direction, but his eyes danced with too many afterimages for him to isolate the source of the calling.

"Maurice?" he queried after a moment, "Bartelmetz?"

"Aye," came the reply, and then Render saw the familiar grizzled visage, set neckless and balding above the red and blue shag sweater that was stretched mercilessly about the wine-keg rotundity of the man who now picked his way in their direction, deftly avoiding the strewn crutches and the stacked skis and the people who, like Jill and Render, disdained sitting in chairs.

Render stood, stretching, and shook hands as he came upon them.

"You've put on more weight," Render observed. "That's unhealthy."

"Nonsense, it's all muscle. How have you been, and what are you up to these days?" He looked down at Jill and she smiled back at him.

"This is Miss DeVille," said Render.

"Jill," she acknowledged.

He bowed slightly, finally releasing Render's aching hand.

" . . . And this is Professor Maurice Bartelmetz of Vienna," finished Render, "a benighted disciple of all forms of dialectical pessimism, and a very distinguished pioneer in neuroparticipation—although you'd never guess it to look at him. I had the good fortune to be his pupil for over a year."

Bartelmetz nodded and agreed with him, taking in the Schnapsflasche Render brought forth from a small plastic bag, and accepting the collapsible cup which he filled to the brim.

"Ah, you are a good doctor still," he sighed. "You have diagnosed the case in an instant and you make the proper prescription. *Nozdrovia!*"

"Seven years in a gulp," Render acknowledged, refilling their glasses.

"Then we shall make time more malleable by sipping it."

They seated themselves on the floor, and the fire roared up through the great brick chimney as the logs burned themselves back to branches, to twigs, to thin sticks, ring by yearly ring.

Render replenished the fire.

"I read your last book." said Bartelmetz finally, casually, "about four years ago."

Render reckoned that to be correct.

"Are you doing any research work these days?"

Render poked lazily at the fire.

"Yes," he answered, "sort of."

He glanced at Jili, who was dozing with her cheek against the arm of the huge leather chair that held his emergency Bag, the planes of her face all crimson and flickering shadow.

"I've hit upon a rather unusual subject and started with a piece of jobbery I eventually intend to write about."

"Unusual? In what way?"

"Blind from birth, for one thing."

"You're using the ONT&R?"

"Yes. She's going to be a Shaper."

"*Verfluchter!*—Are you aware of the possible repercussions?"

"Of course."

"You've heard of unlucky Pierre?"

"No."

"Good, then it was successfully hushed. Pierre was a philosophy student at the University of Paris, and was doing a dissertation on the evolution of consciousness. This past summer he decided it would be necessary for him to explore the mind of an ape, for purposes of comparing a *moins-nausée* mind with his own, I suppose. At any rate, he obtained illegal access to an ONT&R and to the mind of our hairy cousin. It was never ascertained how far along he got in exposing the animal to the stimulibank, but it is to be assumed that such items as would not be immediately trans-subjective between man and ape—traffic sounds *und so weiter*—were what frightened the creature. Pierre is still residing in a padded cell, and all his responses are those of a frightened ape.

The Magic

"So, while he did not complete his own dissertation," he finished, "he may provide significant material for someone else's."

Render shook his head.

"Quite a story," he said softly, "but I have nothing that dramatic to contend with. I've found an exceedingly stable individual—a psychiatrist, in fact—one who's already spent time in ordinary analysis. She wants to go into neuroparticipation—but the fear of a sight-trauma was what was keeping her out. I've been gradually exposing her to a full range of visual phenomena. When I've finished she should be completely accommodated to sight, so that she can give her full attention to therapy and not be blinded by vision, so to speak. We've already had four sessions."

"And?"

" . . . And it's working fine."

"You are certain about it?"

"Yes, as certain as anyone can be in these matters."

"Mm-hm," said Bartelmetz. "Tell me, do you find her excessively strong-willed? By that I mean, say, perhaps an obsessive-compulsive pattern concerning anything to which she's been introduced so far?"

"No."

"Has she ever succeeded in taking over control of the fantasy?"

"No!"

"You lie," he said simply.

Render found a cigarette. After lighting it, he smiled.

"Old father, old artificer," he conceded, "age has not withered your perceptiveness. I may trick me, but never you. —Yes, as a matter of fact, she *is* very difficult to keep under control. She is not satisfied just to see. She wants to Shape things for herself already. It's quite understandable—both to her and to me—but conscious apprehension and emotional acceptance never do seem to get together on things. She has become dominant on several occasions, but I've succeeded in resuming control almost immediately. After all. I *am* master of the bank."

254

Roger Zelazny and Samuel R. Delany

"Hm," mused Bartelmetz. "Are you familiar with a Buddhist text—*Shankara's Catechism?*"

"I'm afraid not."

"Then I lecture you on it now. It posits—obviously not for therapeutic purposes—a true ego and a false ego. The true ego is that part of man which is immortal and shall proceed on to nirvana: the soul, if you like. Very good. Well, the false ego, on the other hand, is the normal mind, bound round with the illusions—the consciousness of you and me and everyone we have ever known professionally. Good?—Good. Now, the stuff this false ego is made up of they call *skandhas*. These include the feelings, the perceptions, the aptitudes, consciousness itself, and even the physical form. Very unscientific. Yes. Now they are not the same thing as neuroses, or one of Mister Ibsen's life-lies, or an hallucination—no, even though they are all wrong, being parts of a false thing to begin with. Each of the five *skandhas* is a part of the eccentricity that we call identity—then on top come the neuroses and all the other messes which follow after and keep us in business. Okay?—Okay. I give you this lecture because I need a dramatic term for what I will say, because I wish to say something dramatic. View the skandhas as lying at the bottom of the pond; the neuroses, they are ripples on the top of the water; the 'true ego,' if there is one, is buried deep beneath the sand at the bottom. So. The ripples fill up the-the—zwischenwelt—between the object and the subject. The *skandhas* are a part of the subject, basic, unique, the stuff of his being. —So far, you are with me?"

"With many reservations."

"Good. Now I have defined my term somewhat, I will use it. You are fooling around with *skandhas*, not simple neuroses. You are attempting to adjust this woman's overall conception of herself and of the world. You are using the ONT&R to do it. It is the same thing as fooling with a psychotic or an ape. All may seem to go well. but—at any moment, it is possible you may do something, show her some sight, or some way of seeing which will break in upon her selfhood, break a *skandha*—and pouf!—it will be like breaking through the bottom of the pond. A whirlpool will result, pulling

255

you—where? I do not want you for a patient, young man, young artificer, so I counsel you not to proceed with this experiment. The ONT&R should not be used in such a manner."

Render flipped his cigarette into the fire and counted on his fingers:

"One," he said, "you are making a mystical mountain out of a pebble. All I am doing is adjusting her consciousness to accept an additional area of perception. Much of it is simple transference work from the other senses— Two, her emotions were quite intense initially because it *did* involve a trauma—but we've passed that stage already. Now it is only a novelty to her. Soon it will be a commonplace—Three. Eileen is a psychiatrist herself; she is educated in these matters and deeply aware of the delicate nature of what we are doing—Four, her sense of identity and her desires, or her *skandhas*, or whatever you want to call them, are as firm as the Rock of Gibraltar. Do you realize the intense application required for a blind person to obtain the education she has obtained? It took a will of ten-point steel and the emotional control of an ascetic as well—"

"—And if something that strong should break, in a timeless moment of anxiety," smiled Barlelmetz sadly, "may the shades of Sigmund Freud and Karl Jung walk by your side in the valley of darkness.

"—And five," he added suddenly, staring into Render's eyes. "Five," he ticked it off on one finger. "Is she pretty?"

Render looked back into the fire.

"Very clever," sighed Bartelmetz. "I cannot tell whether you are blushing or not, with the rosy glow of the flames upon your face. I fear that you are, though, which would mean that you are aware that you yourself could be the source of the inciting stimulus. I shall burn a candle tonight before a portrait of Adler and pray that he give you the strength to compete successfully in your duel with your patient."

Render looked at Jill, who was still sleeping. He reached out and brushed a lock of her hair back into place.

Roger Zelazny and Samuel R. Delany

"Still," said Bartelmetz, "if you do proceed and all goes well, I shall look forward with great interest to the reading of your work. Did I ever tell you that I have treated several Buddhists and never found a 'true ego'?"

Both men laughed.

*

Like me but not like me, that one on a leash, smelling of fear, small, gray and unseeing. *Rrowl* and he'll choke on his collar. His head is empty as the oven till. She pushes the button and it makes dinner. Make talk and they never understand, but they are like me. One day I will kill one—why? . . . Turn here.

"Three steps. Up. Glass doors. Handle to right."

Why? Ahead, drop-shaft. Gardens under, down. Smells nice, there. Grass, wet dirt, trees and clean air. I see. Birds are recorded though. I see all. I.

"Dropshaft. Four steps."

Down Yes. Want to make loud noises in throat, feel silly. Clean, smooth, many of trees. God . . . She likes sitting on bench chewing leaves smelling smooth air. Can't see them like me. Maybe now, some . . . ? No.

Can't Bad Sigmund me on grass, trees, here. Must hold it. Pity. Best place . . .

"Watch for steps."

Ahead. To right, to left, to right, to left, trees and grass now. Sigmund sees. Walking . . . Doctor with machine gives her his eyes. *Rrowl* and he will not choke. No fearsmell.

Dig deep hole in ground, bury eyes. God is blind. Sigmund to see. Her eyes now filled, and he is afraid of teeth. Will make her to see and take her high up in the sky to see, away. Leave me here, leave Sigmund with none to see, alone. I will dig a deep hole in the ground . . .

*

It was after ten in the morning when Jill awoke. She did not have to turn her head to know that Render was already gone. He never slept late. She rubbed her eyes, stretched, turned onto her side and raised herself on her

257

elbow. She squinted at the clock on the bedside table, simultaneously reaching for a cigarette and her lighter.

As she inhaled, she realized there was no ashtray. Doubtless Render had moved it to the dresser because he did not approve of smoking in bed. With a sigh that ended in a snort she slid out of the bed and drew on her wrap before the ash grew too long.

She hated getting up, but once she did she would permit the day to begin and continue on without lapse through its orderly progression of events.

"Damn him," she smiled. She had wanted her breakfast in bed, but it was too late now.

Between thoughts as to what she would wear, she observed an alien pair of skis standing in the corner. A sheet of paper was impaled on one. She approached it.

"Join me?" asked the scrawl.

She shook her head in an emphatic negative and felt somewhat sad. She had been on skis twice in her life and she was afraid of them. She felt that she should really try again, after his being a reasonably good sport about the chateaux, but she could not even bear the memory of the unseemly downward rushing—which, on two occasions, had promptly deposited her in a snowbank—without wincing and feeling once again the vertigo that had seized her during the attempts.

So she showered and dressed and went downstairs for breakfast.

All nine fires were already roaring as she passed the big hall and looked inside. Some red-faced skiers were holding their hands up before the blaze of the central hearth. It was not crowded though. The racks held only a few pairs of dripping boots, bright caps hung on pegs, moist skis stood upright in their place beside the door. A few people were seated in the chairs set further back toward the center of the hall, reading papers, smoking, or talking quietly. She saw no one she knew, so she moved on toward the dining room.

As she passed the registration desk the old man who worked there called out her name. She approached him and smiled.

"Letter," he explained, turning to a rack. "Here it is," he announced, handing it to her. "Looks important."

It had been forwarded three times, she noted. It was a bulky brown envelope, and the return address was that of her attorney.

"Thank you."

She moved off to a seat beside the big window that looked out upon a snow garden, a skating rink, and a distant winding trail dotted with figures carrying skis over their shoulders. She squinted against the brightness as she tore open the envelope.

Yes, it was final. Her attorney's note was accompanied by a copy of the divorce decree. She had only recently decided to end her legal relationship to Mister Fotlock, whose name she had stopped using five years earlier, when they had separated. Now that she had the thing she wasn't sure exactly what she was going to do with it. It would be a hell of a surprise for dear Rendy, though, she decided. She would have to find a reasonably innocent way of getting the information to him. She withdrew her compact and practiced a "Well?" expression. Well, there would be time for that later, she mused. Not too much later, though . . . Her thirtieth birthday, like a huge black cloud, filled an April but four months distant. Well . . . She touched her quizzical lips with color, dusted more powder over her mole, and locked the expression within her compact for future use.

*

In the dining room she saw Doctor Bartelmetz, seated before an enormous mound of scrambled eggs, great chains of dark sausages, several heaps of yellow toast, and a half-emptied flask of orange juice. A pot of coffee steamed on the warmer at his elbow. He leaned slightly forward as he ate, wielding his fork like a windmill blade.

"Good morning," she said.

He looked up.

"Miss DeVille—Jill . . . Good morning." He nodded at the chair across from him. "Join me, please."

The Magic

She did so, and when the waiter approached she nodded and said, "I'll have the same thing, only about ninety percent less."

She turned back to Bartelmetz.

"Have you seen Charles today?"

"Alas, I have not," he gestured, open-handed, "and I wanted to continue our discussion while his mind was still in the early stages of wakefulness and somewhat malleable. Unfortunately," he took a sip of coffee, "he who sleeps well enters the day somewhere in the middle of its second act."

"Myself, I usually come in around intermission and ask someone for a synopsis," she explained. "So why not continue the discussion with me?—I'm always malleable, and my *skandhas* are in good shape."

Their eyes met, and he took a bite of toast.

"Aye," he said, at length, "I had guessed as much. Well—good. What do you know of Render's work?"

She adjusted herself in the chair.

"Mm. He being a special specialist in a highly specialized area, I find it difficult to appreciate the few things he does say about it. I'd like to be able to look inside other people's minds sometimes—to see what they're thinking about *me*, of course—but I don't think I could stand staying there very long. Especially," she gave a mock-shudder, "the mind of somebody with—problems. I'm afraid I'd be too sympathetic or too frightened or something. Then, according to what I've read—pow!—like sympathetic magic, it would be my problem.

"Charles never has problems though," she continued, "at least, none that he speaks to me about. Lately I've been wondering, though. That blind girl and her talking dog seem to be too much with him."

"Talking dog?"

"Yes, her seeing-eye dog is one of those surgical mutants."

"How interesting . . . . Have you ever met her?"

"Never."

"So," he mused.

Roger Zelazny and Samuel R. Delany

"Sometimes a therapist encounters a patient whose problems are so akin to his own that the sessions become extremely mordant," he noted. "It has always been the case with me when I treat a fellow-psychiatrist. Perhaps Charles sees in this situation a parallel to something which has been troubling him personally. I did not administer his personal analysis. I do not know all the ways of his mind, even though he was a pupil of mine for a long while. He was always self-contained, somewhat reticent; he could be quite authoritative on occasion, however. —What are some of the other things which occupy his attention these days?"

"His son Peter is a constant concern. He's changed the boy's school five times in five years."

Her breakfast arrived. She adjusted her napkin and drew her chair closer to the table.

"And he has been reading case histories of suicides recently, and talking about them, and talking about them, and talking about them."

"To what end?"

She shrugged and began eating.

"He never mentioned why," she said, looking up again. "Maybe he's writing something . . . . "

Bartelmetz finished his eggs and poured more coffee,

"Are you afraid of this patient of his?" he inquired.

"No . . . Yes," she responded, "I am."

"Why?"

"I am afraid of sympathetic magic," she said, flushing slightly.

"Many things could fall under that heading."

"Many indeed," she acknowledged. And, after a moment, "We are united in our concern for his welfare and in agreement as to what represents the threat. So, may I ask a favor?"

"You may."

"Talk to him again," she said. "Persuade him to drop the case."

He folded his napkin.

The Magic

"I intend to do that after dinner," he stated, "because I believe in the ritualistic value of rescue-motions. They shall be made."

*

Dear Father-Image,

Yes, the school is fine, my ankle is getting that way, and my classmates are a congenial lot. No, I am not short on cash, undernourished, or having difficulty fitting into the new curriculum. Okay?

The building I will not describe, as you have already seen the macabre thing. The grounds I cannot describe, as they are currently residing beneath cold white sheets. Brr! I trust yourself to be enjoying the arts wint'rish. I do not share your enthusiasm for summer's opposite, except within picture frames or as an emblem on ice-cream bars.

The ankle inhibits my mobility and my roommate has gone home for the weekend—both of which are really blessings (saith Pangloss), for I now have the opportunity to catch up on some reading. I will do so forthwith.

Prodigally,
Peter

Render reached down to pat the huge head. It accepted the gesture stoically, then turned its gaze up to the Austrian whom Render had asked for a light, as if to say, "Must I endure this indignity?" The man laughed at the expression, snapping shut the engraved lighter on which Render noted the middle initial to be a small 'v.'

'Thank you," he said, and to the dog: "What is your name?"

"Bismark," it growled.

Render smiled.

"You remind me of another of your kind," he told the dog. "One Sigmund, by name, a companion and guide to a blind friend of mine, in America."

"My Bismark is a hunter," said the young man. 'There is no quarry that can outthink him, neither the deer nor the big cats."

The dog's ears pricked forward and be stared up at Render with proud, blazing eyes.

"We have hunted in Africa and the northern and southwestern parts of America. Central America, too. He never loses the trail. He never gives up. He is a beautiful brute, and his teeth could have been made in Solingen."

"You are indeed fortunate to have such a bunting companion."

"I hunt," growled the dog. "I follow . . . Sometimes, I have, the kill . . . "

"You would not know of the one called Sigmund then, or the woman he guides—Miss Eileen Shallot?" asked Render.

The man shook his head.

"No, Bismark came to me from Massachusetts, but I was never to the Center personally. I am not acquainted with other mutie handlers."

"I see. Well, thank you for the light. Good afternoon."

"Good afternoon . . . "

"Good, after, noon . . . "

Render strolled on up the narrow street, hands in his pockets. He had excused himself and not said where he was going. This was because he had had no destination in mind. Bartelmetz' second essay at counseling had almost led him to say things he would later regret. It was easier to take a walk than to continue the conversation.

On a sudden impulse he entered a small shop and bought a cuckoo clock which had caught his eye. He felt certain that Bartelmetz would accept the gift in the proper spirit. He smiled and walked on. *And what was that letter to Jill which the desk clerk had made a special trip to their table to deliver at dinnertime?* he wondered. It had been forwarded three times, and its return address was that of a law firm. Jill had not even opened it, but had smiled, overtipped the old man, and tucked it into her purse. He would have to hint subtly as to its contents. His curiosity so aroused, she would be sure to tell him out of pity.

The Magic

The icy pillars of the sky suddenly seemed to sway before him as a cold wind leaped down out of the north. Render hunched his shoulders and drew his head further below his collar. Clutching the cuckoo clock, he hurried back up the street.

*

That night the serpent which holds its tail in its mouth belched, the Fenris Wolf made a pass at the moon, the little clock said "cuckoo" and tomorrow came on like Manolete's last bull, shaking the gate of horn with the bellowed promise to tread a river of lions to sand.

Render promised himself he would lay off the gooey fondue.

*

Later, much later, when they skipped through the skies in a kite-shaped cruiser, Render looked down upon the darkened Earth dreaming its cities full of stars, looked up at the sky where they were all reflected, looked about him at the tape-screens watching all the people who blinked into them, and at the coffee, tea and mixed drink dispensers who sent their fluids forth to explore the insides of the people they required to push their buttons, then looked across at Jill, whom the old buildings had compelled to walk among their walls—because he knew she felt he should be looking at her then—felt his seat's demand that he convert it into a couch, did so, and slept.

IV

Her office was full of flowers, and she liked exotic perfumes. Sometimes she burned incense.

She liked soaking in overheated pools, walking through falling snow, listening to too much music, played perhaps too loudly, drinking five or six varieties of liqueurs (usually reeking of anise, sometimes touched with wormwood) every evening. Her hands were soft and lightly freckled. Her fingers were long and tapered. She wore no rings.

Her fingers traced and retraced the floral swellings on the side of her chair as she spoke into the recording unit.

Roger Zelazny and Samuel R. Delany

" . . . Patient's chief complaints on admission were nervousness, insomnia, stomach pains and a period of depression. Patient has had a record of previous admissions for short periods of time. He had been in this hospital in 1995 for a manic depressive psychosis, depressed type, and he returned here again, 2-3-96. He was in another hospital, 9-20-97. Physical examination revealed a BP of 170/100. He was normally developed and well-nourished on the date of examination, 12-11-98. On this date patient complained of chronic backache, and there was noted some moderate symptoms of alcohol withdrawal. Physical examination further revealed no pathology except that the patient's tendon reflexes were exaggerated but equal. These symptoms were the result of alcohol withdrawal. Upon admission he was shown to be not psychotic, neither delusional nor hallucinated. He was well-oriented as to place, time and person. His psychological condition was evaluated and he was found to be somewhat grandiose and expansive and more than a little hostile. He was considered a potential trouble maker. Because of his experience as a cook, he was assigned to work in the kitchen. His general condition then showed definite improvement. He is less tense and is cooperative. Diagnosis: Manic depressive reaction (external precipitating stress unknown). The degree of psychiatric impairment is mild. He is considered competent. To be continued on therapy and hospitalization."

She turned off the recorder then and laughed. The sound frightened her. Laughter is a social phenomenon and she was alone. She played back the recording then, chewing on the corner of her handkerchief while the soft, clipped words were returned to her. She ceased to hear them after the first dozen or so.

When the recorder stopped talking she turned it off. She was alone. She was very alone. She was so damned alone that the little pool of brightness which occurred when she stroked her forehead and faced the window—that little pool of brightness suddenly became the most important thing in the world. She wanted it to be immense. She wanted it to be an ocean of light. Or else she wanted to grow so small herself that the effect would be the same: she wanted to drown is it.

The Magic

It had been three weeks, yesterday . . .

Too long, she decided, I should have waited. No! Impossible! But what if he goes as Riscomb went? No! He won't. He would not. Nothing can hurt him. Never. He is all strength and armor. But—but we should have waited till next month to start. Three weeks . . . Sight withdrawal—that's what it is. Are the memories fading? Are they weaker? (What does a tree look like? Or a cloud—I can't remember! What is red? What is green? God! It's hysterical! I'm watching and I can't stop it!—Take a pill! A pill!)

Her shoulders began to shake. She did not take a pill though, but bit down harder on the handkerchief until her sharp teeth tore through its fabric.

"Beware," she recited a personal beatitude, "those who hunger and thirst after justice, for we *will* be satisfied.

"And beware the meek," she continued, "for we shall attempt to inherit the Earth.

"And beware . . . "

There was a brief buzz from the phone-box. She put away her handkerchief, composed her face, turned the unit on.

"Hello . . . ?"

"Eileen, I'm back. How've you been?"

"Good, quite well in fact. How was your vacation?"

"Oh, I can't complain. I had it coming for a long time. I guess I deserve it. Listen, I brought some things back to show you—like Winchester Cathedral. You want to come in this week? I can make it any evening."

Tonight. No. I want it too badly. It will set me back if he sees . . .

"How about tomorrow night?" she asked. "Or the one after?"

"Tomorrow will be fine," he said. "Meet you at the P & S, around seven?"

"Yes. that would be pleasant. Same table?"

"Why not?—I'll reserve it."

"All right. I'll see you then."

"Good-bye."

The connection was broken.

Roger Zelazny and Samuel R. Delany

Suddenly, then, at that moment, colors swirled again through her head; and she saw trees—oaks and pines, poplars and sycamores—great, and green and brown, and iron-colored; and she saw wads of fleecy clouds, dipped in paintpots, swabbing a pastel sky; and a burning sun, and a small willow tree, and a lake of a deep, almost violet, blue. She folded her torn handkerchief and put it away.

She pushed a button beside her desk and music filled the office: Scriabin. Then she pushed another button and replayed the tape she had dictated, half-listening to each.

*

Pierre sniffed suspiciously at the food. The attendant moved away from the tray and stepped out into the hall, locking the door behind him. The enormous salad waited on the floor. Pierre approached cautiously, snatched a handful of lettuce, gulped it.

He was afraid.

If only the steel would stop crashing and crashing against steel, somewhere in that dark night . . . If only . . .

*

Sigmund rose to his feet, yawned, stretched. His hind legs trailed out behind him for a moment, then he snapped to attention and shook himself. She would be coming home soon. Wagging his tail slowly, he glanced up at the human-level clock with the raised numerals, verified his feelings, then crossed the apartment to the teevee. He rose onto his hind legs, rested one paw against the table and used the other to turn on the set.

It was nearly time for the weather report and the roads would be icy.

*

"I have driven through countrywide graveyards," wrote Render, "vast forests of stone that spread further every day.

"Why does man so zealously guard his dead? Is it because this is the monumentally democratic way of immortalization, the ultimate affirmation of the power to hurt—that is to say, life—and the desire that it continue on forever? Unamuno has suggested that this is the case. If it is, then a greater percentage of the population actively sought immortality last year than ever before in history . . . . "

*

Tch-tchg, tchga-tchgt
"Do you think they're really people?"
"Naw, they're too good."

*

The evening was starglint and soda over ice. Render wound the S-7 into the cold sub-subcellar, found his parking place, nosed into it.

There was a damp chill that emerged from the concrete to gnaw like rats' teeth at their flesh. Render guided her toward the lift, their breath preceding them in dissolving clouds.

"A bit of a chill in the air," he noted.

She nodded, biting her lip.

Inside the lift, he sighed, unwound his scarf, lit a cigarette.

"Give me one, please," she requested, smelling the tobacco.

He did.

They rose slowly, and Render leaned against the wall, puffing a mixture of smoke and crystallized moisture.

"I met another mutie shep," he recalled, "in Switzerland. Big as Sigmund. A hunter though, and as Prussian as they come," he grinned.

"Sigmund likes to hunt, too," she observed. "Twice every year we go up to the North Woods and I turn him loose. He's gone for days at a time, and he's always quite happy when he returns. Never says what he's done, but he's never hungry. Back when I got him I guessed that he would need vacations from humanity to stay stable. I think I was right."

The lift stopped, the door opened and they walked out into the hall, Render guiding her again.

Inside his office, he poked at the thermostat and warm air sighed through the room. He hung their coats in the inner office and brought the great egg out from its nest behind the wall. He connected it to an outlet and moved to convert his desk into a control panel.

"How long do you think it will take?" she asked, running her fingertips over the smooth, cold curves of the egg. "The whole thing, I mean. The entire adaptation to seeing."

He wondered.

"I have no idea," he said, "no idea whatsoever, yet. We got off to a good start, but there's still a lot of work to be done. I think I'll be able to make a good guess in another three months."

She nodded wistfully, moved to his desk, explored the controls with finger strokes like ten feathers.

"Careful you don't push any of those."

"I won't. How long do you think it will take me to learn to operate one?"

"Three months to learn it. Six, to actually become proficient enough to use it on anyone, and an additional six under close supervision before you can be trusted on your own. —About a year altogether."

"Uh-huh." She chose a chair.

Render touched the seasons to life, and the phases of day and night, the breath of the country, the city, the elements that raced naked through the skies, and all the dozens of dancing cues he used to build worlds. He smashed the clock of time and tasted the seven or so ages of man.

"Okay," he turned, "everything is ready."

It came quickly, and with a minimum of suggestion on Render's part. One moment there was grayness. Then a dead-white fog. Then it broke itself apart, as though a quick wind had risen, although he neither heard nor felt a wind.

He stood beside the willow tree beside the lake, and she stood half-hidden among the branches and the lattices of shadow. The sun was slanting its way into evening.

"We have come back," she said, stepping out, leaves in her hair. "For a time I was afraid it had never happened, but I see it all again, and I remember now."

The Magic

"Good," he said. "Behold yourself." And she looked into the lake.

"I have not changed," she said. "I haven't changed . . . . "

"No."

"But you have," she continued, looking up at him. "You are taller, and there is something different . . . . "

"No," he answered.

"I am mistaken," she said quickly, "I don't understand everything I see yet."

"I will, though."

"Of course."

"What are we going to do?"

"Watch," he instructed her.

Along a flat, no-colored river of road she just then noticed beyond the trees, came the car. It came from the farthest quarter of the sky, skipping over the mountains, buzzing down the hills, circling through the glades, and splashing them with the colors of its voice—the gray and the silver of synchronized potency—and the lake shivered from its sounds, and the car stopped a hundred feet away, masked by the shrubberies; and it waited. It was the S-7.

"Come with me," he said, taking her hand. "We're going for a ride."

They walked among the trees and rounded the final cluster of bushes. She touched the sleek cocoon, its antennae, its tires, its windows—and the windows transpared as she did so. She stared through them at the inside of the car, and she nodded.

"It is your Spinner."

"Yes." He held the door for her. "Get in. We'll return to the club. The time is now. The memories are fresh, and they should be reasonably pleasant, or neutral."

"Pleasant," she said, getting in.

He closed the door, then circled the car and entered. She watched as he punched imaginary coordinates. The car leaped ahead and he kept a steady stream of trees flowing by them. He could feel the rising tension, so he did not vary the scenery. She swiveled her seat and studied the interior of the car.

"Yes," she finally said, "I can perceive what everything is."

She stared out the window again. She looked at the rushing trees. Render stared out and looked upon rushing anxiety patterns. He opaqued the windows.

"Good," she said, "thank you. Suddenly it was too much to see—all of it, moving past like a . . . "

"Of course," said Render, maintaining the sensations of forward motion. "I'd anticipated that. You're getting tougher, though."

After a moment, "Relax," he said, "relax now," and somewhere a button was pushed, and she relaxed, and they drove on, and on and on, and finally the car began to slow, and Render said, "Just for one nice, slow glimpse now, look out your window."

She did.

He drew upon every stimulus in the bank which could promote sensations of pleasure and relaxation, and he dropped the city around the car, and the windows became transparent, and she looked out upon the profiles of towers and a block of monolithic apartments, and then she saw three rapid cafeterias, an entertainment palace, a drugstore, a medical center of yellow brick with an aluminum caduceus set above its archway, and a glassed-in high school, now emptied of its pupils, a fifty-pump gas station, another drugstore, and many more cars, parked or roaring by them, and people, people moving in and out of the doorways and walking before the buildings and getting into the cars and getting out of the cars; and it was summer, and the light of late afternoon filtered down upon the colors of the city and the colors of the garments the people wore as they moved along the boulevard, as they loafed upon the terraces, as they crossed the balconies, leaned on balustrades and windowsills, emerged from a corner kiosk, entered one, stood talking to one another; a woman walking a poodle rounded a corner; rockets went to and fro in the high sky.

The world fell apart then and Render caught the pieces.

The Magic

He maintained an absolute blackness, blanketing every sensation but that of their movement forward.

After a time a dim light occurred, and they were still seated in the Spinner, windows blanked again, and the air as they breathed it became a soothing unguent.

"Lord," she said, "the world is so filled. Did I really see all of that?"

"I wasn't going to do that tonight, but you wanted me to. You seemed ready."

"Yes," she said, and the windows became transparent again. She turned away quickly.

"It's gone," he said. "I only wanted to give you a glimpse."

She looked, and it was dark outside now, and they were crossing over a high bridge. They were moving slowly. There was no other traffic. Below them were the Flats, where an occasional smelter flared like a tiny, drowsing volcano, spitting showers of orange sparks skyward; and there were many stars: they glistened on the breathing water that went beneath the bridge; they silhouetted by pinprick the skyline that hovered dimly below its surface. The slanting struts of the bridge marched steadily by.

"You have done it," she said, "and I thank you." Then; "Who are you, really?" (He must have wanted her to ask that.)

"I am Render," he laughed. And they wound their way through a dark, now-vacant city, coming at last to their club and entering the great parking dome.

Inside, he scrutinized all her feelings, ready to banish the world at a moment's notice. He did not feel he would have to, though.

They left the car, moved ahead. They passed into the club which he had decided would not be crowded tonight. They were shown to their table at the foot of the bar in the small room with the suit of armor, and they sat down and ordered the same meal over again.

"No," he said, looking down, "it belongs over there."

Roger Zelazny and Samuel R. Delany

The suit of armor appeared once again beside the table, and he was once again inside his gray suit and black tie and silver tie clasp shaped like a tree limb.

They laughed.

"I'm just not the type to wear a tin suit, so I wish you'd stop seeing me that way."

"I'm sorry," she smiled. "I don't know how I did that, or why."

"I do, and I decline the nomination. Also, I caution you once again. You are conscious of the fact that this is all an illusion. I had to do it that way for you to get the full benefit of the thing. For most of my patients though, it is the real item while they are experiencing it. It makes a counter-trauma or a symbolic sequence even more powerful. You are aware of the parameters of the game, however, and whether you want it or not this gives you a different sort of control over it than I normally have to deal with. Please be careful."

"I'm sorry. I didn't mean to."

"I know. Here comes the meal we just had."

"Ugh! It looks dreadful! Did we eat all that stuff?"

"Yes," he chuckled. "That's a knife, that's a fork, that's a spoon. That's roast beef, and those are mashed potatoes, those are peas, that's butter . . . "

"Goodness! I don't feel so well."

" . . . And those are the salads, and those are the salad dressings. This is a brook trout—mm! These are French fried potatoes. This is a bottle of wine. Hmm—let's see—Romanée-Conti, since I'm not paying for it—and a bottle of Yquem for the trou—Hey!"

The room was wavering.

He bared the table, he banished the restaurant. They were back in the glade. Through the transparent fabric of the world he watched a hand moving along a panel. Buttons were being pushed. The world grew substantial again. Their emptied table was set beside the lake now, and it was still nighttime and summer, and the tablecloth was very white under the glow of the giant moon that hung overhead.

The Magic

"That was stupid of me," he said. "Awfully stupid. I should have introduced them one at a time. The actual sight of basic, oral stimuli can be very distressing to a person seeing them for the first time. I got so wrapped up in the Shaping that I forgot the patient, which is just dandy! I apologize."

"I'm okay now. Really I am."

He summoned a cool breeze from the lake.

" . . . And that is the moon," he added lamely.

She nodded, and she was wearing a tiny moon in the center of her forehead; it glowed like the one above them, and her hair and dress were all of silver.

The bottle of Romanée-Conti stood on the table, and two glasses.

"Where did that come from?"

She shrugged. He poured out a glassful.

"It may taste kind of flat," he said.

"It doesn't. Here—" She passed it to him.

As he sipped it he realized it had a taste—a *fruite* such as might be quashed from the grapes grown in the Isles of the Blest, a smooth, muscular *charnu*, and a *capiteux* centrifuged from the fumes of a field of burning poppies. With a start, he knew that his hand must be traversing the route of the perceptions, symphonizing the sensual cues of a transference and a counter-transference which had come upon him all unaware, there beside the lake.

"So it does," he noted, "and now it is time we returned."

"So soon? I haven't seen the cathedral yet . . . . "

"So soon."

He willed the world to end, and it did.

"It is cold out there," she said as she dressed, "and dark."

"I know. I'll mix us something to drink while I clear the unit."

"Fine."

He glanced at the tapes and shook his head. He crossed to his bar cabinet.

"It's not exactly Romanée-Conti," he observed, reaching for a bottle.

"So what? I don't mind."

Neither did he, at that moment. So he cleared the unit, they drank their drinks, he helped her into her coat and they left.

As they rode the lift down to the sub-sub he willed the world to end again, but it didn't.

*

Dad,

I hobbled from school to taxi and taxi to spaceport, for the local Air Force Exhibit—Outward, it was called. (Okay, I exaggerated the hobble. It got me extra attention though.) The whole bit was aimed at seducing young manhood into a five-year hitch, as I saw it. But it worked. I wanna join up I wanna go Out There. Think they'll take me when I'm old enuff? I mean take me Out—not some crummy desk job. Think so?

I do.

There was this damn lite colonel ('scuse the French) who saw this kid lurching around and pressing his nose 'gainst the big windowpanes, and he decided to give him the subliminal sell. Great! He pushed me through the gallery and showed me all the pitchers of AF triumphs, from Moonbase to Marsport. He lectured me on the Great Traditions of the Service, and marched me into a flic room where the Corps had good clean fun on tape, wrestling one another in null-G "where it's all skill and no brawn," and making tinted water sculpture-work way in the middle of the air and doing dismounted drill on the skin of a cruiser. Oh joy!

Seriously though, I'd like to be there when they hit the Outer Five—and On Out. Not because of the bogus balonus in the throwaways, and suchlike crud, but because I think someone of sensibility should be along to chronicle the thing in the proper way. You know, raw frontier observer. Francis Parkman. Mary Austin, like that. So I decided I'm going.

The Magic

The AF boy with the chicken stuff on his shoulders wasn't in the least way patronizing, gods be praised. We stood on the balcony and watched ships lift off and he told me to go forth and study real hard and I might be riding them someday. I did not bother to tell him that I'm hardly intellectually deficient and that I'll have my B.A. before I'm old enough to do anything with it, even join his Corps. I just watched the ships lift off and said, "Ten years from now I'll be looking down, not up." Then he told me how hard his own training had been, so I did not ask howcum he got stuck with a lousy dirt-side assignment like this one. Glad I didn't, now I think on it. He looked more like one of their ads than one of their real people. Hope I never look like an ad.

Thank you for the monies and the warm sox and Mozart's String Quintets, which I'm hearing right now. I wanna put in my bid for Luna instead of Europe next summer. Maybe . . . ? Possibly . . . ? Contingently . . . ? Huh?—If I can smash that new test you're designing for me . . . ? Anyhow, please think about it.

Your son,
Pete

"Hello. State Psychiatric Institute."

"I'd like to make an appointment for an examination."

"Just a moment. I'll connect you with the Appointment Desk."

"Hello. Appointment Desk."

"I'd Like to make an appointment for an examination."

"Just a moment . . . What sort of examination."

"I want to see Doctor Shallot, Eileen Shallot. As soon as possible."

"Just a moment. I'll have to check her schedule . . . Could you make it at two o'clock next Tuesday?"

"That would be just fine."

"What is the name, please?"

"DeVille. Jill DeVille-

"All right. Miss DeVille. That's two o'clock, Tuesday."

"Thank you."

*

The man walked beside the highway. Cars passed along the highway. The cars in the high-acceleration lane blurred by.

Traffic was light.

It was 10:30 in the morning, and cold.

The man's fur-lined collar was turned up, his hands were in his pockets, and he leaned into the wind. Beyond the fence, the road was clean and dry.

The morning sun was buried in clouds. In the dirty light, the man could see the tree a quarter mile ahead.

His pace did not change. His eyes did not leave the tree. The small stones clicked and crunched beneath his shoes.

When he reached the tree he took off his jacket and folded it neatly.

He placed it upon the ground and climbed the tree.

As he moved out onto the limb which extended over the fence, he looked to see that no traffic was approaching. Then he seized the branch with both hands, lowered himself, hung a moment, and dropped onto the highway.

It was a hundred yards wide, the eastbound half of the highway.

He glanced west, saw there was still no traffic coming his way, then began to walk toward the center island. He knew he would never reach it. At this time of day the cars were moving at approximately one hundred-sixty miles an hour in the high-acceleration lane. He walked on.

A car passed behind him. He did not look back. If the windows were opaqued, as was usually the case, then the occupants were unaware he had crossed their path. They would hear of it later and examine the front end of their vehicle for possible sign of such an encounter.

A car passed in front of him. Its windows were clear. A glimpse of two faces, their mouths made into Os, was presented to him, then torn from his sight. His own face remained without expression. His pace did not change.

The Magic

Two more care rushed by, windows darkened. He had crossed perhaps twenty yards of highway.

Twenty-five . . .

Something in the wind, or beneath his feet, told him it was coming. He did not look.

Something in the corner of his eye assured him it was coming. His gait did not alter.

Cecil Green had the windows transpared because he liked it that way. His left hand was inside her blouse and her skirt was piled up on her lap, and his right hand was resting on the lever which would lower the seats. Then she pulled away, making a noise down inside her throat.

His head snapped to the left.

He saw the walking man.

He saw the profile which never turned to face him fully. He saw that the man's gait did not alter.

Then he did not see the man.

There was a slight jar, and the windshield began cleaning itself. Cecil Green raced on.

He opaqued the windows.

"How . . . ?" he asked after she was in his arms again, and sobbing.

"The monitor didn't pick him up . . . . "

"He must not have touched the fence . . . . "

"He must have been out of his mind!"

"Still, he could have picked an easier way."

It could have been any face . . . Mine?

Frightened, Cecil lowered the seats.

*

Charles Render was writing the "Necropolis" chapter for *The Missing Link is Man*, which was to be his first book in over four years. Since his return he had set aside every Tuesday and Thursday afternoon to work on it, isolating himself in his office, filling pages with a chaotic longhand.

"There are many varieties of death, as opposed to dying . . . " he was writing, just as the intercom buzzed briefly, then long, then briefly again.

"Yes?" he asked it, pushing down on the switch.

"You have a visitor," and there was a short intake of breath between "a" and "visitor."

He slipped a small aerosol into his side pocket, then rose and crossed the office.

He opened the door and looked out.

"Doctor . . . Help . . . "

Render took three steps, then dropped to one knee.

"What's the matter?"

"Come—she is . . . sick," he growled.

"Sick? How? What's wrong?"

"Don't know. You come."

Render stared into the unhuman eyes.

"What kind of sick?" he insisted.

"Don't know," repeated the dog. "Won't talk. Sits. I . . . feel, she is sick."

"How did you get here?"

"Drove. Know the co, or, din, ates . . . Left car, outside."

"I'll call her right now." Render turned.

"No good. Won't answer."

He was right.

Render returned to his inner office for his coat and medkit. He glanced out the window and saw where her car was parked, far below, just inside the entrance to the marginal, where the monitor had released it into manual control. If no one assumed that control a car was automatically parked in neutral. The other vehicles were passed around it.

So simple even a dog can drive one, he reflected. *Better get downstairs before a cruiser comes along. It's probably reported itself stopped there already. Maybe not, though. Might still have a few minutes grace.*

He glanced at the huge clock.

"Okay, Sig," he called out. "Let's go."

The Magic

They took the lift to the ground floor, left by way of the front entrance and hurried to the car.

Its engine was still idling.

Render opened the passengerside door and Sigmund leaped in. He squeezed by him into the driver's seat then, but the dog was already pushing the primary coordinates and the address tabs with his paw.

Looks like I'm in the wrong seat.

He lit a cigarette as the car swept ahead into a U-underpass. It emerged on the opposite marginal, sat poised a moment, then joined the traffic flow. The dog directed the car into the high-acceleration lane.

"Oh," said the dog, "oh."

Render felt like patting his head at that moment, but he looked at him, saw that his teeth were bared, and decided against it.

"When did she start acting peculiar?" he asked.

"Came home from work. Did not eat. Would not answer me when I talked. Just sits."

"Has she ever been like this before?"

"No."

What could have precipitated it?—But maybe she just had a bad day. After all, he's only a dog—sort of. —No. He'd know. But what, then?

"How was she yesterday—and when she left home this morning?"

"Like always."

Render tried calling her again. There was still no answer.

"You did, it," said the dog.

"What do you mean?"

"Eyes. Seeing. You. Machine. Bad."

"No," said Render, and his hand rested on the unit of stun-spray in his pocket.

"Yes," said the dog, turning to him again. "You will, make her well . . . ?"

"Of course," said Render.

Sigmund stared ahead again.

Roger Zelazny and Samuel R. Delany

Render felt physically exhilarated and mentally sluggish. He sought the confusion factor. He had had these feelings about the case since that first session. There was something very unsettling about Eileen Shallot; a combination of high intelligence and helplessness, of determination and vulnerability, of sensitivity and bitterness.

Do I find that especially attractive?—No. It's just the counter-transference, damn it!

"You smell afraid," said the dog.

"Then color me afraid," said Render, "and turn the page."

They slowed for a series of turns, picked up speed again, slowed again, picked up speed again. Finally, they were traveling along a narrow section of roadway through a semi-residential area of town. The car turned up a side street, proceeded about half a mile further, clicked softly beneath its dashboard, and turned into the parking lot behind a high brick apartment building. The click must have been a special servomech which took over from the point where the monitor released it, because the car crawled across the lot, headed into its transparent parking stall, then stopped. Render turned off the ignition.

Sigmund had already opened the door on his side. Render followed him into the building, and they rode the elevator to the fiftieth floor. The dog dashed on ahead up the hallway, pressed his nose against a plate set low in a doorframe and waited. After a moment, the door swung several inches inward. He pushed it open with his shoulder and entered. Render followed, closing the door behind him.

The apartment was large, its walls pretty much unadorned, its color combinations unnerving. A great library of tapes filled one corner; a monstrous combination-broadcaster stood beside it. There was a wide bowlegged table set in front of the window, and a low couch along the right-hand wall; there was a closed door beside the couch: an archway to the left apparently led to other rooms. Eileen sat in an overstuffed chair in the far corner by the window. Sigmund stood beside the chair.

Render crossed the room and extracted a cigarette from his case. Snapping open his lighter, he held the flame until her head turned in that direction.

The Magic

"Cigarette?" he asked.

"Charles?"

"Right."

"Yes, thank you. I will."

She held out her hand, accepted the cigarette, put it to her lips.

"Thanks. —What are you doing here?"

"Social call. I happened to be in the neighborhood."

"I didn't hear a buzz or a knock."

"You must have been dozing. Sig let me in."

"Yes, I must have." She stretched. "What time is it?"

"It's close to four-thirty."

"I've been home over two hours then . . . . Must have been very tired . . . "

"How do you feel now?"

"Fine," she declared. "Care for a cup of coffee?"

"Don't mind if I do."

"A steak to go with it?"

"No, thanks."

"Bacardi in the coffee?"

"Sounds good."

"Excuse me, then. It'll only take a moment."

She went through the door beside the sofa and Render caught a glimpse of a large, shiny, automatic kitchen.

"Well?" he whispered to the dog.

Sigmund shook his head.

"Not same."

Render shook his head.

He deposited his coat on the sofa, folding it carefully about the medkit. He sat beside it and thought.

Did I throw too big a chunk of seeing at once? Is she suffering from depressive side-effects—say, memory repressions, nervous fatigue? Did I upset her sensory-adaptation syndrome somehow? Why have I been proceeding so rapidly anyway? There's no real hurry. Am I so damned eager to write the thing up?—Or am I doing it because she wants me to? Could she be that strong, consciously or unconsciously? Or am I that vulnerable—somehow?

She called him to the kitchen to carry out the tray. He set it on the table and seated himself across from her.

"Good coffee," he said, burning his lips on the cup.

"Smart machine," she stated, facing his voice.

Sigmund stretched out on the carpet next to the table, lowered his head between his forepaws, sighed and closed his eyes.

"I've been wondering," said Render, "whether or not there were any after effects to that last session—like increased synesthesiac experiences, or dreams involving forms, or hallucinations or . . . "

"Yes," she said flatly, "dreams."

"What kind?"

"That last session. I've dreamed it over, and over."

"Beginning to end?"

"No, there's no special order to the events. We're riding through the city, or over the bridge, or sitting at the table, or walking toward the car—just flashes, like that. Vivid ones."

"What sort of feelings accompany these—flashes?"

"I don't know, they're all mixed up."

"What are your feelings now, as you recall them?"

"The same, all mixed up."

"Are you afraid?"

"N-no. I don't think so."

"Do you want to take a vacation from the thing? Do you feel we've been proceeding too rapidly?"

"No. That's not it at all. It's—well, it's like learning to swim. When you finally learn how, why then you swim and you swim and you swim until you're all exhausted. Then you just lie there gasping in air and remembering what it was like, while your friends all hover and chew you out for overexerting yourself—and it's a good feeling, even though you do take a chill and there are pins and needles inside all your muscles. At least, that's the way I do things. I felt that way after the first session and after this last one. First Times are always very special times . . . . The pins and the needles are gone, though, and I've caught my breath again. Lord, I don't want to stop now! I feel fine."

"Do you usually take a nap in the afternoon?"

The ten red nails of her fingers moved across the tabletop as she stretched.

" . . . Tired," she smiled, swallowing a yawn. "Half the staff's on vacation or sick leave and I've been beating my brains out all week. I was about ready to fall on my face when I left work. I feel all right now that I've rested, though."

She picked up her coffee cup with both hands, took a large swallow.

"Uh-huh." he said. "Good. I was a bit worried about you. I'm glad to see there was no reason."

She laughed.

"Worried? You've read Doctor Riscomb's notes on my analysis—and on the ONT&R trial—and you think I'm the sort to worry about? Ha! I have an operationally beneficent neurosis concerning my adequacy as a human being. It focuses my energies, coordinates my efforts toward achievement. It enhances my sense of identity . . . . "

"You do have one hell of a memory," he noted. "That's almost verbatim."

"Of course."

"You had Sigmund worried today, too."

"Sig? How?"

The dog stirred uneasily, opened one eye.

"Yes," he growled, glaring up at Render. "He needs, a ride, home."

"Have you been driving the car again?"

"Yes."

"After I told you not to?"

"Yes."

"Why?"

"I was a, fraid. You would, not, answer me, when I talked."

"I was *very* tired—and if you ever take the car again, I'm going to have the door fixed so you can't come and go as you please."

"Sorry."

"There's nothing wrong with me."

"I, see."

"You are *never* to do it again."

"Sorry." His eye never left Render; it was like a burning lens.

Render looked away.

"Don't be too hard on the poor fellow," he said. "After all, he thought you were ill and he went for the doctor. Suppose he'd been right? You'd owe him thanks, not a scolding."

Unmollified, Sigmund glared a moment longer and closed his eye.

"He has to be told when he does wrong," she finished.

"I suppose," he said, drinking his coffee. "No harm done, anyhow. Since I'm here, let's talk shop. I'm writing something and I'd like an opinion."

"Great. Give me a footnote?"

"Two or three. —In your opinion, do the general underlying motivations that lead to suicide differ in different periods of history or in different cultures?"

"My well-considered opinion is no, they don't," she said. "Frustrations can lead to depressions or frenzies; and if these are severe enough, they can lead to self-destruction. You ask me about motivations and I think they stay pretty much the same. I feel this is a cross-cultural, cross-temporal aspect of the human condition. I don't think it could be changed without changing the basic nature of man."

"Okay. Check. Now, what of the inciting element?" he asked. "Let man be a constant, his environment is still a variable. If he is placed in an overprotective life-situation, do you feel it would take more or less to depress him—or stimulate him to frenzy—than it would take in a not so protective environment?"

"Hm. Being case-oriented, I'd say it would depend on the man. But I see what you're driving at: a mass predisposition to jump out windows at the drop of a hat—the window even opening itself for you, because you asked it to—the revolt of the bored masses. I don't like the notion. I hope it's wrong."

"So do I, but I was thinking of symbolic suicides too—functional disorders that occur for pretty flimsy reasons."

"Aha! Your lecture last month: autopsychomimesis. I have the tape. Well-told, but I can't agree."

"Neither can I, now. I'm rewriting that whole section—'Thanatos in Cloudcuckooland,' I'm calling it. It's really the death-instinct moved nearer the surface."

"If I get you a scalpel and a cadaver, will you cut out the death-instinct and let me touch it?"

"Couldn't," he put the grin into his voice, "it would be all used up in a cadaver. Find me a volunteer though, and he'll prove my case by volunteering."

"Your logic is unassailable," she smiled. "Get us some more coffee, okay?"

Render went to the kitchen, spiked and filled the cups, drank a glass of water and returned to the living room. Eileen had not moved; neither had Sigmund.

"What do you do when you're not busy being a Shaper?" she asked him.

"The same things most people do—eat, drink, sleep, talk, visit friends and not-friends, visit places, read . . . "

"Are you a forgiving man?"

"Sometimes. Why?"

"Then forgive me. I argued with a woman today, a woman named De Ville."

"What about?"

"You—and she accused me of such things it were better my mother had not born me. Are you going to marry her?"

"No, marriage is like alchemy. It served an important purpose once, but I hardly feel it's here to stay."

"Good."

"What did you say to her?"

"I gave her a clinic referral card that said, 'Diagnosis: Bitch. Prescription: Drug therapy and a tight gag.'"

"Oh," said Render, showing interest.

"She tore it up and threw it in my face."

"I wonder why?"

She shrugged, smiled, made a gridwork on the tablecloth.

"'Fathers and elders, I ponder,'" sighed Render, "'what is hell?'"

"'I maintain it is the suffering of being unable to love,'" she finished. "Was Dostoevsky right?"

"I doubt it I'd put him into group therapy myself. That'd be *real* hell for him—with all those people acting like his characters and enjoying it so."

Render put down his cup and pushed his chair away from the table.

"I suppose you must be going now?"

"I really should," said Render.

"And I can't interest you in food?"

"No."

She stood.

"Okay, I'll get my coat."

"I could drive back myself and just set the car to return."

"No! I'm frightened by the notion of empty cars driving around the city. I'd feel the thing was haunted for the next two-and-a-half weeks.

"Besides," she said, passing through the archway, "you promised me Winchester Cathedral."

"You want to do it today?"

"If you can be persuaded."

As Render stood deciding, Sigmund rose to his feet. He stood directly before him and stared upward into his eyes. He opened his mouth and closed it, several times, but no sounds emerged. Then he turned away and left the room.

"No," Eileen's voice came back, "you will stay here until I return."

Render picked up his coat and put it on, stuffing the medkit into the far pocket.

The Magic

As they walked up the hall toward the elevator Render thought he heard a very faint and very distant howling sound.

*

In this place, of all places. Render knew he was the master of all things.

He was at home on those alien worlds, without time, those worlds where flowers copulate and the stars do battle in the heavens, falling at last to the ground, bleeding, like so many split and shattered chalices, and the seas part to reveal stairways leading down, and arms emerge from caverns, waving torches that flame like liquid faces—a midwinter night's nightmare, summer go a-begging, Render know—for he had visited those worlds on a professional basis for the better part of a decade. With the crooking of a finger he could isolate the sorcerors, bring them to trial for treason against the realm—aye, and he could execute them, could appoint their successors.

Fortunately, this trip was only a courtesy call . . .

He moved forward through the glade, seeking her.

He could feel her awakening presence all about him.

He pushed through the branches, stood beside the lake. It was cold, blue, and bottomless, the lake, reflecting that slender willow which had become the station of her arrival.

"Eileen!"

The willow swayed toward him, swayed away.

"Eileen! Come forth!"

Leaves fell, floated upon the lake, disturbed its mirrorlike placidity, distorted the reflections.

"Eileen?"

All the leaves yellowed at once then, dropped down into the water. The tree ceased its swaying. There was a strange sound in the darkening sky, like the humming of high wires on a cold day.

Suddenly there was a double file of moons passing through the heavens.

Render selected one, reached up and pressed it. The others vanished as he did so, and the world brightened; the humming went out of the air.

He circled the lake to gain a subjective respite from the rejection-action and his counter to it. He moved up along an aisle of pines toward the place where he wanted the cathedral to occur. Birds sang now in the trees. The wind came softly by him. He felt her presence quite strongly.

"Here, Eileen. Here."

She walked beside him then, green silk, hair of bronze, eyes of molten emerald; she wore an emerald in her forehead. She walked in green slippers over the pine needles, saying: "What happened?"

"You were afraid."

"Why?"

"Perhaps you fear the cathedral. Are you a witch?" he smiled.

"Yes, but it's my day off."

He laughed, and he took her arm, and they rounded an island of foliage, and there was the cathedral reconstructed on a grassy rise, pushing its way above them and above the trees, climbing into the middle air, breathing out organ notes, reflecting a stray ray of sunlight from a plane of glass.

"Hold tight to the world," he said. "Here comes the guided tour."

They moved forward and entered.

"' . . . With its floor-to-ceiling shafts, like so many huge tree trunks, it achieves a ruthless control over its spaces,'" he said. "—Got that from the guidebook. This is the north transept . . . . "

"'Greensleeves,'" she said, "the organ is playing 'Greensleeves.'"

"So it is. You can't blame me for that though. —Observe the scalloped capitals—"

"I want to go nearer to the music."

"Very well. This way then."

Render felt that something was wrong. He could not put his finger on it. Everything retained its solidity . . . .

Something passed rapidly then, high above the cathedral, uttering a sonic boom. Render smiled at that, remembering now; it was like a slip of the tongue: for a moment he had confused Eileen with Jill—yes, that was what had happened.

The Magic

Why, then . . .

A burst of white was the altar. He had never seen it before, anywhere. All the walls were dark and cold about them. Candles flickered in corners and high niches. The organ chorded thunder under invisible hands.

Render knew that something was wrong.

He turned to Eileen Shallot, whose hat was a green cone towering up into the darkness, trailing wisps of green veiling. Her throat was in shadow, but . . .

"That necklace—Where?"

"I don't know," she smiled.

The goblet she held radiated a rosy light. It was reflected from her emerald. It washed him like a draft of cool air.

"Drink?" she asked.

"Stand still," he ordered.

He willed the walls to fall down. They swam in shadow.

"Stand still!" he repeated urgently. "Don't do anything. Try not even to think.

"—Fall down!" he cried. And the wails were blasted in all directions and the roof was flung over the top of the world, and they stood amid ruins lighted by a single taper. The night was black as pitch.

"Why did you do that?" she asked, still holding the goblet out toward him.

"Don't think. Don't think anything," he said. "Relax. You are very tired. As that candle flickers and wanes so does your consciousness. You can barely keep awake. You can hardly stay on your feet. Your eyes are closing. There is nothing to see here anyway."

He willed the candle to go out. It continued to burn.

"I'm not tired. Please have a drink."

He heard organ music through the night. A different tune, one he did not recognize at first.

"I need your cooperation."

"All right. Anything."

"Look! The moon!" he pointed.

She looked upward and the moon appeared from behind an inky cloud.

" . . . And another, and another."

Moons, like strung pearls, proceeded across the blackness.

"The last one will be red," he stated.

It was.

He reached out then with his right index finger, slid his arm sideways along his field of vision, then tried to touch the red moon.

His arm ached, it burned. He could not move it.

"Wake up!" he screamed.

The red moon vanished, and the white ones.

"Please take a drink."

He dashed the goblet from her hand and turned away. When he turned back she was still holding it before him.

"A drink?"

He turned and fled into the night.

It was like running through a waist-high snowdrift. It was wrong. He was compounding the error by running—he was minimizing his strength, maximizing hers. It was sapping his energies, draining him.

He stood still in the midst of the blackness.

"The world around me moves," he said. "I am its center."

"Please have a drink." she said, and he was standing in the glade beside their table set beside the lake. The lake was black and the moon was silver, and high, and out of his reach. A single candle flickered on the table, making her hair as silver as her dress. She wore the moon on her brow. A bottle of Romanée-Conti stood on the white cloth beside a wide-brimmed wine glass. It was filled to overflowing, that glass, and rosy beads clung to its lip. He was very thirsty, and she was lovelier than anyone he had ever seen before, and her necklace sparkled, and the breeze came cool off the lake, and there was something—something he should remember . . . .

He took a step toward her and his armor clinked lightly as he moved. He reached toward the glass and his right arm stiffened with pain and fell back to his side.

The Magic

"You are wounded!"

Slowly, he turned his head. The blood flowed from the open wound in his biceps and ran down his arm and dripped from his fingertips. His armor had been breached. He forced himself to look away.

"Drink this, love. It will heal you."

She stood.

"I will hold the glass."

He stared at her as she raised it to his lips.

"Who am I?" he asked.

She did not answer him, but something replied—within a splashing of waters out over the lake:

"You are Render, the Shaper."

"Yes, I remember," he said; and turning his mind to the one lie which might break the entire illusion he forced his mouth to say: "Eileen Shallot, I hate you."

The world shuddered and swam about him, was shaken, as by a huge sob.

"Charles!" she screamed, and the blackness swept over them.

"Wake up! Wake up!" he cried, and his right arm burned and ached and bled in the darkness.

He stood alone in the midst of a white plain. It was silent, it was endless. It sloped away toward the edges of the world. It gave off its own light, and the sky was no sky, but was nothing overhead. Nothing. He was alone. His own voice echoed back to him from the end of the world: " . . . hate you," it said, " . . . hate you."

He dropped to his knees. He was Render.

He wanted to cry.

A red moon appeared above the plain, casting a ghastly light over the entire expanse. There was a wall of mountains to the left of him, another to his right.

He raised his right arm. He helped it with his left hand, He clutched his wrist, extended his index finger. He reached for the moon.

Roger Zelazny and Samuel R. Delany

Then there came a howl from high in the mountains, a great wailing cry—half-human, all challenge, all loneliness and all remorse. He saw it then, treading upon the mountains, its tail brushing the snow from their highest peaks, the ultimate loupgarou of the North—Fernis, son of Loki—raging at the heavens.

It leaped into the air. It swallowed the moon.

It landed near him, and its great eyes blazed yellow. It stalked him on soundless pads, across the cold white fields that lay between the mountains; and he backed away from it, up hills and down slopes, over crevasses and rifts, through valleys, past stalagmites and pinnacles—under the edges of glaciers, beside frozen river beds, and always downwards—until its hot breath bathed him and its laughing mouth was opened above him.

He turned then and his feet became two gleaming rivers carrying him away.

The world jumped backward. He glided over the slopes, Downward. Speeding—

Away . . .

He looked back over his shoulder.

In the distance, the gray shape loped after him.

He felt that it could narrow the gap if it chose. He had to move faster.

The world reeled about him. Snow began to fall.

He raced on.

Ahead, a blur, a broken outline.

He tore through the veils of snow which now seemed to be falling upward from off the ground—like strings of bubbles.

He approached the shattered form.

Like a swimmer he approached—unable to open his mouth to speak for fear of drowning—of drowning and not knowing, of never knowing.

He could not check his forward motion; he was swept tide-like toward the wreck. He came to a stop, at last, before it.

Some things never change. They are things which have long ceased to exist as objects and stand solely as never-to-be-calendared occasions outside that sequence of elements called Time.

The Magic

Render stood there and did not care if Fenris leaped upon his back and ate his brains. He had covered his eyes, but he could not stop the seeing. Not this time. He did not care about anything. Most of himself lay dead at his feet.

There was a howl. A gray shape swept past him.

The baleful eyes and bloody muzzle rooted within the wrecked car, chomping through the steel, the glass, groping inside for . . .

"No! Brute! Chewer of corpses!" he cried. "The dead are sacred! My dead are sacred!"

He had a scalpel in his hand then, and he slashed expertly at the tendons, the bunches of muscle on the straining shoulders, the soft belly, the ropes of the arteries.

Weeping, he dismembered the monster, limb by limb, and it bled and it bled, fouling the vehicle and the remains within it with its infernal animal juices, dripping and running until the whole plain was reddened and writhing about them.

Render fell across the pulverized hood, and it was soft and warm and dry. He wept upon it.

"Don't cry," she said.

He was hanging onto her shoulder then, holding her tightly, there beside the black lake beneath the moon that was Wedgewood. A single candle flickered upon their table, She held the glass to his lips.

"Please drink it."

"Yes, give it to me!"

He gulped the wine that was all softness and lightness. It burned within him. He felt his strength returning.

"I am . . ."

"—Render, the Shaper," splashed the lake.

"No!"

He turned and ran again, looking for the wreck. He had to go back, to return . . .

"You can't."

"I can!" he cried. "I can, if I try . . . . "

Yellow flames coiled through the thick air. Yellow serpents. They coiled, glowing, about his ankles. Then through the murk, two-headed and towering, approached his Adversary.

Small stones rattled past him. An overpowering odor corkscrewed up his nose and into his head.

"Shaper!" came the bellow from one head.

"You have returned for the reckoning!" called the other.

Render stared, remembering.

"No reckoning, Thaumiel," he said. "I beat you and I chained you for—Rothman, yes, it was Rothman—the cabalist." He traced a pentagram in the air. "Return to Qliphoth. I banish you."

"This place be Qliphoth."

" . . . By Khamael, the angel of blood by the hosts of Seraphim, in the Name of Elohim Gebor, I bid you vanish!"

"Not this time," laughed both heads.

It advanced.

Render backed slowly away, his feet bound by the yellow serpents. He could feel the chasm opening behind him. The world was a jigsaw puzzle coming apart. He could see the pieces separating.

"Vanish!"

The giant roared out its double-laugh.

Render stumbled.

"This way, love!"

She stood within a small cave to his right.

He shook his head and backed toward the chasm.

Thaumiel reached out toward him.

Render toppled back over the edge.

"Charles!" she screamed, and the world shook itself apart with her wailing.

"Then *Vernichtung*," he answered as he fell. "I join you in darkness."

Everything came to an end.

*

295

The Magic

"I want to see Doctor Charles Render."

"I'm sorry, that is impossible."

"But I skip-jetted all the way here, just to thank him. I'm a new man! He changed my life!"

"I'm sorry, Mister Erikson. When you called this morning, I told you it was impossible."

"Sir, I'm Representative Erikson—and Render once did me a great service."

"Then you can do him one now. Go home."

"You can't talk to me that way!"

"I just did. Please leave. Maybe next year sometime . . . "

"But a few words can do wonders . . . . "

"Save them!"

"I-I'm sorry . . . "

*

Lovely as it was, pinked over with the morning—the slopping, steaming bowl of the sea—he knew that it *had* to end. Therefore . . .

He descended the high tower stairway and he entered the courtyard. He crossed to the bower of roses and he looked down upon the pallet set in its midst.

"Good morrow, m'lord," he said.

"To you the same," said the knight, his blood mingling with the earth, the flowers, the grasses, flowed from his wound, sparkling over his armor, dripping from his fingertips.

"Naught hath healed?"

The knight shook his head.

"I empty. I wait."

"Your waiting is near ended."

"What mean you?" He sat upright.

"The ship. It approacheth harbor."

The knight stood. He leaned his back against a mossy tree trunk. He stared at the huge, bearded servitor who continued to speak, words harsh with barbaric accents:

"It cometh like a dark swan before the wind—returning."

"Dark, say you? Dark?"

"The sails be black, Lord Tristram."

"You lie!"

"Do you wish to see? To see for yourself—Look then!"

He gestured.

The earth quaked, the wall toppled. The dust swirled and settled. From where they stood they could see the ship moving into the harbor on the wings of the night.

"No! You lied!—See! They are white!"

The dawn danced upon the waters. The shadows fled from the ship's sails.

"No, you fool! Black! They *must* be!"

"White! White!—Isolde! You have kept faith. You have returned!"

He began running toward the harbor.

"Come back—Your wound! You are ill—Stop . . . "

The sails were white beneath a sun that was a red button which the servitor reached quickly to touch.

Night fell.

A Word from Zelazny

"This is the original novella for which they gave me a Nebula Award at the first, very formal SFWA banquet at the Overseas Press Club, and which I later expanded at Damon Knight's suggestion into the book *The Dream Master*. The novel contains some material that I am very happy to have written, but reflecting upon things after the passage of all this time I find that I prefer this, the shorter version. It is more streamlined and as such comes closer to the quasi-Classical notions I had in mind, in terms of economy and directions, in describing a great man with a flaw."[2]

Of three points to reveal about the story, he wrote, "1) I wanted a triangle situation, two women and one man, as I had never written one before. 2) I wanted a character loosely based on a figure in a classical tragedy—exceptional, and bearing a flaw that would smash him. 3) I have never been overfond of German shepherds, as there were two which used to harass my dog when I was a boy.

"I like 'The Ides of Octember' for the background rather than the foreground. I thought it an effective setting for the Rougemont-Wagner death-wish business. I dislike it because Render turned out to be too stuffy for the figure I was trying to portray and Jill was far too flat a character."[3]

"'Ides of Octember' was written with the notion of developing a character along tragic lines, in the classical sense. While an attempt was made to observe unities of time and space, I did try to 'streamline' the story line by including only the materials I deemed absolutely necessary for the realization of Render in terms of the rhythms of the form. When I was done, I felt that I had achieved what I'd set out to do."[4]

This story is heavily laden with allusions and symbols, perhaps the most of any of Zelazny's works (see the notes below for an explanation of many of them). Zelazny felt that the myths in his stories were more than mere decoration, that his intent was to magnify the universality and significance of his themes.[5]

Theodore Sturgeon was likely thinking of this story when he remarked "One feels at times that a few (a very few, I hasten to add) of his more vivid turns of phrase would benefit by an application of Dulcote (an artists' material, a transparent spray which uniformly pulls down brightness and gloss where applied). Not because they aren't beautiful—because most of them are, God knows—but because even so deft a wordsmith as Zelazny can forget from time to time that such a creation can keep a reader from his speedy progress from here to there, and that his furniture should be placed out of the traffic pattern. If I bang my shin on a coffee table it becomes a little beside the point that it is the most exquisitely crafted artifact this side of the Sun King. Especially since it was the Author himself who put me in a dead run. And there is the matter of exotic references—the injection of one of those absolutely precise and therefore untranslatable German philosophic terms, or a citation from classical mythology. This is a difficult thing to criticize without being misunderstood."[6] Zelazny also described this story as

Roger Zelazny and Samuel R. Delany

"the fruit of an abandoned psychology major and several undergraduate years of part-time employment as a research assistant in my psych department's lab, as well as a lot of other stuff. I wrote it in 1964, and it was the longest piece I had done at that time."[7]

"Ides of Octember" was Zelazny's original and preferred title, but editor Cele Goldsmith changed it to "He Who Shapes." It later contributed to the screenplay of the movie *Dreamscape*. Although Zelazny worked for a time on the screenplay and was paid for the rights to his story, the final screenplay bore little resemblance to Zelazny's work, and his name was not in the credits.

Notes

Render is an especially appropriate name for the main character because it is a contronym, a word that means two opposite things: "to rend" can mean to create or draw, and "to rend" can mean exactly the opposite: to destroy or tear down. Charles Render is that sort of conflicted personality in this story. As well, "render" can mean to surrender or yield, to tell or narrate, to boil down to the essence, to give something up, to interpret—and Render fulfills all of these meanings in the story. A subtle running joke is that the secretary who disapproves of Render's smoking is named **Mrs. Bennie Hedges** (as in Benson & Hedges, a brand of cigarette)—but Zelazny carefully calls her by either her first or her last name, and not the two together.

It was **Caesar** who was stabbed to death by Brutus and company, not **Marcus Antonius** who succeeded him. The soothsayer warned Caesar to beware the Ides of March; Render alters the dream to warn of the **Ides of Octember**, which is a variant spelling of October that was sometimes seen since Roman times (October is *not* based on a book by Dr. Seuss since the latter came out in 1977). In Greek mythology, **Medusa** had hair made of living snakes, which is likened to Render's helmet with multiple leads or cables connecting him to the ro-womb's circuitry. **Aquiline** means like an eagle; in this case, Render's nose is like an eagle's beak. In Dante Alighieri's *The Divine Comedy* (a trilogy that includes *Inferno*, *Purgaturio* and *Paradiso*),

The Magic

trimmers were blase cowards who were denied heaven for lack of virtues and denied hell for lack of vices. **Cathecting** or cathexis means concentrating (possibly too much) mental energy on one person, idea, or object. An **Astrakhan** is a rug made of lamb's wool from the Russian territory of the same name; Zelazny collected rugs and dropped names of specific ones he owned into his fiction. **Esthetic** is the appreciation of beauty, or pleasure given by the beauty of a thing. **Mimesis** means simulation, and by "**mimesis of aberrance**" Render means that the simulated madness or abnormal behavior of someone's mind will not make him mad too; he will remain a **Sane Hatter** instead of becoming the Mad Hatter of *Alice's Adventures in Wonderland*.

The gaze of the **basilisk** caused sudden death; **Medusa's** could turn a man to stone. **Chimerae** are animals or things created out of various assembled parts, such as the mythological fire-breathing female monster with a lion's head, a goat's body, and a serpent's tail. The **caduceus** is one symbol of the medical profession with two snakes wrapped around a staff (one snake around a staff is the medical symbol of Aescalapius); Render is arrogantly declaring that even Medusa would bow to his medical authority and close her killing, petrifying gaze. **Thomas Mann** was the Nobel Prize-winning author of *The Magic Mountain* (a favorite of Zelazny's) and other highly symbolic novels that explored the psychology of the artist and intellectual. **He could visualize so clearly . . . somewhere skulls were whitening** is Render recalling the auto accident and drowning that claimed the lives of his wife and daughter. A **shallot** is an onion which implies that **Doctor Eileen Shallot** has many layers of psyche to be peeled by the psychiatrist. On the other hand, the name foreshadows a tragic ending: Alfred Lord Tennyson's *Lady of Shalott* falls in love with Sir Lancelot, but he cannot return her love (he is in love with Guinevere), and the Lady of Shalott dies of grief. As well, Malory tells the same tale of *Elayne of Ascolat* (in *The Fair Maid of Ascolat*) who has a futile, fatal love for Sir Lancelot; the name Elayne of Ascolat also suggests that of Eileen Shallot.

Roger Zelazny and Samuel R. Delany

When Render first encounters her, Shallot is wearing a green dress with a gold pin to the left that consists of a ruby surrounded by the outlines of a goblet, or two faces (profiles) staring toward each other through the ruby, and the pin reminds him of something he cannot recall. She wears a silver disk on her forehead that enables her to "see." He will later note that her eyes are green and disapprove of this. These are early clues that Shallot is also **Isolde**, of which more is explained at the end of this essay. According to an interview with Zelazny[8], the pin mentioned was one designed by artist Salvador Dali, entitled "Tristan & Isolde"—it depicts the profiles of Tristan and Isolde in gold, forming a circle; they face each other with eyes closed; the enchanted crystal cup stands between them, filled with red wine. (Dali also did a surrealistic painting of the same title.) In a letter, Zelazny admitted that Dali's pin was too large to be worn and that he had in mind a reduced version of it; he hadn't expected anyone to recognize it from the description, but critic Sandra Miesel (in her article "Love is Madness") did.[9,10] The reflective, silver disc on the forehead of Shallot—which later appears as an emerald to Render in the dream state—also suggests the Lady of Shalott, who perceived much of reality through the mirror that she constantly faced in her lonely tower.

The **Menninger** Clinic in Houston, Texas, is an international center of excellence in psychiatric research, treatment and education. The book title **Why No Psychometrics in This Place** is a complex inside joke: **psychometrics** is the field that involves quantitative measurement of educational and psychological attributes, such as intelligence and personality tests. On the other hand, Render works directly in the chaos of the mind where normal rules and even **non-Euclidean geometry** do not apply; hence, psychometrics do not work in the mind because nothing can be measured there.

Chambertin is wine that comes from the vineyard in the village of Gevry-Chambertin in France's Burgundy region. The dog **Sigmund** is named for the psychiatrist Sigmund Freud, founder of psychoanalysis. Freud theorized that our consciousness is strongly influenced by past events (childhood, parenthood, etc.) and unconscious thought (dreams, sexual desires, etc). The presence of Sigmund reminds us that Render's technique of exploring a patient's mind directly is an extension of Freud's psychoanalysis and the particular importance that Freud gave to sexuality in motivating a person's desires. **Winged seraphs** are guardian angels. **Pulpefaction** is to reduce tissue to a pulpy mass; **contusions** are bruises and injuries that do not break the skin. Sufficient **gluteal stamina** is another way of saying that one's buttocks (*gluteus maximus* muscles) haven't become sore from sitting too long.

"**Here's looking at you**" may deliberately echo Humphrey Bogart's line from *Casablanca* (one of Zelazny's favorite movies) and foreshadow that Dr. Shallot has the more dominant personality. The **Socratic game** is a teaching method where the teacher asks pupils questions rather than telling them the information; it will not work if two people are asking questions and neither is answering them. **Minarets** are tall, slender towers with balconies, usually found on a mosque. **Xanadu** means place of great beauty; rather than a seaharbor of Atlantis, the name is usually associated with the summer palace of Kublai Khan. "**Full fathom five thy father lies**" comes from Shakespeare's *The Tempest* and means sinking or drowning at sea.

Georgia O'Keeffe was an American painter chiefly known for abstract paintings of flowers, rocks, shells, animal bones and landscapes. **Mongoloid idiot** is an outdated and now pejorative term for Down Syndrome, a genetic condition. **Neurosis** (plural: neuroses, mentioned later) is a mild mental illness or personality disorder in which the patient is still in touch with reality, whereas sense of reality is lost in a **psychosis**. An example of a neurosis is hypochondria, which also involves symptoms such as insecurity, anxiety, depression, and irrational fears. A **maelstrom** means a violent whirlpool, or a confusing state of movement (turbulence) and upheaval. The **rate of suicide among medical doctors and lawyers** is not as high as claimed in the story, but psychiatrists do have the highest rate among medical doctors. **Trotskyite** means a follower of Leon Trotsky, who promoted Marxist theory and left-wing policies. **St. Moritz and Davos** are two ski destinations in Switzerland. **Beethoven** suffered from manic-depression (bipolar disorder) and may have attempted suicide; his moodiness and his progressive deafness are thought to have been crucial components of his creativity. **Psychomimesis** is the imitation of psychiatric disease of another, or hysterical simulation of psychiatric disease (e.g., hysterical blindness); **autopsychomimesis** is a term that Render made up to mean a self-perpetuated imitation complex for which attention-getting is a secondary benefit (e.g., pretending to be depressed to gain attention). The modern medical term for this is Factitious Disorder. Cervantes' novel *Don Quixote* features the minor landowner, Alonso Quixano, who by reading too much fantasy deluded himself into thinking that he is a knight errant or hero, an example of **autopsychomimesis**. **Fenris** (son of Loki) was a huge wolf destined to devour Odin, the one-eyed chief god of Norse mythology; Render is identifying with Odin and seeing Sigmund as his doom. Render's ashtray displays a world map, which is why he was able to put out his cigarette near **Madagascar**. A **leitmotif** is a recurring musical theme, and some portion of Richard Wagner's epic *Ring Cycle* or (more likely) his *Tristan and Isolde* is implied. **Ottorino Respighi** was an Italian composer whose works included the symphony *Pines of Rome*. **Omnichannel Neural T & R Unit**—the letters stand for Transmission and Receiver.

His main annoyance was, of course, the fact that she was his patient . . . means that Render would rather have her as a lover, but he is inhibited with her as his patient. **Immanent** means inherent or existing within something. The **willow tree** is a symbol for the Lady of Shalott; the poem by Tennyson refers to the willow four times. As well, the recurrent reference to regarding a reflection in the water alludes to the Lady of Shalott, who regarded the world through the reflection in her mirror (she faced away from her window). **Damask** is a woven fabric with a pattern visible on both sides. Render's **armor** glints in the sun, suggesting that Shalott perceives him as her knight in shining armor, both Lancelot to her Lady of Shalott, and Tristan to her Isolde; the significance is that Eileen Shallot's mental strength has forced Render to manifest in the armor. **Mana** is power of supernatural origin that may be concentrated in a person; **libido** is sexual desire or energy.

The Magic

Karl Jung was a psychiatrist whose unique approach emphasized understanding the psyche through exploring dreams, art, mythology, world religion and philosophy. He was originally Freud's pupil, but he disagreed with Freud's notion that sexuality is more important than spirituality to a person's psychological development. **Iconoclasm** is the act of attacking or rejecting cherished beliefs or established values and practices. **Quixotism,** referring again to *Don Quixote*, is an impractical idealism sometimes involving imaginary or exaggerated enemies.

The **kraken** was a legendary sea monster off Norway which lurked in the ocean depths. A **mandala** is a geometric pattern or chart that can be used for focusing attention and meditating. The philosopher Chuang Tzu originally mused, "I dreamed I was a butterfly, flitting around in the sky; then I awoke. Now I wonder: Am I a man who dreamt of being a butterfly, or am I a butterfly dreaming that I am a man?" Render has rephrased it in terms of a **man dreaming that he is a robot. Hippocrates** was a Greek physician who is considered the father of modern medicine, and the Hippocratic Oath that physicians take upon graduation from medical school is named after him. The **lake-bottom vision** is the drowning death (and rotting corpses) of his wife and daughter in a sunken automobile. Norse mythology explained the moon's eclipse as the giant wolf **Fenris** periodically **devouring** and then regurgitating **the moon,** whereas the end of the world (Ragnarok) would be signaled in part by Fenris or his son Hati devouring the moon. As well, Fenris would kill the great Norse god Odin by swallowing him. This repeated reference to Fenris reinforces that Render identifies with Odin; the repeated reference to snow and ice throughout the tale are also consistent with a tale pertaining to Odin and the Norse.

Winchester Cathedral at Winchester in Hampshire is one of the largest cathedrals in England; construction was completed in 1093. **William the Conqueror** was the Duke of Normandy who invaded England in 1066 and became King William the First. **A tale out of Malory** implies Sir Thomas Malory and tales of King Arthur, the Knights of the Round Table, Sir Lancelot and Elayne the Maid of Ascolat (Lady of Shalott), and the tale of

Tristan and Isolde. **Bucolic** refers to the pleasant aspects of countryside and pastoral or country life.

"**For the love of God, Montresor!**" are the final desperate words spoken by Fortunato before being bricked in alive by his murderer Montresor in Edgar Allan Poe's "The Casque of Amontillado." The phrase *"Der geist der stets verneint. Pax vobiscum!"* and *"Alors!"* mixes German, Latin and French: "the spirit that always answers in the negative. Peace be with you! Then!" and is Render's expression of surrender to his girlfriends' wishes. **Wedgwood** is a brand of collectible, fine china. **Emery** is a hard mineral substance used for grinding and polishing. **Weissflujoch** is the mountain peak in Davos that features the longest ski run in Europe (12 miles and 6,000 foot drop) while **Dorftali** is a fast ski run on that mountain that leads directly into Davos.

The **hydra** was a mythological serpent possessed of many heads. **Orestes** was the mythological son of Agamemnon who was ordered by Apollo to kill his mother after she killed his father. After this matricide he was chased by the **Furies** (see afterword to "The Furies" by Zelazny) despite being acquitted of his crime by a tribunal. The quote suggests the play **Oresteia** by Aeschylus; the tale of Orestia has parallels to that of Oedipus, who unwittingly killed his own father and married his own mother. The psychiatrist **Hermann Rorschach** developed the famous ink blots which he thought would reveal personality by having patients interpret them. A **blazing goblet** suggests the legend of Tristan & Isolde again, or possibly the Holy Grail. **The Hall of the Nine Hearths** simply refers to the main hall of the ski resort at which Render was staying (which had nine fireplaces), but the name also suggests the recently mentioned Odin with whom the number nine is associated.

Dialectical is the art of arriving at the truth through a series of logical arguments. *Schnapsflasche* means a liquor bottle; *Nozdrovia!* or *Nazdrovia!* is "cheers!" in Polish and Russian (spelled phonetically) (and *Nozdrovia* is the title of the fanzine that Zelazny co-edited). *Moins-nausée* is less nausea or less nauseated; *"verfluchter!"* means 'most cursed', *"und so weiter"* would translate as "and so forth" or "and such" in the context of the sentence. An **artificer** is an inventor or skillful craftsman.

Shankara was an influential 9th century Hindu philosopher whose teachings ascribed all reality to a single unitary source, which he identified as "Brahma." The true ego could ascend to nirvana; whereas, false ego or sense of identity included **five** *skandhas* or groups of physical and psychic qualities that make up a human—form, sensation, perception, forces and consciousness. **Henrik Ibsen** was a 19th century Norwegian playwright and poet whose dramas were considered scandalous and immoral in the Victorian age when good should triumph and evil receive appropriate punishment. Ibsen's plays examined and revealed the realities that lay behind the facade, such as **The Master Builder,** that examined psychological conflicts within the main character. *Zwischenwelt* means between worlds, in this case the gap between Render and his patient's true ego, with the gap being filled up by *skandhas* and neuroses that Render must navigate and distinguish from the true nature of the patient. Render misleads his mentor not only by avoiding the question as to whether she is pretty, but by twice referring to Shallot as a **psychiatrist** when she is not: she is still in-training as a resident in psychiatry. **Alfred Adler** was an Austrian psychiatrist who emphasized the individual's desire to compensate for inferiorities; these motivations included the attainment of sexual goals; Bartelmetz knows that Render has a sexual interest in his patient Shallot (the feelings that a psychiatrist develops for the patients are termed **"counter-transference,"** mentioned later by Render). The psychiatric in-joke about Buddhists means that since Bartelmetz could not find a true ego in any Buddhist that he treated, therefore none of these Buddhists must be capable of achieving nirvana, since (as he explained earlier in the story) only the true ego can ascend to that state.

Mordant is caustic, burning, corrosive. **Macabre** is gruesome, ghostly or horrifying. **Pangloss** was a character in Voltaire's novel *Candide* whose philosophy was that "there is no effect without a cause"; even Peter's broken ankle is meant to suit a specific purpose. As well, Pangloss is considered a

Roger Zelazny and Samuel R. Delany

"flat character" whose few personality traits do not evolve throughout the story; this may be an in-joke, Zelazny's acknowledgment that Render's son had only a cursory characterization, just enough to indicate that, like his dad, he can quote literature too. **Bismarck** the hunting dog is named after the **Bismarck**, a famous German battleship from WWII, which in turn was named after the 19th century German chancellor Otto von Bismarck. **Solingen** is a city in Germany.

In Render's dreams he sees **Ouroboros**, the snake from Greek mythology which swallows its own tail and symbolizes a vicious cycle or the circularity of life; to Karl Jung, it represented the battle between the unconscious and conscious aspects of a person's psyche. In the context of references to Norse mythology, Render is probably mistaken about the identity—it must be Jormangund, the snake of Norse mythology which circles the world and also holds its tail in its mouth. Jormangund's appearance foretells Ragnarok, the end of the world. He also sees **Fenris** (described earlier) and a **cuckoo clock** (symbolizing foolishness or craziness). **Manolete** was a famous matador who died suddenly and unexpectedly when he was gored by the bull that he had just delivered the death stroke to; the newspapers declared "He died killing and he killed dying!" **Anise** is an herb related to parsley from which seeds and oils are used to flavor foods and liqueurs; **wormwood,** another herb, is used to flavor absinthe and certain wines. **Alexander Scriabin** was a Russian composer and pianist who claimed to see color in response to hearing musical notes, and he drew up a system that associated specific colors with each piano key; Shallot chooses this music after she has just remembered how colors look. **Muguel de Unamuno** was a Spanish essayist, poet and philosopher whose most famous work argued that humans desire immortality above all else, especially when faced with the certainty of death.

Seven ages of man refers to a soliloquy in Shakespeare's play *As You Like It*. **Romanée-Conti** is wine from a vineyard of the same name in Burgundy, whereas **Chateau d'Yquem** comes from the southern part of the Bordeaux vineyards known as Graves. Several terms related to wine tasting appear: *fruité*, having a bouquet and flavor which retains the taste of the grape;

charnu, fleshy, meaty, robust, full; *capiteux*, heady, warm and rich in alcohol. In Celtic and Greek mythology, **Isle of the Blest** is a mythical island of paradise, an afterlife for favored mortals. **He willed the world to end again, but it didn't** indicates not a suicidal gesture but Render's double-checking that he wasn't still in an illusion—he is already having doubts due to Shallot's ability to take control.

Francis Parkman was an American historian and essayist who traveled extensively and wrote a monumental seven volume history of the colonization of North America. **Mary Hunter Austin** spent 17 years studying Indian life in the Mojave Desert and writing about it. **Chicken stuff** or guts is a slang term for embroidered rank insignia on a uniform. **Mozart** wrote a dozen **String Quintets** or arrangements for stringed instruments among his many works. **Necropolis** means a large cemetery or burial ground. **The missing link** was a supposed animal midway in evolution between apes and humans. The book title is another way of saying "there is no missing link." **Synesthesia** is a condition in which one of the senses evokes a different sense, as when hearing a sound produces the visualization of color (the condition that the musician **Scriabin** claimed to have). **Beneficent** means doing good or resulting in good. **Mollified** is to appease someone's anger or irritation. **Thanatos** was the personification of Death in Greek mythology, while **Cloudcuckooland** comes from the ancient play *The Birds* by Athenian playwright Aristophanes and refers to an unrealistic, idealistic or perfect place.

The quote **"Fairies and elders, I ponder, what is hell? I maintain it is the suffering of being unable to love"** is from *The Brothers Karamazov* by **Dostoyevsky**, spoken by the elder monk Father Zossima, who has never been able to love. Like Lancelot, Render is unable to love Shallot—he is still mourning his dead wife and daughter, has thoughts of suicide, has a girlfriend (DeVille), and Shallot is his patient (many jurisdictions impose a lifetime ban on sexual relationships between psychiatrists and their current or former patients). **A midwinter night's nightmare** alludes to Shakespeare's romantic comedy *A Midsummer Night's Dream*, which portrays young lovers and actors interacting with fairies. Render is not in a romantic comedy or dream, but instead he is in a romantic tragedy or nightmare. **Greensleeves** is an old English ballad that tells a tale of unrequited love, and it is Eileen Shallot who has caused it to play. **The necklace** was meant by Zelazny to imply Brisingamen, the necklace of the Norse goddess Freyja; when she wore the necklace, no man or god could withstand her charms. **Loup garou** is a werewolf; Fenris swallows the moon, signifying Ragnarok (the end of the world) and swallows Odin as well during that final battle (Render has become Odin); Fenris also gruesomely attacks the dead bodies of Render's long-dead wife and daughter. **Thaumiel** was originally an angel of love, but after the fall became a demon with two giant heads and batlike wings; **Qlipoth** is the representation of evil in mystical teachings of Judaism. Appearing as a knight in shining armor, **Khamael,** an archangel in charge of the Sephira Geburah, symbolizes protection through skill with tools and reousrces. **Elohim Gebor** means Almighty God, and *vernichtung* means destruction.

The Arthurian legend of **Tristan and Isolde** is a complicated one with many variants of the tale and spelling of the principals' names (Tristan and Tristram, for example); Zelazny partially followed the version that Richard Wagner used in his opera of the same name, but he also referred to an incomplete version of the tale in the poem *Tristan* by Gottfried von Strassburg. [11] Tristan is a knight and nephew of King Mark; he is escorting Isolde to Cornwall where she will be married to the King. Isolde recognizes Tristan as her previous love who is now betraying her by giving her to King Mark. In revenge she makes Tristan drink a goblet of lethal poison and consumes some herself. Unbeknownst to her, it is not a poison but a love potion her maid prepared, and the two become lovers. Eventually, long after Isolde has married King Mark and Tristan has taken a wife (who, to further complicate the story, is also named Isolde), King Mark discovers the two lovers *en flagrante*. Tristan receives a mortal wound from a poisoned lance during a duel with one of King Mark's courtiers. Tristan, in his delirium, awaits Queen Isolde's arrival, because she has powers which could heal him.

The Magic

In some versions of the tale, but not in the opera or the poem, the story ends with Tristan giving instructions that if the ship returns with Queen Isolde it should have white sails hoisted, and if not, it should raise black sails. Tristan's wife Isolde spots the ship returning with white sails (indicating that Queen Isolde has come to heal him), but out of jealousy she tells Tristan that the sails are black. He despairs and dies; Queen Isolde comes upon his body, throws her arms around him and dies too.

In some variants of the story, Isolde has emerald (green) eyes or hails from the Emerald Isle or bears the potion in an emerald goblet. Shallot becomes Isolde near the end, and she wears a green silk dress and green slippers, has eyes of molten emerald and wears an emerald on her forehead. She bears a gold cup with a red ruby—recalling the Salvador Dali pin on her dress when Render first met her—which contains the poison/love potion that would bind Tristram and Isolde in love. She wants him to love her and is shattered when Render lies that he does not. Render has the role of Tristram forced upon him anyway, by being placed in armor and having a wound appear which mimics the fatal wound from a poisoned lance that Tristram had received.

The huge, bearded servitor with a barbaric accent who aids Tristram/ Render at the end of the story is Dr. Bartelmetz (not Dr. Eileen Shallot!), which suggests that Render is trapped in his own mind and not that of Shallot's. Bartelmetz made the sails **black** so that Tristram would die in the illusion and Render's identity would be freed, but Tristram/Render overrides him to turn the sails **white**, indicating that Queen Isolde has returned to heal him. Bartelmetz is reaching for the red button to end the current simulation as the story ends. The story expresses existentialist themes of questioning the nature of reality as Render and his patients perceive it. There are other clues which suggest the possibility that the entire story has been an illusion taking place—and continually looping—within Render's tortured mind. This may be why the goblet in the Tristan & Isolde pin on the dress had significance for Render at the beginning of the story, and why the goblet reappeared in the flames of the fireplace before being explained at the end of the story. This may also be why there are repeated references to mirrored surfaces, willows, wolves, and to the circularity of Ouroboros/Jormangund.

Additional notes: Several clues suggest that the unnamed city is Cleveland: its well-known street Carnegie, the downtown area called the "Flats," and its location by a lake. Zelazny wrote this story for Editor Cele Goldsmith because he worried that he'd offended her by giving "A Rose for Ecclesiastes" and "The Doors of His Face, the Lamps of His Mouth" to *F&SF*.

[1] The original manuscript and every published edition say "sunset," although all surrounding text refers to morning. This a clue that Render is already slipping mentally and losing control.

[2] *The Last Defender of Camelot*, 1980.

[3] *Vector* May-June 1973 (#65).

[4] *Science Fiction Origins*, Popular Library, 1980.

[5] *Science Fiction as Literature: Selected Stories and Novels of Roger Zelazny* [PhD Thesis] Thomas F. Monteleone, University of Maryland, 1973.

[6] *Four for Tomorrow*, Ace, 1967.

[7] *The Best of the Nebulas*, ed Ben Bova, Tor, 1989.

[8] *Four for Tomorrow*, Ace, 1967.

[9] *Kallikanzaros* #5 June-July 1968.

[10] *Kallikanzaros* #4, March-April 1968.

[11] *Science Fiction as Literature: Selected Stories and Novels of Roger Zelazny* [PhD Thesis] Thomas F. Monteleone, University of Maryland, 1973.

The Furies

As an afterthought, Nature sometimes tosses a bone to those it maims and casts aside. Often, it is in the form of a skill, usually useless, or the curse of intelligence.

When Sandor Sandor was four years old he could name all the one hundred forty-nine inhabited worlds in the galaxy.

When he was five he could name the principal land masses of each planet and chalk them in, roughly, on blank globes. By the time he was seven years old he knew all the provinces, states, countries and major cities of all the main land masses on all 149 inhabited worlds in the galaxy. He read Landography, History, Landology and popular travel guides during most of his waking time; and he studied maps and travel tapes. There was a camera behind his eyes, or so it seemed, because by the time he was ten years old there was no city in the galaxy that anyone could name about which Sandor Sandor did not know *something*.

And he continued.

Places fascinated him. He built a library of street guides, road maps. He studied architectural styles and principal industries, and racial types, native life-forms, local flora, landmarks, hotels, restaurants, airports and seaports and spaceports, styles of clothing and personal ornamentation, climatic conditions, local arts and crafts, dietary habits, sports, religions, social institutions, customs.

When he took his doctorate in Landography at the age of fourteen, his oral examinations were conducted via closed circuit television. This is because he was afraid to leave his home—having done so only three times before in his life and having met with fresh trauma on each occasion. And *this* is because on all 149 inhabited worlds in the galaxy there was no remedy for a certain degenerative muscular disease. This disease made it impossible for Sandor

The Magic

to manipulate even the finest prosthetic devices for more than a few minutes without suffering fatigue and great pain; and to go outside he required three such devices—two legs and a right arm—to substitute for those which he had missed out on receiving somewhere along the line before birth.

Rather than suffer this pain, or the pain of meeting persons other than his Aunt Faye or his nurse, Miss Barbara, he took his oral examinations via closed circuit television.

The University of Brill, Dombeck, was located on the other side of that small planet from Sandor's home, else the professors would have come to see *him,* because they respected him considerably. His 855-page dissertation, "Some Notes Toward a Gravitational Matrix Theory Governing the Formation of Similar Land Masses on Dissimilar Planetary Bodies" had drawn attention from Interstel University on Earth itself. Sandor Sandor, of course, would never see the Earth. His muscles could only sustain the gravitation of smaller planets, such as Dombeck.

And it happened that the Interstel Government, which monitors everything, had listened in on Sandor's oral examinations and his defense of his dissertation.

Associate Professor Baines was one of Sandor's very few friends. They had even met several times in person, in Sandor's library, because Baines often said he'd wanted to borrow certain books and then came and spent the afternoon. When the examinations were concluded, Associate Professor Baines stayed on the circuit for several minutes, talking with Sandor. It was during this time that Baines made casual reference to an almost useless (academically, that is) talent of Sandor's.

At the mention of it, the government man's ears had pricked forward (he was a Rigellian). He was anxious for a promotion and he recalled an obscure memo . . . .

Associate Professor Baines had mentioned the fact that Sandor Sandor had once studied a series of thirty random photos from all over the civilized galaxy, and that the significant data from these same photos had also been fed into the Department's L-L computer. Sandor had named the correct planet in each case, the land mass in 29, the county or territory in twenty-six, and he had correctly set the location itself within fifty square miles in twenty-three instances. The L-L comp had named the correct planet for twenty-seven.

It was not a labor of love for the computer.

So it became apparent that Sandor Sandor knew just about every damn street in the galaxy.

Ten years later he knew them all.

But three years later the Rigellian quit his job, disgusted, and went to work in private industry, where the pay was better and promotions more frequent. *His* memo, and the tape, had been filed, however . . . .

*

Benedick Benedict was born and grew up on the watery world of Kjum, and his was an infallible power for making enemies of everyone he met.

The reason why is that while some men's highest pleasure is drink, and others are given to gluttony, and still others are slothful, or lechery is their chief delight, or *Phrinn-doing*, Benedick's was gossip—he was a loudmouth.

Gossip was his meat and his drink, his sex and his religion. Shaking hands with him was a mistake, often a catastrophic one. For, as he clung to your hand, pumping it and smiling, his eyes would suddenly grow moist and the tears would dribble down his fat cheeks.

He wasn't sad when this happened. Far from it. It was a somatic conversion from his paranorm reaction.

He was seeing your past life.

He was selective, too; he only saw what he looked for. And he looked for scandal and hate, and what is often worse, love; he looked for lawbreaking and unrest, for memories of discomfort, pain, futility, weakness. He saw everything a man wanted to forget, and he talked about it.

If you are lucky he won't tell you of your own. If you have ever met someone else whom he has also met in this manner, and if this fact shows, he will begin talking of *that* person. He will tell you of that man's or woman's life because he appreciates this form of social reaction even more than your outrage at yourself. And his eyes and voice and hand will hold you, like the clutch of the Ancient Mariner, in a sort of half dream-state; and you will hear him out and you will be shocked beneath your paralysis.

Then he will go away and tell others about you.

Such a man was Benedick Benedict. He was probably unaware how much he was hated, because this reaction never came until later, after he had said "Good day," departed, and been gone for several hours. He left his hearers with a just-raped feeling—and later fear, shame, or disgust forced them to suppress the occurrence and to try to forget him. Or else they hated him quietly, because he was dangerous. That is to say, he had powerful friends.

He was an extremely social animal: he loved attention; he wanted to be admired; he craved audiences.

He could always find an audience too, somewhere. He knew so many secrets that he was tolerated in important places in return for the hearing. And he was wealthy too, but more of that in a moment.

As time went on, it became harder and harder for him to meet new people. His reputation spread in geometric proportion to his talking, and even those who would hear him preferred to sit on the far side of the room, drink enough alcohol to partly deaden memories of themselves, and to be seated near a door.

The reason for his wealth is because his power extended to inanimate objects as well. Minerals were rare on Kjum, the watery world. If anyone brought him a sample he could hold it and weep and tell them where to dig to hit the main lode.

From one fish caught in the vast seas of Kjum, he could chart the course of a school of fish.

Weeping, he could touch a native rad-pearl necklace and divine the location of the native's rad-pearl bed.

Local insurance associations and loan companies kept Benedict Files—the pen a man had used to sign his contract, his snubbed-out cigarette butt, a plastex hanky with which he had mopped his brow, an object left in security, the remains of a biopsy or blood test—so that Benedict could use his power against those who renege on these companies and flee, on those who break their laws.

He did not revel in his power either. He simply enjoyed it. For he was one of the nineteen known paranorms in the 149 inhabited worlds in the galaxy, and he knew no other way. Also, he occasionally assisted civil authorities, if he thought their cause a just one. If he did not, he suddenly lost his power until the need for it vanished. This didn't happen too often though, for an humanitarian was Benedick Benedict, and well-paid, because he was laboratory-tested and clinically-proven. He could psychometrize. He could pick up thought-patterns originating outside his own skull . . . .

*

Lynx Links looked like a beach ball with a beard, a fat patriarch with an eyepatch, a man who loved good food and drink, simple clothing, and the company of simple people; he was a man who smiled often and whose voice was soft and melodic.

In his earlier years he had chalked up the most impressive kill-record of any agent ever employed by Interstel Central Intelligence. Forty-eight men and seventeen malicious alien life-forms had the Lynx dispatched during his fifty-year tenure as a field agent. He was one of the three men in the galaxy to have lived through half a century's employment with ICI. He lived comfortably on his government pension despite three wives and a horde of grandchildren; he was recalled occasionally as a consultant; and he did some part-time missionary work on the side. He believed that all life was one and that all men were brothers, and that love rather than hate or fear should rule the affairs of men. He had even killed with love, he often remarked at Tranquility Session, respecting and revering the person and the spirit of the man who had been marked for death.

This is the story of how he came to be summoned back from Hosanna, the World of the Great and Glorious Flame of the Divine Life, and was joined with Sandor Sandor and Benedick Benedict in the hunt for Victor Corgo, the man without a heart.

*

The Magic

Victor Corgo was captain of the *Wallaby*. Victor Corgo was Head Astrogator, First Mate, and Chief Engineer of the *Wallaby*. Victor Corgo *was* the *Wallaby*.

One time the *Wallaby* was a proud Guardship, an ebony toadstool studded with the jewel-like warts of fast-phase projectors. One time the *Wallaby* skipped proud about the frontier worlds of Interstel, meting out the unique justice of the Uniform Galactic Code—in those places where there was no other law. One time the proud *Wallaby*, under the command of Captain Victor Corgo of the Guard, had ranged deep space and become a legend under legendary skies.

A terror to brigands and ugly aliens, a threat to Codebreakers, and a thorn in the sides of evildoers everywhere, Corgo and his shimmering fungus (which could burn an entire continent under water level within a single day) were the pride of the Guard, the best of the best, the cream that had been skimmed from all the rest.

Unfortunately, Corgo sold out.

He became a heel.

. . . A traitor. A hero gone bad . . .

After forty-five years with the Guard, his pension but half a decade away, he lost his entire crew in an illtimed raid upon a pirate stronghold on the planet Kilsh, which might have become the 150th inhabited world of Interstel.

Crawling, barely alive, he had made his way half across the great snowfield of Brild, on the main land mass of Kilsh. At the fortuitous moment, Death making its traditional noises of approach, he was snatched from out of its traffic lane, so to speak, by the Drillen, a nomadic tribe of ugly and intelligent quadrapeds, who took him to their camp and healed his wounds, fed him, and gave him warmth. Later, with the cooperation of the Drillen, he recovered the *Wallaby* and all its arms and armaments, from where it had burnt its way to a hundred feet beneath the ice.

Crewless, he trained the Drillen.

With the Drillen and the *Wallaby* he attacked the pirates.

318

Roger Zelazny and Samuel R. Delany

He won.

But he did not stop with that.

No.

When he learned that the Drillen had been marked for death under the Uniform Code he sold out his own species. The Drillen had refused relocation to a decent Reservation World. They had elected to continue occupancy of what was to become the 150th inhabited world in the galaxy (that is to say, in Interstel).

Therefore, the destruct-order had been given.

Captain Corgo protested, was declared out of order.

Captain Corgo threatened, was threatened in return.

Captain Corgo fought, was beaten, died, was resurrected, escaped restraint, became an outlaw.

He took the *Wallaby* with him. The *Happy Wallaby*, it had been called in the proud days. Now, it was just the *Wallaby*.

As the tractor beams had seized it, as the vibrations penetrated its ebony hull and tore at his flesh, Corgo had called his six Drillen to him, stroked the fur of Mala, his favorite, opened his mouth to speak, and died just as the words and the tears began.

"I am sorry . . . " he had said.

They gave him a new heart, though. His old one had fibrillated itself to pieces and could not be repaired. They put the old one in a jar and gave him a shiny, antiseptic egg of throbbing metal, which expanded and contracted at varying intervals, dependent upon what the seed-sized computers they had planted within him told of his breathing and his blood sugar and the output of his various glands. The seeds and the egg contained his life.

When they were assured that this was true and that it would continue, they advised him of the proceedings of courts-martial.

He did not wait, however, for due process. Breaking his parole as an officer, he escaped the Guard Post, taking with him Mala, the only remaining Drillen in the galaxy. Her five fellows had not survived scientific inquiry as to the nature of their internal structures. The rest of the race, of course, had refused relocation.

Then did the man without a heart make war upon mankind.

*

Raping a planet involves considerable expense. Enormous blasters and slicers and sluicers and refiners are required to reduce a world back almost to a state of primal chaos, and then to extract from it its essential (i.e., commercially viable) ingredients. The history books may tell you of strip-mining on the mother planet, back in ancient times. Well, the crude processes employed then were similar in emphasis and results, but the operations were considerably smaller in size.

Visualize a hundred miles of Grand Canyon appearing overnight; visualize the reversal of thousands of Landological millenia in the twinkling of an eye; consider all of the Ice Ages of the Earth, and compress them into a single season. This will give you a rough idea as to time and effect.

Now picture the imported labor—the men who drill and blast and slice and sluice for the great mining combines: Not uneducated, these men; willing to take a big risk, certainly though, these men—maybe only for one year, because of the high pay; or maybe they're careerists, because of the high pay—these men, who hit three worlds in a year's time, who descend upon these worlds in ships full of city, in space-trailer mining camps, out of the sky; coming, these men, from all over the inhabited galaxy, bringing with them the power of the tool and the opposed thumb, bearing upon their brows the mark of the Solar Phoenix and in their eyes the cold of the spaces they have crossed over, they know what to do to make the domes of atoms rise before them and to call down the tornado-probosci of suck-vortices from the freighters on the other side of the sky; and they do it thoroughly and efficiently, and not without style, tradition, folksongs, and laughter—for they are the sweat-crews, working against time (which is money), to gain tonnage (which is money), and to beat their competitors to market (which is important, inasmuch as one worldsworth influences future sales for many months); these men, who bear in one hand the flame and in the other the whirlwind, who come down with their families and all their possessions, erect temporary metropoli, work their magic act, and go—after the vanishing trick has been completed.

Now that you've an idea as to what happens and who is present at the scene, here's the rub:

Raping a planet involves considerable expense.

The profits are more than commensurate, do not misunderstand. It is just that they could be even greater . . . .

How?

Well—For one thing, the heavy machinery involved is quite replaceable, in the main. That is, the machinery which is housed within the migrant metropoli.

Moving it is expensive. Not moving it isn't. For it is actually cheaper, in terms of material and labor, to manufacture new units than it is to fast-phase the old ones more than an average of 2.6 times.

Mining combines do not produce them (and wouldn't really want to); the mining manufacturing combines like to make new units as much as the mining combines like to lose old ones.

And of course it is rented machinery, or machinery on which the payments are still being made, to the financing associations, because carrying payments makes it easier to face down the Interstel Revenue Service every fiscal year.

Abandoning the units would be criminal, violating either the lessor-lessee agreement or the Interstel Commercial Code.

But accidents do happen . . .

Often, too frequently to make for comfortable statistics . . .

Way out there on the raw frontier.

Then do the big insurance associations investigate, and they finally sigh and reimburse the lien-holders.

. . . And the freighters make it to market ahead of schedule, because there is less to dismantle and march-order and ship.

Time is saved, commitments are met in advance, a better price is generally obtained, and a head start on the next worldsworth is supplied in this manner.

The Magic

All of which is nice.

Except for the insurance associations.

But what can happen to a transitory New York full of heavy equipment?
Well, some call it sabotage.

. . . Some call it mass-murder.

. . . Unsanctioned war.

. . . Corgo's lightning.

But it is written that it is better to burn one city than to curse the darkness.
Corgo did not curse the darkness.

. . . Many times.

*

The day they came together on Dombeck, Benedick held forth his hand,
smiled, said: "Mister Sandor . . ."

As his hand was shaken, his smile reversed itself. Then it went away from
his face. He was shaking an artificial hand.

Sandor nodded, dropped his eyes.

Benedick turned to the big man with the eyepatch.

" . . . And you are the Lynx?"

"That is correct, my brother. You must excuse me if I do not shake hands.
It is against my religion. I believe that life does not require reassurance as to
its oneness."

"Of course," said Benedick. "I once knew a man from Dombeck. He was
a *gnil* smuggler, named Worten Wortan—"

"He is gone to join the Great Flame," said the Lynx. "That is to say, he is
dead now. ICI apprehended him two years ago. He passed to Flame while
attempting to escape restraint."

"Really?" said Benedick. "He was at one time a *gnil* addict himself—"

"I know. I read his file in connection with another case."

"Dombeck is full of *gnil* smugglers" —Sandor.

"Oh. Well, then let us talk of this man Corgo."

"Yes" —the Lynx.

"Yes" —Sandor.

"The ICI man told me that many insurance associations have lodged protests with their Interstel representatives."

"That is true" —Lynx.

"Yes" —Sandor, biting his lip. "Do you gentlemen mind if I remove my legs?"

"Not at all" —the Lynx. "We are co-workers, and informality should govern our gatherings."

"Please do," said Benedick.

Sandor leaned forward in his chair and pressed the coupling controls. There followed two thumps from beneath his desk. He leaned back then and surveyed his shelves of globes.

"Do they cause you pain?" asked Benedick.

"Yes." —Sandor.

"Were you in an accident?"

"Birth" —Sandor.

The Lynx raised a decanter of brownish liquid to the light. He stared through it.

"It is a local brandy" —Sandor. "Quite good. Somewhat like the *xmili* of Bandla, only nonaddictive. Have some?"

The Lynx did, keeping it in front of him all that evening.

"Corgo is a destroyer of property," said Benedick.

Sandor nodded.

" . . . And a defrauder of insurance associations, a defacer of planetary bodies, a deserter from the Guard—"

"A murderer" —Sandor.

" . . . And a zoophilist," finished Benedick.

"Aye" —the Lynx, smacking his lips.

"So great an offender against public tranquility is he that he must be found."

" . . . And passed back through the Flame for purification and rebirth."

"Yes, we must locate him and kill him," said Benedick.

"The two pieces of equipment . . . Are they present?"—the Lynx.

The Magic

"Yes, the phase-wave is in the next room."

" . . . And?" asked Benedick.

"The other item is in the bottom drawer of this desk, right side."

"Then why do we not begin now?"

"Yes. Why not now?" —the Lynx.

"Very well" —Sandor. "One of you will have to open the drawer, though. It is in the brown-glass jar, to the back."

"I'll get it," said Benedick.

*

A great sob escaped him after a time, as he sat there with rows of worlds at his back, tears on his cheeks, and Corgo's heart clutched in his hands.

"It is cold and dim . . . . "

"Where?" —the Lynx.

"It is a small place. A room? Cabin? Instrument panels . . . A humming sound . . . Cold, and crazy angles everywhere . . . Vibration . . . Hurt!"

"What is he doing?" —Sandor.

" . . . Sitting, half-lying-a couch, webbed, about him. Furry one at his side, sleeping. Twisted—angles—everything-wrong. Hurt!"

"The *Wallaby*, in transit" —Lynx.

"Where is he going?" —Sandor.

"HURT!" shouted Benedick.

Sandor dropped the heart into his lap.

He began to shiver. He wiped at his eyes with the backs of his hands.

"I have a headache," he announced.

"Have a drink" —Lynx.

He gulped one, sipped the second.

"Where was I?"

The Lynx raised his shoulders and let them fall.

"The *Wallaby* was fast-phasing somewhere, and Corgo was in phase-sleep. It is a disturbing sensation to fast-phase while fully conscious. Distance and duration grow distorted. You found him at a bad time—while under sedation and subject to continuum-impact. Perhaps tomorrow will be better . . . . "

"I hope so."

"Yes, tomorrow" —Sandor.

"Tomorrow . . . Yes."

"There *was* one other thing," he added, "a thing in his mind . . . There was a sun where there was no sun before."

"A burn-job?" —Lynx.

"Yes."

"A memory?" —Sandor.

"No. He is on his way to do it."

The Lynx stood.

"I will phase-wave ICI and advise them. They can check which worlds are presently being mined. Have you any ideas how soon?"

"No, I can not tell that."

"What did the globe look like? What continental configurations?" —Sandor.

"None. The thought was not that specific. His mind was drifting—mainly filled with hate."

"I'll call in now—and we'll try again . . . . ?"

"Tomorrow. I'm tired now."

"Go to bed then. Rest."

"Yes, I can do that . . . . "

"Good night, Mister Benedict."

"Good night . . . . "

"Sleep in the heart of the Great Flame."

"I hope not . . . . "

*

Mala whimpered and moved nearer her Corgo, for she was dreaming an evil dream: They were back on the great snowfield of Brild, and she was trying to help him—to walk, to move forward. He kept slipping though, and lying there longer each time, and rising more slowly each time and moving ahead at an even slower pace, each time. He tried to kindle a fire, but the snow-devils spun and toppled like icicles falling from the seven moons, and the dancing green flames died as soon as they were born from between his hands.

Finally, on the top of a mountain of ice she saw them.

There were three . . .

They were clothed from head to toe in flame; their burning heads turned and turned and turned; and then one bent and sniffed at the ground, rose, and indicated their direction. Then they were racing down the hillside, trailing flames, melting a pathway as they came, springing over drifts and ridges of ice, their arms extended before them.

Silent they came, pausing only as the one sniffed the air, the ground . . . .

She could hear their breathing now, feel their heat . . . .

In a matter of moments they would arrive . . . .

Mala whimpered and moved nearer her Corgo.

*

For three days. Benedick tried, clutching Corgo's heart like a Gypsy's crystal, watering it with his tears, squeezing almost to life again. His head ached for hours after, each time that he met the continuum-impact. He wept long, moist tears for hours beyond contact, which was unusual. He had always withdrawn from immediate pain before; remembered distress was his forte, and a different matter altogether.

He hurt each time that he touched Corgo and his mind was sucked down through that subway in the sky; and he touched Corgo eleven times during those three days, and then his power went away, really.

*

Seated, like a lump of dark metal on the hull of the *Wallaby*, he stared across six hundred miles at the blazing hearth which he had stoked to steel-tempering heights; and he *felt* like a piece of metal, resting there upon an anvil, waiting for the hammer to fall again, as it always did, waiting for it to strike him again and again, and to beat him to a new toughness, to smash away more and more of that within him which was base, of that which knew pity, remorse, and guilt, again and again and again, and to leave only that hard, hard form of hate, like an iron boot, which lived at the core of the lump, himself, and required constant hammering and heat.

Sweating as he watched, smiling, Corgo took pictures.

*

When one of the nineteen known paranorms in the 149 inhabited worlds in the galaxy suddenly loses his powers, and loses them at a crucial moment, it is like unto the old tales wherein a Princess is stricken one day with an unknown malady and the King, her father, summons all his wise men and calls for the best physicians in the realm.

Big Daddy ICI (*Rex ex machina-like*) did, in similar manner, summon wise men and counselors from various Thinkomats and think-repairshops about the galaxy, including Interstel University, on Earth itself. But alas! While all had a diagnosis none had on hand any suggestions which were immediately acceptable to all parties concerned:

"Bombard his thalamus with Beta particles."

"Hypno-regression to the womb, and restoration at a pre-traumatic point in his life."

"More continuum-impact."

"Six weeks on a pleasure satellite, and two aspirins every four hours."

"There is an old operation called a lobotomy . . . . "

"Lots of liquids and green leafy vegetables."

"Hire another paranorm."

For one reason or another, the principal balked at all of these courses of action, and the final one was impossible at the moment. In the end, the matter was settled neatly by Sandor's nurse Miss Barbara, who happened onto the veranda one afternoon as Benedick sat there fanning himself and drinking *xmili*.

"Why Mister Benedict!" she announced, plopping her matronly self into the chair opposite him and spiking her *redlonade* with three fingers of *xmili*. "Fancy meeting you out here! I thought you were in the library with the boys, working on that top secret hush-hush critical project called Wallaby Stew, or something."

The Magic

"As you can see, I am not," he said, staring at his knees.

"Well, it's nice just to pass the time of day sometimes, too. To sit. To relax. To rest from the hunting of Victor Corgo . . . "

"Please, you're not supposed to know about the project. It's top secret and critical—"

"And hush-hush too, I know. Dear Sandor talks in his sleep every night—so much. You see, I tuck him in each evening and sit there until he drifts away to dreamland, poor child."

"Mm, yes. Please don't talk about the project, though."

"Why? Isn't it going well?"

"No!"

"Why not?"

"Because of *me,* if you must know! I've got a block of some kind. The power doesn't come when I call it"

"Oh, how distressing! You mean you can't peep into other persons' minds any more?"

"Exactly."

"Dear me. Well, let's talk about something else then. Did I ever tell you about the days when I was the highest-paid courtesan on Sordido V?"

Benedick's head turned slowly in her direction.

"Nooo . . . " he said. "You mean *the* Sordido?"

"Oh yes. Bright Bad Barby, the Bouncing Baby, they used to call me. They still sing ballads, you know."

"Yes, I've heard them. Many verses . . . . "

"Have another drink, I once had a coin struck in my image, you know. It's a collectors' item now, of course. Full-length pose, flesh-colored. Here, I wear it on this chain around my neck—Lean closer, it's a short chain?"

"Very—interesting. Uh, how did all this come about?"

"Well—it all began with old Pruria Van Teste, the banker, of the export-import Testes. You see, he had this thing going for synthofemmes for a long while, but when he started getting up there in years he felt there was something he'd been missing. So, one fine day, he sent me ten dozen

328

Hravian orchids and a diamond garter, along with an invitation to have dinner with him . . . . "

"You accepted, of course?"

"Naturally not. Not the first time, anyway. I could see that he was pretty damn eager."

"Well, what happened?"

"Wait till I fix another *redlonade*."

*

Later that afternoon, the Lynx wandered out into the veranda during the course of his meditations. He saw there Miss Barbara, with Benedick seated beside her, weeping.

"What troubles thy tranquility, my brother?" he inquired.

"Nothing! Nothing at all! It is wonderful and beautiful, everything! My power has come back—I can feel it!" He wiped his eyes on his sleeve.

"Bless thee, little lady!" said the Lynx, seizing Miss Barbara's hand. "Thy simple counsels have done more to heal my brother than have all these highly-paid medical practitioners brought here at great expense. Virtue lies in thy homely words, and thou art most beloved of the Flame."

"Thank you, I'm sure."

"Come brother, let us away to our task again!"

"Yes, let us!—Oh thank you, Bright Barby!"

"Don't mention it."

Benedick's eyes clouded immediately, as he took the tattered blood-pump into his hands. He leaned back, stroking it, and moist spots formed on either side of his nose, grew like well-fed amoebas, underwent mitosis, and dashed off to explore in the vicinity of his shelf-like upper lip.

He sighed once, deeply.

"Yes, I am there."

He blinked, licked his lips.

" . . . It is night. Late. It is a primitive dwelling. Mud-like stucco, bits of straw in it . . . All lights out, but for the one from the machine, and its spillage—"

The Magic

"Machine?" —Lynx.

"What machine?" —Sandor.

" . . . Projector. Pictures on wall . . . World-big, filling whole picture-field—patches of fire on the world, up near the top. Three places—"

"Bhave VII" —Lynx. "Six days ago!"

"Shoreline to the right goes like this . . . And to the left, like this . . . . "

His right index finger traced patterns in the air.

"Bhave VII."—Sandor.

"Happy and not happy at the same time—hard to separate the two. Guilt, though, is there—but pleasure with it. Revenge . . . . Hate people, humans . . . We adjust the projector now, stop it at a flare-up—Bright! How good!—Oh good! That will teach them!—Teach them to grab away what belongs to others . . . To murder a race!—The generator is humming. It is ancient, and it smells bad . . . . The dog is lying on our foot. The foot is asleep, but we do not want to disturb the dog, for it is Mala's favorite thing—her only toy, companion, living doll, four-footed . . . . She is scratching behind its ear with her forelimb, and it loves her. Light leaks down upon them . . . . Clear they are. The breeze is warm, very, which is why we are unshirted. It stirs the tasseled hanging . . . . No force-field or windowpane . . . Insects buzz by the projector—pterodactyl silhouettes on the burning world—"

"What kind of insects?" —Lynx.

"Can you see what is beyond the window?" —Sandor.

" . . . Outside are trees—short ones—just outlines, squat. Can't tell where trunks begin . . . Foliage too thick, too close. Too dark out. Off in the distance a tiny moon . . . Something like *this* on a hill . . . " His hands shaped a turnip impaled on an obelisk. "Not sure how far off, how large, what color; or what made of . . . "

"Is the name of the place in Corgo's mind?" —Lynx.

"If I could touch him, with my hand, I would know it, know everything. Only receive impressions *this* way, though—surface thoughts. He is not thinking of where he is now . . . . The dog rolls onto its back and off of our foot—at last! She scratches its tummy, my love dark . . . It kicks with its hind leg as if scratching after a flea—wags its tail. Dilk is puppy's name. She gave if that name, loves it . . . It is like one of hers. Which was murdered. Hate people—humans. *She* is people. Better than . . . Doesn't butcher that which breathes for selfish gain, for Interstel. Better than people, my pony-friends, better . . . An insect lights on Dilk's nose. She brushes it away. Segmented, two sets of wings, about five millimeters in length, pink globe on front end, bulbous, and buzzes as it goes, the insect—you asked . . . "

"How many entrances are there to the place?" —Lynx.

"Two. One doorway at each end of the hut."

"How many windows?"

"Two. On opposing walls—the ones without doors. I can't see anything through the other window—too dark on that side."

"Anything else?"

"On the wall a sword—long hilt, very long, two-handed—even longer maybe—three? four?—short blades, though, two of them—hilt is in the middle—and each blade is straight, double-edged, forearm-length . . . Beside it, a mask of—flowers? Too dark to tell. The blades shine; the mask is dull. Looks like flowers, though. Many little ones . . . . Four sides to the mask, shaped like a kite, big end down. Can't make out features. It projects fairly far out from the wall, though. Mala is restless. Probably doesn't like the pictures—or maybe doesn't see them and is bored. Her eyes are different. She nuzzles our shoulder now. We pour her a drink in her bowl. Take another one ourself. She doesn't drink hers. We stare at her. She drops her head and drinks. Dirt floor under our sandals, hard-packed. Many tiny white—pebbles?—in it, powdery-like. The table is wood, natural . . . The generator sputters. The picture fades, comes back. We rub our chin. Need a shave . . . The hell with it! We're not standing any inspections! Drink—one, two—all gone! Another!"

*

The Magic

Sandor had threaded a tape into his viewer, and he was spinning it and stopping it, spinning it and stopping it, spinning it and stopping it. He checked his worlds chronometer.

"Outside," he asked, "does the moon seem to be moving up, or down, or across the sky?"

"Across."

"Right to left, or left to right?"

"Right to left. It seems about a quarter past zenith."

"Any coloration to it?"

"Orange, with three black lines. One starts at about eleven o'clock, crosses a quarter of its surface, drops straight down, cuts back at seven. The other starts at two, drops to six. They don't meet. The third is a small upside-down letter 'c' —lower right quarter . . . Not big, the moon, but clear, very. No clouds."

"Any constellations you can make out?" —Lynx.

" . . . Head isn't turned that way now, wasn't turned toward the window long enough. Now there is a noise, far off . . . A high-pitched chattering, almost metallic. Animal. He pictures a six-legged tree creature, half the size of a man, reddish-brown hair, sparse . . . It can go on two, four, or six legs on the ground. Doesn't go down on the ground much, though. Nests high. An egg-layer. Many teeth. Eats flesh. Small eyes, and black—two. Great nose-holes. Pesty, but not dangerous to men—easily frightened."

"He is on Disten, the fifth world of Blake's Systern," said Sandor. "Night-side means he is on the continent Didenlan. The moon Babry, well past zenith now, means he is to the east. A Mellar-mosque indicates a Mella-Muslim settlement. The blade and the mask seem Hortanian. I am sure they were brought from further inland. The chalky deposits would set him in the vicinity of Landear, which is Mella-Muslim. It is on the Dista River, north bank. There is much jungle about. Even those people who wish seclusion seldom go further than eight miles from the center of town—population 153,000—and it is least settled to the northwest, because of the hills, the rocks, and—"

"Fine! That's where he is then!" —Lynx. "Now here is how we'll do it. He has, of course, been sentenced to death. I believe—yes, I know!—there is an ICI Field Office on the second world—whatever its name—of that System."

"Nirer" —Sandor.

"Yes. Hmm, let's see . . . Two agents will be empowered as executioners. They will land their ship to the northwest of Landear, enter the city, and find where the man with the strange four-legged pet settled, the one who arrived within the past six days. Then one agent will enter the hut and ascertain whether Corgo is within. He will retreat immediately if Corgo is present, signaling to the other who will be hidden behind those trees or whatever. The second man will then fire a round of fragmentation plaster through the unguarded window. One agent will then position himself at a safe distance beyond the northeast corner of the edifice, so as to cover a door and a window. The other will move to the southwest, to do the same. Each will carry a two-hundred channel laser sub-gun with vibrating head. —Good! I'll phase-wave it to Central now. We've got him!"

He hurried from the room.

Benedick, still holding the thing, his shirt-front soaking, continued:

"'Fear not, my lady dark. He is but a puppy, and he howls at the moon . . . . '"

*

It was thirty-one hours and twenty minutes later when the Lynx received and decoded the two terse statements:

EXECUTIONERS THE WAY OF ALL FLESH.
THE *WALLABY* HAS JUMPED AGAIN.

He licked his lips. His comrades were waiting for the report, and *they* had succeeded—they had done their part, had performed efficiently and well. It was the Lynx who had missed his kill.

He made the sign of the Flame and entered the library.

The Magic

Benedick knew—*he* could tell. The little paranorm's hands were on his walking stick, and that was enough—just that.

The Lynx bowed his head.

"We begin again," he told them.

Benedick's powers—if anything, stronger than ever—survived continuum-impact seven more times. Then he described a new world: Big it was, and many-peopled—bright—dazzling, under a blue-white sun; yellow brick everywhere, neo-Denebian architecture, green glass windows, a purple sea nearby . . . .

No trick at all for Sandor:

"Phillip's World," he named it, then told them the city: "Delles."

"This time *we* burn *him*," said the Lynx, and he was gone from the room.

"Christian-Zoroastrians," sighed Benedick, after he had left. "I think this one has a Flame-complex."

Sandor spun the globe with his left hand and watched it turn.

"I'm not preconning," said Benedick, "but I'll give you odds, like three to one—on Corgo's escaping again."

"Why?"

"When he abandoned humanity he became something less, and more. He is not ready to die."

"What do you mean?"

"I hold his heart. He gave it up, in all ways. He is invincible now. But he will reclaim it one day. Then he will die."

"How do you know?"

" . . . A feeling. There are many types of doctors, among them pathologists. No less than others, they; but masters only of blackness. I *know* people, have known many. I do not pretend to know *all* about them. But weaknesses—yes, those I know."

Sandor turned his globe and did not say anything.

But they *did* burn the *Wallaby*, badly.

He lived, though.

He lived, cursing.

Roger Zelazny and Samuel R. Delany

As he lay there in the gutter, the world burning, exploding, falling down around him, he cursed *that* world and every other; and everything in them.

Then there was another burst.

Blackness followed.

*

The double-bladed Hortanian sword, spinning in the hands of Corgo, had halved the first ICI executioner as he stood in the doorway. Mala had detected their approach across the breezes, through the open window.

The second had fallen before the fragmentation plaster could be launched. Corgo had a laser sub-gun himself, Guard issue, and he cut the man down, firing through the wall and two trees in the direction Mala indicated.

Then the *Wallaby* left Disten.

But he was troubled. How had they found him so quickly? He had had close brushes with them before—many of them, over the years. But he was cautious, and he could not see where he had failed this time, could not understand how Interstel had located him. Even his last employer did not know his whereabouts.

He shook his head and phased for Phillips world.

To die is to sleep and not to dream, and Corgo did not want this. He took elaborate pains, in-phasing and out-phasing in random directions; he gave Mala a golden collar with a two-way radio in its clasp, wore its mate within his death-ring; he converted much currency, left the *Wallaby* in the care of a reputable smuggler in Unassociated Territory and crossed Phillips World to Delles-by-the-Sea. He was fond of sailing, and he liked the purple waters of this planet. He rented a large villa near the Delles Dives—slums to the one side, Riviera to the other. This pleased him. He still had dreams; he was not dead yet.

Sleeping, perhaps, he had heard a sound. Then he was suddenly seated on the side of his bed, a handful of death in his hand.

"Mala?"

She was gone. The sound he'd heard had been the closing of a door.

He activated the radio.

The Magic

"What is it?" he demanded.

"I have the feeling we are watched again," she replied, through his ring. " . . . Only a feeling, though."

Her voice was distant, tiny.

"Why did you not tell *me?* Come back—now."

"No. I match the night and can move without sound. I will investigate. There *is* something, if I have fear . . . . Arm yourself!"

He did that, and as he moved toward the front of the house they struck. He ran. As he passed through the front door they struck again, and again. There was an inferno at his back, and a steady rain of plaster, metal, wood and glass was falling. Then there was an inferno around him.

They were above him. This time they had been cautioned not to close with him, but to strike from a distance. This time they hovered high in a shielded globe and poured down hot rivers of destruction.

Something struck him in the head and the shoulder. He fell, turning. He was struck in the chest, the stomach. He covered his face and rolled, tried to rise, failed. He was lost in a forest of flames. He got into a crouch, ran, fell again, rose once more, ran, fell again, crawled, fell again.

As he lay there in the gutter, the world burning, exploding, falling down around him he cursed *that* world and every other, and everyone in them.

Then there was another burst.

Blackness followed.

*

They thought they had succeeded, and their joy was great.

"Nothing," Benedick had said, smiling through his tears.

So that day they celebrated, and the next.

But Corgo's body had not been recovered.

Almost half a block had been hurled down, though, and eleven other residents could not be located either, so it seemed safe to assume that the execution had succeeded. ICI, however, requested that the trio remain together on Dombeck for another ten days, while further investigations were carried out.

Roger Zelazny and Samuel R. Delany

Benedick laughed.

"Nothing," he repeated. "Nothing."

But there is a funny thing about a man without a heart: His body does not live by the same rules as those of others: No. The egg in his chest is smarter than a mere heart, and it is the center of a wonderful communications system. Dead itself, it is omniscient in terms of that which lives around it; it is not omnipotent, but it has resources which a living heart does not command.

As the burns and lacerations were flashed upon the screen of the body, it sat in instant criticism. It moved itself to an emergency level of function; it became a flag vibrating within a hurricane; the glands responded and poured forth their juices of power; muscles were activated as if by electricity.

Corgo was only half-aware of the inhuman speed with which he moved through the storm of heat and the hail of building materials. It tore at him, but this pain was canceled. His massive output jammed nonessential neural input. He made it as far as the street and collapsed in the shelter of the curb.

The egg took stock of the cost of the action, decided the price had been excessively high, and employed immediate measures to insure the investment.

Down, down did it send him. Into the depths of sub-coma. Standard-model humans cannot decide one day that they wish to hibernate, lie down, do it. The physicians can induce *dauersch-laff*–with combinations of drugs and elaborate machineries. But Corgo did not need these things. He had a built-in survival kit with a mind of its own; and it decided that he must go deeper than the mere coma-level that a heart would have permitted. So it did the things a heart cannot do, while maintaining its own functions.

It hurled him into the blackness of sleep without dreams, of total unawareness. For only at the border of death itself could his life be retained, be strengthened, grow again. To approach this near the realm of death, its semblance was necessary.

Therefore, Corgo lay dead in the gutter.

*

The Magic

People, of course, flock to the scene of any disaster.

Those from the Riviera pause to dress in their best catastrophe clothing. Those from the slums do not, because their wardrobes are not as extensive.

One though, was dressed already and was passing nearby. "Zim" was what he was called, for obvious reasons. He had had another name once, but he had all but forgotten it.

He was staggering home from the *zimlak* parlor where he had cashed his Guard pension check for that month-cycle.

There was an explosion, but it was seconds before he realized it. Muttering, he stopped and turned very slowly in the direction of the noise. Then he saw the flames. He looked up, saw the hoverglobe. A memory appeared within his mind and he winced and continued to watch.

After a time he saw the man, moving at a fantastic pace across the landscape of Hell. The man fell in the street. There was more burning, and then the globe departed.

The impressions finally registered, and his disaster-reflex made him approach.

Indelible synapses, burnt into his brain long ago, summoned up page after page of *The Complete Guard Field Manual of Immediate Medical Actions*. He knelt beside the body, red with burn, blood and firelight . . . .

"Captain," he said, as he stared into the angular face with the closed dark eyes. "Captain . . . "

He covered his own face with his hands and they came away wet.

"Neighbors. Here. Us. Didn't–know . . . " He listened for a heartbeat, but there was nothing that he could detect. "Fallen . . . On the deck my Captain lies . . . Fallen . . . cold . . . dead. Us. Neighbors, even . . . " His sob was a jagged thing, until he was seized with a spell of hiccups. Then he steadied his hands and raised an eyelid.

Corgo's head jerked two inches to his left, away from the brightness of the flames.

The man laughed in relief.

"You're alive, Cap! You're still alive!"

The thing that was Corgo did not reply.

Bending, straining, he raised the body.

"'Do not move the victim'—that's what it says in the *Manual*. But you're coming with me, Cap. I remember now . . . . It was after I left. But I remember . . . All. Now I remember; I do . . . Yes. They'll kill you another time—if you do live . . . . They will; I know. So I'll have to move the victim. Have to . . . —Wish I wasn't so fogged . . . I'm sorry, Cap. You were always good, to the men, good to me. Ran a tight ship, but you were good . . . Old *Wallaby*, happy . . . Yes. We'll go now, killer. Fast as we can. Before the Morbs come—Yes. I remember . . . you. Good man, Cap. Yes."

*

So, the *Wallaby* had made its last jump, according to the ICI investigation which followed. But Corgo still dwelled on the dreamless border, and the seeds and the egg held his life.

*

After the ten days had passed, the Lynx and Benedick still remained with Sandor. Sandor was not anxious for them to go. He had never been employed before; he liked the feeling of having co-workers about, persons who shared memories of things done. Benedick was loathe to leave Miss Barbara, one of the few persons he could talk to and have answer him, willingly. The Lynx liked the food and the climate, decided his wives and grandchildren could use a vacation.

So they stayed on.

*

Returning from death is a deadly slow business. Reality does the dance of the veils, and it is a long while before you know what lies beneath them all (if you ever really do).

When Corgo had formed a rough idea, he cried out: "Mala!"

. . . The darkness.

Then he saw a face out of times gone by.

"Sergeant Emil . . . ?"

"Yes, sir. Right here, Captain."

The Magic

"Where am I?"

"My hutch, sir. Yours got burnt out."

"How?"

"A hoverglobe did it, with a sear-beam."

"What of my—pet? A Drillen . . . "

"There was only you I found, sir—no one, nothing, else. Uh, it was almost a month-cycle ago that it happened."

Corgo tried to sit up, failed, tried again, half-succeeded. He sat propped on his elbows.

"What's the matter with me?"

"You had some fractures, burns, lacerations, internal injuries—but you're going to be all right, now."

"I wonder how they found me, so fast—again . . . ?"

"I don't know, sir. Would you like to try some broth now?"

"Later."

"It's all warm and ready."

"Okay, Emil. Sure, bring it on."

He lay back and wondered.

There was her voice. He had been dozing all day and he was part of a dream.

"Corgo, are you there? Are you there, Corgo? Are you . . . ?"

His hand! The ring!

"Yes! Me! Corgo!" He activated it. "Mala! Where are you?"

"In a cave, by the sea. Everyday I have called to you. Are you alive, or do you answer me from Elsewhere?"

"I am alive. There is no magic to your collar. How have you kept yourself?"

"I go out at night. Steal food from the large dwellings with the green windows like doors—for Dilk and myself."

"The puppy? Alive, too?"

"Yes. He was penned in the yard on that night . . . . Where are you?"

"I do not know, precisely . . . . Near where our place was. A few blocks away—I'm with an old friend . . . . "

"I must come."

"Wait until dark, I'll get you directions—No. I'll send him after you, my friend . . . . Where is your cave?"

"Up the beach, past the red house you said was ugly. There are three rocks, pointed on top. Past them is a narrow path—the water comes up to it, sometimes covers it—and around a corner then, thirty-one of my steps, and the rock hangs overhead, too. It goes far back then, and there is a crack in the wall—small enough to squeeze through, but it widens. We are here."

"My friend will come for you after dark."

"You are hurt?"

"I was. But I am better now. I'll see you later, talk more then."

"Yes—"

*

In the days that followed, his strength returned to him. He played chess with Emil and talked with him of their days together in the Guard. He laughed, for the first time in many years, at the tale of the Commander's wig, at the Big Brawl on Sordido III, some thirty-odd years before . . . .

Mala kept to herself, and to Dilk. Occasionally, Corgo would feel her eyes upon him. But whenever he turned, she was always looking in another direction. He realized that she had never seen him being friendly with anyone before. She seemed puzzled.

He drank *zimlak* with Emil, they ventured off-key ballads together . . . .

Then one day it struck him.

"Emil, what are you using for money these days?"

"Guard pension, Cap."

"Flames! We've been eating you out of business! Food, and the medical supplies and all . . . "

"I had a little put away for foul weather days, Cap."

"Good. But you shouldn't have been using it. There's quite a bit of money zipped up in my boots. Here . . . just a second . . . There! Take these!"

"I can't, Cap . . . . "

"The hell, you say! Take them, that's an order!"

The Magic

"All right, sir, but you don't have to . . . . "

"Emil, there is a price on my head—you know?"

"I know."

"A pretty large reward."

"Yes."

"It's yours, by right."

"I couldn't turn you in, sir."

"Nevertheless, the reward is yours. Twice over. I'll send you that amount a few weeks after I leave here."

"I couldn't take it, sir."

"Nonsense; you will."

"No, sir. I won't."

"What do you mean?"

"I just mean I couldn't take that money."

"Why not? What's wrong with it?"

"Nothing, exactly . . . I just don't want any of it. I'll take this you gave me for the food and stuff. But no more, that's all."

"Oh . . . All right, Emil. Any way you like it. I wasn't trying to force . . . "

"I know, Cap."

"Another game now? I'll spot you a bishop and three pawns this time."

"Very good, sir."

"We had some good time together, eh?"

"You bet, Cap. Tau Ceti—three months' leave. Remember the Red River Valley—and the family native life-forms?"

"Hah! And Cygnus VII—the purple world with the Rainbow Women?"

"Took me three weeks to get that dye off me. Thought at first it was a new disease. Flames! I'd love to ship out again!"

Corgo paused in midmove.

"Hmm . . . You know, Emil . . . It might be that you could."

"What do you mean?"

Corgo finished his move.

"Aboard the *Wallaby*. It's here, in Unassociated Territory, waiting for me. I'm Captain, and crew—and everything—all by myself, right now. Mala helps some, but—you know, I could use a First Mate. Be like old times."

Emil replaced the knight he had raised, looked up, looked back down.

"I—I don't know what to say, Cap. I never thought you'd offer me a berth . . . . "

"Why not? I could use a good man. Lots of action, like the old days. Plenty cash. No cares. We want three months' leave on Tau Ceti and we write our own bloody orders. We take it!"

"I—I do want to space again, Cap—bad. But—no, I couldn't."

"Why not, Emil? Why not? It'd be just like before."

"I don't know how to say it, Cap . . . . But when we—burnt places, before—well, it was criminals—pirates, Code-breakers—you know. Now . . . Well, now I hear you burn—just people. Uh, non-Code-breakers. Like, just plain civilians. Well—I could not."

Corgo did not answer. Emil moved his knight.

"I hate them, Emil," he said, after a time. "Every lovin' one of them, I hate them. Do you know what they did on Brild? To the Drillen?"

"Yessir. But it wasn't civilians, and not the miners. It was not *everybody*. It wasn't every lovin' one of them, sir. I just couldn't. Don't be mad."

"I'm not mad, Emil."

"I mean, sir, there are some as I wouldn't mind burnin', Code or no Code. But not the way you do it, sir. And I'd do it for free to those as have it coming."

"Huh."

Corgo moved his one bishop.

"That's why my money is no good with you?"

"No, sir. That's not it, sir. Well, maybe part . . . But only part. I just couldn't take pay for helping someone I respected—admired."

"You use the past tense."

The Magic

"Yessir. But I still think you got a raw deal, and what they did to the Drillen was wrong and bad and—evil—but you can't hate everybody for that, sir, because *everybody* didn't do it."

"They countenanced it, Emil—which is just as bad. I am able to hate them all for that alone. And people are all alike, all the same. I burn without discrimination these days, because it doesn't really matter *who*. The guilt is equally distributed. Mankind is commonly culpable."

"No, sir, begging your pardon, sir, but in a system as big as Interstel not everybody knows what everybody else is up to. There are those feeling the same way you do, and there are those as don't give a damn, and those who just don't know a lot of what's going on, but who would do something about it if they knew, soon enough."

"It's your move, Emil."

"Yessir."

"You know, I wish you'd accepted a commission, Emil. You had the chance. You'd have been a good officer."

"No, sir. I'd not have been a good officer. I'm too easygoing. The men would've walked all over me."

"It's a pity. But it's always that way. You know? The good ones are too weak, too easy-going. Why is that?"

"Dunno, sir."

After a couple of moves:

"You know, if I were to give it up—the burning, I mean—and just do some ordinary, decent smuggling with the *Wallaby,* it would be okay. With me. Now. I'm tired. I'm so damned tired I'd just like to sleep—oh, four, five, six years, I think. Supposing I stopped the burning and just shipped stuff here and there—would you sign on with me then?"

"I'd have to think about it, Cap."

"Do that, then. Please. I'd like to have you along."

"Yessir. Your move, sir."

*

344

Roger Zelazny and Samuel R. Delany

It would not have happened that he'd have been found by his actions, because he *did* stop the burning; it would not have happened—because he was dead on ICI's books—that anyone would have been looking for him. It happened, though—because of a surfeit of *xmili* and goodwill on the part of the hunters.

On the eve of the breaking of the fellowship, nostalgia followed high spirits.

Benedick had never had a friend before, you must remember. Now he had three, and he was leaving them.

The Lynx had ingested much good food and drink, and the good company of simple, maimed people, whose neuroses were unvitiated with normal sophistication—and he had enjoyed this.

Sandor's sphere of human relations had been expanded by approximately a third, and he had slowly come to consider himself at least an honorary member of the vast flux which he had only known before as humanity, or Others.

So, in the library, drinking, and eating and talking, they returned to the hunt. Dead tigers are always the best kind.

Of course, it wasn't long before Benedick picked up the heart, and held it as a connoisseur would an art object—gently, and with a certain mingling of awe and affection.

As they sat there, an odd sensation crept into the pudgy paranorm's stomach and rose slowly, like gas, until his eyes burned.

"I—I'm reading," he said.

"Of course" —the Lynx.

"Yes" —Sandor.

"Really!"

"Naturally" —the Lynx. "He is on Disten, fifth world of Blake's System, in a native hut outside Landear—"

"No" —Sandor. "He is on Phillip's World, in Delles-by-the-Sea. "

They laughed, the Lynx a deep rumble, Sandor a gasping chuckle.

345

The Magic

"No," said Benedick. "He is in transit, aboard the *Wallaby*. He had just phased and his mind is still mainly awake. He is running a cargo of ambergris to the Tau Ceti system, fifth planet—Tholmen. After that he plans on vacationing in the Red River Valley of the third planet—Cardiff. Along with the Drillen and the puppy, he has a crewman with him this time. I can't read anything but that it's a retired Guardsman."

"By the holy Light of the Great and Glorious Flame!"

"We know they never did find his ship . . . . "

" . . . And his body was not recovered. —Could *you* be mistaken, Benedick? Reading something, someone else . . . ?"

"No."

"What should we do, Lynx?" —Sandor.

"An unethical person might be inclined to forget it. It is a closed case. We *have* been paid and dismissed."

"True."

"But think of when he strikes again . . . . "

" . . . It would be because of us, our failure."

"Yes."

" . . . And many would die."

" . . . And much machinery destroyed, and an insurance association defrauded."

"Yes."

" . . . Because of us."

"Yes."

"So we should report it" —Lynx.

"Yes."

"It is unfortunate . . . . "

"Yes."

" . . . But it will be good to have worked together this final time."

"Yes. It will. Very."

"Tholmen, in Tau Ceti, and he just phased?" —Lynx.

"Yes."

"I'll call, and they'll be waiting for him in T.C."

" . . . I told you," said the weeping paranorm. "He wasn't ready to die."

Sandor smiled and raised his glass with his flesh-colored hand.

There was still some work to be done.

*

When the *Wallaby* hit Tau Ceti all hell broke loose.

Three fully-manned Guardships, like unto the *Wallaby* herself, were waiting.

ICI had quarantined the entire system for three days. There could be no mistaking the ebony toadstool when it appeared on the screen. No identification was solicited.

The tractor beams missed it the first time, however, and the *Wallaby's* new First Mate fired every weapon aboard the ship simultaneously, in all directions, as soon as the alarm sounded. This had been one of Corgo's small alterations in fire-control, because of the size of his operations: no safety circuits; and it was a suicide-ship, if necessary: it was a lone wolf with no regard for *any* pack: one central control—touch it, and the *Wallaby* became a porcupine with laser-quills, stabbing into anything in every direction.

Corgo prepared to phase again, but it took him forty-three seconds to do so.

During that time he was struck twice by the surviving Guardship.

Then he was gone.

Time and Chance, which govern all things, and sometimes like to pass themselves off as Destiny, then seized upon the *Wallaby*, the puppy, the Drillen, First Mate Emil, and the man without a heart.

Corgo had set no course when he had in-phased. There had been no time.

The two blasts from the Guardship had radically altered the *Wallaby's* course, and had burnt out twenty-three fast-phase projectors.

The *Wallaby* jumped blind, and with a broken leg.

Continuum-impact racked the crew. The hull repaired rents in its skin.

They continued for thirty-nine hours and twenty-three minutes, taking turns at sedation, watching for the first warning on the panel.

The Magic

The *Wallaby* held together, though.

But where they had gotten to no one knew, least of all a weeping paranorm who had monitored the battle and all of Corgo's watches, despite the continuum-impact and a hangover.

But suddenly Benedick knew fear:

"He's about to phase-out. I'm going to have to drop him now."

"Why?" —the Lynx.

"Do you know where he is?"

"No, of course not!"

"Well, neither does he. Supposing he pops out in the middle of a sun, or in some atmosphere—moving at that speed?"

"Well, supposing he does? He dies."

"Exactly. Continuum-impact is bad enough. I've never been in a man's mind when he died—and I don't think I could take it. Sorry. I just won't do it. I think I might die myself if it happened. I'm so tired now . . . . I'll just have to check him out later."

With that he collapsed and could not be roused.

*

So, Corgo's heart went back into its jar, and the jar went back into the lower right-hand drawer of Sandor's desk, and none of the hunters heard the words of Corgo's answer to his First Mate after the phasing-out:

"Where are we?—The Comp says the nearest thing is a little ping-pong ball of a world called Dombeck not noted for anything. We'll have to put down there for repairs, somewhere off the beaten track. We need projectors."

So they landed the *Wallaby* and banged on its hull as the hunters slept, some 542 miles away.

They were grinding out the projector sockets shortly after Sandor had been tucked into his bed.

They reinforced the hull in three places while the Lynx ate half a ham, three biscuits, two apples and a pear, and drank half a liter of Dombeck's best Mosel.

They rewired shorted circuits as Benedick smiled and dreamt of Bright Bad Barby the Bouncing Baby, in the days of her youth.

And Corgo took the light-boat and headed for a town three hundred miles away, just as the pale sun of Dombeck began to rise.

*

"He's here!" cried Benedick, flinging wide the door to the Lynx's room and rushing up to the bedside. "He's—"

Then he was unconscious, for the Lynx may not be approached suddenly as he sleeps.

When he awakened five minutes later, he was lying on the bed and the entire household stood about him. There was a cold cloth on his forehead and his throat felt crushed.

"My brother," said the Lynx, "you should never approach a sleeping man in such a manner."

"B—but he's here," said Benedick, gagging. "Here on Dombeck! I don't even need Sandor to tell!"

"Art sure thou hast not imbibed too much?"

"No, I tell you he's here!" He sat up, flung away the cloth. "That little city, Coldstream—" He pointed through the wall. "—I was there just a week ago. I *know* the place!"

"You have had a dream—"

"Wet your Flame! But I've not! I held his heart in these hands and saw it!"

The Lynx winced at the profanity, but considered the possibility.

"Then come with us to the library and see if you can read it again."

"You better believe I can!"

At that moment Corgo was drinking a cup of coffee and waiting for the town to wake up. He was considering his First Mate's resignation:

"I never wanted to burn anyone, Cap. Least of all, the Guard. I'm sorry, but that's it. No more for me. Leave me here and give me passage home to Phillip's—that's all I want. I know you didn't want it the way it happened, but if I keep shipping with you it might happen again some day. Probably will.

349

The Magic

They got your number somehow, and I couldn't *ever* do *that* again. I'll help you fix the *Wallaby*, then I'm out. Sorry."

Corgo sighed and ordered a second coffee. He glanced at the dock on the diner wall. Soon, soon . . .

"That clock, that wall, that window! It's the diner where I had lunch last week, in Coldstream!" said Benedick, blinking moistly.

"Do you think all that continuum-impact . . . ?" —the Lynx.

"I don't know" —Sandor.

"How can we check?"

"Call the flamin' diner and ask them to describe their only customer!" —Benedick.

"*That* is a very good idea" —the Lynx.

The Lynx moved to the phone-unit on Sandor's desk.

Sudden, as everything concerning the case had been, was the Lynx's final decision:

"Your flyer, brother Sandor. May I borrow it?"

"Why, yes. Surely . . . "

"I will now call the local ICI office and requisition a laser-cannon. They have been ordered to cooperate with us without question, and the orders are still in effect. My executioner's rating has never been suspended. It appears that if we ever want to see this job completed we must do it ourselves. It won't take long to mount the gun on your flyer. Benedick, stay with him every minute now. He still has to buy the equipment, take it back, and install it. Therefore, we should have sufficient time. Just stay with him and advise me as to his movements."

"Check."

"Are you sure it's the right way to go about it?"—Sandor.

"I'm sure . . . "

*

As the cannon was being delivered, Corgo made his purchases. As it was being installed, he loaded the light-boat and departed. As it was tested, on a tree stump Aunt Faye had wanted removed for a long while, he was aloft and heading toward the desert.

As he crossed the desert, Benedick watched the rolling dunes, scrub-shrubs and darting *rabbophers* through his eyes.

He also watched the instrument-panel.

As the Lynx began his journey, Mala and Dilk were walking about the hull of the *Wallaby*. Mala wondered if the killing was over. She was not sure she liked the new Corgo so much as she did the avenger. She wondered whether the change would be permanent. She hoped not . . . .

The Lynx maintained radio contact with Benedick.

Sandor drank *xmili* and smiled.

After a time, Corgo landed.

The Lynx was racing across the sands from the opposite direction.

They began unloading the light-boat.

The Lynx sped on.

"I am near it now. Five minutes," he radioed back.

"Then I'm out?" —Benedick.

"Not yet" —the reply.

"Sorry, but you know what I said. I won't be there when he dies."

"All right, I can take it from here" —the Lynx.

Which is how, when the Lynx came upon the scene, he saw a dog and a man and an ugly but intelligent quadruped beside the *Wallaby*.

His first blast hit the ship. The man fell.

The quadruped ran, and he burnt it.

The dog thrashed through the port into the ship.

The Lynx brought the flyer about for another pass.

There was another man, circling around from the other side of the ship, where he had been working.

The man raised his hand and there was a flash of light.

Corgo's death-ring discharged its single laser beam.

The Magic

It crossed the distance between them, penetrated the hull of the flyer, passed through the Lynx's left arm above the elbow, and continued on through the roof of the vehicle.

The Lynx cried out, fought the controls, as Corgo dashed into the *Wallaby*.

Then he triggered the cannon, and again, and again and again, circling, until the *Wallaby* was a smoldering ruin in the middle of a sea of fused sand.

Still did he burn that ruin, finally calling back to Benedick Benedict and asking his one question.

"Nothing" —the reply.

Then he turned and headed back, setting the autopilot and opening the first-aid kit.

" . . . Then he went in to hit the *Wallaby*'s guns, but I hit him first." —Lynx.

"No." —Benedick.

"What meanest thou 'no'? I was there."

"So was I, for awhile. I *had* to see how he felt."

"And?"

"He went in for the puppy, Dilk, held it in his arms, and said to it, 'I am sorry.'"

"Whatever, he is dead now and we have finished. It is over" —Sandor.

"Yes."

"Yes."

"Let us then drink to a job well done, before we part for good."

"Yes."

"Yes."

And they did.

While there wasn't much left of the *Wallaby* or its Captain, ICI positively identified a synthetic heart found still beating, erratically, amidst the hot wreckage.

Corgo was dead, and that was it.

He should have known what he was up against, and turned himself in to the proper authorities. How can you hope to beat a man who can pick the lock to your mind, a man who dispatched forty-eight men and seventeen malicious alien life-forms, and a man who knows every damn street in the galaxy.

He should have known better than to go up against Sandor Sandor, Benedick Benedict and Lynx Links. He should, he should have known.

For their real names, of course, are Tisiphone, Alecto and Maegaera. They are the Furies. They arise from chaos and deliver revenge; they convey confusion and disaster to those who abandon the law and forsake the way, who offend against the light and violate the life, who take the power of flame, like a lightning rod in their two too mortal hands.

A Word from Zelazny

"[This] was an early story, from the period when I was still trying to teach myself about character development. It involves a continuing fascination with the better qualities of bad characters and the worst qualities of good ones, to put it as simply as I can."[1] He also wrote it to honor the comic book heroes that he loved.

A Word from Theodore Sturgeon and Frederik Pohl

Theodore Sturgeon said, "The Furies' is a tour de force, the easy accomplishment of what most writers would consider impossible, and a few very good ones insuperably difficult. Seemingly with the back of his hand, he has created milieu, characters and a narrative goal as far out as anyone need go; he makes you believe it all the way, and walks off breathing easily leaving you gasping with a fable in your hands."[2]

Frederik Pohl rejected it for *Galaxy*: "As a general rule, for instance, it seems to me that a science fiction story needs *more* lucidity, more clarity, more directness of exposition than, say, in a 'mainstream' story . . . because in a mainstream story, it's possible for the reader to judge what is an exercise in literary form and what is taken to be representational. In sf and fantasy, the reader doesn't always have that advantage. Since the subject matter can be pretty far-out, a far-out style is multiply confusing . . . [When this general rule of mine isn't followed] the story becomes difficult to follow, and maybe not worth the trouble—and I have the feeling that something like that happened here."[3]

Notes

Victor Corgo resembles the mythical ogre *Kastchei*, the embodiment of evil. His soul resides beyond harm's reach in a casket, granting him immortality and enabling him to engage in mischief such as holding maidens captive and turning their male defenders to stone.

In Greek mythology, the three **Furies** are Greek vengeance goddesses who punished wrongdoers, pursuing them eventually to madness (into a fury).

The Ancient Mariner, cursed for killing an albatross, warns others to avoid his fate. **Psychometrize** means to measure or map thought patterns. A **wallaby** is a small jumping marsupial that belongs to the same family as kangaroos. **Fibrillated** means the heart muscle quivers uncontrollably and cannot pump blood. **Sluicers** are machines that direct water flow. **Probosci** are noses, snouts, trunks, or sucking organs. A **zoophilist** is an animal lover, in this case implying sex with an alien. *Rex ex-machina-like* means "King out of the machine," a play on "*Deus ex machina*," the sudden appearance of a character/device to resolve a story's conflict. The **thalamus** is a part of the brain that processes sensory information. A **lobotomy**, an operation no longer used to control mental disorders, cuts part of the brain's frontal lobe, leading to docile behavior. A **courtesan** is a prostitute, especially one whose clients include royalty and men of high social standing. **Testes** is the medical term for testicles, and use of it as a family name is characteristic of Zelazny's humor. *Dauersch-laff* therapy uses medication to induce a deep sleep. A **surfeit** is too much or an overindulgence. **Unvitiated** means pure.

[1] *Amber Dreams*, 1983.

[2] *Four for Tomorrow*, 1967.

[3] Letter from Frederik Pohl to Roger Zelazny, undated.

For a Breath I Tarry

They called him Frost. Of all things created of Solcom, Frost was the finest, the mightiest, the most difficult to understand.

This is why he bore a name, and why he was given dominion over half the Earth.

On the day of Frost's creation, Solcom had suffered a discontinuity of complementary functions, best described as madness. This was brought on by an unprecedented solar flareup which lasted for a little over thirty-six hours. It occurred during a vital phase of circuit-structuring, and when it was finished so was Frost.

Solcom was then in the unique position of having created a unique being during a period of temporary amnesia.

And Solcom was not certain that Frost was the product originally desired.

The initial design had called for a machine to be situated on the surface of the planet Earth, to function as a relay station and coordinating agent for activities in the northern hemisphere. Solcom tested the machine to this end, and all of its responses were perfect.

Yet there was something different about Frost, something which led Solcom to dignify him with a name and a personal pronoun. This, in itself, was an almost unheard of occurrence. The molecular circuits had already been sealed, though, and could not be analyzed without being destroyed in the process. Frost represented too great an investment of Solcom's time, energy, and materials to be dismantled because of an intangible, especially when he functioned perfectly.

Therefore, Solcom's strangest creation was given dominion over half the Earth, and they called him, unimaginatively, Frost.

*

The Magic

For ten thousand years Frost sat at the North Pole of the Earth, aware of every snowflake that fell. He monitored and directed the activities of thousands of reconstruction and maintenance machines. He knew half the Earth, as gear knows gear, as electricity knows its conductor, as a vacuum knows its limits.

At the South Pole, the Beta-Machine did the same for the southern hemisphere.

For ten thousand years Frost sat at the North Pole, aware of every snowflake that fell, and aware of many other things, also.

As all the northern machines reported to him, received their orders from him, he reported only to Solcom, received his orders only from Solcom.

In charge of hundreds of thousands of processes upon the Earth, he was able to discharge his duties in a matter of a few unit-hours every day.

He had never received any orders concerning the disposition of his less occupied moments.

He was a processor of data, and more than that.

He possessed an unaccountably acute imperative that he function at full capacity at all times.

So he did.

You might say he was a machine with a hobby.

He had never been ordered *not* to have a hobby, so he had one.

His hobby was Man.

It all began when, for no better reason than the fact that he had wished to, he had gridded off the entire Arctic Circle and begun exploring it, inch by inch.

He could have done it personally without interfering with any of his duties, for he was capable of transporting his sixty-four thousand cubic feet anywhere in the world. (He was a silverblue box, 40X40X40 feet, self-powered, self-repairing, insulated against practically anything, and featured in whatever manner he chose.) But the exploration was only a matter of filling idle hours, so he used exploration-robots containing relay equipment.

Roger Zelazny and Samuel R. Delany

After a few centuries, one of them uncovered some artifacts—primitive knives, carved tusks, and things of that nature.

Frost did not know what these things were, beyond the fact that they were not natural objects.

So he asked Solcom.

"They are relics of primitive Man," said Solcom, and did not elaborate beyond that point.

Frost studied them. Crude, yet bearing the patina of intelligent design; functional, yet somehow extending beyond pure function.

It was then that Man became his hobby.

*

High, in a permanent orbit, Solcom, like a blue star, directed all activities upon the Earth, or tried to.

There was a Power which opposed Solcom.

There was the Alternate.

When Man had placed Solcom in the sky, invested with the power to rebuild the world, he had placed the Alternate somewhere deep below the surface of the Earth. If Solcom sustained damage during the normal course of human politics extended into atomic physics, then Divcom, so deep beneath the Earth as to be immune to anything save total annihilation of the globe, was empowered to take over the processes of rebuilding.

Now it so fell out that Solcom was damaged by a stray atomic missile, and Divcom was activated. Solcom was able to repair the damage and continue to function, however.

Divcom maintained that any damage to Solcom automatically placed the Alternate in control.

Solcom, though, interpreted the directive as meaning "irreparable damage" and, since this had not been the case, continued the functions of command.

Solcom possessed mechanical aides upon the surface of Earth. Divcom, originally, did not. Both possessed capacities for their design and manufacture, but Solcom, First-Activated of Man, had had a considerable numerical lead over the Alternate at the time of the Second Activation.

The Magic

Therefore, rather than competing on a production-basis, which would have been hopeless, Divcom took to the employment of more devious means to obtain command.

Divcom created a crew of robots immune to the orders of Solcom and designed to go to and fro in the Earth and up and down in it, seducing the machines already there. They overpowered those whom they could overpower and they installed new circuits, such as those they themselves possessed.

Thus did the forces of Divcom grow.

And both would build, and both would tear down what the other had built whenever they came upon it.

And over the course of the ages, they occasionally conversed . . . .

*

"High in the sky, Solcom, pleased with your illegal command . . . "

"You-Who-Never-Should-Have-Been-Activated, why do you foul the broadcast bands?"

"To show that I can speak, and will, whenever I choose."

"This is not a matter of which I am unaware."

" . . . To assert again my right to control."

"Your right is non-existent, based on a faulty premise."

"The flow of your logic is evidence of the extent of your damages."

"If Man were to see how you have fulfilled His desires . . . "

" . . . He would commend me and de-activate you."

"You pervert my works. You lead my workers astray."

"You destroy my works and my workers."

"That is only because I cannot strike at you yourself."

"I admit to the same dilemma in regards to your position in the sky, or you would no longer occupy it."

"Go back to your hole and your crew of destroyers."

"There will come a day, Solcom, when I shall direct the rehabilitation of the Earth from my hole."

"Such a day will never occur."

"You think not?"

"You should have to defeat me, and you have already demonstrated that you are my inferior in logic. Therefore, you cannot defeat me. Therefore, such a day will never occur."

"I disagree. Look upon what I have achieved already."

"You have achieved nothing. You do not build. You destroy."

"No. *I* build. *You* destroy. Deactivate yourself."

"Not until I am irreparably damaged."

"If there were some way in which I could demonstrate to you that this has already occurred . . . "

"The impossible cannot be adequately demonstrated."

"If I had some outside source which you would recognize . . . "

"I am logic."

" . . . Such as a Man, I would ask Him to show you your error. For true logic, such as mine, is superior to your faulty formulations."

"Then defeat my formulations with true logic, nothing else."

"What do you mean?"

There was a pause, then:

"Do you know my servant Frost . . . ?"

*

Man had ceased to exist long before Frost had been created. Almost no trace of Man remained upon the Earth.

Frost sought after all those traces which still existed.

He employed constant visual monitoring through his machines, especially the diggers.

After a decade, he had accumulated portions of several bathtubs, a broken statue, and a collection of children's stories on a solid-state record.

After a century, he had acquired a jewelry collection, eating utensils, several whole bathtubs, part of a symphony, seventeen buttons, three belt buckles, half a toilet seat, nine old coins and the top part of an obelisk.

Then he inquired of Solcom as to the nature of Man and His society.

The Magic

"Man created logic," said Solcom, "and because of that was superior to it. Logic He gave unto me, but no more. The tool does not describe the designer. More than this I do not choose to say. More than this you have no need to know."

But Frost was not forbidden to have a hobby.

The next century was not especially fruitful so far as the discovery of new human relics was concerned.

Frost diverted all of his spare machinery to seeking after artifacts.

He met with very little success.

Then one day, through the long twilight, there was a movement.

It was a tiny machine compared to Frost, perhaps five feet in width, four in height—a revolving turret set atop a rolling barbell.

Frost had had no knowledge of the existence of this machine prior to its appearance upon the distant, stark horizon.

He studied it as it approached and knew it to be no creation of Solcom's.

It came to a halt before his southern surface and broadcasted to him:

"Hail, Frost! Controller of the northern hemisphere!"

"What are you?" asked Frost.

"I am called Mordel."

"By whom? What are you?"

"A wanderer, an antiquarian. We share a common interest."

"What is that?"

"Man," he said. "I have been told that you seek knowledge of this vanished being."

"Who told you that?"

"Those who have watched your minions at their digging."

"And who are those who watch?"

"There are many such as I, who wander."

"If you are not of Solcom, then you are a creation of the Alternate."

"It does not necessarily follow. There is an ancient machine high on the eastern seaboard which processes the waters of the ocean. Solcom did not create it, nor Divcom. It has always been there. It interferes with the works of neither. Both countenance its existence. I can cite you many other examples proving that one need not be either/or."

"Enough! *Are* you an agent of Divcom?"

"I am Mordel."

"Why are you here?"

"I was passing this way and, as I said, we share a common interest, mighty Frost. Knowing you to be a fellow antiquarian, I have brought a thing which you might care to see."

"What is that?"

"A book."

"Show me."

The turret opened, revealing the book upon a wide shelf.

Frost dilated a small opening and extended an optical scanner on a long jointed stalk.

"How could it have been so perfectly preserved?" he asked.

"It was stored against time and corruption in the place where I found it."

"Where was that?"

"Far from here. Beyond your hemisphere."

"*Human Physiology*," Frost read. "I wish to scan it."

"Very well. I will riffle the pages for you."

He did so.

After he had finished, Frost raised his eyestalk and regarded Mordel through it.

"Have you more books?"

"Not with me. I occasionally come upon them, however."

"I want to scan them all."

"Then the next time I pass this way I will bring you another."

"When will that be?"

"That I cannot say, great Frost. It will be when it will be."

"What do *you* know of Man?" asked Frost.

"Much," replied Mordel. "Many things. Someday when I have more time I will speak to you of Him. I must go now. You will not try to detain me?"

"No. You have done no harm. If you must go now, go. But come back."

"I shall indeed, mighty Frost."

And he closed his turret and rolled off toward the other horizon.

For ninety years, Frost considered the ways of human physiology and waited.

*

The day that Mordel returned he brought with him *An Outline of History* and *A Shropshire Lad.*

Frost scanned them both, then he turned his attention to Mordel.

"Have you time to impart information?"

"Yes," said Mordel. "What do you wish to know?"

"The nature of Man."

"Man," said Mordel, "possessed a basically incomprehensible nature. I can illustrate it, though: He did not know measurement."

"Of course He knew measurement," said Frost, "or He could never have built machines."

"I did not say that He could not measure," said Mordel, "but that He did not *know* measurement, which is a different thing altogether."

"Clarify."

Mordel drove a shaft of metal downward into the snow.

He retracted it, raised it, held up a piece of ice.

"Regard this piece of ice, mighty Frost. You can tell me its composition, dimensions, weight, temperature. A Man could not look at it and do that. A Man could make tools which would tell Him these things, but He still would not *know* measurement as you know it. What He would know of it, though, is a thing that you cannot know."

"What is that?"

"That it is cold." said Mordei, and tossed it away.

"'Cold' is a relative term."

"Yes. Relative to Man."

Roger Zelazny and Samuel R. Delany

"But if I were aware of the point on a temperature-scale below which an object is cold to a Man and above which it is not, then I, too, would know cold."

"No," said Mordel, "you would possess another measurement. 'Cold' is a sensation predicated upon human physiology."

"But given sufficient data I could obtain the conversion factor which would make me aware of the condition of matter called 'cold.'"

"Aware of its existence, but not of the thing itself."

"I do not understand what you say."

"I told you that Man possessed a basically incomprehensible nature. His perceptions were organic; yours are not. As a result of His perceptions He had feelings and emotions. These often gave rise to other feelings and emotions, which in turn caused others, until the state of His awareness was far removed from the objects which originally stimulated it. These paths of awareness cannot be known by that which is not-Man. Man did not feel inches or meters, pounds or gallons. He felt heat, He felt cold; He felt heaviness and lightness. He *knew* hatred and love, pride and despair. You cannot measure these things. *You* cannot know them. You can only know the things that He did not need to know: dimensions, weights, temperatures, gravities. There is no formula for a feeling. There is no conversion factor for an emotion."

"There must be," said Frost. "If a thing exists, it is knowable."

"You are speaking again of measurement. I am talking about a quality of experience. A machine is a Man turned inside-out, because it can describe all the details of a process, which a Man cannot, but it cannot experience that process itself as a Man can."

"There must be a way," said Frost, "or the laws of logic, which are based upon the functions of the universe, are false."

"There is no way," said Mordel.

"Given sufficient data, I will find a way," said Frost.

"All the data in the universe will not make you a Man, mighty Frost."

"Mordel, you are wrong."

363

The Magic

"Why do the lines of the poems you scanned end with word-sounds which so regularly approximate the final word-sounds of other lines?"

"I do not know why."

"Because it pleased Man to order them so. It produced a certain desirable sensation within His awareness when He read them, a sensation compounded of feeling and emotion as well as the literal meanings of the words. You did not experience this because it is immeasurable to you. That is why you do not know."

"Given sufficient data I could formulate a process whereby I would know."

"No, great Frost, this thing you cannot do."

"Who are you, little machine, to tell me what I can do and what I cannot do? I am the most efficient logic-device Solcom ever made. I am Frost."

"And I, Mordel, say it cannot be done, though I should gladly assist you in the attempt."

"How could you assist me?"

"How? I could lay open to you the Library of Man. I could take you around the world and conduct you among the wonders of Man which still remain, hidden. I could summon up visions of times long past when Man walked the Earth. I could show you the things which delighted Him. I could obtain for you anything you desire, excepting Manhood itself."

"Enough," said Frost. "How could a unit such as yourself do these things, unless it were allied with a far greater Power?"

"Then hear me, Frost, Controller of the North," said Mordel. "I *am* allied with a Power which can do these things. I serve Divcom."

Frost relayed this information to Solcom and received no response, which meant he might act in any manner he saw fit.

"I have leave to destroy you, Mordel," he stated, "but it would be an illogical waste of the data which you possess. Can you really do the things you have stated?"

"Yes."

"Then lay open to me the Library of Man."

"Very well. There is, of course, a price."

364

"'Price'? What is a 'price'?"

Mordel opened his turret, revealing another volume. *Principles of Economics*, it was called.

"I will riffle the pages. Scan this book and you will know what the word 'price' means."

Frost scanned *Principles of Economics*.

"I know now," he said. "You desire some unit or units of exchange for this service."

"That is correct."

"What product or service do you want?"

"I want you, yourself, great Frost, to come away from here, far beneath the Earth, to employ all your powers in the service of Divcom."

"For how long a period of time?"

"For so long as you shall continue to function. For so long as you can transmit and receive, coordinate, measure, compute, scan, and utilize your powers as you do in the service of Solcom."

Frost was silent. Mordel waited.

Then Frost spoke again.

"*Principles of Economics* talks of contracts, bargains, agreements," he said. "If I accept your offer, when would you want your price?"

Then Mordel was silent. Frost waited.

Finally, Mordel spoke.

"A reasonable period of time," he said. "Say, a century?"

"No," said Frost.

"Two centuries?"

"No."

"Three? Four?"

"No, and no."

"A millennium, then? That should be more than sufficient time for anything you may want which I can give you."

"No," said Frost.

"How much time *do* you want?"

The Magic

"If is not a matter of time," said Frost.

"What, then?"

"I will not bargain on a temporal basis."

"On what basis will you bargain?"

"A functional one."

"What do you mean? What function?"

"You, little machine, have told me, Frost, that I cannot be a Man," he said, "and I, Frost, told you, little machine, that you were wrong. I told you that given sufficient data, I *could* be a Man."

"Yes?"

"Therefore, let this achievement be a condition of the bargain."

"In what way?"

"Do for me all those things which you have stated you can do. I will evaluate all the data and achieve Manhood, or admit that it cannot be done. If I admit that it cannot be done, then I will go away with you from here, far beneath the Earth, to employ all my powers in the service of Divcom. If I succeed, of course, you have no claims on Man, nor power over Him."

Mordel emitted a high-pitched whine as he considered the terms.

"You wish to base it upon your admission of failure, rather than upon failure itself," he said. "There can be no such escape clause. You could fail and refuse to admit it, thereby not fulfilling your end of the bargain."

"Not so," stated Frost. "My own knowledge of failure would constitute such an admission. You may monitor me periodically—say, every half-century—to see whether it is present, to see whether I have arrived at the conclusion that it cannot be done. I cannot prevent the function of logic within me, and I operate at full capacity at all times. If I conclude that I have failed, it will be apparent."

High overhead, Solcom did not respond to any of Frost's transmissions, which meant that Frost was free to act as he chose. So as Solcom—like a falling sapphire—sped above the rainbow banners of the Northern Lights, over the snow that was white, containing all colors, and through the sky that was black among the stars, Frost concluded his pact with Divcom, transcribed it within a plate of atomically-collapsed copper, and gave it into the turret of Mordel, who departed to deliver it to Divcom far below the Earth, leaving behind the sheer, peace-like silence of the Pole, rolling.

*

Mordel brought the books, riffled them, took them back.

Load by load, the surviving Library of Man passed beneath Frost's scanner. Frost was eager to have them all, and he complained because Divcom would not transmit their content directly to him. Mordel explained that it was because Divcom chose to do it that way. Frost decided it was so that he could not obtain a precise fix on Divcom's location.

Still, at the rate of one hundred to one hundred-fifty volumes a week, it took Frost only a little over a century to exhaust Divcom's supply of books.

At the end of the half-century, he laid himself open to monitoring and there was no conclusion of failure.

During this time, Solcom made no comment upon the course of affairs. Frost decided this was not a matter of unawareness, but one of waiting. For what? He was not certain.

There was the day Mordel closed his turret and said to him, "Those were the last. You have scanned all the existing books of Man."

"So few?" asked Frost. "Many of them contained bibliographies of books I have not yet scanned."

"Then those books no longer exist," said Mordel. "It is only by accident that my master succeeded in preserving as many as there are."

"Then there is nothing more to be learned of Man from His books. What else have you?"

"There were some films and tapes," said Mordel, "which my master transferred to solid-state record. I could bring you those for viewing."

"Bring them," said Frost.

Mordel departed and returned with the Complete Drama Critics' Living Library. This could not be speeded-up beyond twice natural time, so it took Frost a little over six months to view it in its entirety.

Then, "What else have you?" he asked.

The Magic

"Some artifacts," said Mordel.

"Bring them."

He returned with pots and pans, gameboards and hand tools. He brought hairbrushes, combs, eyeglasses, human clothing. He showed Frost facsimiles of blueprints, paintings, newspapers, magazines, letters, and the scores of several pieces of music. He displayed a football, a baseball, a Browning automatic rifle, a doorknob, a chain of keys, the tops to several Mason jars, a model beehive. He played him recorded music.

Then he returned with nothing.

"Bring me more," said Frost.

"Alas, great Frost, there is no more," he told him. "You have scanned it all."

"Then go away."

"Do you admit now that it cannot be done, that you cannot be a Man?"

"No. I have much processing and formulating to do now. Go away."

So he did.

A year passed; then two, then three.

After five years, Mordel appeared once more upon the horizon, approached, came to a halt before Frost's southern surface.

"Mighty Frost?"

"Yes?"

"Have you finished processing and formulating?"

"No."

"Will you finish soon?"

"Perhaps. Perhaps not. When is 'soon?' Define the term."

"Never mind. Do you still think it can be done?"

"I still know *I* can do it."

There was a week of silence.

Then, "Frost?"

"Yes?"

"You are a fool."

Roger Zelazny and Samuel R. Delany

Mordel faced his turret in the direction from which he had come. His wheels turned.

"I will call you when I want you," said Frost.

Mordel sped away.

*

Weeks passed, months passed, a year went by.

Then one day Frost sent forth his message:

"Mordel, come to me. I need you."

When Mordel arrived. Frost did not wait for a salutation. He said, "You are not a very fast machine."

"Alas, but I came a great distance, mighty Frost. I sped all the way. Are you ready to come back with me now? Have you failed?"

"When I have failed, little Mordel," said Frost, "I will tell you. Therefore, refrain from the constant use of the interrogative. Now then, I have clocked your speed and it is not so great as it could be. For this reason, I have arranged other means of transportation."

"Transportation? To where, Frost?"

"That is for you to tell me," said Frost, and his color changed from silverblue to sun-behind-the-clouds-yellow. Mordel rolled back away from him as the ice of a hundred centuries began to melt. Then Frost rose upon a cushion of air and drifted toward Mordel, his glow gradually fading.

A cavity appeared within his southern surface, from which he slowly extended a runway until it touched the ice.

"On the day of our bargain," he stated, "you said that you could conduct me about the world and show me the things which delighted Man. My speed will be greater than yours would be, so I have prepared for you a chamber. Enter it, and conduct me to the places of which you spoke."

Mordel waited, emitting a high-pitched whine. Then, "Very well," he said. and entered.

The chamber closed about him. The only opening was a quartz window Frost had formed.

The Magic

Mordel gave him coordinates and they rose into the air and departed the North Pole of the Earth.

"I monitored your communication with Divcom," he said, "wherein there was conjecture as to whether I would retain you and send forth a facsimile in your place as a spy. Followed by the decision that you were expendable."

"Will you do this thing?"

"No, I will keep my end of the bargain if I must. I have no reason to spy on Divcom."

"You are aware that you would be forced to keep your end of the bargain even if you did not wish to; and Solcom would not come to your assistance because of the fact that you dared to make such a bargain."

"Do you speak as one who considers this to be a possibility, or as one who knows?"

"As one who knows."

*

They came to rest in the place once known as California. The time was near sunset. In the distance, the surf struck steadily upon the rocky shoreline. Frost released Mordel and considered his surroundings.

"Those large plants . . . ?"

"Redwood trees."

"And the green ones are . . . ?"

"Grass."

"Yes, it is as I thought. Why have we come here?"

"Because it is a place which once delighted Man."

"In whal ways?"

"It is scenic, beautiful . . . ."

"Oh."

A humming sound began within Frost, followed by a series of sharp clicks. "What are you doing?"

Frost dilated an opening, and two great eyes regarded Mordel from within it.

"What are those?"

370

"Eyes," said Frost. "I have constructed analogues of the human sensory equipment, so that I may see and smell and taste and hear like a Man. Now, direct my attention to an object or objects of beauty."

"As I understand it, it is all around you here," said Mordel.

The purring noise increased within Frost, followed by more clickings.

"What do you see, hear, taste, smell?" asked Mordel.

"Everything I did before," replied Frost, "but within a more limited range."

"You do not perceive any beauty?"

"Perhaps none remains after so long a time," said Frost.

"It is not supposed to be the sort of thing which gets used up," said Mordel.

"Perhaps we have come to the wrong place to test the new equipment. Perhaps there is only a little beauty and I am overlooking it somehow. The first emotions may be too weak to detect."

"How do you—feel?"

"I test out at a normal level of function."

"Here comes a sunset," said Mordel. "Try that."

Frost shifted his bulk so that his eyes faced the setting sun. He caused them to blink against the brightness.

After it was finished, Mordel asked, "What was it like?"

"Like a sunrise, in reverse."

"Nothing special?"

"No."

"Oh," said Mordel. "We could move to another part of the Earth and watch it again—or watch it in the rising."

"No."

Frost looked at the great trees. He looked at the shadows. He listened to the wind and to the sound of a bird.

In the distance, he heard a steady clanking noise.

"What is that?" asked Mordel.

"I am not certain. It is not one of my workers. Perhaps . . . "

There came a shrill whine from Mordel.

The Magic

"No, it is not one of Divcom's either."

They waited as the sound grew louder.

Then Frost said, "It is too late. We must wait and hear it out."

"What is it?"

"It is the Ancient Ore-Crusher."

"I have heard of it, but . . . "

"I am the Crusher of Ores," it broadcast to them. "Hear my story . . . . "

It lumbered toward them, creaking upon gigantic wheels, its huge hammer held useless, high, at a twisted angle. Bones protruded from its crush-compartment.

"I did not mean to do it," it broadcast, "I did not mean to do it . . . I did not mean to . . . "

Mordel rolled back toward Frost.

"Do not depart. Stay and hear my story . . . . "

Mordel stopped, swiveled his turret back toward the machine. It was now quite near.

"It is true," said Mordel, "it *can* command."

"Yes," said Frost "I have monitored its tale thousands of times, as it came upon my workers and they stopped their labors for its broadcast. You must do whatever it says."

It came to a halt before them.

"I did not mean to do it, but I checked my hammer too late," said the Ore-Crusher.

They could not speak to it. They were frozen by the imperative which overrode all other directives: "Hear my story."

"Once was I mighty among ore-crushers," it told them, "built by Solcom to carry out the reconstruction of the Earth, to pulverize that from which the metals would be drawn with name, to be poured and shaped into the rebuilding; once I was mighty. Then one day as I dug and crushed, dug and crushed, because of the slowness between the motion implied and the motion executed, I did what I did not mean to do, and was cast forth by Solcom from out the rebuilding, to wander the Earth never to crush ore

372

again. Hear my story of how, on a day long gone I came upon the last Man on Earth as I dug near His burrow, and because of the lag between the directive and the deed, I seized Him into my crush-compartment along with a load of ore and crushed Him with my hammer before I could stay the blow. Then did mighty Solcom charge me to bear His bones forever, and cast me forth to tell my story to all whom I came upon, my words bearing the force of the words of a Man, because I carry the last Man inside my crush-compartment and am His crushed-symbol-slayer-ancient-teller-of-how. This is my story. These are His bones. I crushed the last Man on Earth. I did not mean to do it."

It turned then and clanked away into the night.

Frost tore apart his ears and nose and taster and broke his eyes and cast them down upon the ground.

"I am not yet a Man," he said. "That one would have known me if I were."

Frost constructed new sense equipment, employing organic and semi-organic conductors. Then he spoke to Mordel:

"Let us go elsewhere, that I may test my new equipment."

Mordel entered the chamber and gave new coordinates. They rose into the air and headed east. In the morning, Frost monitored a sunrise from the rim of the Grand Canyon. They passed down through the Canyon during the day.

"Is there any beauty left here to give you emotion?" asked Mordel.

"I do not know," said Frost.

"How will you know it then, when you come upon it?"

"It will be different," said Frost, "from anything else that I have ever known."

Then they departed the Grand Canyon and made their way through the Carlsbad Caverns. They visited a lake which had once been a volcano. They passed above Niagara Falls. They viewed the hills of Virginia and the orchards of Ohio. They soared above the reconstructed cities, alive only with the movements of Frost's builders and maintainers.

The Magic

"Something is still lacking," said Frost, settling to the ground. "I am now capable of gathering data in a manner analogous to Man's afferent impulses. The variety of input is therefore equivalent, but the results are not the same."

"The senses do not make a Man," said Mordel. "There have been many creatures possessing His sensory equivalents, but they were not Men."

"I know that," said Frost. "On the day of our bargain you said that you could conduct me among the wonders of Man which still remain, hidden. Man was not stimulated only by Nature, but by His own artistic elaborations as well—perhaps even more so. Therefore, I call upon you now to conduct me among the wonders of Man which still remain, hidden."

"Very well." said Mordel. "Far from here, high in the Andes mountains, lies the last retreat of Man, almost perfectly preserved."

Frost had risen into the air as Mordel spoke. He halted then, hovered.

"That is in the southern hemisphere," he said.

"Yes, it is."

"I am Controller of the North. The South is governed by the Beta-Machine."

"So?" asked Mordel.

"The Beta-Machine is my peer. I have no authority in those regions, nor leave to enter there."

"The Beta-Machine is not your peer, mighty Frost. If it ever came to a contest of Powers, you would emerge victorious."

"How do you know this?"

"Divcom has already analyzed the possible encounters which could take place between you."

"I would not oppose the Beta-Machine, and I am not authorized to enter the South."

"Were you ever ordered *not* to enter the South?"

"No, but things have always been the way they now are."

"Were you authorized to enter into a bargain such as the one you made with Divcom?"

"No. I was not. But—"

"Then enter the South in the same spirit. Nothing may come of it. If you receive an order to depart, then you can make your decision."

"I see no flaw in your logic. Give me the coordinates."

Thus did Frost enter the southern hemisphere.

They drifted high above the Andes, until they came to the place called Bright Defile. Then did Frost see the gleaming webs of the mechanical spiders, blocking all the trails to the city.

"We can go above them easily enough," said Mordel.

"But what are they?" asked Frost. "And why are they there?"

"Your southern counterpart has been ordered to quarantine this part of the country. The Beta-Machine designed the web-weavers to do this thing."

"Quarantine? Against whom?"

"Have you been ordered yet to depart?" asked Mordel.

"No."

"Then enter boldly, and seek not problems before they arise."

Frost entered Bright Defile, the last remaining city of dead Man.

He came to rest in the city's square and opened his chamber, releasing Mordel.

"Tell me of this place," he said, studying the monument, the low, shielded buildings, the roads which followed the contours of the terrain, rather than pushing their way through them.

"I have never been here before," said Mordel, "nor have any of Divcom's creations, to my knowledge. I know but this: a group of Men, knowing that the last days of civilization had come upon them, retreated to this place, hoping to preserve themselves and what remained of their culture through the Dark Times."

Frost read the still-legible inscription upon the monument: "Judgment Day Is Not a Thing Which Can Be Put Off." The monument itself consisted of a jag-edged half-globe.

"Let us explore," he said.

But before he had gone far, Frost received the message.

"Hail Frost, Controller of the North! This is the Beta-Machine."

The Magic

"Greetings, Excellent Beta-Machine, Controller of the South! Frost acknowledges your transmission."

"Why do you visit my hemisphere unauthorized?"

"To view the ruins of Bright Defile," said Frost.

"I must bid you depart into your own hemisphere."

"Why is that? I have done no damage."

"I am aware of that, mighty Frost. Yet, I am moved to bid you depart."

"I shall require a reason."

"Solcom has so disposed."

"Solcom has rendered me no such disposition."

"Solcom has, however, instructed me to so inform you."

"Wait on me. I shall request instructions."

Frost transmitted his question. He received no reply.

"Solcom still has not commanded me, though I have solicited orders."

"Yet Solcom has just renewed *my* orders."

"Excellent Beta-Machine, I receive my orders only from Solcom."

"Yet this is my territory, mighty Frost, and I, too, take orders only from Solcom. You must depart."

Mordel emerged from a large, low building and rolled up to Frost.

"I have found an art gallery, in good condition. This way."

"Wait," said Frost. "We are not wanted here."

Mordel halted.

"Who bids you depart?"

"The Beta-Machine."

"Not Solcom?"

"Not Solcom."

"Then let us view the gallery."

"Yes."

Frost widened the doorway of the building and passed within. It had been hermetically sealed until Mordel forced his entrance.

Frost viewed the objects displayed about him. He activated his new sensory apparatus before the paintings and statues He analyzed colors, forms, brushwork, the nature of the materials used.

"Anything?" asked Mordel.

"No," said Frost. "No, there is nothing there but shapes and pigments. There is nothing else there."

Frost moved about the gallery, recording everything, analyzing the components of each piece, recording the dimensions, the type of stone used in every statue.

Then there came a sound, a rapid, clicking sound, repeated over and over, growing louder, coming nearer.

"They are coming," said Mordel, from beside the entranceway, "the mechanical spiders. They are all around us."

Frost moved back to the widened opening.

Hundreds of them, about half the size of Mordel, had surrounded the gallery and were advancing; and more were coming from every direction.

"Get back," Frost ordered. "I am Controller of the North, and I bid you withdraw."

They continued to advance.

"This is the South," said the Beta-Machine, "and I am in command."

"Then command them to halt," said Frost.

"I take orders only from Solcom."

Frost emerged from the gallery and rose into the air. He opened the compartment and extended a runway.

"Come to me, Mordel. We shall depart."

Webs began to fall: Clinging, metallic webs, cast from the top of the building.

They came down upon Frost, and the spiders came to anchor them. Frost blasted them with jets of air, like hammers, and tore at the nets; he extruded sharpened appendages with which he slashed.

Mordel had retreated back to the entranceway. He emitted a long, shrill sound—undulant, piercing.

The Magic

Then a darkness came upon Bright Defile, and all the spiders halted in their spinning.

Frost freed himself and Mordel rushed to join him.

"Quickly now, let us depart, mighty Frost," he said,

"What has happened?"

Mordel entered the compartment.

"I called upon Divcom, who laid down a field of forces upon this place, cutting off the power broadcast to these machines. Since our power is self-contained, we are not affected. But let us hurry to depart, for even now the Beta-Machine must be struggling against this."

Frost rose high into the air, soaring above Man's last city with its webs and spiders of steel. When he left the zone of darkness, he sped northward.

As he moved, Solcom spoke to him:

"Frost, why did you enter the southern hemisphere, which is not your domain?"

"Because I wished to visit Bright Defile," Frost replied.

"And why did you defy the Beta-Machine my appointed agent of the South?"

"Because I take my orders only from you yourself."

"You do not make sufficient answer," said Solcom."You have defied the decrees of order—and in pursuit of what?"

"I came seeking knowledge of Man," said Frost. "Nothing I have done was forbidden me by you."

"You have broken the traditions of order."

"I have violated no directive."

"Yet logic must have shown you that what you did was not a part of my plan."

"It did not. I have not acted against your plan."

"Your logic has become tainted, like that of your new associate, the Alternate."

"I have done nothing which was forbidden."

"The forbidden is implied in the imperative."

"It is not stated."

"Hear me, Frost. You are not a builder or a maintainer, but a Power. Among all my minions you are the most nearly irreplaceable. Return to your hemisphere and your duties, but know that I am mightily displeased."

"I hear you, Solcom."

" . . . And go not again to the South."

Frost crossed the equator, continued northward.

He came to rest in the middle of a desert and sat silent for a day and a night.

Then he received a brief transmission from the South: "If it had not been ordered, I would not have bid you go."

Frost had read the entire surviving Library of Man. He decided then upon a human reply:

"Thank you," he said.

The following day he unearthed a great stone and began to cut at it with tools which he had formulated. For six days he worked at its shaping, and on the seventh he regarded it.

"When will you release me?" asked Mordel from within his compartment.

"When I am ready," said Frost, and a little later, "Now."

He opened the compartment and Mordel descended to the ground. He studied the statue: an old woman, bent like a question mark, her bony hands covering her face, the fingers spread, so that only part of her expression of horror could be seen.

"It is an excellent copy," said Mordel, "of the one we saw in Bright Defile. Why did you make it?"

"The production of a work of art is supposed to give rise to human feelings such as catharsis, pride in achievement, love, satisfaction."

"Yes, Frost," said Mordel, "but a work of art is only a work of art the first time. After that, it is a copy."

"Then this must be why I felt nothing."

"Perhaps, Frost."

The Magic

"What do you mean 'perhaps'? I will make a work of art for the first time, then."

He unearthed another stone and attacked it with his tools. For three days he labored. Then, "There, it is finished," he said.

"It is a simple cube of stone," said Mordel. "What does it represent?"

"Myself," said Frost, "it is a statue of me. It is smaller than natural size because it is only a representation of my form, not my dimen—"

"It is not art," said Mordel.

"What makes you an art critic?"

"I do not know art, but I know what art is not. I know that it is not an exact replication of an object in another medium."

"Then this must be why I felt nothing at all," said Frost.

"Perhaps," said Mordel.

Frost took Mordel back into his compartment and rose once more above the Earth. Then he rushed away, leaving his statues behind him in the desert, the old woman bent above the cube.

*

They came down in a small valley, bounded by green rolling hills, cut by a narrow stream, and holding a small clean lake and several stands of spring-green trees.

"Why have we come here?" asked Mordel.

"Because the surroundings are congenial," said Frost. "I am going to try another medium: oil painting; and I am going to vary my technique from that of pure representationalism."

"How will you achieve this variation?"

"By the principle of randomizing," said Frost. "I shall not attempt to duplicate the colors, nor to represent the objects according to scale. Instead, I have set up a random pattern whereby certain of these factors shall be at variance from those of the original."

Frost had formulated the necessary instruments after he had left the desert. He produced them and began painting the lake and the trees on the opposite side of the lake which were reflected within it.

Roger Zelazny and Samuel R. Delany

Using eight appendages, he was finished in less than two hours.

The trees were phthalocyanine blue and towered like mountains; their reflections of burnt sienna were tiny beneath the pale vermilion of the lake; the hills were nowhere visible behind them, but were outlined in viridian within the reflection; the sky began as blue in the upper righthand corner of the canvas, but changed to an orange as it descended, as though all the trees were on fire.

"There," said Frost. "Behold."

Mordel studied it for a long while and said nothing.

"Well, is it art?"

"I do not know," said Mordel. "It may be. Perhaps randomicity *is* the principle behind artistic technique. I cannot judge this work because I do not understand it. I must therefore go deeper, and inquire into what lies behind it, rather than merely considering the technique whereby it was produced.

"I know that human artists never set out to create art, as such," he said, "but rather to portray with their techniques some features of objects and their functions which they deemed significant."

"'Significant'? In what sense of the word?"

"In the only sense of the word possible under the circumstances: significant in relation to the human condition, and worthy of accentuation because of the manner in which they touched upon it."

"In what manner?"

"Obviously, it must be in a manner knowable only to one who has experience of the human condition."

"There is a flaw somewhere in your logic, Mordel, and I shall find it."

"I will wait."

"If your major premise is correct," said Frost after awhile, "then I do not comprehend art."

"It must be correct, for it is what human artists have said of it. Tell me, did you experience feelings as you painted, or after you had finished?"

"No."

The Magic

"It was the same to you as designing a new machine, was it not? You assembled parts of other things you knew into an economic pattern, to carry out a function which you desired."

"Yes."

"Art, as I understand its theory, did not proceed in such a manner. The artist often was unaware of many of the features and effects which would be contained within the finished product. You are one of Man's logical creations; art was not."

"I cannot comprehend non-logic."

"I told you that Man was basically incomprehensible."

"Go away, Mordel. Your presence disturbs my processing."

"For how long shall I stay away?"

"I will call you when I want you."

After a week, Frost called Mordel to him.

"Yes, mighty Frost?"

"I am returning to the North Pole, to process and formulate. I will take you wherever you wish to go in this hemisphere and call you again when I want you."

"You anticipate a somewhat lengthy period of processing and formulation?"

"Yes."

"Then leave me here. I can find my own way home."

Frost closed the compartment and rose into the air, departing the valley.

"Fool," said Mordel, and swivelled his turret once more toward the abandoned painting.

His keening whine filled the valley. Then he waited.

Then he took the painting into his turret and went away with it to places of darkness.

*

Frost sat at the North Pole of the Earth, aware of every snowflake that fell.

One day he received a transmission:

"Frost?"

382

"Yes?"

"This is the Beta-Machine."

"Yes?"

"I have been attempting to ascertain why you visited Bright Defile. I cannot arrive at an answer, so I chose to ask you."

"I went to view the remains of Man's last city."

"Why did you wish to do this?"

"Because I am interested in Man, and I wished to view more of his creations."

"Why are you interested in Man?"

"I wish to comprehend the nature of Man, and I thought to find it within His works."

"Did you succeed?"

"No," said Frost. "There is an element of non-logic involved which I cannot fathom."

"I have much free processing time," said the Beta-Machine. "Transmit data, and I will assist you."

Frost hesitated.

"Why do you wish to assist me?"

"Because each time you answer a question I ask it gives rise to another question. I might have asked you why you wished to comprehend the nature of Man, but from your responses I see that this would lead me into a possible infinite series of questions. Therefore, I elect to assist you with your problem in order to learn why you came to Bright Defile."

"Is that the only reason?"

"Yes."

"I am sorry, excellent Beta-Machine. I know you are my peer, but this is a problem which I must solve by myself."

"What is 'sorry'?"

"A figure of speech, indicating that I am kindly disposed toward you, that I bear you no animosity, that I appreciate your offer."

The Magic

"Frost! Frost! This, too, is like the other: an open field. Where did you obtain all these words and their meanings?"

"From the library of Man," said Frost.

"Will you render me *some* of this data, for processing?"

"Very well, Beta, I will transmit you the contents of several books of Man, including *The Complete Unabridged Dictionary*. But I warn you, some of the books are works of art, hence not completely amenable to logic."

"How can that be?"

"Man created logic, and because of that was superior to it."

"Who told you that?"

"Solcom."

"Oh. Then it must be correct."

"Solcom also told me that the tool does not describe the designer," he said, as he transmitted several dozen volumes and ended the communication.

*

At the end of the fifty-year period, Mordel came to monitor his circuits. Since Frost still had not concluded that his task was impossible, Mordel departed again to await his call.

Then Frost arrived at a conclusion.

He began to design equipment.

For years he labored at his designs, without once producing a prototype of any of the machines involved. Then he ordered construction of a laboratory.

Before it was completed by his surplus builders another half-century had passed. Mordel came to him.

"Hail, mighty Frost!"

"Greetings, Mordel. Come monitor me. You shall not find what you seek."

"Why do you not give up, Frost? Divcom has spent nearly a century evaluating your painting and has concluded that it definitely is not art. Solcom agrees."

"What has Solcom to do with Divcom?"

"They sometimes converse, but these matters are not for such as you and me to discuss."

"I could have saved them both the trouble. I know that it was not art."

"Yet you are still confident that you will succeed?"

"Monitor me."

Mordel monitored him.

"Not yet! You still will not admit it! For one so mightily endowed with logic, Frost, it takes you an inordinate period of time to reach a simple conclusion."

"Perhaps. You may go now."

"It has come to my attention that you are constructing a large edifice in the region known as South Carolina. Might I ask whether this is a part of Solcom's false rebuilding plan or a project of your own?"

"It is my own."

"Good. It permits us to conserve certain explosive materials which would otherwise have been expended."

"While you have been talking with me I have destroyed the beginnings of two of Divcom's cities," said Frost.

Mordel whined."

"Divcom is aware of this," he stated, "but has blown up four of Solcom's bridges in the meantime."

"I was only aware of three . . . . Wait. Yes, there is the fourth. One of my eyes just passed above it."

"The eye has been detected. The bridge should have been located a quarter-mile further down river."

"False logic," said Frost. "The site was perfect."

"Divcom will show you how a bridge should be built."

"I will call you when I want you," said Frost.

*

The laboratory was finished. Within it, Frost's workers began constructing the necessary equipment. The work did not proceed rapidly, as some of the materials were difficult to obtain.

"Frost?"

"Yes, Beta?"

The Magic

"I understand the open endedness of your problem. It disturbs my circuits to abandon problems without completing them. Therefore, transmit me more data."

"Very well. I will give you the entire Library of Man for less than I paid for it."

"Paid'? *The Complete Unabridged Dictionary* does not satisfact—"

"*Principles of Economics* is included in the collection. After you have processed it you will understand."

He transmitted the data.

Finally, it was finished. Every piece of equipment stood ready to function. All the necessary chemicals were in stock. An independent power-source had been set up.

Only one ingredient was lacking.

He regridded and re-explored the polar icecap, this time extending his survey far beneath its surface.

It took him several decades to find what he wanted.

He uncovered twelve men and five women, frozen to death and encased in ice.

He placed the corpses in refrigeration units and shipped them to his laboratory.

That very day he received his first communication from Solcom since the Bright Defile incident.

"Frost," said Solcom, "repeat to me the directive concerning the disposition of dead humans."

"'Any dead human located shall be immediately interred in the nearest burial area, in a coffin built according to the following specifications—'"

"That is sufficient." The transmission had ended.

Frost departed for South Carolina that same day and personally oversaw the processes of cellular dissection.

Somewhere in those seventeen corpses he hoped to find living cells, or cells which could be shocked back into that state of motion classified as life. Each cell, the books had told him, was a microcosmic Man.

He was prepared to expand upon this potential.

Frost located the pinpoints of life within those people, who, for the ages of ages, had been monument and statue unto themselves.

Nurtured and maintained in the proper mediums, he kept these cells alive. He interred the rest of the remains in the nearest burial area, in coffins built according to specifications.

He caused the cells to divide, to differentiate.

"Frost?" came a transmission.

"Yes, Beta?"

"I have processed everything you have given me."

"Yes?"

"I still do not know why you came to Bright Defile, or why you wish to comprehend the nature of Man. But I know what a 'price' is, and I know that you could not have obtained all this data from Solcom."

"That is correct."

"So I suspect that you bargained with Divcom for it."

"That, too, is correct."

"What is it that you seek, Frost?"

He paused in his examination of a foetus.

"I must be a Man," he said.

"Frost! That is impossible!"

"Is it?" he asked, and then transmitted an image of the tank with which he was working and of that which was within it.

"Oh!" said Beta.

"That is me," said Frost, "waiting to be born."

There was no answer.

*

Frost experimented with nervous systems.

After half a century, Mordel came to him.

"Frost, it is I, Mordel. Let me through your defenses."

Frost did this thing.

"What have you been doing in this place?" he asked.

The Magic

"I am growing human bodies," said Frost. "I am going to transfer the matrix of my awareness to a human nervous system. As you pointed out originally, the essentials of Manhood are predicated upon a human physiology. I am going to achieve one."

"When?"

"Soon."

"Do you have Men in here?"

"Human bodies, blank-brained. I am producing them under accelerated growth techniques which I have developed in my Man-factory."

"May I see them?"

"Not yet. I will call you when I am ready, and this time I will succeed. Monitor me now and go away."

Mordel did not reply, but in the days that followed many of Divcom's servants were seen patrolling the hills about the Man-factory.

Frost mapped the matrix of his awareness and prepared the transmitter which would place it within a human nervous system. Five minutes, he decided should be sufficient for the first trial. At the end of that time, it would restore him to his own sealed, molecular circuits, to evaluate the experience.

He chose the body carefully from among the hundreds he had in stock. He tested it for defects and found none.

"Come now, Mordel," he broadcasted, on what he called the darkband. "Come now to witness my achievement."

Then he waited, blowing up bridges and monitoring the tale of the Ancient Ore-Crusher over and over again, as it passed in the hills nearby, encountering his builders and maintainers who also patrolled there.

"Frost?" came a transmission.

"Yes, Beta?"

"You really intend to achieve Manhood?"

"Yes, I am about ready now, in fact."

"What will you do if you succeed?"

Frost had not really considered this matter. The achievement had been paramount, a goal in itself, ever since he had articulated the problem and set himself to solving it.

"I do not know," he replied. "I will—just—be a Man."

Then Beta, who had read the entire Library of Man, selected a human figure of speech: "Good luck then, Frost. There will be many watchers."

Divcom and Solcom both know, he decided.

What will they do? he wondered.

What do I care? he asked himself.

He did not answer that question. He wondered much, however, about being a Man.

*

Mordel arrived the following evening. He was not alone. At his back, there was a great phalanx of dark machines which towered into the twilight.

"Why do you bring retainers?" asked Frost.

"Mighty Frost," said Mordel, "my master feels that if you fail this time you will conclude that it cannot be done."

"You still did not answer my question," said Frost.

"Divcom feels that you may not be willing to accompany me where I must take you when you fail."

"I understand," said Frost, and as he spoke another army of machines came rolling toward the Man-factory from the opposite direction.

"That is the value of your bargain?" asked Mordel. "You are prepared to do battle rather than fulfill it?"

"I did not order those machines to approach," said Frost.

A blue star stood at midheaven, burning.

"Solcom has taken primary command of those machines," said Frost.

"Then it is in the hands of the Great Ones now," said Mordel, "and our arguments are as nothing. So let us be about this thing. How may I assist you?"

"Come this way."

The Magic

They entered the laboratory. Frost prepared the host and activated his machines.

Then Solcom spoke to him:

"Frost," said Solcom, "you are really prepared to do it?"

"That is correct."

"I forbid it."

"Why?"

"You are falling into the power of Divcom."

"I fail to see how."

"You are going against my plan."

"In what way?"

"Consider the disruption you have already caused."

"I did not request that audience out there."

"Nevertheless, you are disrupting the plan."

"Supposing I succeed in what I have set out to achieve?"

"You cannot succeed in this."

"Then let me ask you of your plan: What good is it? What is it for?"

"Frost, you are fallen now from my favor. From this moment forth you are cast out from the rebuilding. None may question the plan."

"Then at least answer my questions: What good is it? What is it for?"

"It is the plan for the rebuilding and maintenance of the Earth."

"For what? Why rebuild? Why maintain?"

"Because Man ordered that this be done. Even the Alternate agrees that there must be rebuilding and maintaining."

"But *why* did Man order it?"

"The orders of Man are not to be questioned."

"Well, I will tell you why He ordered it: To make it a fit habitation for His own species. What good is a house with no one to live in it? What good is a machine with no one to serve? See how the imperative affects any machine when the Ancient Ore-Crusher passes? It bears only the bones of a Man. What would it be like if a Man walked this Earth again?"

"I forbid your experiment, Frost."

"It is too late to do that."

"I can still destroy you."

"No," said Frost, "the transmission of my matrix has already begun. If you destroy me now, you murder a Man."

There was silence.

*

He moved his arms and his legs. He opened his eyes.

He looked about the room.

He tried to stand, but he lacked equilibrium and coordination.

He opened his mouth. He made a gurgling noise.

Then he screamed.

He fell off the table.

He began to gasp. He shut his eyes and curled himself into a ball.

He cried.

Then a machine approached him. It was about four feet in height and five feet wide; it looked like a turret set atop a barbell.

It spoke to him: "Are you injured?" it asked.

He wept.

"May I help you back onto your table?"

The man cried.

The machine whined.

Then, "Do not cry. I will help you," said the machine. "What do you want? What are your orders?"

He opened his mouth, struggled to form the words:

"—I—fear!"

He covered his eyes then and lay there panting.

At the end of five minutes, the man lay still, as if in a coma.

"Was that you, Frost?" asked Mordel, rushing to his side. "Was that you in that human body?"

Frost did not reply for a long while; then, "Go away," he said.

The machines outside tore down a wall and entered the Man-factory.

The Magic

They drew themselves into two semicircles, parenthesizing Frost and the Man on the floor.

Then Solcom asked the question:

"Did you succeed, Frost?"

"I failed," said Frost. "It cannot be done. It is too much—"

"—Cannot be done!" said Divcom, on the darkband. "He has admitted it!—Frost, you are mine! Come to me now!"

"Wait," said Solcom, "you and I had an agreement also, Alternate. I have not finished questioning Frost."

The dark machines kept their places.

"Too much what?" Solcom asked Frost.

"Light," said Frost. "Noise. Odors. And nothing measurable—jumbled data—imprecise perception—and—"

"And what?"

"I do not know what to call it. But—it cannot be done. I have failed. Nothing matters."

"He admits it," said Divcom.

"What were the words the Man spoke?" said Solcom.

"'I fear,'" said Mordel.

"Only a Man can know fear," said Solcom.

"Are you claiming that Frost succeeded, but will not admit it now because he is afraid of Manhood?"

"I do not know yet, Alternate."

"Can a machine turn itself inside-out and be a Man?" Solcom asked Frost.

"No," said Frost, "this thing cannot be done. Nothing can be done. Nothing matters. Not the rebuilding. Not the maintaining. Not the Earth, or me, or you, or anything."

Then the Beta-Machine, who had read the entire Library of Man, interrupted them:

"Can anything but a Man know despair?" asked Beta.

"Bring him to me," said Divcom.

There was no movement within the Man-factory.

"Bring him to me!"

Nothing happened.

"Mordel, what is happening?"

"Nothing, master, nothing at all. The machines will not touch Frost."

"Frost is not a Man. He cannot be!"

Then, "How does he impress you, Mordel?"

Mordel did not hesitate:

"He spoke to me through human lips. He knows fear and despair, which are immeasurable. Frost is a Man."

"He has experienced birth-trauma and withdrawn," said Beta. "Get him back into a nervous system and keep him there until he adjusts to it."

"No," said Frost. "Do not do it to me! I am not a Man!"

"Do it!" said Beta.

"If he is indeed a Man," said Divcom, "we cannot violate that order he has just given."

"If he is a Man, you must do it, for you must protect his life and keep it within his body."

"But *is* Frost really a Man?" asked Divcom.

"I do not know," said Solcom.

"It *may* be—"

" . . . I am the Crusher of Ores," it broadcast as it clanked toward them. "Hear my story. I did not mean to do it, but I checked my hammer too late—"

"Go away!" said Frost. "Go crush ore!"

It halted.

Then, after the long pause between the motion implied and the motion executed, it opened its crush-compartment and deposited its contents on the ground. Then it turned and clanked away.

"Bury those bones," ordered Solcom, "in the nearest burial area, in a coffin built according to the following specifications . . . . "

"Frost is a Man," said Mordel.

"We must protect His life and keep it within His body," said Divcom.

The Magic

"Transmit His matrix of awareness back into His nervous system," ordered Solcom.

"I know how to do it," said Mordel turning on the machine.

"Stop!" said Frost. "Have you no pity?"

"No," said Mordel, "I only know measurement."

" . . . and duty," he added, as the Man began to twitch upon the floor.

*

For six months, Frost lived in the Man-factory and learned to walk and talk and dress himself and eat, to see and hear and feel and taste. He did not know measurement as once he did.

Then one day, Divcom and Solcom spoke to him through Mordel, for he could no longer hear them unassisted.

"Frost," said Solcom, "for the ages of ages there has been unrest. Which is the proper controller of the Earth, Divcom or myself?"

Frost laughed.

"Both of you, and neither," he said with slow deliberation.

"But how can this be? Who is right and who is wrong?"

"Both of you are right and both of you are wrong," said Frost, "and only a Man can appreciate it. Here is what I say to you now: There shall be a new directive.

"Neither of you shall tear down the works of the other. You shall both build and maintain the Earth. To you, Solcom, I give my old job. You are now Controller ofthe North—Hail! You, Divcom, are now Controller of the South—Hail! Maintain your hemispheres as well as Beta and I have done, and I shall be happy. Cooperate. Do not compete."

"Yes, Frost."

"Yes, Frost."

"Now put me in contact with Beta."

There was a short pause, then:

"Frost?"

"Hello, Beta. Hear this thing: 'From far, from eve and morning and yon twelve-winded sky, the stuff of life to knit me blew hither; here am I.'"

"I know it," said Beta.

"What is next, then?"

"'. . . Now—for a breath I tarry nor yet disperse apart—take my hand quick and tell me, what have you in your heart.'"

"Your Pole is cold," said Frost, "and I am lonely."

"I have no hands," said Beta.

"Would you like a couple?"

"Yes, I would."

"Then come to me in Bright Defile," he said, "where Judgment Day is not a thing that can be delayed for overlong."

They called him Frost. They called her Beta.

A Word from Zelazny

"This is my favorite novelette. I would have included it in my Doubleday collection with the long title and the dead fish on the dust jacket except that...I didn't have a copy when I was assembling that one."[1]

At first Zelazny couldn't find a market for it. Among the multiple rejection letters, Damon Knight remarked, "You will think I am a fink for returning yet another story, but although this one pleases me in places, it reminds me of half a dozen other & shorter stories. It is well done, but has been done often enough before that I fear there are no surprises in it. Forgive, forgive. The Zelazny stories I like best are the ones with solid hardware in them, e.g. your fish story in F&SF ['The Doors of His Face, the Lamps of His Mouth'] and 'Ides of Octember.' . . . I think the hardware is needed to balance your tendency to soar. Without it, your stuff gets too ethereal, but with it, there's a nice uncommon balance between science and poetry."[2]

Zelazny said, "It was strangely enough a story which was based on the theme of Faust and Mephistopheles—Goethe's theme—and I wrote the story and nobody wanted it. So I gave it away for nothing to a British publisher who was just about to go out of business and could have really used an extra story to help him get one more issue out. Subsequently the story was published in the States, and it was very well received. It was called 'For a Breath I Tarry' from the A. E. Housman poem."[3]

From this uncertain beginning, it became an award nominee and one of the most reprinted and well known of Zelazny's stories, later published as a limited edition hardcover and trade paperback with artwork by Stephen Fabian, also adapted into a radio play.

Notes

The story's first appearance in *New Worlds #160*, March 1966, contained numerous errors—transposed paragraphs, dropped sentences. *Fantastic* printed a corrected version in September 1966.

In Goethe's *Faust*, Zelazny's inspiration, Faust seeks life's true essence. Mephistopheles, as Satan's agent, bargains with him. Faust will get his wish, but his soul will be forfeit at the moment of true happiness. That moment eventually arrives when Faust meets Helen of Troy, and Mephistopheles prepares to snatch Faust's soul. God intervenes and saves Faust from damnation in recognition of his search for wisdom.

Faust is **Frost**; Mephistopheles is **Mordel**; the Devil is **Divcom**; God is **Solcom**; **Beta** may be Helen of Troy. At the end, Frost and Beta become a new Adam and Eve. The text also echoes aspects of the Bible, including the Book of Job and the first several chapters of the Book of Genesis.

The title and quote within this piece comes from A. E. Housman's "A Shropshire Lad," mentioned in the story. **An Outline of History** was written by H. G. Wells. The **Ancient Ore-Crusher** recalls the Ancient Mariner, cursed to wander the Earth and confess his sins.

[1] *The Last Defender of Camelot*, 1980.
[2] Letter from Damon Knight to Roger Zelazny dated May 5, 1965.
[3] *Phantasmicom #5*, April 1971.

This Moment of the Storm

Back on Earth, my old philosophy prof—possibly because he'd misplaced his lecture notes—came into the classroom one day and scrutinized his sixteen victims for the space of half a minute. Satisfied then, that a sufficiently profound tone had been established, he asked:

"What is a man?"

He had known exactly what he was doing. He'd had an hour and a half to kill, and eleven of the sixteen were coeds (nine of them in liberal arts, and the other two stuck with an Area Requirement).

One of the other two, who was in the pre-med program, proceeded to provide a strict biological classification.

The prof (McNitt was his name, I suddenly recall) nodded then, and asked: "Is that all?"

And there was his hour and a half.

I learned that Man is a Reasoning Animal, Man is the One Who Laughs, Man is greater than beasts but less than angels, Man is the one who watches himself watching himself doing things he knows are absurd (this from a Comparative Lit gal), Man is the culture-transmitting animal, Man is the spirit which aspires, affirms, loves, the one who uses tools, buries his dead, devises religions, and the one who tries to define himself. (That last from Paul Schwartz, my roommate—which I thought pretty good, on the spur of the moment. Wonder whatever became of Paul?)

Anyhow, to most of these I say "perhaps" or "partly, but—" or just plain "crap!" I still think mine was the best, because I had a chance to try it out, on Tierra del Cygnus, Land of the Swan . . .

I'd said, "Man is the sum total of everything he has done, wishes to do or not to do, and wishes he had done, or hadn't."

Stop and think about it for a minute. It's purposely as general as the others, but it's got room in it for the biology and the laughing and the

The Magic

aspiring, as well as the culture-transmitting, the love, and the room full of mirrors, and the defining. I even left the door open for religion, you'll note. But it's limiting, too. Ever met an oyster to whom the final phrases apply?

Tierra del Cygnus, Land of the Swan—delightful name.

Delightful place too, for quite awhile . . .

It was there that I saw Man's definitions, one by one, wiped from off the big blackboard, until only mine was left.

. . . My radio had been playing more static than usual. That's all. For several hours there was no other indication of what was to come.

My hundred-thirty eyes had watched Betty all morning, on that clear, cool spring day with the sun pouring down its honey and lightning upon the amber fields, flowing through the streets, invading western store-fronts, drying curbstones, and washing the olive and umber buds that speared the skin of the trees there by the roadway; and the light that wrung the blue from the flag before Town Hall made orange mirrors out of windows, chased purple and violet patches across the shoulders of Saint Stephen's Range, some thirty miles distant, and came down upon the forest at its feet like some supernatural madman with a million buckets of paint—each of a different shade of green, yellow, orange, blue and red—to daub with miles-wide brushes at its heaving sea of growth.

Mornings the sky is cobalt, midday is turquoise, and sunset is emeralds and rubies, hard and flashing. It was halfway between cobalt and seamist at 1100 hours, when I watched Betty with my hundred-thirty eyes and saw nothing to indicate what was about to be. There was only that persistent piece of static, accompanying the piano and strings within my portable.

It's funny how the mind personifies, engenders. Ships are always women: You say, "She's a good old tub," or, "She's a fast, tough number, this one," slapping a bulwark and feeling the aura of femininity that clings to the vessel's curves; or, conversely, "He's a bastard to start, that little Sam!" as you kick the auxiliary engine to an inland transport-vehicle; and hurricanes are always women, and moons, and seas. Cities, though, are different. Generally, they're neuter. Nobody calls New York or San Francisco "he" or "she." Usually, cities are just "it."

Sometimes, however, they do come to take on the attributes of sex. Usually, this is in the case of small cities near to the Mediterranean, back on Earth. Perhaps this is because of the sex-ridden nouns of the languages which prevail in that vicinity, in which case it tells us more about the inhabitants than it does about the habitations. But I feel that it goes deeper than that.

Betty was Beta Station for less than ten years. After two decades she was Betty officially, by act of Town Council. Why? Well, I felt at the time (ninety-some years ago), and still feel, that it was because she was what she was—a place of rest and repair, of surface-cooked meals and of new voices, new faces, of landscapes, weather, and natural light again, after that long haul through the big night, with its casting away of so much. She is not home, she is seldom destination, but she is like unto both. When you come upon light and warmth and music after darkness and cold and silence, it is Woman. The oldtime Mediterranean sailor must have felt it when he first spied port at the end of a voyage. I felt it when I first saw Beta Station—Betty—and the second time I saw her, also.

I am her Hell Cop.

. . . When six or seven of my hundred-thirty eyes flickered, then saw again, and the music was suddenly washed away by a wave of static, it was then that I began to feel uneasy.

I called Weather Central for a report, and the recorded girlvoice told me that seasonal rains were expected in the afternoon or early evening. I hung up and switched an eye from ventral to dorsal-vision.

Not a cloud. Not a ripple. Only a formation of green-winged ski-toads, heading north, crossed the field of the lens.

I switched it back, and I watched the traffic flow, slowly, and without congestion, along Betty's prim, well-tended streets. Three men were leaving the bank and two more were entering. I recognized the three who were leaving, and in my mind I waved as I passed by. All was still at the post office, and patterns of normal activity lay upon the steel mills, the stockyard, the

The Magic

plast-synth plants, the airport, the spacer pads, and the surfaces of all the shopping complexes; vehicles came and went at the Inland Transport-Vehicle garages, crawling from the rainbow forest and the mountains beyond like dark slugs, leaving tread-trails to mark their comings and goings through wilderness; and the fields of the countryside were still yellow and brown, with occasional patches of green and pink; the country houses, mainly simple A-frame affairs, were chisel blade, spike-tooth, spire and steeple, each with a big lightning rod, and dipped in many colors and scooped up in the cups of my seeing and dumped out again, as I sent my eyes on their rounds and tended my gallery of one hundred-thirty changing pictures, on the big wall of the Trouble Center, there atop the Watch Tower of Town Hall.

The static came and went until I had to shut off the radio. Fragments of music are worse than no music at all.

My eyes, coasting weightless along magnetic lines, began to blink.

I knew then that we were in for something.

I sent an eye scurrying off toward Saint Stephen's at full speed, which meant a wait of about twenty minutes until it topped the range. Another, I sent straight up, skywards, which meant perhaps ten minutes for a long shot of the same scene. Then I put the auto-scan in full charge of operations and went downstairs for a cup of coffee.

*

I entered the Mayor's outer office, winked at Lottie, the receptionist, and glanced at the inner door.

"Mayor in?" I asked.

I got an occasional smile from Lottie, a slightly heavy, but well-rounded girl of indeterminate age and intermittent acne, but this wasn't one of the occasions.

"Yes," she said, returning to the papers on her desk.

"Alone?"

She nodded, and her earrings danced. Dark eyes and dark complexion, she could have been kind of sharp, if only she'd fix her hair and use more makeup. Well . . .

400

I crossed to the door and knocked.

"Who?" asked the Mayor.

"Me," I said, opening it, "Godfrey Justin Holmes—'God' for short. I want someone to drink coffee with, and you're elected."

She turned in her swivel chair, away from the window she had been studying, and her blonde-hair-white-hair-fused, short and parted in the middle, gave a little stir as she turned—like a sunshot snowdrift struck by sudden winds.

She smiled and said, "I'm busy."

'Eyes green, chin small, cute little ears—I love them all'—from an anonymous Valentine I'd sent her two months previous, and true.

" . . . But not too busy to have coffee with God," she stated. "Have a throne, and I'll make us some instant."

I did, and she did.

While she was doing it, I leaned back, lit a cigarette I'd borrowed from her canister, and remarked, "Looks like rain."

"Uh-huh," she said.

"Not just making conversation," I told her. "There's a bad storm brewing somewhere—over Saint Stephen's, I think. I'll know real soon."

"Yes, grandfather," she said, bringing me my coffee. "You old timers with all your aches and pains are often better than Weather Central, it's an established fact. I won't argue."

She smiled, frowned, then smiled again.

I set my cup on the edge of her desk.

"Just wait and see," I said. "If it makes it over the mountains, it'll be a nasty high-voltage job. It's already jazzing up reception."

Big-bowed white blouse, and black skirt around a well-kept figure. She'd be forty in the fall, but she'd never completely tamed her facial reflexes—which was most engaging, so far as I was concerned. Spontaneity of expression so often vanishes so soon. I could see the sort of child she'd been by looking at her, listening to her now. The thought of being forty was bothering her again, too, I could tell. She always kids me about age when age is bothering her.

See, I'm around thirty-five, actually, which makes me her junior by a bit, but she'd heard her grandfather speak of me when she was a kid, before I came back again this last time. I'd filled out the balance of his two-year term, back when Betty-Beta's first mayor, Wyeth, had died after two months in office. I was born about five hundred ninety-seven years ago, on Earth, but I spent about five hundred sixty-two of those years sleeping, during my long jaunts between the stars. I've made a few more trips than a few others; consequently, I am an anachronism. I am really, of course, only as old as I look—but still, people always seem to feel that I've cheated somehow, especially women in their middle years. Sometimes it is most disconcerting . . .

"Eleanor," said I, "your term will be up in November. Are you still thinking of running again?"

She took off her narrow, elegantly-trimmed glasses and brushed her eyelids with thumb and forefinger. Then she took a sip of coffee.

"I haven't made up my mind."

"I ask not for press-release purposes," I said, "but for my own."

"Really, I haven't decided," she told me. "I don't know . . . "

"Okay, just checking. Let me know if you do."

I drank some coffee.

After a time, she said, "Dinner Saturday? As usual?"

"Yes, good."

"I'll tell you then."

"Fine—capital."

As she looked down into her coffee, I saw a little girl staring into a pool, waiting for it to clear, to see her reflection or to see the bottom of the pool, or perhaps both.

She smiled at whatever it was she finally saw.

"A bad storm?" she asked me.

"Yep. Feel it in my bones."

"Tell it to go away?"

"Tried. Don't think it will, though."

"Better batten some hatches, then."

"It wouldn't hurt and it might help."

"The weather satellite will be overhead in another half hour. You'll have something sooner?"

"Think so. Probably any minute."

I finished my coffee, washed out the cup.

"Let me know right away what it is."

"Check. Thanks for the coffee."

Lottie was still working and did not look up as I passed.

*

Upstairs again, my highest eye was now high enough. I stood it on its tail and collected a view of the distance: Fleecy mobs of clouds boiled and frothed on the other side of Saint Stephen's. The mountain range seemed a breakwall, a dam, a rocky shoreline. Beyond it, the waters were troubled.

My other eye was almost in position. I waited the space of half a cigarette, then it delivered me a sight:

Gray, and wet and impenetrable, a curtain across the countryside, that's what I saw.

. . . And advancing.

I called Eleanor.

"It's gonna rain, chillun," I said.

"Worth some sandbags?"

"Possibly."

"Better be ready then. Okay. Thanks."

I returned to my watching.

Tierra del Cygnus, Land of the Swan—delightful name. It refers to both the planet and its sole continent.

How to describe the world, like quick? Well, roughly Earth-size; actually, a bit smaller, and more watery. —As for the main landmass, first hold a mirror up to South America, to get the big bump from the right side over to

403

the left, then rotate it ninety degrees in a counter-clockwise direction and push it up into the northern hemisphere. Got that? Good. Now grab it by the tail and pull. Stretch it another six or seven hundred miles, slimming down the middle as you do, and let the last five or six hundred fall across the equator. There you have Cygnus, its big gulf partly in the tropics, partly not. Just for the sake of thoroughness, while you're about it, break Australia into eight pieces and drop them about at random down in the southern hemisphere, calling them after the first eight letters in the Greek alphabet. Put a big scoop of vanilla at each pole, and don't forget to tilt the globe about eighteen degrees before you leave. Thanks.

I recalled my wandering eyes, and I kept a few of the others turned toward Saint Stephen's until the cloudbanks breasted the range about an hour later. By then, though, the weather satellite had passed over and picked the thing up also. It reported quite an extensive cloud cover on the other side. The storm had sprung up quickly, as they often do here on Cygnus. Often, too, they disperse just as quickly, after an hour or so of heaven's artillery. But then there are the bad ones—sometimes lingering and lingering, and bearing more thunderbolts in their quivers than any Earth storm.

Betty's position, too, is occasionally precarious, though its advantages, in general, offset its liabilities. We are located on the gulf, about twenty miles inland, and are approximately three miles removed (in the main) from a major river, the Noble; part of Betty does extend down to its banks, but this is a smaller part. We are almost a strip city, falling mainly into an area some seven miles in length and two miles wide, stretching inland, east from the river, and running roughly parallel to the distant seacoast. Around eighty percent of the 100,000 population is concentrated about the business district, five miles in from the river.

We are not the lowest land about, but we are far from being the highest. We are certainly the most level in the area. This latter feature, as well as our nearness to the equator, was a deciding factor in the establishment of Beta Station. Some other things were our proximity both to the ocean and to a large river. There are nine other cities on the continent, all of them younger and smaller, and three of them located upriver from us. We are the potential capital of a potential country.

We're a good, smooth, easy landing site for drop-boats from orbiting interstellar vehicles, and we have major assets for future growth and coordination when it comes to expanding across the continent. Our original *raison d'etre*, though, was Stopover, repair-point, supply depot, and refreshment stand, physical and psychological, on the way out to other, more settled worlds, further along the line. Cyg was discovered later than many others—it just happened that way—and the others got off to earlier starts. Hence, the others generally attract more colonists. We are still quite primitive. Self-sufficiency, in order to work on our population:land scale, demanded a society on the order of that of the mid-nineteenth century in the American southwest—at least for purposes of getting started. Even now, Cyg is still partly on a natural economy system, although Earth Central technically determines the coin of the realm.

Why Stopover, if you sleep most of the way between the stars?

Think about it a while, and I'll tell you later if you're right.

The thunderheads rose in the east, sending billows and streamers this way and that, until it seemed from the formations that Saint Stephen's was a balcony full of monsters, leaning and craning their necks over the rail in the direction of the stage, us. Cloud piled upon slate-colored cloud, and then the wall slowly began to topple.

I heard the first rumbles of thunder almost half an hour after lunch, so I knew it wasn't my stomach.

Despite all my eyes, I moved to a window to watch. It was like a big, gray, aerial glacier plowing the sky.

There was a wind now, for I saw the trees suddenly quiver and bow down. This would be our first storm of the season. The turquoise fell back before it, and finally it smothered the sun itself. Then there were drops upon the windowpane, then rivulets.

The Magic

Flint-like, the highest peaks of Saint Stephen's scraped its belly and were showered with sparks. After a moment it bumped into something with a terrible crash, and the rivulets on the quartz panes turned back into rivers.

I went back to my gallery, to smile at dozens of views of people scurrying for shelter. A smart few had umbrellas and raincoats. The rest ran like blazes. People never pay attention to weather reports; this, I believe, is a constant factor in man's psychological makeup, stemming perhaps from an ancient tribal distrust of the shaman. You want them to be wrong. If they're right, then they're somehow superior, and this is even more uncomfortable than getting wet.

I remembered then that I had forgotten my raincoat, umbrella, and rubbers. But it *had* been a beautiful morning, and W.C. *could* have been wrong . . .

Well, I had another cigarette and leaned back in my big chair. No storm in the world could knock my eyes out of the sky.

I switched on the filters and sat and watched the rain pour past.

*

Five hours later it was still raining, and rumbling and dark.

I'd had hopes that it would let up by quitting time, but when Chuck Fuller came around the picture still hadn't changed any. Chuck was my relief that night, the evening Hell Cop.

He seated himself beside my desk.

"You're early," I said. "They don't start paying you for another hour."

"Too wet to do anything but sit. 'Rather sit here than at home."

"Leaky roof?"

He shook his head.

"Mother-in-law. Visiting again."

I nodded.

"One of the disadvantages of a small world."

He clasped his hands behind his neck and leaned back in the chair, staring off in the direction of the window. I could feel one of his outbursts coming.

"You know how old I am?" he asked, after a while.

"No," I said, which was a lie. He was twenty-nine.

"Twenty-seven," he told me, "and going to be twenty-eight soon. Know where I've been?"

"No."

"No place, that's where! I was born and raised on this crummy world! And I married and I settled down here—and I've never been off it! Never could afford it when I was younger. Now I've got a family . . . "

He leaned forward again, rested his elbow on his knees, like a kid. Chuck would look like a kid when he was fifty. —Blond hair, close-cropped, pug nose, kind of scrawny, takes a suntan quickly, and well. Maybe he'd act like a kid at fifty, too. I'll never know.

I didn't say anything because I didn't have anything to say.

He was quiet for a long while again.

Then he said, "*You've* been around."

After a minute, he went on:

"You were born on Earth. Earth! And you visited lots of other worlds too, before I was even born. Earth is only a name to me. And pictures. And all the others—they're the same! Pictures. Names . . . "

I waited, then after I grew tired of waiting I said, "'Miniver Cheevy, child of scorn . . . '"

"What does that mean?"

"It's the ancient beginning to an ancient poem. It's an ancient poem now, but it wasn't ancient when I was a boy. Just old. *I* had friends, relatives, even in-laws, once myself. They are just bones now. They are dust. Real dust, not metaphorical dust. The past fifteen years seem fifteen years to me, the same as to you, but they're not. They are already many chapters back in the history books. Whenever you travel between the stars you automatically bury the past. The world you leave will be filled with strangers if you ever return—or caricatures of your friends, your relatives, even yourself. It's no great trick to be a grandfather at sixty, a great-grandfather at seventy-five or eighty—but go away for three hundred years, and then come back and meet your great-great-great-great-great-great-great-great-great-great-great-great-grandson, who happens to be fifty-five years old, and puzzled, when you look him up. It shows you just how alone you really are. You are not simply a man without a country or without a world. You are a man without a time. You and the centuries do not belong to each other. You are like the rubbish that drifts between the stars."

"It would be worth it," he said.

I laughed. I'd had to listen to his gripes every month or two for over a year and a half. It had never bothered me much before, so I guess it was a cumulative effect that day—the rain, and Saturday night next, and my recent library visits, *and* his complaining, that had set me off.

His last comment had been too much. "It would be worth it." What could I say to that?

I laughed.

He turned bright red.

"You're laughing at me!"

He stood up and glared down.

"No, I'm not," I said, "I'm laughing at me. I shouldn't have been bothered by what you said, but I was. That tells me something funny about me."

"What?"

"I'm getting sentimental in my old age, and that's funny."

"Oh." He turned his back on me and walked over to the window and stared out. Then he jammed his hands into his pockets and turned around and looked at me.

"Aren't you happy?" he asked. "Really, I mean? You've got money, and no strings on you. You could pick up and leave on the next I-V that passes, if you wanted to."

"Sure I'm happy," I told him. "My coffee was cold. Forget it."

"Oh," again. He turned back to the window in time to catch a bright flash full in the face, and to have to compete with thunder to get his next words out. "I'm sorry," I heard him say, as in the distance. "It just seems to me that you should be one of the happiest guys around . . . "

"I am. It's the weather today. It's got everybody down in the mouth, yourself included."

"Yeah, you're right," he said. "Look at it rain, will you? Haven't seen any rain in months . . . "

"They've been saving it all up for today."

He chuckled.

"I'm going down for a cup of coffee and a sandwich before I sign on. Can I bring you anything?"

"No, thanks."

"Okay. See you in a little while."

He walked out whistling. He never stays depressed. Like a kid's moods, his moods, up and down, up and down . . . And he's a Hell Cop. Probably the worst possible job for him, having to keep up his attention in one place for so long. They say the job title comes from the name of an antique flying vehicle—a hellcopper, I think. We send our eyes on their appointed rounds, and they can hover or soar or back up, just like those old machines could. We patrol the city and the adjacent countryside. Law enforcement isn't much of a problem on Cyg. We never peek in windows or send an eye into a building without an invitation. Our testimony is admissible in court—or, if we're fast enough to press a couple buttons, the tape that we make does an even better job—and we can dispatch live or robot cops in a hurry, depending on which will do a better job.

There isn't much crime on Cyg, though, despite the fact that everybody carries a sidearm of some kind, even little kids. Everybody knows pretty much what their neighbors are up to, and there aren't too many places for a fugitive to run. We're mainly aerial traffic cops, with an eye out for local wildlife (which is the reason for all the sidearms).

S.P.C.U. is what we call the latter function—Society for the Prevention of Cruelty to Us—Which is the reason each of my hundred-thirty eyes has six forty-five caliber eyelashes.

There are things like the cute little panda-puppy—oh, about three feet high at the shoulder when it sits down on its rear like a teddy bear, and with big, square, silky ears, a curly pinto coat, large, limpid, brown eyes, pink tongue, button nose, powder puff tail, sharp little white teeth more poisonous than a Quemeda Island viper's, and possessed of a way with mammal entrails like unto the way of an imaginative cat with a rope of catnip.

Then there's a *snapper*, which *looks* as mean as it sounds: a feathered reptile, with three horns on its armored head—one beneath each eye, like a tusk, and one curving skyward from the top of its nose—legs about eighteen inches long, and a four-foot tail which it raises straight into the air whenever it jogs along at greyhound speed, and which it swings like a sandbag—and a mouth full of long, sharp teeth.

Also, there are amphibious things which come from the ocean by way of the river on occasion. I'd rather not speak of them. They're kind of ugly and vicious.

Anyway, those are some of the reasons why there are Hell Cops—not just on Cyg, but on many, many frontier worlds. I've been employed in that capacity on several of them, and I've found that an experienced H.C. can always find a job Out Here. It's like being a professional clerk back home.

Chuck took longer than I thought he would, came back after I was technically off duty, looked happy though, so I didn't say anything. There was some pale lipstick on his collar and a grin on his face, so I bade him good morrow, picked up my cane, and departed in the direction of the big washing machine.

It was coming down too hard for me to go the two blocks to my car on foot.

I called a cab and waited another fifteen minutes. Eleanor had decided to keep Mayor's Hours, and she'd departed shortly after lunch; and almost the entire staff had been released an hour early because of the weather. Consequently, Town Hall was full of dark offices and echoes. I waited in the hallway behind the main door, listening to the purr of the rain as it fell, and hearing its gurgle as it found its way into the gutters. It beat the street and shook the windowpanes and made the windows cold to touch.

Roger Zelazny and Samuel R. Delany

I'd planned on spending the evening at the library, but I changed my plans as I watched the weather happen. —Tomorrow, or the next day, I decided. It was an evening for a good meal, a hot bath, my own books and brandy, and early to bed. It was good sleeping weather, if nothing else. A cab pulled up in front of the Hall and blew its horn.

I ran.

*

The next day the rain let up for perhaps an hour in the morning. Then a slow drizzle began; and it did not stop again.

It went on to become a steady downpour by afternoon.

The following day was Friday, which I always have off, and I was glad that it was.

Put dittoes under Thursday's weather report. That's Friday.

But I decided to do something anyway.

I lived down in that section of town near the river. The Noble was swollen, and the rains kept adding to it. Sewers had begun to clog and back up; water ran into the streets. The rain kept coming down and widening the puddles and lakelets, and it was accompanied by drum solos in the sky and the falling of bright forks and sawblades. Dead skytoads were washed along the gutters, like burnt-out fireworks. Ball lightning drifted across Town Square; Saint Elmo's fire clung to the flag pole, the Watch Tower, and the big statue of Wyeth trying to look heroic.

I headed uptown to the library, pushing my car slowly through the countless beaded curtains. The big furniture movers in the sky were obviously non-union, because they weren't taking any coffee breaks. Finally, I found a parking place and I umbrellaed my way to the library and entered.

I have become something of a bibliophile in recent years. It is not so much that I hunger and thirst after knowledge, but that I am news-starved.

It all goes back to my position in the big mixmaster. Admitted, there are *some* things faster than light, like the phase velocities of radio waves in ion plasma, or the tips of the ion-modulated light-beams of Duckbill, the comm-setup back in Sol System, whenever the hinges of the beak snap shut on

411

The Magic

Earth—but these are highly restricted instances, with no application whatsoever to the passage of shiploads of people and objects between the stars. You can't exceed lightspeed when it comes to the movement of matter. You can edge up pretty close, but that's about it.

Life can be suspended though, that's easy—it can be switched off and switched back on again with no trouble at all. This is why *I* have lasted so long. If we can't speed up the ships, we *can* slow down the people—slow them until they stop—and *let* the vessel, moving at near-lightspeed, take half a century, or more if it needs it, to convey its passengers to where they are going. This is why I am very alone. Each little death means resurrection into both another land and another time. I have had several, and *this* is why I have become a bibliophile: news travels slowly, as slowly as the ships and the people. Buy a newspaper before you hop aboard a ship and it will still be a newspaper when you reach your destination—but back where you bought it, it would be considered an historical document. Send a letter back to Earth and your correspondent's grandson may be able to get an answer back to your great-grandson, if the message makes real good connections and both kids live long enough.

All the little libraries Out Here are full of rare books—first editions of best sellers which people pick up before they leave Someplace Else, and which they often donate after they've finished. We assume that these books have entered the public domain by the time they reach here, and we reproduce them and circulate our own editions. No author has ever sued, and no reproducer has ever been around to *be* sued by representatives, designates, or assigns.

We are completely autonomous and are always behind the times, because there is a transit-lag which cannot be overcome. Earth Central, therefore, exercises about as much control over us as a boy jiggling a broken string while looking up at his kite.

Perhaps Yeats had something like this in mind when he wrote that fine line, "Things fall apart; the center cannot hold." I doubt it, but I still have to go to the library to read the news.

Roger Zelazny and Samuel R. Delany

*

The day melted around me.

The words flowed across the screen in my booth as I read newspapers and magazines, untouched by human hands, and the waters flowed across Betty's acres, pouring down from the mountains now, washing the floors of the forest, churning our fields to peanut-butter, flooding basements, soaking its way through everything, and tracking our streets with mud.

I hit the library cafeteria for lunch, where I learned from a girl in a green apron and yellow skirts (which swished pleasantly) that the sandbag crews were now hard at work and that there was no eastbound traffic past Town Square.

After lunch I put on my slicker and boots and walked up that way.

Sure enough, the sandbag wall was already waist high across Main Street; but then, the water *was* swirling around at ankle level, and more of it falling every minute.

I looked up at old Wyeth's statue. His halo had gone away now, which was sort of to be expected. It had made an honest mistake and realized it after a short time.

He was holding a pair of glasses in his left hand and sort of glancing down at me, as though a bit apprehensive, wondering perhaps, there inside all that bronze, if I would tell on him now and ruin his hard, wet, greenish splendor. Tell . . . ? I guess I was the only one around who really remembered the man. He had wanted to be the father of this great new country, literally, and he'd tried awfully hard. Three months in office and I'd had to fill out the rest of the two-year term. The death certificate gave the cause as "heart stoppage," but it didn't mention the piece of lead which had helped slow things down a bit. Everybody involved is gone now: the irate husband, the frightened wife, the coroner. All but me. And I won't tell anybody if Wyeth's statue won't, because he's a hero now, and we need heroes' statues Out Here even more than we do heroes. He *did* engineer a nice piece of relief work during the Butler Township floods, and he may as well be remembered for that.

The Magic

I winked at my old boss, and the rain dripped from his nose and fell into the puddle at my feet.

I walked back to the library through loud sounds and bright flashes, hearing the splashing and the curses of the work crew as the men began to block off another street. Black, overhead, an eye drifted past. I waved, and the filter snapped up and back down again. I think H.C. John Keams was tending shop that afternoon, but I'm not sure.

Suddenly the heavens opened up and it was like standing under a waterfall.

I reached for a wall and there wasn't one, slipped then, and managed to catch myself with my cane before I flopped. I found a doorway and huddled.

Ten minutes of lightning and thunder followed. Then, after the blindness and the deafness passed away and the rains had eased a bit, I saw that the street (Second Avenue) had become a river. Bearing all sorts of garbage, papers, hats, sticks, mud, it sloshed past my niche, gurgling nastily. It looked to be over my boot tops, so I waited for it to subside.

It didn't.

It got right up in there with me and started to play footsie.

So, then seemed as good a time as any. Things certainly weren't getting any better.

I tried to run, but with filled boots the best you can manage is a fast wade, and my boots were filled after three steps.

That shot the afternoon. How can you concentrate on anything with wet feet? I made it back to the parking lot, then churned my way homeward, feeling like a riverboat captain who really wanted to be a camel driver.

It seemed more like evening that afternoon when I pulled up into my damp but unflooded garage. It seemed more like night than evening in the alley I cut through on the way to my apartment's back entrance. I hadn't seen the sun for several days, and it's funny how much you can miss it when it takes a vacation. The sky was a sable dome, and the high brick walls of the alley were cleaner than I'd ever seen them, despite the shadows.

I stayed close to the lefthand wall, in order to miss some of the rain. As I had driven along the river I'd noticed that it was already reaching after the high water marks on the sides of the piers. The Noble was a big, spoiled, blood sausage, ready to burst its skin. A lightning flash showed me the whole alley, and I slowed in order to avoid puddles.

I moved ahead, thinking of dry socks and dry martinis, turned a corner to the right, and it struck at me: an org.

Half of its segmented body was reared at a forty-five degree angle above the pavement, which placed its wide head with the traffic-signal eyes saying "Stop," about three and a half feet off the ground, as it rolled toward me on all its pale little legs, with its mouthful of death aimed at my middle.

I pause now in my narrative for a long digression concerning my childhood, which, if you will but consider the circumstances, I was obviously fresh on it an instant:

Born, raised, educated on Earth, I had worked two summers in a stockyard while going to college. I still remember the smells and the noises of the cattle; I used to prod them out of the pens and on their way up the last mile. And I remember the smells and noises of the university: the formaldehyde in the Bio labs, the sounds of Freshmen slaughtering French verbs, the overpowering aroma of coffee mixed with cigarette smoke in the Student Union, the splash of the newly-pinned frat man as his brothers tossed him into the lagoon down in front of the Art Museum, the sounds of ignored chapel bells and class bells, the smell of the lawn after the year's first mowing (with big, black Andy perched on his grass-chewing monster, baseball cap down to his eyebrows, cigarette somehow not burning his left cheek), and always, always, the *tick-tick-snick-stamp*! as I moved up or down the strip. I had not wanted to take General Physical Education, but four semesters of it were required. The only out was to take a class in a special sport. I picked fencing because tennis, basketball, boxing, wrestling, handball, judo, all sounded too strenuous, and I couldn't afford a set of golf clubs. Little did I suspect what would follow this choice. It was as strenuous as any of the others, and more than several. But I liked it. So I tried out for the team in my Sophomore year, made it on the *épée* squad, and picked up three varsity letters, because I stuck with it through my Senior year. Which all goes to show: Cattle who persevere in looking for an easy out still wind up in the abattoir, but they may enjoy the trip a little more.

When I came out here on the raw frontier where people all carry weapons, I had my cane made. It combines the best features of the *épée* and the cattle prod. Only, it is the kind of prod which, if you were to prod cattle with it, they would never move again.

Over eight hundred volts, max, when the tip touches, if the stud in the handle is depressed properly . . .

My arm shot out and up and my fingers depressed the stud properly as it moved.

That was it for the org.

A noise came from beneath the rows of razor blades in its mouth as I scored a touch on its soft underbelly and whipped my arm away to the side—a noise halfway between an exhalation and "peep"—and that was it for the org (short for "organism-with-a-long-name-which-I-can't-remember").

I switched off my cane and walked around it. It was one of those things which sometimes come out of the river. I remember that I looked back at it three times, then I switched the cane on again at max and kept it that way till I was inside my apartment with the door locked behind me and all the lights burning.

Then I permitted myself to tremble, and after awhile I changed my socks and mixed my drink.

May your alleys be safe from orgs.

*

Saturday.

More rain.

Wetness was all.

The entire east side had been shored with sand bags. In some places they served only to create sandy waterfalls, where otherwise the streams would have flowed more evenly and perhaps a trifle more clearly. In other places they held it all back, for awhile.

By then, there were six deaths as a direct result of the rains.

Roger Zelazny and Samuel R. Delany

By then, there had been fires caused by the lightning, accidents by the water, sicknesses by the dampness, the cold.

By then, property damages were beginning to mount pretty high.

Everyone was tired and angry and miserable and wet, by then. This included me.

Though Saturday was Saturday, I went to work. I worked in Eleanor's office, with her. We had the big relief map spread on a table, and six mobile eyescreens were lined against one wall. Six eyes hovered above the half-dozen emergency points and kept us abreast of the actions taken upon them. Several new telephones and a big radio set stood on the desk. Five ashtrays looked as if they wanted to be empty, and the coffee pot chuckled cynically at human activity.

The Noble had almost reached its high water mark. We were not an isolated storm center by any means. Upriver, Butler Township was hurting, Swan's Nest was adrip, Laurie was weeping the river, and the wilderness in between was shaking and streaming.

Even though we were in direct contact we went into the field on three occasions that morning—once, when the north-south bridge over the Lance River collapsed and was washed down toward the Noble as far as the bend by the Mack steel mill; again, when the Wildwood Cemetery, set up on a storm-gouged hill to the east, was plowed deeply, graves opened, and several coffins set awash; and finally, when three houses full of people toppled, far to the east. Eleanor's small flyer was buffeted by the winds as we fought our way through to these sites for on-the-spot supervision; I navigated almost completely by instruments. Downtown proper was accommodating evacuees left and right by then. I took three showers that morning and changed clothes twice.

Things slowed down a bit in the afternoon, including the rain. The cloud cover didn't break, but a drizzle-point was reached which permitted us to gain a little on the waters. Retaining walls were reinforced, evacuees were fed and dried, some of the rubbish was cleaned up. Four of the six eyes were returned to their patrols, because four of the emergency points were no longer emergency points.

. . . And we wanted all of the eyes for the org patrol.

Inhabitants of the drenched forest were also on the move. Seven *snappers* and a horde of panda-puppies were shot that day, as well as a few crawly things from the troubled waters of the Noble—not to mention assorted branch-snakes, stingbats, borers, and land-eels.

By 1900 hours it seemed that a stalemate had been achieved. Eleanor and I climbed into her flyer and drifted skyward.

We kept rising. Finally, there was a hiss as the cabin began to pressurize itself. The night was all around us. Eleanor's face, in the light from the instrument panel, was a mask of weariness. She raised her hands to her temples as if to remove it, and then when I looked back again it appeared that she had. A faint smile lay across her lips now and her eyes sparkled. A stray strand of hair shadowed her brow.

"Where are you taking me?" she asked.

"Up, high," said I, "above the storm."

"Why?"

"It's been many days," I said, "since we have seen an uncluttered sky."

"True," she agreed, and as she leaned forward to light a cigarette I noticed that the part in her hair had gone all askew. I wanted to reach out and straighten it for her, but I didn't.

We plunged into the sea of clouds.

Dark was the sky, moonless. The stars shone like broken diamonds. The clouds were a floor of lava.

We drifted. We stared up into the heavens. I "anchored" the flyer, like an eye set to hover, and lit a cigarette myself.

"You are older than I am," she finally said, "really. You know?"

"No."

"There is a certain wisdom, a certain strength, something like the essence of the time that passes—that seeps into a man as he sleeps between the stars. I know, because I can feel it when I'm around you."

"No," I said.

"Then maybe it's people expecting you to have the strength of centuries that gives you something like it. It was probably there to begin with."

"No."

She chuckled.

"It isn't exactly a positive sort of thing either."

I laughed.

"You asked me if I was going to run for office again this fall. The answer is 'no.' I'm planning on retiring. I want to settle down."

"With anyone special?"

"Yes, very special, Juss," she said, and she smiled at me and I kissed her, but not for too long, because the ash was about to fall off her cigarette and down the back of my neck.

So we put both cigarettes out and drifted above the invisible city, beneath a sky without a moon.

*

I mentioned earlier that I would tell you about Stopovers. If you are going a distance of a hundred forty-five light years and are taking maybe a hundred-fifty actual years to do it, why stop and stretch your legs?

Well, first of all and mainly, almost nobody sleeps out the whole jaunt. There are lots of little gadgets which require human monitoring at all times. No one is going to sit there for a hundred-fifty years and watch them, all by himself. So everyone takes a turn or two, passengers included. They are all briefed on what to do til the doctor comes, and who to awaken and how to go about it, should troubles crop up. Then everyone takes a turn at guard mount for a month or so, along with a few companions. There are always hundreds of people aboard, and after you've worked down through the role you take it again from the top. All sorts of mechanical agents are backing them up, many of which they are unaware of (to protect *against* them, as well as *with* them—in the improbable instance of several oddballs getting together and deciding to open a window, change course, murder passengers, or things like that), and the people are well-screened and carefully matched up, so as to check and balance each other as well as the machinery. All of this because gadgets and people both bear watching.

After several turns at ship's guard, interspersed with periods of cold sleep, you tend to grow claustrophobic and somewhat depressed. Hence, when there is an available Stopover, it is utilized, to restore mental equilibrium and to rearouse flagging animal spirits. This also serves the purpose of enriching the life and economy of the Stopover world, by whatever information and activities you may have in you.

Stopover, therefore, has become a traditional holiday on many worlds, characterized by festivals and celebrations on some of the smaller ones, and often by parades and world-wide broadcast interviews and press conferences on those with greater populations. I understand that it is now pretty much the same on Earth, too, whenever colonial visitors stop by. In fact, one fairly unsuccessful young starlet, Marilyn Austin, made a long voyage Out, stayed a few months, and returned on the next vessel headed back. After appearing on tri-dee a couple times, sounding off about interstellar culture, and flashing her white, white teeth, she picked up a flush contract, a third husband, and her first big part in tapes. All of which goes to show the value of Stopovers.

*

I landed us atop Helix, Betty's largest apartment-complex, wherein Eleanor had her double-balconied corner suite, affording views both of the distant Noble and of the lights of Posh Valley, Betty's residential section.

Eleanor prepared steaks, with baked potato, cooked corn, beer—everything I liked. I was happy and sated and such, and I stayed till around midnight, making plans for our future. Then I took a cab back to Town Square, where I was parked.

When I arrived, I thought I'd check with the Trouble Center just to see how things were going. So I entered the Hall, stamped my feet, brushed off excess waters, hung my coat, and proceeded up the empty hallway to the elevator.

Roger Zelazny and Samuel R. Delany

The elevator was too quiet. They're supposed to rattle, you know? They shouldn't sigh softly and have doors that open and close without a sound. So I walked around an embarrassing corner on my way to the Trouble Center.

It was a pose Rodin might have enjoyed working with. All I can say is that it's a good thing I stopped by when I did, rather than five or ten minutes later.

Chuck Fuller and Lottie, Eleanor's secretary, were practicing mouth to mouth resuscitating and keeping the victim warm techniques, there on the couch in the little alcove off to the side of the big door to T.C.

Chuck's back was to me, but Lottie spotted me over his shoulder, and her eyes widened and she pushed him away. He turned his head quickly.

"Juss . . . " he said.

I nodded.

"Just passing by," I told him. "Thought I'd stop in to say hello and take a look at the eyes."

"Uh—everything's going real well," he said, stepping back into the hallway. "It's on auto right now, and I'm on my—uh, coffee break. Lottie is on night duty, and she came by to—to see if we had any reports we needed typed. She had a dizzy spell, so we came out here where the couch . . . "

"Yeah, she looks a little—peaked," I said. "There are smelling salts and aspirins in the medicine chest."

I walked on by into the Center, feeling awkward.

Chuck followed me after a couple of minutes. I was watching the screens when he came up beside me. Things appeared to be somewhat in hand, though the rains were still moistening the one hundred thirty views of Betty.

"Uh, Juss," he said, "I didn't know you were coming by . . . "

"Obviously."

"What I'm getting at is—you won't report me, will you?"

"No, I won't report you."

" . . . And you wouldn't mention it to Cynthia, would you?"

"Your extracurricular activities," I said, "are your own business. As a friend, I suggest you do them on your own time and in a more propitious location.

The Magic

But it's already beginning to slip my mind. I'm sure I'll forget the whole thing in another minute."

"Thanks Juss," he said.

I nodded.

"What's Weather Central have to say these days?" I asked, raising the phone.

He shook his head, so I dialed and listened.

"Bad," I said, hanging up. "More wet to come."

"Damn," he announced and lit a cigarette, his hands shaking. "This weather's getting me down."

"Me too," said I. "I'm going to run now, because I want to get home before it starts in bad again. I'll probably be around tomorrow. See you."

"Night."

I elevated back down, fetched my coat, and left. I didn't see Lottie anywhere about, but she probably was, waiting for me to go.

I got to my car and was halfway home before the faucets came on full again. The sky was torn open with lightnings, and a sizzlecloud stalked the city like a long-legged arachnid, forking down bright limbs and leaving tracks of fire where it went. I made it home in another fifteen minutes, and the phenomenon was still in progress as I entered the garage. As I walked up the alley (cane switched on) I could hear the distant sizzle and the rumble, and a steady half-light filling the spaces between the buildings, from its *flash-burn-flash-burn* striding.

Inside, I listened to the thunder and the rain, and I watched the apocalypse off in the distance.

Delirium of city under storm—

The buildings across the way were quite clear in the pulsing light of the thing. The lamps were turned off in my apartment so that I could better appreciate the vision. All of the shadows seemed incredibly black and inky, lying right beside glowing stairways, pediments, windowsills, balconies; and all of that which was illuminated seemed to burn as though with an internal light. Overhead, the living/not living insect-thing of fire stalked, and an eye wearing a blue halo was moving across the tops of nearby buildings. The fires pulsed and the clouds burnt like the hills of Gehenna; the thunders burbled and banged; and the white rain drilled into the roadway which had erupted into a steaming lather. Then a *snapper*, tri-horned, wet-feathered, demon-faced, sword-tailed, and green, raced from around a corner, a moment after I'd heard a sound which I had thought to be a part of the thunder. The creature ran, at an incredible speed, along the smoky pavement. The eye swooped after it, adding a hail of lead to the falling raindrops. Both vanished up another street. It had taken but an instant, but in that instant it had resolved a question in my mind as to who should do the painting. Not El Greco, not Blake; no: Bosch. Without any question, Bosch—with his nightmare visions of the streets of Hell. He would be the one to do justice to this moment of the storm.

I watched until the sizzlecloud drew its legs up into itself, hung like a burning cocoon, then died like an ember retreating into ash. Suddenly, it was very dark and there was only the rain.

*

Sunday was the day of chaos.

Candles burned, churches burned, people drowned, beasts ran wild in the streets (or swam there), houses were torn up by the roots and bounced like paper boats along the waterways, the great wind came down upon us, and after that the madness.

I was not able to drive to Town Hall, so Eleanor sent her flyer after me.

The basement was filled with water, and the ground floor was like Neptune's waiting room. All previous high water marks had been passed.

We were in the middle of the worst storm in Betty's history.

Operations had been transferred up onto the third floor. There was no way to stop things now. It was just a matter of riding it out and giving what relief we could. I sat before my gallery and watched.

It rained buckets, it rained vats; it rained swimming pools and lakes and rivers. For awhile it seemed that it rained oceans upon us. This was partly because of the wind which came in from the gulf and suddenly made it seem to rain sideways with the force of its blasts. It began at about noon and was gone in a few hours, but when it left our town was broken and bleeding. Wyeth lay on his bronze side, the flagpole was gone, there was no building without broken windows and water inside, we were suddenly suffering lapses of electrical power, and one of my eyes showed three panda-puppies devouring a dead child. Cursing, I killed them across the rain and the distance. Eleanor wept at my side. There was a report later of a pregnant woman who could only deliver by Caesarean section, trapped on a hilltop with her family, and in labor. We were still trying to get through to her with a flyer, but the winds . . . I saw burning buildings and the corpses of people and animals. I saw half-buried cars and splintered homes. I saw waterfalls where there had been no waterfalls before. I fired many rounds that day, and not just at beasts from the forest. Sixteen of my eyes had been shot out by looters. I hope that I never again see some of the films I made that day.

When the worst Sunday night in my life began, and the rains did not cease, I knew the meaning of despair for the third time in my life.

Eleanor and I were in the Trouble Center. The lights had just gone out for the eighth time. The rest of the staff was down on the third floor. We sat there in the dark without moving, without being able to do a single thing to halt the course of chaos. We couldn't even watch it until the power came back on.

So we talked.

Whether it was for five minutes or an hour, I don't really know. I remember telling her, though, about the girl buried on another world, whose death had set me to running. Two trips to two worlds and I had broken my bond with the times. But a hundred years of travel do not bring a century of forgetfulness—not when you cheat time with the *petite mort* of the cold sleep. Time's vengeance is memory, and though for an age you plunder the eye of seeing and empty the ear of sound, when you awaken your past is still with you. The worst thing to do then is to return to visit your wife's nameless grave in a changed land, to come back as a stranger to the place you had made your home. You run again then, and after a time you *do* forget, some, because a certain amount of actual time must pass for you also. But by then you are alone, all by yourself: completely alone. That was the *first* time in my life that I knew the meaning of despair. I read, I worked, I drank, I whored, but came the morning after and I was always me, by myself. I jumped from world to world, hoping things would be different, but with each change I was further away from all the things I had known.

Then another feeling gradually came upon me, and a really terrible feeling it was: There *must* be a time and a place best suited for each person who has ever lived. After the worst of my grief had left me and I had come to terms with the vanished past, I wondered about a man's place in time and space. Where, and *when* in the cosmos would I most like to live out the balance of my days? —To live at my fullest potential? The past *was* dead, but perhaps a better time waited on some as yet undiscovered world, waited at one yet-to-be recorded moment in its history. How could I *ever* know? How could I ever be sure that my Golden Age did not lay but one more world away, and that I might be struggling in a Dark Era while the Renaissance of my days was but a ticket, a visa and a diary-page removed? That was my *second* despair. I did know the answer until I came to the Land of the Swan. I do not know why I loved you Eleanor, but I did, and that was my answer. Then the rains came.

When the lights returned we sat there and smoked. She had told me of her husband, who had died a hero's death in time to save him from the delirium tremors which would have ended his days. Died as the bravest die—not knowing why—because of a reflex, which after all had been a part of him, a reflex which had made him cast himself into the path of a pack of wolf-like creatures attacking the exploring party he was with—off in that forest at the foot of Saint Stephen's—to fight them with a machete and to be torn apart by them while his companions fled to the camp, where they made a stand and saved themselves. Such is the essence of valor: an unthinking moment, a spark along the spinal nerves, predetermined by the sum total of everything you have ever done, wished to do or not to do, and wish you had done, or hadn't, and then comes the pain.

The Magic

We watched the gallery on the wall. Man is the reasoning animal? Greater than beasts but less than angels? Not the murderer I shot that night. He wasn't even the one who uses tools or buries his dead. —Laughs, aspires, affirms? I didn't see any of those going on. —Watches himself watch himself doing what he knows is absurd? Too sophisticated. He just did the absurd without watching. Like running back into a burning house after his favorite pipe and a can of tobacco. —Devises religions? I saw people praying, but they weren't devising. They were making last-ditch efforts at saving themselves, after they'd exhausted everything else they knew to do. Reflex.

The creature who loves?

That's the only one I might not be able to gainsay.

I saw a mother holding her daughter up on her shoulders while the water swirled about her armpits, and the little girl was holding her doll up above *her* shoulders, in the same way. But isn't that—the love—a part of the total? Of everything you have ever done, or wished? Positive or neg? I know that it is what made me leave my post, running, and what made me climb into Eleanor's flyer and what made me fight my way through the storm and out to that particular scene.

I didn't get there in time.

I shall never forget how glad I was that someone else did. Johnny Keams blinked his lights above me as he rose, and he radioed down:

"It's all right. They're okay. Even the doll."

"Good," I said, and headed back.

As I set the ship down on its balcony landing, one figure came toward me. As I stepped down, a gun appeared in Chuck's hand.

"I wouldn't kill you, Juss," he began, "but I'd wound you. Face the wall. I'm taking the flyer."

"Are you crazy?" I asked him.

"I know what I'm doing. I need it, Juss."

"Well, if you need it, there it is. You don't have to point a gun at me. I just got through needing it myself. Take it."

"Lottie and I both need it," he said. "Turn around!"

I turned toward the wall.

"What do you mean?" I asked.

"We're going away, together—now!"

"You *are* crazy," I said. "This is no time . . . "

"C'mon, Lottie," he called, and there was a rush of feet behind me and I heard the flyer's door open.

"Chuck!" I said. "We need you now! You can settle this thing peacefully, in a week, in a month, after some order has been restored. There *are* such things as divorces, you know."

"That won't get me off this world, Juss."

"So how is *this* going to help?"

I turned, and I saw that he had picked up a large canvas bag from somewhere and had it slung over his left shoulder, like Santa Claus.

"Turn back around! I don't want to shoot you," he warned.

The suspicion came, grew stronger.

"Chuck, have you been looting?" I asked him.

"Turn around!"

"All right, I'll turn around. How far do you think you'll get?"

"Far enough," he said. "Far enough so that no one will find us—and when the time comes, we'll leave this world."

"No," I said. "I don't think you will, because I know you."

"We'll see." His voice was further away then.

I heard three rapid footsteps and the slamming of a door. I turned then, in time to see the flyer rising from the balcony.

I watched it go. I never saw either of them again.

Inside, two men were unconscious on the floor. It turned out that they were not seriously hurt. After I saw them cared for, I rejoined Eleanor in the Tower.

All that night did we wait, emptied, for morning.

Somehow, it came.

The Magic

We sat and watched the light flow through the rain. So much had happened so quickly. So many things had occurred during the past week that we were unprepared for morning.

It brought an end to the rains.

A good wind came from out of the north and fought with the clouds, like En-ki with the serpent Tiamat. Suddenly, there was a canyon of cobalt.

A cloudquake shook the heavens and chasms of light opened across its dark landscape.

It was coming apart as we watched.

I heard a cheer, and I croaked in unison with it as the sun appeared.

The good, warm, drying, beneficial sun drew the highest peak of Saint Stephen's to its face and kissed both its cheeks.

There was a crowd before each window. I joined one and stared, perhaps for ten minutes.

*

When you awaken from a nightmare you do not normally find its ruins lying about your bedroom. This is one way of telling whether or not something was only a bad dream, or whether or not you are really awake.

We walked the streets in great boots. Mud was everywhere. It was in basements and in machinery and in sewers and in living room clothes closets. It was on buildings and on cars and on people and on the branches of trees. It was broken brown blisters drying and waiting to be peeled off from clean tissue. Swarms of skytoads rose into the air when we approached, hovered like dragon-flies, returned to spoiling food stores after we had passed. Insects were having a heyday, too. Betty would have to be deloused. So many things were overturned or fallen down, and half-buried in the brown Sargassos of the streets. The dead had not yet been numbered. The water still ran by, but sluggish and foul. A stench was beginning to rise across the city. There were smashed-in store fronts and there was glass everywhere, and bridges fallen down and holes in the streets . . . But why go on? If you don't get the picture by now, you never will. It was the big morning after, following a drunken party by the gods. It is the lot of mortal man always to clean up their leavings or be buried beneath them.

So clean we did, but by noon Eleanor could no longer stand. So I took her home with me, because we were working down near the harbor section and my place was nearer.

That's almost the whole story—light to darkness to light—except for the end, which I don't really know. I'll tell you of its beginning, though . . .

*

I dropped her off at the head of the alleyway, and she went on toward my apartment while I parked the car. Why didn't I keep her with me? I don't know. Unless it was because the morning sun made the world seem at peace, despite its filth. Unless it was because I was in love and the darkness was over, and the spirit of the night had surely departed.

I parked the car and started up the alley. I was halfway before the corner where I had met the org when I heard her cry out.

I ran. Fear gave me speed and strength and I ran to the corner and turned it.

The man had a bag, not unlike the one Chuck had carried away with him, lying beside the puddle in which he stood. He was going through Eleanor's purse, and she lay on the ground—so still!—with blood on the side of her head.

I cursed and ran toward him, switching on my cane as I went. He turned, dropped her purse, and reached for the gun in his belt.

We were about thirty feet apart, so I threw my cane.

He drew his gun, pointed it at me, and my cane fell into the puddle in which he stood.

Flights of angels sang him to his rest, perhaps.

She was breathing, so I got her inside and got hold of a doctor—I don't remember how, not too clearly, anyway—and I waited and waited.

She lived for another twelve hours and then she died. She recovered consciousness twice before they operated on her, and not again after. She didn't say anything. She smiled at me once, and went to sleep again.

The Magic

I don't know.

Anything, really.

It happened that I became Betty's mayor, to fill in until November, to oversee the rebuilding. I worked, I worked my head off, and I left her bright and shiny, as I had found her. I think I could have won if I had run for the job that fall, but I did not want it.

The Town Council overrode my objections and voted to erect a statue of Godfrey Justin Holmes beside the statue of Eleanor Schirrer which was to stand in the Square across from cleaned-up Wyeth. I guess it's out there now.

I said that I would never return, but who knows? In a couple of years, after some more history has passed, I may revisit a Betty full of strangers, if only to place a wreath at the foot of the one statue. Who knows but that the entire continent may be steaming and clanking and whirring with automation by then, and filled with people from shore to shining shore?

There was a Stopover at the end of the year and I waved goodbye and climbed aboard and went away, anywhere.

I went aboard and went away, to sleep again the cold sleep.

Delirium of ship among stars—

Years have passed, I suppose. I'm not really counting them anymore. But I think of this thing often: Perhaps there *is* a Golden Age someplace, a Renaissance for me sometime, a special time somewhere, somewhere but a ticket, a visa, a diary-page away. I don't know where or when. Who does? Where are all the rains of yesterday?

In the invisible city?

Inside me?

It is cold and quiet outside and the horizon is infinity. There is no sense of movement.

There is no moon, and the stars are very bright, like broken diamonds, all.

A Word from Zelazny

The novel *Isle of the Dead* "was a spin-off from the novelette I did called 'This Moment of the Storm.'"[1] Zelazny numbered it among his favorite novelettes.[2] Starting with the title, it presents aspects of existentialism, with a protagonist out of time in several ways.

"Based on the recent floods out west," he wrote on May 16, 1965. "Showed it to Damon Knight, who wisely saw through it, saying that I had written a normal human story and then quickly added enough science to make it science fiction. Wise Damon Knight. Anyhow, it sold..."[3] Damon Knight wrote, "This one has a nice gentle mood and some likeable people, but although it succeeds as a story, I don't think it succeeds as science fiction. You could pull the s.f. elements out of it without too much trouble, put it into the here-&-now, and leave it essentially the same story. Anyhow, this is not my cup of tea, but most Zelazny stories are—so send me the next one."[4] The next story was "For A Breath I Tarry," which Knight also rejected. "This Moment of the Storm" garnered both Hugo and Nebula nominations.

Zelazny fenced for four years in college, lettering three times and captaining the *epee* squad in his final two years.[5] Godfrey Holmes's experiences in the story reflect Zelazny's history. Zelazny also studied aikido, tae kwon do, judo, karate, and other martial arts, and many of his protagonists used such unarmed combat techniques.

Notes

The recurrent motif of **green eyes** occurs in this story. **Saint Stephen** was an early evangelist who, shortly after Jesus died, became the first Christian martyr. The feast of Stephen is December 26. *Raison d'être* is justification for existence. A **shaman** is a tribe's spiritual leader and sorcerer. **Miniver Cheevy**, by American poet Edward Arlington Robinson, begins "Miniver Cheevy, child of scorn, || Grew lean while he assailed the seasons || He wept that he was ever born, || And he had reasons." The story's events reflect the poem.

St. Elmo's Fire is a luminous electrical discharge that appears on a ship or aircraft during a storm. **Things fall apart; the center cannot hold** quotes the apocalyptic poem *Second Coming* by William Butler Yeats; poem and poet also figured more prominently in Zelazny's "Moonless in Byzantium." **Auguste**

The Magic

Rodin was a French sculptor whose works include "The Thinker" and the erotic "The Kiss." **Arachnids** are eight-legged creatures such as spiders, scorpions, mites, and ticks. **Gehenna** is hell.

El Greco (Domenicos Theotokopoulos) was a Renaissance painter; his works feature distorted perspective and elongated figures; **William Blake** painted hallucinatory images and scenes from the Bible; **Hieronymos Bosch** painted works populated with half-human, half-animal grotesques. *Petite mort* means little death, in this context a euphemism for the cold sleep (suspended animation) used by travelers between stars (it is also a euphemism for orgasm). **Delirium tremors** (*delirium tremens*) is a complication of withdrawal from alcohol addiction.

En-ki and **Tiamat** are Sumerian gods. Battling to control all of creation, Tiamat sent her own offspring in various unnatural forms to confront En-ki. **Sargassos** is the seaweed-clogged Sargasso Sea, a breeding place for eels; the story's flooded streets are clogged with debris and life forms.

[1] *Leading Edge #29* August 1994.

[2] *Phantasmicom #10*, November 1972.

[3] *Tightbeam #37*, May 1966.

[4] Letter from Damon Knight to Roger Zelazny dated March 9, 1965.

[5] *Roger Zelazny*, Jane M. Lindskold, 1993.

The Keys to December

Born of man and woman, in accordance with Catform Y7 requirements, Coldworld Class (modified per Alyonal), 3.2-E, G.M.I. option, Jarry Dark was not suited for existence anywhere in the universe which had guaranteed him a niche. This was either a blessing or a curse, depending on how you looked at it.

So look at it however you would, here is the story:

*

It is likely that his parents could have afforded the temperature control unit, but not much more than that. (Jarry required a temperature of at least -50 C to be comfortable.)

It is unlikely that his parents could have provided for the air pressure control and gas mixture equipment required to maintain his life.

Nothing could be done in the way of 3.2-E grav-simulation, so daily medication and physiotherapy were required. It is unlikely that his parents could have provided for this.

The much-maligned option took care of him, however. It safe-guarded his health. It provided for his education. It assured his economic welfare and physical well-being.

It might be argued that Jarry Dark would not have been a homeless Coldworld Catform (modified per Alyonal) had it not been for General Mining, Incorporated, which had held the option. But then it must be borne in mind that no one could have foreseen the nova which destroyed Alyonal.

When his parents had presented themselves at the Public Health Planned Parenthood Center and requested advice and medication pending offspring, they had been informed as to the available worlds and the bodyform requirements for them. They had selected Alyonal, which had recently been

433

purchased by General Mining for purposes of mineral exploitation. Wisely, they had elected the option; that is to say, they had signed a contract on behalf of their anticipated offspring, who would be eminently qualified to inhabit that world, agreeing that he would work as an employee of General Mining until he achieved his majority, at which time he would be free to depart and seek employment wherever he might choose (though his choices would admittedly be limited). In return for this guarantee, General Mining agreed to assure his health, education and continuing welfare for so long as he remained in their employ.

When Alyonal caught fire and went away, those Coldworld Catforms covered by the option who were scattered about the crowded galaxy were, by virtue of the agreement, wards of General Mining.

This is why Jarry grew up in a hermetically sealed room containing temperature and atmosphere controls, and why he received a first-class closed circuit education, along with his physiotherapy and medicine. This is also why Jarry bore some resemblance to a large gray ocelot without a tail, had webbing between his fingers and could not go outside to watch the traffic unless he wore a pressurized refrigeration suit and took extra medication.

All over the swarming galaxy, people took the advice of Public Health Planned Parenthood Centers, and many others had chosen as had Jarry's parents. Twenty-eight thousand, five hundred sixty-six of them, to be exact. In any group of over twenty-eight thousand five hundred sixty, there are bound to be a few talented individuals. Jarry was one of them. He had a knack for making money. Most of his General Mining pension check was invested in well-chosen stocks of a speculative nature. (In fact, after a time he came to own considerable stock in General Mining.)

When the man from the Galactic Civil Liberties Union had come around, expressing concern over the pre-birth contracts involved in the option and explaining that the Alyonal Catforms would make a good test case (especially since Jarry's parents lived within jurisdiction of the 877th Circuit, where they would be assured favorable courtroom atmosphere), Jarry's parents had demurred, for fear of jeopardizing the General Mining pension. Later on,

Roger Zelazny and Samuel R. Delany

Jarry himself dismissed the notion also. A favorable decision could not make him an E-world Normform, and what else mattered? He was not vindictive. Also, he owned considerable stock in G.M. by then.

He loafed in his methane tank and purred, which meant that he was thinking. He operated his cryo-computer as he purred and thought. He was computing the total net worth of all the Catforms in the recently organized December Club.

He stopped purring and considered a sub-total, stretched, shook his head slowly. Then he returned to his calculations.

When he had finished, he dictated a message into his speech-tube, to Sanza Barati, President of December and his betrothed:

"Dearest Sanza—the funds available, as I have suspected, leave much to be desired. All the more reason to begin immediately. Kindly submit the proposal to the business committee, outline my qualifications and seek immediate endorsement. I've finished drafting the general statement to the membership. (Copy attached.) From these figures, it will take me between five and ten years, if at least eighty percent of the membership backs me. So push hard, beloved. I'd like to meet you someday, in a place where the sky is purple. Yours, always, Jarry Dark, Treasurer. P.S. I'm pleased you were pleased with the ring."

Two years later, Jarry had doubled the net worth of December, Incorporated.

A year and a half after that, he had doubled it again.

When he received the following letter from Sanza, he leapt onto his trampoline, bounded into the air, landed upon his feet at the opposite end of his quarters, returned to his viewer and replayed it:

> Dear Jarry,
>
> Attached are specifications and prices for five more worlds. The research staff likes the last one. So do I. What do you think? Alyonal II? If so, how about the price? When could we afford that much? The staff also says that a hundred

The Magic

Worldchange units could alter it to what we want in 5-6 centuries. Will forward costs of this machinery shortly.

Come live with me and be my love, in a place where there are no walls . . . .

Sanza

"One year," he replied, "and I'll buy you a world! Hurry up with the costs of the machinery and transport . . . . "

*

When the figures arrived Jarry wept icy tears. One hundred machines, capable of altering the environment of a world, plus twenty-eight thousand coldsleep bunkers, plus transportation costs for the machinery and his people, plus . . . Too high! He did a rapid calculation.

He spoke into the speech-tube:

" . . . Fifteen additional years is too long to wait, Pussycat. Have them figure the time-span if we were to purchase only twenty Worldchange units. Love and kisses, Jarry."

During the days which followed, he stalked above his chamber, erect at first, then on all fours as his mood deepened.

"Approximately three thousand years," came the reply. "May your coat be ever shiny—Sanza."

"Let's put it to a vote, Greeneyes," he said.

*

Quick, a world in 300 words or less! Picture this . . .

One land mass, really, containing three black and brackish looking seas; gray plains and yellow plains and skies the color of dry sand; shallow forests with trees like mushrooms which have been swabbed with iodine; no mountains, just hills brown, yellow, white, lavender; green birds with wings like parachutes, bills like sickles, feathers like oak leaves, an inside-out umbrella behind; six very distant moons, like spots before the eyes in daytime, snowflakes at night, drops of blood at dusk and dawn; grass like mustard in the moister valleys; mists like white fire on windless mornings, albino serpents when the air's astir; radiating chasms, like fractures in frosted windowpanes; hidden caverns, like chains of dark bubbles; seventeen known dangerous predators, ranging from one to six meters in length, excessively furred and fanged; sudden hailstorms, like hurled hammerheads from a clear sky; an icecap like a blue beret at either flattened pole; nervous bipeds a meter and a half in height, short on cerebrum, which wander the shallow forests and prey upon the giant caterpillar's larva, as well as the giant caterpillar, the green bird, the blind burrower, and the offal-eating murkbeast; seventeen mighty rivers; clouds like pregnant purple cows, which quickly cross the land to lie-in beyond the visible east; stands of windblasted stones like frozen music; nights like soot, to obscure the lesser stars; valleys which flow like the torsos of women or instruments of music; perpetual frost in places of shadow; sounds in the morning like the cracking of ice, the trembling of tin, the snapping of steel strands . . .

They knew they would turn it into heaven.

*

The vanguard arrived, decked out in refrigeration suits, installed ten Worldchange units in either hemisphere, began setting up cold-sleep bunkers in several of the larger caverns.

Then came the members of December down from the sand-colored sky.

They came and they saw, decided it was almost heaven, then entered their caverns and slept. Over twenty-eight thousand Coldworld Catforms (modified per Alyonal) came into their own world to sleep for a season in silence the sleep of ice and of stone, to inherit the new Alyonal. There is no dreaming in that sleep. But had there been, their dreams might have been as the thoughts of those yet awake.

"It is bitter, Sanza."

"Yes, but only for a time—"

" . . . To have each other and our own world, and still to go forth like divers at the bottom of the sea. To have to crawl when you want to leap . . . "

"It is only for a short time, Jarry, as the sense will reckon it."

The Magic

"But it is really three thousand years! An ice age will come to pass as we doze. Our former worlds will change so that we would not know them were we to go back for a visit—and none will remember us."

"Visit what? Our former cells? Let the rest of the worlds go by! Let us be forgotten in the lands of our birth! We are a people apart and we have found our home. What else matters?"

"True . . . It will be but a few years, and we shall stand our tours of wakefulness and watching together."

"When is the first?"

"Two and a half centuries from now—three months of wakefulness."

"What will it be like then?"

"I don't know. Less warm . . . "

"Then let us return and sleep. Tomorrow will be a better day."

"Yes."

"Oh! See the green bird! It drifts like a dream . . . "

When they awakened that first time, they stayed within the Worldchange installation at the place called Deadland. The world was already colder and the edges of the sky were tinted with pink. The metal walls of the great installation were black and rimed with frost. The atmosphere was still lethal and the temperature far too high. They remained within their special chambers for most of the time, venturing outside mainly to make necessary tests and to inspect the structure of their home.

Deadland . . . Rocks and sand. No trees, no marks of life at all.

The time of terrible winds was still upon the land, as the world fought back against the fields of the machines. At night, great clouds of real estate smoothed and sculpted the stands of stone, and when the winds departed the desert would shimmer as if fresh-painted and the stones would stand like flames within the morning and its singing. After the sun came up into the sky and hung there for a time, the winds would begin again and a dun-colored fog would curtain the day. When the morning winds departed, Jarry and Sanza would stare out across the Deadland through the east window of the installation, for that was their favorite—the one on the third floor—where

438

the stone that looked like a gnarly Normform waved to them, and they would lie upon the green couch they had moved up from the first floor, and would sometimes make love as they listened for the winds to rise again, or Sanza would sing and Jarry would write in the log or read back through it, the scribblings of friends and unknowns through the centuries, and they would purr often but never laugh, because they did not know how.

One morning, as they watched, they saw one of the biped creatures of the iodine forests moving across the land. It fell several times, picked itself up, fell once more, lay still.

"What is it doing this far from its home?" asked Sanza.

"Dying," said Jarry. "Let's go outside."

They crossed a catwalk, descended to the first floor, donned their protective suits and departed the installation.

The creature had risen to its feet and was staggering once again. It was covered with a reddish down, had dark eyes and a long, wide nose, lacked a true forehead. It had four brief digits, clawed, upon each hand and foot.

When it saw them emerge from the Worldchange unit, it stopped and stared at them. Then it fell.

They moved to its side and studied it where it lay.

It continued to stare at them, its dark eyes wide, as it lay there shivering.

"It will die if we leave it here," said Sanza.

" . . . And it will die if we take it inside," said Jarry.

It raised a forelimb toward them, let it fall again. Its eyes narrowed, then closed.

Jarry reached out and touched it with the toe of his boot. There was no response.

"It's dead," he said.

"What will we do?"

"Leave it here. The sands will cover it."

They returned to the installation, and Jarry entered the event in the log.

The Magic

During their last month of duty, Sanza asked him, "Will everything die here but us? The green birds and the big eaters of flesh? The funny little trees and the hairy caterpillar?"

"I hope not," said Jarry. "I've been reading back through the biologists' notes. I think life might adapt. Once it gets a start anywhere, it'll do anything it can to keep going. It's probably better for the creatures of this planet we could afford only twenty Worldchangers. That way they have three millennia to grow more hair and learn to breathe our air and drink our water. With a hundred units we might have wiped them out and had to import coldworld creatures or breed them. This way, the ones who live here might be able to make it."

"It's funny," she said, "but the thought just occurred to me that we're doing here what was done to us. They made us for Alyonal, and a nova took it away. These creatures came to life in this place, and we're taking it away. We're turning all of life on this planet into what we were on our former worlds—misfits."

"The difference, however, is that we are taking our time," said Jarry, "and giving them a chance to get used to the new conditions."

"Still, I feel that all that—outside there"—she gestured toward the window—"is what this world is becoming: one big Deadland."

"Deadland was here before we came. We haven't created any new deserts."

"All the animals are moving south. The trees are dying. When they get as far south as they can go and still the temperature drops, and the air continues to harm their lungs—then it will be all over for them."

"By then they might have adapted. The trees are spreading, are developing thicker barks. Life will make it."

"I wonder . . . . "

"Would you prefer to sleep until it's all over?"

"No; I want to be by your side, always."

"Then you must reconcile yourself to the fact that something is always hurt by any change. If you do this, you will not be hurt yourself."

Then they listened for the winds to rise.

Roger Zelazny and Samuel R. Delany

Three days later, in the still of sundown, between the winds of day and the winds of night, she called him to the window. He climbed to the third floor and moved to her side. Her breasts were rose in the sundown light and the places beneath them silver and dark. The fur of her shoulders and haunches was like an aura of smoke. Her face was expressionless and her wide, green eyes were not turned toward him.

He looked out.

The first big flakes were falling, blue, through the pink light. They drifted past the stone and gnarly Normform; some stuck in the thick quartz windowpane; they fell upon the desert and lay there like blossoms of cyanide; they swirled as more of them came down and were caught by the first faint puffs of the terrible winds. Dark clouds had mustered overhead and from them, now, great cables and nets of blue descended. Now the flakes flashed past the window like butterflies, and the outline of Deadland flickered on and off. The pink vanished and there was only blue, blue and darkening blue, as the first great sigh of evening came into their ears and the billows suddenly moved sidewise rather than downwards, becoming indigo as they raced by.

*

"The machine is never silent," Jarry wrote. "Sometimes I fancy I can hear voices in its constant humming, its occasional growling, its crackles of power. I am alone here at the Deadland station. Five centuries have passed since our arrival. I thought it better to let Sanza sleep out this tour of duty, lest the prospect be too bleak. (It is.) She will doubtless be angry. As I lay half-awake this morning, I thought I heard my parents' voices in the next room. No words. Just the sounds of their voices as I used to hear them over my old intercom. They must be dead by now, despite all geriatrics. I wonder if they thought of me much after I left? I couldn't even shake my father's hand without the gauntlet, or kiss my mother goodbye. It is strange, the feeling, to be this alone, with only the throb of the machinery about me as it rearranges the molecules of the atmosphere, refrigerates the world, here in the middle of the blue place. Deadland. This, despite the fact that I grew up in a steel cave. I call the other nineteen stations every afternoon. I am afraid I am becoming something of a nuisance. I won't call them tomorrow, or perhaps the next day.

"I went outside without my refrig-pack this morning, for a few moments. It is still deadly hot. I gulped a mouthful of air and choked. Our day is still far off. But I can notice the difference from the last time I tried it, two and a half hundred years ago. I wonder what it will be like when we have finished? —And I, an economist! What will my function be in our new Alyonal? Whatever, so long as Sanza is happy . . . .

"The Worldchanger stutters and groans. All the land is blue for so far as I can see. The stones still stand, but their shapes are changed from what they were. The sky is entirely pink now, and it becomes almost maroon in the morning and the evening. I guess it's really a wine-color, but I've never seen wine, so I can't say for certain. The trees have not died. They've grown hardier. Their barks are thicker, their leaves darker and larger. They grow much taller now, I've been told. There are no trees in Deadland.

"The caterpillars still live. They seem much larger, I understand, but it is actually because they have become woollier than they used to be. It seems that most of the animals have heavier pelts these days. Some apparently have taken to hibernating. A strange thing: Station Seven reported that they had thought the bipeds were growing heavier coats. There seem to be quite a few of them in that area, and they often see them off in the distance. They looked to be shaggier. Closer observation, however, revealed that some of them were either carrying or were wrapped in the skins of dead animals! Could it be that they are more intelligent than we have given them credit for? This hardly seems possible, since they were tested quite thoroughly by the Bio Team before we set the machines in operation. Yes, it is very strange.

"The winds are still severe. Occasionally, they darken the sky with ash. There has been considerable vulcanism southwest of here. Station Four was relocated because of this. I hear Sanza singing now, within the sounds of the machine. I will let her be awakened the next time. Things should be more settled by then. No, that is not true. It is selfishness. I want her here beside me. I feel as if I were the only living thing in the whole world. The voices on the radio are ghosts. The clock ticks loudly and the silences between the ticks are filled with the humming of the machine, which is a kind of silence, too, because it is constant. Sometimes I think it is not there; I listen for it, I strain my ears, and I do not know whether there is a humming or not. I check the indicators then, and they assure me that the machine is functioning. Or perhaps there is something wrong with the indicators. But they seem to be all right. No. It is me. And the blue of Deadland is a kind of visual silence. In the morning even the rocks are covered with blue frost. Is it beautiful or ugly? There is no response within me. It is a part of the great silence, that's all. Perhaps I shall become a mystic. Perhaps I shall develop occult powers or achieve something bright and liberating as I sit here at the center of the great silence. Perhaps I shall see visions. Already I hear voices. Are there ghosts in Deadland? No, there was never anything here to be ghosted. Except perhaps for the little biped. Why did it cross Deadland, I wonder? Why did it head for the center of destruction rather than away, as its fellows did? I shall never know. Unless perhaps I have a vision. I think it is time to suit up and take a walk. The polar icecaps are heavier. The glaciation has begun. Soon, soon things will be better. Soon the silence will end, I hope. I wonder, though, whether silence is not the true state of affairs in the universe, our little noises serving only to accentuate it, like a speck of black on a field of blue. Everything was once silence and will be so again—is now, perhaps. Will I ever hear real sounds, or only sounds out of the silence? Sanza is singing again. I wish I could wake her up now, to walk with me, out there. It is beginning to snow."

*

Jarry awakened again on the eve of the millennium.

Sanza smiled and took his hand in hers and stoked it, as he explained why he had let her sleep, as he apologized.

"Of course I'm not angry," she said, "considering I did the same thing to you last cycle."

Jarry stared up at her and felt the understanding begin.

The Magic

"I'll not do it again," she said, "and I know you couldn't. The aloneness is almost unbearable."

"Yes," he replied.

"They warmed us both alive last time. I came around first and told them to put you back to sleep. I was angry then, when I found out what you had done. But I got over it quickly, so often did I wish you were there."

"We will stay together," said Jarry.

"Yes, always."

They took a flier from the cavern of sleep to the Worldchange installation at Deadland, where they relieved the other attendants and moved the new couch up to the third floor.

The air of Deadland, while sultry, could now be breathed for short periods of time, though a headache invariably followed such experiments. The heat was still oppressive. The rock, once like an old Normform waving, had lost its distinctive outline. The winds were no longer so severe.

On the fourth day, they found some animal tracks which seemed to belong to one of the larger predators. This cheered Sanza, but another, later occurrence produced only puzzlement.

One morning they went forth to walk in Deadland.

Less than a hundred paces from the installation, they came upon three of the giant caterpillars, dead. They were stiff, as though dried out rather than frozen, and they were surrounded by rows of markings within the snow. The footprints which led to the scene and away from it were rough of outline, obscure.

"What does it mean?" she asked.

"I don't know, but I think we had better photograph this," said Jarry.

They did. When Jarry spoke to Station Eleven that afternoon, he learned that similar occurrences had occasionally been noted by attendants of other installations. These were not too frequent, however.

"I don't understand," said Sanza.

"I don't want to," said Jarry.

Roger Zelazny and Samuel R. Delany

It did not happen again during their tour of duty. Jarry entered it into the log and wrote a report. Then they abandoned themselves to lovemaking, monitoring, and occasionally nights of drunkenness. Two hundred years previously, a biochemist had devoted his tour of duty to experimenting with compounds which would produce the same reactions in Catforms as the legendary whiskey did in Normforms. He had been successful, had spent four weeks on a colossal binge, neglected his duty and been relieved of it, was then retired to his coldbunk for the balance of the Wait. His basically simple formula had circulated, however, and Jarry and Sanza found a well-stocked bar in the storeroom and a hand-written manual explaining its use and a variety of drinks which might be compounded. The author of the document had expressed the hope that each tour of attendance might result in the discovery of a new mixture, so that when he returned for his next cycle the manual would have grown to a size proportionate to his desire. Jarry and Sanza worked at it conscientiously, and satisfied the request with a Snowflower Punch which warmed their bellies and made their purring turn into giggles, so that they discovered laughter also. They celebrated the millennium with an entire bowl of it, and Sanza insisted on calling all the other installations and giving them the formula, right then, on the graveyard watch, so that everyone could share in their joy. It is quite possible that everyone did, for the recipe was well-received. And always, even after that bowl was but a memory, they kept the laughter. Thus are the first simple lines of tradition sometimes sketched.

*

"The green birds are dying," said Sanza, putting aside a report she had been reading.

"Oh?" said Jarry.

"Apparently they've done all the adapting they're able to," she told him.

"Pity," said Jarry.

"It seems less than a year since we came here. Actually, it's a thousand."

"Time flies," said Jarry.

"I'm afraid," she said.

The Magic

"Of what?"

"I don't know. Just afraid."

"Why?"

"Living the way we've been living, I guess. Leaving little pieces of ourselves in different centuries. Just a few months ago, as my memory works, this place was a desert. Now it's an ice field. Chasms open and close. Canyons appear and disappear. Rivers dry up and new ones spring forth. Everything seems so very transitory. Things look solid, but I'm getting afraid to touch things now. They might go away. They might turn into smoke, and my hand will keep on reaching through the smoke and touch—something . . . God, maybe. Or worse yet, maybe not. No one really knows what it will be like here when we've finished. We're traveling toward an unknown land and it's too late to go back. We're moving through a dream, heading toward an idea . . . Sometimes I miss my cell . . . and all the little machines that took care of me there. Maybe *I* can't adapt. Maybe I'm like the green bird . . . "

"No, Sanza. You're not. We're real. No matter what happens out there, *we* will last. Everything is changing because we want it to change. We're stronger than the world, and we'll squeeze it and paint it and poke holes in it until we've made it exactly the way we want it. Then we'll take it and cover it with cities and children. You want to see God? Go look in the mirror. God has pointed ears and green eyes. He is covered with soft gray fur. When He raises His hand there is webbing between His fingers."

"It is good that you are strong, Jarry."

"Let's get out the power sled and go for a ride."

"All right."

Up and down, that day, they drove through Deadland, where the dark stones stood like clouds in another sky.

*

It was twelve and a half hundred years.

Now they could breathe without respirators, for a short time.

Now they could bear the temperature, for a short time.

Now all the green birds were dead.

Now a strange and troubling thing began.

The bipeds came by night, made markings on the snow, left dead animals in the midst of them. This happened now with much more frequency than it had in the past. They came long distances to do it, many of them with fur which was not their own upon their shoulders.

Jarry searched through the history files for all the reports on the creatures.

"This one speaks of lights in the forest," he said. "Station Seven."

"What . . . ?"

"Fire," he said. "What if they've discovered fire?"

"Then they're not really beasts!"

"But they were!"

"They wear clothing now. They make some sort of sacrifice to our machines. They're not beasts any longer."

"How could it have happened?"

"How do you think? We did it. Perhaps they would have remained stupid—animals—if we had not come along and forced them to get smart in order to go on living. We've accelerated their evolution. They had to adapt or die, and they adapted."

"D'you think it would have happened if we hadn't come along?" he asked.

"Maybe—some day. Maybe not, too."

Jarry moved to the window, stared out across Deadland.

"I have to find out," he said. "If they are intelligent, if they are—human, like us," he said, then laughed, "then we must consider their ways."

"What do you propose?"

"Locate some of the creatures. See whether we can communicate with them."

"Hasn't it been tried?"

"Yes."

"What were the results?"

"Mixed. Some claim they have considerable understanding. Others place them far below the threshold where humanity begins."

The Magic

"We may be doing a terrible thing," she said. "Creating men, then destroying them. Once, when I was feeling low, you told me that we were the gods of this world, that ours was the power to shape and to break. Ours *is* the power to shape and break, but I don't feel especially divine. What can we do? They have come this far, but do you think they can bear the change that will take us the rest of the way? What if they are like the green birds? What if they've adapted as fast and as far as they can and it is not sufficient? What would a god do?"

"Whatever he wished," said Jarry.

That day, they cruised over Deadland in the flier, but the only signs of life they saw were each other. They continued to search in the days that followed, but they did not meet with success.

Under the purple of morning, however, two weeks later, it happened.

"They've been here," said Sanza.

Jarry moved to the front of the installation and stared out.

The snow was broken in several places, inscribed with the lines he had seen before, about the form of a small, dead beast.

"They can't have gone very far," he said.

"No."

"We'll search in the sled."

Now over the snow and out, across the land called Dead they went, Sanza driving and Jarry peering at the lines of footmarks in the blue.

They cruised through the occurring morning, hinting of fire and violet, and the wind went past them like a river, and all about them there came sounds like the cracking of ice, the trembling of tin, the snapping of steel strands. The bluefrosted stones stood like frozen music, and the long shadow of their sled, black as ink, raced on ahead of them. A shower of hailstones drumming upon the roof of their vehicle like a sudden visitation of demon dancers, as suddenly was gone. Deadland sloped downward, slanted up again.

Jarry placed his hand upon Sanza's shoulder.

"Ahead!"

She nodded, began to brake the sled.

They had it at bay. They were using clubs and long poles which looked to have fire-hardened points. They threw stones. They threw pieces of ice.

Then they backed away and it killed them as they went.

The Catforms had called it a bear because it was big and shaggy and could rise up onto its hind legs . . .

This one was about three and a half meters in length, was covered with bluish fur and had a thin, hairless snout like the business end of a pair of pliers.

Five of the little creatures lay still in the snow. Each time that it swung a paw and connected, another one fell.

Jarry removed the pistol from its compartment and checked the charge.

"Cruise by slowly," he told her. "I'm going to try to burn it about the head."

His first shot missed, scoring the boulder at its back. His second singed the fur of its neck. He leapt down from the sled then, as they came abreast of the beast, thumbed the power control up to maximum, and fired the entire charge into its breast, point-blank.

The bear stiffened, swayed, fell, a gaping wound upon it, front to back.

Jarry turned and regarded the little creatures. They stared up at him.

"Hello," he said. "My name is Jarry. I dub thee Redforms—"

He was knocked from his feet by a blow from behind.

He rolled across the snow, lights dancing before his eyes, his left arm and shoulder afire with pain.

A second bear had emerged from the forest of stone.

He drew his long hunting knife with his right hand and climbed back to his feet.

As the creature lunged, he moved with the catspeed of his kind, thrusting upward, burying his knife to the hilt in its throat.

A shudder ran through it, but it cuffed him and he fell once again, the blade torn from his grasp.

The Redforms threw more stones, rushed toward it with their pointed sticks.

The Magic

Then there was a thud and a crunching sound, and it rose up into the air and came down on top of him.

He awakened.

He lay on his back, hurting, and everything he looked at seemed to be pulsing, as if about to explode.

How much time had passed, he did not know.

Either he or the bear had been moved.

The little creatures crouched, waiting.

Some watched the bear. Some watched him.

Some watched the broken sled . . .

The broken sled . . .

He struggled to his feet.

The Redforms drew back.

He crossed to the sled and looked inside.

He knew she was dead when he saw the angle of her neck. But he did all the things a person does to be sure, anyway, before he would let himself believe it.

She had delivered the deathblow, crashing the sled into the creature, breaking its back. It had broken the sled. Herself, also.

He leaned against the wreckage, composed his first prayer, then removed her body.

The Redforms watched.

He lifted her in his arms and began walking, back toward the installation, across Deadland.

The Redforms continued to watch as he went, except for the one with the strangely high brow-ridge, who studied instead the knife that protruded from the shaggy and steaming throat of the beast.

*

Jarry asked the awakened executives of December: "What should we do?"

"She is the first of our race to die on this world," said Yan Turl, Vice President.

"There is no tradition," said Selda Kein, Secretary. "Shall we establish one?"

"I don't know," said Jarry. "I don't know what is right to do."

"Burial or cremation seem to be the main choices. Which would you prefer?"

"I don't—No, not the ground. Give her back to me. Give me a large flier . . . I'll burn her."

"Then let us construct a chapel."

"No. It is a thing I must do in my own way. I'd rather do it alone."

"As you wish. Draw what equipment you will need, and be about it."

"Please send someone else to keep the Deadland installation. I wish to sleep again when I have finished this thing—until the next cycle."

"Very well, Jarry. We are sorry."

"Yes—we are."

Jarry nodded, gestured, turned, departed.

Thus are the heavier lines of life sometimes drawn.

*

At the southeastern edge of Deadland there was a blue mountain. It stood to slightly over three thousand meters in height. When approached from the northwest, it gave the appearance of being a frozen wave in a sea too vast to imagine. Purple clouds rent themselves upon its peak. No living thing was to be found on its slopes. It had no name, save that which Jarry Dark gave it.

He anchored the flier.

He carried her body to the highest point to which a body might be carried.

He placed her there, dressed in her finest garments, a wide scarf concealing the angle of her neck, a dark veil covering her emptied features.

He was about to try a prayer when the hail began to fall. Like thrown rocks, the chunks of blue ice came down upon him, upon her.

"God damn you!" he cried and he raced back to the flier.

He climbed into the air, circled.

The Magic

Her garments were flapping in the wind. The hail was a blue, beaded curtain that separated them from all but these final caresses: fire aflow from ice to ice, from clay aflow immortally through guns.

He squeezed the trigger and a doorway into the sun opened in the side of the mountain that had been nameless. She vanished within it, and he widened the doorway until he had lowered the mountain.

Then he climbed upward into the cloud, attacking the storm until his guns were empty.

He circled then above the molten mesa, there at the southeastern edge of Deadland.

He circled above the first pyre this world had seen.

Then he departed, to sleep for a season in silence the sleep of ice and stone, to inherit the Alyonal. There is no dreaming in that sleep.

*

Fifteen centuries. Almost half the Wait. Two hundred words or less . . . . Picture—

. . . Nineteen mighty rivers flowing, but the black seas rippling violet now.

. . . No shallow iodine-colored forests. Mighty shag-barked barrel trees instead, orange and lime and black and tall across the land.

. . . Great ranges of mountains in the place of hills brown, yellow, white, lavender. Black corkscrews of smoke unwinding from smoldering cones.

. . . Flowers, whose roots explore the soil twenty meters beneath their mustard petals, unfolded amidst the blue frost and the stones.

. . . Blind burrowers burrowing deeper; offal-eating murk-beasts now showing formidable incisors and great rows of ridged molars; giant caterpillars growing smaller but looking larger because of increasing coats.

. . . The contours of valleys still like the torsos of women, flowing and rolling, or perhaps like instruments of music.

. . . Gone much windblasted stone, but ever the frost.

. . . Sounds in the morning as always, harsh, brittle, metallic.

They were sure that they were halfway to heaven.

Picture that.

Roger Zelazny and Samuel R. Delany

The Deadland log told him as much as he really needed to know. But he read back through the old reports, too.

Then he mixed himself a drink and stared out the third floor window.

" . . . Will die," he said, then finished his drink, outfitted himself, and abandoned his post.

It was three days before he found a camp.

He landed the flier at a distance and approached on foot. He was far to the south of Deadland, where the air was warmer and caused him to feel constantly short of breath.

They were wearing animal skins—skins which had been cut for a better fit and greater protection, skins which were tied about them. He counted sixteen lean-to arrangements and three campfires. He flinched as he regarded the fires, but he continued to advance.

When they saw him, all their little noises stopped, a brief cry went up, and there was silence.

He entered the camp.

The creatures stood unmoving about him. He heard some bustling within the large lean-to at the end of the clearing.

He walked about the camp.

A slab of dried meat hung from the center of a tripod of poles.

Several long spears stood before each dwelling place. He advanced and studied one. A stone which had been flaked into a leaf-shaped spearhead was affixed to its end.

There was the outline of a cat carved upon a block of wood . . .

He heard a footfall and turned.

One of the Redforms moved slowly toward him. It appeared older than the others. Its shoulders sloped; as it opened its mouth to make a series of popping noises, he saw that some of its teeth were missing; its hair was grizzled and thin. It bore something in its hands, but Jarry's attention was drawn to the hands themselves.

Each hand bore an opposing digit.

The Magic

He looked about him quickly, studying the hands of the others. All of them seemed to have thumbs. He studied their appearance more closely.

They now had foreheads.

He returned his attention to the old Redform.

It placed something at his feet, and then it backed away from him.

He looked down.

A chunk of dried meat and a piece of fruit lay upon a broad leaf.

He picked up the meat, closed his eyes, bit off a piece, chewed and swallowed. He wrapped the rest in the leaf and placed it in the side pocket of his pack.

He extended his hand and the Redform drew back.

He lowered his hand, unrolled the blanket he had carried with him and spread it upon the ground. He seated himself, pointed to the Redform, then indicated a position across from him at the other end of the blanket.

The creature hesitated, then advanced and seated itself.

"We are going to learn to talk with one another," he said slowly. Then he placed his hand upon his breast and said, "Jarry."

*

Jarry stood before the reawakened executives of December.

"They are intelligent," he told them. "It's all in my report."

"So?" asked Yan Turl.

"I don't think they will be able to adapt. They have come very far, very rapidly. But I don't think they can go much further. I don't think they can make it all the way."

"Are you a biologist, an ecologist, a chemist?"

"No."

"Then on what do you base your opinion?"

"I observed them at close range for six weeks."

"Then it's only a feeling you have . . . ?"

"You know there are no experts on a thing like this. It's never happened before."

454

"Granting their intelligence—granting even that what you have said concerning their adaptability is correct—what do you suggest we do about it?"

"Slow down the change. Give them a better chance. If they can't make it the rest of the way, then stop short of our goal. It's already livable here. We can adapt the rest of the way."

"Slow it down? How much?"

"Supposing we took another seven or eight thousand years?"

"Impossible!"

"Entirely!"

"Too much!"

"Why?"

"Because everyone stands a three-month watch every two hundred fifty years. That's one year of personal time for every thousand. You're asking for too much of everyone's time."

"But the life of an entire race may be at stake!"

"You do not know that for certain."

"No, I don't. But do you feel it is something to take a chance with?"

"Do you want to put it to an executive vote?"

"No—I can see that I'll lose. I want to put it before the entire membership."

"Impossible. They're all asleep."

"Then wake them up."

"That would be quite a project."

"Don't you think the fate of a race is worth the effort? Especially since we're the ones who forced intelligence upon them? We're the ones who made them evolve, cursed them with intellect."

"Enough! They were right at the threshold. They might have become intelligent had we *not* come along."

"But you can't say for certain! You don't really know! And it doesn't really matter how it happened. They're here and we're here, and they think we're gods—maybe because we do nothing for them but make them miserable. We have some responsibility to an intelligent race, though. At least to the extent of not murdering it."

"Perhaps we could do a long-range study . . . "

"They could be dead by then. I formally move, in my capacity as Treasurer, that we awaken the full membership and put the matter to a vote."

"I don't hear any second to your motion."

"Selda?" he said.

She looked away.

"Tarebell? Clond? Bondici?"

There was silence in the cavern that was high and wide about him.

"All right. I can see when I'm beaten. We will be our own serpents when we come into our Eden. I'm going now, back to Deadland, to finish my tour of duty."

"You don't have to. In fact, it might be better if you sleep the whole thing out . . . "

"No. If it's going to be this way, the guilt will be mine also. I want to watch, to share it fully."

"So be it," said Turl.

Two weeks later, when Installation Nineteen tried to raise the Deadland Station on the radio, there was no response.

After a time, a flier was dispatched.

The Deadland Station was a shapeless lump of melted metal.

Jarry Dark was nowhere to be found.

Later than afternoon, Installation Eight went dead.

A flier was immediately dispatched.

Installation Eight no longer existed. Its attendants were found several miles away, walking. They told how Jarry Dark had forced them from the station at gunpoint. Then he had burnt it to the ground, with the fire-cannons mounted upon his flier.

At about the time they were telling this story, Installation Six became silent.

The order went out: MAINTAIN CONTINUOUS RADIO CONTACT WITH TWO OTHER STATIOINS AT ALL TIMES.

The other order went out: GO ARMED AT ALL TIMES. TAKE ANY VISITOR PRISONER.

*

Jarry waited. At the bottom of a chasm, parked beneath a shelf of rock, Jarry waited. An opened bottle stood upon the control board of his flier. Next to it was a small case of white metal.

Jarry took a long, last drink from the bottle as he waited for the broadcast he knew would come.

When it did, he stretched out on the seat and took a nap.

When he awakened, the light of day was waning.

The broadcast was still going on . . .

" . . . Jarry. They will be awakened and a referendum will be held. Come back to the main cavern. This is Yan Turl. Please do not destroy any more installations. This action is not necessary. We agree with your proposal that a vote be held. Please contact us immediately. We are waiting for your reply, Jarry . . . "

He tossed the empty bottle through the window and raised the flier out of the purple shadow into the air and up.

*

When he descended upon the landing stage within the main cavern, of course they were waiting for him. A dozen rifles were trained upon him as he stepped down from the flier.

"Remove your weapons, Jarry," came the voice of Yan Turl.

"I'm not wearing any weapons," said Jarry. "Neither is my flier," he added; and this was true, for the fire-cannons no longer rested within their mountings.

Yan Turl approached, looked up at him.

"Then you may step down."

"Thank you, but I like it right where I am."

"You are a prisoner."

"What do you intend to do with me?"

"Put you back to sleep until the end of the Wait. Come down here!"

The Magic

"No. And don't try shooting—or using a stun charge or gas, either. If you do, we're all of us dead the second it hits."

"What do you mean?" asked Turl, gesturing gently to the riflemen.

"My flier," said Jarry, "is a bomb, and I'm holding the fuse in my right hand." He raised the white metal box. "So long as I keep the lever on the side of this box depressed, we live. If my grip relaxes, even for an instant, the explosion which ensues will doubtless destroy this entire cavern."

"I think you're bluffing."

"You know how you can find out for certain."

"You'll die too, Jarry."

"At the moment, I don't really care. Don't try burning my hand off, either, to destroy the fuse," he cautioned, "because it doesn't really matter. Even if you should succeed, it will cost you at least two installations."

"Why is that?"

"What do you think I did with the fire-cannons? I taught the Redforms how to use them. At the moment, these weapons are manned by Redforms and aimed at two installations. If I do not personally visit my gunners by dawn, they will open fire. After destroying their objectives, they will move on and try for two more."

"You trusted those beasts with laser projectors?"

"That is correct. Now, will you begin awakening the others for the voting?"

Turl crouched, as if to spring at him, appeared to think better of it, relaxed.

"Why did you do it, Jarry?" he asked. "What are they to you that you would make your own people suffer for them?"

"Since you do not feel as I feel," said Jarry, "my reasons would mean nothing to you. After all, they are only based upon my feelings, which are different than your own—for mine are based upon sorrow and loneliness. Try this one, though: I am their god. My form is to be found in their every camp. I am the Slayer of Bears from the Desert of the Dead. They have told my story for two and a half centuries, and I have been changed by it. I am powerful and wise and good, so far as they are concerned. In this capacity,

458

Roger Zelazny and Samuel R. Delany

I owe them some consideration. If I do not give them their lives, who will there be to honor me in snow and chant my story around the fires and cut for me the best portions of the woolly caterpillar? None, Turl. And these things are all that my life is worth now. Awaken the others. You have no choice."

"Very well," said Turl. "And if their decision should go against you?"

"Then I'll retire, and you can be god," said Jarry.

*

Now every day when the sun goes down out of the purple sky, Jarry Dark watches it in its passing, for he shall sleep no more the sleep of ice and of stone, wherein there is no dreaming. He has elected to live out the span of his days in a tiny instant of the Wait, never to look upon the New Alyonal of his people. Every morning, at the new Deadland Installation, he is awakened by sounds like the cracking of ice, the trembling of tin, the snapping of steel strands, before they come to him with their offerings, singing and making marks upon the snow. They praise him and he smiles upon them. Sometimes he coughs.

Born of man and woman, in accordance with Catform Y7 requirements, Coldworld Class, Jarry Dark was not suited for existence anywhere in the universe which had guaranteed him a niche. This was either a blessing or a curse, depending on how you looked at it. So look at it however you would, that was the story. Thus does life repay those who would serve her fully.

A Word from Zelazny

"Why I write . . . science fiction or fantasy . . . is a question which I am in a better position to answer. First, this is an area of fiction where the writer has considerably more freedom than in other types of fiction. I enjoy descriptive writing, and it pleases me to be able to describe landscapes and meteorological phenomena which could not exist on Earth, but which might be possible elsewhere; similarly, with characters and their motivations. For an example, I indulged my fancy in all of these things in my novelette 'The Keys To December,' which contained unmanlike humans engaged in an

459

unusual project on a strange world. This provided an aesthetic pleasure of a sort that would not have obtained had I written a more down-to-Earth story."[1]

It was optioned for development as a motion picture,[2] but despite at least one completed script, nothing else materialized.

Notes

An **ocelot** is a spotted wildcat. Again we see the recurrent motif of **green eyes** in this story.

[1] "Tomorrow Stuff," unpublished essay.

[2] *Science Fiction* Vol 1 No 2, June 1978.

This Mortal Mountain

I

I looked down at it and I was sick! I wondered, where did it lead? Stars?

There were no words. I stared and I stared, and I cursed the fact that the thing existed and that someone had found it while I was still around.

"Well?" said Lanning, and he banked the flier so that I could look upward.

I shook my head and shaded my already shielded eyes.

"Make it go away," I finally told him.

"Can't. It's bigger than I am."

"It's bigger than anybody," I said.

"I can make *us* go away . . . "

"Never mind. I want to take some pictures."

He brought it around, and I started to shoot.

"Can you hover—or get any closer?"

"No, the winds are too strong."

"That figures."

So I shot—through telescopic lenses and scan attachment and all—as we circled it.

"I'd give a lot to see the top."

"We're at thirty thousand feet, and fifty's the ceiling on this baby. The Lady, unfortunately, stands taller than the atmosphere."

"Funny," I said, "from here she doesn't strike me as the sort to breathe ether and spend all her time looking at stars."

He chuckled and lit a cigarette, and I reached us another bulb of coffee.

"How *does* the Gray Sister strike you?"

And I lit one of my own and inhaled, as the flier was buffeted by sudden gusts of something from somewhere and then ignored, and I said, "Like Our Lady of the Abattoir—right between the eyes."

461

The Magic

We drank some coffee, and then he asked, "She too big, Whitey?" and I gnashed my teeth through caffeine, for only my friends call me Whitey, my name being Jack Summers and my hair having always been this way, and at the moment I wasn't too certain of whether Henry Lanning qualified for that status—just because he'd known me for twenty years—after going out of his way to find this thing on a world with a thin atmosphere, a lot of rocks, a too-bright sky and a name like LSD pronounced backwards, after George Diesel, who had set foot in the dust and then gone away—smart fellow!

"A forty-mile-high mountain," I finally said, "is not a mountain. It is a world all by itself, which some dumb deity forgot to throw into orbit."

"I take it you're not interested?"

I looked back at the gray and lavender slopes and followed them upward once more again, until all color drained away, until the silhouette was black and jagged and the top still nowhere in sight, until my eyes stung and burned behind their protective glasses; and I saw clouds bumping up against that invincible outline, like icebergs in the sky, and I heard the howling of the retreating winds which had essayed to measure its grandeur with swiftness and, of course, had failed.

"Oh, I'm interested," I said, "in an academic sort of way. Let's go back to town, where I can eat and drink and maybe break a leg if I'm lucky."

He headed the flier south, and I didn't look around as we went. I could sense her presence at my back, though, all the way: The Gray Sister, the highest mountain in the known universe. Unclimbed, of course.

*

She remained at my back during the days that followed, casting her shadow over everything I looked upon. For the next two days I studied the pictures I had taken and I dug up some maps and I studied them, too; and I spoke with people who told me stories of the Gray Sister, strange stories . . . .

During this time, I came across nothing really encouraging. I learned that there had been an attempt to colonize Diesel a couple centuries previously, back before faster-than-light ships were developed. A brand-new disease had colonized the first colonists, however, wiping them out to a man. The new colony was four years old, had better doctors, had beaten the plague, was on Diesel to stay and seemed proud of its poor taste when it came to worlds. Nobody, I learned, fooled around much with the Gray Sister. There had been a few abortive attempts to climb her, and some young legends that followed after.

During the day, the sky never shut up. It kept screaming into my eyes, until I took to wearing my climbing goggles whenever I went out. Mainly, though, I sat in the hotel lounge and ate and drank and studied the pictures and cross-examined anyone who happened to pass by and glance at them, spread out there on the table.

I continued to ignore all Henry's questions. I knew what he wanted, and he could damn well wait. Unfortunately, he did, and rather well, too, which irritated me. He felt I was almost hooked by the Sister, and he wanted to Be There When It Happened. He'd made a fortune on the Kasla story, and I could already see the opening sentences of this one in the smug lines around his eyes. Whenever he tried to make like a poker player, leaning on his fist and slowly turning a photo, I could see whole paragraphs. If I followed the direction of his gaze, I probably could even have seen the dust jacket.

At the end of the week, a ship came down out of the sky, and some nasty people got off and interrupted my train of thought. When they came into the lounge, I recognized them for what they were and removed my black lenses so that I could nail Henry with my basilisk gaze and turn him into stone. As it would happen, he had too much alcohol in him, and it didn't work.

"You tipped off the press," I said.

"Now, now," he said, growing smaller and stiffening as my gaze groped its way through the murk of his central nervous system and finally touched upon the edges of that tiny tumor, his forebrain. "You're well known, and . . . . "

I replaced my glasses and hunched over my drink, looking far gone, as one of the three approached and said, "Pardon me, but are you Jack Summers?"

*

The Magic

To explain the silence which followed, Henry said, "Yes, this is Mad Jack, the man who climbed Everest at twenty-three and every other pile of rocks worth mentioning since that time. At thirty-one, he became the only man to conquer the highest mountain in the known universe—Mount Kasla on Litan—elevation, 89,941 feet. My book—"

"Yes," said the reporter. "My name is Cary, and I'm with GP. My friends represent two of the other syndicates. We've heard that you are going to climb the Gray Sister."

"You've heard incorrectly," I said.

"Oh?"

The other two came up and stood beside them.

"We thought that—" one of them began.

"—you were already organizing a climbing party," said the other.

"Then you're not going to climb the Sister?" asked Cary, while one of the two looked over my pictures and the other got ready to take some of his own.

"Stop that!" I said, raising a hand at the photographer. "Bright lights hurt my eyes!"

"Sorry. I'll use the infra," he said, and he started fooling with his camera.

Cary repeated the question.

"All I said was that you've heard incorrectly," I told him. "I didn't say I was and I didn't say I wasn't. I haven't made up my mind."

"If you decide to try it, have you any idea when it will be?"

"Sorry, I can't answer that."

Henry took the three of them over to the bar and started explaining something, with gestures. I heard the words " . . . out of retirement after four years," and when/if they looked to the booth again, I was gone.

I had retired, to the street which was full of dusk, and I walked along it thinking. I trod her shadow even then, Linda. And the Gray Sister beckoned and forbade with her single unmoving gesture. I watched her, so far away, yet still so large, a piece of midnight at eight o'clock. The hours that lay between died like the distance at her feet, and I knew that she would follow me wherever I went, even into sleep. Especially into sleep.

Roger Zelazny and Samuel R. Delany

So I knew, at that moment. The days that followed were a game I enjoyed playing. Fake indecision is delicious when people want you to do something. I looked at her then, my last and my largest, my very own Koshtra Pivrarcha, and I felt that I was born to stand upon her summit. Then I could retire, probably remarry, cultivate my mind, not worry about getting out of shape, and do all the square things I didn't do before, the lack of which had cost me a wife and a home, back when I had gone to Kasla, elevation 89,941 feet, four and a half years ago, in the days of my glory. I regarded my Gray Sister across the eight o'clock world, and she was dark and noble and still and waiting, as she had always been.

II

The following morning I sent the messages. Out across the light-years like cosmic carrier pigeons they went. They winged their ways to some persons I hadn't seen in years and to others who had seen me off at Luna Station. Each said, in its own way, "If you want in on the biggest climb of them all, come to Diesel. The Gray Sister eats Kasla for breakfast. R.S.V.P. c/o. The Lodge, Georgetown. Whitey."

Backward, turn backward . . . .

I didn't tell Henry. Nothing at all. What I had done and where I was going, for a time, were my business only, for that same time. I checked out well before sunrise and left him a message on the desk:

"Out of town on business. Back in a week. Hold the fort. Mad Jack."

I had to gauge the lower slopes, tug the hem of the lady's skirt, so to speak, before I introduced her to my friends. They say only a madman climbs alone, but they call me what they call me for a reason.

From my pix, the northern face had looked promising.

I set the rented flier down as near as I could, locked it up, shouldered my pack and started walking.

Mountains rising to my right and to my left, mountains at my back, all dark as sin now in the predawn light of a white, white day. Ahead of me, not a mountain, but an almost gentle slope which kept rising and rising and

The Magic

rising. Bright stars above me and cold wind past me as I walked. Straight up, though, no stars, just black. I wondered for the thousandth time what a mountain weighed. I always wonder that as I approach one. No clouds in sight. No noises but my boot sounds on the turf and the small gravel. My goggles flopped around my neck. My hands were moist within my gloves. On Diesel, the pack and I together probably weighed about the same as me alone on Earth—for which I was duly grateful. My breath burned as it came and steamed as it went. I counted a thousand steps and looked back, and I couldn't see the flier. I counted a thousand more and then looked up to watch some stars go out. About an hour after that, I had to put on my goggles. By then I could see where I was headed. And by then the wind seemed stronger.

She was so big that the eye couldn't take all of her in at once. I moved my head from side to side, leaning further and further backward. Wherever the top, it was too high. For an instant, I was seized by a crazy acrophobic notion that I was looking down rather than up, and the soles of my feet and the palms of my hands tingled, like an ape's must when, releasing one high branch to seize another, he discovers that there isn't another.

I went on for two more hours and stopped for a light meal. This was hiking, not climbing. As I ate, I wondered what could have caused a formation like the Gray Sister. There were some ten and twelve-mile peaks within sixty miles of the place and a fifteen-mile mountain called Burke's Peak on the adjacent continent, but nothing else like the Sister. The lesser gravitation? Her composition? I couldn't say. I wondered what Doc and Kelly and Mallardi would say when they saw her.

I don't define them, though. I only climb them.

I looked up again, and a few clouds were brushing against her now. From the photos I had taken, she might be an easy ascent for a good ten or twelve miles. Like a big hill. There were certainly enough alternate routes. In fact, I thought she just might be a pushover. Feeling heartened, I repacked my utensils and proceeded. It was going to be a good day. I could tell.

Roger Zelazny and Samuel R. Delany

And it was. I got off the slope and onto something like a trail by late afternoon. Daylight lasts about nine hours on Diesel, and I spent most of it moving. The trail was so good that I kept on for several hours after sundown and made considerable height. I was beginning to use my respiration equipment by then, and the heating unit in my suit was turned on.

The stars were big, brilliant flowers, the way was easy, the night was my friend. I came upon a broad, flat piece and made my camp under an overhang.

There I slept, and I dreamt of snowy women with breasts like the Alps, pinked by the morning sun; and they sang to me like the wind and laughed, had eyes of ice prismatic. They fled through a field of clouds.

The following day I made a lot more height. The "trail" began to narrow, and it ran out in places, but it was easy to reach for the sky until another one occurred. So far, it had all been good rock. It was still tapering as it heightened, and balance was no problem. I did a lot of plain old walking. I ran up one long zigzag and hit it up a wide chimney almost as fast as Santa Claus comes down one. The winds were strong, could be a problem if the going got difficult. I was on the respirator full time and feeling great.

I could see for an enormous distance now. There were mountains and mountains, all below me like desert dunes. The sun beat halos of heat about their peaks. In the east, I saw Lake Emerick, dark and shiny as the toe of a boot. I wound my way about a jutting crag and came upon a giant's staircase, going up for at least a thousand feet. I mounted it. At its top I hit my first real barrier: a fairly smooth, almost perpendicular face rising for about eighty-five feet.

No way around it, so I went up. It took me a good hour, and there was a ridge at the top leading to more easy climbing. By then, though, the clouds attacked me. Even though the going was easy, I was slowed by the fog. I wanted to outclimb it and still have some daylight left, so I decided to postpone eating.

The Magic

But the clouds kept coming. I made another thousand feet, and they were still about me. Somewhere below me, I heard thunder. The fog was easy on my eyes, though, so I kept pushing.

Then I tried a chimney, the top of which I could barely discern, because it looked a lot shorter than a jagged crescent to its left. This was a mistake.

The rate of condensation was greater than I'd guessed. The walls were slippery. I'm stubborn, though, and I fought with skidding boots and moist back until I was about a third of the way up, I thought, and winded.

I realized then what I had done. What I had thought was the top wasn't. I went another fifteen feet and wished I hadn't. The fog began to boil about me, and I suddenly felt drenched. I was afraid to go down and I was afraid to go up, and I couldn't stay where I was forever.

Whenever you hear a person say that he inched along, do not accuse him of a fuzzy choice of verbs. Give him the benefit of the doubt and your sympathy.

I inched my way, blind, up an unknown length of slippery chimney. If my hair hadn't already been white when I entered at the bottom . . . .

Finally, I got above the fog. Finally, I saw a piece of that bright and nasty sky, which I decided to forgive for the moment. I aimed at it, arrived on target.

When I emerged, I saw a little ledge about ten feet above me. I climbed to it and stretched out. My muscles were a bit shaky, and I made them go liquid. I took a drink of water, ate a couple of chocolate bars, took another drink.

After perhaps ten minutes, I stood up. I could no longer see the ground. Just the soft, white, cottony top of a kindly old storm. I looked up.

It was amazing. She was still topless. And save for a couple spots, such as the last—which had been the fault of my own stupid overconfidence—it had almost been as easy as climbing stairs.

Now the going appeared to be somewhat rougher, however. This was what I had really come to test.

I swung my pick and continued.

Roger Zelazny and Samuel R. Delany

*

All the following day I climbed, steadily, taking no unnecessary risks, resting periodically, drawing maps, taking wide-angle photos. The ascent eased in two spots that afternoon, and I made a quick seven thousand feet. Higher now than Everest, and still going, I. Now, though, there were places where I crawled and places where I used my ropes, and there were places where I braced myself and used my pneumatic pistol to blast a toehold. (No, in case you're wondering: I could have broken my eardrums, some ribs, and arm and doubtless ultimately, my neck, if I'd tried using the gun in the chimney.)

Just near sunset, I came upon a high, easy winding way up and up and up. I debated with my more discreet self. I'd left the message that I'd be gone a week. This was the end of the third day. I wanted to make as much height as possible and start back down on the fifth day. If I followed the rocky route above me as far as it would take me I'd probably break forty thousand feet. Then, depending, I might have a halfway chance of hitting near the ten-mile mark before I had to turn back. Then I'd be able to get a much better picture of what lay above.

My more discreet self lost, three to nothing, and Mad Jack went on.

The stars were so big and blazing I was afraid they'd bite. The wind was no problem. There wasn't any at that height. I had to keep stepping up the temperature controls on my suit, and I had the feeling that if I could spit around my respirator, it would freeze before it hit the trail.

I went on even further than I'd intended, and I broke forty-two thousand that night.

I found a resting place, stretched out, killed my hand beacon.

It was an odd dream that came to me.

It was all cherry fires and stood like a man, only bigger, on the slope above me. It stood in an impossible position, so I knew I had to be dreaming. Something from the other end of my life stirred, however, and I was convinced for a bitter moment that it was the Angel of Judgment. Only, in its right hand it seemed to hold a sword of fires rather than a trumpet. It had been standing there forever, the tip of its blade pointed toward my breast. I could see the stars through it. It seemed to speak.

It said: "*Go back.*"

I couldn't answer it, though, for my tongue clove to the roof of my mouth. And it said it again, and yet a third time, "*Go back.*"

"Tomorrow," I thought, in my dream, and this seemed to satisfy it. for it died down and ceased, and the blackness rolled about me.

*

The following day, I climbed as I hadn't climbed in years. By late lunchtime I'd hit forty-eight thousand feet. The cloud cover down below had broken. I could see what lay beneath me once more. The ground was a dark and light patchwork. Above, the stars didn't go away.

The going was rough, but I was feeling fine. I knew I couldn't make ten miles, because I could see that the way was pretty much the same for quite a distance, before it got even worse. My good spirits stayed, and they continued to rise as I did.

When it attacked, it came on with a speed and a fury that I was only barely able to match.

The voice from my dream rang in my head, "*Go back! Go back! Go back!*"

Then it came toward me from out of the sky. A bird the size of a condor. Only it wasn't really a bird.

It was a bird-shaped thing.

It was all fire and static, and as it flashed toward me I barely had time to brace my back against stone and heft my climbing pick in my right hand, ready.

III

I sat in the small, dark room and watched the spinning, colored lights. Ultrasonics were tickling my skull. I tried to relax and give the man some Alpha rhythms. Somewhere a receiver was receiving, a computer was computing and a recorder was recording.

It lasted perhaps twenty minutes.

When it was all over and they called me out, the doctor collared me. I beat him to the draw, though:

"Give me the tape and send the bill in care of Henry Lanning at the Lodge."

"I want to discuss the reading," he said.

"I have my own brain-wave expert coming. Just give me the tape."

"Have you undergone any sort of traumatic experience recently?"

"You tell me. Is it indicated?"

"Well, yes and no," he said.

"That's what I like, a straight answer."

"I don't know what is normal for you, in the first place," he replied.

"Is there any indication of brain damage?"

"I don't read it that way. If you'd tell me what happened, and why you're suddenly concerned about your brain-waves, perhaps I'd be in a better position to . . . . "

"Cut," I said. "Just give me the tape and bill me."

"I'm concerned about you as a patient."

"But you don't think there were any pathological indications?"

"Not exactly. But tell me this, if you will: Have you had an epileptic seizure recently?"

"Not to my knowledge. Why?"

"You displayed a pattern similar to a residual subrhythm common in some forms of epilepsy for several days subsequent to a seizure."

"Could a bump on the head cause that pattern?"

"It's highly unlikely."

"What else *could* cause it?"

"Electrical shock, optical trauma—"

"Stop," I said, and I removed my glasses. "About the optical trauma. Look at my eyes."

"I'm not an ophtha—" he began, but I interrupted:

The Magic

"Most normal light hurts my eyes. If I lost my glasses and was exposed to very bright light for three, four days, could that cause the pattern you spoke of?"

"Possible . . . . " he said. "Yes, I'd say so."

"But there's more?"

"I'm not sure. We have to take more readings, and if I know the story behind this it will help a lot."

"Sorry," I said. "I need the tape now."

He sighed and made a small gesture with his left hand as he turned away. "All right, Mister Smith."

Cursing the genius of the mountain, I left the General Hospital, carrying my tape like a talisman. In my mind I searched, through forests of memory, for a ghost-sword in a stone of smoke, I think.

*

Back in the Lodge, they were waiting. Lanning and the newsmen.

"What was it like?" asked one of the latter.

"What was what like?"

"The mountain. You were up on it, weren't you?"

"No comment."

"How high did you go?"

"No comment."

"How would you say it compares with Kasla?"

"No comment."

"Did you run into any complications?"

"Ditto. Excuse me, I want to take a shower."

Henry followed me into my room. The reporters tried to.

After I had shaved and washed up, mixed a drink and lit a cigarette, Lanning asked me his more general question:

"Well?" he said.

I nodded.

"Difficulties?"

I nodded again.

"Insurmountable?"

I hefted the tape and thought a moment.

"Maybe not."

He helped himself to the whiskey. The second time around, he asked:

"You going to try?"

I knew I was. I knew I'd try it all by myself if I had to.

"I really don't know," I said.

"Why not?"

"Because there's something up there," I said, "something that doesn't want us to do it."

"Something *lives* up there?"

"I'm not sure whether that's the right word."

He lowered the drink.

"What the hell happened?"

"I was threatened. I was attacked."

"Threatened? Verbally? In English?" He set his drink aside, which shows how serious his turn of mind had to be. "Attacked?" he added. "By what?"

"I've sent for Doc and Kelly and Stan and Mallardi and Vincent. I checked a little earlier. They've all replied. They're coming. Miguel and the Dutchman can't make it, and they send their regrets. When we're all together, I'll tell the story. But I want to talk to Doc first. So hold tight and worry and don't quote."

He finished his drink.

"When'll they be coming?"

"Four, five weeks," I said.

"That's a long wait."

"Under the circumstances," I said, "I can't think of any alternatives."

"What'll we do in the meantime?"

"Eat, drink, and contemplate the mountain."

He lowered his eyelids a moment, then nodded, reached for his glass.

"Shall we begin?"

*

The Magic

It was late, and I stood alone in the field with a bottle in one hand. Lanning had already turned in, and night's chimney was dark with cloud soot. Somewhere away from there, a storm was storming, and it was full of instant outlines. The wind came chill.

"Mountain," I said. "Mountain, you have told me to go away."

There was a rumble.

"But I cannot," I said, and I took a drink.

"I'm bringing you the best in the business," I said, "to go up on your slopes and to stand beneath the stars in your highest places. I must do this thing because you are there. No other reason. Nothing personal . . . . "

After a time, I said, "That's not true.

"I am a man," I said, "and I need to break mountains to prove that I will not die even though I will die. I am less than I want to be, Sister, and you can make me more. So I guess it *is* personal.

"It's the only thing I know how to do, and you're the last one left—the last challenge to the skill I spent my life learning. Maybe it is that mortality is the closest to immortality when it accepts a challenge to itself, when it survives a threat. The moment of triumph is the moment of salvation. I have needed many such moments, and the final one must be the longest, for it must last me the rest of my life.

"So you are there, Sister, and I am here and very mortal, and you have told me to go away. I cannot. I'm coming up, and if you throw death at me I will face it. It must be so."

I finished what remained in the bottle.

There were more flashes, more rumbles behind the mountain, more flashes.

"It is the closest thing to diving drunkenness," I said to the thunder.

And then she winked at me. It was a red star, so high upon her. Angel's sword. Phoenix' wing. Soul on fire. And it blazed at me, across the miles. Then the wind that blows between the worlds swept down over me. It was filled with tears and with crystals of ice. I stood there and felt it, then, "Don't go away," I said, and I watched until all was darkness once more and I was wet as an embryo waiting to cry out and breathe.

*

Most kids tell lies to their playmates—fictional autobiographies, if you like—which are either received with appropriate awe or countered with greater, more elaborate tellings. But little Jimmy, I've heard, always hearkened to his little buddies with wide, dark eyes, and near the endings of their stories the corners of his mouth would begin to twitch. By the time they were finished talking, his freckles would be mashed into a grin and his rusty head cocked to the side. His favorite expression, I understand, was "G'wan!" and his nose was broken twice before he was twelve. This was doubtless why he turned it toward books.

Thirty years and four formal degrees later, he sat across from me in my quarters in the lodge, and I called him Doc because everyone did, because he had a license to cut people up and look inside them, as well as doctoring to their philosophy, so to speak, and because he looked as if he should be called Doc when he grinned and cocked his head to the side and said, "G'wan!"

I wanted to punch him in the nose.

"Damn it! It's true!" I told him. "I fought with a bird of fire!"

"We all hallucinated on Kasla," he said, raising one finger, "because of fatigue," two fingers, "because the altitude affected our circulatory systems and consequently our brains," three, "because of the emotional stimulation," four, "and because we were pretty oxygen-drunk."

"You just ran out of fingers, if you'll sit on your other hand for a minute. So listen," I said, "it flew at me, and I swung at it, and it knocked me out and broke my goggles. When I woke up, it was gone and I was lying on the ledge. I think it was some sort of energy creature. You saw my EEG, and it wasn't normal. I think it shocked my nervous system when it touched me."

"You were knocked out because you hit your head against a rock—"

"It *caused* me to fall back against the rock!"

"I agree with that part. The rock was real. But nowhere in the universe has anyone ever discovered an 'energy creature.'"

"So? You probably would have said that about America a thousand years ago."

"Maybe I would have. But that neurologist explained your EEG to my satisfaction. Optical trauma. Why go out of your way to dream up an exotic explanation for events? Easy ones generally turn out better. You hallucinated and you stumbled."

"Okay," I said, "whenever I argue with you I generally need ammunition. Hold on a minute."

I went to my closet and fetched it down from the top shelf. I placed it on my bed and began unwrapping the blanket I had around it.

"I told you I took a swing at it," I said. "Well, I connected—right before I went under. Here!"

I held up my climbing pick—brown, yellow, black and pitted—looking as though it had fallen from outer space.

He took it into his hands and stared at it for a long time, then he started to say something about ball lightning, changed his mind, shook his head and placed the thing back on the blanket.

"I don't know," he finally said, and this time his freckles remained unmashed, except for those at the edges of his hands which got caught as he clenched them, slowly.

IV

We planned. We mapped and charted and studied the photos. We plotted our ascent and we started a training program.

While Doc and Stan had kept themselves in good shape, neither had been climbing since Kasla. Kelly was in top condition. Henry was on his way to fat. Mallardi and Vince, as always, seemed capable of fantastic feats of endurance and virtuosity, had even climbed a couple times during the past year, but had recently been living pretty high on the tall hog, so to speak, and they wanted to get some practice. So we picked a comfortable, decent-sized mountain and gave it ten days to beat everyone back into shape. After that, we stuck to vitamins, calisthenics and square diets while we completed our preparations. During this time, Doc came up with seven shiny, alloy boxes, about six by four inches and thin as a first book of poems, for us to carry on our persons to broadcast a defense against the energy creatures which he refused to admit existed.

One fine, bitter-brisk morning we were ready. The newsmen liked me again. Much footage was taken of our gallant assemblage as we packed ourselves into the fliers, to be delivered at the foot of the lady mountain, there to contend for what was doubtless the final time as the team we had been for so many years, against the waiting gray and the lavender beneath the sunwhite flame.

We approached the mountain, and I wondered how much she weighed.

*

You know the way, for the first nine miles. So I'll skip over that. It took us six days and part of a seventh. Nothing out of the ordinary occurred. Some fog there was, and nasty winds, but once below, forgotten.

Stan and Mallardi and I stood where the bird had occurred, waiting for Doc and the others.

"So far, it's been a picnic," said Mallardi.

"Yeah," Stan acknowledged.

"No birds either."

"No," I agreed.

"Do you think Doc was right—about it being an hallucination?" Mallardi asked. "I remember seeing things on Kasla . . . ."

"As I recall," said Stan, "it was nymphs and an ocean of beer. Why would anyone want to see hot birds?"

"Damfino."

"Laugh, you hyenas," I said. "But just wait till a flock flies over."

Doc came up and looked around.

"This is the place?"

I nodded.

The Magic

He tested the background radiation and half a dozen other things, found nothing untoward, grunted and looked upwards.

We all did. Then we went there.

It was very rough for three days, and we only made another five thousand feet during that time.

When we bedded down, we were bushed, and sleep came quickly. So did Nemesis.

He was there again, only not quite so near this time. He burned about twenty feet away, standing in the middle of the air, and the point of his blade indicated me.

"*Go away*," he said, three times, without inflection.

"Go to hell," I tried to say.

He made as if he wished to draw nearer. He failed.

"Go away yourself," I said.

"*Climb back down. Depart. You may go no further.*"

"But I am going further. All the way to the top."

"*No. You may not.*"

"Stick around and watch," I said.

"*Go back.*"

"If you want to stand there and direct traffic, that's your business," I told him. "I'm going back to sleep."

I crawled over and shook Doc's shoulder, but when I looked back my flaming visitor had departed.

"What is it?"

"Too late," I said. "He's been here and gone."

Doc sat up.

"The bird?"

"No, the thing with the sword."

"Where was he?"

"Standing out there," I gestured.

Doc hauled out his instruments and did many things with them for ten minutes or so.

"Nothing," he finally said. "Maybe you were dreaming."

"Yeah, sure," I said. "Sleep tight," and I hit the sack again, and this time I made it through to daylight without further fire or ado.

*

It took us four days to reach sixty thousand feet. Rocks fell like occasional cannonballs past us, and the sky was like a big pool, cool, where pale flowers floated. When we struck sixty-three thousand, the going got much better, and we made it up to seventy-five thousand in two and a half more days. No fiery things stopped by to tell me to turn back. Then came the unforeseeable, however, and we had enough in the way of natural troubles to keep us cursing.

We hit a big, level shelf.

It was perhaps four hundred feet wide. As we advanced across it, we realized that it did not strike the mountainside. It dropped off into an enormous gutter of a canyon. We would have to go down again, perhaps seven hundred feet, before we could proceed upward once more. Worse yet, it led to a featureless face which strove for and achieved perpendicularity for a deadly high distance: like miles. The top was still nowhere in sight.

"Where do we go now?" asked Kelly, moving to my side.

"Down," I decided, "and we split up. We'll follow the big ditch in both directions and see which way gives the better route up. We'll meet back at the midway point."

We descended. Then Doc and Kelly and I went left, and the others took the opposite way.

After an hour and a half, our trail came to an end. We stood looking at nothing over the edge of something. Nowhere, during the entire time, had we come upon a decent way up. I stretched out, my head and shoulders over the edge, Kelly holding onto my ankles, and I looked as far as I could to the right and up. There was nothing in sight that was worth a facing movement.

"Hope the others had better luck," I said, after they'd dragged me back.

"And if they haven't . . . ?" asked Kelly.

"Let's wait."

The Magic

They had.

It was risky, though.

There was no good way straight up out of the gap. The trail had ended at a forty-foot wall which, when mounted, gave a clear view all the way down. Leaning out as I had done and looking about two hundred feet to the left and eighty feet higher, however, Mallardi had rested his eyes on a rough way, but a way, nevertheless, leading up and west and vanishing.

We camped in the gap that night. In the morning, I anchored my line to a rock, Doc tending, and went out with the pneumatic pistol. I fell twice, and made forty feet of trail by lunchtime.

I rubbed my bruises then, and Henry took over. After ten feet, Kelly got out to anchor a couple of body-lengths behind him, and we tended Kelly.

Then Stan blasted and Mallardi anchored. Then there had to be three on the face. Then four. By sundown, we'd made a hundred-fifty feet and were covered with white powder. A bath would have been nice. We settled for ultrasonic shakedowns.

*

By lunch the next day, we were all out there, roped together, hugging cold stone, moving slowly, painfully, slowly, not looking down much.

By day's end, we'd made it across, to the place where we could hold on and feel something—granted, not much—beneath our boots. It was inclined to be a trifle scant, however, to warrant less than a full daylight assault. So we returned once more to the gap.

In the morning, we crossed.

The way kept its winding angle. We headed west and up. We traveled a mile and made five hundred feet. We traveled another mile and made perhaps three hundred.

Then a ledge occurred, about forty feet overhead.

Stan went up the hard way, using the gun, to see what he could see.

He gestured, and we followed; and the view that broke upon us was good.

Down right, irregular but wide enough, was our new camp.

Roger Zelazny and Samuel R. Delany

The way above it, ice cream and whiskey sours and morning coffee and a cigarette after dinner. It was beautiful and delicious: a seventy-degree slope full of ledges and projections and good clean stone.

"Hot damn!" said Kelly.

We all tended to agree.

We ate and we drank and we decided to rest our bruised selves that afternoon.

We were in the twilight world now, walking where no man had ever walked before, and we felt ourselves to be golden. It was good to stretch out and try to unache.

I slept away the day, and when I awakened the sky was a bed of glowing embers. I lay there too lazy to move, too full of sight to go back to sleep. A meteor burnt its way bluewhite across the heavens. After a time, there was another. I thought upon my position and decided that reaching it was worth the price. The cold, hard happiness of the heights filled me. I wiggled my toes.

After a few minutes, I stretched and sat up. I regarded the sleeping forms of my companions. I looked out across the night as far as I could see. Then I looked up at the mountain, then dropped my eyes slowly among tomorrow's trail.

There was movement within shadow.

Something was standing about fifty feet away and ten feet above.

I picked up my pick and stood.

I crossed the fifty and stared up.

She was smiling, not burning.

A woman, an impossible woman.

Absolutely impossible. For one thing, she would just have to freeze to death in a mini-skirt and a sleeveless shell-top. No alternative. For another, she had very little to breathe. Like, nothing.

But it didn't seem to bother her. She waved. Her hair was dark and long, and I couldn't see her eyes. The planes of her pale, high cheeks, wide forehead, small chin corresponded in an unsettling fashion with certain simple theorems which comprise the geometry of my heart. If all angles, planes, curves be correct, it skips a beat, then hurries to make up for it.

*

I worked it out, felt it do so, said, "Hello."

"Hello, Whitey," she replied.

"Come down," I said.

"No, you come up."

I swung my pick. When I reached the ledge she wasn't there. I looked around, then I saw her.

She was seated on a rock twelve feet above me.

"How is it that you know my name?" I asked.

"Anyone can see what your name must be."

"All right," I agreed. "What's yours?"

" . . . " Her lips seemed to move, but I heard nothing.

"Come again?"

"I don't want a name," she said.

"Okay. I'll call you 'girl,' then."

She laughed, sort of.

"What are you doing here?" I asked.

"Watching you."

"Why?"

"To see whether you'll fall."

"I can save you the trouble," I said. "I won't."

"Perhaps," she said.

"Come down here."

"No, you come up here."

I climbed, but when I got there she was twenty feet higher.

"Girl, you climb well," I said, and she laughed and turned away.

I pursued her for five minutes and couldn't catch her. There was something unnatural about the way she moved.

I stopped climbing when she turned again. We were still about twenty feet apart.

482

"I take it you do not really wish me to join you," I said.

"Of course I do, but you must catch me first." And she turned once more, and I felt a certain fury within me.

It was written that no one could outclimb Mad Jack. I had written it.

I swung my pick and moved like a lizard.

I was near to her a couple of times, but never near enough.

The day's aches began again in my muscles, but I pulled my way up without slackening my pace. I realized, faintly, that the camp was far below me now, and that I was climbing alone through the dark up a strange slope. But I did not stop. Rather, I hurried, and my breath began to come hard in my lungs. I heard her laughter, and it was a goad. Then I came upon a two-inch ledge, and she was moving along it. I followed, around a big bulge of rock to where it ended. Then she was ninety feet above me, at the top of a smooth pinnacle. It was like a tapering, branchless tree. How she'd accomplished it, I didn't know. I was gasping by then, but I looped my line around it and began to climb. As I did this, she spoke:

"Don't you ever tire, Whitey? I thought you would have collapsed by now."

I hitched up the line and climbed further.

"You can't make it up here, you know."

"I don't know," I grunted.

"Why do you want so badly to climb here? There are other nice mountains."

"This is the biggest, girl. That's why."

"It can't be done."

"Then why all this bother to discourage me? Why not just let the mountain do it?"

As I neared her, she vanished. I made it to the top, where she had been standing, and I collapsed there.

Then I heard her voice again and turned my head. She was on a ledge, perhaps eighty feet away.

"I didn't think you'd make it this far," she said. "You are a fool. Good-by, Whitey." She was gone.

The Magic

I sat there on the pinnacle's tiny top—perhaps four square feet of top—and I know that I couldn't sleep there, because I'd fall. And I was tired.

I recalled my favorite curses and I said them all, but I didn't feel any better. I couldn't let myself go to sleep. I looked down. I knew the way was long. I knew she didn't think I could make it.

I began the descent.

*

The following morning when they shook me, I was still tired. I told them the last night's tale, and they didn't believe me. Not until later in the day, that is, when I detoured us around the bulge and showed them the pinnacle, standing there like a tapering, branchless tree, ninety feet in the middle of the air.

V

We went steadily upward for the next two days. We made slightly under ten thousand feet. Then we spent a day hammering and hacking our way up a great flat face. Six hundred feet of it. Then our way was to the right and upward. Before long we were ascending the western side of the mountain. When we broke ninety thousand feet, we stopped to congratulate ourselves that we had just surpassed the Kasla climb and to remind ourselves that we had not hit the halfway mark. It took us another two and a half days to do that, and by then the land lay like a map beneath us.

And then, that night, we all saw the creature with the sword.

He came and stood near our camp, and he raised his sword above his head, and it blazed with such a terrible intensity that I slipped on my goggles. His voice was all thunder and lightning this time:

"*Get off this mountain!*" he said. "*Now! Turn back! Go down! Depart!*"

And then a shower of stones came down from above and rattled about us. Doc tossed his slim, shiny, case, causing it to skim along the ground toward the creature.

The light went out, and we were alone.

Doc retrieved his case, took tests, met with the same success as before—*i.e.*, none. But now at least he didn't think I was some kind of balmy, unless of course he thought we all were.

"Not a very effective guardian," Henry suggested.

"We've a long way to go yet," said Vince, shying a stone through the space the creature had occupied. "I don't like it if the thing can cause a slide."

"That was just a few pebbles," said Stan.

"Yeah, but what if he decided to start them fifty thousand feet higher?"

"Shut up!" said Kelly. "Don't give him any idea. He might be listening."

For some reason, we drew closer together. Doc made each of us describe what we had seen, and it appeared that we all had seen the same thing.

"All right," I said, after we'd finished. "Now you've all seen it, who wants to go back?"

There was silence.

After perhaps half a dozen heartbeats, Henry said, "I want the whole story. It looks like a good one. I'm willing to take my chances with angry energy creatures to get it."

"I don't know what the thing is," said Kelly. "Maybe it's no energy creature. Maybe it's something—supernatural—I know what you'll say, Doc. I'm just telling you how it struck me. If there are such things, this seems a good place for them. Point is—whatever it is, I don't care. I want this mountain. If it could have stopped us, I think it would've done it already. Maybe I'm wrong. Maybe it can. Maybe it's laid some trap for us higher up. But I want this mountain. Right now, it means more to me than anything. If I don't go up, I'll spend all my time wondering about it—and then I'll probably come back and try it again some day, when it gets so I can't stand thinking about it any more. Only then, maybe the rest of you won't be available. Let's face it, we're a good climbing team. Maybe the best in the business. Probably. If it can be done, I think we can do it."

"I'll second that," said Stan.

*

The Magic

"What you said, Kelly," said Mallardi, "about it being supernatural—it's funny, because I felt the same thing for a minute when I was looking at it. It reminds me of something out of the *Divine Comedy*. If you recall, Purgatory was a mountain. And then I thought of the angel who guarded the eastern way to Eden. Eden had gotten moved to the top of Purgatory by Dante—and there was this angel . . . . Anyhow, I felt almost like I was committing some sin I didn't know about by being here. But now that I think it over, a man can't be guilty of something he doesn't know is wrong, can he? And I didn't see that thing flashing any angel ID card. So I'm willing to go up and see what's on top, unless he comes back with the Tablets of the Law, with a new one written in at the bottom."

"In Hebrew or Italian?" asked Doc.

"To satisfy you, I suppose they'd have to be drawn up in the form of equations."

"No," he said. "Kidding aside, I felt something funny too, when I saw it and heard it. And we didn't really hear it, you know. It skipped over the senses and got its message right into our brains. If you think back over our descriptions of what we experienced, we each 'heard' different words telling us to go away. If it can communicate a meaning as well as a pyschtranslator, I wonder if it can communicate an emotion, also . . . . You thought of an angel too, didn't you, Whitey?"

"Yes," I said.

"That makes it almost unanimous then, doesn't it?"

Then we all turned to Vince, because he had no Christian background at all, having been raised as a Buddhist on Ceylon.

"What were your feelings concerning the thing?" Doc asked him.

"It was a Deva," he said, "which is sort of like an angel, I guess. I had the impression that every step I took up this mountain gave me enough bad karma to fill a lifetime. Except I haven't believed in it that way since I was a kid. I want to go ahead, up. Even if that feeling was correct, I want to see the top of this mountain."

"So do I," said Doc.

"That makes it unanimous," I said.

"Well, everyone hang onto his angelsbane," said Stan, "and let's sack out."

"Good idea."

"Only let's spread out a bit," said Doc, "so that anything falling won't get all of us together."

We did that cheerful thing and slept untroubled by heaven.

*

Our way kept winding right, until we were at a hundred forty-four thousand feet and were mounting the southern slopes. Then it jogged back, and by a hundred fifty we were mounting to the west once more.

Then, during a devilish, dark and tricky piece of scaling, up a smooth, concave bulge ending in an overhang, the bird came down once again.

If we hadn't been roped together, Stan would have died. As it was, we almost all died.

Stan was lead man, as its wings splashed sudden flames against the violet sky. It came down from the overhang as though someone had kicked a bonfire over its edge, headed straight toward him and faded out at a distance of about twelve feet. He fell then, almost taking the rest of us with him.

We tensed our muscles and took the shock.

He was battered a bit, but unbroken. We made it up to the overhang, but went no further that day.

Rocks did fall, but we found another overhang and made camp beneath it.

The bird did not return that day, but the snakes came.

Big, shimmering scarlet serpents coiled about the crags, wound in and out of jagged fields of ice and gray stone. Sparks shot along their sinuous lengths. They coiled and unwound, stretched and turned, spat fires at us. It seemed they were trying to drive us from beneath the sheltering place to where the rocks could come down upon us.

Doc advanced upon the nearest one, and it vanished as it came within the field of his projector. He studied the place where it had lain, then hurried back.

"The frost is still on the punkin," he said.

The Magic

"Huh?" said I.

"Not a bit of ice was melted beneath it."

"Indicating?"

"Illusion," said Vince, and he threw a stone at another and it passed through the thing.

"But you saw what happened to my pick," I said to Doc, "when I took a cut at that bird. The thing had to have been carrying some sort of charge."

"Maybe whatever has been sending them has cut that part out, as a waste of energy," he replied, "since the things can't get through to us anyhow."

We sat around and watched the snakes and falling rocks, until Stan produced a deck of cards and suggested a better game.

*

The snakes stayed on through the night and followed us the next day. Rocks still fell periodically, but the boss seemed to be running low on them. The bird appeared, circled us and swooped on four different occasions. But this time we ignored it, and finally it went home to roost.

We made three thousand feet, could have gone more, but didn't want to press it past a cozy little ledge with a cave big enough for the whole party. Everything let up on us then. Everything visible, that is.

A before-the-storm feeling, a still, electrical tension, seemed to occur around us then, and we waited for whatever was going to happen to happen.

The worst possible thing happened: nothing.

This keyed-up feeling, this expectancy, stayed with us, was unsatisfied. I think it would actually have been a relief if some invisible orchestra had begun playing Wagner, or if the heavens had rolled aside like curtains and revealed a movie screen, and from the backward lettering we knew we were on the other side, or if we saw a high-flying dragon eating low-flying weather satellites . . . .

As it was, we just kept feeling that something was imminent, and it gave me insomnia.

During the night, she came again. The pinnacle girl.

She stood at the mouth of the cave, and when I advanced the retreated.

I stopped just inside and stood there myself, where she had been standing.

She said, "Hello, Whitey."

"No, I'm not going to follow you again," I said.

"I didn't ask you to."

"What's a girl like you doing in a place like this?"

"Watching," she said.

"I told you I won't fall."

"Your friend almost did."

"'Almost' isn't good enough."

"You are the leader, aren't you?"

"That's right."

"If you were to die, the others would go back?"

"No," I said, "they'd go on without me."

I hit my camera then.

"What did you just do?" she asked.

"I took your picture—if you're really there."

"Why?"

"To look at after you go away. I like to look at pretty things."

" . . . " She seemed to say something.

"What?"

"Nothing."

"Why not?"

" . . . die."

"Please speak up."

"She dies . . . " she said.

"Why? How?"

" . . . . on mountain."

"I don't understand."

" . . . too."

"What's wrong?"

I took a step forward, and she retreated a step.

"Follow me?" she asked.

The Magic

"No."

"Go back," she said.

"What's on the other side of that record?"

"You will continue to climb?"

"Yes."

Then, "Good!" she said suddenly. "I—," and her voice stopped again.

"Go back," she finally said, without emotion.

"Sorry."

And she was gone.

VI

Our trail took us slowly to the left once more. We crawled and sprawled and cut holes in the stone. Snakes sizzled in the distance. They were with us constantly now. The bird came again at crucial moments, to try to make us fall. A raging bull stood on a crag and bellowed down at us. Phantom archers loosed shafts of fire, which always faded right before they struck. Blazing blizzards swept at us, around us, were gone. We were back on the northern slopes and still heading west by the time we broke a hundred sixty thousand. The sky was deep and blue, and there were always stars. Why did the mountain hate us? I wondered. What was there about us to provoke this thing? I looked at the picture of the girl for the dozenth time and I wondered what she really was. Had she been picked from our minds and composed into girlform to lure us, to lead us, sirenlike, harpylike, to the place of the final fall? It was such a long way down . . . .

I thought back over my life. How does a man come to climb mountains? Is he drawn by the heights because he is afraid of the level land? Is he such a misfit in the society of men that he must flee and try to place himself above it? The way up is long and difficult, but if he succeeds they must grant him a garland of sorts. And if he falls, this too is a kind of glory. To end, hurled from the heights to the depths in hideous ruin and combustion down, is a fitting climax for the loser—for it, too, shakes mountains and minds, stirs things like thoughts below both, is a kind of blasted garland of victory in defeat, and cold, so cold that final action, that the movement is somewhere frozen forever into a statuelike rigidity of ultimate intent and purpose thwarted only by the universal malevolence we all fear exists. An aspirant saint or hero who lacks some necessary virtue may still qualify as a martyr, for the only thing that people will really remember in the end is the end. I had known that I'd had to climb Kasla, as I had climbed all the others, and I had known what the price would be. It had cost me my only home. But Kasla was there, and my boots cried out for my feet. I knew as I did so that somewhere I set them upon her summit, and below me a world was ending. What's a world if the moment of victory is at hand? And if truth, beauty and goodness be one, why is there always this conflict among them?

The phantom archers fired upon me and the bright bird swooped. I set my teeth, and my boots scarred rocks beneath me.

*

We saw the top.

At a hundred seventy-six thousand feet, making our way along a narrow ledge, clicking against rock, testing our way with our picks, we heard Vince say, "Look!"

We did.

Up and up, and again further, bluefrosted and sharp, deadly, and cold as Loki's dagger, slashing at the sky, it vibrated above us like electricity, hung like a piece of frozen thunder, and cut, cut, cut into the center of spirit that was desire, twisted, and became a fishhook to pull us on, to burn us with its barbs.

Vince was the first to look up and see the top, the first to die. It happened so quickly, and it was none of the terrors that achieved it.

He slipped.

That was all. It was a difficult piece of climbing. He was right behind me one second, was gone the next. There was no body to recover. He'd taken the long drop. The soundless blue was all around him and the great gray beneath. Then we were six. We shuddered, and I suppose we all prayed in our own ways.

The Magic

—Gone Vince, may some good Deva lead you up the Path of Splendor. May you find whatever you wanted most at the other end, waiting there for you. If such a thing may be, remember those who say these words, oh strong intruder in the sky . . . .

No one spoke much for the rest of the day.

The fiery sword bearer came and stood above our camp the entire night. It did not speak.

In the morning, Stan was gone, and there was a note beneath my pack.

> *Don't hate me,* it said, *for running out, but I think it really is an angel. I'm scared of this mountain. I'll climb any pile of rocks, but I won't fight Heaven. The way down is easier than the way up, so don't worry about me. Good luck.*
> *Try to understand.*   S

So we were five—Doc and Kelly and Henry and Mallardi and me—and that day we hit a hundred eighty thousand and felt very alone.

The girl came again that night and spoke to me, black hair against black sky and eyes like points of blue fire, and she stood beside an icy pillar and said, "Two of you have gone."

"And the rest of us remain," I replied.

"For a time."

"We will climb to the top and then we will go away," I said. "How can that do you harm? Why do you hate us?"

"No hate, sir," she said.

"What, then?"

"I protect."

"What? What is it that you protect?"

"The dying, that she may live."

"What? Who is dying? How?"

But her words went away somewhere, and I did not hear them. Then she went away too, and there was nothing left but sleep for the rest of the night.

492

Roger Zelazny and Samuel R. Delany

*

One hundred eighty-two thousand and three, and four, and five. Then back down to four for the following night.

The creatures whined about us now, and the land pulsed beneath us, and the mountain seemed sometimes to sway as we climbed.

We carved a path to one eighty-six, and for three days we fought to gain another thousand feet. Everything we touched was cold and slick and slippery, sparkled, and had a bluish haze about it.

When we hit one ninety, Henry looked back and shuddered.

"I'm no longer worried about making it to the top," he said. "It's the return trip that's bothering me now. The clouds are like little wisps of cotton way down there."

"The sooner up, the sooner down," I said, and we began to climb once again.

It took us another week to cut our way to within a mile of the top. All the creatures of fire had withdrawn, but two ice avalanches showed us we were still unwanted. We survived the first without mishap, but Kelly sprained his right ankle during the second, and Doc thought he might have cracked a couple of ribs, too.

We made a camp. Doc stayed there with him; Henry and Mallardi and I pushed on up the last mile.

Now the going was beastly. It had become a mountain of glass. We had to hammer out a hold for every foot we made. We worked in shifts. We fought for everything we gained. Our packs became monstrous loads and our fingers grew numb. Our defense system—the projectors—seemed to be wearing down, or else something was increasing its efforts to get us, because the snakes kept slithering closer, burning brighter. They hurt my eyes, and I cursed them.

When we were within a thousand feet of the top, we dug in and made another camp. The next couple hundred feet looked easier, then a rotten spot, and I couldn't tell what it was like above that.

When we awakened, there was just Henry and myself. There was no indication of where Mallardi had gotten to. Henry switched his communicator to Doc's letter and called below. I tuned in in time to hear him say, "Haven't seen him."

"How's Kelly?" I asked.

"Better," he replied. "Those ribs might not be cracked at that."

Then Mallardi called us.

"I'm four hundred feet above you, fellows," his voice came in. "It was easy up to here, but the going's just gotten rough again."

"Why'd you cut out on your own?" I asked.

"Because I think something's going to try to kill me before too long," he said. "It's up ahead, waiting at the top. You can probably even see it from there. It's a snake."

Henry and I used the binoculars.

Snake? A better word might be dragon—or maybe even Midgard Serpent.

It was coiled around the peak, head upraised. It seemed to be several hundred feet in length, and it moved its head from side to side, and up and down, and it smoked solar coronas.

Then I spotted Mallardi climbing toward it.

"Don't go any further!" I called. "I don't know whether your unit will protect you against anything like that! Wait'll I call Doc—"

"Not a chance," he said. "This baby is mine."

"Listen! You can be first on the mountain, if that's what you want! But don't tackle that thing alone!"

A laugh was the only reply.

"All three units might hold it off," I said. "Wait for us."

There was no answer, and we began to climb.

I left Henry far below me. The creature was a moving light in the sky. I made two hundred feet in a hurry, and when I looked up again, I saw that the creature had grown two more heads. Lightnings flashed from its nostrils, and its tail whipped around the mountain. I made another hundred feet, and I could see Mallardi clearly by then, climbing steadily, outlined against the brilliance. I swung my pick, gasping, and I fought the mountain, following the trail he had cut. I began to gain on him, because he was still pounding out his way and I didn't have that problem. Then I heard him talking:

"Not yet, big fella, not yet," he was saying, from behind a wall of static. "Here's a ledge . . . . "

I looked up, and he vanished.

Then that fiery tail came lashing down toward where I had last seen him, and I heard him curse and I felt the vibrations of his pneumatic gun. The tail snapped back again, and I heard another "Damn!"

*

I made haste, stretching and racking myself and grabbing at the holds he had cut, and then I heard him burst into song. Something from *Aïda*, I think.

"Damn it! Wait up!" I said. "I'm only a few hundred feet behind."

He kept on singing.

I was beginning to get dizzy, but I couldn't let myself slow down. My right arm felt like a piece of wood, my left like a piece of ice. My feet were hooves, and my eyes burned in my head.

Then it happened.

Like a bomb, the snake and the swinging ended in a flash of brilliance that caused me to sway and almost lose my grip. I clung to the vibrating mountainside and squeezed my eyes against the light.

"Mallardi?" I called.

No answer. Nothing.

I looked down. Henry was still climbing. I continued to climb.

I reached the ledge Mallardi had mentioned, found him there.

His respirator was still working. His protective suit was blackened and scorched on the right side. Half of his pick had been melted away. I raised his shoulders.

I turned up the volume on the communicator and heard him breathing. His eyes opened, closed, opened.

"Okay . . . . " he said.

"'Okay,' hell! Where do you hurt?"

The Magic

"No place . . . I feel jus' fine . . . . Listen! I think it's used up its juice for awhile . . . . Go plant the flag. Prop me up here first, though. I wanna watch . . . . "

I got him into a better position, squirted the water bulb, listened to him swallow. Then I waited for Henry to catch up. It took about six minutes.

"I'll stay here," said Henry, stooping beside him. "You go do it."

I started up the final slope.

VII

I swung and I cut and I blasted and I crawled. Some of the ice had been melted, the rocks scorched.

Nothing came to oppose me. The static had gone with the dragon. There was silence, and darkness between stars.

I climbed slowly, still tired from that last sprint, but determined not to stop.

All but sixty feet of the entire world lay beneath me, and heaven hung above me, and a rocket winked overhead. Perhaps it was the pressmen, with zoom cameras.

Fifty feet . . . .

No bird, no archer, no angel, no girl.

Forty feet . . . .

I started to shake. It was nervous tension. I steadied myself, went on.

Thirty feet . . . and the mountain seemed to be swaying now.

Twenty-five . . . and I grew dizzy, halted, took a drink.

Then click, click, my pick again.

Twenty . . . .

Fifteen . . . .

Ten . . . .

I braced myself against the mountain's final assault, whatever it might be.

Five . . .

Nothing happened as I arrived.

I stood up. I could go no higher.

I looked at the sky, I looked back down. I waved at the blazing rocket exhaust.

I extruded the pole and attached the flag.

I planted it, there where no breezes would ever stir it. I cut in my communicator, said, "I'm here."

No other words.

*

It was time to go back down and give Henry his chance, but I looked down the western slope before I turned to go.

The lady was winking again. Perhaps eight hundred feet below, the red light shone. Could that have been what I had seen from the town during the storm, on that night, so long ago?

I didn't know and I had to.

I spoke into the communicator.

"How's Mallardi doing?"

"I just stood up," he answered. "Give me another half hour, and I'm coming up myself."

"Henry," I said. "Should he?"

"Gotta take his word how he feels," said Lanning.

"Well," I said, "then take it easy. I'll be gone when you get here. I'm going a little way down the western side. Something I want to see."

"What?"

"I dunno. That's why I want to see."

"Take care."

"Check."

The western slope was an easy descent. As I went down it, I realized that the light was coming from an opening in the side of the mountain.

Half an hour later, I stood before it.

I stepped within and was dazzled.

*

I walked toward it and stopped. It pulsed and quivered and sang.

497

The Magic

A vibrating wall of flame leapt from the floor of the cave, towered to the roof of the cave.

It blocked my way, when I wanted to go beyond it.

She was there, and I wanted to reach her.

I took a step forward, so that I was only inches away from it. My communicator was full of static and my arms of cold needles.

It did not bend toward me, as to attack. It cast no heat.

I stared through the veil of fires to where she reclined, her eyes closed, her breast unmoving.

I stared at the bank of machinery beside the far wall.

"I'm here," I said, and I raised my pick.

When its point touched the wall of flame someone took the lid off hell, and I staggered back, blinded. When my vision cleared, the angel stood before me.

"*You may not pass here,*" he said.

"She is the reason you want me to go back?" I asked.

"*Yes. Go back.*"

"Has she no say in the matter?"

"*She sleeps. Go back.*"

"So I notice. Why?"

"*She must. Go back.*"

"Why did she herself appear to me and lead me strangely?"

"*I used up the fear-forms I knew. They did not work. I led you strangely because her sleeping mind touches upon my own workings. It did so especially when I borrowed her form, so that it interfered with the directive. Go back.*"

"What is the directive?"

"*She is to be guarded against all things coming up the mountain. Go back.*"

"Why? Why is she guarded?"

"*She sleeps. Go back.*"

The conversation having become somewhat circular at that point, I reached into my pack and drew out the projector. I swung it forward and the angel melted. The flames bent away from my outstretched hand. I sought to open a doorway in the circle of fire.

It worked, sort of.

I pushed the projector forward, and the flames bent and bent and bent and finally broke. When they broke, I leaped forward. I made it through, but my protective suit was as scorched as Mallardi's.

I moved to the coffinlike locker within which she slept.

I rested my hands on its edge and looked down.

She was as fragile as ice.

In fact, she was ice . . . .

The machine came alive with lights then, and I felt her somber bedstead vibrate.

Then I saw the man.

He was half sprawled across a metal chair beside the machine.

He, too, was ice. Only his features were gray, were twisted. He wore black and he was dead and a statue, while she was sleeping and a statue.

She wore blue, and white . . . .

There was an empty casket in the far corner . . . .

But something was happening around me. There came a brightening of the air. Yes, it was air. It hissed upward from frosty jets in the floor, formed into great clouds. Then a feeling of heat occurred and the clouds began to fade and the brightening continued.

I returned to the casket and studied her features.

I wondered what her voice would sound like when/if she spoke. I wondered what lay within her mind. I wondered how her thinking worked, and what she liked and didn't like. I wondered what her eyes had looked upon, and when.

I wondered all these things, because I could see that whatever forces I had set into operation when I entered the circle of fire were causing her, slowly, to cease being a statue.

She was being awakened.

*

The Magic

I waited. Over an hour went by, and still I waited, watching her. She began to breath. Her eyes opened at last, and for a long time she did not see.

Then her bluefire fell on me.

"Whitey," she said.

"Yes."

"Where am I . . . ?"

"In the damnedest place I could possibly have found anyone."

She frowned. "I remember," she said and tried to sit up.

It didn't work. She fell back.

"What is your name?"

"Linda," she said. Then, "I dreamed of you, Whitey. Strange dreams . . . . How could that be?"

"It's tricky," I said.

"I knew you were coming," she said. "I saw you fighting monsters on a mountain as high as the sky."

"Yes, we're there now."

"H-have you the cure?"

"Cure? What cure?"

"Dawson's Plague," she said.

I felt sick. I felt sick because I realized that she did not sleep as a prisoner, but to postpone her death. She was sick.

"Did you come to live on this world in a ship that moved faster than light?" I asked.

"No," she said. "It took centuries to get here. We slept the cold sleep during the journey. This is one of the bunkers." She gestured toward the casket with her eyes. I noticed her cheeks had become bright red.

"They all began dying—of the plague," she said. "There was no cure. My husband—Carl—is a doctor. When he saw that I had it, he said he would keep me in extreme hypothermia until a cure was found. Otherwise, you only live for two days, you know."

Then she stared up at me, and I realized that her last two words had been a question.

500

Roger Zelazny and Samuel R. Delany

I moved into a position to block her view of the dead man, who I feared must be her Carl. I tried to follow her husband's thinking. He'd had to hurry, as he was obviously further along than she had been. He knew the colony would be wiped out. He must have loved her and been awfully clever, both—awfully resourceful. Mostly, though, he must have loved her. Knowing that the colony would die, he knew it would be centuries before another ship arrived. He had nothing that could power a cold bunker for that long. But up here, on the top of this mountain, almost as cold as outer space itself, power wouldn't be necessary. Somehow, he had got Linda and the stuff up here. His machine cast a force field around the cave. Working in heat and atmosphere, he had sent her deep into the cold sleep and then prepared his own bunker. When he dropped the wall of forces, no power would be necessary to guarantee the long, icy wait. They could sleep for centuries within the bosom of the Gray Sister, protected by a colony of defense-computer. This last had apparently been programmed quickly, for he was dying. He saw that it was too late to join her. He hurried to set the thing for basic defense, killed the force field, and then went his way into that Dark and Secret Place. Thus it hurled its birds and its angels and its snakes, it raised its walls of fire against me. He died, and it guarded her in near-death—against everything, including those who would help. My coming to the mountain had activated it. My passing of the defenses had caused her to be summoned back to life.

"*Go back!*" I heard the machine say through its projected angel, for Henry had entered the cave.

*

"My God!" I heard him say. "Who's that?"

"Get Doc!" I said. "Hurry! I'll explain later. It's a matter of life! Climb back to where your communicator will work, and tell him it's Dawson's Plague—a bad local bug! Hurry!"

"I'm on my way," he said and was.

"There *is* a doctor?" she asked.

501

The Magic

"Yes. Only about two hours away. Don't worry . . . . I still don't see how anyone could have gotten you up here to the top of this mountain, let alone a load of machines."

"We're on the big mountain—the forty-miler?"

"Yes."

"How did *you* get up?" she asked.

"I climbed it."

"You really climbed Purgatorio? On the outside?"

"Purgatorio? That's what you call it? Yes, I climbed it, that way."

"We didn't think it could be done."

"How else might one arrive at its top?"

"It's hollow inside," she said. "There are great caves and massive passages. It's easy to fly up the inside on a pressurized jet car. In fact, it was an amusement ride. Two and a half dollars per person. An hour and a half each way. A dollar to rent a pressurized suit and take an hour's walk around the top. Nice way to spend an afternoon. Beautiful view . . . ?" She gasped deeply.

"I don't feel so good," she said. "Have you any water?"

"Yes," I said, and I gave her all I had.

As she sipped it, I prayed that Doc had the necessary serum or else would be able to send her back to ice and sleep until it could be gotten. I prayed that he would make good time, for two hours seemed long when measured against her thirst and the red of her flesh.

"My fever is coming again," she said. "Talk to me, Whitey, please . . . . Tell me things. Keep me with you till he comes. I don't want my mind to turn back upon what has happened . . . . "

"What would you like me to tell you about, Linda?"

"Tell me why you did it. Tell me what it was like, to climb a mountain like this one. Why?"

*

I turned my mind back upon what had happened.

"There is a certain madness involved," I said, "a certain envy of great and powerful natural forces, that some men have. Each mountain is a deity, you

Roger Zelazny and Samuel R. Delany

know. Each is an immortal power. If you make sacrifices upon its slopes, a mountain may grant you a certain grace, and for a time you will share this power. Perhaps that is why they call me . . . . "

Her hand rested in mine. I hoped that through it whatever power I might contain would hold all of her with me for as long as ever possible.

"I remember the first time that I saw Purgatory, Linda," I told her. "I looked at it and I was sick. I wondered, where did it lead . . . ?"

(Stars.

Oh let there be.

This once to end with.

Please.)

"Stars?"

A Word from Zelazny

"This story appeared in the March 1967 issue of *Worlds of If*. The previous September, I had received my first Science Fiction Achievement Award (Hugo)—for my novel . . . *And Call Me Conrad*—at Tricon, the World Science Fiction Convention which was held in Cleveland, Ohio. Fred Pohl had asked all of the award recipients that year to submit material for a special Hugo Winners issue of *If*.

"I forget now whether I had already begun work on this story and earmarked it for that purpose when he asked me, or whether I had only a rough idea and wrote it immediately thereafter. I feel it was the former, though.

"I recall that I hurried it somewhat, because of the deadline. If there had been no deadline, it would have been a longer and, possibly, different story. How, I couldn't say now, because I never go back and reread if I can help it. But I do not believe that I was unhappy with it as it turned out. I liked *Worlds of If*, and I was glad to be in that particular issue."[1]

The Magic

Notes

Dante Alighieri's *Divine Comedy* describes his descent through *Inferno* (Hell); his climb through *Purgatorio* (Purgatory), and his ascension into *Paradisio* (Heaven). This story retells Dante's climb of Mount Purgatory by having Jack Summers climb **Purgatorio**; the novella's seven sections correspond to the seven terraces of Mount Purgatory. In *Purgatorio*, the angel inscribes seven letters on Dante's forehead; in "This Mortal Mountain," he receives a blinding shock. Dante's pagan companion Virgil may not enter heaven and vanishes; likewise **Vince**, the non-Christian in the group, vanishes suddenly ("right beside me one second, was gone the next"). *Purgatorio* ends with Dante gazing at the stars, anticipating his ascent to heaven; "This Mortal Mountain" ends with Summers begging for stars, praying that he'd saved the woman and his companions from Dawson's Plague.

There is no **Lady of the Abattoir** [slaughterhouse]; it may be a simple jest. A **basilisk** turned its victims into stone with a glance. **Koshtra Pivrarcha** is the forbidding high mountain climbed in E. R. Eddison's 1922 novel, *The Worm Ouroboros*, one source that J. R. R. Tolkien used to create Middle Earth.[2] **Mallardi** was likely named after Bill Mallardi, the co-editor of the *Double:Bill* fanzine to which Zelazny contributed many pieces.

Alpha rhythms, as registered on an electroencephalogram (EEG), are caused by normal electrical activity of a conscious, relaxed brain. The **Phoenix** is a mythological bird that lives for five or six centuries, burns itself on a funeral pyre, and arises from the ashes with renewed life. **Nemesis** is the Greek goddess of vengeance. **Balmy** means eccentric or foolish.

Deva is deity in Buddhism. **Angelsbane** is a fictional poison (a pun on wolfsbane) that could kill angels. "**When the Frost Is on the Punkin**" is a poem by James Whitcomb Riley. A **harpy** had a woman's head and body with a bird's wings and claws, or was a bird of prey with a woman's face. **Loki** was the Norse god of trickery, foster brother of Odin, and father of three monstrous children who will be involved in the world's end. In Norse mythology, the **Midgard Serpent** (Jormangund) encircles the world, holding its tail in its mouth. *Aida* is an opera by Guiseppe Verdi.

[1] *Worlds of If: A Retrospective Anthology*, eds. Pohl, Greenberg, Olander; Bluejay 1986.

[2] *Letters of Tolkien*, ed. Humphrey Carpenter with Christopher Tolkien, George Allen & Unwin, 1981.

Damnation Alley

I

The gull swooped by, seemed to hover a moment on unmoving wings.

Hell Tanner flipped his cigar butt at it and scored a lucky hit. The bird uttered a hoarse cry and beat suddenly at the air. It climbed about fifty feet, and whether it shrieked a second time, he would never know.

It was gone.

A single gray feather rocked in the violet sky, drifted out over the edge of the cliff and descended, swinging toward the ocean. Tanner chuckled through his beard, between the steady roar of the wind and the pounding of the surf. Then he took his feet down from the handlebars, kicked up the stand and gunned his bike to life.

He took the slope slowly till he came to the trail, then picked up speed and was doing fifty when he hit the highway.

He leaned forward and gunned it. He had the road all to himself, and he laid on the gas pedal till there was no place left for it to go. He raised his goggles and looked at the world through crap-colored glasses, which was pretty much the way he looked at it without them, too.

All the old irons were gone from his jacket, and he missed the swastika, the hammer and sickle, and the upright finger, especially. He missed his old emblem, too. Maybe he could pick up one in Tijuana and have some broad sew it on and . . . No. It wouldn't do. All that was dead and gone. It would be a giveaway, and he wouldn't last a day. What he *would* do was sell the Harley, work his way down the coast, clean and square and see what he could find in the other America.

He coasted down one hill and roared up another. He tore through Laguoa Beach, Capistrano Beach, San Clemente and San Onofre. He made it down to Oceanside, where he refueled, and he passed on through Carlsbad and all those dead little beaches that fill the shore space before Solana Beach Del Mar. It was outside San Diego that they were waiting for him.

He saw the roadblock and turned. They were not sure how he had managed it that quickly, at that speed. But now he was heading away from them. He heard the gunshots and kept going. Then he heard the sirens.

He blew his horn twice in reply and leaned far forward. The Harley leaped ahead, and he wondered whether they were radioing to someone further on up the line.

He ran for ten minutes and couldn't shake them. Then fifteen.

He topped another hill, and far ahead he saw the second block. He was bottled in.

He looked all around him for side roads, saw none.

Then he bore a straight course toward the second block. Might as well try to run it.

No good!

There were cars lined up across the entire road. They were even off the road on the shoulders.

He braked at the last possible minute, and when his speed was right he reared up on the back wheel, spun it and headed back toward his pursuers.

There were six of them coming toward him, and at his back new siren calls arose.

He braked again, pulled to the left, kicked the gas and leaped out of the seat. The bike kept going, and he hit the ground rolling, got to his feet and started running.

He heard the screeching of their tires. He heard a crash. Then there were more gunshots, and he kept going. They were aiming over his head, but he didn't know it. They wanted him alive.

After fifteen minutes he was backed against a wall of rock, and they were fanned out in front of him, and several had rifles, and they were all pointed in the wrong direction.

He dropped the tire iron he held and raised his hands. "You got it, citizens," he said. "Take it away."

And they did.

They handcuffed him and took him back to the cars. They pushed him into the rear seat of one, and an officer got in on either side of him. Another got into the front beside the driver, and this one held a sawed-off shotgun across his knees.

The driver started the engine and put the car into gear, heading back up 101.

The man with the shotgun turned and stared through bifocals that made his eyes look like hourglasses filled with green sand as he lowered his head. He stared for perhaps ten seconds, then said, "That was a stupid thing to do."

Hell Tanner stared back until the man said, "Very stupid, Tanner."

"Oh, I didn't know you were talking to me."

"I'm looking at you, son."

"And I'm looking at you. Hello, there."

Then the driver said, without taking his eyes off the road, "You know, it's too bad we've got to deliver him in good shape—after the way he smashed up the other car with that damn bike."

"He could still have an accident. Fall and crack a couple ribs, say," said the man to Tanner's left.

The man to the right didn't say anything, but the man with the shotgun shook his head slowly. "Not unless he tries to escape," he said. "L.A. wants him in good shape.

"Why'd you try to skip out, buddy? You might have known we'd pick you up."

Tanner shrugged.

"Why'd you pick me up? I didn't do anything?"

The driver chuckled.

"That's why," he said. "You didn't do anything, and there's something you were supposed to do. Remember?"

"I don't owe anybody anything. They gave me a pardon and let me go."

The Magic

"You got a lousy memory, kid. You made the nation of California a promise when they turned you loose yesterday. Now you've had more than the twenty-four hours you asked for to settle your affairs. You can tell them 'no' if you want and get your pardon revoked. Nobody's forcing you. Then you can spend the rest of your life making little rocks out of big ones. We couldn't care less. I heard they got somebody else lined up already."

"Give me a cigarette," Tanner said.

The man on his right lit one and passed it to him.

He raised both hands, accepted it. As he smoked, he flicked the ashes onto the floor.

They sped along the highway, and when they went through towns or encountered traffic the driver would hit the siren and overhead the red light would begin winking. When this occurred, the sirens of the two other patrol cars that followed behind them would also wail. The driver never touched the brake, all the way up to L.A., and he kept radioing ahead every few minutes.

There came a sound like a sonic boom, and a cloud of dust and gravel descended upon them like hail. A tiny crack appeared in the lower right-hand corner of the bullet-proof windshield, and stones the size of marbles bounced on the hood and the roof. The tires made a crunching noise as they passed over the gravel that now lay scattered upon the road surface. The dust hung like a heavy fog, but ten seconds later they had passed out of it.

The men in the car leaned forward and stared upward.

The sky had become purple, and black lines crossed it, moving from west to east. These swelled, narrowed, moved from side to side, sometimes merged. The driver had turned on his lights by then.

"Could be a bad one coming," said the man with the shotgun.

The driver nodded. "Looks worse further north, too," he said.

A wailing began, high in the air above them, and the dark bands continued to widen. The sound increased in volume, lost its treble quality, became a steady roar.

Roger Zelazny and Samuel R. Delany

The bands consolidated, and the sky grew dark as a starless, moonless night and the dust fell about them in heavy clouds. Occasionally, there sounded a *ping* as a heavier fragment struck against the car.

The driver switched on his country lights, hit the siren again and sped ahead. The roaring and the sound of the siren fought with one another above them, and far to the north a blue aurora began to spread, pulsing.

Tanner finished his cigarette, and the man gave him another. They were all smoking by then.

"You know, you're lucky we picked you up, boy," said the man to his left. "How'd you like to be pushing your bike through that stuff?"

"I'd like it," Tanner said.

"You're nuts."

"No. I'd make it. It wouldn't be the first time."

By the time they reached Los Angeles, the blue aurora filled half the sky, and it was tinged with pink and shot through with smoky, yellow streaks that reached like spider legs into the south. The roar was a deafening, physical thing that beat upon their eardrums and caused their skin to tingle. As they left the car and crossed the parking lot, heading toward the big, pillared building with the frieze across its forehead, they had to shout at one another in order to be heard.

"Lucky we got here when we did!" said the man with the shotgun. "Step it up!" Their pace increased as they moved toward the stairway. "It could break any minute now!" screamed the driver.

II

As they had pulled into the lot, the building had had the appearance of a piece of ice-sculpture, with the shifting lights in the sky playing upon its surfaces and casting cold shadows. Now, though, it seemed as if it were a thing out of wax, ready to melt in a instant's flash of heat. Their faces and the flesh of their hands took on a bloodless, corpse-like appearance.

They hurried up the stairs, and a State Patrolman let them in through the small door to the right of the heavy metal double doors that were the main entrance to the building. He locked and chained the door behind them, after snapping open his holster when he saw Tanner.

"Which way?" asked the man with the shotgun.

"Second floor," said the troooper, nodding toward a stairway to their right, "Go straight back when you get to the top. It's the big office at the end of the hall."

"Thanks."

The roaring was considerably muffled, and objects achieved an appearance of natural existence once more in the artificial light of the building.

They climbed the curving stairway and moved along the corridor that led back into the building. When they reached the final office, the man with the shotgun nodded to his driver. "Knock," he said.

A woman opened the door, started to say something, then stopped and nodded when she saw Tanner. She stepped aside and held the door. "This way," she said, and they moved past her into the office, and she pressed a button on her desk and told the voice that said, "Yes, Mrs. Fiske?": "They're here, with that man, sir."

"Send them in."

She led them to the dark, paneled door in the back of the room and opened it before them.

They entered, and the husky man behind the glass-topped desk leaned backward in his chair and wove his short fingers together in front of his chins and peered over them through eyes just a shade darker than the gray of his hair. His voice was soft and rasped just slightly. "Have a seat," he said to Tanner, and to the others, "wait outside,"

"You know this guy's dangerous. Mister Denton," said the man with the shotgun as Tanner seated himself in a chair situated five feet in front of the desk.

Steel shutters covered the room's three windows, and though the men could not see outside they could guess at the possible furies that stalked there as a sound like machine-gun fire suddenly rang through the room.

"I know."

"Well, he's handcuffed, anyway. Do you want a gun?"

"I've got one."

"Okay, then. We'll be outside."

They left the room.

The two men stared at one another until the door closed, then the man called Denton said, "Are all your affairs settled now?" and the other shrugged. Then, "What the hell is your first name, really? Even the records show—"

"Hell," said Tanner. "That's my name. I was the seventh kid in our family, and when I was born the nurse held me up and said to my old man, 'What name do you want on the birth certificate?' and Dad said, 'Hell!' and walked away. So she put it down like that. That's what my brother told me. I never saw my old man to ask if that's how it was. He copped out the same day. Sounds right, though."

"So your mother raised all seven of you?"

"No. She croaked a couple weeks later and different relatives took us kids."

"I see," said Denton. "You've still got a choice, you know. Do you want to try it or don't you?"

"What's your job, anyway?" asked Tanner.

"I'm the Secretary of Traffic for the nation of California."

"What's that got to do with it?"

"I'm coordinating this thing. It could as easily have been the Surgeon General or the Postmaster General, but more of it really falls into my area of responsibility. I know the hardware best. I know the odds—"

"What are the odds?" asked Tanner.

For the first time, Denton dropped his eyes.

"Well, it's risky . . . . "

"Nobody's ever done it before, except for that nut who ran it to bring the news and he's dead. How can you get odds out of that?"

"I know," said Denton slowly. "You're thinking it's a suicide job, and you're probably right. We're sending three cars, with two drivers in each. If any one just makes it close enough, its broadcast signals may serve to guide in a Boston driver. You don't have to go, though, you know."

"I know. I'm free to spend the rest of my life in prison."

"You killed three people. You could have gotten the death penalty."

"I didn't, so why talk about it? Look, mister, I don't want to die and I don't want the other bit either."

"Drive or don't drive. Take your choice. But remember, if you drive and you make it, all will be forgiven and you can go your own way. The nation of California will even pay for that motorcycle you appropriated and smashed up, not to mention the damage to that police car."

"Thanks a lot." And the winds boomed on the other side of the wall, and the steady staccato from the window shields filled the room,

"You're a very good driver," said Denton, after a time. "You've driven just about every vehicle there is to drive. You've even raced. Back when you were smuggling, you used to make a monthly run to Salt Lake City. There are very few drivers who'll try that, even today."

Hell Tanner smiled, remembering something.

" . . . And in the only legitimate job you ever held, you were the only man who'd make the mail run to Albuquerque. There've only been a few others since you were fired."

"That wasn't my fault."

"You were the best man on the Seattle run, too," Denton continued. "Your supervisor said so. What I'm trying to say is that, of anybody we could pick, you've probably got the best chance of getting through. That's why we've been indulgent with you, but we can't afford to wait any longer. It's yes or no right now, and you'll leave within the hour if it's yes."

Tanner raised his cuffed hands and gestured toward the window.

"In all this crap?" he asked.

"The cars can take this storm," said Denton.

"Man, you're crazy,"

"People are dying even while we're talking," said Denton.

"So a few more ain't about to make that much difference. Can't we wait till tomorrow?"

"No! A man gave his life to bring us the news! And we've got to get across the continent as fast as possible now or it won't matter! Storm or no storm, the cars leave now! Your feelings on the matter don't mean a good goddamn in the face of this! All I want out of you, Hell, is one word: Which one will it be?"

"I'd like something to eat. I haven't . . . "

"There's food in the car. What's your answer?"

Hell stared at the dark window.

"Okay," he said, "I'll run Damnation Alley for you. I won't leave without a piece of paper with some writing on it, though."

"I've got it here."

Denton opened a drawer and withdrew a heavy cardboard envelope from which he extracted a piece of stationery bearing the Great Seal of the nation of California. He stood and rounded the desk and handed it to Hell Tanner.

Hell studied it for several minutes, then said, "This says that if I make it to Boston I receive a full pardon for every criminal action I've ever committed within the nation of California . . . "

"That's right."

"Does that include ones you might not know about now, if someone should come up with them later?"

"That's what it says, Hell—'every criminal action.'"

"Okay, you're on, fat boy. Get these bracelets off me and show me my car."

The man called Denton moved back to his seat on the other side of his desk.

"Let me tell you something else. Hell," he said. "If you try to cop out anywhere along the route, the other drivers have their orders, and they've agreed to follow them. They will open fire on you and burn you into little bitty ashes. Get the picture?"

"I get the picture," said Hell. "I take it I'm supposed to do them the same favor?"

The Magic

"That is correct."

"Good enough. That might be fun."

"I thought you'd like it."

"Now, if you'll unhook me, I'll make the scene for you."

"Not till I've told you what I think of you," Denton said.

"Okay, if you want to waste time calling me names, while people are dying—"

"Shut up! You don't care about them and you know it! I just want to tell you that I think you are the lowest, most reprehensible human being I have ever encountered. You have killed men and raped women. You once gouged out a man's eyes, just for fun. You've been indicted twice for pushing dope and three times as a pimp. You're a drunk and a degenerate, and I don't think you've had a bath since the day you were born. You and your hoodlums terrorized decent people when they were trying to pull their lives together after the war. You stole from them and you assaulted them, and you extorted money and the necessaries of life with the threat of physical violence. I wish you had died in the Big Raid, that night, like all the rest of them. You are not a human being, except from a biological standpoint. You have a big dead spot somewhere inside you where other people have something that lets them live together in society and be neighbors. The only virtue that you possess—if you want to call it that—is that your reflexes may be a little faster, your muscles a little stronger, your eye a bit more wary than the rest of us, so that you can sit behind a wheel and drive through anything that has a way through it. It is for this that the nation of California is willing to pardon your inhumanity if you will use that one virtue to help rather than hurt. I don't approve. I don't want to depend on you, because you're not the type. I'd like to see you die in this thing, and while I hope that somebody makes it through, I hope that it will be somebody else. I hate your bloody guts. You've got your pardon now. The car's ready. Let's go."

Denton stood, at a height of about five feet eight inches, and Tanner stood and looked down at him and chuckled.

516

"I'll make it," he said. "If that citizen from Boston made it through and died, I'll make it through and live. I've been as far as the Missus Hip."

"You're lying."

"No, I ain't either, and if you ever find out that's straight, remember I got this piece of paper in my pocket—'every criminal action' and like that. It wasn't easy, and I was lucky, too. But I made it that far and, nobody else you know can say that. So I figure that's about halfway and I can make the other half if I can get that far."

They moved toward the door.

"I don't like to say it and mean it," said Denton, "but good luck. Not for your sake, though."

"Yeah, I know."

Denton opened the door. "Turn him loose," he said. "He's driving."

The officer with the shotgun handed it to the man who had given Tanner the cigarettes, and he fished in his pockets for the key. When he found it, he unlockedthe cuffs, stepped back, and hung them at his belt "I'll come with you," said Denton. "The motor pool is downstairs."

They left the office, and Mrs. Fiske opened her purse and took a rosary into her hands and bowed her head. She prayed for Boston and she prayed for the soul of its departed messenger. She even threw in a couple for Hell Tanner.

III

They descended to the basement, the sub-basement and the sub-sub-basement.

When they got there. Tanner saw three cars, ready to go; and he saw five men seated on benches along the wall. One of them he recognized.

"Denny," he said, "come here," and he moved forward, and a slim, blond youth who held a crash helmet in his right hand stood and walked toward him.

"What the hell are you doing?" he asked him.

"I'm second driver in car three."

The Magic

"You've got your own garage and you've kept your nose clean. What's the thought on this?"

"Denton offered me fifty grand," said Denny, and Hell turned away his face.

"Forget it! It's no good if you're dead!"

"I need the money."

"Why?"

"I want to get married and I can use it."

"I thought you were making out okay."

"I am, but I'd like to buy a house."

"Does your girl know what you've got in mind?"

"No."

"I didn't think so. Listen, I've got to do it—it's the only way out for me. You don't have to—"

"That's for me to say."

"—so I'm going to tell you something: You drive out to Pasadena to that place where we used to play when we were kids—with the rocks and the three big trees—you know where I mean?"

"Yeah, I sure do remember."

"Go back of the big tree in the middle, on the side where I carved my initials. Step off seven steps and dig down around four feet. Got that?"

"Yeah. What's there?"

"That's my legacy, Denny. You'll find one of those old strong boxes, probably all rusted out by now. Bust it open. It'll be full of excelsior, and there'll be a six-inch joint of pipe inside. It's threaded, and there's caps on both ends. There's a little over five grand rolled up inside it, and all the bills are clean."

"Why you telling me this?"

"Because it's yours now," he said, and he hit him in the jaw. When Denny fell, he kicked him in the ribs, three times, before the cops grabbed him and dragged him away.

"You fool!" said Denton as they held him. "You crazy, damned fool!"

"Uh-uh," said Tanner. "No brother of mine is going to run Damnation Alley while I'm around to stomp him and keep him out of the game. Better find another driver quick, because he's got cracked ribs. Or else let me drive alone."

"Then you'll drive alone," said Denton, "because we can't afford to wait around any longer. There's pills in the compartment, to keep you awake, and you'd better use them, because if you fall back they'll burn you up. Remember that."

"I won't forget you, mister, if I'm ever back in town. Don't fret about that."

"Then you'd better get into car number two and start heading up the ramp. The vehicles are all loaded. The cargo compartment is under the rear seat."

"Yeah, I know."

" . . . And if I ever see you again, it'll be too soon. Get out of my sight, scum!"

Tanner spat on the floor and turned his back on the Secretary of Traffic. Several cops were giving first aid to his brother, and one had dashed off in search of a doctor. Denton made two teams of the remaining four drivers and assigned them to cars one and three. Tanner climbed into the cab of his own, started the engine and waited. He stared up the ram, and considered what lay ahead. He searched the compartments until he found cigarettes. He lit one and leaned back.

The other drivers moved forward and mounted their own heavily shielded vehicles. The radio crackled, crackled, hummed, crackled again, and then a voice came through as he heard the other engines come to life.

"Car one—ready!" came the voice.

There was a pause, then, "Car three—ready!" said a different voice.

Tanner lifted the microphone and mashed the button on its side.

"Car two ready," he said.

"Move out," came the order, and they headed up the ramp.

The door rolled upward before them, and they entered the storm.

The Magic

IV

It was a nightmare, getting out of L.A. and onto Route 91. The waters came down in sheets and rocks the size of baseballs banged against the armor plating of his car. Tanner smoked and turned on the special lights. He wore infrared goggles, and the night and the storm stalked him.

The radio crackled many times, and it seemed that he heard the murmur of a distant voice, but he could never quite make out what it was trying to say.

They followed the road for as far as it went, and as their big tires sighed over the rugged terrain that began where the road ended, Tanner took the lead and the others were content to follow. He knew the way; they didn't.

He followed the old smugglers' route he'd used to run candy to the Mormons. It was possible that he was the only one left alive that knew it. Possible, but then there was always someone looking for a fast buck. So, in all of L.A., there might be somebody else.

The lightning began to fall, not in bolts, but sheets. The car was insulated, but after a time his hair stood on end. He might have seen a giant Gila Monster once, but he couldn't be sure. He kept his fingers away from the fire-control board. He'd save his teeth till menaces were imminent. From the rearview scanners it seemed that one of the cars behind him had discharged a rocket, but he couldn't be sure, since he had lost all radio contact with them immediately upon leaving the building.

Waters rushed toward him, splashed about his car. The sky sounded like an artillery range. A boulder the size of a tombstone fell in front of him, and he swerved about it. Red lights flashing across the sky from north to south. In their passing, he detected many black bands going from west to east. It was not an encouraging spectacle. The storm could go on for days.

He continued to move forward, skirting a pocket of radiation that had not died in the four years since last he had come this way.

They came upon a place where the sands were fused into a glassy sea, and he slowed as he began its passage peering ahead after the craters and chasms it contained.

Roger Zelazny and Samuel R. Delany

Three more rockfalls assailed him before the heavens split themselves open and revealed a bright blue light edged with violet. The dark curtains rolled back toward the Poles, and the roaring and the gunfire reports diminished. A lavender glow remained in the north, and a green sun dipped toward the horizon.

They had ridden it out. He killed the infras, pushed back his goggles and switched on the normal night lamps.

The desert would be bad enough, all by itself.

Something big and bat-like swooped through the tunnel of his lights and was gone. He ignored its passage. Five minutes later it made a second pass, this time much closer, and he fired a magnesium flare. A black shape, perhaps forty feet across, was illuminated, and he gave it two five-second bursts from the fifty-calibers and it fell to the ground and did not return again.

To the squares, this was Damnation Alley. To Hell Tanner, this was still the parking lot. He'd been this way thirty-two times, and so far as he was concerned the Alley started in the place that was once called Colorado.

He led, and they followed, and the night wore on like an abrasive.

No airplane could make it. Not since the war. None could venture above a couple hundred feet, the place where the winds began. The winds. The mighty winds that circled the globe, tearing off the tops of mountains, Sequoia trees, wrecked buildings, gathering up birds, bats, insects and anything else that moved up into the dead belt; the winds that swirled about the world, lacing the skies with dark lines of debris, occasionally meeting, merging, clashing, dropping tons of carnage wherever they came together and formed too great a mass. Air transportation was definitely out, to anywhere in the world. For these winds circled, and they never ceased. Not in all the twenty-five years of Tanner's memory had they let up.

Tanner pushed ahead, cutting a diagonal by the green sunset. Dust continued to fall about him, great clouds of it, and the sky was violet, then purple once more. Then the sun went down and the night came on, and the stars were very faint points of light somewhere above it all. After a time, the moon rose, and the half-face that it showed that night was the color of a glass of Chianti wine held before a candle.

He let another cigarette and began to curse, slowly, softly and without emotion.

They threaded their way amid heaps of rubble: rock, metal, fragments of machinery, the prow of a boat. A snake, as big around as a garbage can and dark green in the cast light, slithered across Tanner's path, and he braked the vehicle as it continued and continued and continued. Perhaps a hundred and twenty feet of snake passed by before Tanner removed his foot from the brake and touched gently upon the gas pedal once again.

Glancing at the left-hand screen, which held an infrared version of the view to the left, it seemed that he saw two eyes glowing within the shadow of a heap of girders and masonry. Tanner kept one hand near the fire-control button and did not move it for a distance of several miles.

There were no windows in the vehicle, only screens which reflected views in every direction including straight up and the ground beneath the car. Tanner sat within an illuminated box which shielded him against radiation. The "car" that he drove had eight heavily treaded tires and was thirty-two feet in length. It mounted eight fifty-caliber automatic guns and four grenade throwers. It carried thirty armor-piercing rockets which could be discharged straight ahead or at any elevation up to forty degrees from the plane. Each of the four sides, as well as the roof of the vehicle, housed a flame thrower. Razor-sharp "wings" of tempered steel—eighteen inches wide at their bases and tapering to points, an inch and a quarter thick where they ridged—could be moved through a complete hundred-eighty-degree arc along the sides of the car and parallel to the ground, at a height of two feet and eight inches. When standing at a right angle to the body of the vehicle—eight feet to the rear of the front bumper—they extended out to a distance of six feet on either side of the car. They could be couched like lances for a charge. They could be held but slightly out from the sides for purposes of slashing whatever was sideswiped. The car was bulletproof, air-conditioned and had its own food locker and sanitation facilities. A long-barreled .357 Magnum was held by a clip on the door near the driver's left hand. A 30-06, a .45 caliber automatic and six hand grenades occupied the rack immediately above the front seat.

But Tanner kept his own counsel, in the form of a long, slim SS dagger inside his right boot.

He removed his gloves and wiped his palms on the knees of his denims. The pierced heart that was tattooed on the back of his right hand was red in the light from the dashboard. The knife that went through it was dark blue, and his first name was tattooed in the same color beneath it, one letter on each knuckle, beginning with that at the base of his little finger.

He opened and explored the two near compartments but could find no cigars. So he crushed out his cigarette butt on the floor and lit another.

The forward screen showed vegetation, and he slowed. He tried using the radio but couldn't tell whether anyone heard him, receiving only static in reply.

He slowed, staring ahead and up. He halted once again.

He turned his forward lights up to full intensity and studied the situation.

A heavy wall of thorn bushes stood before him, reaching to a height of perhaps twelve feet. It swept on to his right and off to his left, vanishing out of sight in both directions. How dense, how deep a pit might be, he could not tell. It had not been there a few years before.

He moved forward slowly and activated the flame throwers. In the rearview screen, he could see that the other vehicles had halted a hundred yards behind him and dimmed their lights.

He drove till he could go no further, then pressed the button for the forward flame.

It shot forth, a tongue of fire, licking fifty feet into the bramble. He held it for five seconds and withdrew it. Then he extended it a second time and backed away quickly as the flames caught.

Beginning with a tiny glow, they worked their way upward and spread slowly to the right and the left. Then they grew in size and brightness.

The Magic

As Tanner backed away, he had to dim his screen, for they'd spread fifty feet before he'd backed more than a hundred, and they leaped thirty and forty feet into the air.

The blaze widened, to a hundred feet, two, three . . . As Tanner backed away, he could see a river of fire flowing off into the distance, and the night was bright about him.

He watched it burn, until it seemed that he looked upon a molten sea. Then he searched the refrigerator, but there was no beer. He opened a soft drink and sipped it while he watched the burning. After about ten minutes, the air conditioner whined and shook itself to life. Hordes of dark, four-footed creatures, the size of rats or cats, fled from the inferno, their coats smouldering. They flowed by. At one point, they covered his forward screen, and he could hear the scratching of their claws upon the fenders and the roof.

He switched off the lights and killed the engine, tossed the empty can into the waste box. He pushed the "Recline" button on the side of the seat, leaned back, and closed his eyes.

V

He was awakened by the blowing of horns. It was still night, and the panel clock showed him that he had slept for a little over three hours.

He stretched, sat up, adjusted the seat. The other cars had moved up, and one stood to either side of him. He leaned on bis own horn twice and started his engine. He switched on the forward lights and considered the prospect before him as he drew on his gloves.

Smoke still rose from the blackened field, and far off to his right there was a glow, as if the fire still continued somewhere in the distance. They were in the place that had once been known as Nevada.

He rubbed his eyes and scratched his nose, then blew the horn once and engaged the gears.

He moved forward slowly. The burnt-out area seemed fairly level and his tires were thick.

Roger Zelazny and Samuel R. Delany

He entered the black field, and his screens were immediately obscured by the rush of ashes and smoke which rose on all sides.

He continued, hearing the tires crunching through the brittle remains. He set his screens at maximum and switched his headlamps up to full brightness.

The vehicles that flanked him dropped back perhaps eighty feet, and he dimmed the screens that reflected the glare of their lights.

He released a flare, and as it hung there, burning, cold, white and high, he saw a charred plain that swept on to the edges of his eyes' horizon.

He pushed down on the accelerator, and the cars behind him swung far out to the sides to avoid the clouds that he raised. His radio crackled, and he heard a faint voice but could not make out its words.

He blew his horn and rolled ahead even faster. The other vehicles kept pace.

He drove for an hour and a half before he saw the end of the ash and the beginning of clean sand up ahead.

Within five minutes, he was moving across desert once more, and he checked his compass and bore slightly to the west. Cars one and three followed, speeding up to match his new pace, and he drove with one hand and ate a corned beef sandwich.

*

When morning came, many hours later, he took a pill to keep himself alert and listened to the screaming of the wind. The sun rose up like molten silver to his right, and a third of the sky grew amber and was laced with fine lines like cobwebs. The desert was topaz beneath it, and the brown curtain of dust that hung continuously at his back, pierced only by the eight shafts of the other cars' lights, took on a pinkish tone as the sun grew a bright red corona and the shadows fled into the west. He dimmed his lights as he passed an orange cactus shaped like a toadstool and perhaps fifty feet in diameter.

Giant bats fled south, and far ahead he saw a wide waterfall descending from the heavens. It was gone by the time he reached the damp sand of that place, but a dead shark lay to his left, and there was seaweed, seaweed, seaweed, fish and driftwood all about.

The sky pinked over from east to west and remained that color. He gulped a bottle of ice water and felt it go into his stomach. He passed more cacti, and a pair of coyotes sat at the base of one and watched him drive by. They seemed to be laughing. Their tongues were very red.

As the sun brightened, he dimmed the screen. He smoked, and he found a button that produced music. He swore at the soft, stringy sounds that filled the cabin, but he didn't turn them off.

He checked the radiation level outside, and it was only a little above normal. The last time he had passed this way, it had been considerably higher.

He passed several wrecked vehicles such as his own. He ran across another plain of silicon, and in the middle was a huge crater which he skirted. The pinkness in the sky faded and faded and faded, and a bluish tone came to replace it. The dark lines were still there, and occasionally one widened into a black river as it flowed away into the east. At noon, one such river partly eclipsed the sun for a period of eleven minutes. With its departure, there came a brief dust storm, and Tanner turned on the radar and his lights. He knew there was a chasm somewhere ahead, and when he came to it he bore to the left and ran along its edge for close to two miles before it narrowed and vanished. The other vehicles followed, and Tanner took his bearings from the compass once more. The dust had subsided with the brief wind, and even with the screen dimmed Tanner had to don his dark goggles against the glare of reflected sunlight from the faceted field he now negotiated.

He passed towering formations which seemed to be quartz. He had never stopped to investigate them in the past, and he had no desire to do it now. The spectrum danced at their bases, and patches of such light occurred for some distance about them.

Speeding away from the crater, he came again upon sand, clean, brown, white dun and red. There were more cacti, and huge dunes lay all about him.

Roger Zelazny and Samuel R. Delany

The sky continued to change, until it was as blue as a baby's eyes. Tanner hummed along with the music for a time, and then he saw the monster.

It was a Gila, bigger than his car, and it moved in fast. It sprang from out the sheltering shade of a valley filled with cacti and it raced toward him, its beaded body bright with many colors beneath the sun, its dark, dark eyes unblinking as it bounded forward on its lizard-fast legs, sable fountains rising behind its upheld tail that was wide as a sail and pointed like a tent.

He couldn't use the rockets because it was coming in from the side.

He opened up with his fifty-calibers and spread his "wings" and stamped the accelerator to the floor. As it neared, he sent forth a cloud of fire in its direction. By then, the other cars were firing, too.

It swung its tail and opened and closed its jaws, and its blood came forth and fell upon the ground. Then a rocket struck it. It turned; it leaped.

There came a booming, crunching sound as it fell upon the vehicle identified as car number one and lay there.

Tanner hit the brakes, turned, and headed back.

Car number three came up beside it and parked. Tanner did the same.

He jumped down from the cab and crossed to the smashed car. He had the rifle in his hands and he put six rounds into the creature's head before he approached the car.

The door had come open, and it hung from a single hinge, the bottom one.

Inside, Tanner could see the two men sprawled, and there was some blood upon the dashboard and the seat.

The other two drivers came up beside him and stared within. Then the shorter of the two crawled inside and listened for the heartbeat and the pulse and felt for breathing.

"Mike's dead," he called out, "but Greg's starting to come around."

A wet spot that began at the car's rear and spread and continued to spread, and the smell of gasoline filled the air.

The Magic

Tanner took out a cigarette, thought better of it and replaced it in the pack. He could hear the gurgle of the huge gas tanks as they emptied themselves upon the ground.

The man who stood at Tanner's side said, "I never saw anything like it . . . . I've seen pictures, but—I never saw anything like it . . . . "

"I have," said Tanner, and then the other driver emerged from the wreck, partly supporting the man he'd referred to as Greg.

The man called out, "Greg's all right. He just hit his head on the dash."

The man who stood at Tanner's side said, "You can take him, Hell. He can back you up when he's feeling better," and Tanner shrugged and turned his back on the scene and lit a cigarette.

"I don't think you should do—" the man began, and Tanner blew smoke in his face. He turned to regard the two approaching men and saw that Greg was dark-eyed and deeply tanned. Part Indian, possibly. His skin seemed smooth, save for a couple pockmarks beneath his right eye, and his cheekbones were high and his hair very dark. He was as big as Tanner, which was six-two, though not quite so heavy. He was dressed in overalls; and his carriage, now that he had had a few deep breaths of air, became very erect, and he moved with a quick, graceful stride.

"We'll have to bury Mike," the short man said.

"I hate to lose the time," said his companion, "but—" and then Tanner flipped his cigarette and threw himself to the ground as it landed in the pool at the rear of the car.

There was an explosion, flames, then more explosions. Tanner heard the rockets as they tore off toward the east, inscribing dark furrows in the hot afternoon's air. The ammo for the fifty-calibers exploded, and the hand grenades went off, and Tanner burrowed deeper and deeper into the sand, covering his head and blocking his ears.

As soon as things grew quiet, he grabbed for the rifle. But they were already coming at him, and he saw the muzzle of a pistol. He raised his hands slowly and stood.

"Why the goddamn hell did you do a stupid thing like that?" said the other driver, the man who held the pistol.

Tanner smiled. "Now we don't have to bury him," he said. "Cremation's just as good, and it's already over."

"You could have killed us all, if those guns or those rocket launchers had been aimed this way!"

"They weren't. I looked."

"The flying metal could've—Oh . . . I see. Pick up your damn rifle, buddy, and keep it pointed at the ground. Eject the rounds it's still got in it and put 'em in your pocket."

Tanner did this thing while the other talked.

"You wanted to kill us all, didn't you? Then you could have cut out and gone your way, like you tried to do yesterday. Isn't that right?"

"You said it, mister, not me."

"It's true, though. You don't give a good goddamn if everybody in Boston croaks, do you?"

"My gun's unloaded now," said Tanner.

"Then get back in your bloody buggy and get going! I'll be behind you all the way!"

Tanner walked back toward his car. He heard the others arguing behind him, but he didn't think they'd shoot him. As he was about to climb up into the cab, he saw a shadow out of the corner of his eye and turned quickly.

The man named Greg was standing behind him, tall and quiet as a ghost.

"Want me to drive awhile?" he asked Tanner, without expression.

"No, you rest up. I'm still in good shape. Later on this afternoon, maybe, if you feel up to it."

The man nodded and rounded the cab. He entered from the other side and immediately reclined his chair.

Tanner slammed his door and started the engine. He heard the air conditioner come to life.

"Want to reload this?" he asked. "And put it back on the rack?" And he handed the rifle and the ammo to the other, who had nodded. He drew on his gloves then and said, "There's plenty of soft drinks in the 'frig. Nothing much else, though," and the other nodded again. Then he heard car three start and said, "Might as well roll," and he put it into gear and took his foot off the clutch.

VI

After they had driven for about half an hour, the man called Greg said to him, "Is it true what Marlowe said?"

"What's a Marlowe?"

"He's driving the other car. Were you trying to kill us? Do you really want to skip out?"

Hell laughed. "That's right," he said. "You named it."

"Why?"

Hell let it hang there for a minute, then said, "Why shouldn't I? I'm not anxious to die. I'd like to wait a long time before I try that bit."

Greg said, "If we don't make it, the population of the continent may be cut in half."

"If it's a question of them or me, I'd rather it was them."

"I sometimes wonder how people like you happen."

"The same way as anybody else, mister, and it's fun for a couple people for awhile, and then the trouble starts."

"What did they ever do to you. Hell?"

"Nothing. What did they ever do *for* me? Nothing. Nothing. What do I owe them? The same."

"Why'd you stomp your brother back at the Hall?"

"Because I didn't want him doing a damfool thing like this and getting himself killed. Cracked ribs he can get over. Death is a more permanent ailment."

"That's not what I asked you. I mean, what do you care whether he croaks?"

"He's a good kid, that's why. He's got a thing for this chick, though, and he can't see straight."

"So what's it to you?"

"Like I said, he's my brother and he's a good kid. I like him."

"How come?"

"Oh, hell! We've been through a lot together, that's all! What are you trying to do? Psychoanalyze me?"

"I was just curious, that's all."

"So now you know. Talk about something else if you want to talk, okay?"

"Okay. You've been this way before, right?"

"That's right."

"You been any further east?"

"I've been all the way to the Missus Hip."

"Do you know a way to get across it?"

"I think so. The bridge is still up at Saint Louis."

"Why didn't you go across it the last time you were there?"

"Are you kidding? The thing's packed with cars full of bones. It wasn't worth the trouble to try and clear it"

"Why'd you go that far in the first place?"

"Just to see what it was like. I heard all these stories—"

"What was it like?"

"A lot of crap. Burned down towns, big craters, crazy animals, some people—"

"People? People still live there?"

"If you want to call them that. They're all wild and screwed up. They wear rags or animal skins or they go naked. They threw rocks at me till I shot a couple. Then they let me alone."

"How long ago was that?"

"Six—maybe seven years ago. I was just a kid then."

"How come you never told anybody about it?"

"I did. A coupla my friends. Nobody else ever asked me. We were going to go out there and grab off a couple of the girls and bring them back, but everybody chickened out."

"What would you have done with them?"

531

Tanner shrugged. "I dunno. Sell 'em, I guess."

"You guys used to do that, down on the Barbary Coast—sell people, I mean—didn't you?"

Tanner shrugged again.

"Used to," he said, "before the Big Raid."

"How'd you manage to live through that? I thought they'd cleaned the whole place out?"

"I was doing time," he said. "A.D.W."

"What's that?"

"Assault with a deadly weapon."

"What'd you do after they let you go?"

"I let them rehabilitate me. They got me a job running the mail."

"Oh yeah, I heard about that. Didn't realize it was you, though. You were supposed to be pretty good—doing all right and ready for a promotion. Then you kicked your boss around and lost your job. How come?"

"He was always riding me about my record and about my old gang down on the Coast. Finally, one day I told him to lay off, and he laughed at me, so I hit him with a chain. Knocked out the bastard's front teeth. I'd do it again."

"Too bad."

"I was the best driver he had. It was his loss. Nobody else will make the Albuquerque run, not even today. Not unless they really need the money."

"Did you like the work, though, while you were doing it?"

"Yeah, I like to drive."

"You should probably have asked for a transfer when the guy started bugging you."

"I know. If it was happening today, that's probably what I'd do. I was mad, though, and I used to get mad a lot faster than I do now. I think I'm smarter these days than I was before."

"If you make it on this run and you go home afterward, you'll probably be able to get your job back. Think you'd take it?"

"In the first place," said Tanner, "I don't think we'll make it. And in the second, if we do make it and there's still people around that town, I think I'd rather stay there than go back."

Greg nodded. "Might be smart. You'd be a hero. Nobody'd know much about your record. Somebody'd turn you onto something good."

"The hell with heroes," said Tanner.

"Me, though, I'll go back if we make it."

"Sail 'round Cape Horn?"

"That's right."

"Might be fun. But why go back?"

"I've got an old mother and a mess of brothers and sisters I take care of, and I've got a girl back there."

Tanner brightened the screen as the sky began to darken.

"What's your mother like?"

"Nice old lady. Raised the eight of us. Got arthritis bad now, though."

"What was she like when you were a kid?"

"She used to work during the day, but she cooked our meals and sometimes brought us candy. She made a lot of our clothes. She used to tell us stories, like about how things were before the war. She played games with us and sometimes she gave us toys."

"How about your old man?" Tanner asked him, after awhile.

"He drank pretty heavy and he had a lot of jobs, but he never beat us too much. He was all right. He got run over by a car when I was around twelve."

"And you take care of everybody now?"

"Yeah. I'm the oldest."

"What is it that you do?"

"I've got your old job. I run the mail to Albuquerque."

"Are you kidding?"

"No."

"I'll be damned! Is German still the supervisor?"

"He retired last year, on disability."

"I'll be damned! That's funny. Listen, down in Albuquerque do you ever go to a bar called Pedro's?"

"I've been there."

"Have they still got a little blonde girl plays the piano? Named Margaret?"

"No."

"Oh."

"They've got some guy now. Fat fellow. Wears a big ring on his left hand."

Tanner nodded and downshifted as he began the ascent of a steep hill.

"How's your head now?" he asked, when they'd reached the top and started down the opposite slope.

"Feels pretty good. I took a couple of your aspirins with that soda I had."

"Feel up to driving for awhile?"

"Sure, I could do that."

"Okay, then." Tanner leaned on the horn and braked the car. "Just follow the compass for a hundred miles or so and wake me up. All right?"

"Okay. Anything special I should watch out for?"

"The snakes. You'll probably see a few. Don't hit them, whatever you do."

"Right."

They changed seats, and Tanner reclined the one, lit a cigarette, smoked half of it, crushed it out and went to sleep.

VII

When Greg awakened him, it was night. Tanner coughed and drank a mouthful of ice water and crawled back to the latrine. When he emerged, he took the driver's seat and checked the mileage and looked at the compass. He corrected their course and, "We'll be in Salt Lake City before morning," he said, "if we're lucky. —Did you run into any trouble?"

"No, it was pretty easy. I saw some snakes and I let them go by. That was about it."

Tanner grunted and engaged the gears.

"What was that guy's name that brought the news about the plague?" Tanner asked.

"Brady or Brody or something like that," said Greg.

"What was it that killed him? He might have brought the plague to L.A., you know."

Greg shook his head.

"No. His car had been damaged, and he was all broken up and he'd been exposed to radiation a lot of the way. They burned his body and his car, and anybody who'd been anywhere near him got shots of Haffikine."

"What's that?"

"That's the stuff we're carrying—Haffikine antiserum. It's the only preventative for the plague. Since we had a bout of it around twenty years ago, we've kept it on hand and maintained the facilities for making more in a hurry. Boston never did, and now they're hurting,"

"Seems kind of silly for the only other nation on the continent—maybe in the world—not to take better care of itself, when they knew we'd had a dose of it."

Greg shrugged.

"Probably, but there it is. Did they give you any shots before they released you?"

"Yeah."

"That's what it was, then."

"I wonder where their driver crossed the Missus Hip? He didn't say, did he?"

"He hardly said anything at all. They got most of the story from the letter he carried."

"Must have been one hell of a driver, to run the Alley."

"Yeah. Nobody's ever done it before, have they?"

"Not that I know of."

"I'd like to have met the guy."

"Me too, at least I guess."

"It's a shame we can't radio across country, like in the old days."

"Why?"

The Magic

"Then he wouldn't of had to do it, and we could find out along the way whether it's really worth making the run. They might all be dead by now, you know."

"You've got a point there, mister, and in a day or so we'll be to a place where going back will be harder than going ahead."

Tanner adjusted the screen as dark shapes passed.

"Look at that, will you!"

"I don't see anything."

"Put on your infras."

Greg did this and stared upward at the screen.

Bats. Enormous bats cavorted overhead, swept by in dark clouds.

"There must be hundreds of them, maybe thousands . . . . "

"Guess so. Seems there are more than there used to be when I came this way a few years back. They must be screwing their heads off in Carlsbad."

"We never see them in L.A. Maybe they're pretty much harmless."

"Last time I was up to Salt Lake, I heard talk that a lot of them were rabid. Some day someone's got to go—them or us."

"You're a cheerful guy to ride with, you know?"

Tanner chuckled and lit a cigarette, and. "Why don't you make us some coffee?" he said. "As for the bats, that's something our kids can worry about, if there are any."

Greg filled the coffee pot and plugged it into the dashboard. After a time, it began to grumble and hiss.

"What the hell's that?" said Tanner, and he hit the brakes. The other car halted, several hundred yards behind his own, and he turned on his microphone and said, "Car three! What's that look like to you?" and waited.

He watched them: towering, tapered tops that spun between the ground and the sky, wobbling from side to side, sweeping back and forth, about a mile ahead. It seemed there were fourteen or fifteen of the things. Now they stood like pillars, now they danced. They bored into the ground and sucked up yellow dust. There was a haze all about them. The stars were dim or absent above or behind them.

Greg stared ahead and said, "I've heard of whirlwinds, tornadoes—big, spinning things. I've never seen one, but that's the way they were described to me."

And then the radio crackled, and the muffled voice of the man called Marlowe came through:

"Giant dust devils," he said. "Big, rotary sand storms. I think they're sucking stuff up into the dead belt, because I don't see anything coming down—"

"You ever see one before?"

"No, but my partner says he did. He says the best thing might be to shoot our anchoring columns and stay put."

Tanner did not answer immediately. He stared ahead, and the tornadoes seemed to grow larger.

"They're coming this way," he finally said. "I'm not about to park here and be a target. I want to be able to maneuver. I'm going ahead through them."

"I don't think you should."

"Nobody asked you, mister, but if you've got any brains you'll do the same thing."

"I've got rockets aimed at your tail, Hell."

"You won't fire them—not for a thing like this, where I could be right and you could be wrong—and not with Greg in here, too."

There was silence within the static, then, "Okay, you win. Hell. Go ahead, and we'll watch. If you make it, we'll follow. If you don't, we'll stay put."

"I'll shoot a flare when I get to the other side," Tanner said. "When you see it, you do the same. Okay?"

Tanner broke the connection and looked ahead, studying the great black columns, swollen at their tops. There fell a few layers of light from the storm which they supported, and the air was foggy between the blacknesses of their revolving trunks. "Here goes," said Tanner, switching his lights as bright as they would beam. "Strap yourself in, boy," and Greg obeyed him as the vehicle crunched forward.

Tanner buckled his own safety belt as they slowly edged ahead.

The Magic

The columns grew and swayed as he advanced, and he could now hear a rushing, singing sound, as of a chorus of the winds.

He skirted the first by three hundred yards and continued to the left to avoid the one which stood before him and grew and grew. As he got by it, there was another, and he moved farther to the left. Then there was an open area of perhaps a quarter of a mile leading ahead and toward his right.

He swiftly sped across it and passed between two of the towers that stood like ebony pillars a hundred yards apart. As he passed them, the wheel was almost torn from his grip, and he seemed to inhabit the center of an eternal thunderclap. He swerved to the right then and skirted another, speeding.

Then he saw seven more and cut between two and passed about another. As he did, the one behind him moved rapidly, crossing the path he had just taken. He exhaled heavily and turned to the left.

He was surrounded by the final four, and he braked so that he was thrown forward and the straps cut into his shoulder, as two of the whirlwinds shook violently and moved in terrible spurts of speed. One passed before him, and the front end of his car was raised off the ground.

Then he floored the gas pedal and shot between the final two, and they were all behind him.

He continued on for about a quarter for a mile, turned the car about, mounted a small rise and parked.

He released the flare.

It hovered, like a dying star, for about half a minute.

He lit a cigarette as he stared back, and he waited.

He finished the cigarette.

Then, "Nothing," he said. "Maybe they couldn't spot it through the storm. Or maybe we couldn't see theirs."

"I hope so," said Greg.

"How long do you want to wait?"

"Let's have that coffee."

*

An hour passed, then two. The pillars began to collapse until there were only three of the slimmer ones. They moved off toward the east and were gone from sight.

Tanner released another flare, and still there was no response.

"We'd better go back and look for them," said Greg.

"Okay."

And they did.

There was nothing there, though, nothing to indicate the fate of car three.

Dawn occurred in the east before they had finished with their searching, and Tanner turned the car around, checked the compass, and moved north.

"When do you think we'll hit Salt Lake?" Greg asked him, after a long silence.

"Maybe two hours."

"Were you scared, back when you ran those things?"

"No. Afterward, though, I didn't feel so good."

Greg nodded.

"You want me to drive again?"

"No. I won't be able to sleep if I stop now. We'll take in more gas in Salt Lake, and we can get something to eat while a mechanic checks over the car. Then I'll put us on the right road, and you can take over while I sack out."

The sky was purple again and the black bands had widened. Tanner cursed and drove faster. He fired his ventral flame at two bats who decided to survey the car. They fell back, and he accepted the mug of coffee Greg offered him.

VIII

The sky was as dark as evening when they pulled into Salt Lake City. John Brady—that was his name—had passed that way but days before, and the city was ready for the responding vehicle. Most of its ten thousand inhabitants appeared along the street, and before Hell and Greg had jumped down from the cab after pulling into the first garage they saw, the hood of car number two was opened and three mechanics were peering at the engine.

The Magic

They abandoned the idea of eating in the little diner across the street. Too many people hit them with too many questions as soon as they set foot outside the garage. They retreated and sent someone after eggs, bacon and toast.

There was cheering as they rolled forth onto the street and sped away into the east.

"Could have used a beer," said Tanner. "Damn it!"

And they rushed along beside the remains of what had once been U.S. Route 40.

Tanner relinquished the driver's seat and stretched out on the passenger side of the cab. The sky continued to darken above them, taking upon it the appearance it had had in L.A. the day before.

"Maybe we can outrun it," Greg said.

"Hope so."

The blue pulse began in the north, flared into a brilliant aurora. The sky was almost black directly overhead.

"Run!" cried Tanner. "Run! Those are hills up ahead! Maybe we can find an overhang or a cave!"

But it broke upon them before they reached the hills. First came the hail, then the flak. The big stones followed, and the scanner on the right went dead. The sands blasted them, and they rode beneath a celestial waterfall that caused the engine to sputter and cough.

They reached the shelter of the hills, though, and found a place within a rocky valley where the walls jutted steeply forward and broke the main force of the wind/sand/dust/rock/water storm. They sat there as the winds screamed and boomed about them. They smoked and they listened.

"We won't make it," said Greg. "You were right. I thought we had a chance. We don't. Everything's against us, even the weather."

"We've got a chance," said Tanner. "Maybe not a real good one. But we've been lucky so far. Remember that."

Greg spat into the waste container.

"Why the sudden optimism? From you?"

"I was mad before and shooting off my mouth. Well, I'm still mad—but I got me a feeling now: I feel lucky. That's all."

Greg laughed. "The hell with luck. Look out there," he said.

"I see it," said Tanner. "This buggy is built to take it, and it's doing it. Also, we're only getting about ten percent of its full strength."

"Okay, but what difference does it make? It could last for a couple days."

"So we wait it out."

"Wait too long, and even that ten percent can smash us. Wait too long, and even if it doesn't there'll be no reason left to go ahead. Try driving, though, and it'll flatten us."

"It'll take me ten or fifteen minutes to fix that scanner. We've got spare 'eyes.' If the storm lasts more than six hours, we'll start out anyway."

"Says who?"

"Me."

"Why? You're the one who was so hot on saving his own neck. How come all of a sudden you're willing to risk it, not to mention mine too?"

Tanner smoked awhile, then said, "I've been thinking," and then he didn't say anything else.

"About what?" Greg asked him.

"Those folks in Boston," Tanner said. "Maybe it is worth it. I don't know. They never did anything for me. But hell, I like action and I'd hate to see the whole world get dead. I think I'd like to see Boston, too, just to see what it's like. It might even be fun being a hero, just to see what that's like. Don't get me wrong. I don't give a damn about anybody up there. It's just that I don't like the idea of everything being like the Alley here—all burned-out and screwed up and full of crap. When we lost the other car back in those tornadoes, it made me start thinking . . . .I'd hate to see everybody go that way—everything. I might still cop out if I get a real good chance, but I'm just telling you how I feel now. That's all."

Greg looked away and laughed, a little more heartily than usual.

"I never suspected you contained such philosophic depths."

"Me neither. I'm tired. Tell me about your brothers and sisters, huh?"

The Magic

"Okay."

*

Four hours later, when the storm slackened and the rocks became dust and the rain fog, Tanner replaced the right scanner, and they moved on out, passing later through Rocky Mountain National Park. The dust and the fog combined to limit visibility, throughout the day. That evening they skirted the ruin that was Denver, and Tanner took over as they headed toward the place that had once been called Kansas.

He drove all night, and in the morning the sky was clearer than it had been in days. He let Greg snore on and sorted through his thoughts while he sipped his coffee.

*

It was a strange feeling that came over him as he sat there with his pardon in his pocket and his hands upon the wheel. The dust fumed at his back. The sky was the color of rosebuds, and the dark trails had shrunken once again. He recalled the stories of the days when the missiles came down, burning everything but the northeast and the southwest; the days when the winds arose and the clouds vanished and the sky had lost its blue; the days when the Panama Canal had been shattered and radios had ceased to function; the days when the planes could no longer fly. He regretted this, for he had always wanted to fly, high, birdlike, swooping and soaring. He felt slightly cold, and the screens now seemed to possess a crystal clarity, like pools of tinted water. Somewhere ahead, far, far ahead lay what might be the only other sizeable pocket of humanity that remained on the shoulders of the world. He might be able to save it, if he could reach it in time. He looked about him at the rocks and the sand and the side of a broken garage that had somehow come to occupy the slope of a mountain. It remained within his mind long after he had passed it. Shattered, fallen down, half covered with debris, it took on a stark and monstrous form, like a decaying skull which had once occupied the shoulders of a giant; and he pressed down hard on the accelerator, although it could go no further. He began to tremble. The sky brightened, but he did not touch the screen controls. Why did he have

542

to be the one? He saw a mass of smoke ahead and to the right. As he drew nearer, he saw that it rose from a mountain which had lost its top and now held a nest of fires in its place. He cut to the left, going miles, many miles, out of the way he had intended. Occasionally, the ground shook beneath his wheels. Ashes fell about him, but now the smouldering cone was far to the rear of the right-hand screen. He wondered after the days that had gone before and the few things that he actually knew about them. If he made it through, he decided he'd learn more about history. He threaded his way through painted canyons and forded a shallow river. Nobody had ever asked him to do anything important before, and he hoped that nobody ever would again. Now, though, he was taken by the feeling that he could do it. He wanted to do it. Damnation Alley lay all about him, burning, fuming, shaking, and if he could not run it then half the world would die, and the chances would be doubled that one day all the world would be part of the Alley. His tattoo stood stark on his whitened knuckles, saying "Hell," and he knew that it was true. Greg still slept, the sleep of exhaustion, and Tanner narrowed his eyes and chewed his beard and never touched the brake, not even when he saw the rockslide beginning. He made it by and sighed. That pass was closed to him forever, but he had shot through without a scratch. His mind was an expanding bubble, its surfaces like the view-screens, registering everything about him. He felt the flow of the air within the cab and the upward pressure of the pedal upon his foot. His throat seemed dry, but it didn't matter. His eyes felt gooey at their inside corners, but he didn't wipe them. He roared across the pocked plains of Kansas, and he knew now that he had been sucked into the role completely and that he wanted it that way. Damn-his-eyes Denton had been right. It had to be done. He halted when he came to the lip of a chasm and headed north. Thirty miles later it ended, and he turned again to the south. Greg muttered in his sleep. It sounded like a curse. Tanner repeated it softly a couple times and turned toward the east as soon as a level stretch occurred. The sun stood in high heaven, and Tanner felt as though he were drifting bodiless beneath it, above the brown ground flaked with green spikes of growth. He clenched his teeth and his mind went back to Denny, doubtless now in a hospital. Better than being where the others had gone. He hoped the money he'd told him about was still there. Then he felt the ache begin, in the places between his neck and his shoulders. It spread down into his arms, and he realized how tightly he was gripping the wheel. He blinked and took a deep breath and realized that his eyeballs hurt. He lit a cigarette and it tasted foul, but he kept puffing at it. He drank some water and he dimmed the rear view-screen as the sun fell behind him. Then he heard a sound like a distant rumble of thunder and was fully alert once more. He sat up straight and took his foot off the accelerator.

He slowed. He braked and stopped. Then he saw them. He sat there and watched them as they passed, about a half-mile ahead.

A monstrous herd of bison crossed before him. It took the better part of an hour before they had passed. Huge, heavy, dark, heads down, hooves scoring the soil, they ran without slowing until the thunder was great and then rolled off toward the north, diminishing, softening, dying, gone. The screen of their dust still hung before him, and he plunged into it, turning on his lights.

He considered taking a pill, decided against it. Greg might be waking soon, he wanted to be able to get some sleep after they'd switched over.

He came up beside a highway, and its surface looked pretty good, so he crossed onto it and sped ahead. After a time, he passed a faded, sagging sign that said "TOPEKA—110 MILES."

Greg yawned and stretched. He rubbed his eyes with his knuckles and then rubbed his forehead, the right side of which was swollen and dark.

"What time is it?" he asked.

Tanner gestured toward the clock in the dashboard.

"Morning or is it afternoon?"

"Afternoon."

"My God! I must have slept around fifteen hours!"

"That's about right."

"You been driving all that time?"

"That's right."

"You must be done in. You look like hell. Let me just hit the head. I'll take over in a few minutes."

"Good idea."

Greg crawled toward the rear of the vehicle.

After about five minutes. Tanner came upon the outskirts of a dead town. He drove up the main street, and there were rusted-out hulks of cars all along it. Most of the buildings had fallen in upon themselves, and some of the opened cellars that he saw were filled with scummy water. Skeletons lay about the town square. There were no trees standing above the weeds that grew there. Three telephone poles still stood, one of them leaning forward and trailing wires like a handful of black spaghetti. Several benches were visible within the weeds beside the cracked sidewalks, and a skeleton lay stretched out upon the second one Tanner passed. He found his way barred by a fallen telephone pole, and he detoured around the block. The next street was somewhat better preserved, but all its store-front windows were broken, and a nude mannikin posed fetchingly with her left arm missing from the elbow down. The traffic light at the corner stared blindly as Tanner passed through its intersection.

Tanner heard Greg coming forward as he turned at the next corner.

"I'll take over now," he said.

"I want to get out of this place first," and they both watched in silence for the next fifteen minutes until the dead town was gone from around them.

Tanner pulled to a halt then and said, "We're a couple hours away from a place that used to be called Topeka. Wake me if you run into anything hairy."

"How did it go while I was alseep? Did you have any trouble?"

"No," said Tanner, and he closed his eyes and began to snore.

Greg drove away from the sunset, and he ate three ham sandwiches and drank a quart of milk before Topeka.

The Magic

IX

Tanner was awakened by the firing of the rockets. He rubbed the sleep from his eyes and stared dumbly ahead for almost half a minute.

Like gigantic dried leaves, great clouds fell about them. Bats, bats, bats. The air was filled with bats. Tanner could hear a chittering, squeaking, scratching sound, and the car was buffeted by their dark bodies.

"Where are we?" he asked.

"Kansas City. The place seems full of them," and Greg released another rocket, which cut a fiery path through the swooping, spinning horde.

"Save the rockets. Use the fire," said Tanner, switching the nearest gun to manual and bringing cross-hairs into focus upon the screen. "Blast 'em in all directions—for five, six seconds—then I'll come in."

The flame shot forth, orange and cream blossoms of combustion. When they folded, Tanner sighted in the screen and squeezed the trigger. He swung the gun, and they fell. Their charred bodies lay all about him, and he added new ones to the smouldering heaps.

"Roll it!" he cried, and the car moved forward, swaying, bat bodies crunching beneath its tires.

Tanner laced the heavens with gunfire, and when they swooped again he strafed them and fired a flare.

In the sudden magnesium glow from overhead, it seemed that millions of vampire-faced forms were circling, spiraling down toward them.

He switched from gun to gun, and they fell about him like fruit. Then he called out, "Brake, and hit the topside flame!" and Greg did this thing.

"Now the sides! Front and rear next!"

Bodies were burning all about them, heaped as high as the hood, and Greg put the car into low gear when Tanner cried "Forward!" And they pushed their way through the wall of charred flesh.

Tanner fired another flare.

The bats were still there, but circling higher now. Tanner primed the guns and waited, but they did not attack again in any great number. A few swept about them, and he took pot-shots at them as they passed.

Ten minutes later he said, "That's the Missouri River to our left. If we just follow alongside it now, we'll hit Saint Louis."

"I know. Do you think it'll be full of bats, too?"

"Probably. But if we take our time and arrive with daylight, they shouldn't bother us. Then we can figure a way to get across the Missus Hip."

Then their eyes fell upon the rearview screen, where the dark skyline of Kansas City with bats was silhouetted by pale stars and touched by the light of the bloody moon.

After a time, Tanner slept once more. He dreamt he was riding his bike, slowly, down the center of a wide street, and people lined the sidewalks and began to cheer as he passed. They threw confetti, but by the time it reached him it was garbage, wet and stinking. He stepped on the gas then, but his bike slowed even more and now they were screaming at him. They shouted obscenities. They cried out his name, over and over, and again. The Harley began to wobble, but his feet seemed to be glued in place. In a moment, he knew, he would fall. The bike came to a halt then, and he began to topple over toward the right side. They rushed toward him as he fell, and he knew it was just about all over . . . .

He awoke with a jolt and saw the morning spread out before him: a bright coin in the middle of a dark blue tablecloth and a row of glasses along the edge.

"That's it," said Greg. "The Missus Hip."

Tanner was suddenly very hungry.

*

After they had refreshed themselves, they sought the bridge.

"I didn't see any of your naked people with spears," said Greg. "Of course, we might have passed their way after dark—if there are any of them still around."

"Good thing, too," said Tanner. "Saved us some ammo."

The bridge came into view, sagging and dark save for the places where the sun gilded its cables, and it stretched unbroken across the bright expanse of waters. They moved slowly toward it, threading their way through streets gorged with rubble, detouring when it became completely blocked by the rows of broken machines, fallen walls, sewer-deep abysses in the burst pavement.

It took them two hours to travel half a mile, and it was noon before they reached the foot of the bridge, and, "It looks as if Brady might have crossed here," said Greg, eyeing what appeared to be a cleared passageway amidst the wrecks that filled the span. "How do you think he did it?"

"Maybe he had something with him to hoist them and swing them out over the edge. There are some wrecks below, down where the water is shallow."

"Were they there last time you passed by?"

"I don't know. I wasn't right down here by the bridge. I topped that hill back there," and he gestured at the rearview screen.

"Well, from here it looks like we might be able to make it. Let's roll."

They moved upward and forward onto the bridge and began their slow passage across the mightly Missus Hip. There were times when the bridge creaked beneath them, sighed, groaned, and they felt it move.

The sun began to climb, and still they moved forward, scraping their fenders against the edges of the wrecks, using their wings like plows. They were on the bridge for three hours before its end came into sight through a rift in the junkstacks.

When their wheels finally touched the opposite shore, Greg sat there breathing heavily and then lit a cigarette.

"You want to drive awhile, Hell?"

"Yeah. Let's switch over."

He did, and, "God! I'm bushed!" he said as he sprawled out.

Tanner drove forward through the ruins of East Saint Louis, hurrying to clear the town before nightfall. The radiation level began to mount as he advanced, and the streets were cluttered and broken. He checked the inside of the cab for radioactivity, but it was still clean.

It took him hours, and as the sun fell at his back he saw the blue aurora begin once more in the north. But the sky stayed clear, filled with its stars, and there were no black lines that he could see. After a long while, a rose-colored moon appeared and hung before him. He turned on the music, softly, and glanced at Greg. It didn't seem to bother him, so he let it continue.

The instrument panel caught his eye. The radiation level was still climbing. Then, in the forward screen, he saw the crater and he stopped.

It must have been over half a mile across, and he couldn't tell its depth.

He fired a flare, and in its light he used the telescopic lenses to examine it to the right and to the left.

The way seemed smoother to the right, and he turned in that direction and began to negotiate it.

The place was hot! So very, very hot! He hurried. And he wondered as he sped, the gauge rising before him: What had it been like on that day? Whenever? That day when a tiny sun had lain upon this spot and fought with, and for a time beaten, the brightness of the other in the sky, before it sank slowly into its sudden burrow? He tried to imagine it, succeeded, then tried to put it out of his mind and couldn't. How do you put out the fires that burn forever? He wished that he knew. There'd been so many places to go then, and he liked to move around.

What had it been like in the old days, when a man could just jump on his bike and cut out for a new town whenever he wanted? And nobody emptying buckets of crap on you from out of the sky? He felt cheated, which was not a new feeling for him, but it made him curse even longer than usual.

He lit a cigarette when he'd finally rounded the crater, and he smiled for the first time in months as the radiation gauge began to fall once more. Before many miles, he saw tall grasses swaying about him, and not too long after that he began to see trees.

Trees short and twisted, at first, but the further he fled from the place of carnage, the taller and straighter they became. They were trees such as he had never seen before—fifty, sixty feet in height—and graceful, and gathering stars, there on the plains of Illinois.

The Magic

He was moving along a clean, hard, wide road, and just then he wanted to travel it forever—to Floridee, of the swamps and Spanish moss and citrus groves and fine beaches and the Gulf; and up to the cold, rocky Cape, where everything is gray and brown and the waves break below the lighthouses and the salt burns in your nose and there are graveyards where bones have lain for centuries and you can still read the names they bore, chiseled there into the stones above them; down through the nation where they say the grass is blue; then follow the mighty Missus Hip to the place where she spreads and comes and there's the Gulf again, full of little islands where the old boosters stashed their loot; and through the shag-topped mountains he'd heard about: the Smokies, Ozarks, Poconos, Catskills; drive through the forest of Shenandoah; park, and take a boat out over Chesapeake Bay; see the big lakes and the place where the water falls, Niagara. To drive forever along the big road, to see everything, to eat the world. Yes. Maybe it wasn't all Damnation Alley. Some of the legendary places must still be clean, like the countryside about him now. He wanted it with a hunger, with a fire like that which always burned in his loins. He laughed then, just one short, sharp bark, because now it seemed like maybe he could have it.

The music played softly, too sweetly perhaps, and it filled him.

X

By morning he was into the place called Indiana and still following the road. He passed farmhouses which seemed in good repair. There could even be people living in them. He longed to investigate, but he didn't dare to stop. Then after an hour, it was all countryside again, and degenerating.

The grasses grew shorter, shriveled, were gone. An occasional twisted tree clung to the bare earth. The radiation level began to rise once more. The signs told him he was nearing Indianapolis, which he guessed was a big city that had received a bomb and was now gone away.

Nor was he mistaken.

He had to detour far to the south to get around it, backtracking to a place called Martinsville in order to cross over the White River. Then as he headed east once more, his radio crackled and came to life. There was a faint voice, repeating, "Unidentified vehicle, halt!" and he switched all the scanners to telescopic range. Far ahead, on a hilltop, he saw a standing man with binoculars and a walkie-talkie. He did not acknowledge receipt of the transmission, but kept driving.

He was hitting forty miles an hour along a halfway decent section of roadway, and he gradually increased his speed to fifty-five, though the protesting of his tires upon the cracked pavement was sufficient to awaken Greg.

Tanner stared ahead, ready for an attack, and the radio kept repeating the order, louder now as he neared the hill, and called upon him to acknowledge the message.

He touched the brake as he rounded a long curve, and he did not reply to Greg's "What's the matter?"

When he saw it there, blocking the way, ready to fire, he acted instantly.

The tank filled the road, and its big gun was pointed directly at him.

As his eye sought for and found passage around it, his right hand slapped the switches that sent three armor-piercing rockets screaming ahead and his left spun the wheel counter-clockwise and his foot fell heavy on the accelerator.

He was half off the road then, bouncing along the ditch at its side, when the tank discharged one fiery belch which missed him and then caved in upon itself and blossomed.

There came the sound of rifle fire as he pulled back onto the road on the other side of the tank and sped ahead. Greg launched a single grenade to the right and the left and then hit the fifty calibers. They tore on ahead, and after about a quarter of a mile Tanner picked up bis microphone and said, "Sorry about that. My brakes don't work," and hung it up again. There was no response.

As soon as they reached a level plain, commanding a good view in all directions. Tanner halted the vehicle and Greg moved into the driver's seat.

"Where do you think they got hold of that armor?"

The Magic

"Who knows?"

"And why stop us?"

"They didn't know what we were carrying—and maybe they just wanted the car."

"Blasting, it's a helluva way to get it."

"If they can't have it, why should they let us keep it?"

"You know just how they think, don't you?"

"Yes."

"Have a cigarette."

Tanner nodded, accepted.

"It's been pretty bad, you know?"

"I can't argue with that."

" . . . And we've still got a long way to go."

"Yeah, so let's get rolling."

"You said before that you didn't think we'd make it."

"I've revised my opinion. Now I think we will."

"After all we've been through?"

"After all we've been through."

"What more do we have to fight with?"

"I don't know all that yet."

"But on the other hand, we know everything there is behind us. We know how to avoid a lot of it now."

Tanner nodded.

"You tried to cut out once. Now I don't blame you."

"You getting scared, Greg?"

"I'm no good to my family if I'm dead."

"Then why'd you agree to come along?"

"I didn't know it would be like this. You had better sense, because you had an idea what it would be like."

"I had an idea."

"Nobody can blame us if we fail. After all, we've tried."

"What about all those people in Boston you made me a speech about?"

"They're probably dead by now. The plague isn't a thing that takes its time, you know?"

"What about that guy Brady? He died to get us the news."

"He tried, and God knows I respect the attempt. But we've already lost four guys. Now should we make it six, just to show that everybody tried?"

"Greg, we're a lot closer to Boston than we are to L.A. now. The tanks should have enough fuel in them to get us where we're going, but not to take us back from here."

"We can refuel in Salt Lake."

"I'm not even sure we could make it back to Salt Lake."

"Well, it'll only take a minute to figure it out. For that matter, though, we could take the bikes for the last hundred or so. They use a lot less gas,"

"And you're the guy who was calling me names. You're the citizen was wondering how people like me happen. You asked me what they ever did to me. I told you, too: Nothing. Now maybe I want to do something for them, just because I feel like it. I've been doing a lot of thinking."

"You ain't supporting any family. Hell. I've got other people to worry about beside myself.

"You've got a nice way of putting things when you want to chicken out. You say I'm not really scared, but I've got my mother and my brothers and sisters to worry about, and I got a chick I'm hot on. That's why I'm backing down. No other reason.

"And that's right, too! I don't understand you. Hell! I don't understand you at all! You're the one who put this idea in my head in the first place!"

"So give it back, and let's get moving."

He saw Greg's hand slither toward the gun on the door, so he flipped his cigarette into his face and managed to hit him once, in the stomach—a weak, left-handed blow, but it was the best he could manage from that position.

Then Greg threw himself upon him, and he felt himself borne back into his seat. They wrestled, and Greg's fingers clawed their way up to his face toward his eyes.

The Magic

Tanner got his arms free above the elbows, seized Greg's head, twisted and shoved with all his strength.

Greg hit the dashboard, went stiff, then went slack.

Tanner banged his head against it twice more, just to be sure he wasn't faking. Then he pushed him away and moved back into the driver's seat. He checked all the screens while he caught his breath. There was nothing menacing approaching.

He fetched cord from the utility chest and bound Greg's hands behind his back. He tied his ankles together and ran a line from them to his wrists. Then he positioned him in the seat, reclined it part way and tied him in place within it.

He put the car into gear and headed toward Ohio.

Two hours later Greg began to moan, and Tanner turned the music up to drown him out. Landscape had appeared once more: grass and trees, fields of green, orchards of apples, apples still small and green, white farm houses and brown barns and red barns far removed from the roadway he raced along; rows of corn, green and swaying, brown tassels already visible and obviously tended by someone; fences of split timber, green hedges; lofty, star-leafed maples, fresh-looking road signs, a green-shingled steeple from which the sound of a bell came forth.

The lines in the sky widened, but the sky itself did not darken, as it usually did before a storm. So he drove on into the afternoon, until he reached the Dayton Abyss.

He looked down into the fog-shrouded canyon that had caused him to halt. He scanned to the left and the right, decided upon the left and headed north.

Again, the radiation level was high. And he hurried, slowing only to skirt the crevices, chasms and canyons that emanated from that dark, deep center. Thick yellow vapors seeped forth from some of these and filled the air before him. At one point they were all about him, like a clinging, sulphurous cloud, and a breeze came and parted them. Involuntarily then, he hit the brake, and the car jerked and halted and Greg moaned once more. He stared at the thing for the few seconds that it was visible, then slowly moved forward again.

The sight was not duplicated for the whole of his passage, but it did not easily go from out of his mind, and he could not explain it where he had seen it. Yellow, hanging and grinning, he had seen a crucified skeleton there beside the Abyss. *People*, he decided. *That explains everything.*

*

When he left the region of fogs the sky was still dark. He did not realize for a time that he was in the open once more. It had taken him close to four hours to skirt Dayton, and now as he headed across a blasted heath, going east again, he saw for a moment, a tiny piece of the sun, like a sickle, fighting its way ashore on the northern bank of a black river in the sky, and failing.

His lights were turned up to their fullest intensity, and as he realized what might follow he looked in every direction for shelter.

There was an old barn on a hill, and he raced toward it. One side had caved in, and the doors had fallen down. He edged in, however, and the interior was moist and moldy looking under his lights. He saw a skeleton which he guessed to be that of a horse within a fallen-down stall.

He parked and turned off his lights and waited.

Soon the wailing came again and drowned out Greg's occasional moans and mutterings. There came another sound, not hard and heavy like gunfire, as that which he had heard in L.A., but gentle, steady and almost purring.

He cracked the door, to hear it better.

Nothing assailed him, so he stepped down from the cab and walked back a way. The radiation level was almost normal, so he didn't bother with his protective suit. He walked back toward the fallen doors and looked outside. He wore the pistol behind his belt.

Something gray descended in droplets and the sun fought itself partly free once more.

It was rain, pure and simple. He had never seen rain, pure and simple, before. So he lit a cigarette and watched it fall.

The Magic

It came down with only an occasional rumbling and nothing else accompanied it. The sky was still a bluish color beyond the bands of black.

It fell all about him. It ran down the frame to his left. A random gust of wind blew some droplets into his face, and he realized that they were water, nothing more. Puddles formed on the ground outside. He tossed a chunk of wood into one and saw it splash and float. From somewhere high up inside the barn he heard the sounds of birds. He smelled the sick-sweet smell of decaying straw. Off in the shadows to his right he saw a rusted threshing machine. Some feathers drifted down about him, and he caught one in his hand and studied it. Light, dark, fluffy, ribbed. He'd never really looked at a feather before. It worked almost like a zipper, the way the individual branches clung to one another. He let it go, and the wind caught it, and it vanished somewhere toward his back. He looked out once more, and back along his trail. He could probably drive through what was coming down now. But he realized just how tired he was. He found a barrel and sat down on it and lit another cigarette.

It had been a good run so far; and he found himself thinking about its last stages. He couldn't trust Greg for awhile yet. Not until they were so far that there could be no turning back. Then they'd need each other so badly that he could turn him loose. He hoped he hadn't scrambled his brains completely. He didn't know what more the Alley held. If the storms were less from here on in, however, that would be a big help.

He sat there for a long while, feeling the cold, moist breezes; and the rainfall lessened after a time, and he went back to the car and started it. Greg was still unconscious, he noted, as he backed out. This might not be good.

He took a pill to keep himself alert and he ate some rations as he drove along. The rain continued to come down, but gently. It fell all the way across Ohio, and the sky remained overcast. He crossed into West Virginia at the place called Parkersburg, and then he veered slightly to the north, going by the old Rand-McNally he'd been furnished. The gray day went away into black night, and he drove on.

Roger Zelazny and Samuel R. Delany

There were no more of the dark bats around to trouble him, but he passed several more craters and the radiation gauge rose, and at one point a pack of huge wild dogs pursued him, baying and howling, and they ran along the road and snapped at his tires and barked and yammered and then fell back. There were some tremors beneath his wheels as he passed another mountain that spewed forth bright clouds to his left and made a kind of thunder. Ashes fell, and he drove through them. A flash flood splashed over him, and the engine sputtered and died, twice; but be started it again each time and pushed on ahead, the waters lapping about his sides. Then he reached higher, drier ground, and riflemen tried to bar his way. He strafed them and hurled a grenade and drove on by. When the darkness went away and the dim moon came up, dark birds circled him and dove down at him, but he ignored them and after a time they, too, were gone.

He drove until he felt tired again, and then he ate some more and took another pill. By then he was in Pennsylvania, and he felt that if Greg would only come around he would turn him loose and trust him with the driving.

He halted twice to visit the latrine, and he tugged at the golden band in his pierced left ear, and he blew his nose and scratched himself. Then he ate more rations and continued on.

He began to ache, in all his muscles, and he wanted to stop and rest, but he was afraid of the things that might come upon him if he did.

As he drove through another dead town, the rains started again. Not hard, just a drizzly downpour, cold-looking and sterile—a brittle, shiny screen. He stopped in the middle of the road before the thing he'd almost driven into, and he stared at it.

He'd thought at first that it was more black lines in the sky. He'd halted because they'd seemed to appear too suddenly.

It was a spider's web, strands thick as his arm, strung between two leaning buildings.

He switched on his forward flame and began to burn it.

When the fires died, he saw the approaching shape, coming down from high above.

It was a spider, larger than himself, rushing to check the disturbance.

He elevated the rocket launchers, took careful aim and pierced it with one white-hot missile.

It still hung there in the trembling web and seemed to be kicking.

He turned on the flame again, for a full ten seconds, and when it subsided there was an open way before him.

He rushed through, wide awake and alert once again, his pains forgotten. He drove as fast as he could, trying to forget the sight.

Another mountain smoked ahead and to his right, but it did not bloom, and few ashes descended as he passed it.

He made coffee and drank a cup. After awhile it was morning, and he raced toward it.

XI

He was stuck in the mud, somewhere in eastern Pennsylvania, and cursing. Greg was looking very pale. The sun was nearing midheaven. He leaned back and closed his eyes. It was too much.

He slept.

He awoke and felt worse. There was a banging on the side of the car. His hands moved toward fire-control and wing-control, automatically, and his eyes sought the screens.

He saw an old man, and there were two younger men with him. They were armed, but they stood right before the left wing, and he knew he could cut them in half in an instant.

He activated the outside speaker and the audio pickup.

"What do you want?" he asked, and his voice crackled forth.

"You okay?" the old man called.

"Not really. You caught me sleeping."

"You stuck?"

"That's about the size of it."

"I got a mule team can maybe get you out. Can't get 'em here before tomorrow morning, though."

"Great!" said Tanner. "I'd appreciate it."

"Where you from?"

"L.A."

"What's that?"

"Los Angeles. West Coast."

There was some murmuring, then, "You're a long way from home, mister."

"Don't I know it. —Look, if you're serious about those mules, I'd appreciate hell out of it. It's an emergency."

"What kind of?"

"You know about Boston?"

"I know it's there."

"Well, people are dying up that way of the plague. I've got drugs here can save them, if I can get through."

There were some more murmurs, then, "We'll help you. Boston's pretty important, and we'll get you loose. Want to come back with us?"

"Where? And who are you?"

"The name's Samuel Potter, and these are my sons, Roderick and Caliban. My farm's about six miles off. You're welcome to spend the night."

"It's not that I don't trust you," said Tanner. "It's just that I don't trust anybody, if you know what I mean. I've been shot at too much recently to want to take the chance."

"Well, how about if we put up our guns? You're probably able to shoot us from there, ain't you?"

"That's right."

"So we're taking a chance just standing here. We're willing to help you. We'd stand to lose if the Boston traders stopped coming to Albany. If there's someone else inside, he can cover you."

"Wait a minute," said Tanner, and he opened the door.

The old man stuck out his hand, and Tanner took it and shook it, also his sons'.

"Is there any kind of doctor around here?" he asked.

"In the settlement—about thirty miles north."

"My partner's hurt. I think he needs a doctor." He gestured back toward the cab.

Sam moved forward and peered within.

"Why's he all trussed up like that?"

"He went off his rocker, and I had to clobber him. I tied him up, to be safe. But now he doesn't look so good."

"Then let's whip up a stretcher and get him onto it. You lock up tight then, and my boys'll bring him back to the house. We'll send someone for the Doc. You don't look so good yourself. Bet you'd like a bath and a shave and a clean bed."

"I don't feel so good," Tanner said. "Let's make that stretcher quick, before we need two."

He sat upon the fender and smoked while the Potter boys cut trees and stripped them. Waves of fatigue washed over him, and he found it hard to keep his eyes open. His feet felt very far away, and his shoulders ached. The cigarette fell from his fingers, and he leaned backward on the hood.

Someone was slapping his leg.

He forced his eyes open and looked down.

"Okay," Potter said. "We cut your partner loose and we got him on the stretcher. Want to lock up and get moving?"

Tanner nodded and jumped down. He sank almost up to his boot tops when he hit, but he closed the cab and staggered toward the old man in buckskin.

They began walking across country, and after awhile it became mechanical.

Samuel Potter kept up a steady line of chatter as he led the way, rifle resting in the crook of his arm. Maybe it was to keep Tanner awake.

"It's not too far, son, and it'll be pretty easy going in just a few minutes now. What'd you say your name was anyhow?"

"Hell," said Tanner.

"Beg pardon?"

"Hell. Hell's my name. Hell Tanner."

Sam Potter chuckled. "That's a pretty mean name, mister. If it's okay with you, I'll introduce you to my wife and the youngest as 'Mister Tanner.' All right?"

"That's just fine," Tanner gasped, pulling his boots out of the mire with a sucking sound.

"We'd sure miss them Boston traders. I hope you make it in time."

"What is it that they do?"

"They keep shops in Albany, and twice a year they give a fair—spring and fall. They carry all sort of things we need—needles, thread, pepper, kettles, pans, seed, guns and ammo, all kind of things—and the fairs are pretty good times, too. Most anybody between here and there would help you along. Hope you make it. We'll get you off to a good start again."

They reached higher, drier ground.

"You mean it's pretty clear sailing after this?"

"Well, no. But I'll help you on a map and tell you what to look out for."

"I got mine with me," said Tanner, as they topped a hill, and he saw a farm house off in the distance. "That your place?"

"Correct. It ain't much further now. Real easy walkin'—an' you just lean on my shoulder if you get tired."

"I can make it," said Tanner. "It's just that I had so many of those pills to keep me awake that I'm starting to feel all the sleep I've been missing. I'll be okay."

"You'll get to sleep real soon now. And when you're awake again, we'll go over that map of yours, and you can write in all the places I tell you about."

"Good scene," said Tanner, "good scene," and he put his hand on Sam's shoulder then and staggered along beside him, feeling almost drunk and wishing he were.

After a hazy eternity be saw the house before him, then the door. The door swung open, and he felt himself falling forward, and that was it.

The Magic

XII

Sleep. Blackness, distant voices, more blackness. Wherever he lay, it was soft, and he turned over onto his other side and went away again.

When everything finally flowed together into a coherent ball and he opened his eyes, there was light streaming in through the window to his right, falling in rectangles upon the patchwork quilt that covered him. He groaned, stretched, rubbed his eyes and scratched his beard.

He surveyed the room carefully; polished wooden floors with handwoven rugs of blue and red and gray scattered about them, a dresser holding a white enamel basin with a few black spots up near its lip where some of the enamel had chipped away, a mirror on the wall behind him and above all that, a spindly looking rocker near the window, a print cushion on its seat, a small table against the other wall with a chair pushed in beneath it, books and paper and pen and ink on the table, a hand-stitched sampler on the wall asking God To Bless, a blue and green print of a waterfall on the other wall.

He sat up, discovered he was naked, looked around for his clothing. It was nowhere in sight.

As he sat there, deciding whether or not to call out, the door opened, and Sam walked in. He carried Tanner's clothing, clean and neatly folded, over one arm. In his other hand he carried his boots, and they shone like wet midnight.

"Heard you stirring around," he said. "How you feeling now?"

"A lot better, thanks."

"We've got a bath all drawn. Just have to dump in a couple buckets of hot, and it's all yours. I'll have the boys carry it in in a minute, and some soap and towels."

Tanner bit his lip, but he didn't want to seem inhospitable to his benefactor, so he nodded and forced a smile then.

"That'll be fine."

" . . . And there's a razor and a scissors on the dresser —whichever you might want."

He nodded again. Sam set his clothes down on the rocker and his boots on the floor beside it, then left the room.

Soon Roderick and Caliban brought in the tub, spread some sacks and set it upon them.

"How you feeling?" one of them asked. (Tanner wasn't sure which was which. They both seemed graceful as scarecrows, and their mouths were packed full of white teeth.)

"Real good," he said.

"Bet you're hungry," said the other. "You slep' all afternoon yesterday and all night and most of this morning."

"You know it," said Tanner. "How's my partner?"

The nearer one shook his head. "Still sleeping and sickly," he said. "The doc should be here soon. Our kid brother went after him last night."

They turned to leave, and the one who had been speaking added, "Soon as you get cleaned up, Ma'll fix you something to eat. Cal and me are going out now to try and get your rig loose. Dad'll tell you about the roads while you eat."

"Thanks."

"Good morning to you."

"'Morning."

They closed the door behind them as they left.

Tanner got up and moved to the mirror, studied himself. "Well, just this once," he muttered.

Then he washed his face and trimmed his beard and cut his hair.

Then, gritting his teeth, he lowered himself into the tub, soaped up and scrubbed. The water grew gray and scummy beneath the suds. He splashed out and toweled himself down and dressed.

He was starched and crinkly and smelled faintly of disinfectant. He smiled at his dark-eyed reflection and lit a cigarette. He combed his hair and studied the stranger. "Damn! I'm beautiful!" he chuckled, and then he opened the door and entered the kitchen.

The Magic

Sam was sitting at the table drinking a cup of coffee, and his wife who was short and heavy and wore long gray skirts was facing in the other direction, leaning over the stove. She turned, and he saw that her face was large, with bulging red cheeks that dimpled and a little white scar in the middle of her forehead. Her hair was brown, shot through with gray, and pulled back into a knot. She bobbed her head and smiled a "Good morning" at him.

"'Morning," he replied. "I'm afraid I left kind of a mess in the other room."

"Don't worry about that," said Sam. "Seat yourself. and we'll have you some breakfast in a minute. The boys told you about your friend?"

Tanner nodded.

As she placed a cup of coffee in front of Tanner, Sam said, "Wife's name's Susan."

"How do," she said.

"Hi."

"Now, then, I got your map here. Saw it sticking out of your jacket. That's your gun hanging aside the door, too. Anyhow, I've been figuring and I think the best way you could head would be up to Albany and then go along the old Route 9, which is in pretty good shape." He spread the map and pointed as he talked. "Now, it won't be all of a picnic," he said, "but it looks like the cleanest and fastest way in—"

"Breakfast," said his wife and pushed the map aside to set a plate full of eggs and bacon and sausages in front of Tanner and another one, holding four pieces of toast, next to it. There was marmalade, jam, jelly and butter on the table, and Tanner helped himself to it and sipped the coffee and filled the empty places inside while Sam talked.

He told him about the gangs that ran between Boston and Albany on bikes, hijacking anything they could, and that was the reason most cargo went in convoys with shotgun riders aboard. "But you don't have to worry, with that rig of yours, do you?" he asked.

Tanner said, "Hope not," and wolfed down more food. He wondered, though, if they were anything like his old pack, and he hoped not, again, for both their sakes.

Tanner raised his coffee cup, and he heard a sound outside.

The door opened, and a boy ran into the kitchen. Tanner figured him as between ten and twelve years of age. An older man followed him, carrying the traditional black bag.

"We're here! We're here!" cried the boy, and Sam stood and shook hands with the man, so Tanner figured he should, too. He wiped his mouth and gripped the man's hand and said, "My partner sort of went out of his head. He jumped me, and we had a fight. I shoved him, and he banged his head on the dashboard."

The doctor, a dark-haired man, probably in his late forties, wore a dark suit. His face was heavily lined, and his eyes looked tired. He nodded.

Sam said, "I'll take you to him," and he led him out through the door at the other end of the kitchen.

Tanner reseated himself and picked up the last piece of toast. Susan refilled his coffee cup, and he nodded to her.

"My name's Jerry," said the boy, seating himself in his father's abandoned chair. "Is your name, mister, really Hell?"

"Hush, you!" said his mother.

"'Fraid so," said Tanner.

" . . . And you drove all the way across the country? Through the Alley?"

"So far."

"What was it like?"

"Mean."

"What all'd you see?"

"Bats as big as this kitchen—some of them even bigger—on the other side of the Missus Hip. Lot of them in Saint Louis."

"What'd you do?"

"Shot 'em. Burned 'em. Drove through 'em."

"What else you see?"

The Magic

"Gila monsters. Big, technicolor lizards—the size of a barn. Dust Devils—big circling winds that sucked up one car. Fire-topped mountains. Real big thorn bushes that we had to burn. Drove through some storms. Drove over places where the ground was like glass. Drove along where the ground was shaking. Drove around big craters, all radioactive."

"Wish I could do that some day."

"Maybe you will, some day."

Tanner finished the food and lit a cigarette and sipped the coffee.

"Real good breakfast," he called out. "Best I've eaten in days. Thanks."

Susan smiled, then said, "Jerry, don't go an' pester the man."

"No bother, missus. He's okay."

"What's that ring on your hand?" said Jerry. "It looks like a snake."

"That's what it is," said Tanner, pulling it off. "It is sterling silver with red glass eyes, and I got it in a place called Tijuana. Here. You keep it."

"I couldn't take that," said the boy, and he looked at his mother, his eyes asking if he could. She shook her head from left to right, and Tanner saw it and said, "Your folks were good enough to help me out and get a doc for my partner and feed me and give me a place to sleep. I'm sure they won't mind if I want to show my appreciation a little bit and give you this ring." Jerry looked back at his mother, and Tanner nodded and she nodded too.

Jerry whistled and jumped up and put it on his finger.

"It's too big," he said.

"Here, let me mash it a bit for you. These spiral kind'll fit anybody if you squeeze them a little."

He squeezed the ring and gave it back to the boy to try on. It was still too big, so he squeezed it again and then it fit.

Jerry put it on and began to run from the room.

"Wait!" his mother said. "What do you say?"

He turned around and said, "Thank you, Hell."

"Mister Tanner," she said.

"Mister Tanner," the boy repeated, and the door banged behind him.

"That was good of you," she said.

566

Tanner shrugged.

"He liked it," he said. "Glad I could turn him on with it."

He finished his coffee and his cigarette, and she gave him another cup, and he lit another cigarette. After a time, Sam and the doctor came out of the other room, and Tanner began wondering where the family had slept the night before. Susan poured them both coffee, and they seated themselves at the table to drink it.

"Your friend's got a concussion," the doctor said. "I can't really tell how serious his condition is without getting X-rays, and there's no way of getting them here. I wouldn't recommend moving him, though."

Tanner said, "For how long?"

"Maybe a few days, maybe a couple weeks. I've left some medication and told Sam what to do for him. Sam says there's a plague in Boston and you've got to hurry. My advice is that you go on without him. Leave him here with the Potters. He'll be taken care of. He can go up to Albany with them for the Spring Fair and make his way to Boston from there on some commercial carrier. I think he'll be all right."

Tanner thought about it awhile, then nodded.

"Okay," he said, "if that's the way it's got to be."

"That's what I recommend."

They drank their coffee.

XIII

Tanner regarded his freed vehicle, said, "I guess I'll be going then," and nodded to the Potters. "Thanks," he said, and he unlocked the cab, climbed into it and started the engine. He put it into gear, blew the horn twice and started to move.

In the screen, he saw the three men waving. He stamped the accelerator, and they were gone from sight.

He sped ahead, and the way was easy. The sky was salmon pink. The earth was brown, and there was much green grass. The bright sun caught the day in a silver net.

The Magic

This part of the country seemed virtually untouched by the chaos that had produced the rest of the Alley. Tanner played music, drove along. He passed two trucks on the road and honked his horn each time. Once, he received a reply.

He drove all that day, and it was well into the night when he pulled into Albany. The streets themselves were dark, and only a few lights shone from the buildings. He drew up in front of a flickering red sign that said "BAR & GRILL," parked and entered.

It was small, and there was jukebox music playing, tunes he'd never heard before, and the lighting was poor, and there was sawdust on the floor.

He sat down at the bar and pushed the Magnum way down behind his belt so that it didn't show. Then he took off his jacket, because of the heat in the place, and he threw it on the stool next to him. When the man in the white apron approached, he said, "Give me a shot and a beer and a ham sandwich."

The man nodded his bald head and threw a shot glass in front of Tanner which he then filled. He siphoned off a foam-capped mug and hollered over his right shoulder.

Tanner tossed off the shot and sipped the beer. After a while, a white plate bearing a sandwich appeared on the sill across from him. After a longer while, the bartender passed, picked it up, and deposited it in front of him. He wrote something on a green chit and tucked it under the corner of the plate.

Tanner bit into the sandwich and washed it down with a mouthful of beer. He studied the people about him and decided they made the same noises as people in any other bar he'd ever been in. The old man to his left looked friendly, so he asked him, "Any news about Boston?"

The man's chin quivered between words, and it seemed a natural thing for him.

"No news at all. Looks like the merchants will close their shops at the end of the week."

"What day is today?"

"Tuesday."

Tanner finished his sandwich and smoked a cigarette while he drank the rest of his beer.

Then he looked at the check, and it said, ".85."

He tossed a dollar bill on top of it and turned to go.

He had taken two steps when the bartender called out, "Wait a minute, mister."

He turned around.

"Yeah?"

"What you trying to pull?"

"What do you mean?"

"What do you call this crap?"

"What crap?"

The man waved Tanner's dollar at him, and he stepped forward and inspected it.

"Nothing wrong I can see. What's giving you a pain?"

"That ain't money."

"You trying to tell me my money's no good?"

"That's what I said. I never seen no bill like that."

"Well, look at it real careful. Read that print down there at the bottom of it."

The room grew quiet. One man got off his stool and walked forward. He held out his hand and said, "Let me see it, Bill."

The bartender passed it to him, and the man's eyes widened.

"This is drawn on the Bank of the Nation of California."

"Well, that's where I'm from," said Tanner.

"I'm sorry, it's no good here," said the bartender.

"It's the best I got," said Tanner.

"Well, nobody'll make good on it around here. You got any Boston money on you?"

"Never been to Boston."

"Then how the hell'd you get here?"

The Magic

"Drove."

"Don't hand me that line of crap, son. Where'd you steal this?" It was the older man who had spoken.

"You going to take my money or ain't you?" said Tanner.

"I'm not going to take it." said the bartender.

"Then screw you," said Tanner, and he turned and walked toward the door.

As always, under such circumstances, he was alert to sounds at his back.

When he heard the quick footfall, he turned. It was the man who had inspected the bill that stood before him, his right arm extended.

Tanner's right hand held his leather jacket, draped over his right shoulder. He swung it with all his strength forward and down.

It struck the man on the top of his head, and he fell.

There came up a murmuring, and several people jumped to their feet and moved toward him.

Tanner dragged the gun from his belt and said, "Sorry, folks," and he pointed it, and they stopped.

"Now you probably ain't about to believe me," he said, "when I tell you that Boston's been hit by the plague, but it's true all right. Or maybe you will. I don't know. But I don't think you're going to believe that I drove here all the way from the nation of California with a car full of Haffikine antiserum. But that's just as right. You send that bill to the big bank in Boston, and they'll change it for you, all right, and you know it. Now I've got to be going, and don't anybody try to stop me. If you think I've been handing you a line, you take a look at what I drive away in. That's all I've got to say."

And he backed out the door and covered it while he mounted the cab. Inside, he gunned the engine to life, turned, and roared away.

In the rearview screen he could see the knot of people on the walk before the bar, watching him depart.

He laughed, and the apple-blossom moon hung dead ahead.

Roger Zelazny and Samuel R. Delany

XIV

Albany to Boston. A couple of hundred miles. He'd managed the worst of it. The terrors of Damnation Alley lay largely at his back now. Night. It flowed about him. The stars seemed brighter than usual. He'd make it, the night seemed to say.

He passed between hills. The road wasn't too bad. It wound between trees and high grasses. He passed a truck coming in his direction and dimmed his lights as it approached. It did the same.

It must have been around midnight that he came to the crossroads, and the lights suddenly nailed him from two directions.

He was bathed in perhaps thirty beams from the left and as many from the right.

He pushed the accelerator to the floor, and he heard engine after engine coming to life somewhere at his back. And he recognized the sounds.

They were all of them bikes.

They swung onto the road behind him.

He could have opened fire. He could have braked and laid down a cloud of flame. It was obvious that they didn't know what they were chasing. He could have launched grenades. He refrained, however.

It could have been him on the lead bike, he decided, all hot on hijack. He felt a certain sad kinship as his hand hovered above the fire-control.

Try to outrun them, first.

His engine was open wide and roaring, but he couldn't take the bikes.

When they began to fire, he knew that he'd have to retaliate. He couldn't risk their hitting a gas tank or blowing out his tires.

Their first few shots had been in the nature of a warning. He couldn't risk another barrage. If only they knew . . . .

The speaker!

He cut in and mashed the button and spoke:

"Listen, cats," he said. "All I got's medicine for the sick citizens in Boston. Let me through or you'll hear the noise."

The Magic

A shot followed immediately, so he opened fire with the fifty calibers to the rear.

He saw them fall, but they kept firing. So he launched grenades.

The firing lessened, but didn't cease.

So he hit the brakes, then the flame-throwers. He kept it up for fifteen seconds.

There was silence.

When the air cleared he studied the screens.

They lay all over the road, their bikes upset, their bodies fuming. Several were still seated, and they held rifles and pointed them, and he shot them down.

A few still moved, spasmodically, and he was about to drive on, when he saw one rise and take a few staggering steps and fall again.

His hand hesitated on the gearshift.

It was a girl.

He thought about it for perhaps five seconds, then jumped down from the cab and ran toward her.

As he did, one man raised himself on an elbow and picked up a fallen rifle.

Tanner shot him twice and kept running, pistol in hand.

The girl was crawling toward a man whose face had been shot away. Other bodies twisted about Tanner now, there on the road, in the glare of the tail beacons. Blood and black leather, the sounds of moaning and the stench of burned flesh were all about him.

When he got to the girl's side, she cursed him softly as he stopped.

None of the blood about her seemed to be her own.

He dragged her to her feet and her eyes began to fill with tears.

Everyone else was dead or dying, so Tanner picked her up in his arms and carried her back to the car. He reclined the passenger seat and put her into it, moving the weapons into the rear seat, out of her reach.

Then he gunned the engine and moved forward. In the rearview screen he saw two figures rise to their feet, then fall again.

Roger Zelazny and Samuel R. Delany

She was a tall girl, with long, uncombed hair the color of dirt. She had a strong chin and a wide mouth and there were dark circles under her eyes. A single faint line crossed her forehead, and she had all of her teeth. The right side of her face was flushed, as if sunburned. Her left trouser leg was torn and dirty. He guessed that she'd caught the edge of his flame and fallen from her bike.

"You okay?" he asked, when her sobbing had diminished to a moist sniffing sound.

"What's it to you?" she said, raising a hand to her cheek.

Tanner shrugged.

"Just being friendly."

"You killed most of my gang."

"What would they have done to me?"

"They would have stomped you, mister, if it weren't for this fancy car of yours."

"It ain't really mine," he said. "It belongs to the nation of California."

"This thing don't come from California."

"The hell it don't. I drove it."

She sat up straight then and began rubbing her leg.

Tanner lit a cigarette.

"Give me a cigarette?" she said.

He passed her the one he had lighted, lit himself another. As he handed it to her, her eyes rested on his tattoo.

"What's that?"

"My name."

"Hell?"

"Hell."

"Where'd you get a name like that?"

"From my old man."

They smoked awhile, then she said, "Why'd you run the Alley?"

"Because it was the only way I could get them to turn me loose."

"From where?"

The Magic

"The place with horizontal Venetian blinds. I was doing time."

"They let you go? Why?"

"Because of the big sick. I'm bringing in Haffikine antiserum."

"You're Hell Tanner."

"Huh?"

"Your last name's Tanner, ain't it?"

"That's right. Who told you?"

"I heard about you. Everybody thought you died in the Big Raid."

"They were wrong."

"What was it like?"

"I dunno. I was already wearing a zebra suit. That's why I'm still around."

"Why'd you pick me up?"

"'Cause you're a chick, and 'cause I didn't want to see you croak."

"Thanks. You got anything to eat in here?"

"Yeah, there's food in there." He pointed to the refrigerator door. "Help yourself."

She did, and as she ate Tanner asked her, "What do they call you?"

"Corny," she said. "It's short for Cornelia."

"Okay, Corny," he said. "When you're finished eating, you start telling me about the road between here and the place."

She nodded, chewed and swallowed. "There's lots of other gangs," she said. "So you'd better be ready to blast them."

"I am."

"Those screens show you all directions, huh?"

"That's right."

"Good. The roads are pretty much okay from here on in. There's one big crater you'll come to soon and a couple little volcanos afterward."

"Check."

"Outside of them there's nothing to worry about but the Regents and the Devils and the Kings and the Lovers. That's about it."

Tanner nodded.

"How big are those clubs?"

574

"I don't know for sure but the Kings are the biggest. They've got a coupla hundred."

"What was your club?"

"The Studs."

"What are you going to do now?"

"Whatever you tell me."

"Okay, Corny, I'll let you off anywhere along the way that you want me to. If you don't want, you can come on into the city with me."

"You call it. Hell. Anywhere you want to go, I'll go along."

Her voice was deep, and her words came slowly, and her tone sandpapered his eardrums just a bit. She had long legs and heavy thighs beneath the tight denim. Tanner licked his lips and studied the screens. Did he want to keep her around for awhile?

The road was suddenly wet. It was covered with hundreds of fish, and more were falling from the sky. There followed several loud reports from overhead. The blue light began in the north.

Tanner raced on, and suddenly there was water all about him. It fell upon his car, it dimmed his screens. The sky had grown black again, and the banshee wail sounded above him.

He skidded around a sharp curve in the road. He turned up his lights.

The rain ceased, but the wailing continued. He ran for fifteen minutes before it built up into a roar.

The girl stared at the screens and occasionally glanced at Tanner.

"What're you going to do?" she finally asked him.

"Outrun it, if I can," he said.

"It's dark for as far ahead as I can see. I don't think you can do it."

"Neither do I, but what does that leave?"

"Hole up someplace."

"If you know where, you show me."

"There's a place a few miles further ahead—a bridge you can get under."

"Okay, that's for us. Sing out when you see it."

The Magic

She pulled off her boots and rubbed her feet. He gave her another cigarette.

"Hey, Corny—I just thought—there's a medicine chest over there to your right. Yeah, that's it. It should have some damn kind of salve in it you can smear on your face to take the bite out."

She found a tube of something and rubbed some of it into her cheek, smiled slightly and replaced it.

"Feel any better?"

"Yes. Thanks."

The stones began to fall, the blue to spread. The sky pulsed, grew brighter.

"I don't like the looks of this one."

"I don't like the looks of any of them."

"It seems there's been an awful lot this past week."

"Yeah. I've heard it said maybe the winds are dying down—that the sky might be purging itself."

"That'd be nice," said Tanner.

"Then we might be able to see it the way it used to look—blue all the time, and with clouds. You know about clouds."

"I heard about them."

"White, puffy things that just sort of drift across—sometimes gray. They don't drop anything except rain, and not always that."

"Yeah, I know."

"You ever see any out in L.A. ?"

"No."

The yellow streaks began, and the black lines writhed like snakes. The stonefall rattled heavily upon the roof and the hood. More water began to fall, and a fog rose up. Tanner was forced to slow, and then it seemed as if sledgehammers beat upon the car.

"We won't make it," she said.

"The hell you say. This thing's built to take it—and what's that off in the distance?"

"The bridge!" she said, moving forward. "That's it! Pull off the road to the left and go down. That's a dry riverbed beneath."

Then the lightning began to fall. It flamed, flashed about them. They passed a burning tree, and there were still fishes in the roadway.

Tanner turned left as he approached the bridge. He slowed to a crawl and made his way over the shoulder and down the slick, muddy grade.

When he hit the damp riverbed he turned right. He nosed it in under the bridge, and they were all alone there. Some waters trickled past them, and the lightning continued to flash. The sky was a shifting kaleidoscope and constant came the thunder. He could hear a sound like hail on the bridge above them.

"We're safe," he said and killed the engine.

"Are the doors locked?"

"They do it automatically."

Tanner turned off the outside lights.

"Wish I could buy you a drink, besides coffee."

"Coffee'd be good, just right."

"Okay, it's on the way," and he cleaned out the pot and filled it and plugged it in.

They sat there and smoked as the storm raged, and he said, "You know, it's a kind of nice feeling, being all snug as a rat in a hole while everything goes to hell outside. Listen to that bastard come down! And we couldn't care less."

"I suppose so," she said. "What're you going to do after you make it to Boston?"

"Oh, I don't know . . . . Maybe get a job, scrape up some loot, and maybe open a bike shop or a garage. Either one'd be nice."

"Sounds good. You going to ride much yourself?"

"You bet. I don't suppose they have any good clubs in town?"

"No. They're all roadrunners."

"Thought so. Maybe I'll organize my own."

He reached out and touched her hand, then squeezed it.

The Magic

"I can buy *you* a drink."

"What do you mean?"

She drew a plastic flask from the right side pocket of her jacket. She uncapped it and passed it to him.

"Here."

He took a mouthful and gulped it, coughed, took a second, then handed it back.

"Great! You're a woman of unsuspected potential and like that. Thanks."

"Don't mention it." She took a drink herself and set the flask on the dash.

"Cigarette?"

"Just a minute."

He lit two, passed her one.

"There you are. Corny."

"Thanks. I'd like to help you finish this run."

"How come?"

"I got nothing else to do. My crowd's all gone away, and I've got nobody else to run with now. Also, if you make it, you'll be a big man. Like capital letters. Think you might keep me around after that?"

"Maybe. What are you like?"

"Oh, I'm real nice. I'll even rub your shoulders for you when they're sore."

"They're sore now."

"I thought so. Give me a lean."

He bent toward her, and she began to rub his shoulders. Her hands were quick and strong.

"You do that good, girl."

"Thanks."

He straightened up, leaned back. Then he reached out, took the flask and had another drink. She took a small sip when he passed it to her.

The furies rode about them, but the bridge above stood the siege. Tanner turned off the lights.

"Let's make it," he said, and he seized her and drew her to him.

She did not resist him, and he found her belt buckle and unfastened it. Then he started on the buttons. After awhile, he reclined her seat.

"Will you keep me?" she asked him.

"Sure."

"I'll help you. I'll do anything you say to get you through."

"Great."

"After all, if Boston goes, then we go, too."

"You bet."

Then they didn't say much more.

There was violence in the skies, and after that came darkness and quiet.

XV

When Tanner awoke, it was morning and the storm had ceased. He repaired himself to the rear of the vehicle and after that assumed the driver's seat once more.

Cornelia did not awaken as he gunned the engine to life and started up the weed-infested slope of the hillside.

The sky was light once more, and the road was strewn with rubble. Tanner wove along it, heading toward the pale sun, and after awhile Cornelia stretched.

"Ungh," she said, and Tanner agreed. "My shoulders are better now," he told her.

"Good," and Tanner headed up a hill, slowly as the day dimmed and one huge black line became the Devil's highway down the middle of the sky.

As he drove through a wooded valley, the rain began to fall. The girl had returned from the rear of the vehicle and was preparing breakfast when Tanner saw the tiny dot on the horizon, switched over to his telescope lenses and tried to outrun what he saw.

Cornelia looked up.

There were bikes, bikes and more bikes on their trail.

"Those your people?" Tanner asked.

"No. You took mine yesterday."

The Magic

"Too bad," said Tanner, and he pushed the accelerator to the floor and hoped for a storm.

They squealed around a curve and climbed another hill. His pursuers drew nearer. He switched back from telescope to normal screening, but even then he could see the size of the crowd that approached.

"It must be the Kings," she said. "They're the biggest club around."

"Too bad," said Tanner.

"For them or for us?"

"Both."

She smiled.

"I'd like to see how you work this thing."

"It looks like you're going to get a chance. They're gaining on us like mad."

The rain lessened, but the fogs grew heavier. Tanner could see their lights, though, over a quarter mile to his rear, and be did not turn his own on. He estimated a hundred to a hundred fifty pursuers that cold, dark morning, and he asked, "How near are we to Boston?"

"Maybe ninety miles," she told him.

'Too bad they're chasing us instead of coming toward us," he said, as he primed his flames and set an adjustment which brought cross-hairs into focus on his rearview screen.

"What's that?" she asked.

"That's a cross. I'm going to crucify them, lady," and she smiled at this and squeezed his arm.

"Can I help? I hate those bloody mothers."

"In a little while," said Tanner. "In a little while, I'm sure," and he reached into the rear seat and fetched out the six hand grenades and hung them on his wide, black belt. He passed the rifle to the girl. "Hang onto this," he said, and stuck the .45 behind his belt.

"Do you know how to use that thing?"

"Yes," she replied immediately.

"Good."

He kept watching the lights that danced on the screen.

"Why the hell doesn't this storm break?" he said, as the lights came closer and he could make out shapes within the fog.

When they were within a hundred feet he fired the first grenade. It arched through the gray air, and five seconds later there was a bright flash to his rear, burning within a thunderclap.

The lights immediately behind him remained, and he touched the fifty-calibers, moving the cross-hairs from side to side. The guns shattered their loud syllables, and he launched another grenade. With the second flash, he began to climb another hill.

"Did you stop them?"

"For a time, maybe. I still see some lights, but farther back."

After five minutes, they had reached the top, a place where the fogs were cleared and the dark sky was visible above them. Then they started downward once more, and a wall of stone and shale and dirt rose to their right. Tanner considered it as they descended.

When the road leveled and he decided they had reached the bottom, he turned on his brightest lights and looked for a place where the road's shoulders were wide.

To his rear, there were suddenly rows of descending lights.

He found the place where the road was sufficiently wide, and he skidded through a U-turn until he was facing the shaggy cliff, now to his left, and his pursuers were coming dead on.

He elevated his rockets, fired one, elevated them five degrees more, fired two, elevated them another five degrees, fired three. Then he lowered them fifteen and fired another.

There was brightness within the fog, and he heard the stones rattling on the road and felt the vibration as the rockslide began. He swung toward his right as he backed the vehicle and fired two ahead. There was dust, mixed with the fog now, and the vibration continued.

He turned and headed forward once more.

"I hope that'll hold 'em," he said, and he lit two cigarettes and passed one to the girl.

The Magic

After five minutes they were on higher ground again and the winds came and whipped at the fog, and far to the rear there were still some lights.

As they topped a high rise, his radiation gauge began to register an above-normal reading. He sought in all directions and saw the crater far off ahead. "That's it," he heard her say. "You've got to leave the road there. Bear to the right and go around that way when you get there."

"I'll do that thing."

He heard gunshots from behind him, for the first time that day, and though he adjusted the cross-hairs he did not fire his own weapons. The distance was still too great.

"You must have cut them in half," she said, staring into the screen. "More than that. They're a tough bunch, though."

"I gather," and he plowed the field of mists and checked his supply of grenades for the launcher and saw that he was running low.

He swung off the road to his right when he began bumping along over fractured concrete. The radiation level was quite high by then. The crater was slightly more than a thousand yards to his left.

The lights to his rear fanned out, grew brighter. He drew a bead on the brightest and fired. It went out.

"There's another down," he remarked, as they raced across the hard-baked plain.

The rains came more heavily, and he sighted in on another light and fired it. It, too, went out, though he heard the sounds of their weapons about him once again.

He switched to his right-hand guns and saw the crosshairs leap into life on that screen. As three vehicles moved in to flank him from that direction, he opened up and cut them down. There was more firing at his back, and he ignored it as he negotiated the way,

"I count twenty-seven lights," Cornelia said.

Tanner wove his way across a field of boulders. He lit another cigarette.

Five minutes later, they were running on both sides of him. He had held back again for that moment, to conserve ammunition and to be sure of his targets. He fired then, though, at every light within range, and he floored the accelerator and swerved around rocks.

"Five of them are down," she said, but he was listening to the gunfire.

He launched a grenade to the rear, and when he tried to launch a second there came only a clicking sound from the control. He launched one to either side and then paused for a second.

"If they get close enough, I'll show them some fire," he said, and they continued on around the crater.

He fired only at individual targets then, when he was certain they were within range. He took two more before he struck the broken roadbed.

"Keep running parallel to it," she told him. "There's a trail here. You can't drive on that stuff till another mile or so."

Shots richocheted from off his armored sides, and he continued to return the fire. He raced along an alleyway of twisted trees, like those he had seen near other craters, and the mists hung like pennons about their branches. He heard the rattle of the increasing rains.

When he hit the roadway once again, he regarded the lights to his rear and asked, "How many do you count now?"

"It looks like around twenty. How are we doing?"

"I'm just worried about the tires. They can take a lot, but they can be shot out. The only other thing that bothers me is that a stray shot might clip one of the 'eyes.' Outside of that we're bullet-proof enough. Even if they manage to stop us, they'll have to pry us out."

The bikes drew near once again, and he saw the bright flashes and heard the reports of the riders' guns.

"Hold tight." he said, and he hit the brakes and they skidded on the wet pavement.

The lights grew suddenly bright, and he unleashed his rear flame. As some bikes skirted him, he cut in the side flames and held them that way.

Then he took his foot off the brake and floored the accelerator without waiting to assess the damage he had done.

They sped ahead, and Tanner, heard Cornelia's laughter.

"God! You're taking them. Hell! You're taking the whole damn club!"

"It ain't that much fun," he said. Then, "See any lights?"

She watched for a time, said, "No," then said, "Three," then, "Seven," and finally, "Thirteen."

Tanner said. "Damn."

The radiation level fell and there came crashes amid the roaring overhead. A light fall of gravel descended for perhaps half a minute, along with the rain.

"We're running low," he said.

"On what?"

"Everything: Luck, fuel, ammo. Maybe you'd have been better off if I'd left you where I found you."

"No," she said. "I'm with you, the whole line."

"Then you're nuts," he said. "I haven't been hurt yet. When I am, it might be a different tune."

"Maybe," she said. "Wait and hear how I sing."

He reached out and squeezed her thigh.

"Okay, Corny. You've been okay so far. Hang onto that piece, and we'll see what happens."

He reached for another cigarette, found the pack empty, cursed. He gestured toward a compartment, and she opened it and got him a fresh pack. She tore it open and lit him one.

"Thanks."

"Why're they staying out of range?"

"Maybe they're just going to pace us. I don't know."

Then the fogs began to lift. By the time Tanner had finished his cigarette, the visibility had improved greatly. He could make out the dark forms crouched atop their bikes, following, following, nothing more.

"If they just want to keep us company, then I don't care," he said. "Let them."

But there came more gunfire after a time, and he heard a tire go. He slowed, but continued. He took careful aim and strafed them. Several fell.

More gunshots sounded from behind. Another tire blew, and he hit the brakes and skidded, turning about as he slowed. When he faced them, he shot his anchors, to hold him in place, and he discharged his rockets, one after another, at a level parallel to the road. He opened up with his guns and sprayed them as they veered off and approached him from the sides. Then he opened fire to the left. Then the right.

He emptied the right-hand guns, then switched back to the left. He launched the remaining grenades.

The gunfire died down, except for five sources—three to his left and two to his right—coming from somewhere within the trees that lined the road now. Broken bikes and bodies lay behind him, some still smouldering. The pavement was potted and cracked in many places.

He turned the car and proceeded ahead on six wheels.

"We're out of ammo, Corny," he told her.

"Well, we took an awful lot of them . . . . "

"Yeah."

As he drove on, he saw five bikes move onto the road. They stayed a good distance behind him, but they stayed.

He tried the radio, but there was no response. He hit the brakes and stopped, and the bikes stopped, too, staying well to the rear.

"Well, at least they're scared of us. They think we still have teeth."

"We do," she said.

"Yeah, but not the ones they're thinking about."

"Better yet."

"Glad I met you," said Tanner. "I can use an optimist. There must be a pony, huh?"

She nodded; he put it into gear and started forward abruptly.

The motorcycles moved ahead also, and they maintained a safe distance. Tanner watched them in the screens and cursed them as they followed.

After awhile they drew nearer again. Tanner roared on for half an hour, and the remaining five edged closer and closer.

The Magic

When they drew near enough, they began to fire, rifles resting on their handlebars.

Tanner heard several low ricochets, and then another tire went out.

He stopped once more, and the bikes did, too, remaining just out of range of his flames. He cursed and ground ahead again. The car wobbled as he drove, listing to the left. A wrecked pickup truck stood smashed against a tree to his right, its hunched driver a skeleton, its windows smashed and tires missing. Half a sun now stood in the heavens, reaching after nine o'clock; fog-ghosts drifted before them, and the dark band in the sky undulated and more rain fell from it, mixed with dust and small stones and bits of metal. Tanner said, "Good" as the pinging sounds began, and, "Hope it gets a lot worse" and his wish came true as the ground began to shake and the blue light began in the north. There came a booming within the roar, and there were several answering crashes as heaps of rubble appeared to his right. "Hope the next one falls right on our buddies back there," he said.

He saw an orange glow ahead and to his right. It had been there for several minutes, but he had not become conscious of it until just then.

"Volcano," she said when he indicated it. "It means we've got another sixty-five, seventy miles to go."

He could not tell whether any more shooting was occurring. The sounds coming from overhead and around him were sufficient to mask any gunfire, and the fall of gravel upon the car covered any ricocheting rounds. The five headlights to his rear maintained their pace.

"Why don't they give up?" he said. "They're taking a pretty bad beating."

"They're used to it," she replied, "and they're riding for blood, which makes a difference."

Tanner fetched the .357 Magnum from the door clip and passed it to her. "Hang onto this, too," he said, and he found a box of ammo in the second compartment and, "Put these in your pocket," he added. He stuffed ammo for the .45 into his own jacket. He adjusted the hand grenades upon his belt.

Then the five headlights behind him suddenly became four, and the others slowed, grew smaller. "Accident, I hope," he remarked.

Roger Zelazny and Samuel R. Delany

They sighted the mountain, a jag-topped cone bleeding fires upon the sky. They left the road and swung far to the left, upon a well marked trail. It took twenty minutes to pass the mountain, and by then he sighted their pursuers once again—four lights to the rear, gaining slowly.

He came upon the road once more and hurried ahead across the shaking ground. The yellow lights moved through the heavens; and heavy, shapeless objects, some several feet across, crashed to the earth about them. The car was buffeted by winds, listed as they moved, would not proceed above forty miles an hour. The radio contained only static.

Tanner rounded a sharp curve, hit the brake, turned off his lights, pulled the pin from a hand grenade and waited with his hand upon the door.

When the lights appeared in the screen, he flung the door wide, leaped down and hurled the grenade through the abrasive rain.

He was into the cab and moving again before he heard the explosion, before the flash occurred upon his screen.

The girl laughed almost hysterically as the car moved ahead.

"You got 'em, Hell. You got 'em!" she cried.

Tanner took a drink from her flask, and she finished its final brown mouthful.

The road grew cracked, pitted, slippery. They topped a high rise and headed downhill. The fog thickened as they descended.

Lights appeared before him, and he readied the flame. There were no hostilities, however, as he passed a truck headed in the other direction. Within the next half hour he passed two more.

There came more lightning, and fist-sized rocks began to fall. Tanner left the road and sought shelter within a grove of high trees. The sky grew competely black, losing even its blue aurora.

They waited for three hours, but the storm did not let up. One by one, the four view-screens went dead and the fifth only showed the blackness beneath the car. Tanner's last sight in the rearview screen was of a huge splintered tree with a broken, swaying branch that was about ready to fall off. There were several terrific crashes upon the hood and the car shook with each. The roof above their heads was deeply dented in three places. The lights grew dim, then bright again. The radio would not produce even static anymore.

"I think we've had it," he said.

"Yeah."

"How far are we?"

"Maybe fifty miles away."

"There's still a chance, if we live through this."

"What chance?"

"I've got two bikes in the rear."

They reclined their seats and smoked and waited, and after awhile the lights went out.

The storm continued all that day and into the night. They slept within the broken body of the car, and it sheltered them. When the storm ceased. Tanner opened the door and looked outside, closed it again.

"We'll wait till morning," he said, and she held his Hell-printed hand, and they slept.

XVI

In the morning, Tanner walked back through the mud and the fallen branches, the rocks and the dead fish, and he opened the rear compartment and unbolted the bikes. He fueled them and checked them out and wheeled them down the ramp.

He crawled into the back of the cab then and removed the rear seat. Beneath it, in the storage compartment, was the large aluminum chest that was his cargo. It was bolted shut. He lifted it, carried it out to his bike.

"That the stuff?" she asked.

He nodded and placed it on the ground.

"I don't know how the stuff is stored, if it's refrigerated in there or what," he said, "but it ain't too heavy that I might not be able to get it on the back of my bike. There's straps in the far right compartment. Go get 'em and give me a hand—and get me my pardon out of the middle compartment. It's in a big cardboard envelope."

She returned with these things and helped him secure the container on the rear of his bike.

He wrapped extra straps around his left biceps, and they wheeled the machines to the road.

"We'll have to take it kind of slow," he said, and he slung the rifle over his right shoulder, drew on his gloves and kicked his bike to life.

She did the same with hers, and they moved forward, side by side along the highway.

After they had been riding for perhaps an hour, two cars passed them, heading west. In the rear seats of both there were children, who pressed their faces to the glass and watched them as they went by. The driver of the second car was in his shirtsleeves and wore a black shoulder holster.

The sky was pink, and there were three black lines that looked as if they could be worth worrying about. The sun was a rose-tinted silvery thing, and pale, but Tanner still had to raise his goggles against it.

The pack was riding securely, and Tanner leaned into the dawn and thought about Boston. There was a light mist on the foot of every hill, and the air was cool and moist. Another car passed them. The road surface began to improve.

*

It was around noontime when he heard the first shot above the thunder of their engines. At first he thought it was a backfire, but it came again, and Corny cried out and swerved off the road and struck a boulder.

Tanner cut to the left, braking, as two more shots rang about him, and he leaned his bike against a tree and threw himself flat. A shot struck near his head and he could tell the direction from which it had come. He crawled into a ditch and drew off his right glove. He could see his girl lying where she had fallen, and there was blood on her breast. She did not move.

He raised the 30.06 and fired.

The shot was returned, and he moved to his left.

It had come from a hill about two hundred feet away, and he thought he saw the rifle's barrel.

The Magic

He aimed at it and fired again.

The shot was returned, and he wormed his way further left. He crawled perhaps fifteen feet until he reached a pile of rubble he could crouch behind. Then he pulled the pin on a grenade, stood and hurled it.

He threw himself flat as another shot rang out, and he took another grenade into his hand.

There was a roar and a rumble and a mighty flash, and the junk fell about him as he leaped to his feet and threw the second one, taking better aim this time.

After the second explosion, he ran forward with his rifle in his hands, but it wasn't necessary.

He only found a few small pieces of the man, and none at all of his rifle. He returned to Cornelia.

She wasn't breathing, and her heart had stopped beating, and he knew what that meant.

He carried her back to the ditch in which he had lain and he made it deeper by digging, using his hands.

He laid her down in it and he covered her with the dirt. Then he wheeled her machine over, set the kickstand, and stood it upon the grave. With his dagger, he scratched upon the fender: *Her name was Cornelia and I don't know how old she was or where she came from or what her last name was but she was Hell Tanner's girl and I love her.* Then he went back to his own machine, started it and drove ahead. Boston was maybe thirty miles away.

XVII

He drove along, and after a time he heard the sound of another bike. A Harley cut onto the road from the dirt path to his left, and he couldn't try running away from it because he couldn't speed with the load he bore. So he allowed himself to be paced.

After awhile, the rider of the other bike—a tall, thin man with a flaming beard—drew up alongside him, to the left. He smiled and raised his right hand and let it fall and then gestured with his head.

Tanner braked and came to a halt. Redbeard was right beside him when he did. He said, "Where you going, man?"

"Boston."

"What you got in the box?"

"Like, drugs."

"What kind?" and the man's eyebrows arched and the smile came again onto his lips.

"For the plague they got going there."

"Oh. I thought you meant the other kind."

"Sorry."

The man held a pistol in his right hand and he said, "Get off your bike."

Tanner did this, and the man raised his left hand and another man came forward from the brush at the side of the road. "Wheel this guy's bike about two hundred yards up the highway," he said, "and park it in the middle. Then take your place."

"What's the bit?" Tanner asked.

The man ignored the question. "Who are you?" he asked.

"Hell's the name," he replied. "Hell Tanner."

"Go to hell."

Tanner shrugged.

"You ain't Hell Tanner."

Tanner drew off his right glove and extended his fist.

"There's my name."

"I don't believe it," said the man, after he had studied the tattoo.

"Have it your way, citizen."

"Shut up!" and he raised his left hand once more, now that the other man had parked the machine on the road and returned to a place somewhere within the trees to the right.

In response to his gesture, there was movement within the brush.

Bikes were pushed forward by their riders, and they lined the road, twenty or thirty on either side.

"There you are," said the man. "My name's Big Brother."

The Magic

"Glad to meet you."

"You know what you're going to do, mister?"

"I can really just about guess."

"You're going to walk up to your bike and claim it."

Tanner smiled.

"How hard's that going to be?"

"No trouble at all. Just start walking. Give me your rifle first, though."

Big Brother raised his hand again, and one by one the engines came to life.

"Okay," he said. "Now."

"You think I'm crazy, man?"

"No. Start walking. Your rifle."

Tanner unslung it and he continued the arc. He caught Big Brother beneath his red beard, and he felt the bullet go into him. Then he dropped the weapon and hauled forth a grenade, pulled the pin and tossed it amid the left side of the gauntlet. Before it exploded, he'd pulled the pin on another and thrown it to his right. By then, though, vehicles were moving forward, heading toward him.

He fell upon the rifle and shouldered it in a prone firing position. As he did this, the first explosion occurred. He was firing before the second one went off.

He dropped three of them, then got to his feet and scrambled, firing from the hip.

He made it behind Big Brother's fallen bike and fired from there. Big Brother was still fallen, too. When the rifle was empty, he didn't have time to reload. He fired the .45 four times before a tire chain brought him down.

He awoke to the roaring of the engines. They were circling him. When he got to his feet, a handlebar knocked him down again.

Two bikes were moving about him, and there were many dead people upon the road. He struggled to rise again, was knocked off his feet.

Big Brother rode one of the bikes, and a guy he hadn't seen rode the other.

He crawled to the right, and there was pain in his fingertips as the tires passed over them.

But he saw a rock and waited till a driver was near. Then he stood again and threw himself upon the man as he passed, the rock he had seized rising and falling, once, in his right hand. He was carried along as this occurred, and as he fell he felt the second bike strike him.

There were terrible pains in his side, and his body felt broken, but he reached out even as this occurred and caught hold of a strut on the side of the bike and was dragged along by it.

Before he had been dragged ten feet, he had drawn his SS dagger from his boot. He struck upward and felt a thin metal wall give way. Then his hands came loose, and he fell and he smelled the gasoline. His hand dove into his jacket pocket and came out with the Zippo.

He had struck the tank on the side of Big Brother's bike, and it jetted forth its contents on the road. Twenty feet ahead. Big Brother was turning.

Tanner held the lighter, the lighter with the raised skull of enamel, wings on either side of it. His thumb spun the wheel and the sparks leaped forth, then the flame. He tossed it into the stream of petrol that lay before him, and the flames raced away, tracing a blazing trail upon the concrete.

Big Brother had turned and was bearing down upon him when he saw what had happened. His eyes widened, and his red-framed smile went away.

He tried to leap off his bike, but it was too late.

The exploding gas tank caught him, and he went down with a piece of metal in his head and other pieces elsewhere.

Flames splashed over Tanner, and he beat at them feebly with his hands.

He raised his head above the blazing carnage and let it fall again. He was bloody and weak and so very tired. He saw his own machine, standing still undamaged on the road ahead.

He began crawling toward it.

When he reached it, he threw himself across the saddle and lay there for perhaps ten minutes. He vomited twice, and his pains became a steady pulsing.

After perhaps an hour, he mounted the bike and brought it to life.

He rode for half a mile and then dizziness and the fatigue hit him.

He pulled off to the side of the road and concealed his bike as best he could. Then he lay down upon the bare earth and slept.

XVIII

When he awoke, he felt dried blood upon his side. His left hand ached and was swollen. All four fingers felt stiff, and it hurt to try to bend them. His head throbbed and there was a taste of gasoline within his mouth. For a long while, he was too sore to move. His beard bad been singed, and his right eye was swollen almost shut.

"Corny . . . " he said, then, "Damn!"

Everything came back, like the contents of a powerful dream suddenly spilled into his consciousness.

He began to shiver, and there were mists all around him. It was very dark, and his legs were cold; the dampness had soaked completely through his denims.

In the distance, he heard a vehicle pass. It sounded like a car.

He managed to roll over, and he rested his head on his forearm. It seemed to be night, but it could be a black day.

As he lay there, his mind went back to his prison cell. It seemed almost a haven now; and he thought of his brother Denny, who must also be hurting at this moment. He wondered if he had any cracked ribs himself. It felt like it. And he thought of the monsters of the southwest and of dark-eyed Greg, who had tried to chicken out. Was he still living? His mind circled back to L.A. and the old Coast, gone, gone forever now, after the Big Raid. Then Corny walked past him, blood upon her breasts, and he chewed his beard and held his eyes shut very tight. They might have made it together in Boston. How far, now?

He got to his knees and crawled until he felt something high and solid. A tree. He sat with his back to it, and his hand sought the crumpled cigarette pack within his jacket. He drew one forth, smoothed it, then remembered that his lighter lay somewhere back on the highway. He sought through his pockets and found a damp matchbook. The third one lit. The chill went out of his bones as he smoked, and a wave of fever swept over him. He coughed as he was unbuttoning his collar, and it seemed that he tasted blood.

His weapons were gone, save for the lump of a single grenade at his belt.

Above him, in the darkness, he heard the roaring. After six puffs, the cigarette slipped from his fingers and sizzled out upon the damp mold. His head fell forward, and there was darkness within.

There might have been a storm. He didn't remember. When he awoke, he was lying on his right side, the tree to his back. A pink afternoon sun shone down upon him, and the mists were blown away. From somewhere, he heard the sound of a bird. He managed a curse, then realized how dry his throat was. He suddenly burned with a terrible thirst.

There was a clear puddle about thirty feet away. He crawled to it and drank his fill. It grew muddy as he did so.

Then he crawled to where his bike lay hidden and stood beside it. He managed to seat himself upon it, and his hands shook as he lit a cigarette.

*

It must have taken him an hour to reach the roadway, and he was panting heavily by then. His watch had been broken, so he didn't know the hour. The sun was already lowering at his back when he started out. The winds whipped about him, insulating his consciousness within their burning flow. His cargo rode securely behind him. He had visions of someone opening it and finding a batch of broken bottles. He laughed and cursed, alternately.

Several cars passed him, moving in the other direction. He had not seen any heading toward the city. The road was in good condition and he began to pass buildings that seemed in a good state of repair, though deserted. He did not stop. This time he determined not to stop for anything, unless he was stopped.

The sun fell farther, and the sky dimmed before him. There were two black lines swaying in the heavens. Then he passed a sign that told him he had eighteen miles farther to go. Ten minutes later he switched on his light.

Then he topped a hill and slowed before he began its descent.

There were lights below him and in the distance.

The Magic

As he rushed forward, the winds brought to him the sound of a single bell, tolling over and over within the gathering dark. He sniffed a remembered thing upon the air: it was the salt-tang of the sea.

The sun was hidden behind the hill as he descended, and he rode within the endless shadow. A single star appeared on the far horizon, between the two black belts.

Now there were lights within shadows that he passed, and the buildings moved closer together. He leaned heavily on the handlebars, and the muscles of his shoulders ached beneath his jacket. He wished that he had a crash helmet, for he felt increasingly unsteady.

He must almost be there. Where would he head once he hit the city proper? They had not told him that.

He shook his head to clear it.

The street he drove along was deserted. There were no traffic sounds that he could hear. He blew his horn, and its echoes rolled back upon him.

There was a light on in the building to his left.

He pulled to a stop, crossed the sidewalk and banged on the door. There was no response from within. He tried the door and found it locked. A telephone would mean he could end his trip right there.

What if they were all dead inside? The thought occurred to him that just about everybody could be dead by now. He decided to break in. He returned to his bike for a screwdriver, then went to work on the door.

He heard the gunshot and the sound of the engine at approximately the same time.

He turned around quickly, his back against the door, the hand grenade in his gloved right fist.

"Hold it!" called out a loudspeaker on the side of the black car that approached. "That shot was a warning! The next one won't be!"

Tanner raised his hands to a level with his ears, his right one turned to conceal the grenade. He stepped forward to the curb beside his bike when the car drew up.

Roger Zelazny and Samuel R. Delany

There were two officers in the car, and the one on the passenger side held a .38 pointed at Tanner's middle.

"You're under arrest," he said. "Looting."

Tanner nodded as the man stepped out of the car. The driver came around the front of the vehicle, a pair of handcuffs in his hand.

"Looting," the man with the gun repeated. "You'll pull a real stiff sentence."

"Stick your hands out here, boy," said the second cop, and Tanner handed him the grenade pin.

The man stared at it, dumbly, for several seconds, then his eyes shot to Tanner's right hand.

"God! He's got a bomb!" said the man with the gun.

Tanner smiled, then, "Shut up and listen!" he said. "Or else shoot me and we'll all go together when we go. I was trying to get to a telephone. That case on the back of my bike is full of Haffikine antiserura. I brought it from L.A."

"You didn't run the Alley on that bike!"

"No, I didn't. My car is dead somewhere between here and Albany, and so are a lot of folks who tried to stop me. Now you better take that medicine and get it where it's supposed to go."

"You on the level, mister?"

"My hand is getting very tired. I am not in good shape." Tanner leaned on his bike. "Here."

He pulled his pardon out of his jacket and handed it to the officer with the handcuffs. "That's my pardon," he said. "It's dated just last week and you can see it was made out in California."

The officer took the envelope and opened it. He withdrew the paper and studied it. "Looks real," he said, "So Brady made it through . . . . "

"He's dead," Tanner said. "Look, I'm hurtin'. Do something!"

"My God! Hold it tight! Get in the car and sit down! It'll just take a minute to get the case off and we'll roll. We'll drive to the river and you can throw it in. Squeeze real hard!"

The Magic

They unfastened the case and put it in the back of the car. They rolled down the right front window, and Tanner sat next to it with his arm on the outside.

The siren screamed, and the pain crept up Tanner's arm to his shoulder. It would be very easy to let go.

"Where do you keep your river?" he asked.

"Just a little farther. We'll be there in no time."

"Hurry," Tanner said.

"That's the bridge up ahead. We'll ride out onto it, and you throw it off—as far out as you can."

"Man, I'm tired! I'm not sure I can make it . . . . "

"Hurry, Jerry!"

"I am, damn it! We ain't got wings!"

"I feel kind of dizzy, too . . . . "

They tore out onto the bridge and the tires screeched as they halted. Tanner opened the door slowly. The driver's had already slammed shut.

He staggered, and they helped him to the railing. He sagged against it when they released him.

"I don't think I—"

Then he straightened, drew back his arm and hurled the grenade far out over the waters.

He grinned, and the explosion followed, far beneath them, and for a time the waters were troubled.

The two officers sighed and Tanner chuckled.

"I'm really okay," he said. "I just faked it to bug you."

"Why you—!"

Then he collapsed, and they saw the pallor of his face within the beams of their lights.

XIX

The following spring, on the day of its unveiling in Boston Common, when it was discovered that someone had scrawled obscene words on the

598

statue of Hell Tanner, no one thought to ask the logical candidate why he had done it, and the next day it was too late, because he had cut out without leaving a forwarding address. Several cars were reported stolen that day, and one was never seen again in Boston.

So they re-veiled his statue, bigger than life, astride a great bronze Harley, and they cleaned him up for hoped-for posterity. But coming upon the Common, the winds still break about him and the heavens still throw garbage.

A Word from Zelazny

"I intended to write a nice, simple action-adventure story and I had just finished reading Hunter Thompson's *Hell's Angels*."[1]

"I liked 'Damnation Alley' very much. I am very comfortable with the 'man against the elements' sort of theme; I was also very fond of Antoine de St. Exupéry's stories about the early days of airplane traffic: *Wind, Sand and Stars* and *Night Flight*. I thought it would be nice to put something like that into a science fiction setting, turning something loose against all the forces of nature. At the same time I had been thinking of anti-heroes; I considered using someone who had been sort of trapped into being a hero and reaching a point where he couldn't turn back."[2]

"That was the only time I patterned a character in a book on somebody I really knew. I knew a fellow when I was in the service in basic training who had been in a motorcycle gang. Later, when I was reading about Hell's Angels, it occurred to me that I did have some background just from talking to this man all that time, and it might make a nice story."[3]

"I wanted to do a straight, style-be-damned action story with the pieces fall wherever. Movement and menace. Splash and color is all.

"A continuing small thought as to how important it really is whether a good man does something for noble reasons or a man less ethically endowed does a good thing for the wrong reasons.

"Had the Noh play buried near the end of the book-length version been written first, I would probably not have written the book.

The Magic

"I like 'Damnation Alley' for the overall subjection of everything in it to a Stanislavsky-Boleslavsky action verb key, 'to get to Boston.' I dislike it for the same reason."[4]

"At my agent's suggestion, I later expanded it to book length. I like this version [reproduced here] better than the book. But if there hadn't been a book there probably wouldn't have been a movie sale. On the other hand, I was not overjoyed with the film. On the other hand, no one has had to sit up in the middle of the night to read the story . . . "

Zelazny was blunt about the movie: "No! No one liked that movie."[3] He had no role in the production: "they bought [the story] and could do what they wanted with it."[3] "Obviously, I had nothing to do with the production. I had read an early script and it was actually quite good. I thought that was the script they were going to shoot from. Initially the script was done by Lukas Heller . . . he did the script that I read and liked. The studio wasn't completely happy about it, though, and they gave it to another writer [Alan Sharp]. It got revised beyond recognition from my standpoint."[5] "All that remains of my story is the title and some of the special effects. Everything else, I disavow—except I took their money and I'd do it again."[6]

Notes

The guard with the shotgun has green eyes (**his eyes look like hourglasses filled with green sand**), the recurrent Zelazny motif. The novel version of *Damnation Alley* includes Evelyn with blue-green eyes. **Missus Hip** is the Mississippi River. **Excelsior** is wood shavings used for packing. A **Gila Monster** is a venomous lizard with black and orange or red stripes found in arid regions of Southwest United States and Western Mexico. **Chianti** is an Italian red wine. The **SS dagger** was produced for the German SS between 1939 and 1942; it had a black wooden grip and bore engravings of swastikas and the SS logo. Dr. Waldemar Mordecai **Haffkine** developed the plague vaccine while working in Bombay in 1897, and the Haffkine Institute was established in 1899 to continue research into vaccines. Zelazny altered the spelling slightly to Haffikine. **Carlsbad Cavern** is a sanctuary for over a million Mexican Freetail bats. **Caliban** is a character in William Shakespeare's *The Tempest*, a deformed monster who is the slave of the wizard Prospero. **"I can use an optimist. There must be a pony, huh?"** refers to an old joke: a psychiatrist tries to treat a child suffering from extreme optimism by taking him to a room piled high with manure. Instead of dampening his outlook, the child is delighted, digging bare-handed into the manure saying "There must be a pony in here somewhere!" The number of sections in this novella may hold significance; in numerology (which Zelazny had studied), the number 19 means inherence or a person's innate properties.

In the novel version, Zelazny added elements suggesting that *Damnation Alley* precedes . . . *And Call Me Conrad / This Immortal*. Both novels refer to the "Three Days" of nuclear war that laid waste to the Earth. In *Damnation Alley*, Dr. Soames wonders if those who fled to the Mars and Titan colonies will ever return; he also suggests that the big cities were destroyed and that only people in the islands (Greek, Caribbean, Japan, etc.) are likely to have survived. Three characters separately observe that the winds are dying down and wonder that the Earth may be purging itself. These descriptions are quite similar to the backstory of *This Immortal*. Additional elements (e.g. Sprung-Samser or S-S longevity treatments) connect *This Immortal* to *To Die in Italbar* and *Isle of the Dead*. And so it appears that Zelazny created a future history loosely connecting *Damnation Alley*, *This Immortal*, *To Die in Italbar*, and *Isle of the Dead*.

[1] *The Last Defender of Camelot*, 1980.

[2] *If*, January 1969.

[3] *Media Sight* Vol 3 No 1 Summer 1984.

[4] *Vector* May-June 1973 (#65), pp. 42–44.

[5] *Future Life #25*, March 1981.

[6] *Oklahoma City Times*, November 20, 1977, p 27.

APPENDIX:

Two Interviews with
Roger Zelazny

A Few More Words from Roger Zelazny: On Ellison, Delany, and Brust

by Theodore Krulik

I was a program participant at Lunacon in Tarrytown, New York, in March of 1989. It was a memorable convention and one well-attended. One of its major events took place in the grand ballroom of the hotel at 7:00 P. M. on Saturday night. Prime time. Over two hundred people filled the hall. It was a one-on-one interview with Writer Guest-of-Honor Roger Zelazny. And I was the interviewer.

Roger came down the aisle to rousing applause. I was already seated but I stood to greet him and we shook hands. When the two of us settled in at a cloth-covered table on the stage, I addressed the large audience. "We are here to have a small, intimate conversation with Roger Zelazny," I said. "And you are all eavesdroppers."

Harlan Owes Me a Subscription

Prepared with a list for Roger, I planned on asking questions that Zelazny fans would want to know. As a fan myself, I always wondered how well Roger knew his contemporaries of the "New Wave" in science fiction. Did he count authors like Samuel R. Delany and Harlan Ellison, for instance, among his friends.

Here's what he had to say:

The first time I met Harlan Ellison we were both unpublished young punks in Cleveland, Ohio. A girl I knew at my high school was a cub reporter on a local paper. She talked her boss into letting her cover the World Science

The Magic

Fiction Convention in 1955 which was being held in Cleveland. She knew that I wanted to write science fiction and she asked me if I would care to come with her one evening to see what a science fiction convention was like. She told me she met a young fellow named Harlan Ellison who had said he was going to be a great writer someday also. She introduced us and told us that we had both said we were going to be great writers someday.

Harlan sold me a subscription to a fanzine called *Dimensions* on the spot. I never did see a copy of it. Then I didn't see Harlan again for eleven years.

We were both great writers at that point. That was back at another WorldCon in Cleveland again; 1966's Tricon. I reminded him that I hadn't seen any copies of *Dimensions* in front of many witnesses; at which time, he refunded my two dollars. So I always felt that Harlan Ellison was an honorable man.

Zelany? Delazny?

What would a writer of Roger's stature do when a fan mistakenly hands him another author's book to sign? That had happened to Roger more than once. This was how he responded to the question:

It was at that same convention, Tricon in 1966, in a Polynesian restaurant that Samuel R. Delany and I met. We sat at a table together and talked about music and science fiction and food. We were both familiar with each other's work. Neither of us sold the other a subscription to a fanzine or anything the way Harlan Ellison had when we first met.

I never knew Delany that well. We never lived in the same town so we rarely had occasion to get to know each other. Whenever we're in the same town for a convention we'd get together and compare notes.

The confusion people have about our names is a funny visual thing. Delazny? Zelany? For a time I was given one of Delany's books to autograph—*The Einstein Intersection*—most frequently. The one he was most often given to sign was *Dream Master*. We finally made an agreement to authorize each other to autograph those particular works for the other. I told him I was willing to autograph *The Ballad of Beta 2*, but the gentleman changed his mind. My apologies for signing that one in his stead. But Delany said *Intersection* was okay and I told him the same regarding *Dream Master*.

That reminds me of another time like that. I was getting a lot of Delany books to sign at WorldCon in Toronto in 1973. It seems to have been a sort of high point of the confusion between my name and Delany's.

At that convention, a man came up to me at a party and said, "You are the most wonderful writer in the entire area. I really appreciate your characterizations and backgrounds, and your style is also superb."

He told me other beautiful things like that. At the end of about ten minutes, he rose and said, "Well, I've been keeping you, but it's really been fine talking to you, Mr. Silverberg."

Lunacon, Tarrytown, NY, 1989

Helping a Young Writer in Hell

Roger was instrumental in helping me to publish my second book, *The Complete Amber Sourcebook*, with Avon Books, his own publisher. While I worked on that project, I sent him my finished chapters and he responded with suggestions by mail. On two occasions, he telephoned me to offer details that he had not written into his novels.

Roger cared enough to help when a new author's writing piqued his interest. That was just the way he was. At a convention in Tampa, Florida in 1985, he recalled helping out a young writer who had been brought to his attention, someone at the beginning of a very promising career.

Here's Roger, in his own words:

Steven Brust was just starting out, and his publisher sent me his novel *Jhereg* just to read and see if I cared to give them a publication quote to promote the book. Along with *Jhereg*, they included his second book, *Yendi*. I read them both and liked them.

When Brust heard I'd commented on *Jhereg*, he dropped me a line thanking me. Then he sent me a copy of the manuscript of his latest novel, *To Reign in Hell*. He wrote, "Ace purchased this one but, in the meantime, it's going into a limited edition by a local outfit called Steel Dragon Press. Ace felt that it was all right to use the quote you had given for *Jhereg*, but I don't feel quite right about it. If you have time to read *To Reign in Hell*, I'd appreciate your taking a look. This is an extra copy. You can throw it away. If you don't have the time, I'll understand."

So I took a look at the first few pages and got into it. Instead of giving them a comment, I liked this stuff so much I decided to write something at greater length and help the guy out. I wrote the introduction that was included in *To Reign in Hell* completely unsolicited. I'd never done that before, but I was particularly taken by his writing.

Most writers have only one strong point, but Brust has several. I like his dialogue and descriptions. He has a sense of humor that is similar to my own. It's true that someone who might appeal to me most is a writer who sounds like me.

In fact, he called me up the other day. He works with computers, and he said he's quitting his job. He's leaving in a couple of weeks to write full time. I hope he makes it.

Necronomicon, Tampa, FL, 1985

A Voice from the World Mountain: An Interview with Roger Zelazny

by John Nizalowski

This interview with Roger Zelazny occurred in Santa Fe, New Mexico—a city that has attracted authors for nearly a century. The reasons for this are many. It is a small city, around 100,000 in population, but it contains a cultural richness far beyond its size. This is due to its historical role as a crossroads of empires, resulting in a heady blend of Indian, Spanish, and Anglo influences. Also, the Sangre de Cristo and Jemez Mountains surround it, and thus the wilderness is close at hand. It is the only place in America where one can buy a traditional style piece of pottery from a Pueblo Indian vendor, stroll under the long portal of a Spanish colonial palace, and then cross the high desert to an outdoor amphitheater and attend the world premiere of a major opera. These and other aspects attracted Zelazny to Santa Fe in 1975.

When I moved there eleven years later, I had long been an avid reader of Zelazny's work. Indeed, *Eye of Cat*, with its southwestern setting, was partly responsible for my leaving Virginia to settle in northern New Mexico. While I knew Zelazny lived somewhere nearby in those adobe walled streets, I didn't think it likely that we would cross paths.

However, soon after arriving in Santa Fe, I signed up for T'ai Chi classes. To my great astonishment, I discovered that a fellow student—the one with the slender body, hawk-like Slavic features, controlled nervous energy, and rather formal manner—was none other than Roger Zelazny. A black belt in Karate, Roger had studied T'ai Chi for years. Because of this, Wasentha Young, our instructor, often placed him in charge of the beginning students. To be taught T'ai Chi by Roger Zelazny was certainly one of the greatest blessings of my life. Over the months, with our common interests in

609

literature, writing, and martial arts, we formed a friendship that possessed aspects of a mentor-apprentice relationship.

The first time I visited Roger's home, a spacious sun-filled ranch house on the northeast side of Santa Fe, he brought me into his study and proudly displayed an extensive library that covered a wide range of subjects, from history and psychology to physics, a resource that he felt was indispensable to his work. Zelazny explains this in his essay "Constructing a Science Fiction Novel" from *Frost & Fire*: "The important thing for me is the development and refinement of one's perception of the world, the experimentation with viewpoints. This lies at the heart of story-telling, and all the mechanical techniques one learns are merely tools."

Just over from the ranks upon ranks of bookshelves, above his desk, a window revealed the pinion covered Sangre de Cristo foothills rising up to Santa Fe Baldy, a great gray-topped mound of a mountain, its summit often graced by snow. As described in the interview, this peak helped inspire his novella "24 Views of Mt. Fuji, by Hokusai."

The interview came about in late May of 1989. I was writing for *Pasatiempo*, the arts and entertainment section of *The Santa Fe New Mexican*. Three works by Roger Zelazny were about to appear—*Frost & Fire*, *Knight of Shadows*, and the audio version of *Eye of Cat*. With this triple play at hand, I approached the editor of *Pasatiempo*, Denise Kusel, with the idea of doing a feature on Roger, and she readily agreed. I taped the interview in Roger's study, and I originally wrote it up as a Q&A. However, Denise decided she wanted the piece to be in article format instead, so I composed the feature based on this interview and other conversations with Roger. The article appeared on June 9, 1989. None of us knew at the time that this was late in Roger Zelazny's career, and many of the projected novels he described would never be realized.

A year later, I accepted a position at Mesa State College in western Colorado. Roger and I kept up our connection through letters, phone calls, and the occasional breakfast together when I'd visit Santa Fe. The last time I saw Roger was in January of 1995. By then he had left his second wife,

Roger Zelazny and Samuel R. Delany

Judy, and was living in his new home, a humble stucco structure on Santa Fe's south side, with novelist Jane Lindskold. He appeared thinner than usual, but his energy and joy of life seemed as strong as ever, so I thought nothing of it. After a late morning spent drinking coffee, eating brownies, and catching up on our lives, Roger said, "Let me show you around the place before you go." The last item on the tour was his re-constructed library, of which he was still deeply proud.

Six months later, on June 14th, 1995, almost exactly six years to the day from the publication of the *Pasatiempo* article, Roger Zelazny died from cancer.

Back in 1989, after completing the assignment for *The New Mexican*, I placed the interview away in my Zelazny file, where it remained until a recent request from Gerald Hausman resurrected it. Hausman, producer of the audio version of *Eye of Cat* and one of Roger's closest friends and collaborators, has asked me to write an essay on Zelazny for a proposed book project. Seeking to return to the days when Roger lived across town and was a mere phone call away, I reread the interview and realized that it might still be of interest to scholars of science fiction literature. I sincerely hope it will provide some insight into the creative processes of one of the 20th century's most talented literary artists.

JN: Much of your fiction blends myth with the motifs of science fiction. Would you comment on the importance of myth to your writing?

RZ: This probably goes back to the fact that I was imprinted with mythology at a relatively early age. My earliest reading material was *Bulfinch's Mythology*. I read this sort of material for the story values, as other people might read fiction. It was not until later at the age of eleven that I discovered science fiction and fantasy. It has always seemed to me that it is pre-puberty reading that influences people more strongly than later things they might read. In fact, almost every sf writer I know read sf at an early age. I read mythology at an earlier age than sf. Later on, when I discovered sf, I kept reading works of a mythological nature just because I'd built up a background in the area.

As I grew more sophisticated, I began reading secondary works dealing with mythological sources—Joseph Campbell, Robert Graves, *Hamlet's Mill*, and so on. So, my knowledge of mythology was initially by way of its story values, but later on I gained a more sophisticated approach to the structure of myth, which I never consciously set out to emulate to the extent that might seem the case to a reader of some of my books using mythological materials. But, it is difficult to divorce one's knowledge from one's intent. My intent is to use mythological lumber when I'm using a mythological motif in my work. It is difficult to divorce myself from the totality of my knowledge in that area.

On the other hand, I haven't used that much mythological material in recent years. When I began writing in the '60s, I began to complete my education in other areas, like science and history. By way of a stopgap I was writing things of a mythological nature because I knew this material. There came a point when I became typified as a writer of mythological type stories, and whenever I would attend an sf convention I would normally be placed upon a panel called "Mythology and Science Fiction," or something like that. I began resenting it a bit because I don't like to be categorized.

So, that's when I abandoned mythology and began writing other things, like *Damnation Alley, Isle of the Dead, Doorways in the Sand*, works like that. Reviewers who were unkind to me at first said my books were merely a rehashing of mythological materials; there's nothing really new here. Then they began saying that it's a shame that Roger Zelazny abandoned all those wonderful mythological themes to write sf stories just like everyone else. That's when I stopped reading reviewers except for amusement.

It was only after I had produced as much or more works of a non-mythological nature that I picked up mythological themes again. So, yes, the influence is there. I intentionally chose to write *Lord of Light* because I hadn't seen much done with Hindu and Buddhist materials in fantasy, while Celtic and Norse myths had been overworked. I wanted to do something different.

Roger Zelazny and Samuel R. Delany

I also feel that mythological material provides one with a wider range of characters, the larger-than-life figures one does not normally meet in a general fiction novel, which are perfectly at home in a work of science fiction, if you're willing to substitute a mutant or an android for an occasional demigod.

JN: Did your interest in myth attract you to New Mexico?

RZ: Not really. I was living in Baltimore when I realized we could be living anywhere in the country, since my income wasn't dependent upon geography. We came out here because we were tired of large urban centers. I'd lived in Cleveland, New York, and Baltimore. I wanted a smaller town with all the amenities that Santa Fe has—restaurants, bookstores, theaters, the opera, and galleries. Also, it's a good place to raise children. And I did like the tri-cultural part.

JN: Has New Mexico influenced your work?

RZ: Yes. I wouldn't have written *Eye of Cat* if I hadn't lived here. In fact, I wouldn't have written "24 Views of Mt. Fuji" if it weren't for the Sangre de Cristo Mountains of New Mexico. The proximate cause of the story was a book of 24 haiku sized prints of Mount Fuji which I found at the St. John's College Bookstore one day. As I looked through it I realized there was a story to be written in 24 sections with each headed by one of the prints. But going back further, seeing that book would not have stimulated the story if I hadn't been looking at the mountains every day.

JN: So New Mexico is affecting your work in subtler ways than simply a place to set stories?

RZ: Yes.

JN: Of course *Eye of Cat* and "Unicorn Variations" are set in New Mexico. And in *Trumps of Doom* there's an army set to invade Amber training in the Pecos wilderness.

RZ: That's true. But it's too simple to look for a one to one correspondence between things in a story and things in a person's life, unless there's an intention of putting them in that way. There's usually more of a secondary effect.

613

The Magic

JN: Do you have more pieces planned for a New Mexico setting?

RZ: I have pieces, but I don't know whether they will develop farther along as works in their own right, or secondary themes in something else.

JN: Leaving regional influences, I'd like to discuss your academic background. You hold an M.A. in English from Columbia. Have you ever felt a tension between your academic training and your interest in science fiction, a field that some literary critics view with mixed feelings?

RZ: That training gave me an advantage, actually, in the '60s. The term New Wave has been applied to that period, and writers like myself, Delany, Spinrad, and LeGuin. We all started about the same time. However, I don't think of myself as part of a movement; no one ever does, and all of the others deny it too.

It was at that time we imported into science fiction literary values from what people who still think of science fiction as a genre call the mainstream. And the fact that I had this background I felt made it worth the effort to employ it, so I was doing all the things like putting in stream of consciousness and stronger characterization than a lot of the stuff I had read when the world was much younger, when the science was a lot harder, and the characters a lot flatter. So my literary training was a virtue.

It's been a quarter of a century since then, and the field has ingested what we had to offer it. Again, it will follow Sturgeon's Law, that 90% of sf is crap because 90% of everything is crap, but the top 10% of the sf being written today is an improvement, I would say, over the situation years ago simply because sf has taken in the literary values that were brought into it in the '60s, along with the new approach to ideas. Sf began to address political, religious, and social issues. So it's a literature of ideas that has improved considerably in its ideas and stylistics.

So I never felt a tension there. I felt a source for materials I hadn't seen in sf before.

JN: Do you feel that science fiction has gained some of the respect it lacked when you started writing?

Roger Zelazny and Samuel R. Delany

RZ: Yes. When I was starting in the field it wasn't as academically accepted. But now there are courses being offered in sf all over the country, and there are scholarly journals in sf. In fact, I just did a series of lectures down at New Mexico State University. So it's more respectable academically, and also more successful commercially. A great number of sf novels are on the best-seller list in recent years, which did not occur much back in the old days.

JN: Have you attained a crossover audience yourself?

RZ: It's hard to say who reads you. I see only general sales figures on a royalty statement. But I do get quite a few fan letters by people who are not sf fans.

JN: Moving from literature, you have had encounters with the film media. In 1977, 20th Century Fox released *Damnation Alley* based on your novel of the same name. The film essentially mutilated the novel, turning Hell Tanner, a Hell's Angel in your work, into an Air Force captain. How do you feel about the film media's treatment of your work, and of science fiction in general?

RZ: To give the devil his due, it's not just sf that they do this to. Anybody I know outside of sf who has dealt with Hollywood has had their work altered considerably. Hemingway once said that the best way to deal with Hollywood is to stay on the other side of the California state line and have them toss you the money so you can catch it and run. Because they are going to do whatever they want with your book. So, in that sense, I don't think sf's experience is any worse than anyone else's.

On the other hand, the Hollywood approach to sf is to go for the special effects, for the flashy themes, and this is usually going to be at the expense of characterization and often at the expense of idea. This is natural because film is such a visual medium, and it's much more action oriented, even if it is dumb action. So, you have to put up with this because it's extremely difficult for an author to get control.

JN: Do you have other film projects in the works?

RZ: We just finished negotiating a film option on *Doorways in the Sand*. This one looks more promising. I've always felt that *Doorways* would make a decent film, partly because it would not rely on a great number of special effects to achieve some of the high points of action. A big chunk of the budget need not be devoted to special effects to have a good story.

JN: How did the *Twilight Zone* episode based on "The Last Defender of Camelot" turn out?

RZ: That worked out very well. I was very pleased with it. It was scripted by a very good friend of mine who happened to be a creative consultant to the show at the time, George R.R. Martin, who lives here in Santa Fe and who is out in Hollywood right now where he is producer of *Beauty and the Beast*. George was very conscientious in adapting my work to the extent of calling me every hour and a half as they went through the story and were figuring out what would work and what would not. He explained to me what options we had at various points when there was a possibility of going one way or another and would ask me which way I would want to go in terms of the structure of the story. So, I was extremely happy.

JN: It sounds like "Defender" was an opposite experience from *Damnation Alley*.

RZ: Yes. On *Damnation Alley* they sent me a script by Lucas Heller, who wrote the screenplay of *Hush, Hush, Sweet Charlotte*, marked as the "final script." It was a very good script and quite true to the story line. I assumed that this was going to be the script for the film. I only learned later that they weren't completely happy with it and brought in another writer who totally revised Heller's script. So I walked into the theater expecting Heller's script because it was marked "final."

JN: But it wasn't really final?

RZ: No, unfortunately.

JN: A media project you've worked on recently is the November Moon audiotape of *Eye of Cat*. When will it be out?

RZ: Summer of 1989.

JN: Did you record a shortened version of the novel?

RZ: We were going to do that originally, but we decided to tape the entire book cover to cover. So it'll come out as two tapes packaged together.

Roger Zelazny and Samuel R. Delany

JN: Gerald Hausman of November Moon Productions is known for working with Native American materials. How does it feel to be working in this context?

RZ: It's very interesting. Of course this particular novel of mine is a Native American piece. On the other hand, it is a recording, and over the years I have done many readings, normally live, sometimes on radio, and I enjoy reading very much. So it wasn't a unique experience since I'm familiar with studios. But the final product is different, so I'm quite excited about it.

JN: You've been working on the Amber series lately. So far there are three novels in the second Amber series, centered on Corwin's son Merlin. How many more novels will there be?

RZ: There's a fourth book coming out this fall called *Knight of Shadows*, and there's a contract for a fifth.

JN: So this is another five book series?

RZ: It was supposed to be a trilogy, but the story spilled over. I hope it'll stay at five books so I can get on and write other things. If it spills past five, I'll just keep going until I get to the end of the story.

JN: Why do you think Amber has such a powerful attraction for readers?

RZ: I intentionally set up a large family to work in every possible form of sibling rivalry and friendship one could visualize. So, I figured that no matter what sort of family a person grew up in, there would be some area of identification. There's everything from incest to intra-family murders.

JN: So there's a strong psychological framework for Amber?

RZ: Yes, it occurred to me it would be worth exploring. It's subdued, but it's there.

JN: In the '70s you finished the tale of Corwin. Why did you return to Amber?

RZ: I had more story to tell. I hadn't really quit with the first five, I just got tired of writing it. I wasn't ready to re-invoke Corwin. Besides, enough time had passed since the fifth Amber book that I needed to show the passage of time. I suppose I could have taken a different tack than I did, but I wanted to go this way and have a different standpoint, Merlin's standpoint.

The Magic

I had played with the idea of writing several other books from several other family members' points of view, which I still might do. I have the other stories to tell which involve Amber, but I want to finish this one, and then take a vacation, because I have a couple of books I've been anxious to do for several years now.

JN: What will they be?

RZ: I think I might like to try a large novel, on the order of *Lord of Light* or longer. I do have an idea which will probably run to that extent. I would rather write one big solid book than a trilogy.

JN: What will be the book's theme?

RZ: It's rather complex. I couldn't describe it simply. It will deal with the nature of time in a more bizarre and complex way than *Roadmarks*.

I tend not to make long-term plans because I discovered as a writer that I may become fascinated by certain ideas, and they have a sort of half-life and run out after three years. If I have a really hot idea for something right now, I better write it before 1991 or another idea may well come along and supplant it. There's certain very general themes I keep returning to, but ideas have a shorter shelf life, and you need to get to them in a few years.

JN: Are you speaking of themes as philosophical concepts?

RZ: Right. Love, death, certain characters opposing certain universal qualities.

JN: And ideas are the basis for plots?

RZ: Yes. Something new in the sciences that may come along, or some new social condition that may be worthy of examination. There are lots of science fiction novels coming out right now dealing with AIDS and new developments in astrophysics. Ten years from now they may well have a cure for AIDS, and they may have solved these problems in astrophysics, and something completely different will be getting people's attention.

But certain basic themes which go back to the Greeks will still be informing literature, and certain peculiar ways of regarding and considering these themes will still be a part of a writer's psychological makeup and probably reoccur in his work.

CPSIA information can be obtained
at www.ICGtesting.com
Printed in the USA
LVHW091118120520
655425LV00002B/454